JAMIE SMART'S

BUNNY VS MONKEY

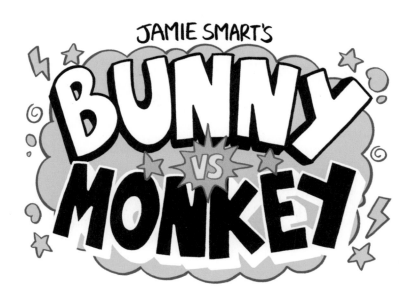

Dedicated to everyone who helped to bring this book together.

union square kids

NEW YORK

UNION SQUARE KIDS and the distinctive Union Square Kids logo are trademarks of Union Square & Co., LLC.

Union Square & Co., LLC, is a subsidiary of Sterling Publishing Co., Inc.

Text and illustrations © 2020 Jamie Smart

This edition first published in North America in 2023 by Union Square & Co., LLC. First published in Great Britain in 2020 by David Fickling Books.

ISBN 978-1-4549-5032-5 (hardcover)
ISBN 978-1-4549-5033-2 (paperback)
ISBN 978-1-4549-5034-9 (e-book)

For information about custom editions, special sales, and premium purchases, please contact specialsales@unionsquareandco.com.

Printed in China

Lot #:
2 4 6 8 10 9 7 5 3 1

05/23

unionsquareandco.com

Adaptation design by Laura Bentley, additional artwork and colors by Sammy Borras
Cover and interior design by Paul Duffield and Julie Robine
Production assistance by Chris Dickey

JAMIE SMART'S
BUNNY vs MONKEY

union
square
kids

NEW YORK

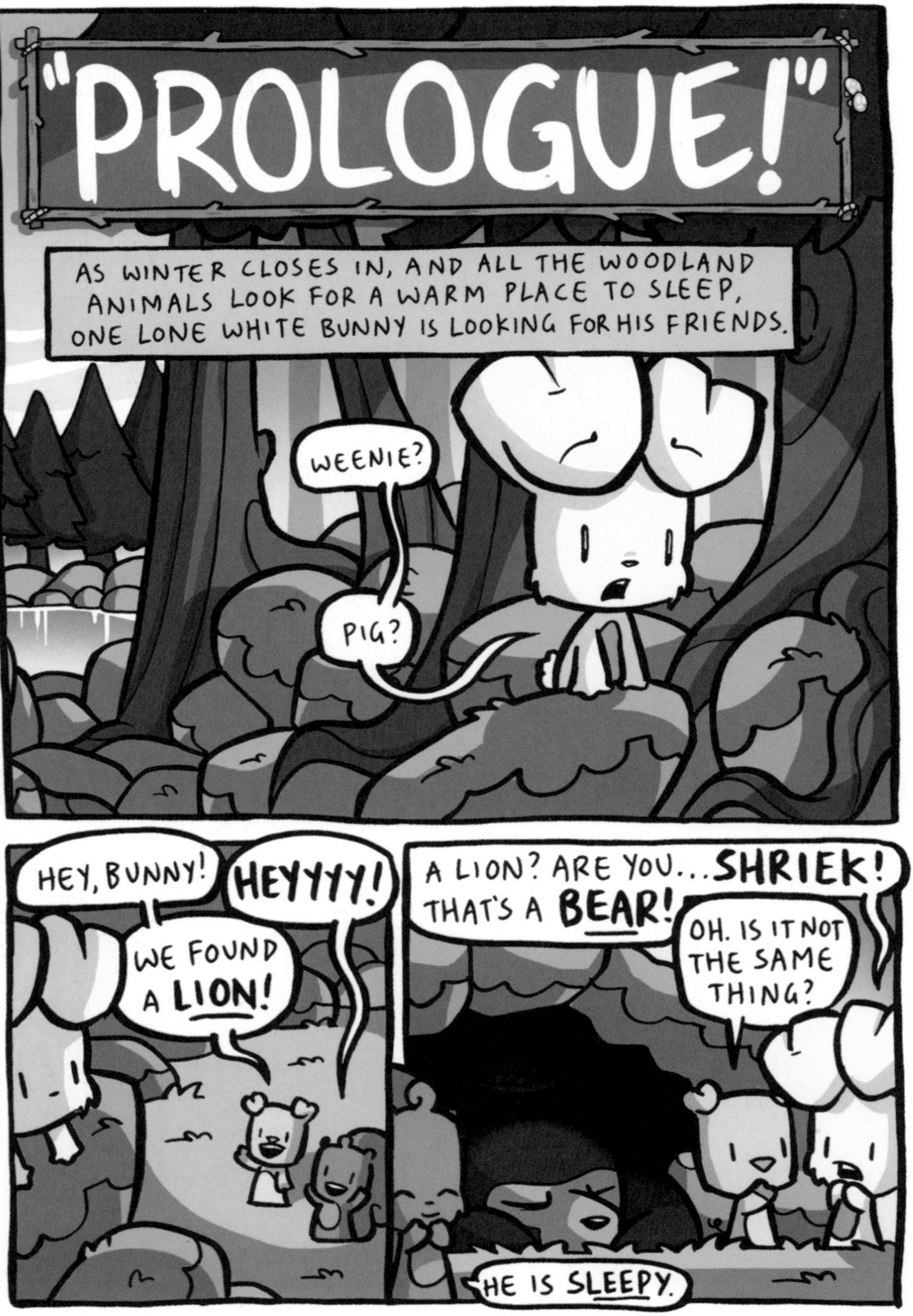
"PROLOGUE!"
AS WINTER CLOSES IN, AND ALL THE WOODLAND ANIMALS LOOK FOR A WARM PLACE TO SLEEP, ONE LONE WHITE BUNNY IS LOOKING FOR HIS FRIENDS.
WEENIE?
PIG?
HEY, BUNNY!
HEYYYY!
WE FOUND A LION!
A LION? ARE YOU... SHRIEK! THAT'S A BEAR!
OH. IS IT NOT THE SAME THING?
HE IS SLEEPY.

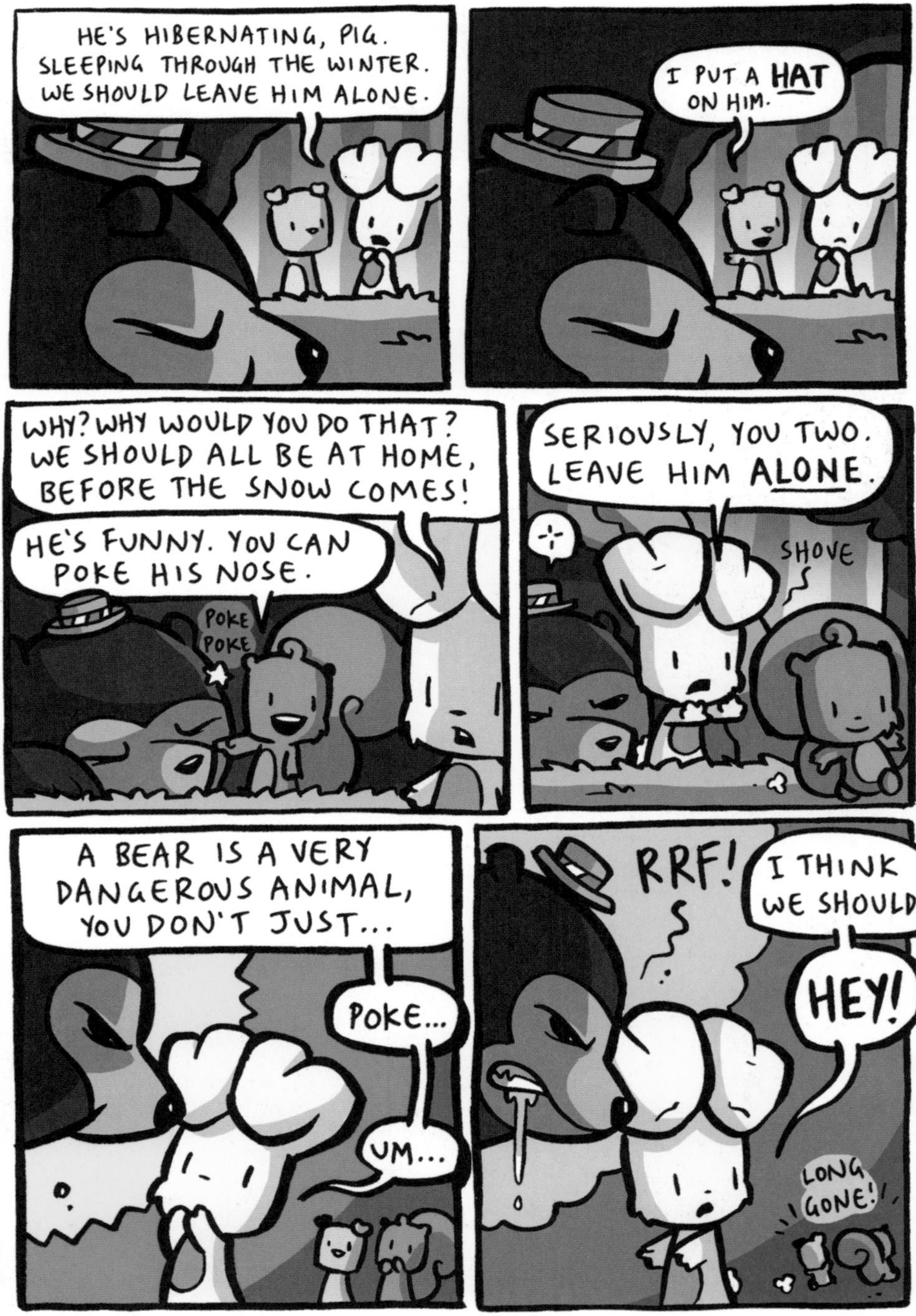
HE'S HIBERNATING, PIG. SLEEPING THROUGH THE WINTER. WE SHOULD LEAVE HIM ALONE.
I PUT A **HAT** ON HIM.
WHY? WHY WOULD YOU DO THAT? WE SHOULD ALL BE AT HOME, BEFORE THE SNOW COMES!
HE'S FUNNY. YOU CAN POKE HIS NOSE.
POKE POKE
SERIOUSLY, YOU TWO. LEAVE HIM **ALONE**.
SHOVE
A BEAR IS A VERY DANGEROUS ANIMAL, YOU DON'T JUST...
POKE...
UM...
RRF!
I THINK WE SHOULD...
HEY!
LONG GONE!

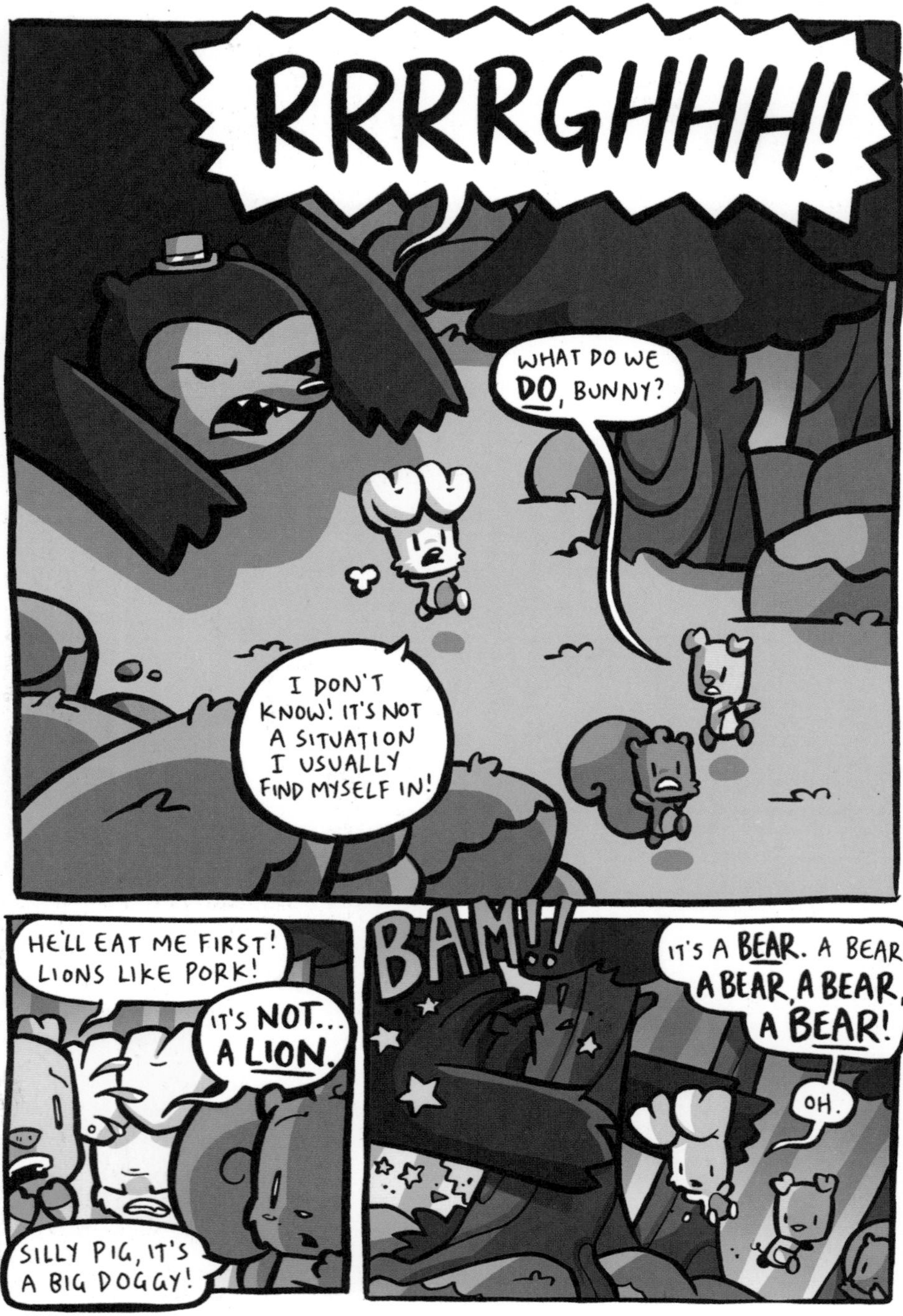
RRRRGHHH!
WHAT DO WE DO, BUNNY?
I DON'T KNOW! IT'S NOT A SITUATION I USUALLY FIND MYSELF IN!
HE'LL EAT ME FIRST! LIONS LIKE PORK!
IT'S NOT... A LION.
SILLY PIG, IT'S A BIG DOGGY!
BAM!!
IT'S A BEAR. A BEAR! A BEAR, A BEAR, A BEAR!
OH.

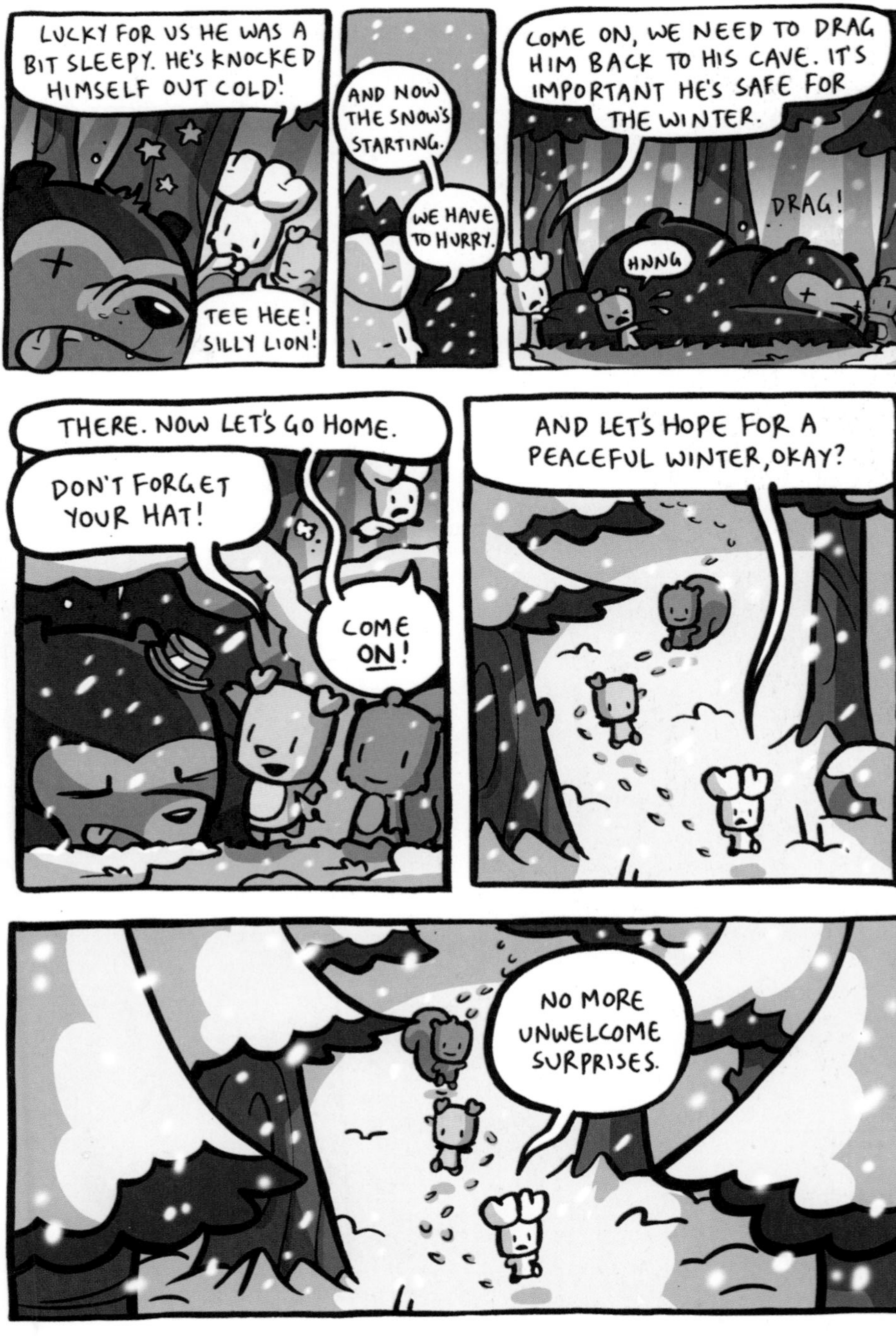
LUCKY FOR US HE WAS A BIT SLEEPY. HE'S KNOCKED HIMSELF OUT COLD!
TEE HEE! SILLY LION!
AND NOW THE SNOW'S STARTING.
WE HAVE TO HURRY.
COME ON, WE NEED TO DRAG HIM BACK TO HIS CAVE. IT'S IMPORTANT HE'S SAFE FOR THE WINTER.
DRAG!
HNNG
THERE. NOW LET'S GO HOME.
DON'T FORGET YOUR HAT!
COME ON!
AND LET'S HOPE FOR A PEACEFUL WINTER, OKAY?
NO MORE UNWELCOME SURPRISES.

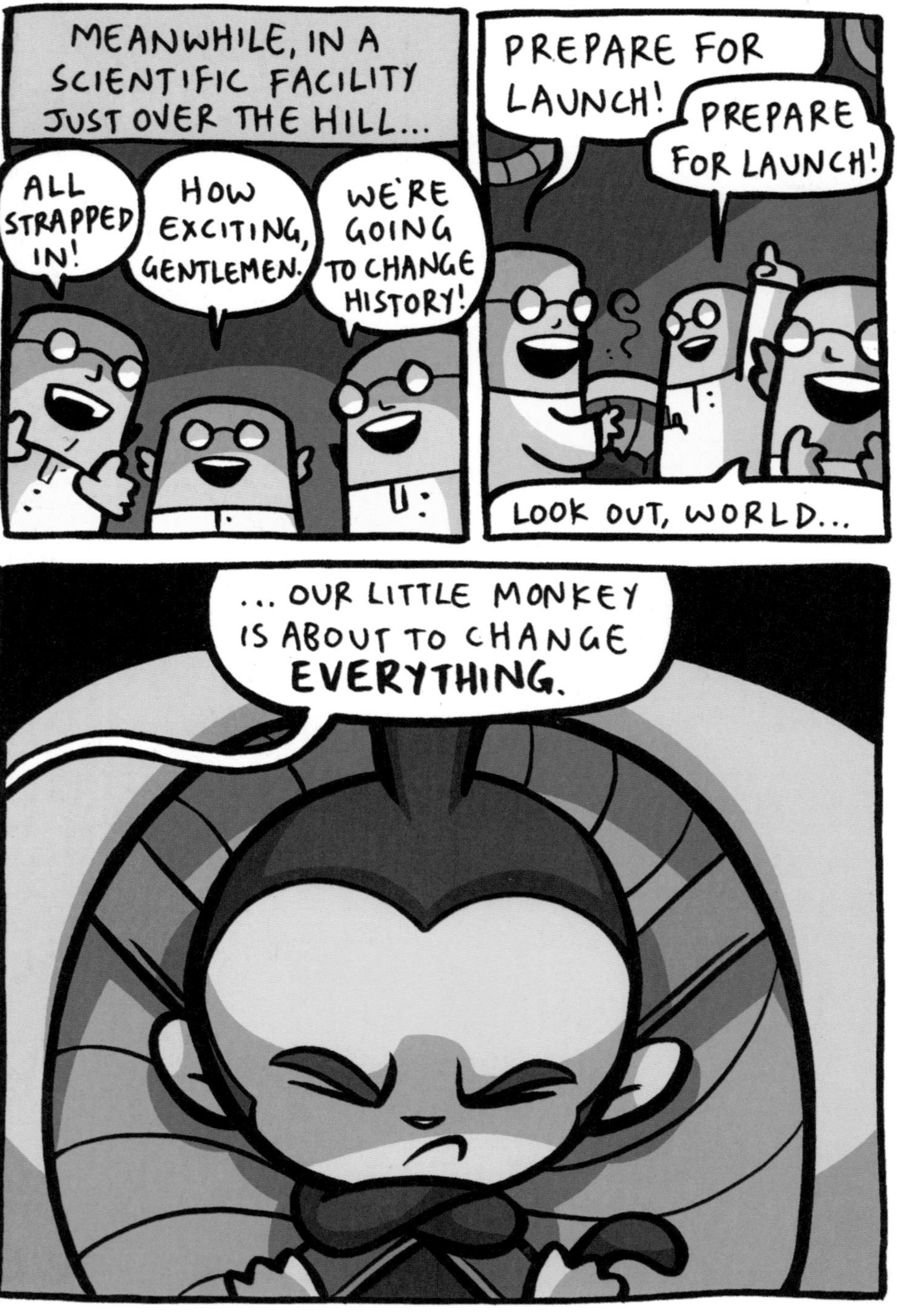
MEANWHILE, IN A SCIENTIFIC FACILITY JUST OVER THE HILL...
ALL STRAPPED IN!
HOW EXCITING, GENTLEMEN.
WE'RE GOING TO CHANGE HISTORY!
PREPARE FOR LAUNCH!
PREPARE FOR LAUNCH!
LOOK OUT, WORLD...
... OUR LITTLE MONKEY IS ABOUT TO CHANGE **EVERYTHING.**

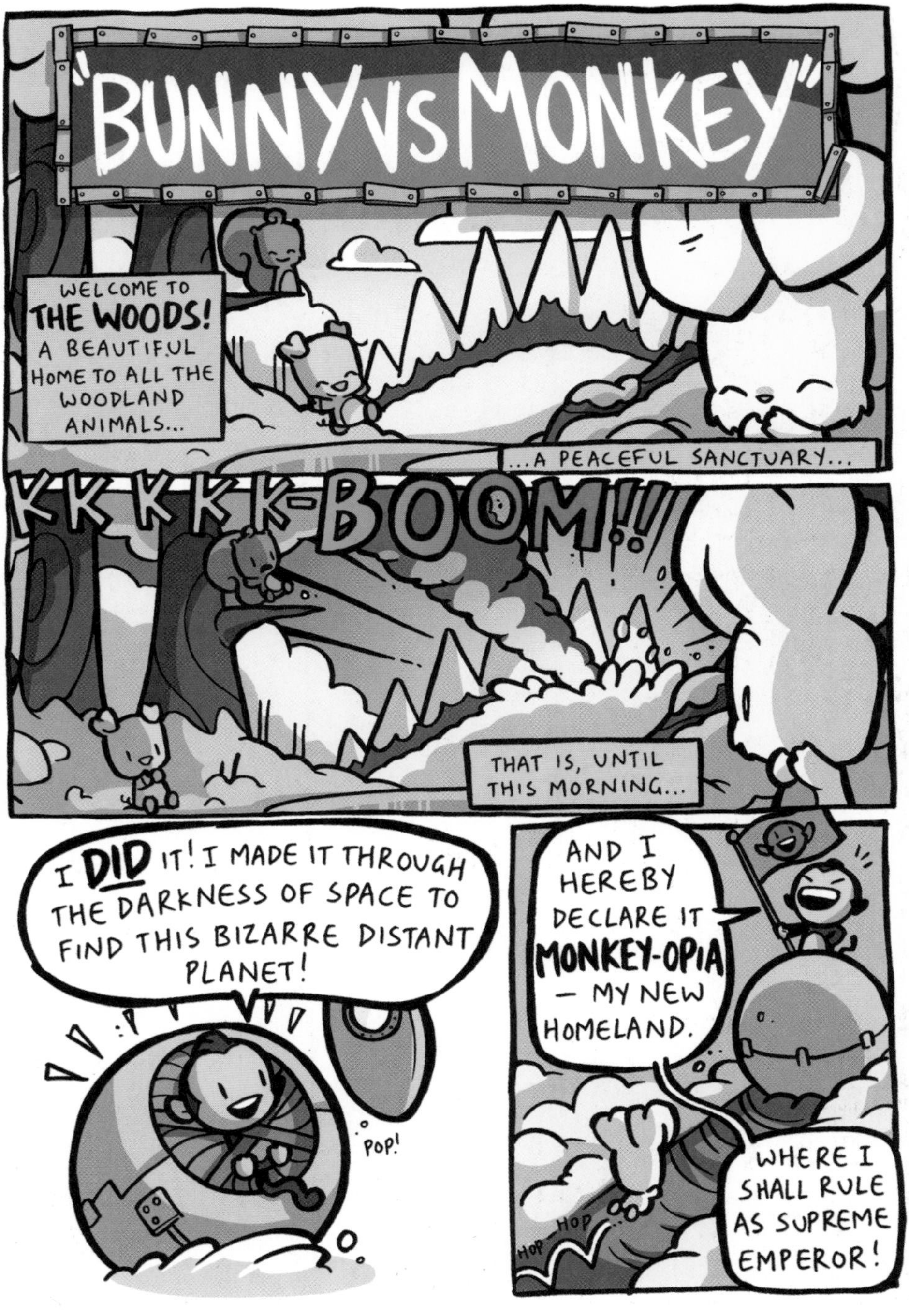
"BUNNY VS MONKEY"
WELCOME TO THE WOODS! A BEAUTIFUL HOME TO ALL THE WOODLAND ANIMALS...
...A PEACEFUL SANCTUARY...
KKKKK-BOOM!!!
THAT IS, UNTIL THIS MORNING...
I DID IT! I MADE IT THROUGH THE DARKNESS OF SPACE TO FIND THIS BIZARRE DISTANT PLANET!
POP!
AND I HEREBY DECLARE IT MONKEY-OPIA — MY NEW HOMELAND.
WHERE I SHALL RULE AS SUPREME EMPEROR!
HOP HOP

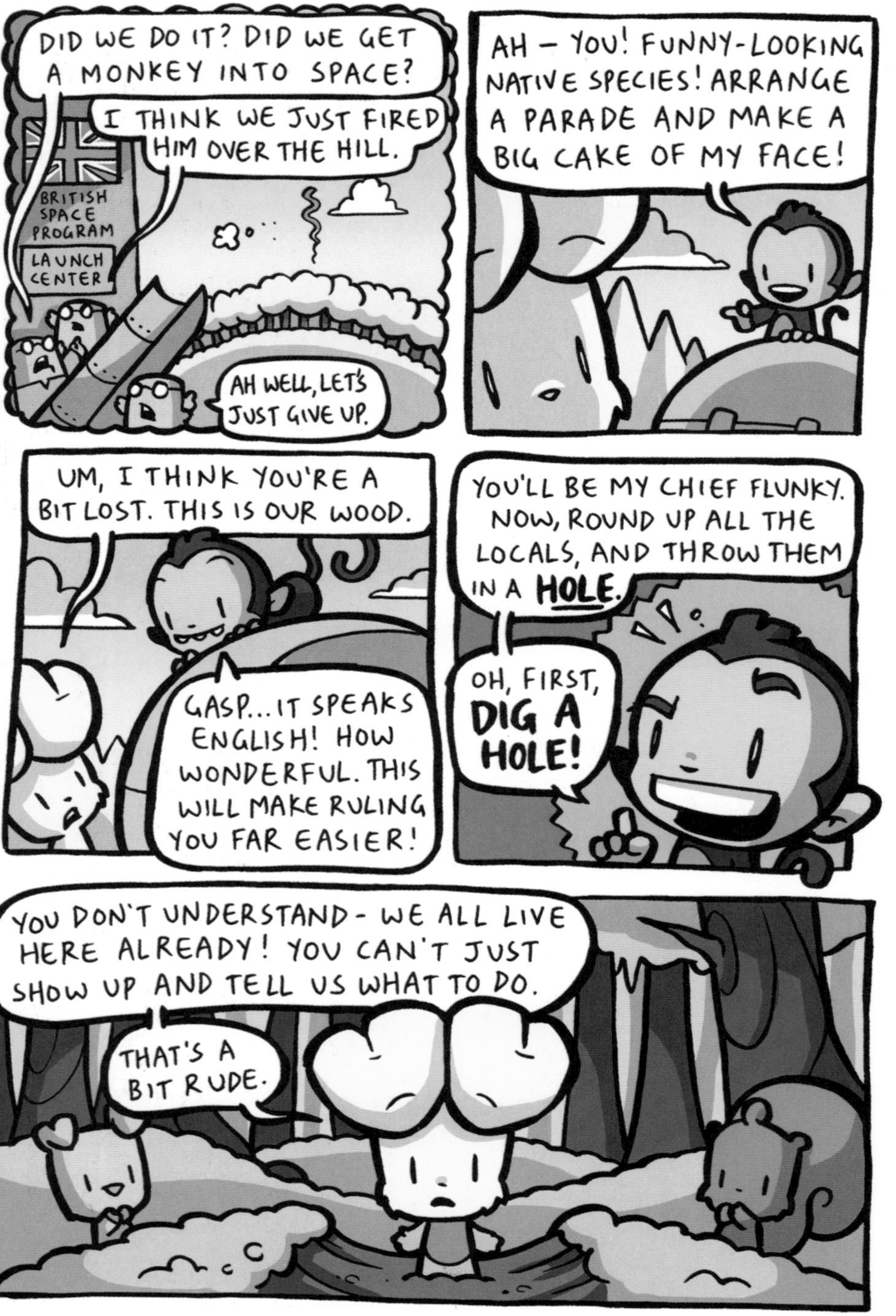
DID WE DO IT? DID WE GET A MONKEY INTO SPACE?
I THINK WE JUST FIRED HIM OVER THE HILL.
BRITISH SPACE PROGRAM
LAUNCH CENTER
AH WELL, LET'S JUST GIVE UP.
AH – YOU! FUNNY-LOOKING NATIVE SPECIES! ARRANGE A PARADE AND MAKE A BIG CAKE OF MY FACE!
UM, I THINK YOU'RE A BIT LOST. THIS IS OUR WOOD.
GASP... IT SPEAKS ENGLISH! HOW WONDERFUL. THIS WILL MAKE RULING YOU FAR EASIER!
YOU'LL BE MY CHIEF FLUNKY. NOW, ROUND UP ALL THE LOCALS, AND THROW THEM IN A HOLE.
OH, FIRST, DIG A HOLE!
YOU DON'T UNDERSTAND - WE ALL LIVE HERE ALREADY! YOU CAN'T JUST SHOW UP AND TELL US WHAT TO DO.
THAT'S A BIT RUDE.

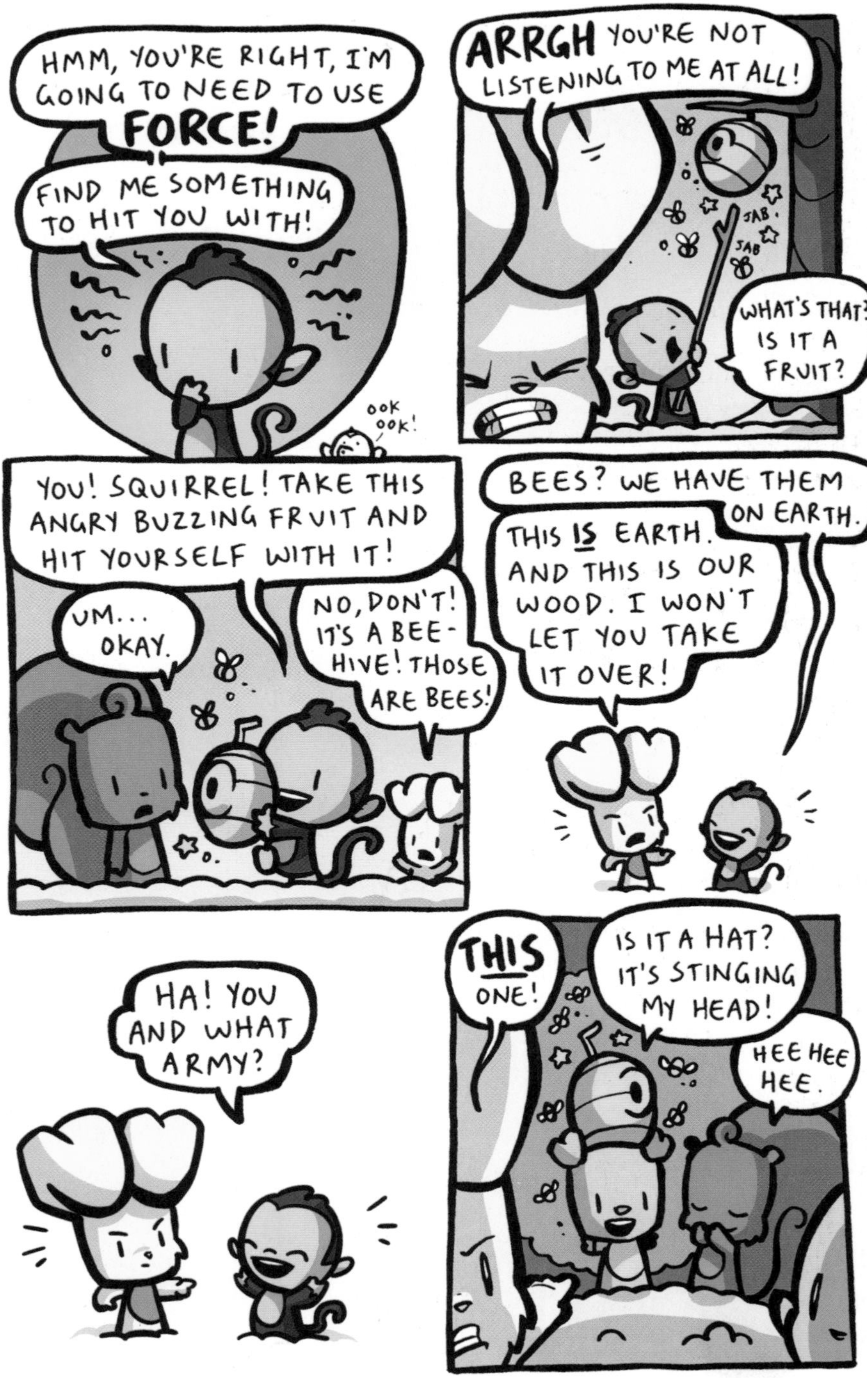
HMM, YOU'RE RIGHT, I'M GOING TO NEED TO USE FORCE!
FIND ME SOMETHING TO HIT YOU WITH!
OOK OOK!
ARRGH YOU'RE NOT LISTENING TO ME AT ALL!
JAB
JAB
WHAT'S THAT? IS IT A FRUIT?
YOU! SQUIRREL! TAKE THIS ANGRY BUZZING FRUIT AND HIT YOURSELF WITH IT!
UM... OKAY.
NO, DON'T! IT'S A BEE-HIVE! THOSE ARE BEES!
BEES? WE HAVE THEM ON EARTH.
THIS IS EARTH. AND THIS IS OUR WOOD. I WON'T LET YOU TAKE IT OVER!
HA! YOU AND WHAT ARMY?
THIS ONE!
IS IT A HAT? IT'S STINGING MY HEAD!
HEE HEE HEE.

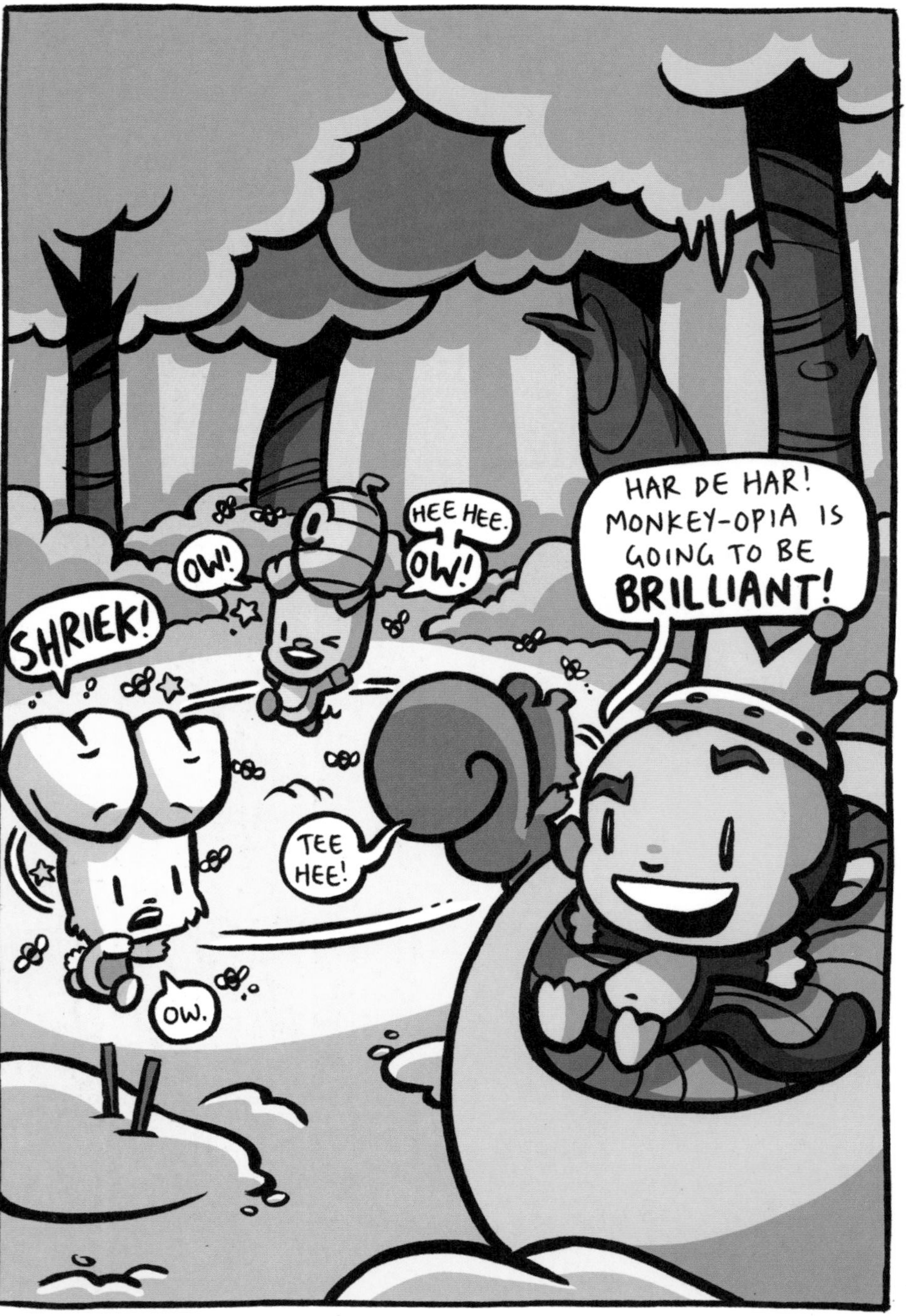
SHRIEK!
OW!
HEE HEE.
OW!
HAR DE HAR! MONKEY-OPIA IS GOING TO BE BRILLIANT!
TEE HEE!
OW.

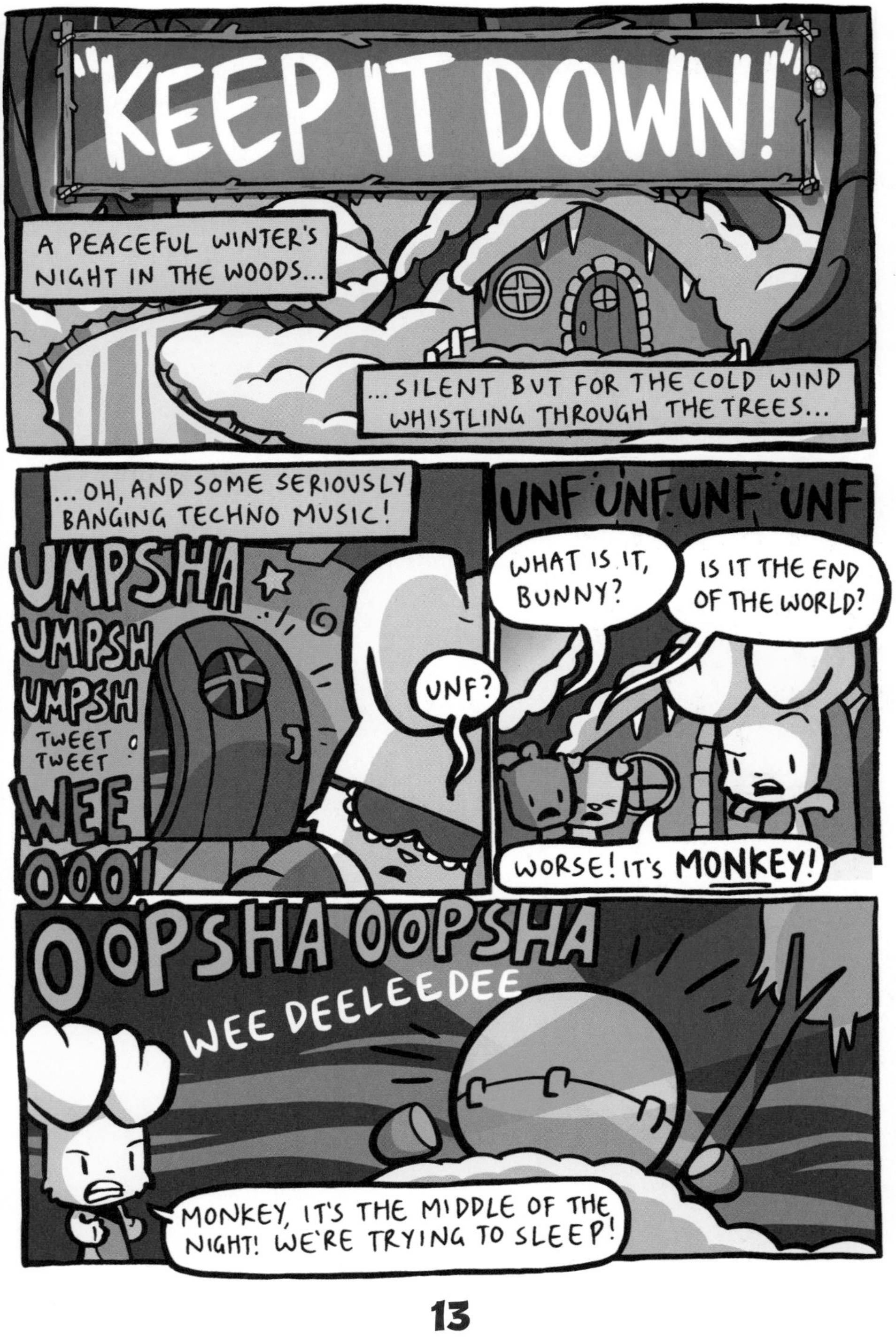
"KEEP IT DOWN!"
A PEACEFUL WINTER'S NIGHT IN THE WOODS...
...SILENT BUT FOR THE COLD WIND WHISTLING THROUGH THE TREES...
...OH, AND SOME SERIOUSLY BANGING TECHNO MUSIC!
UMPSHA
UMPSH
UMPSH
TWEET TWEET
WEE
OOO!
UNF?
UNF UNF UNF UNF
WHAT IS IT, BUNNY?
IS IT THE END OF THE WORLD?
WORSE! IT'S MONKEY!
OOPSHA OOPSHA
WEE DEELEEDEE
MONKEY, IT'S THE MIDDLE OF THE NIGHT! WE'RE TRYING TO SLEEP!

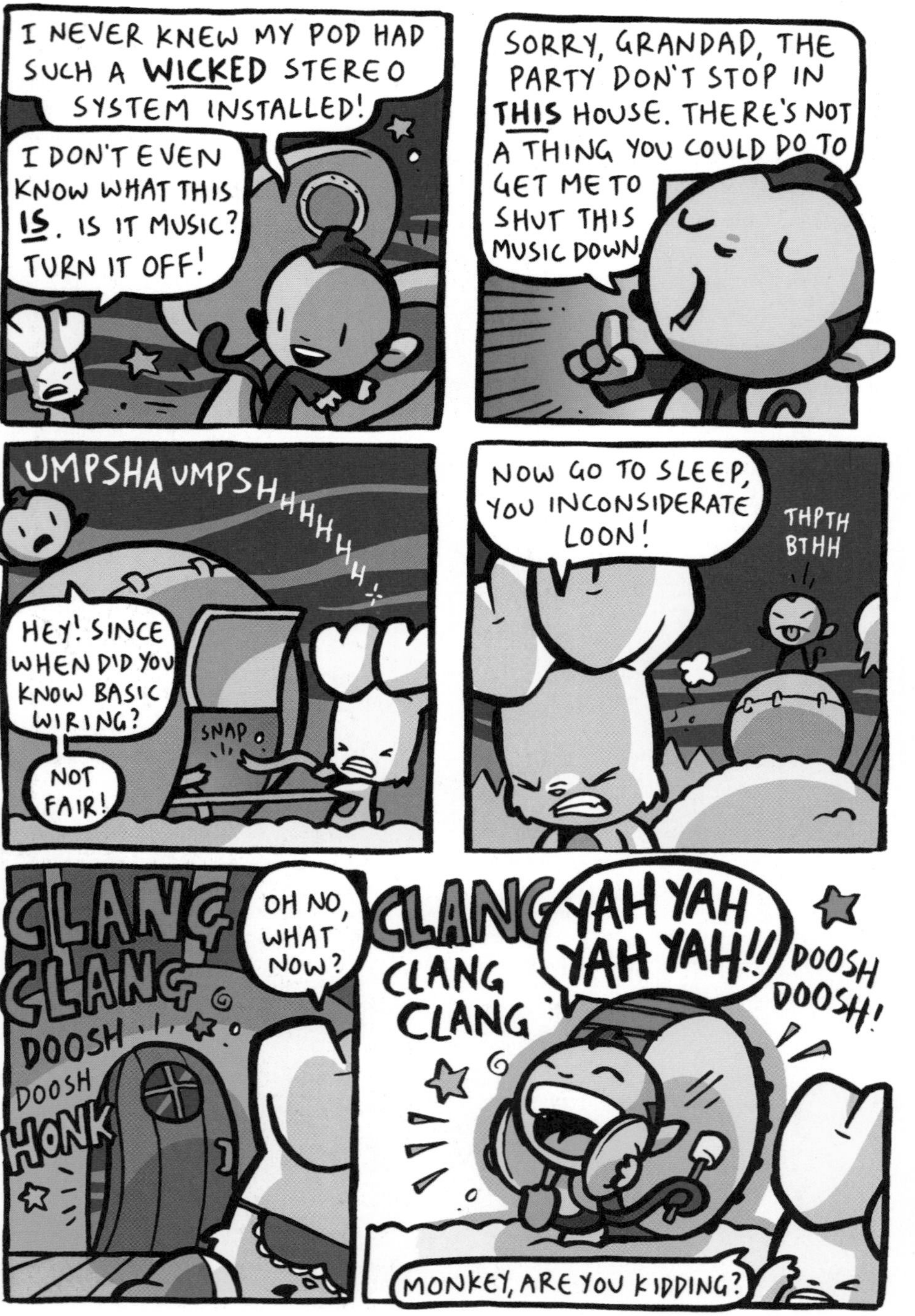
I NEVER KNEW MY POD HAD SUCH A WICKED STEREO SYSTEM INSTALLED!
I DON'T EVEN KNOW WHAT THIS IS. IS IT MUSIC? TURN IT OFF!
SORRY, GRANDAD, THE PARTY DON'T STOP IN THIS HOUSE. THERE'S NOT A THING YOU COULD DO TO GET ME TO SHUT THIS MUSIC DOWN.
UMPSHA UMPSHHHHHHH
HEY! SINCE WHEN DID YOU KNOW BASIC WIRING?
NOT FAIR!
SNAP
NOW GO TO SLEEP, YOU INCONSIDERATE LOON!
THPTH BTHH
CLANG CLANG
DOOSH DOOSH
HONK
OH NO, WHAT NOW?
CLANG
CLANG CLANG
YAH YAH YAH YAH!!
DOOSH DOOSH!
MONKEY, ARE YOU KIDDING?

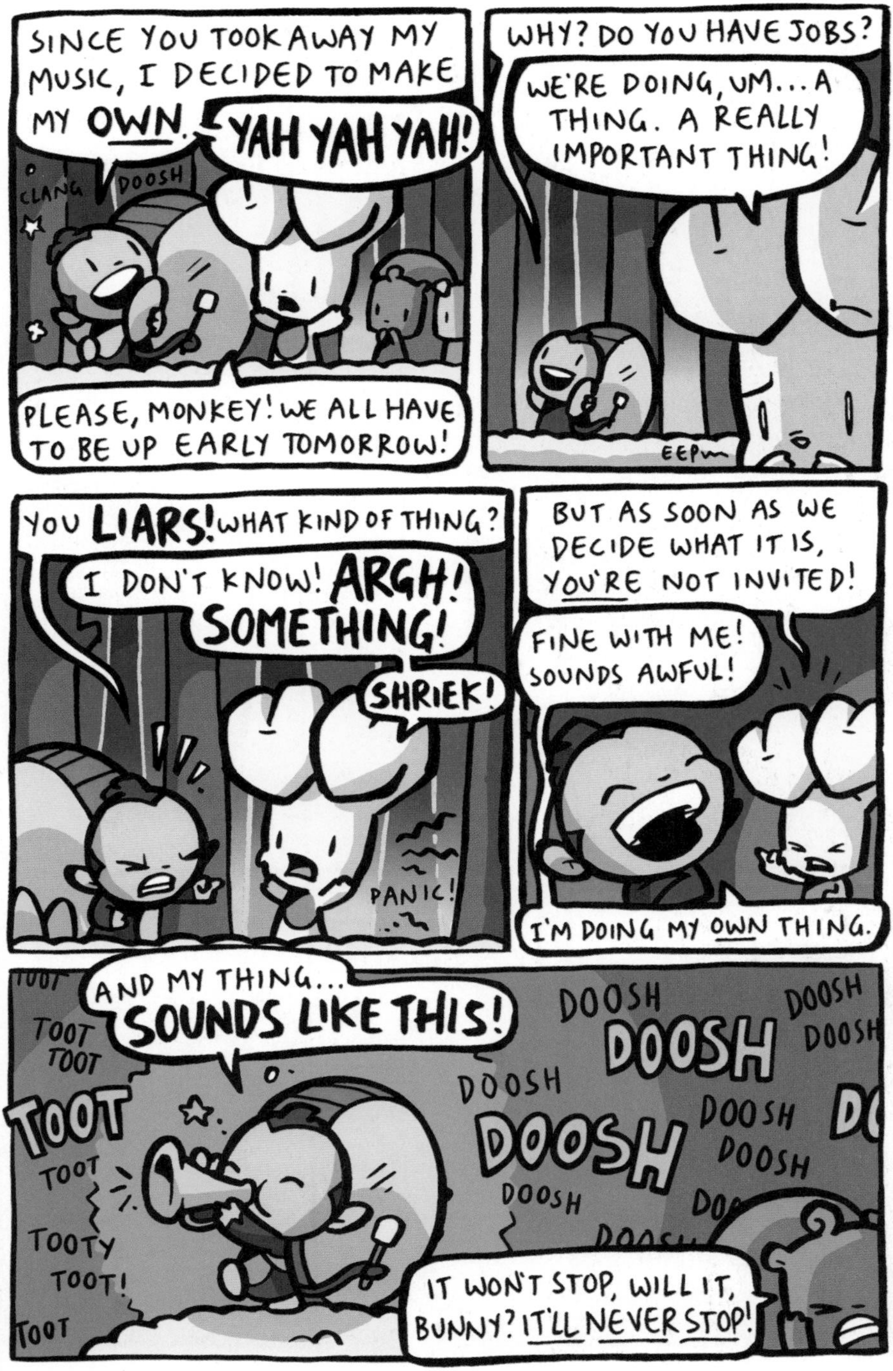
SINCE YOU TOOK AWAY MY MUSIC, I DECIDED TO MAKE MY OWN.
YAH YAH YAH!
CLANG
DOOSH
PLEASE, MONKEY! WE ALL HAVE TO BE UP EARLY TOMORROW!
WHY? DO YOU HAVE JOBS?
WE'RE DOING, UM... A THING. A REALLY IMPORTANT THING!
EEP
YOU LIARS! WHAT KIND OF THING?
I DON'T KNOW! ARGH! SOMETHING!
SHRIEK!
PANIC!
BUT AS SOON AS WE DECIDE WHAT IT IS, YOU'RE NOT INVITED!
FINE WITH ME! SOUNDS AWFUL!
I'M DOING MY OWN THING.
AND MY THING... SOUNDS LIKE THIS!
TOOT TOOT
TOOT
TOOT
TOOTY TOOT!
TOOT
DOOSH
DOOSH
DOOSH
DOOSH
DOOSH
DOOSH
DOOSH
DOOSH
DOOSH
IT WON'T STOP, WILL IT, BUNNY? IT'LL NEVER STOP!

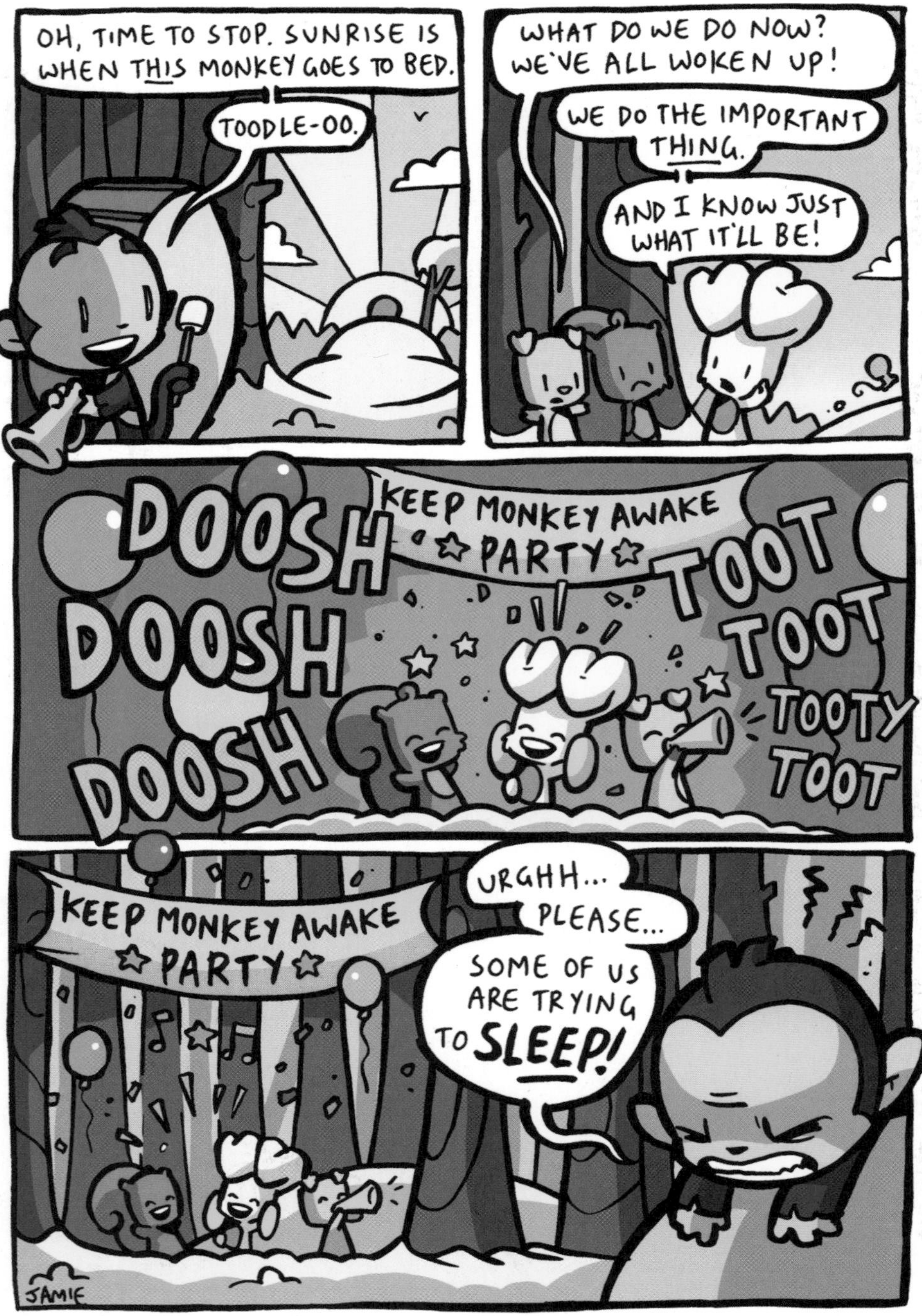
OH, TIME TO STOP. SUNRISE IS WHEN THIS MONKEY GOES TO BED.
TOODLE-OO.
WHAT DO WE DO NOW? WE'VE ALL WOKEN UP!
WE DO THE IMPORTANT THING.
AND I KNOW JUST WHAT IT'LL BE!
DOOSH
KEEP MONKEY AWAKE PARTY
TOOT
DOOSH
TOOT
DOOSH
TOOTY TOOT
KEEP MONKEY AWAKE PARTY
URGHH... PLEASE...
SOME OF US ARE TRYING TO SLEEP!
JAMIE

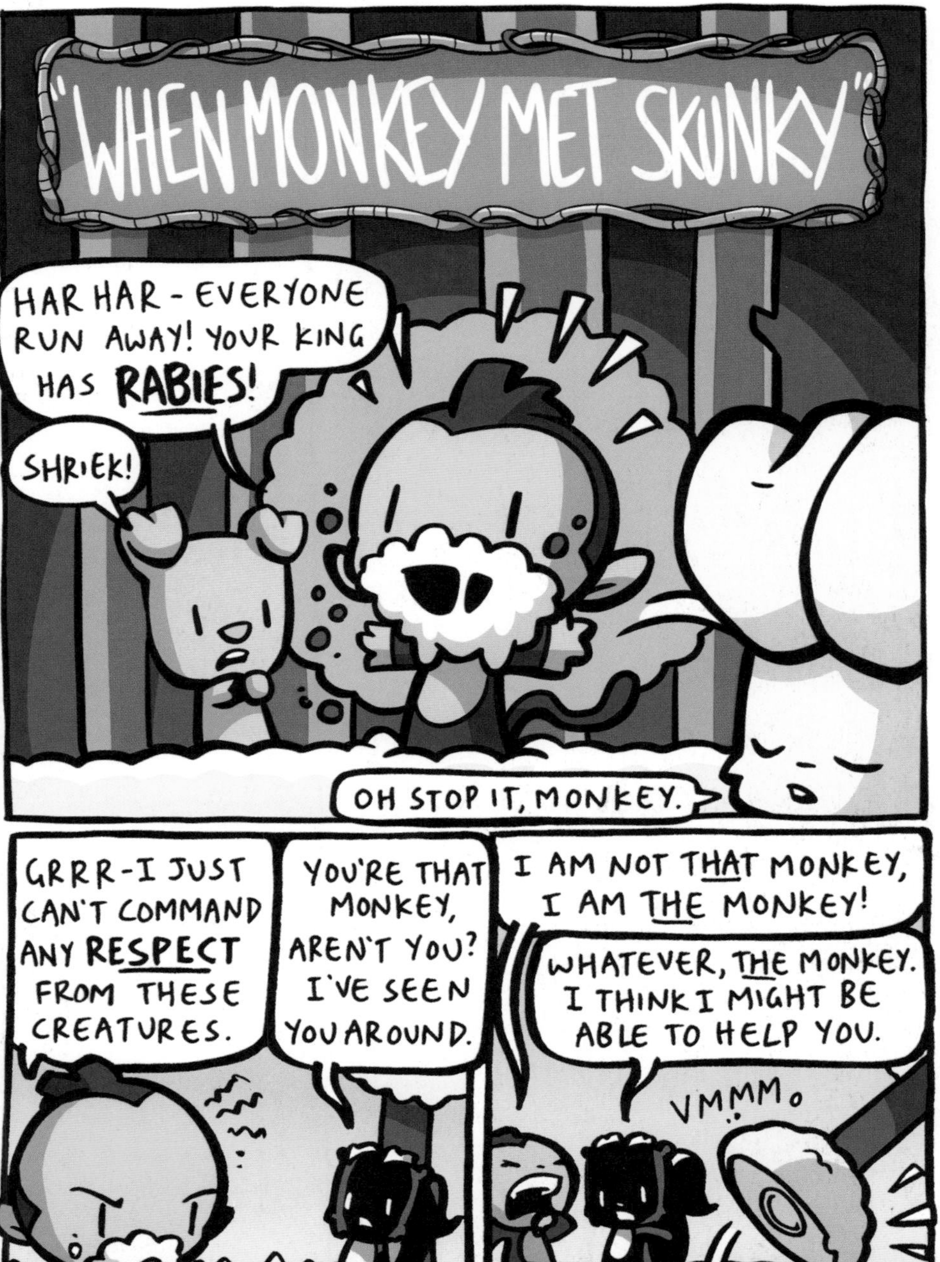
"WHEN MONKEY MET SKUNKY"
HAR HAR - EVERYONE RUN AWAY! YOUR KING HAS RABIES!
SHRIEK!
OH STOP IT, MONKEY.
GRRR-I JUST CAN'T COMMAND ANY RESPECT FROM THESE CREATURES.
TOOTH PASTE
YOU'RE THAT MONKEY, AREN'T YOU? I'VE SEEN YOU AROUND.
I AM NOT THAT MONKEY, I AM THE MONKEY!
WHATEVER, THE MONKEY. I THINK I MIGHT BE ABLE TO HELP YOU.
VMMM

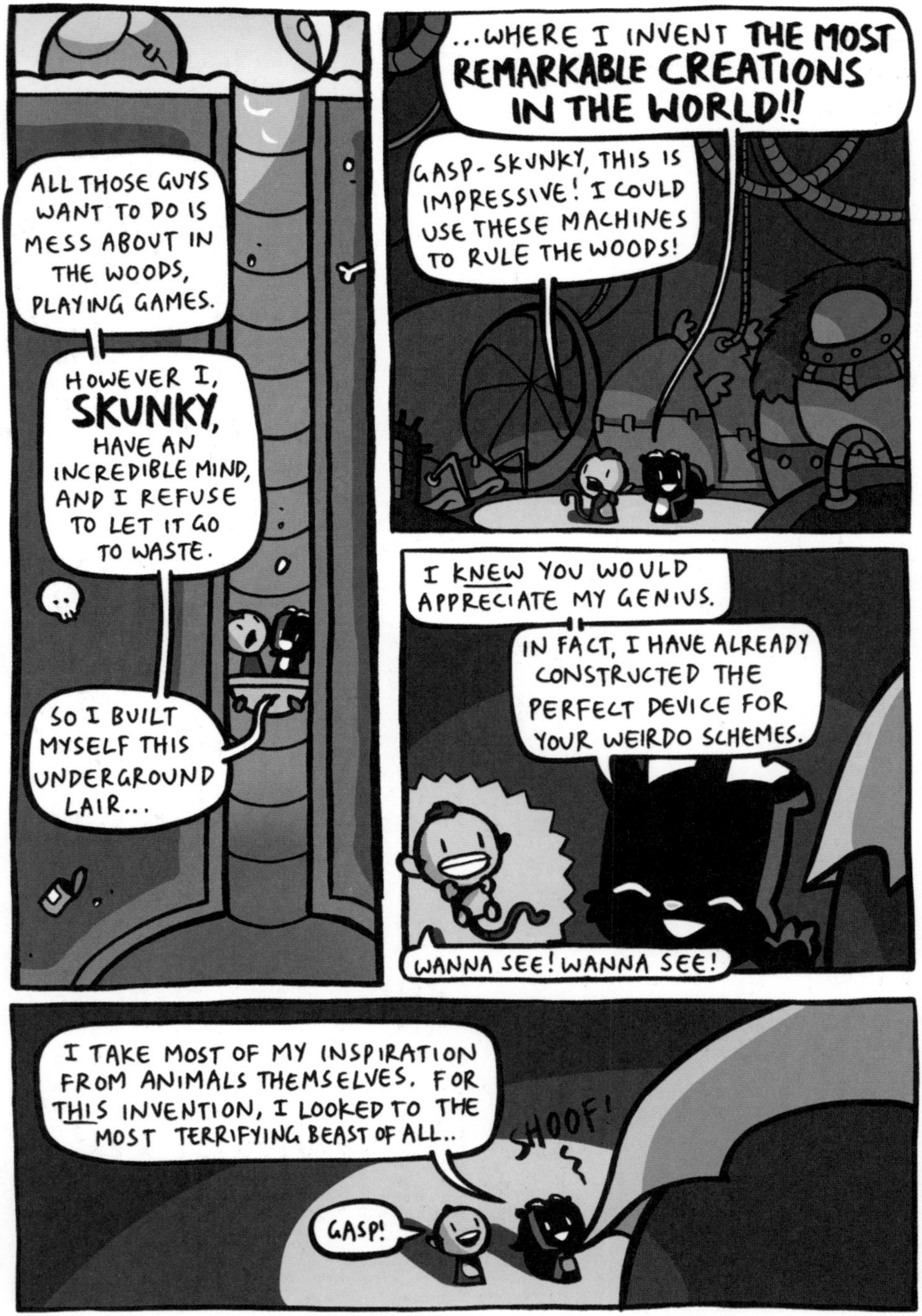
ALL THOSE GUYS WANT TO DO IS MESS ABOUT IN THE WOODS, PLAYING GAMES.
HOWEVER I, SKUNKY, HAVE AN INCREDIBLE MIND, AND I REFUSE TO LET IT GO TO WASTE.
SO I BUILT MYSELF THIS UNDERGROUND LAIR...
...WHERE I INVENT THE MOST REMARKABLE CREATIONS IN THE WORLD!!
GASP- SKUNKY, THIS IS IMPRESSIVE! I COULD USE THESE MACHINES TO RULE THE WOODS!
I KNEW YOU WOULD APPRECIATE MY GENIUS.
IN FACT, I HAVE ALREADY CONSTRUCTED THE PERFECT DEVICE FOR YOUR WEIRDO SCHEMES.
WANNA SEE! WANNA SEE!
I TAKE MOST OF MY INSPIRATION FROM ANIMALS THEMSELVES. FOR THIS INVENTION, I LOOKED TO THE MOST TERRIFYING BEAST OF ALL..
SHOOF!
GASP!

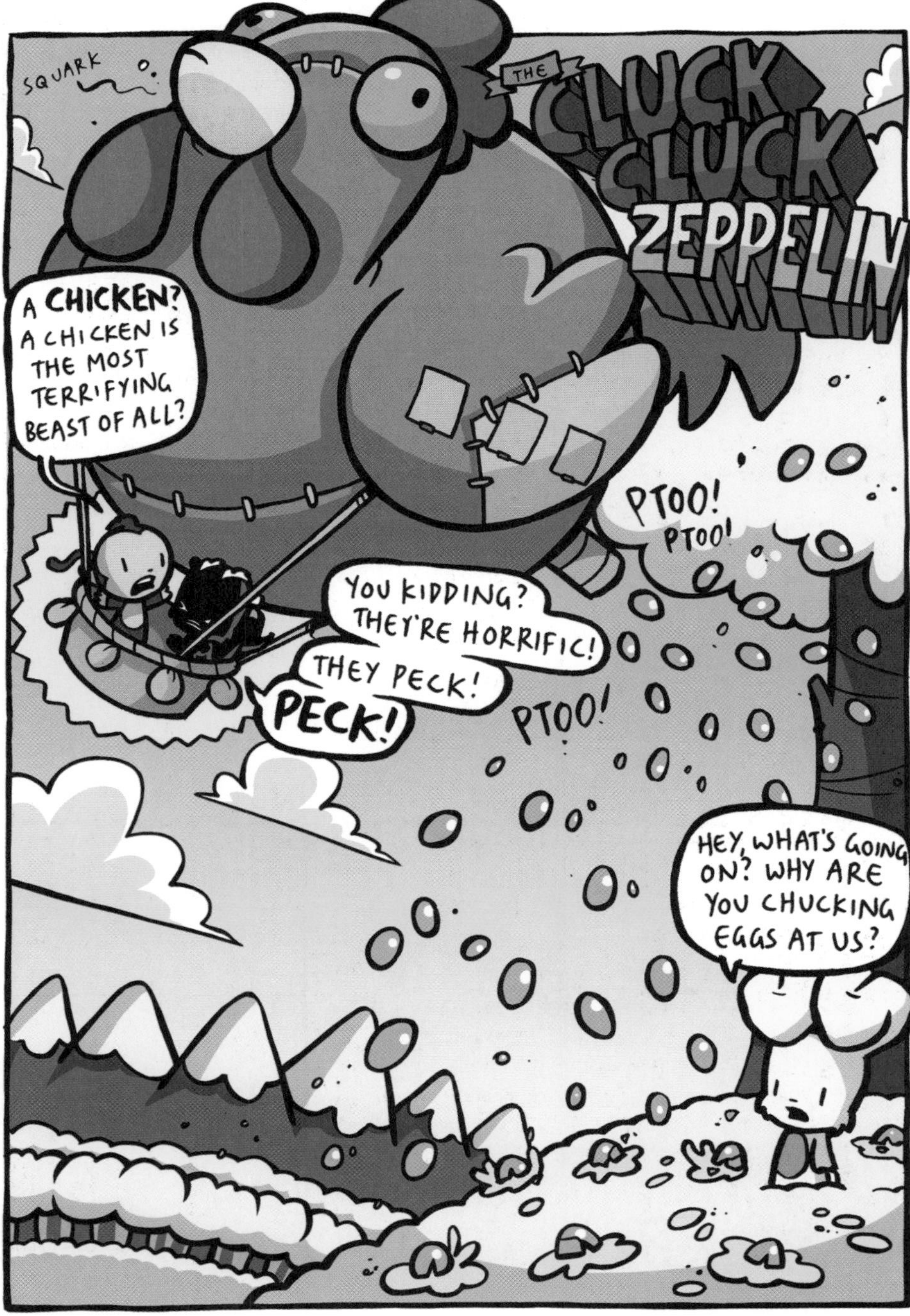
SQUARK
THE CLUCK CLUCK ZEPPELIN
A CHICKEN? A CHICKEN IS THE MOST TERRIFYING BEAST OF ALL?
PTOO! PTOO!
YOU KIDDING? THEY'RE HORRIFIC!
THEY PECK!
PECK!
PTOO!
HEY, WHAT'S GOING ON? WHY ARE YOU CHUCKING EGGS AT US?

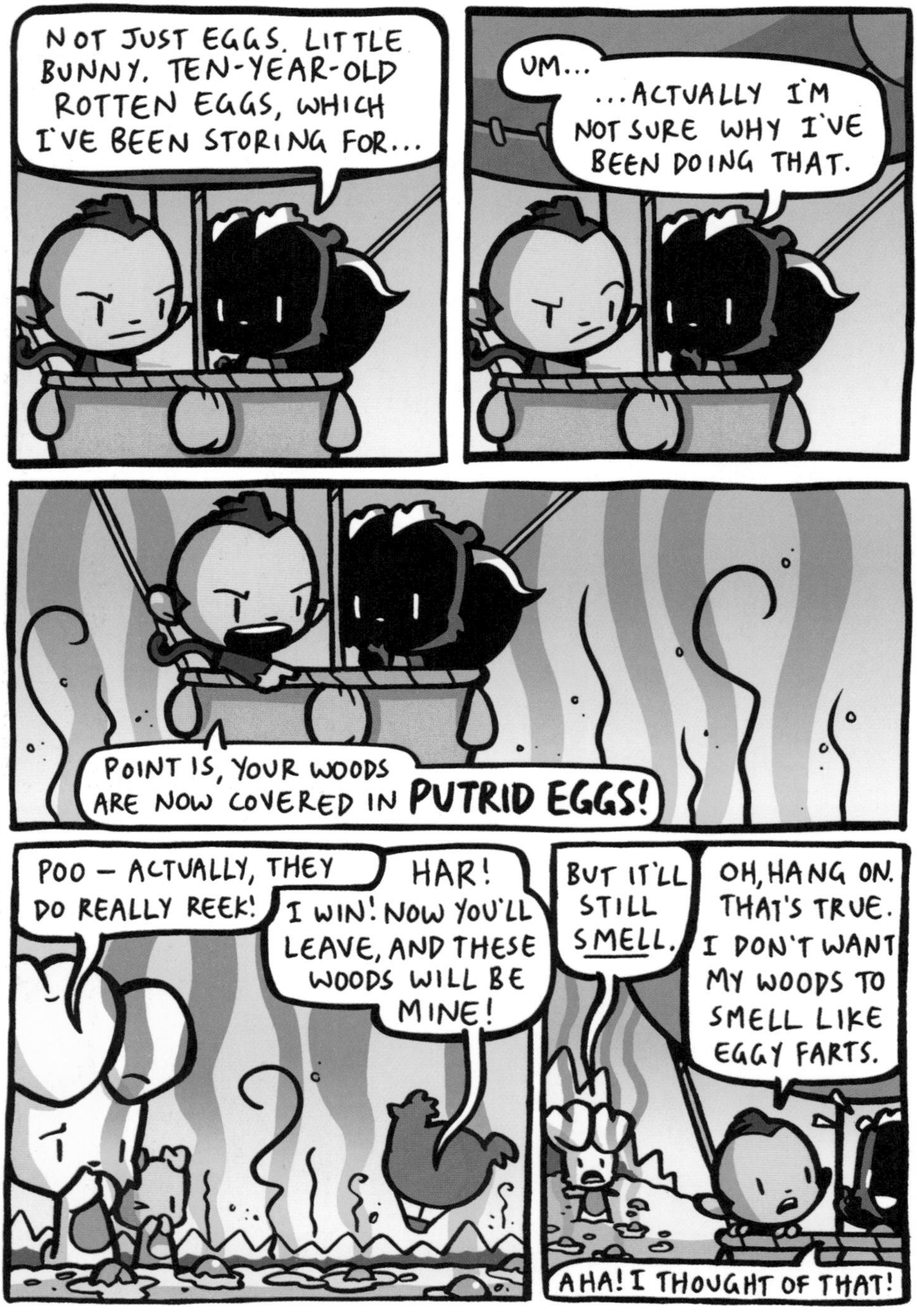

NOT JUST EGGS, LITTLE BUNNY. TEN-YEAR-OLD ROTTEN EGGS, WHICH I'VE BEEN STORING FOR...
UM...
...ACTUALLY I'M NOT SURE WHY I'VE BEEN DOING THAT.
POINT IS, YOUR WOODS ARE NOW COVERED IN PUTRID EGGS!
POO – ACTUALLY, THEY DO REALLY REEK!
HAR! I WIN! NOW YOU'LL LEAVE, AND THESE WOODS WILL BE MINE!
BUT IT'LL STILL SMELL.
OH, HANG ON. THAT'S TRUE. I DON'T WANT MY WOODS TO SMELL LIKE EGGY FARTS.
AHA! I THOUGHT OF THAT!

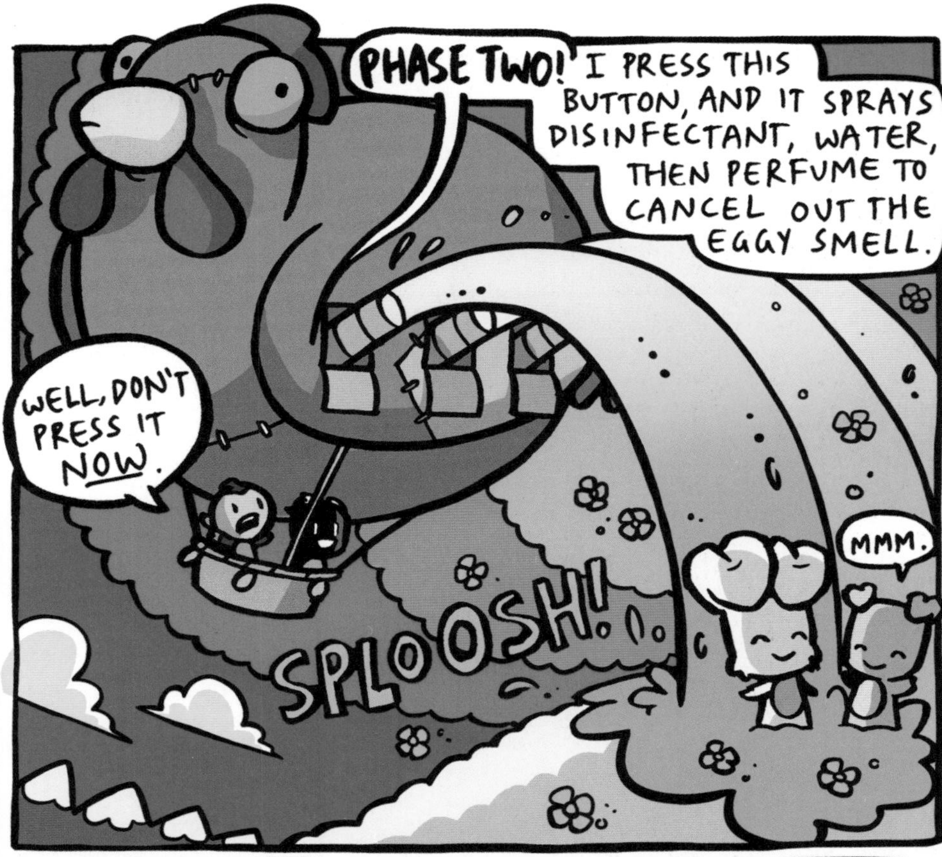
PHASE TWO! I PRESS THIS BUTTON, AND IT SPRAYS DISINFECTANT, WATER, THEN PERFUME TO CANCEL OUT THE EGGY SMELL.
WELL, DON'T PRESS IT NOW.
SPLOOSH!
MMM.

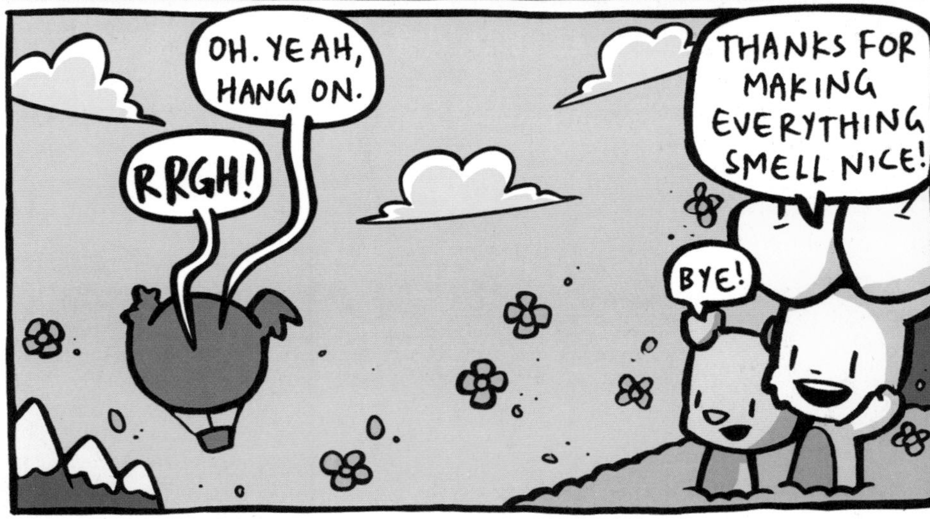
THANKS FOR MAKING EVERYTHING SMELL NICE!
OH. YEAH, HANG ON.
RRGH!
BYE!

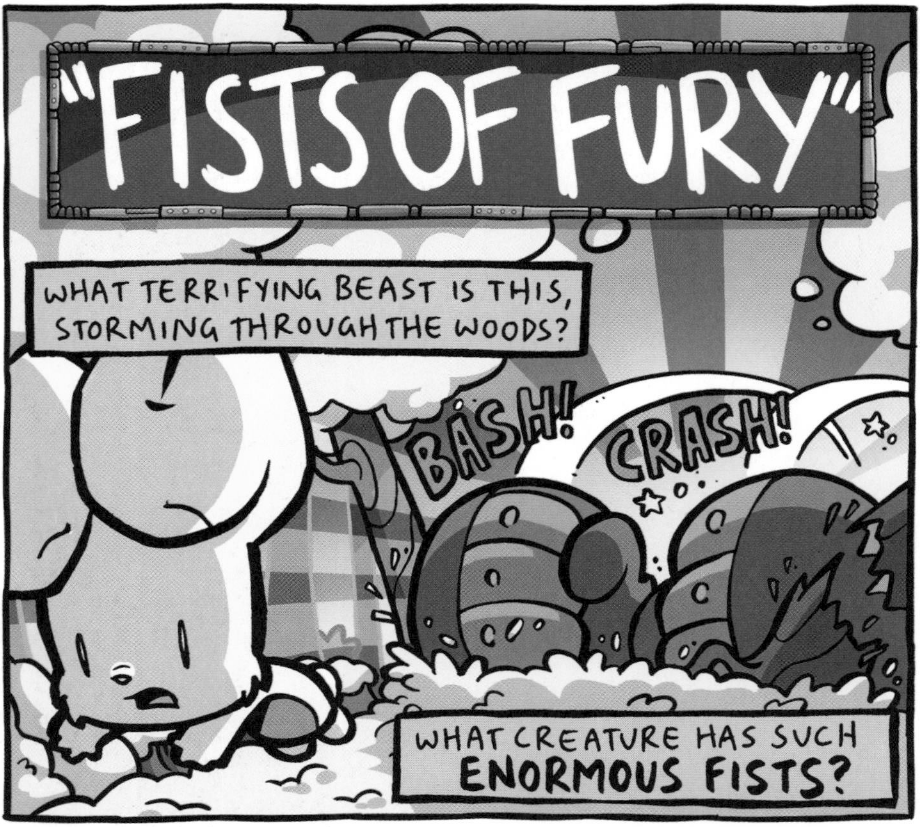
"FISTS OF FURY"
WHAT TERRIFYING BEAST IS THIS, STORMING THROUGH THE WOODS?
BASH!
CRASH!
WHAT CREATURE HAS SUCH ENORMOUS FISTS?

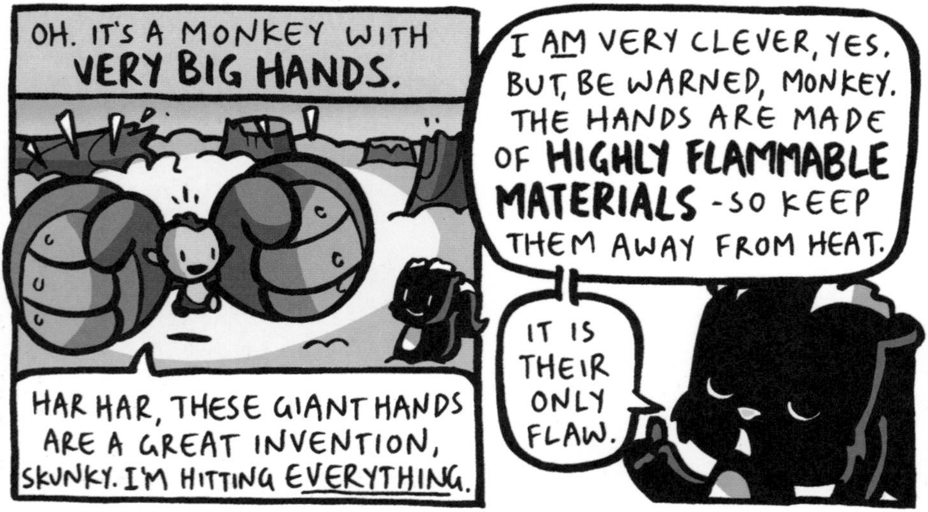
OH. IT'S A MONKEY WITH VERY BIG HANDS.
HAR HAR, THESE GIANT HANDS ARE A GREAT INVENTION, SKUNKY. I'M HITTING EVERYTHING.
I AM VERY CLEVER, YES. BUT, BE WARNED, MONKEY. THE HANDS ARE MADE OF HIGHLY FLAMMABLE MATERIALS - SO KEEP THEM AWAY FROM HEAT.
IT IS THEIR ONLY FLAW.

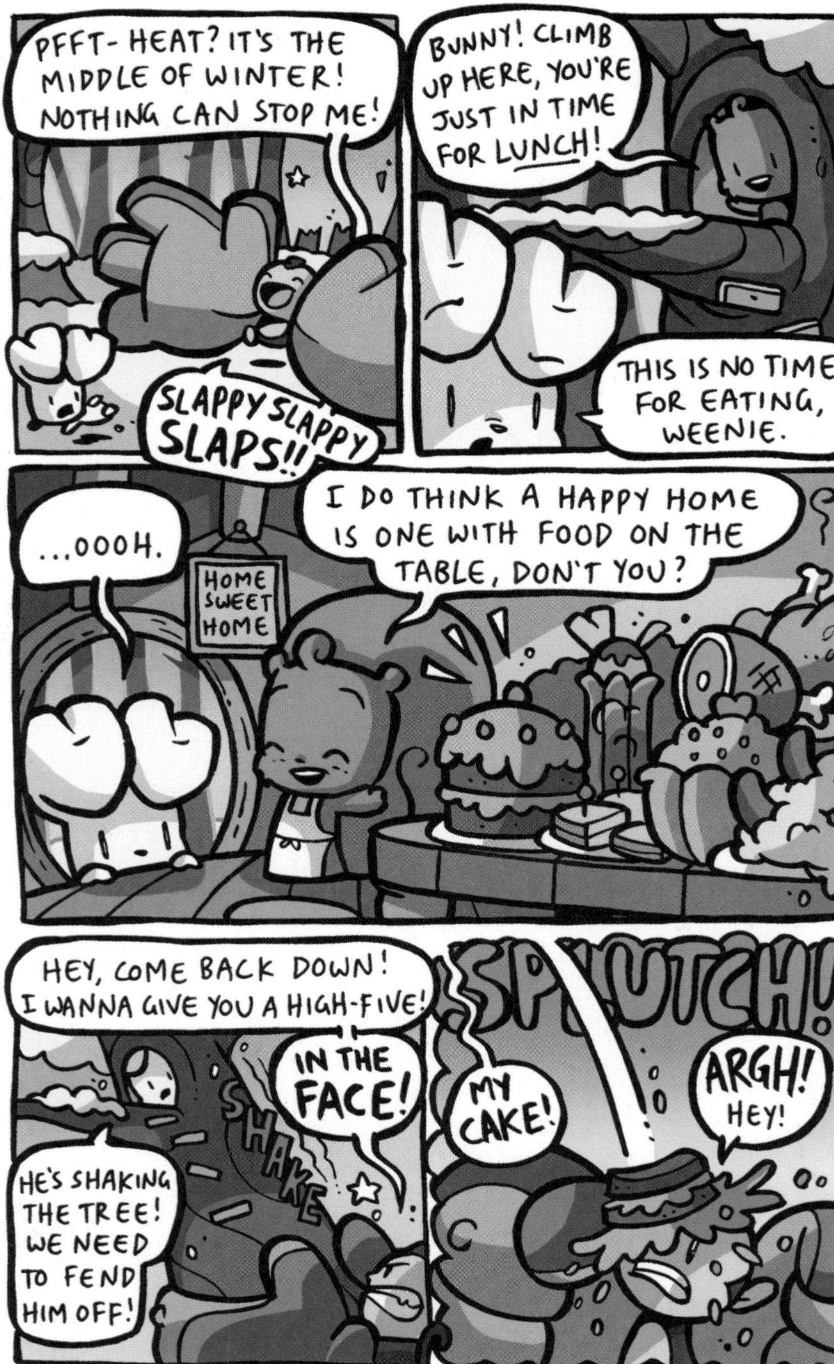
PFFT- HEAT? IT'S THE MIDDLE OF WINTER! NOTHING CAN STOP ME!
SLAPPY SLAPPY SLAPS!!
BUNNY! CLIMB UP HERE, YOU'RE JUST IN TIME FOR LUNCH!
THIS IS NO TIME FOR EATING, WEENIE.
...OOOH.
HOME SWEET HOME
I DO THINK A HAPPY HOME IS ONE WITH FOOD ON THE TABLE, DON'T YOU?
HEY, COME BACK DOWN! I WANNA GIVE YOU A HIGH-FIVE!
IN THE FACE!
SHAKE
HE'S SHAKING THE TREE! WE NEED TO FEND HIM OFF!
MY CAKE!
ARGH! HEY!

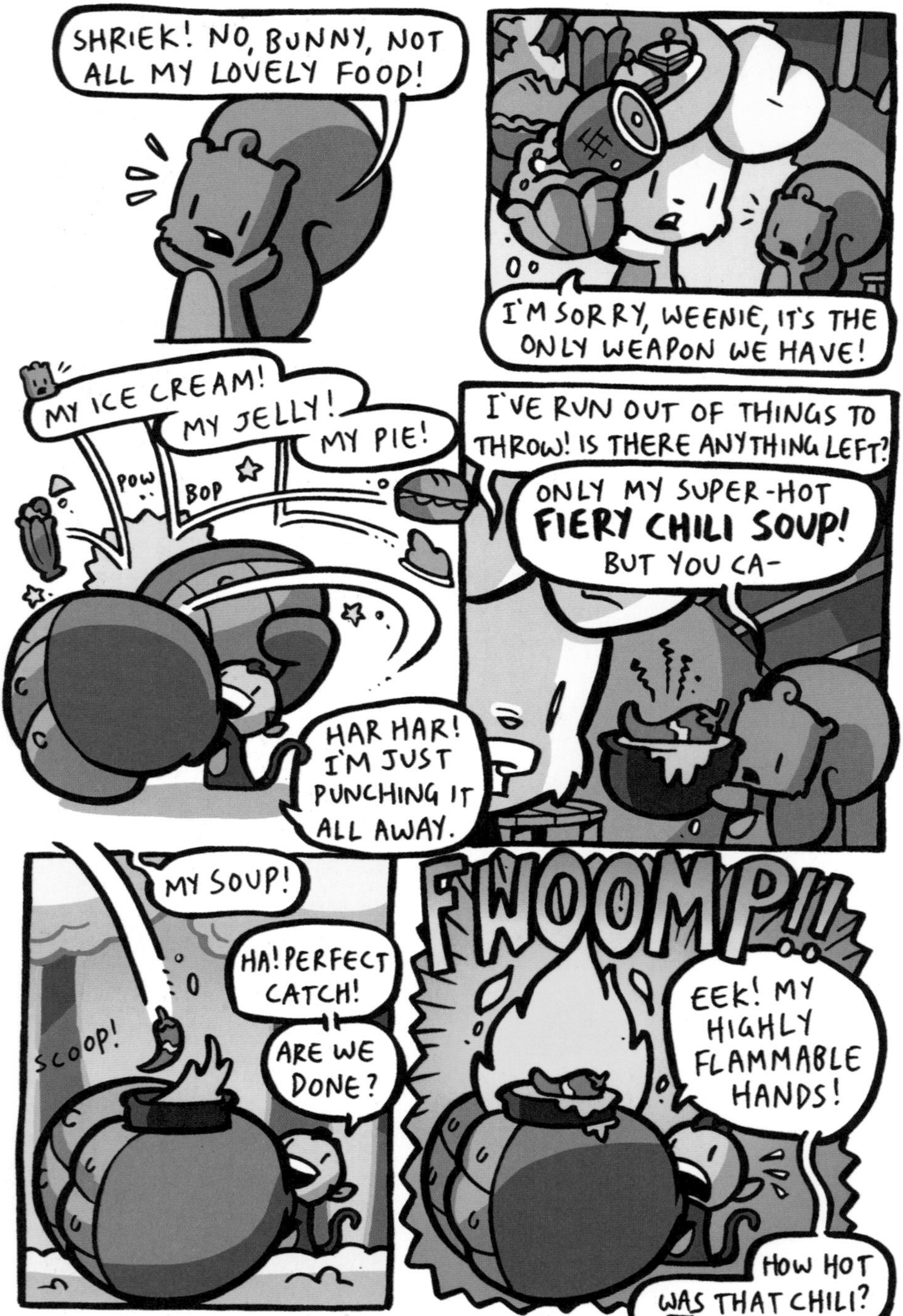
SHRIEK! NO, BUNNY, NOT ALL MY LOVELY FOOD!
I'M SORRY, WEENIE, IT'S THE ONLY WEAPON WE HAVE!
MY ICE CREAM!
MY JELLY!
MY PIE!
POW
BOP
HAR HAR! I'M JUST PUNCHING IT ALL AWAY.
I'VE RUN OUT OF THINGS TO THROW! IS THERE ANYTHING LEFT?
ONLY MY SUPER-HOT FIERY CHILI SOUP! BUT YOU CA-
MY SOUP!
HA! PERFECT CATCH!
ARE WE DONE?
SCOOP!
FWOOMP!!
EEK! MY HIGHLY FLAMMABLE HANDS!
HOW HOT WAS THAT CHILI?

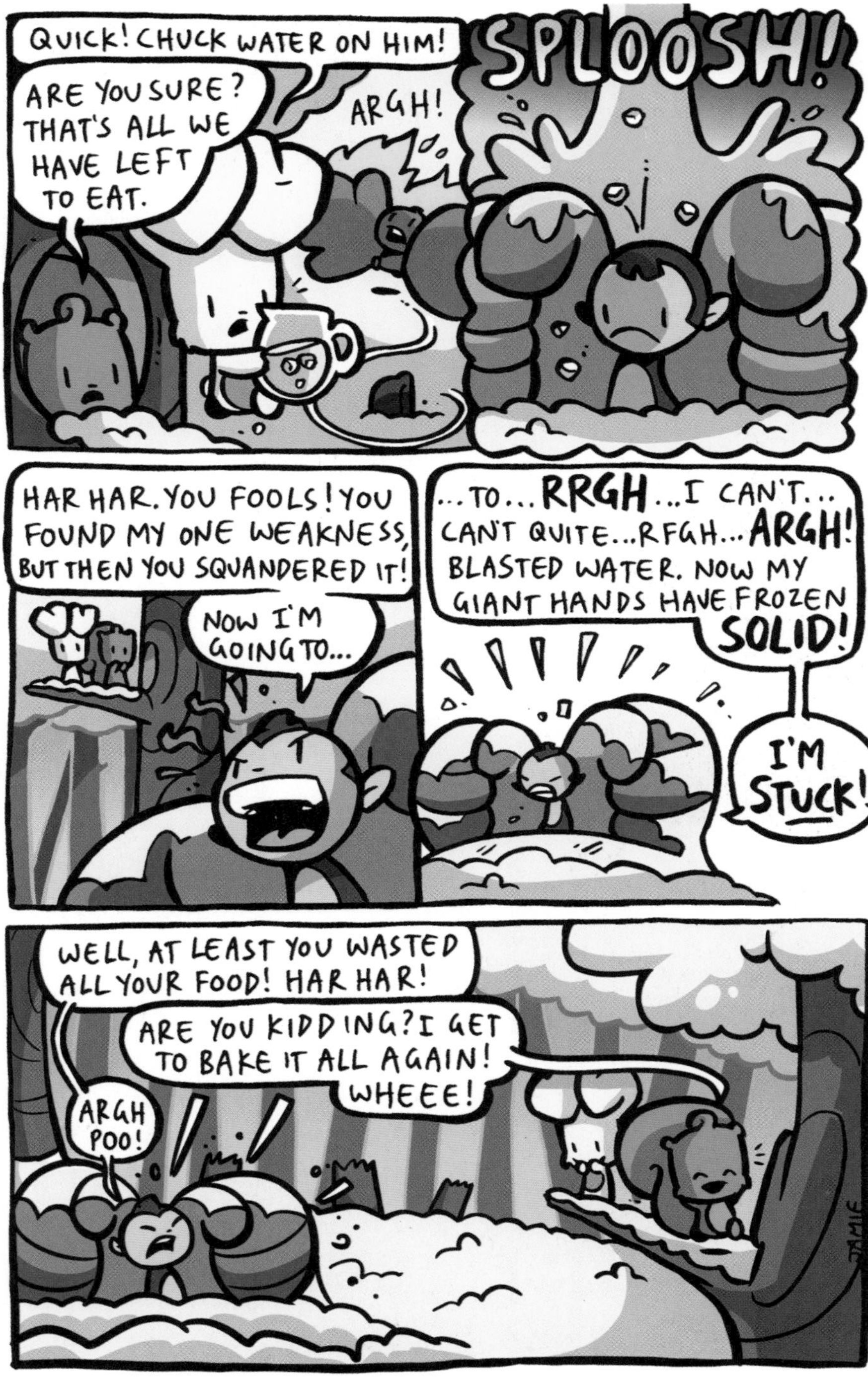
QUICK! CHUCK WATER ON HIM!
ARE YOU SURE? THAT'S ALL WE HAVE LEFT TO EAT.
ARGH!
SPLOOSH!
HAR HAR. YOU FOOLS! YOU FOUND MY ONE WEAKNESS, BUT THEN YOU SQUANDERED IT!
NOW I'M GOING TO...
...TO... RRGH ...I CAN'T... CAN'T QUITE...RFGH... ARGH! BLASTED WATER. NOW MY GIANT HANDS HAVE FROZEN SOLID!
I'M STUCK!
WELL, AT LEAST YOU WASTED ALL YOUR FOOD! HAR HAR!
ARE YOU KIDDING? I GET TO BAKE IT ALL AGAIN! WHEEE!
ARGH POO!
JAMIE

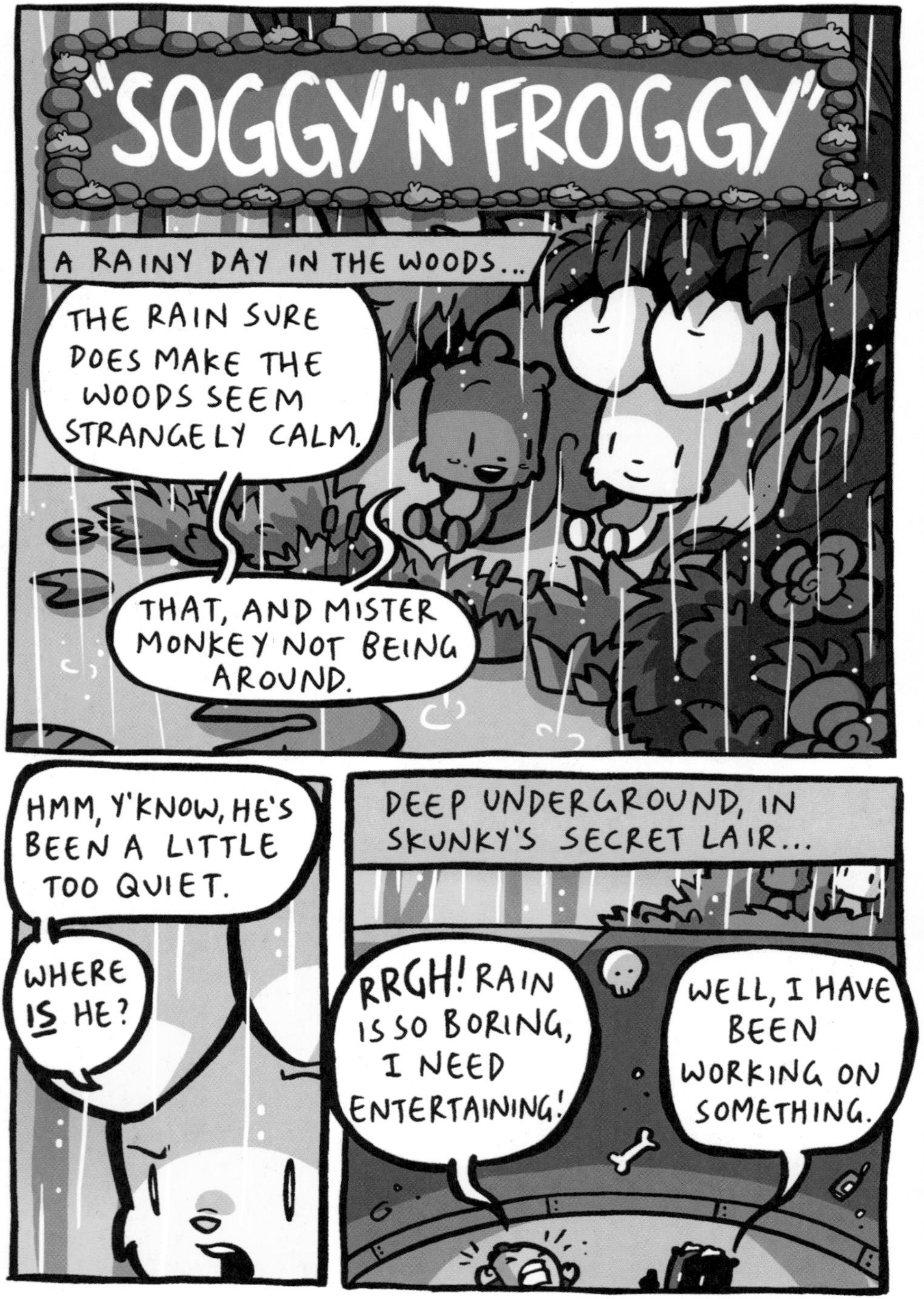
"SOGGY"N"FROGGY"
A RAINY DAY IN THE WOODS...
THE RAIN SURE DOES MAKE THE WOODS SEEM STRANGELY CALM.
THAT, AND MISTER MONKEY NOT BEING AROUND.
HMM, Y'KNOW, HE'S BEEN A LITTLE TOO QUIET.
WHERE IS HE?
DEEP UNDERGROUND, IN SKUNKY'S SECRET LAIR...
RRGH! RAIN IS SO BORING, I NEED ENTERTAINING!
WELL, I HAVE BEEN WORKING ON SOMETHING.

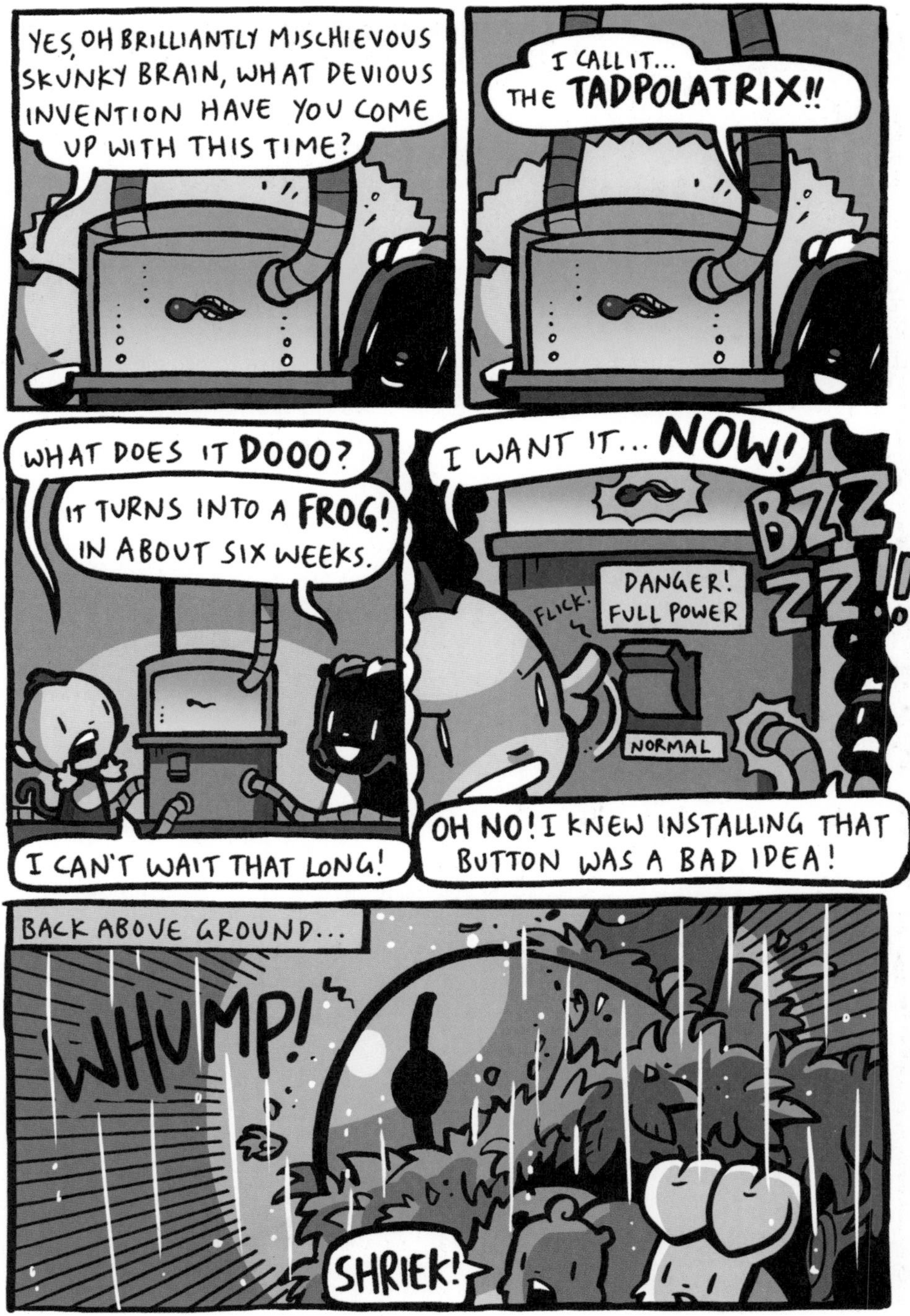
YES, OH BRILLIANTLY MISCHIEVOUS SKUNKY BRAIN, WHAT DEVIOUS INVENTION HAVE YOU COME UP WITH THIS TIME?
I CALL IT... THE TADPOLATRIX!!
WHAT DOES IT DOOO?
IT TURNS INTO A FROG! IN ABOUT SIX WEEKS.
I CAN'T WAIT THAT LONG!
I WANT IT... NOW!
DANGER! FULL POWER
FLICK!
NORMAL
BZZZZ!!
OH NO! I KNEW INSTALLING THAT BUTTON WAS A BAD IDEA!
BACK ABOVE GROUND...
WHUMP!
SHRIEK!

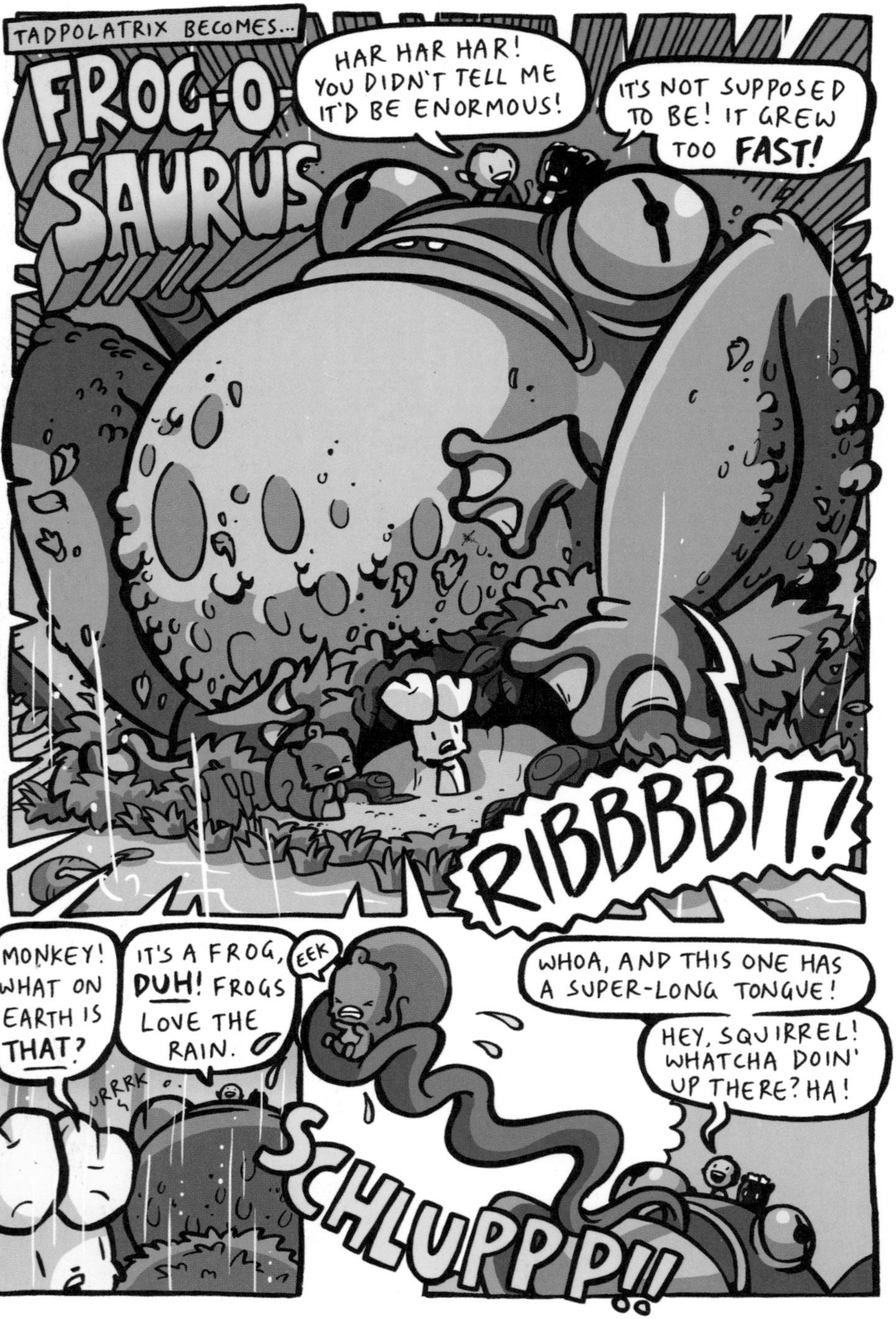
TADPOLATRIX BECOMES...
FROG-O-SAURUS
HAR HAR HAR! YOU DIDN'T TELL ME IT'D BE ENORMOUS!
IT'S NOT SUPPOSED TO BE! IT GREW TOO **FAST!**
RIBBBBIT!
MONKEY! WHAT ON EARTH IS THAT?
IT'S A FROG, DUH! FROGS LOVE THE RAIN.
EEK
URRRK
WHOA, AND THIS ONE HAS A SUPER-LONG TONGUE!
HEY, SQUIRREL! WHATCHA DOIN' UP THERE? HA!
SCHLUPPP!!

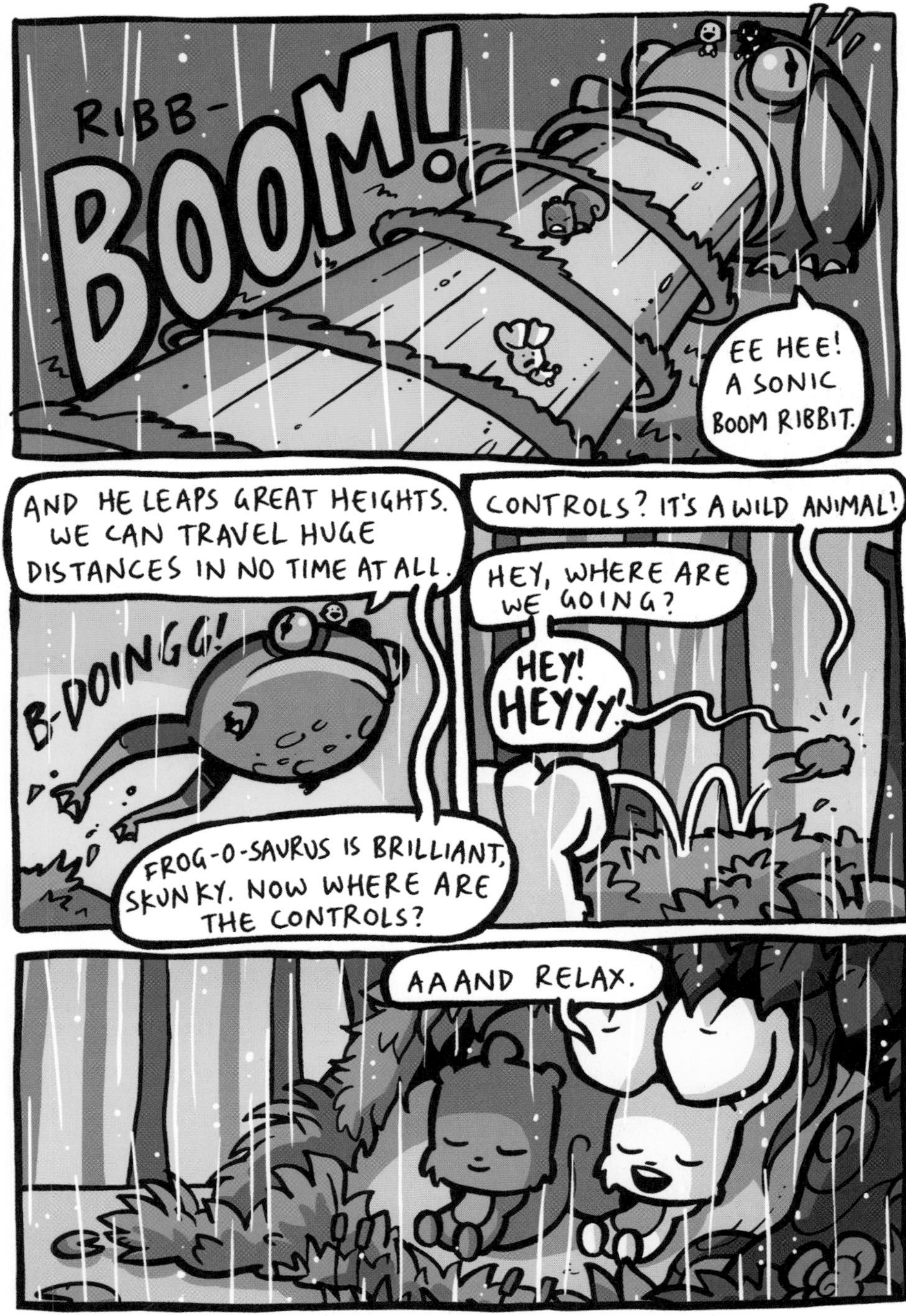
RIBB-
BOOM!
EE HEE! A SONIC BOOM RIBBIT.
AND HE LEAPS GREAT HEIGHTS. WE CAN TRAVEL HUGE DISTANCES IN NO TIME AT ALL.
B-DOINGG!
FROG-O-SAURUS IS BRILLIANT, SKUNKY. NOW WHERE ARE THE CONTROLS?
CONTROLS? IT'S A WILD ANIMAL!
HEY, WHERE ARE WE GOING?
HEY! HEYYY!
AAAND RELAX.

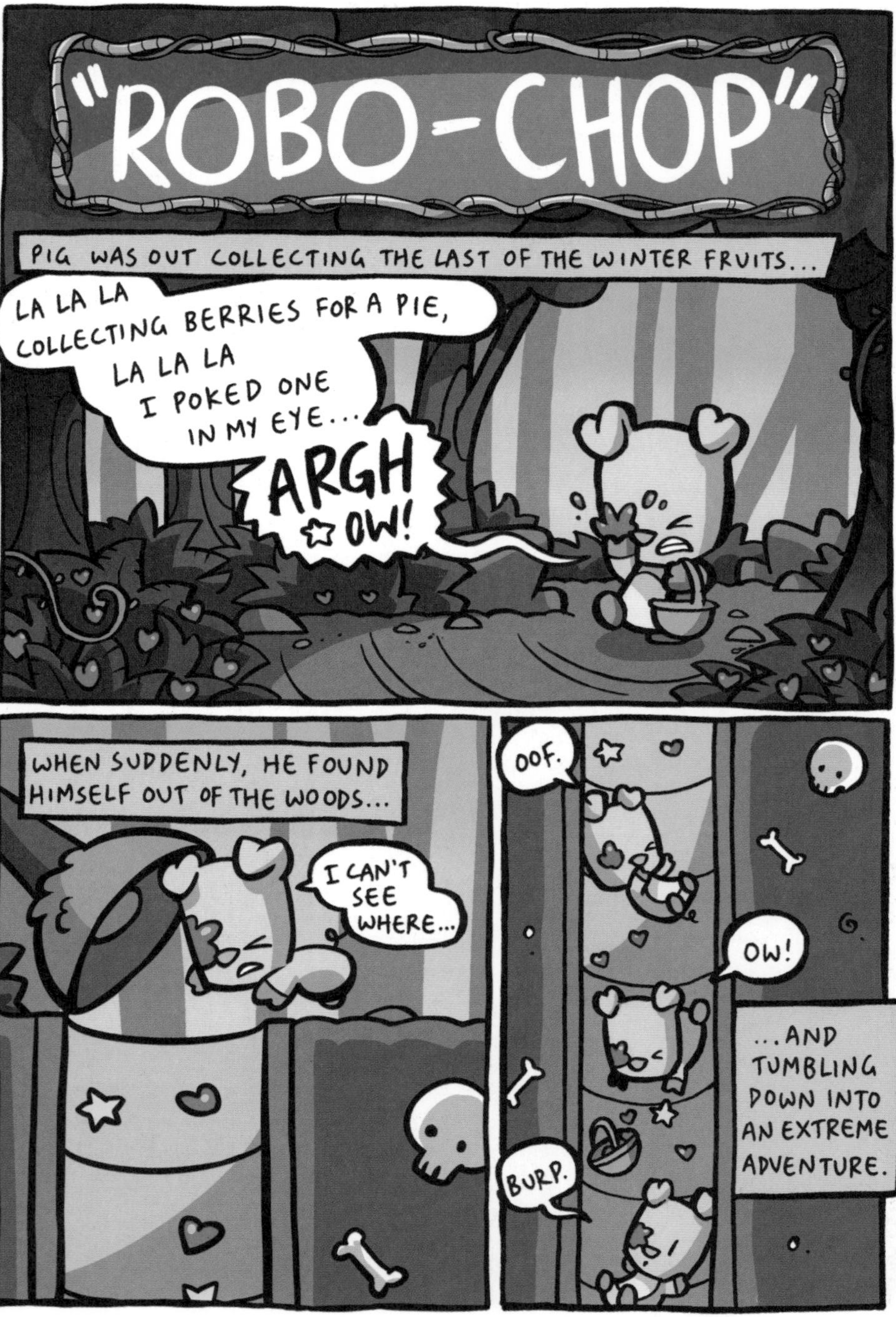
"ROBO-CHOP"
PIG WAS OUT COLLECTING THE LAST OF THE WINTER FRUITS...
LA LA LA
COLLECTING BERRIES FOR A PIE,
LA LA LA
I POKED ONE
IN MY EYE...
ARGH
OW!
WHEN SUDDENLY, HE FOUND HIMSELF OUT OF THE WOODS...
I CAN'T SEE WHERE...
OOF.
OW!
...AND TUMBLING DOWN INTO AN EXTREME ADVENTURE.
BURP.

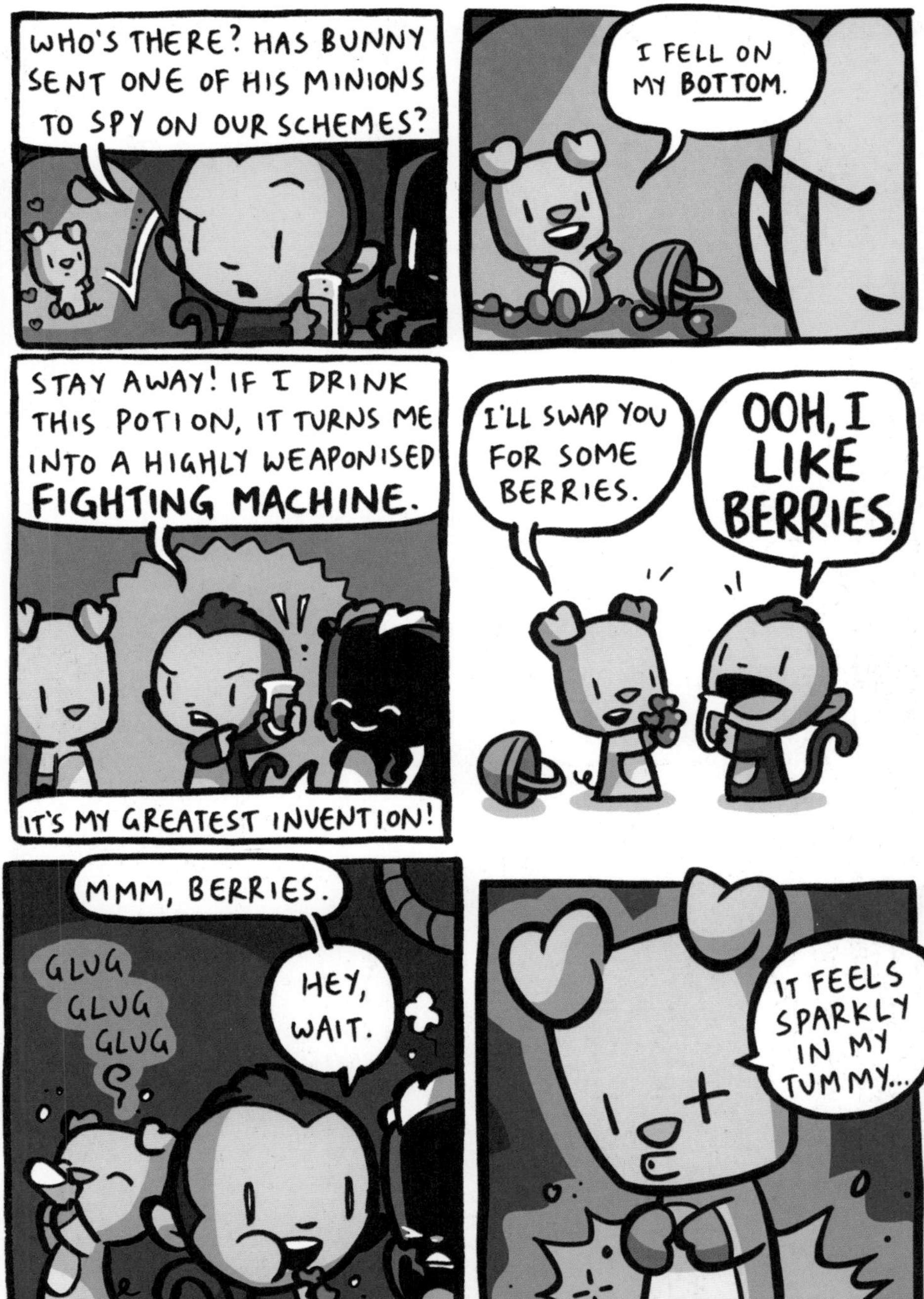
WHO'S THERE? HAS BUNNY SENT ONE OF HIS MINIONS TO SPY ON OUR SCHEMES?
I FELL ON MY BOTTOM.
STAY AWAY! IF I DRINK THIS POTION, IT TURNS ME INTO A HIGHLY WEAPONISED FIGHTING MACHINE.
IT'S MY GREATEST INVENTION!
I'LL SWAP YOU FOR SOME BERRIES.
OOH, I LIKE BERRIES.
MMM, BERRIES.
GLUG GLUG GLUG
HEY, WAIT.
IT FEELS SPARKLY IN MY TUMMY...

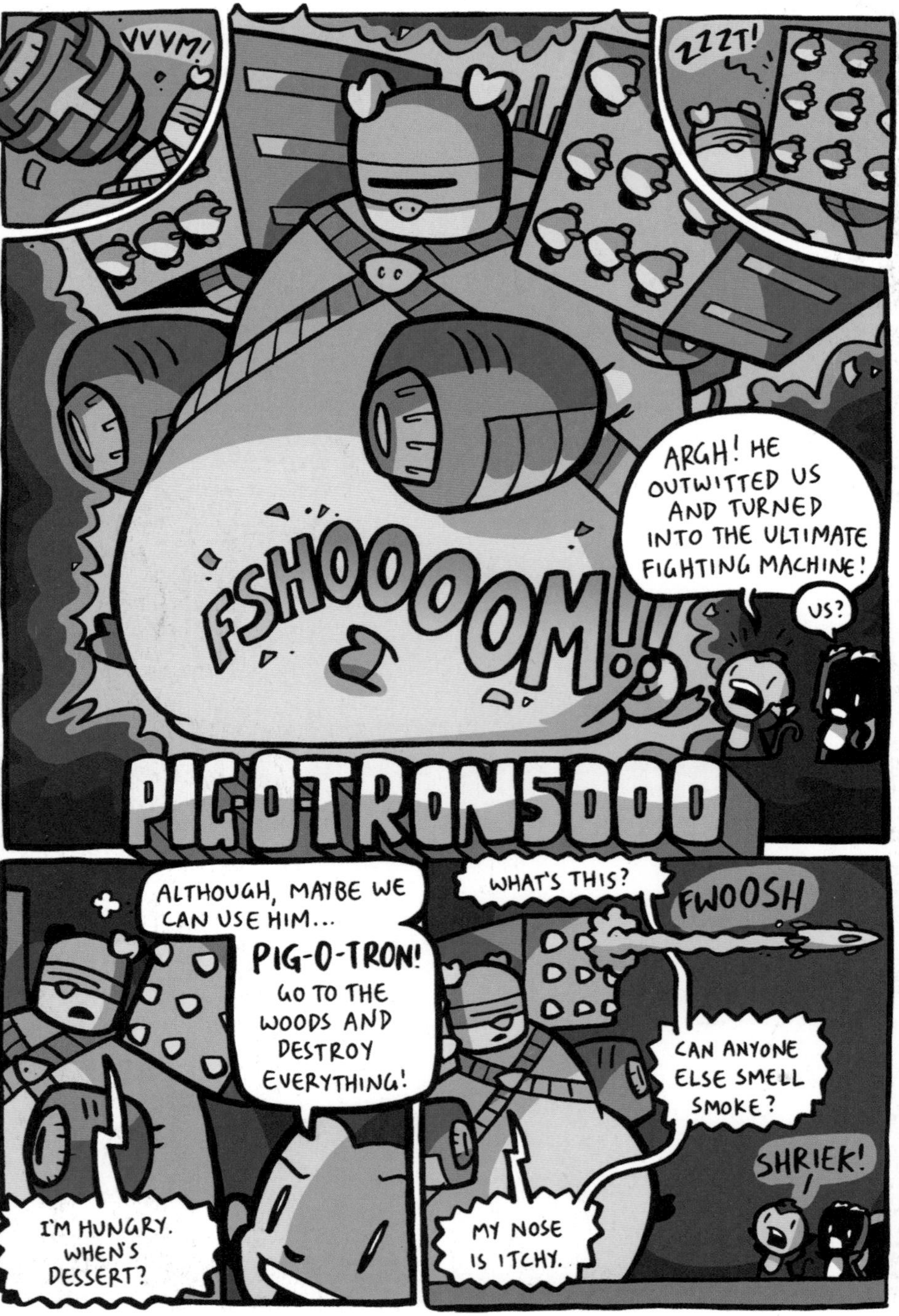
VVVM!
ZZZT!
FSHOOOOM!!!
ARGH! HE OUTWITTED US AND TURNED INTO THE ULTIMATE FIGHTING MACHINE!
US?
PIG-O-TRON 5000
ALTHOUGH, MAYBE WE CAN USE HIM...
PIG-O-TRON! GO TO THE WOODS AND DESTROY EVERYTHING!
I'M HUNGRY. WHEN'S DESSERT?
WHAT'S THIS?
FWOOSH
CAN ANYONE ELSE SMELL SMOKE?
MY NOSE IS ITCHY.
SHRIEK!

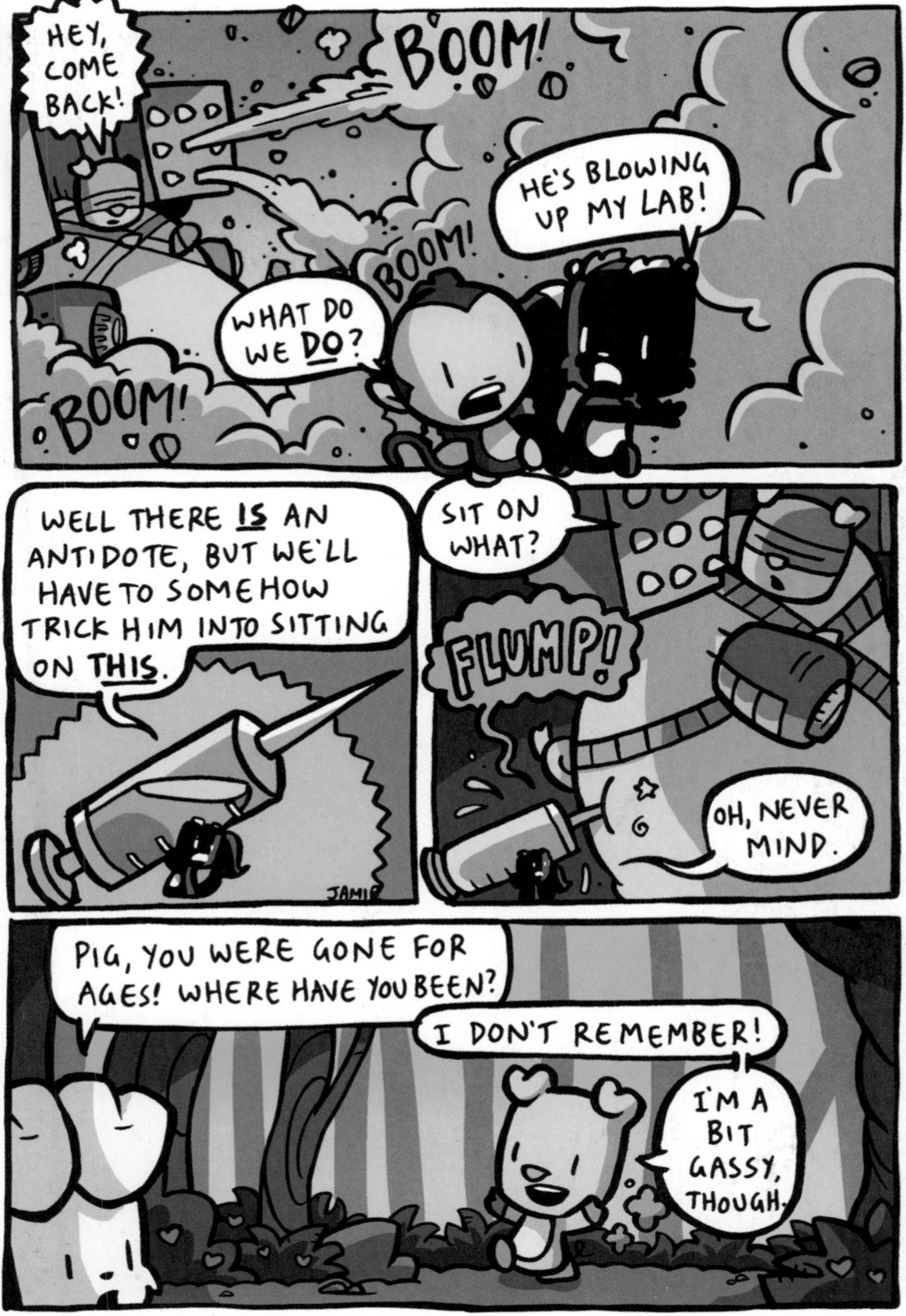
HEY, COME BACK!
BOOM!
HE'S BLOWING UP MY LAB!
BOOM!
WHAT DO WE DO?
BOOM!
WELL THERE IS AN ANTIDOTE, BUT WE'LL HAVE TO SOMEHOW TRICK HIM INTO SITTING ON THIS.
JAMIE
SIT ON WHAT?
FLUMP!
OH, NEVER MIND.
PIG, YOU WERE GONE FOR AGES! WHERE HAVE YOU BEEN?
I DON'T REMEMBER!
I'M A BIT GASSY, THOUGH.

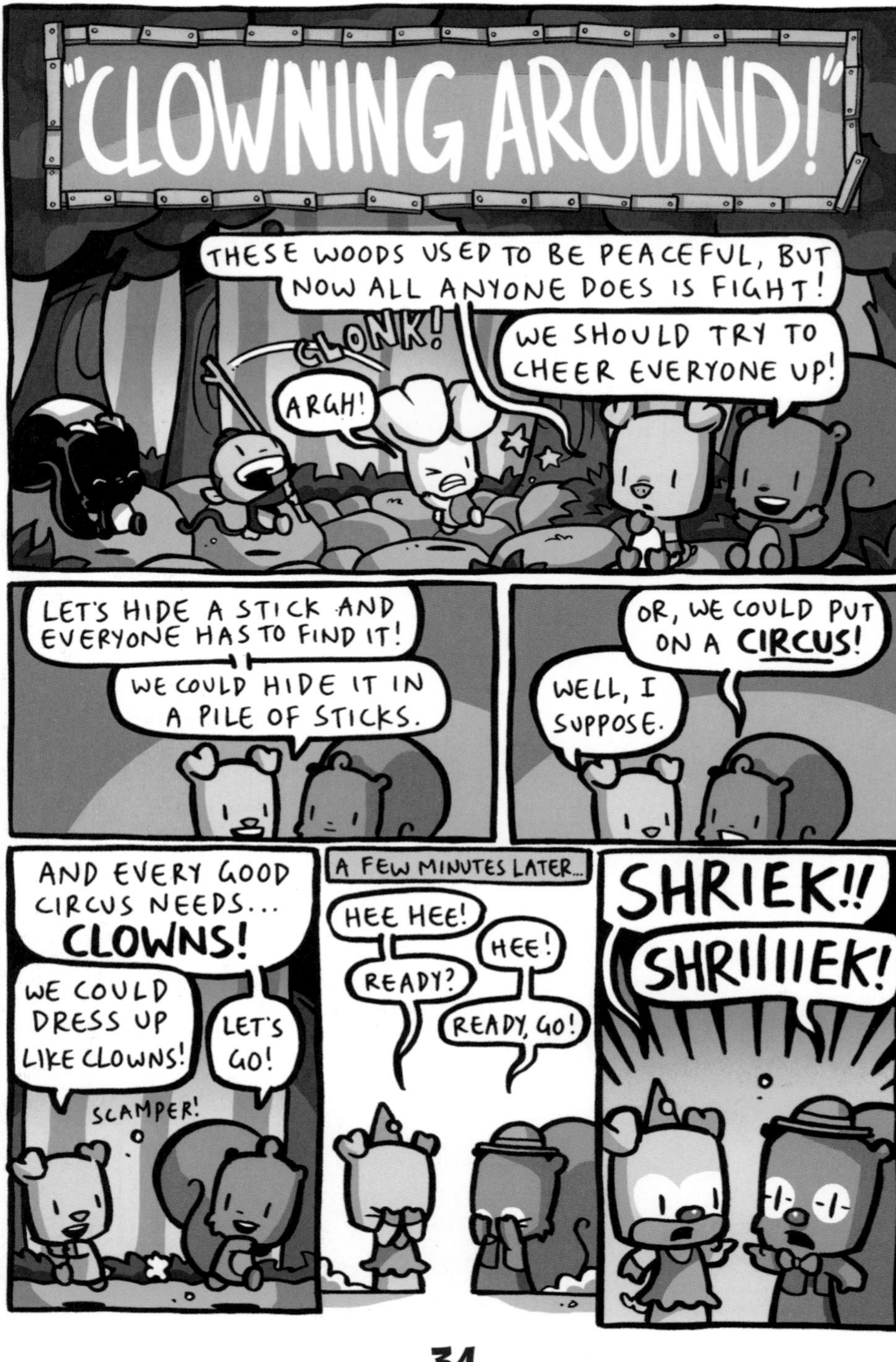
"CLOWNING AROUND!"
THESE WOODS USED TO BE PEACEFUL, BUT NOW ALL ANYONE DOES IS FIGHT!
CLONK!
ARGH!
WE SHOULD TRY TO CHEER EVERYONE UP!
LET'S HIDE A STICK AND EVERYONE HAS TO FIND IT!
WE COULD HIDE IT IN A PILE OF STICKS.
OR, WE COULD PUT ON A CIRCUS!
WELL, I SUPPOSE.
AND EVERY GOOD CIRCUS NEEDS... CLOWNS!
WE COULD DRESS UP LIKE CLOWNS!
LET'S GO!
SCAMPER!
A FEW MINUTES LATER...
HEE HEE!
READY?
HEE!
READY, GO!
SHRIEK!!
SHRIIIIEK!

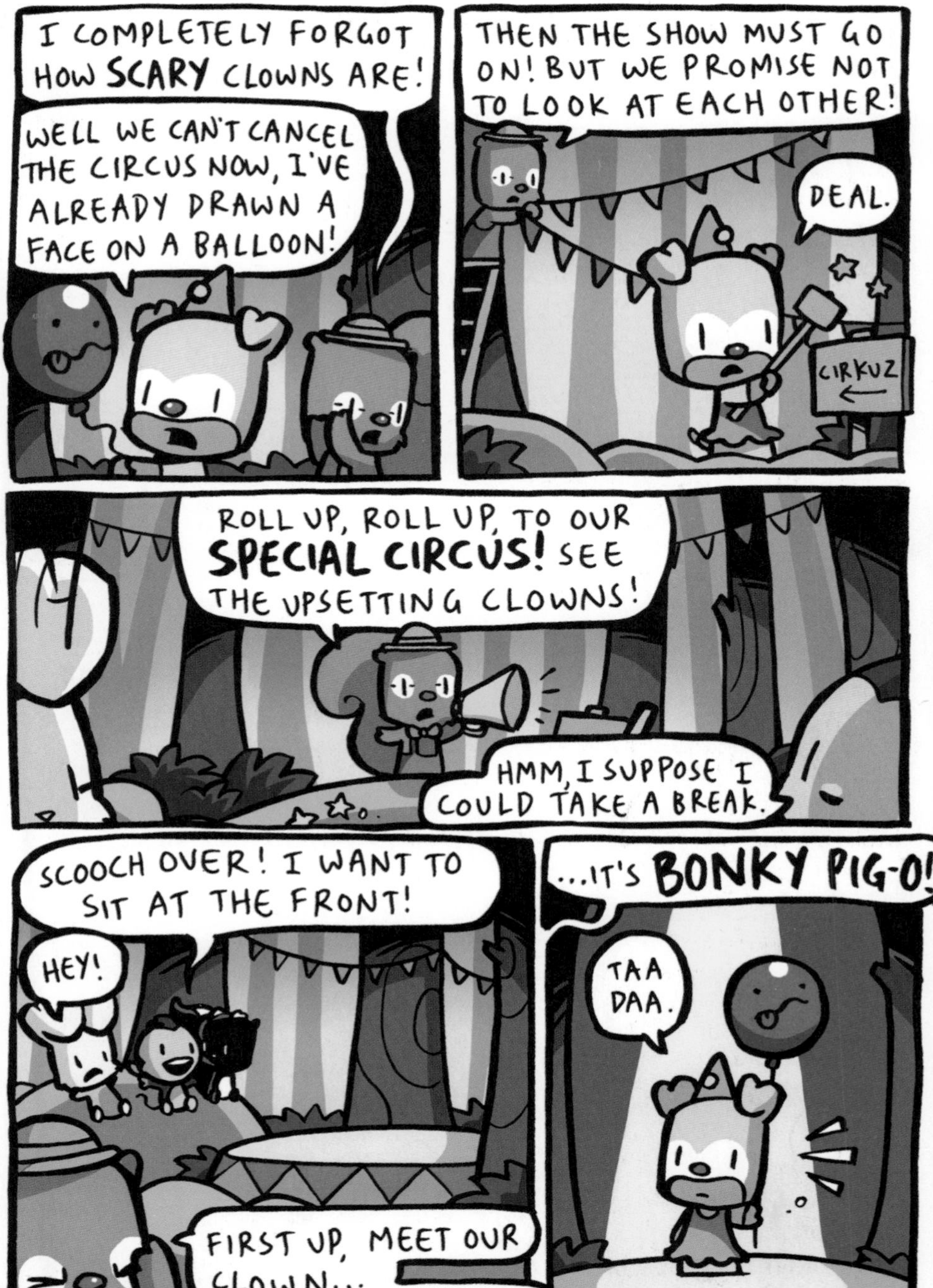
I COMPLETELY FORGOT HOW SCARY CLOWNS ARE!
WELL WE CAN'T CANCEL THE CIRCUS NOW, I'VE ALREADY DRAWN A FACE ON A BALLOON!
THEN THE SHOW MUST GO ON! BUT WE PROMISE NOT TO LOOK AT EACH OTHER!
DEAL.
CIRKUZ
ROLL UP, ROLL UP, TO OUR SPECIAL CIRCUS! SEE THE UPSETTING CLOWNS!
HMM, I SUPPOSE I COULD TAKE A BREAK.
SCOOCH OVER! I WANT TO SIT AT THE FRONT!
HEY!
FIRST UP, MEET OUR CLOWN...
I CAN'T LOOK...
...IT'S BONKY PIG-O!
TAA DAA.

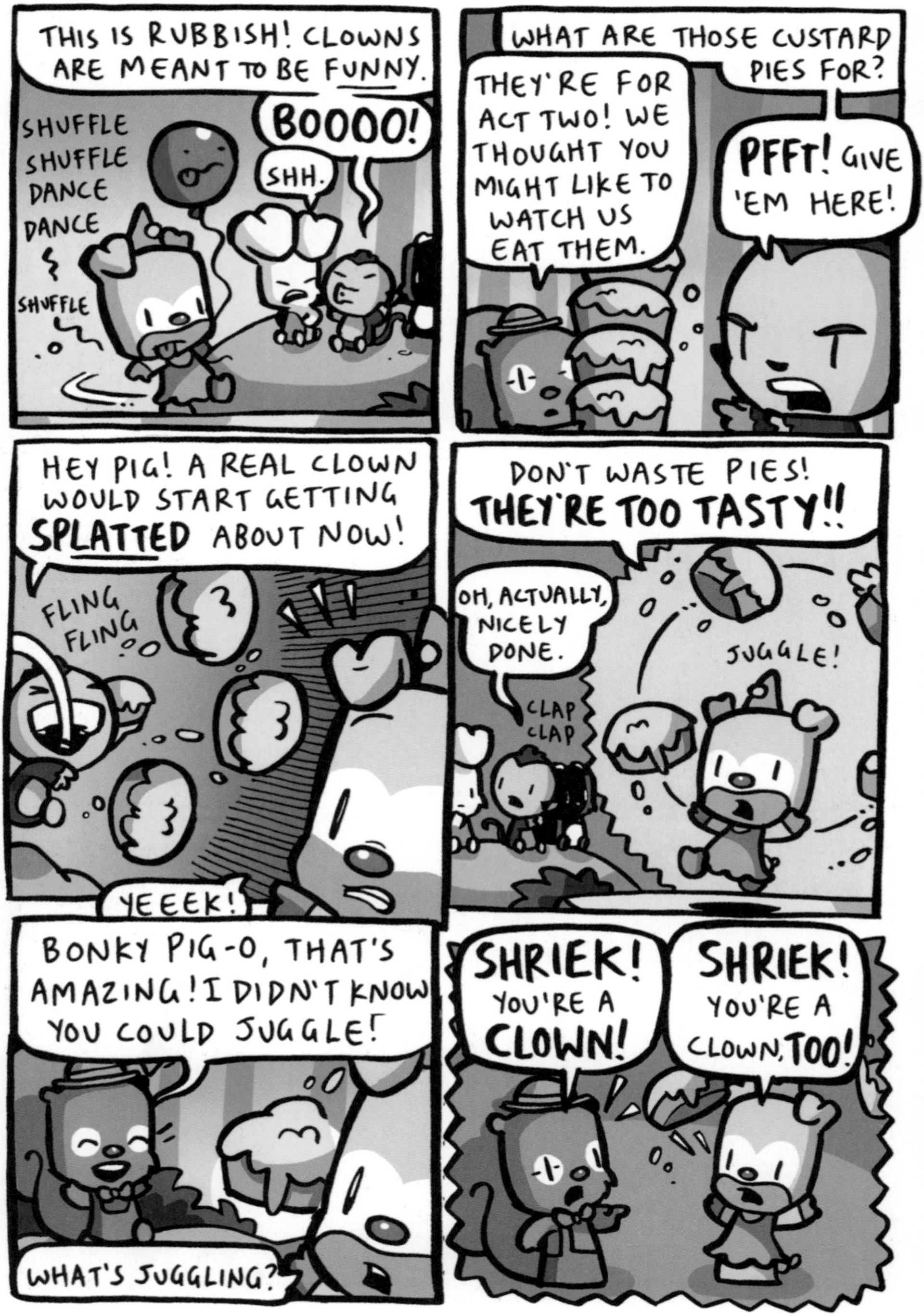
THIS IS RUBBISH! CLOWNS ARE MEANT TO BE FUNNY.
SHUFFLE SHUFFLE DANCE DANCE SHUFFLE
BOOOO!
SHH.
WHAT ARE THOSE CUSTARD PIES FOR?
THEY'RE FOR ACT TWO! WE THOUGHT YOU MIGHT LIKE TO WATCH US EAT THEM.
PFFT! GIVE 'EM HERE!
HEY PIG! A REAL CLOWN WOULD START GETTING SPLATTED ABOUT NOW!
FLING FLING
YEEEK!
DON'T WASTE PIES! THEY'RE TOO TASTY!!
OH, ACTUALLY, NICELY DONE.
CLAP CLAP
JUGGLE!
BONKY PIG-O, THAT'S AMAZING! I DIDN'T KNOW YOU COULD JUGGLE!
WHAT'S JUGGLING?
SHRIEK! YOU'RE A CLOWN!
SHRIEK! YOU'RE A CLOWN, TOO!

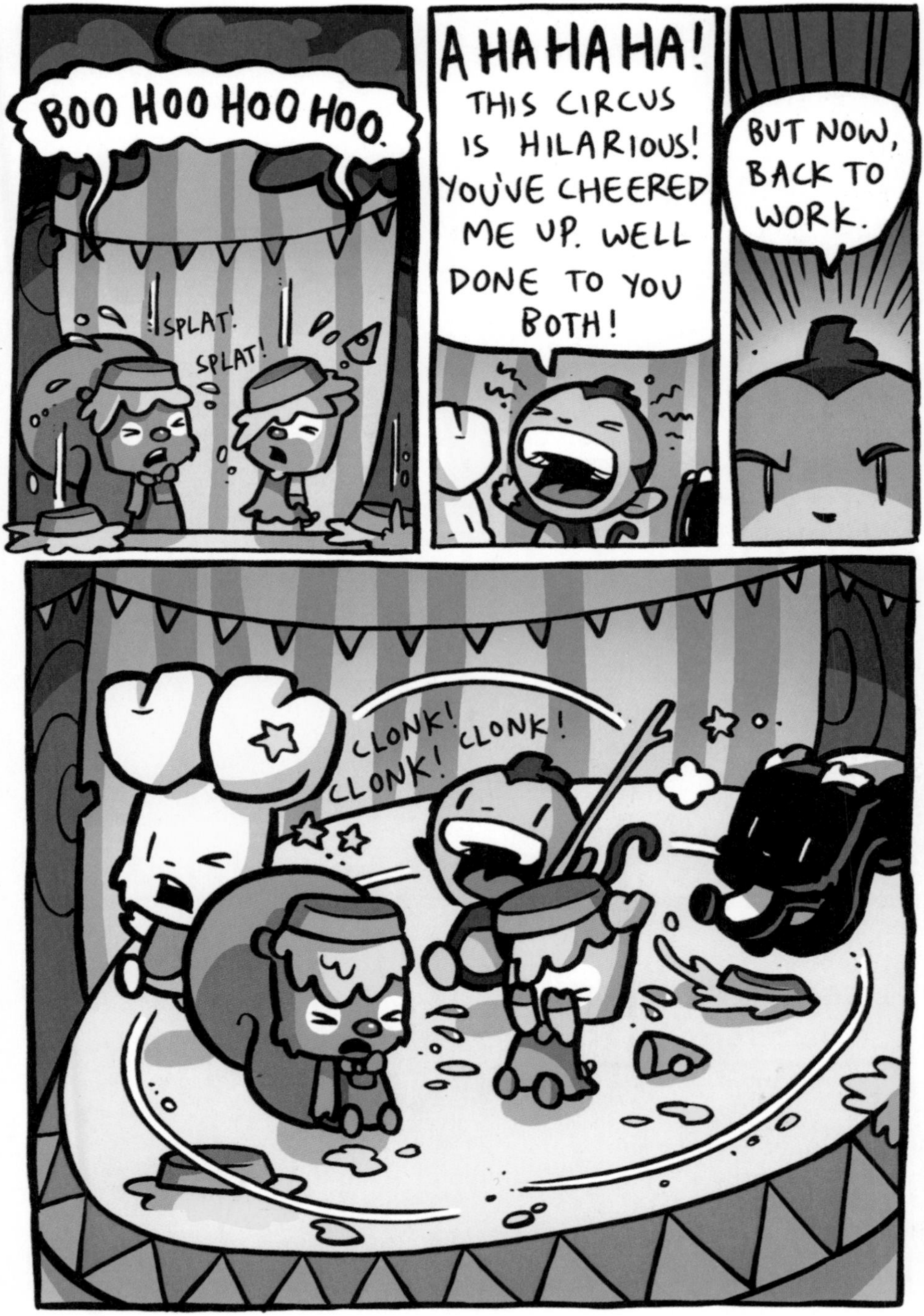
BOO HOO HOO HOO.
SPLAT!
SPLAT!
A HA HA HA HA! THIS CIRCUS IS HILARIOUS! YOU'VE CHEERED ME UP. WELL DONE TO YOU BOTH!
BUT NOW, BACK TO WORK.
CLONK! CLONK! CLONK!

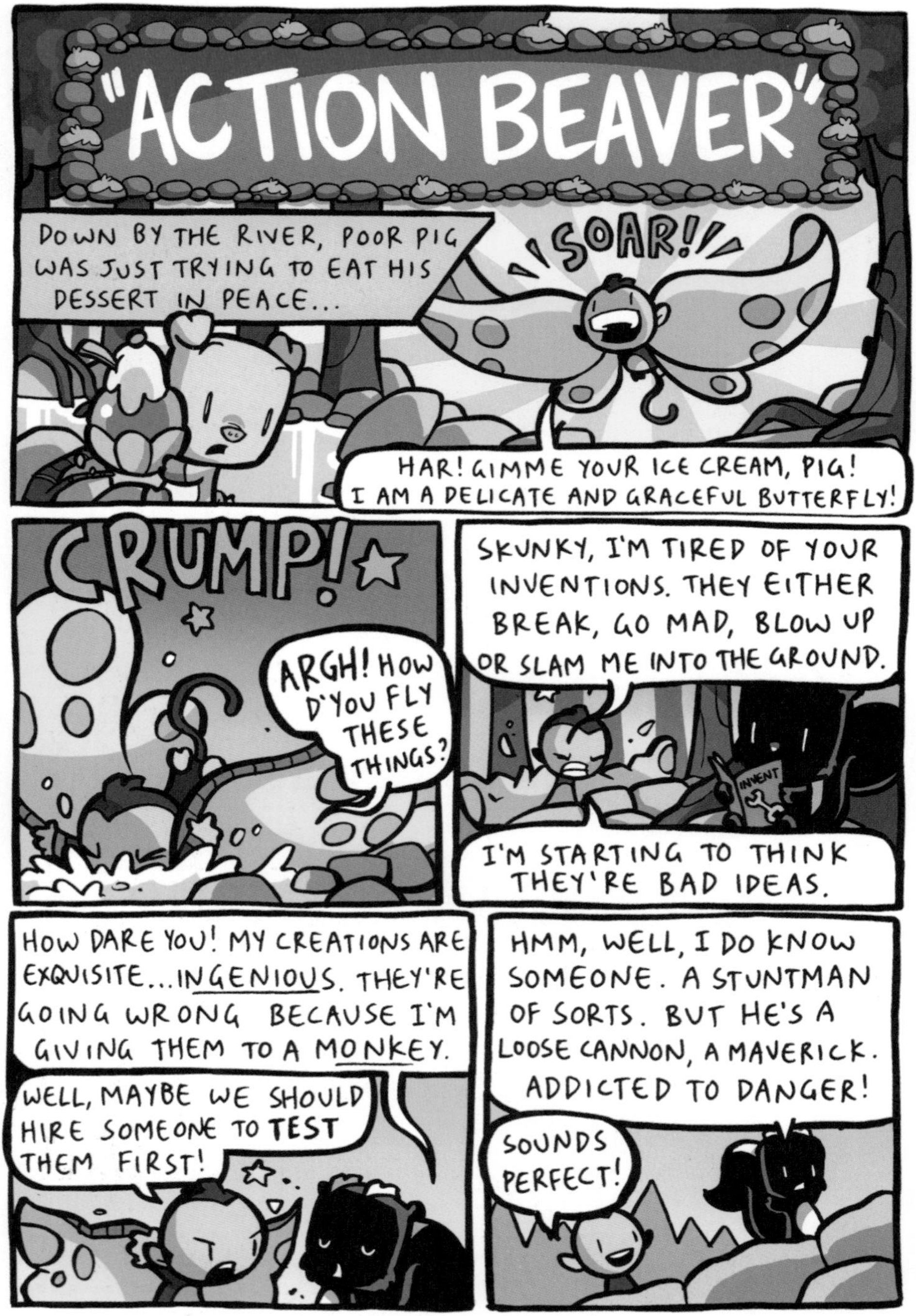
"ACTION BEAVER"
DOWN BY THE RIVER, POOR PIG WAS JUST TRYING TO EAT HIS DESSERT IN PEACE...
SOAR!
HAR! GIMME YOUR ICE CREAM, PIG! I AM A DELICATE AND GRACEFUL BUTTERFLY!
CRUMP!
ARGH! HOW D'YOU FLY THESE THINGS?
SKUNKY, I'M TIRED OF YOUR INVENTIONS. THEY EITHER BREAK, GO MAD, BLOW UP OR SLAM ME INTO THE GROUND.
INVENT
I'M STARTING TO THINK THEY'RE BAD IDEAS.
HOW DARE YOU! MY CREATIONS ARE EXQUISITE...INGENIOUS. THEY'RE GOING WRONG BECAUSE I'M GIVING THEM TO A MONKEY.
WELL, MAYBE WE SHOULD HIRE SOMEONE TO TEST THEM FIRST!
HMM, WELL, I DO KNOW SOMEONE. A STUNTMAN OF SORTS. BUT HE'S A LOOSE CANNON, A MAVERICK. ADDICTED TO DANGER!
SOUNDS PERFECT!

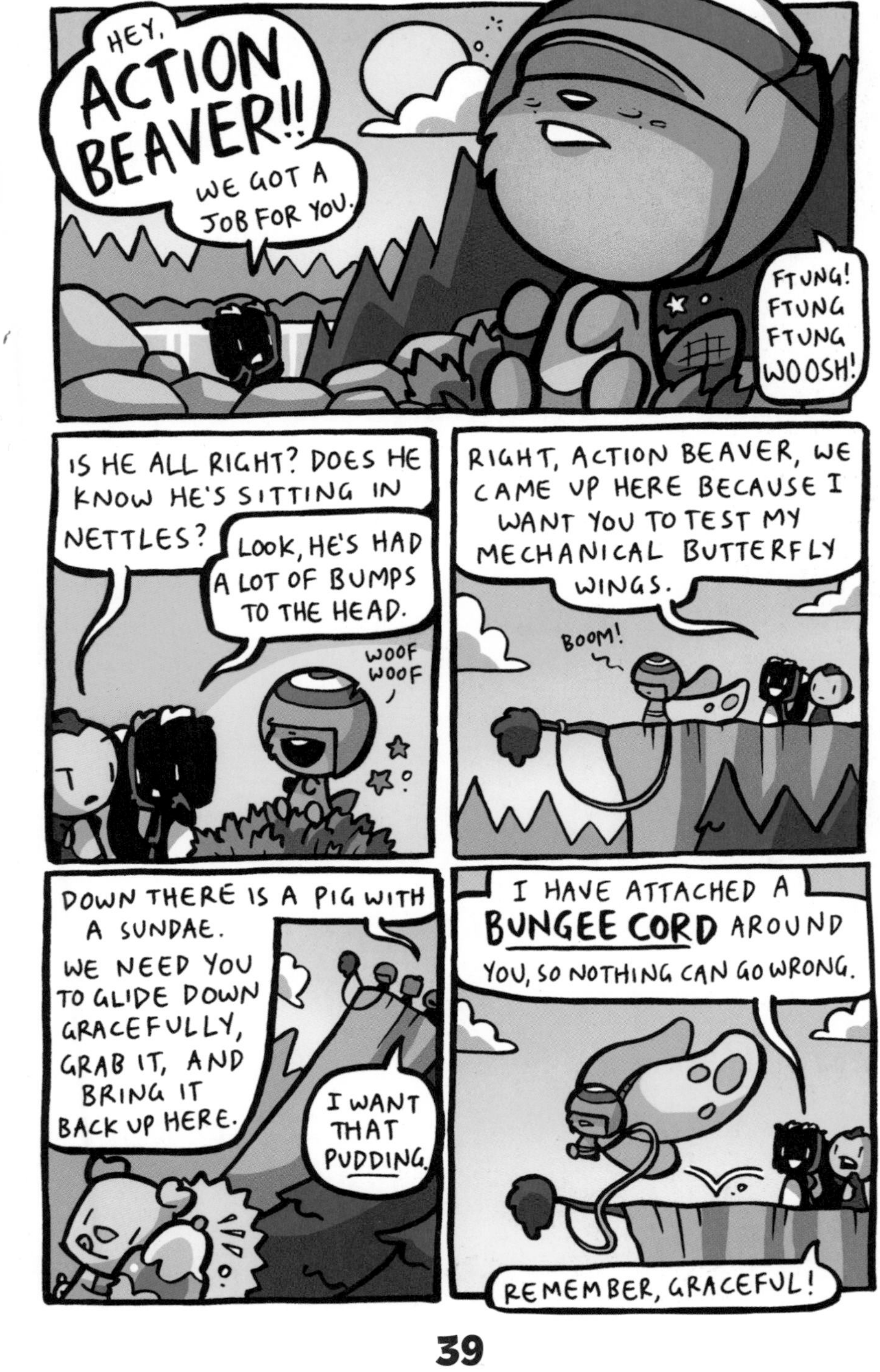

HEY, ACTION BEAVER!!
WE GOT A JOB FOR YOU.
FTUNG! FTUNG FTUNG WOOSH!
IS HE ALL RIGHT? DOES HE KNOW HE'S SITTING IN NETTLES?
LOOK, HE'S HAD A LOT OF BUMPS TO THE HEAD.
WOOF WOOF
RIGHT, ACTION BEAVER, WE CAME UP HERE BECAUSE I WANT YOU TO TEST MY MECHANICAL BUTTERFLY WINGS.
BOOM!
DOWN THERE IS A PIG WITH A SUNDAE.
WE NEED YOU TO GLIDE DOWN GRACEFULLY, GRAB IT, AND BRING IT BACK UP HERE.
I WANT THAT PUDDING.
I HAVE ATTACHED A BUNGEE CORD AROUND YOU, SO NOTHING CAN GO WRONG.
REMEMBER, GRACEFUL!

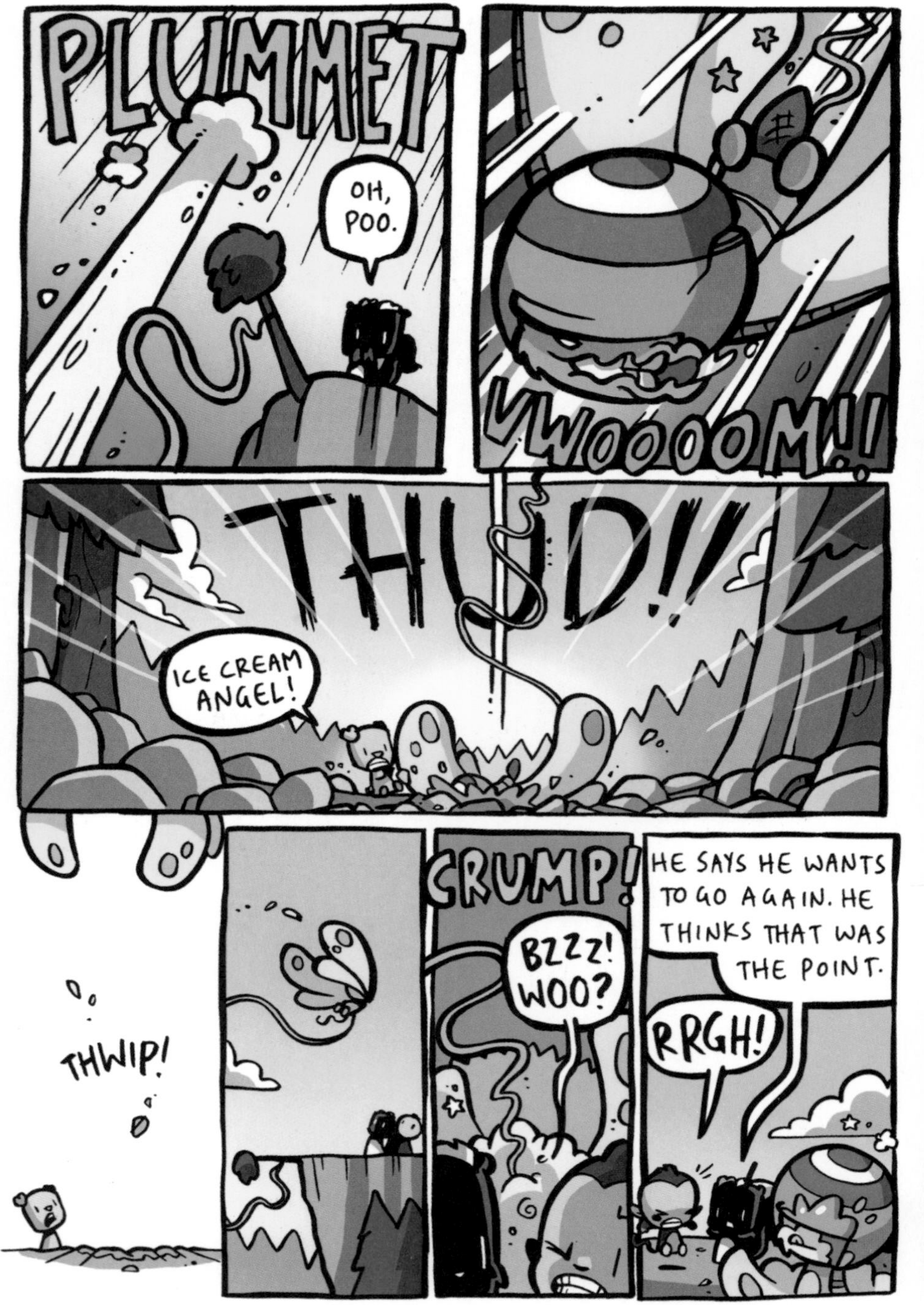
PLUMMET
OH, POO.
VWOOOOM!!
THUD!!
ICE CREAM ANGEL!
THWIP!
CRUMP!
BZZZ! WOO?
HE SAYS HE WANTS TO GO AGAIN. HE THINKS THAT WAS THE POINT.
RRGH!

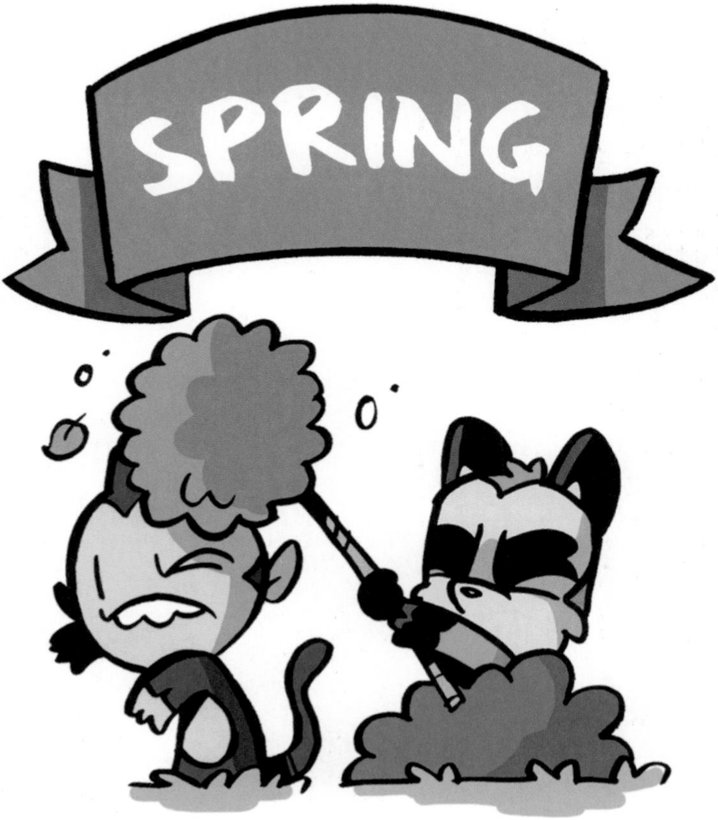
SPRING

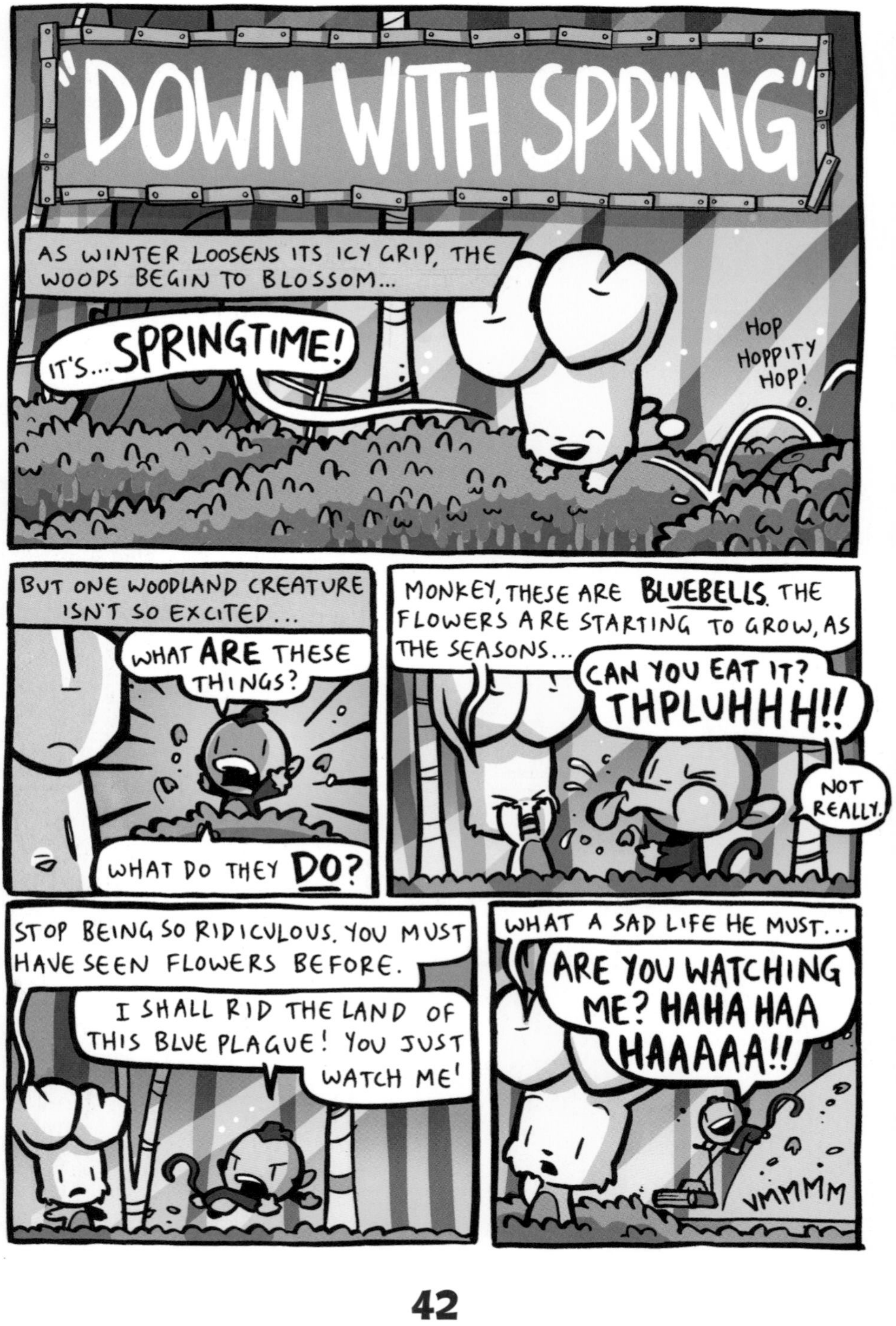
"DOWN WITH SPRING"
AS WINTER LOOSENS ITS ICY GRIP, THE WOODS BEGIN TO BLOSSOM...
IT'S... SPRINGTIME!
HOP HOPPITY HOP!
BUT ONE WOODLAND CREATURE ISN'T SO EXCITED...
WHAT ARE THESE THINGS?
WHAT DO THEY DO?
MONKEY, THESE ARE BLUEBELLS. THE FLOWERS ARE STARTING TO GROW, AS THE SEASONS...
CAN YOU EAT IT? THPLUHHH!!
NOT REALLY.
STOP BEING SO RIDICULOUS. YOU MUST HAVE SEEN FLOWERS BEFORE.
I SHALL RID THE LAND OF THIS BLUE PLAGUE! YOU JUST WATCH ME!
WHAT A SAD LIFE HE MUST...
ARE YOU WATCHING ME? HAHA HAA HAAAAA!!
VMMMM

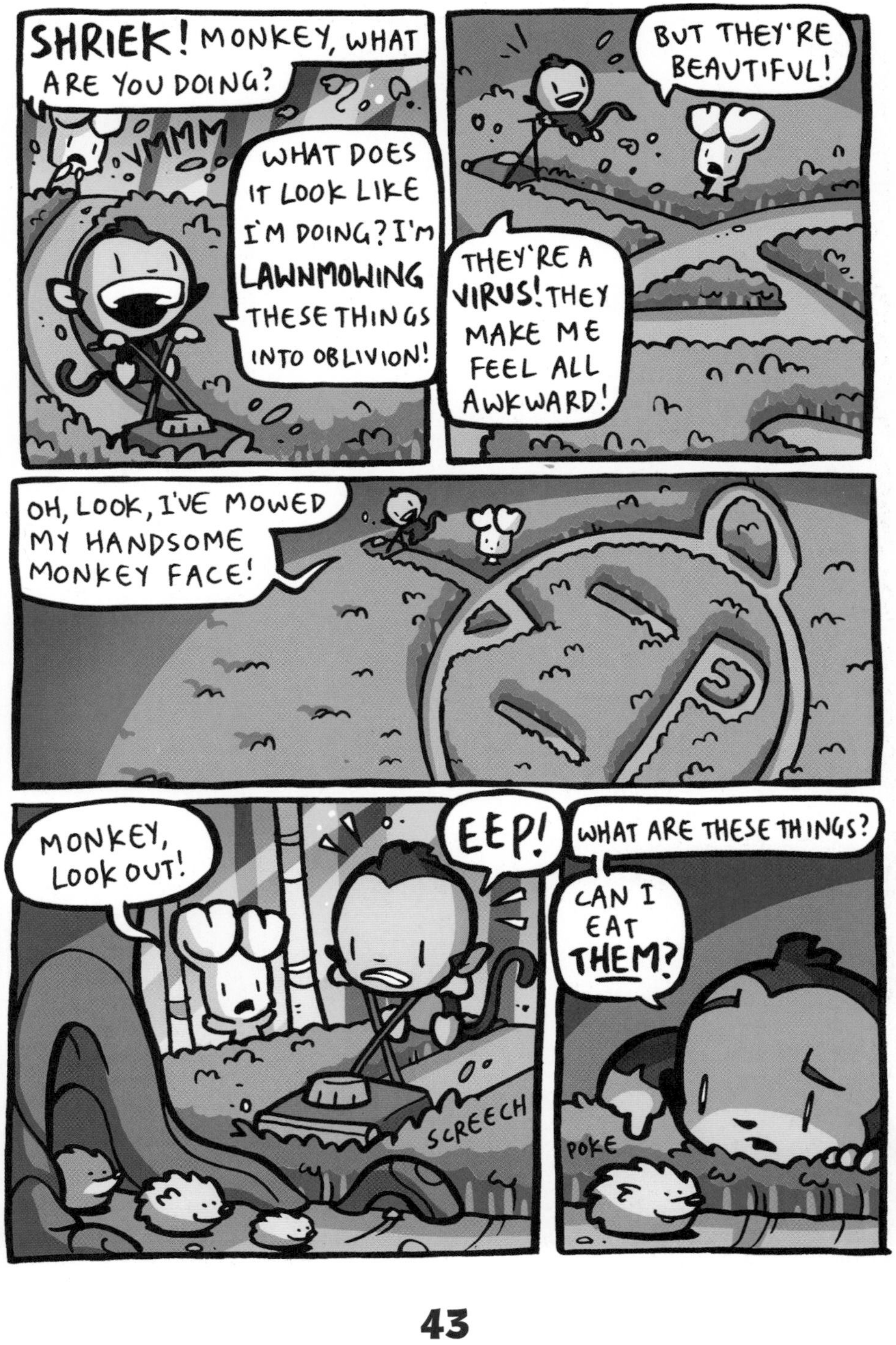

SHRIEK! MONKEY, WHAT ARE YOU DOING?
VMMMM
WHAT DOES IT LOOK LIKE I'M DOING? I'M LAWNMOWING THESE THINGS INTO OBLIVION!
BUT THEY'RE BEAUTIFUL!
THEY'RE A VIRUS! THEY MAKE ME FEEL ALL AWKWARD!
OH, LOOK, I'VE MOWED MY HANDSOME MONKEY FACE!
MONKEY, LOOK OUT!
EEP!
SCREECH
WHAT ARE THESE THINGS?
CAN I EAT THEM?
POKE

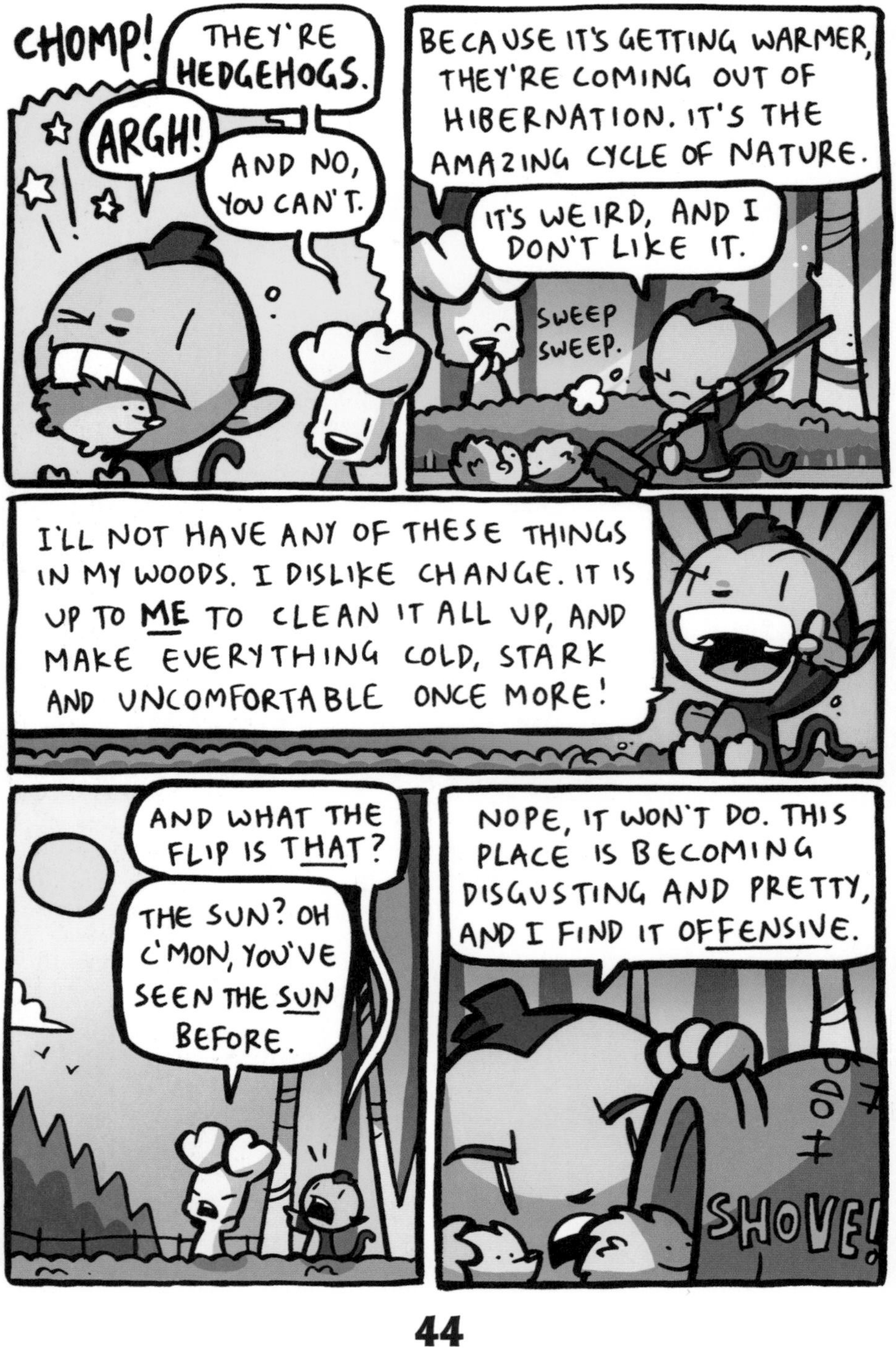
CHOMP!
THEY'RE HEDGEHOGS.
ARGH!
AND NO, YOU CAN'T.
BECAUSE IT'S GETTING WARMER, THEY'RE COMING OUT OF HIBERNATION. IT'S THE AMAZING CYCLE OF NATURE.
IT'S WEIRD, AND I DON'T LIKE IT.
SWEEP SWEEP.
I'LL NOT HAVE ANY OF THESE THINGS IN MY WOODS. I DISLIKE CHANGE. IT IS UP TO ME TO CLEAN IT ALL UP, AND MAKE EVERYTHING COLD, STARK AND UNCOMFORTABLE ONCE MORE!
AND WHAT THE FLIP IS THAT?
THE SUN? OH C'MON, YOU'VE SEEN THE SUN BEFORE.
NOPE, IT WON'T DO. THIS PLACE IS BECOMING DISGUSTING AND PRETTY, AND I FIND IT OFFENSIVE.
SHOVE!

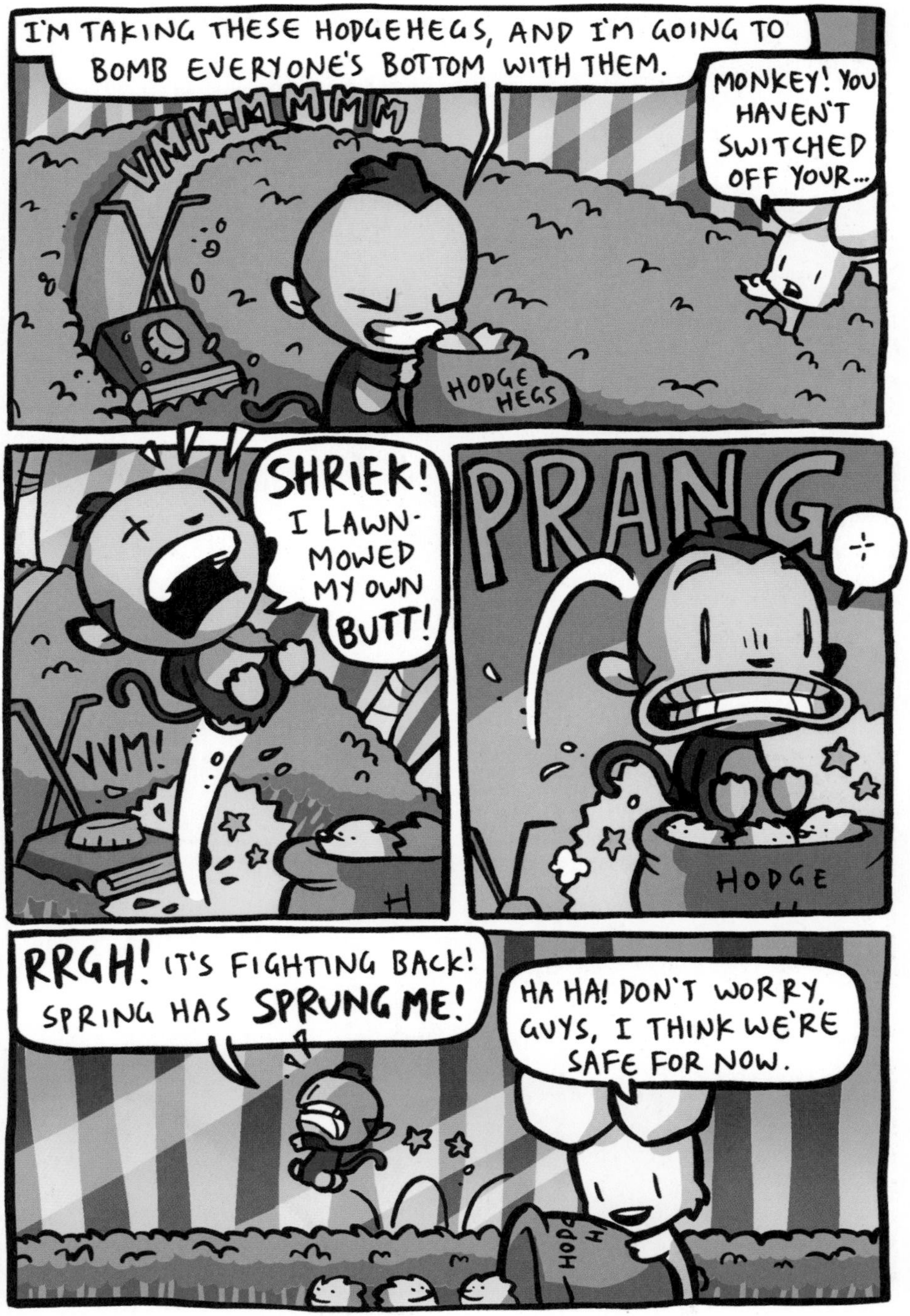
I'M TAKING THESE HODGEHEGS, AND I'M GOING TO BOMB EVERYONE'S BOTTOM WITH THEM.
VMMMMMMMM
MONKEY! YOU HAVEN'T SWITCHED OFF YOUR...
HODGE HEGS
SHRIEK! I LAWN-MOWED MY OWN BUTT!
VVM!
PRANG
HODGE
RRGH! IT'S FIGHTING BACK! SPRING HAS SPRUNG ME!
HA HA! DON'T WORRY, GUYS, I THINK WE'RE SAFE FOR NOW.

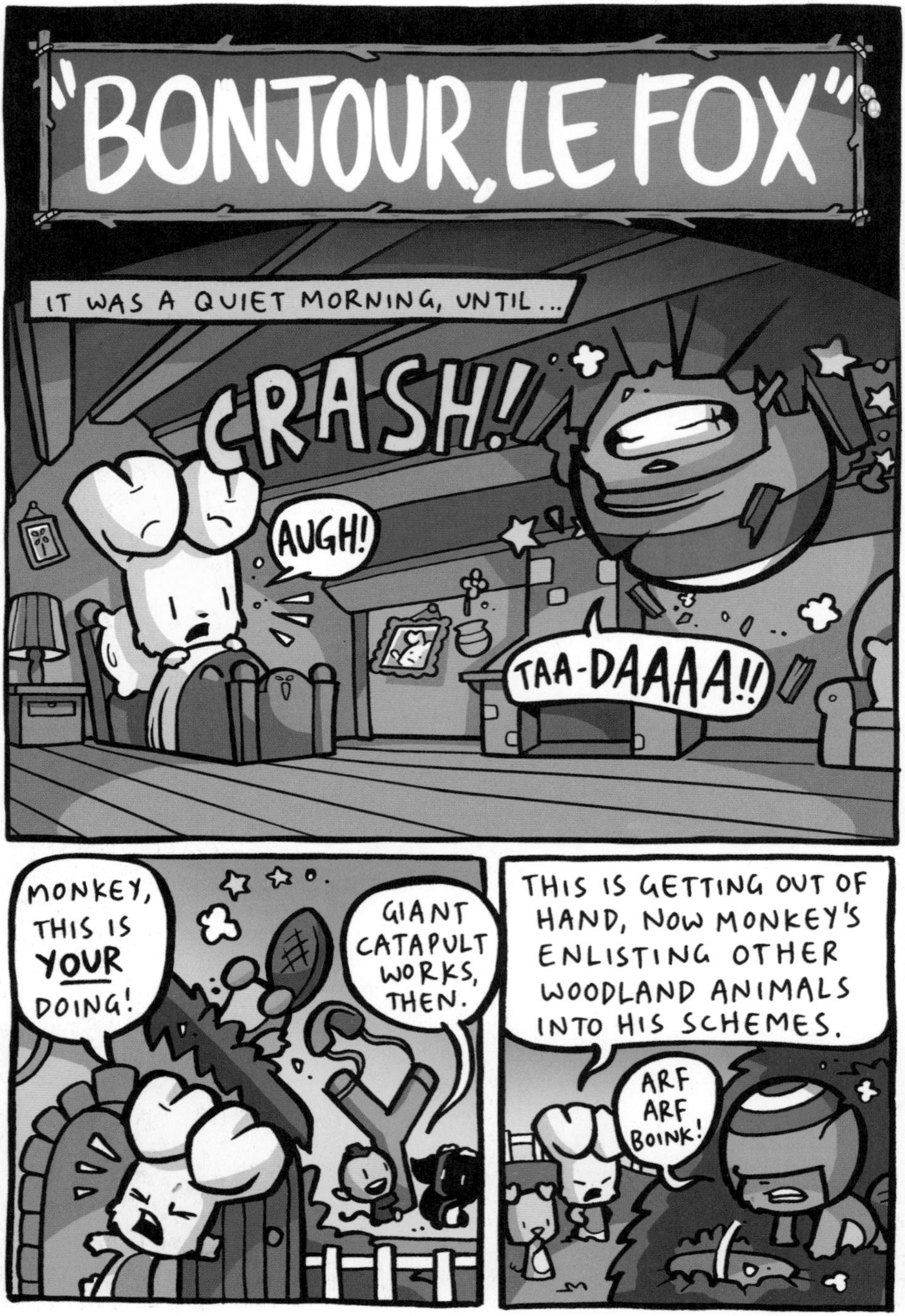
"BONJOUR, LE FOX"
IT WAS A QUIET MORNING, UNTIL...
CRASH!!
AUGH!
TAA-DAAAA!!
MONKEY, THIS IS YOUR DOING!
GIANT CATAPULT WORKS, THEN.
THIS IS GETTING OUT OF HAND, NOW MONKEY'S ENLISTING OTHER WOODLAND ANIMALS INTO HIS SCHEMES.
ARF ARF BOINK!

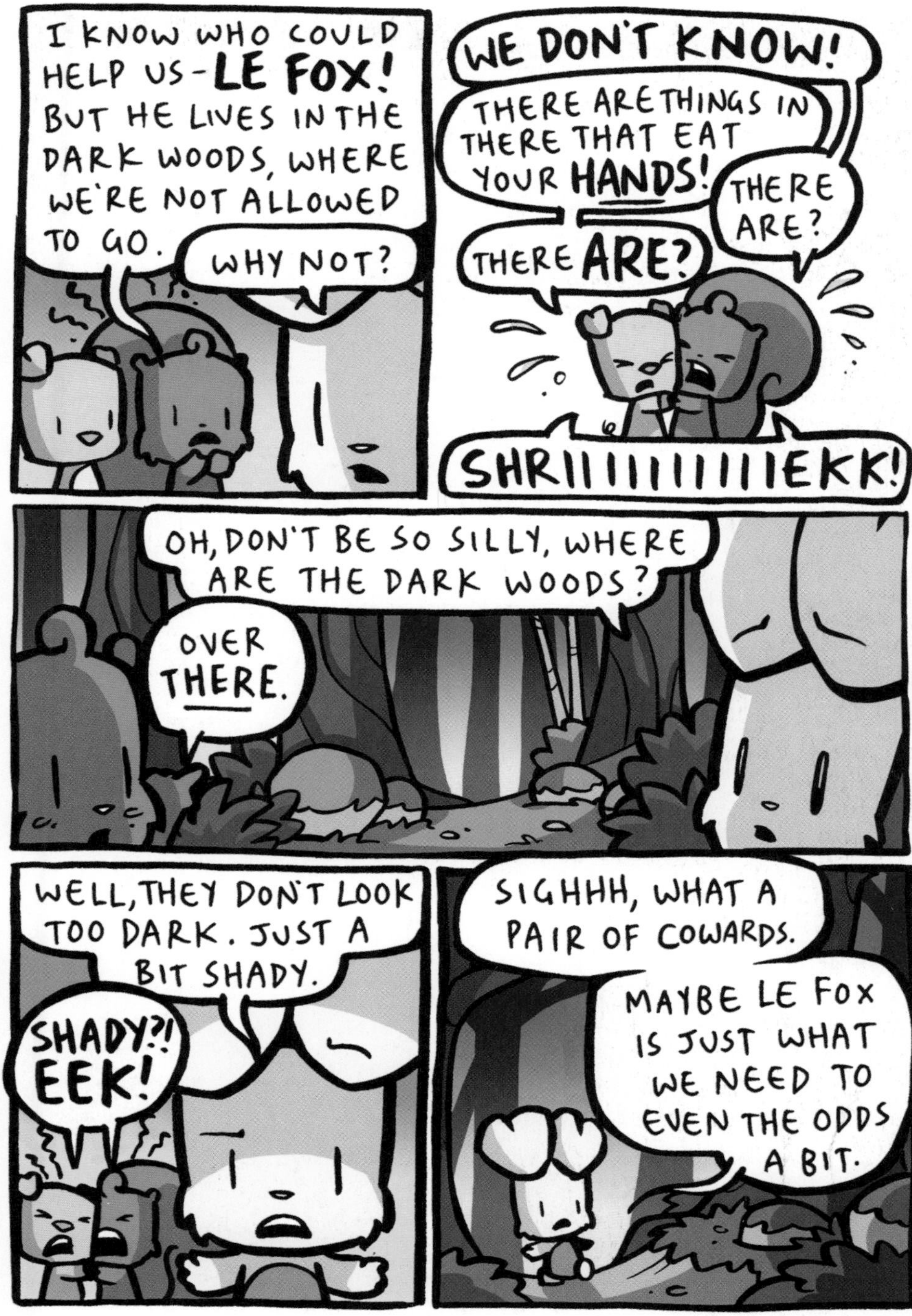
I KNOW WHO COULD HELP US-LE FOX! BUT HE LIVES IN THE DARK WOODS, WHERE WE'RE NOT ALLOWED TO GO.
WHY NOT?
WE DON'T KNOW!
THERE ARE THINGS IN THERE THAT EAT YOUR HANDS!
THERE ARE?
THERE ARE?
SHRIIIIIIIIIIIEKK!
OH, DON'T BE SO SILLY, WHERE ARE THE DARK WOODS?
OVER THERE.
WELL, THEY DON'T LOOK TOO DARK. JUST A BIT SHADY.
SHADY?! EEK!
SIGHHH, WHAT A PAIR OF COWARDS.
MAYBE LE FOX IS JUST WHAT WE NEED TO EVEN THE ODDS A BIT.

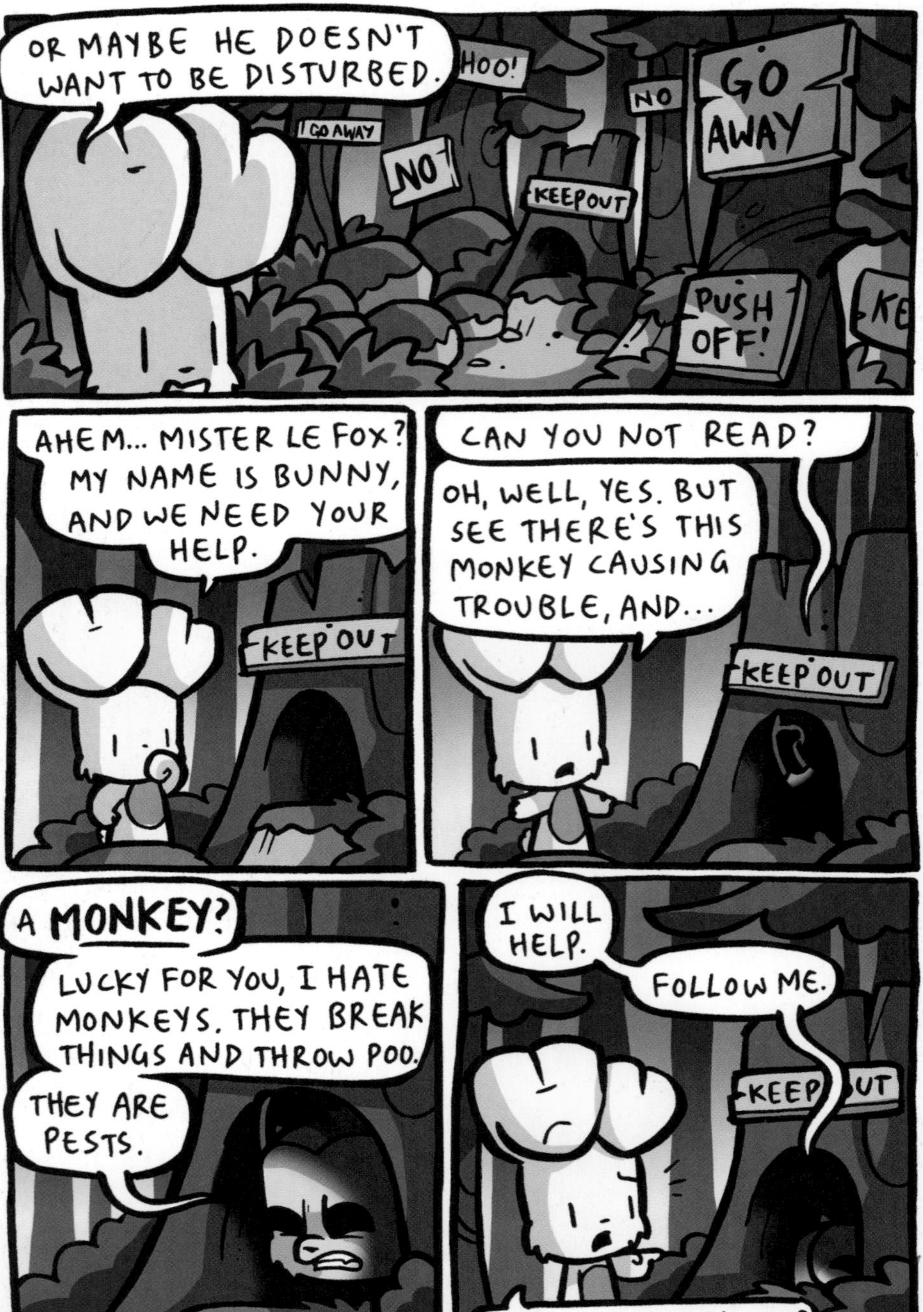
OR MAYBE HE DOESN'T WANT TO BE DISTURBED.
HOO!
I GO AWAY
NO
NO
KEEP OUT
GO AWAY
PUSH OFF!
AHEM... MISTER LE FOX? MY NAME IS BUNNY, AND WE NEED YOUR HELP.
KEEP OUT
CAN YOU NOT READ?
OH, WELL, YES. BUT SEE THERE'S THIS MONKEY CAUSING TROUBLE, AND...
KEEP OUT
A MONKEY?
LUCKY FOR YOU, I HATE MONKEYS. THEY BREAK THINGS AND THROW POO.
THEY ARE PESTS.
I WILL HELP.
FOLLOW ME.
UM... DOWN THERE?

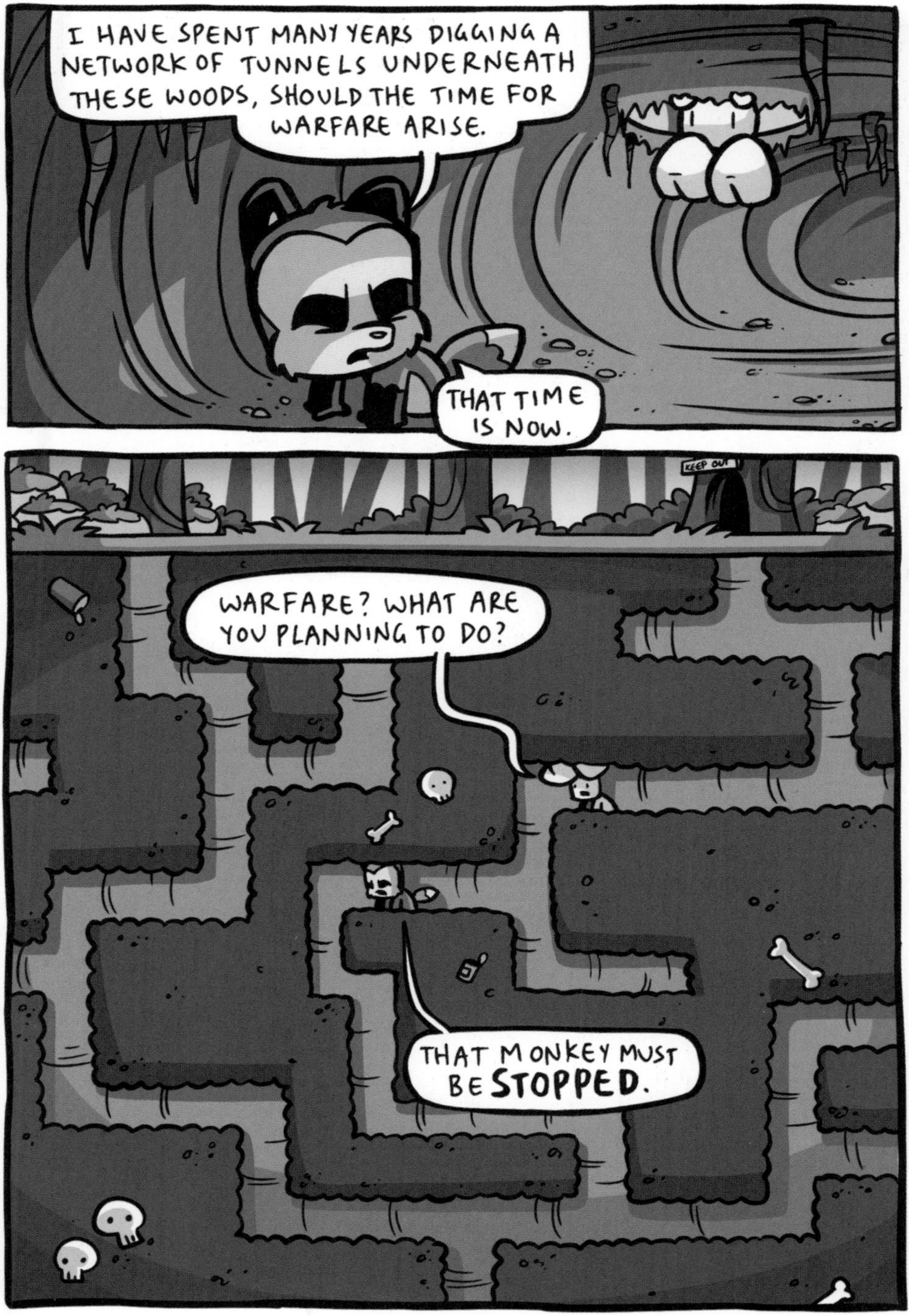
I HAVE SPENT MANY YEARS DIGGING A NETWORK OF TUNNELS UNDERNEATH THESE WOODS, SHOULD THE TIME FOR WARFARE ARISE.
THAT TIME IS NOW.
KEEP OUT
WARFARE? WHAT ARE YOU PLANNING TO DO?
THAT MONKEY MUST BE STOPPED.

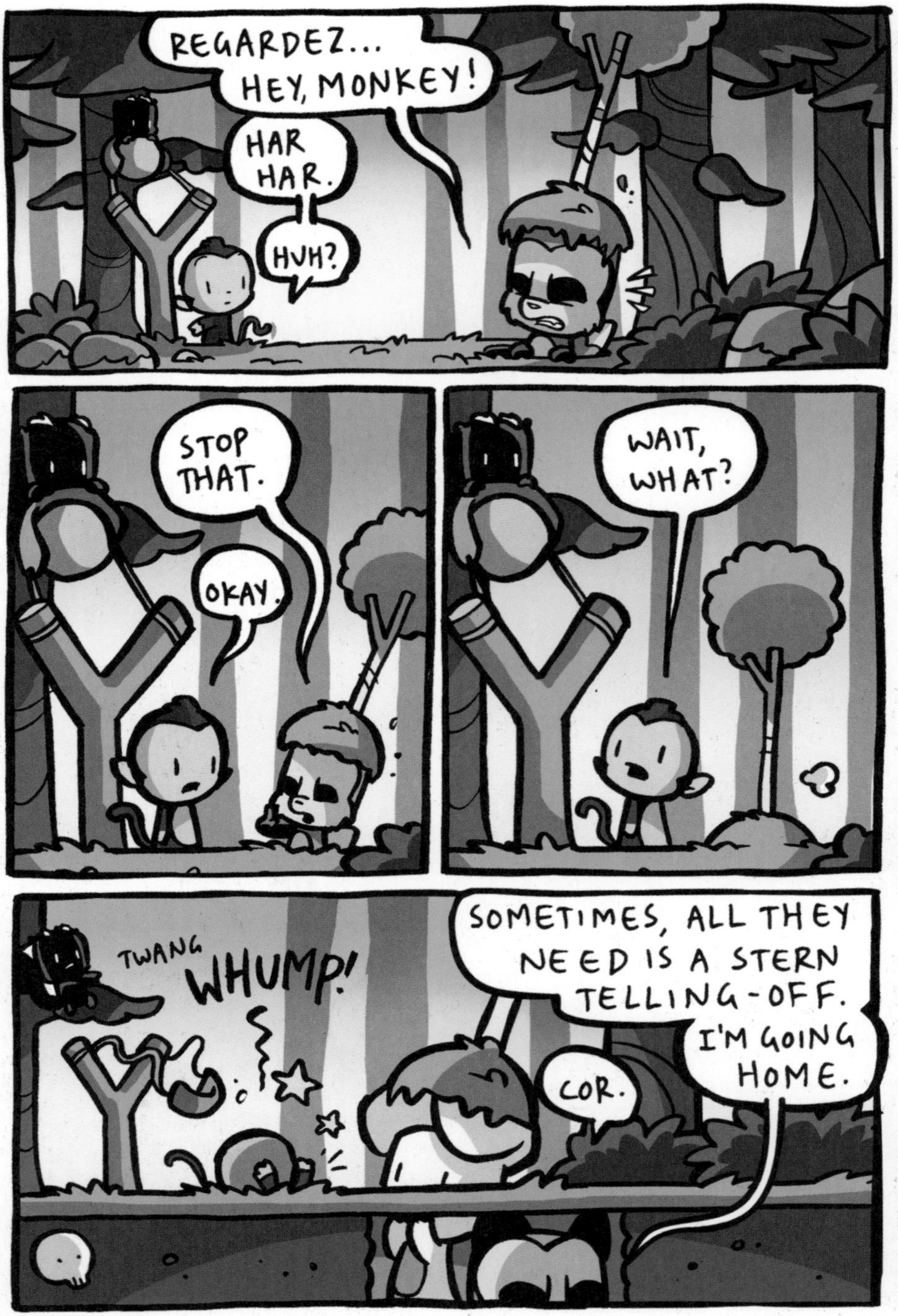
REGARDEZ... HEY, MONKEY!
HAR HAR.
HUH?
STOP THAT.
OKAY.
WAIT, WHAT?
TWANG
WHUMP!
SOMETIMES, ALL THEY NEED IS A STERN TELLING-OFF.
COR.
I'M GOING HOME.

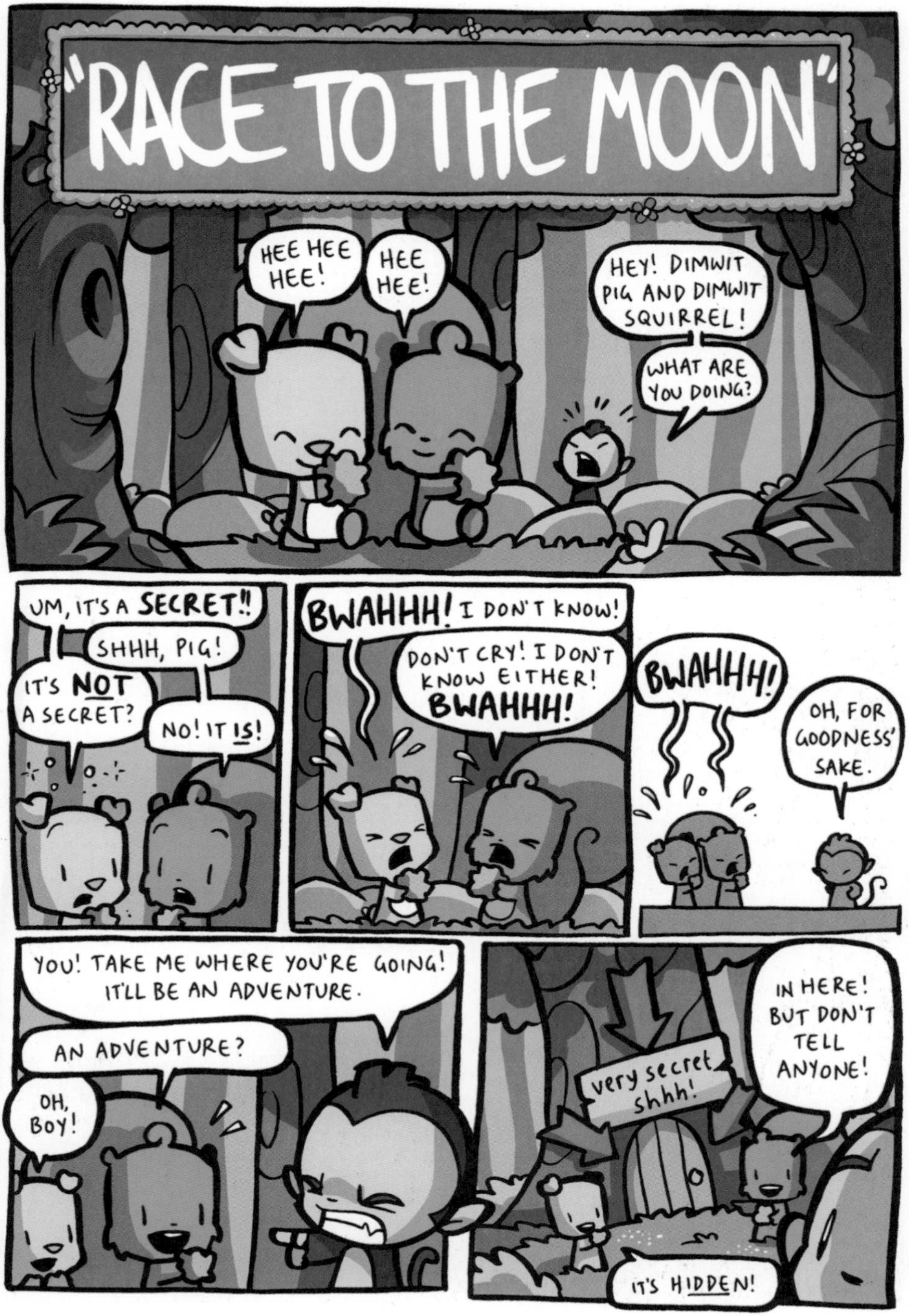
"RACE TO THE MOON"
HEE HEE HEE!
HEE HEE!
HEY! DIMWIT PIG AND DIMWIT SQUIRREL!
WHAT ARE YOU DOING?
UM, IT'S A SECRET!!
SHHH, PIG!
IT'S NOT A SECRET?
NO! IT IS!
BWAHHH! I DON'T KNOW!
DON'T CRY! I DON'T KNOW EITHER! BWAHHH!
BWAHHH!
OH, FOR GOODNESS' SAKE.
YOU! TAKE ME WHERE YOU'RE GOING! IT'LL BE AN ADVENTURE.
AN ADVENTURE?
OH, BOY!
very secret shhh!
IN HERE! BUT DON'T TELL ANYONE!
IT'S HIDDEN!

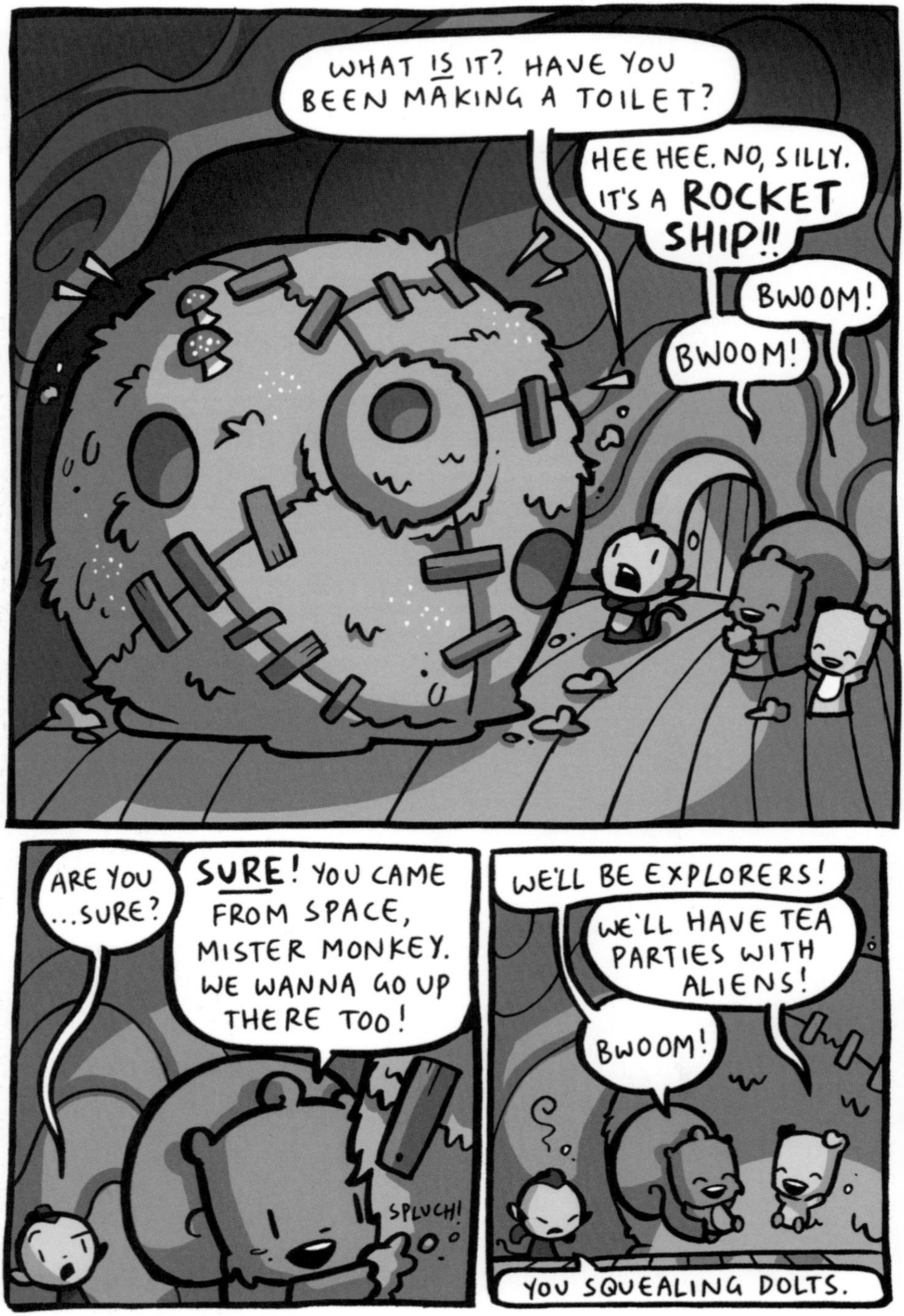
WHAT IS IT? HAVE YOU BEEN MAKING A TOILET?
HEE HEE. NO, SILLY. IT'S A ROCKET SHIP!!
BWOOM!
BWOOM!
ARE YOU ...SURE?
SURE! YOU CAME FROM SPACE, MISTER MONKEY. WE WANNA GO UP THERE TOO!
SPLUCH!
WE'LL BE EXPLORERS!
WE'LL HAVE TEA PARTIES WITH ALIENS!
BWOOM!
YOU SQUEALING DOLTS.

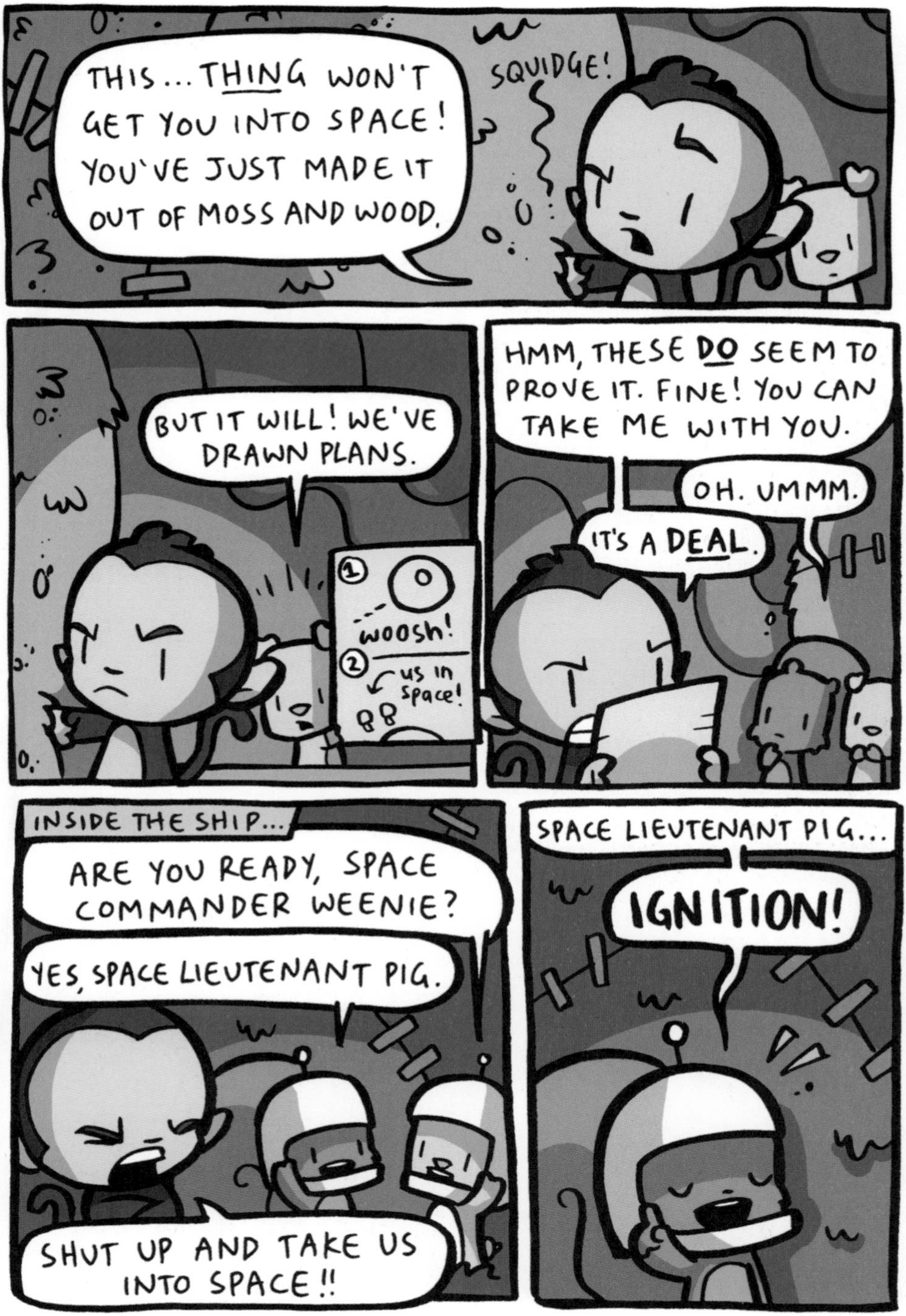
THIS... THING WON'T GET YOU INTO SPACE! YOU'VE JUST MADE IT OUT OF MOSS AND WOOD.
SQUIDGE!
BUT IT WILL! WE'VE DRAWN PLANS.
① woosh!
② us in space!
HMM, THESE DO SEEM TO PROVE IT. FINE! YOU CAN TAKE ME WITH YOU.
OH. UMMM.
IT'S A DEAL.
INSIDE THE SHIP...
ARE YOU READY, SPACE COMMANDER WEENIE?
YES, SPACE LIEUTENANT PIG.
SHUT UP AND TAKE US INTO SPACE!!
SPACE LIEUTENANT PIG...
IGNITION!

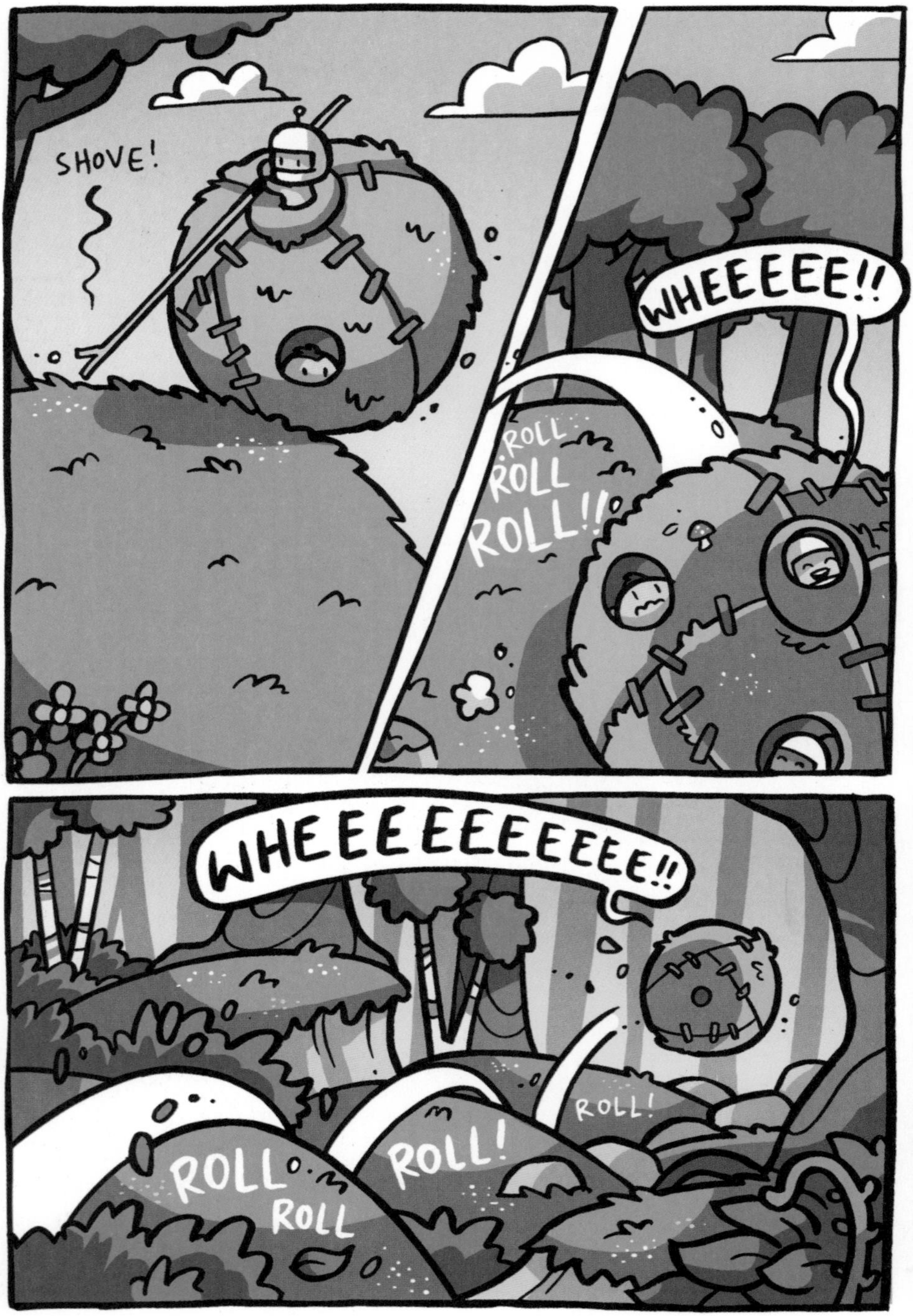
SHOVE!
WHEEEEE!!
ROLL
ROLL
ROLL!!
WHEEEEEEEEEE!!
ROLL
ROLL
ROLL!
ROLL!

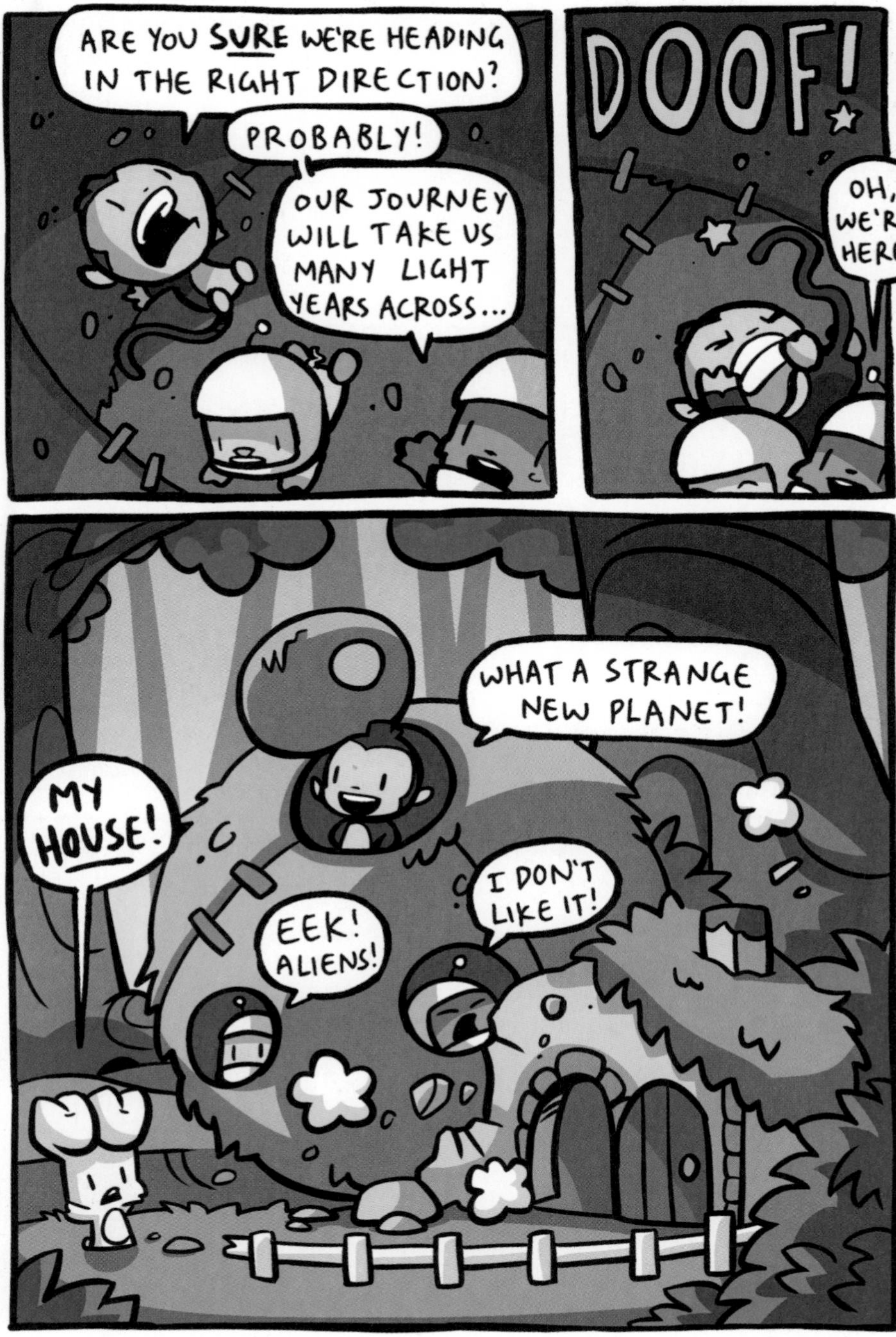
ARE YOU SURE WE'RE HEADING IN THE RIGHT DIRECTION?
PROBABLY!
OUR JOURNEY WILL TAKE US MANY LIGHT YEARS ACROSS...
DOOF!
OH, WE'RE HERE.
WHAT A STRANGE NEW PLANET!
MY HOUSE!
I DON'T LIKE IT!
EEK! ALIENS!

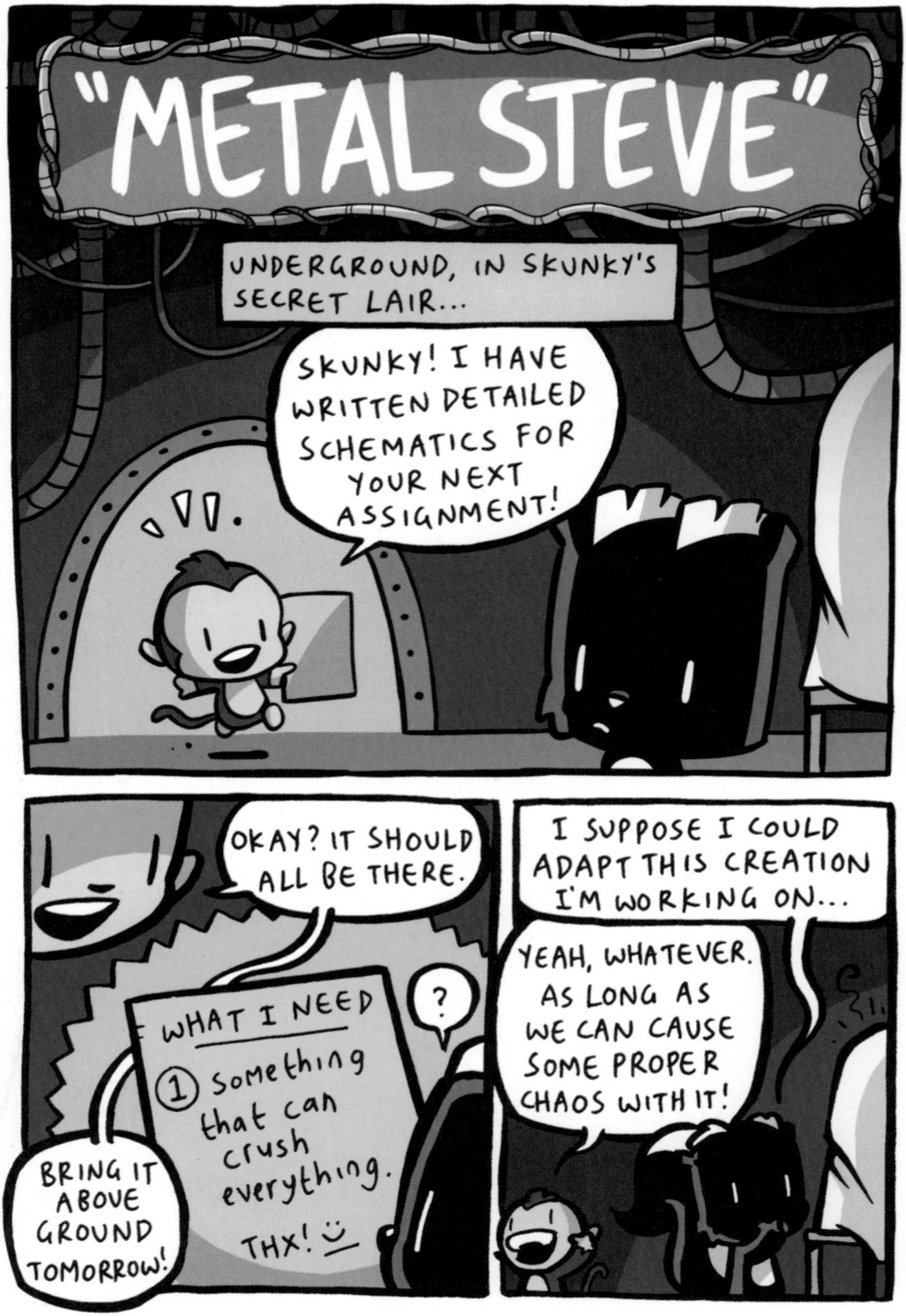
"METAL STEVE"
UNDERGROUND, IN SKUNKY'S SECRET LAIR...
SKUNKY! I HAVE WRITTEN DETAILED SCHEMATICS FOR YOUR NEXT ASSIGNMENT!
OKAY? IT SHOULD ALL BE THERE.
WHAT I NEED
1 Something that can crush everything.
THX!
?
BRING IT ABOVE GROUND TOMORROW!
I SUPPOSE I COULD ADAPT THIS CREATION I'M WORKING ON...
YEAH, WHATEVER. AS LONG AS WE CAN CAUSE SOME PROPER CHAOS WITH IT!

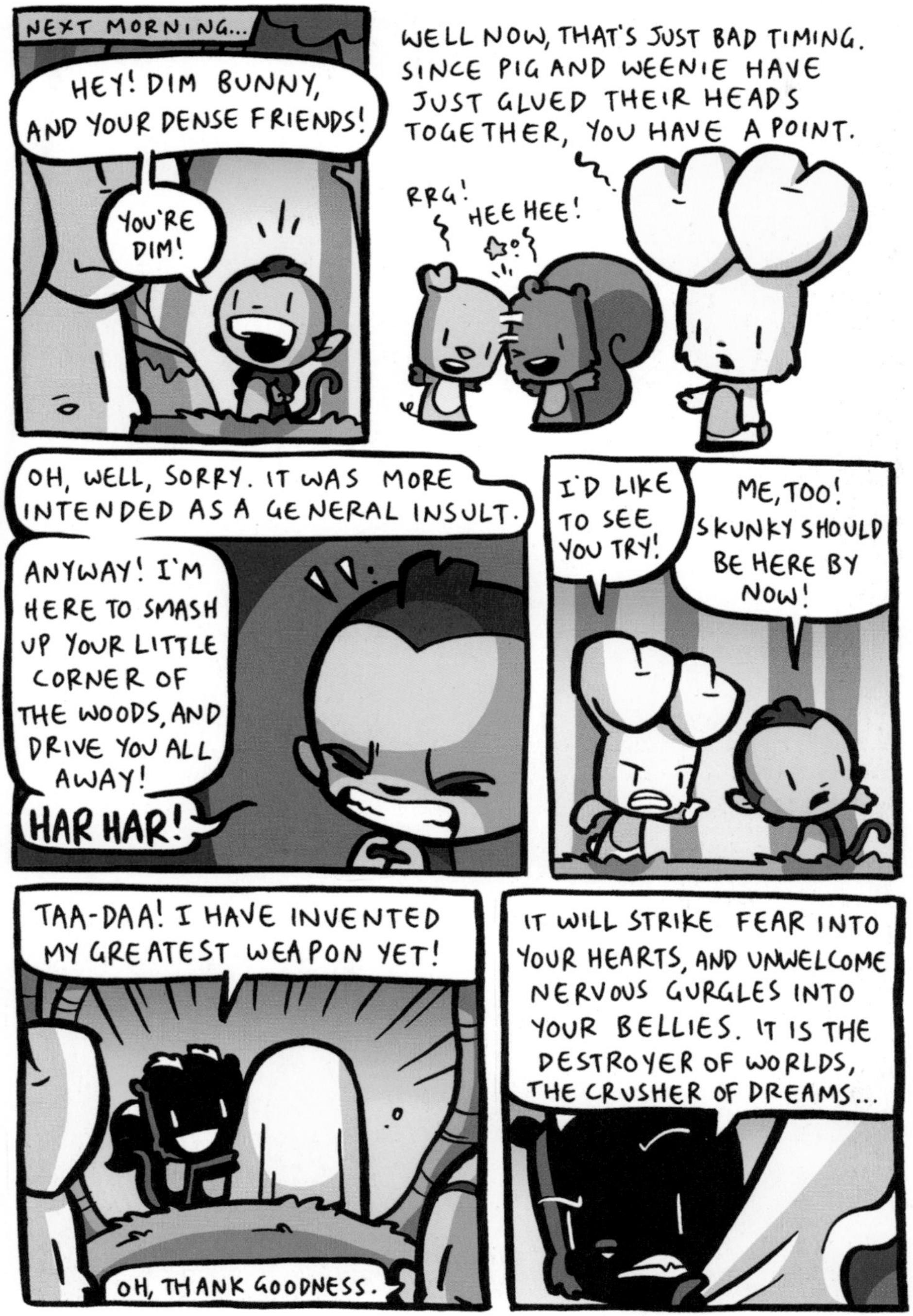
NEXT MORNING...
HEY! DIM BUNNY, AND YOUR DENSE FRIENDS!
YOU'RE DIM!
WELL NOW, THAT'S JUST BAD TIMING. SINCE PIG AND WEENIE HAVE JUST GLUED THEIR HEADS TOGETHER, YOU HAVE A POINT.
RRG!
HEE HEE!
OH, WELL, SORRY. IT WAS MORE INTENDED AS A GENERAL INSULT.
ANYWAY! I'M HERE TO SMASH UP YOUR LITTLE CORNER OF THE WOODS, AND DRIVE YOU ALL AWAY!
HAR HAR!
I'D LIKE TO SEE YOU TRY!
ME, TOO! SKUNKY SHOULD BE HERE BY NOW!
TAA-DAA! I HAVE INVENTED MY GREATEST WEAPON YET!
OH, THANK GOODNESS.
IT WILL STRIKE FEAR INTO YOUR HEARTS, AND UNWELCOME NERVOUS GURGLES INTO YOUR BELLIES. IT IS THE DESTROYER OF WORLDS, THE CRUSHER OF DREAMS...

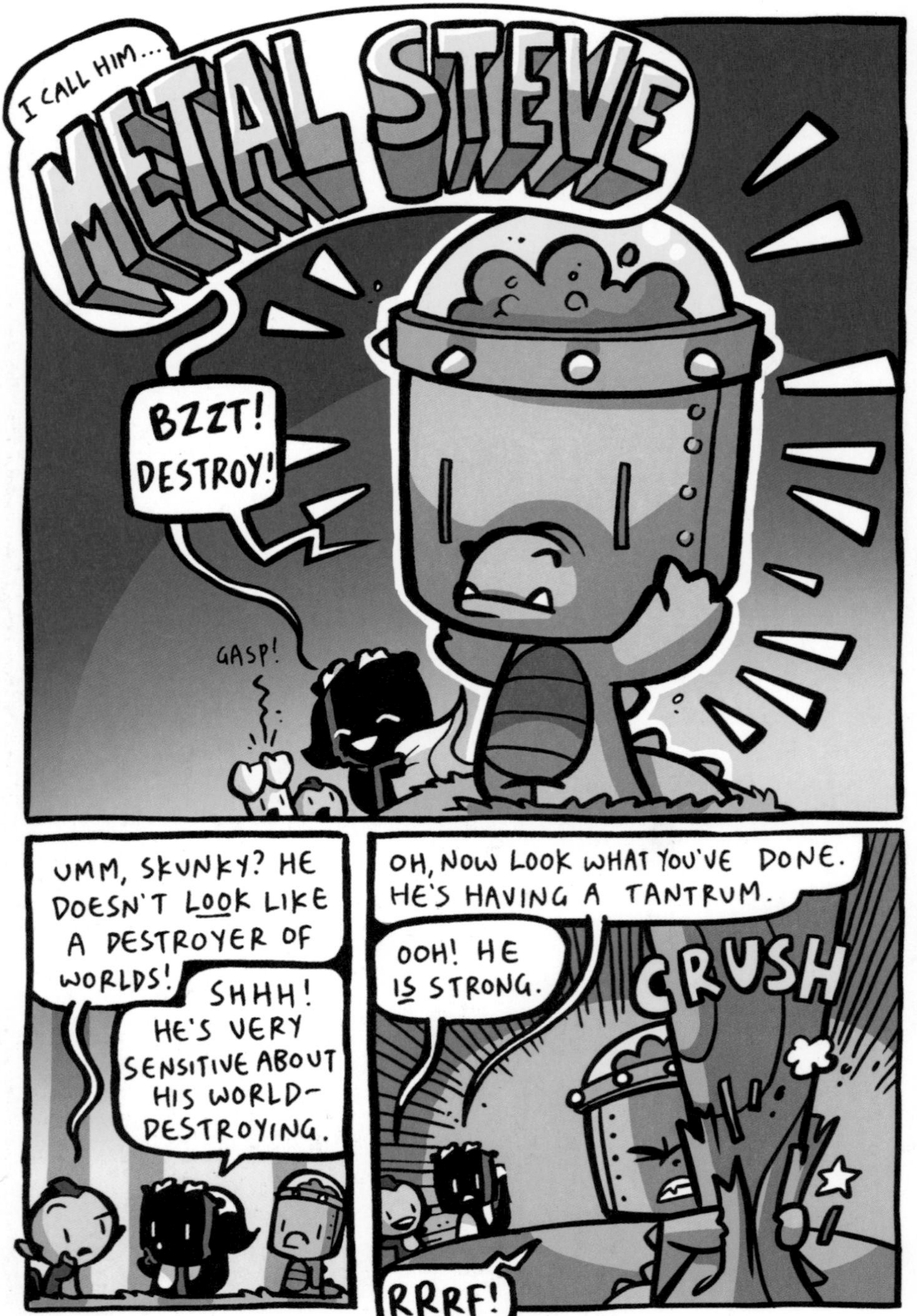
I CALL HIM....
METAL STEVE
BZZT! DESTROY!
GASP!
UMM, SKUNKY? HE DOESN'T LOOK LIKE A DESTROYER OF WORLDS!
SHHH! HE'S VERY SENSITIVE ABOUT HIS WORLD-DESTROYING.
OH, NOW LOOK WHAT YOU'VE DONE. HE'S HAVING A TANTRUM.
OOH! HE IS STRONG.
CRUSH
RRRF!

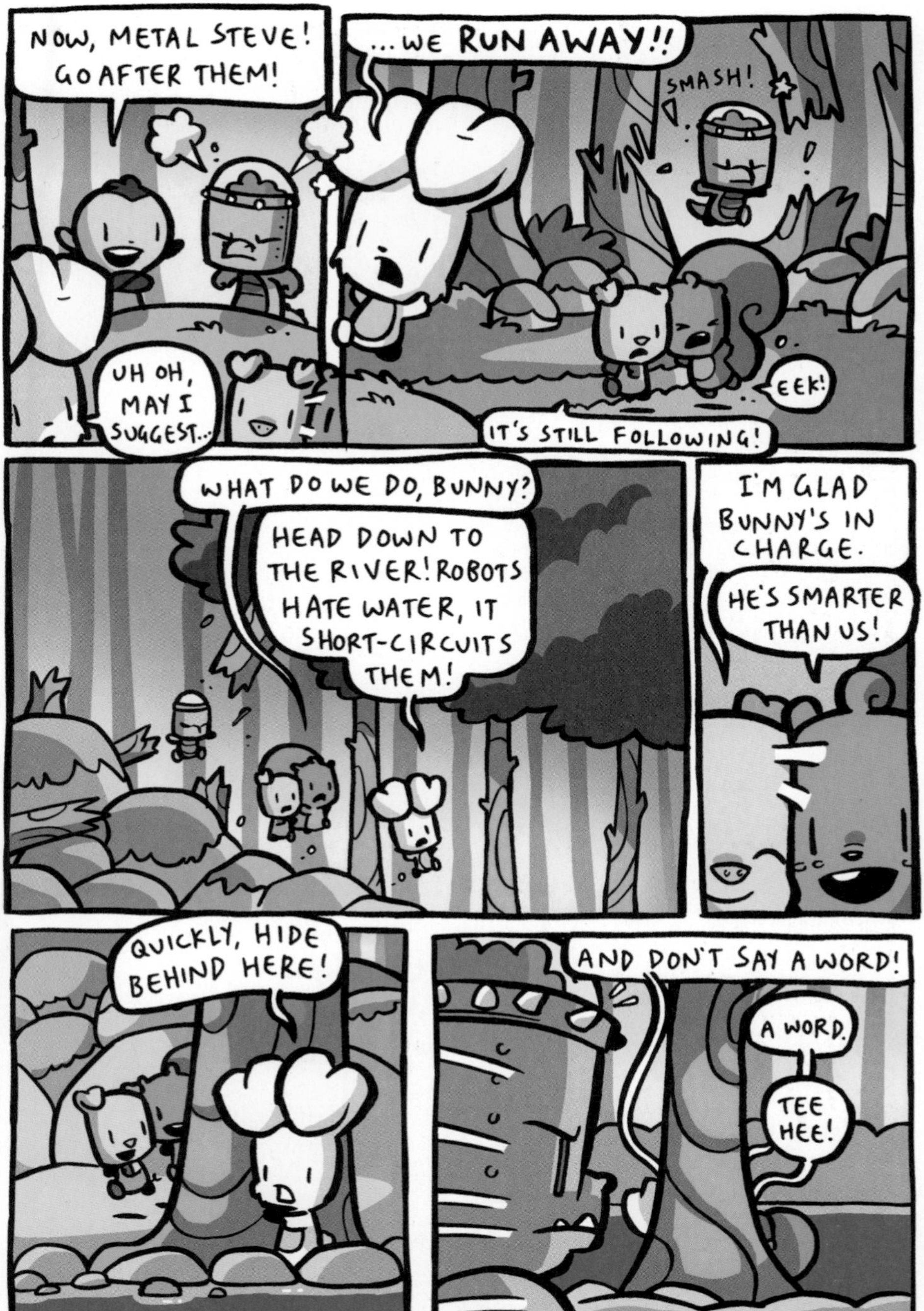
NOW, METAL STEVE! GO AFTER THEM!
UH OH, MAY I SUGGEST...
...WE RUN AWAY!!
SMASH!
EEK!
IT'S STILL FOLLOWING!
WHAT DO WE DO, BUNNY?
HEAD DOWN TO THE RIVER! ROBOTS HATE WATER, IT SHORT-CIRCUITS THEM!
I'M GLAD BUNNY'S IN CHARGE.
HE'S SMARTER THAN US!
QUICKLY, HIDE BEHIND HERE!
AND DON'T SAY A WORD!
A WORD.
TEE HEE!

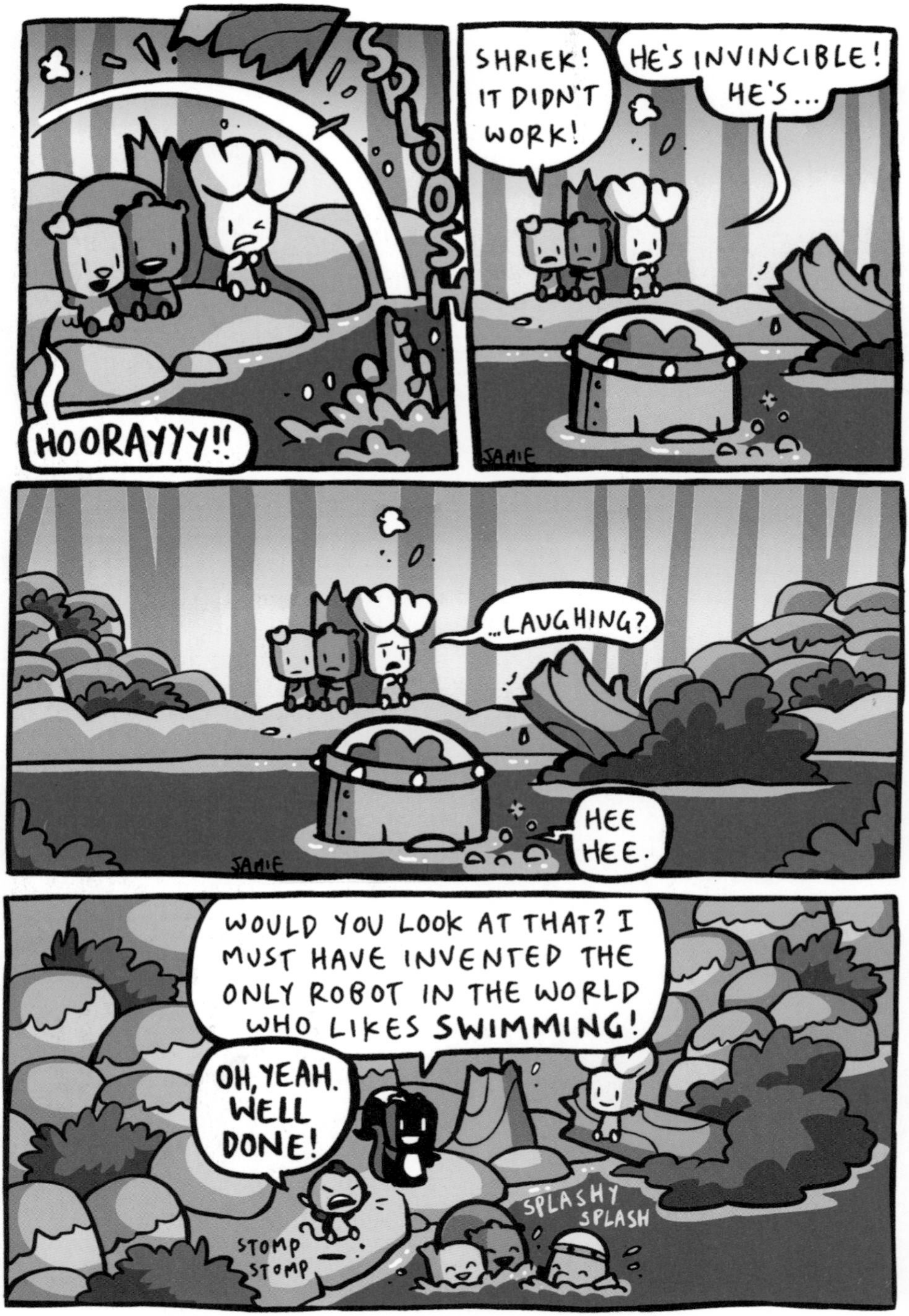
SPLOOSH
HOORAYYY!!
SHRIEK! IT DIDN'T WORK!
HE'S INVINCIBLE! HE'S...
JAMIE
...LAUGHING?
HEE HEE.
JAMIE
WOULD YOU LOOK AT THAT? I MUST HAVE INVENTED THE ONLY ROBOT IN THE WORLD WHO LIKES SWIMMING!
OH, YEAH. WELL DONE!
SPLASHY SPLASH
STOMP STOMP

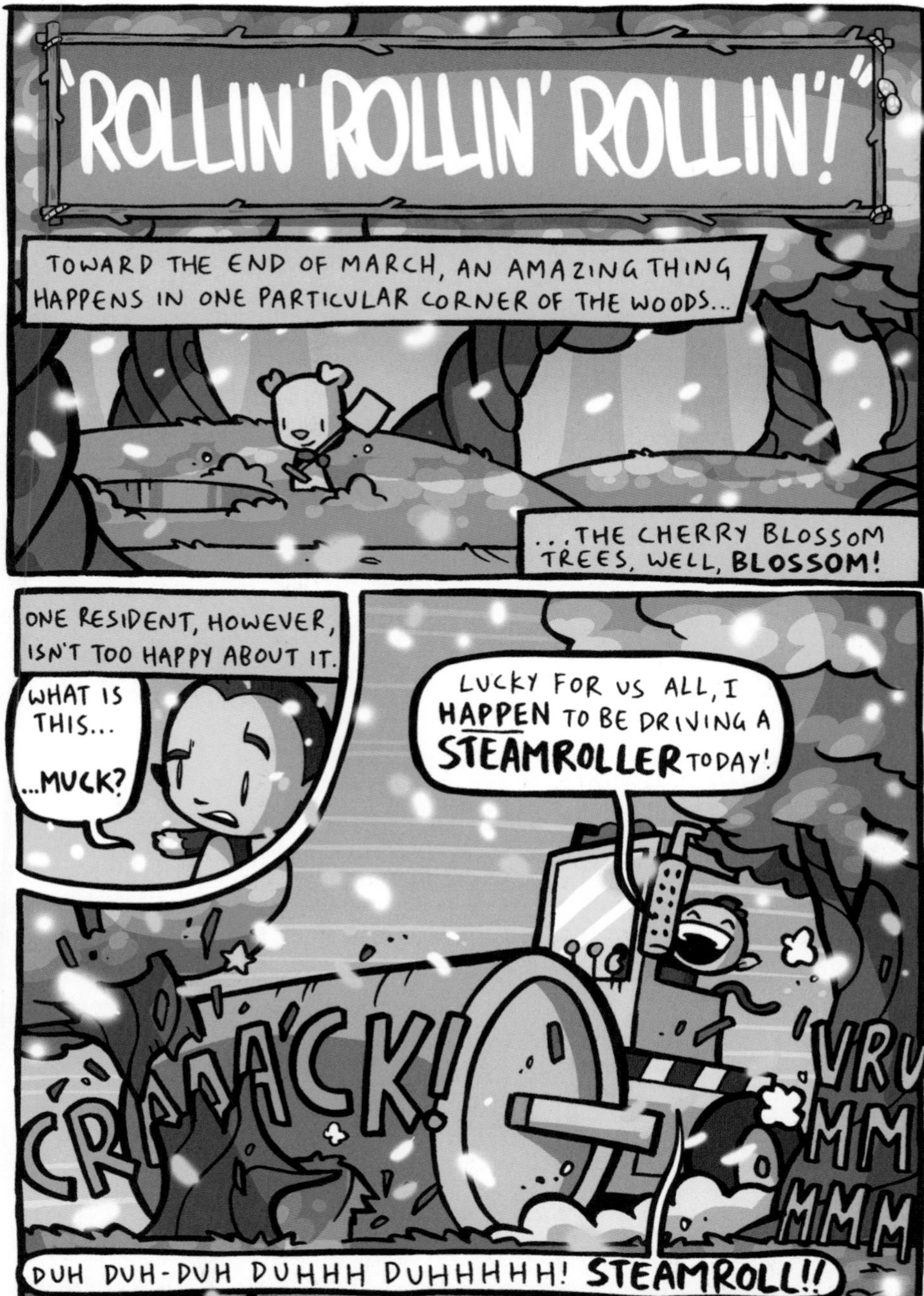
"ROLLIN' ROLLIN' ROLLIN'!"
TOWARD THE END OF MARCH, AN AMAZING THING HAPPENS IN ONE PARTICULAR CORNER OF THE WOODS...
...THE CHERRY BLOSSOM TREES, WELL, BLOSSOM!
ONE RESIDENT, HOWEVER, ISN'T TOO HAPPY ABOUT IT.
WHAT IS THIS... ...MUCK?
LUCKY FOR US ALL, I HAPPEN TO BE DRIVING A STEAMROLLER TODAY!
CRAAACK!
VRUMMMMMM
DUH DUH-DUH DUHHH DUHHHHH! STEAMROLL!!

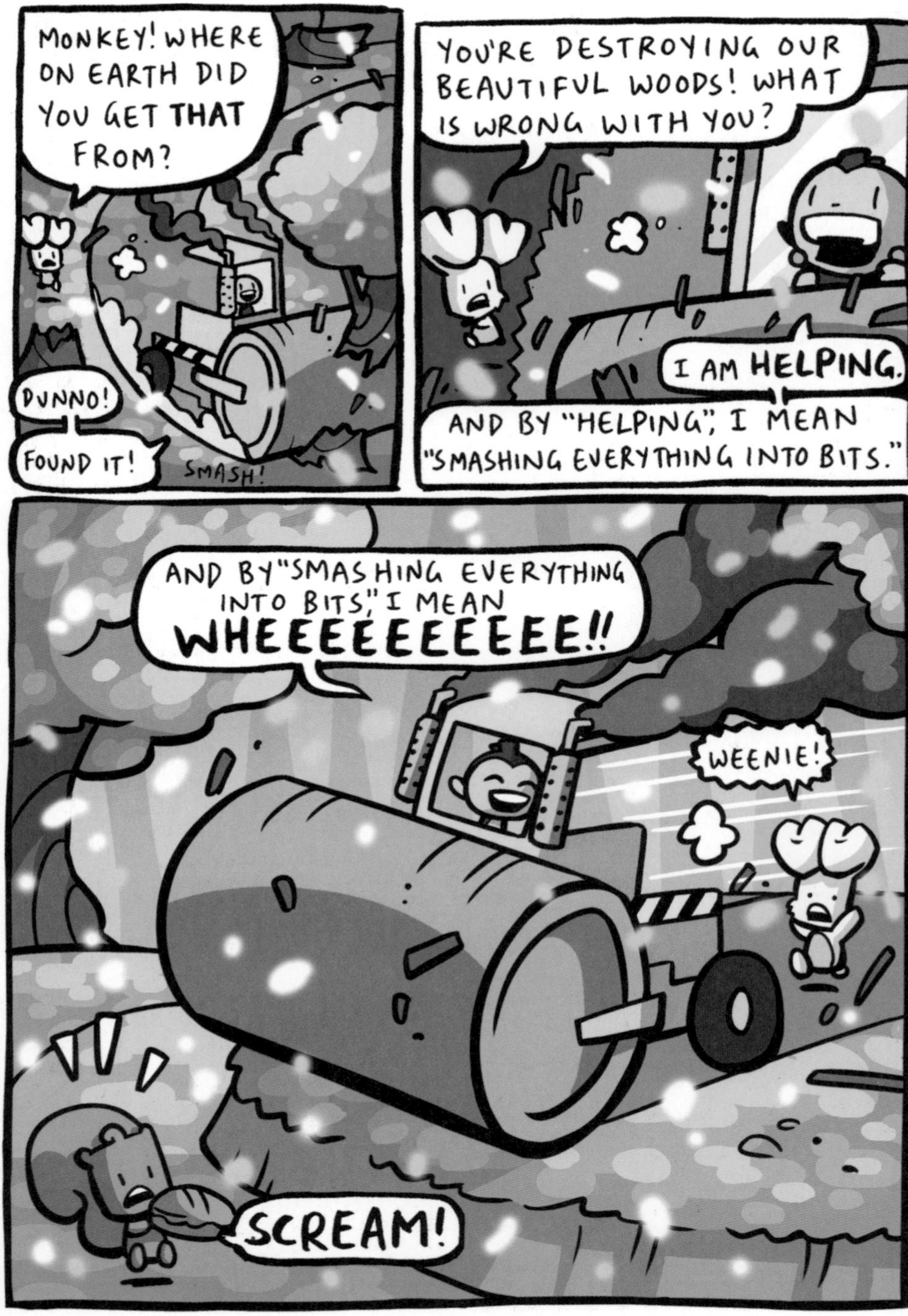
MONKEY! WHERE ON EARTH DID YOU GET THAT FROM?
DUNNO!
FOUND IT!
SMASH!
YOU'RE DESTROYING OUR BEAUTIFUL WOODS! WHAT IS WRONG WITH YOU?
I AM HELPING.
AND BY "HELPING", I MEAN "SMASHING EVERYTHING INTO BITS."
AND BY "SMASHING EVERYTHING INTO BITS," I MEAN WHEEEEEEEEEE!!
WEENIE!
SCREAM!

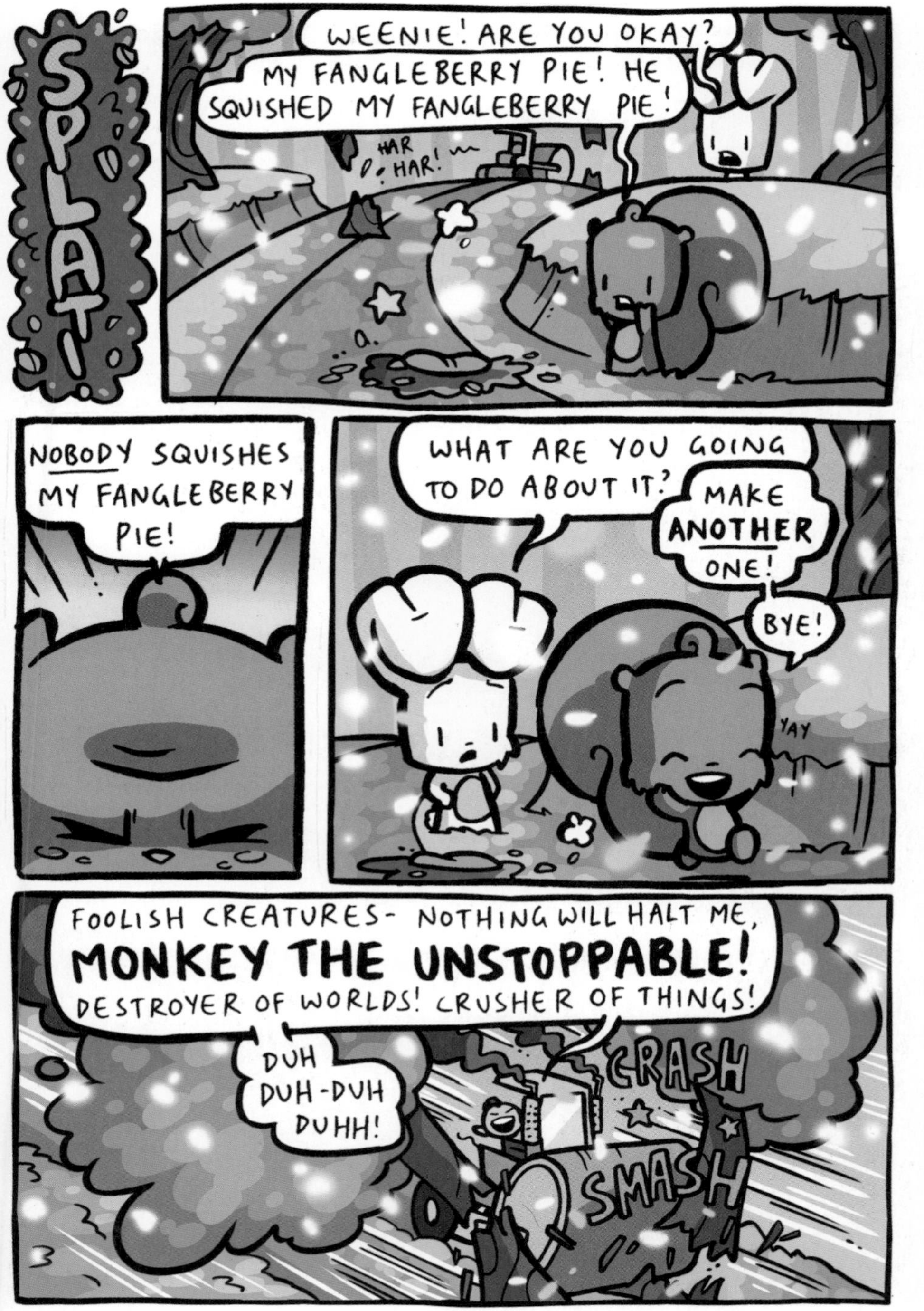
SPLAT!
WEENIE! ARE YOU OKAY?
MY FANGLEBERRY PIE! HE SQUISHED MY FANGLEBERRY PIE!
HAR HAR!
NOBODY SQUISHES MY FANGLEBERRY PIE!
WHAT ARE YOU GOING TO DO ABOUT IT?
MAKE ANOTHER ONE!
BYE!
YAY
FOOLISH CREATURES- NOTHING WILL HALT ME, MONKEY THE UNSTOPPABLE! DESTROYER OF WORLDS! CRUSHER OF THINGS!
DUH DUH-DUH DUHH!
CRASH
SMASH

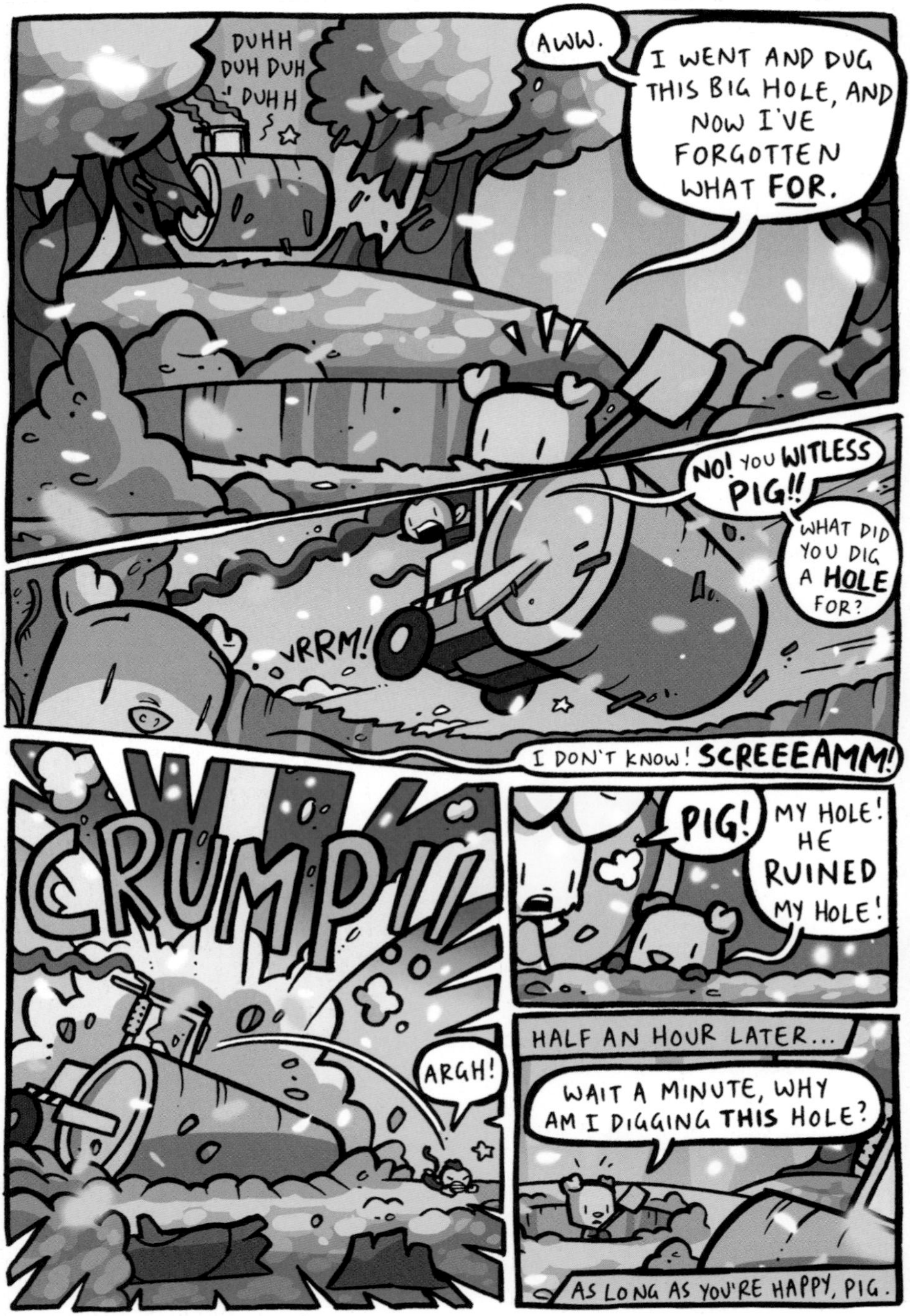
DUHH DUH DUH DUHH
AWW.
I WENT AND DUG THIS BIG HOLE, AND NOW I'VE FORGOTTEN WHAT FOR.
NO! YOU WITLESS PIG!!
WHAT DID YOU DIG A HOLE FOR?
VRRM!
I DON'T KNOW! SCREEEAMM!
CRUMP!!
ARGH!
PIG!
MY HOLE! HE RUINED MY HOLE!
HALF AN HOUR LATER...
WAIT A MINUTE, WHY AM I DIGGING THIS HOLE?
AS LONG AS YOU'RE HAPPY, PIG.

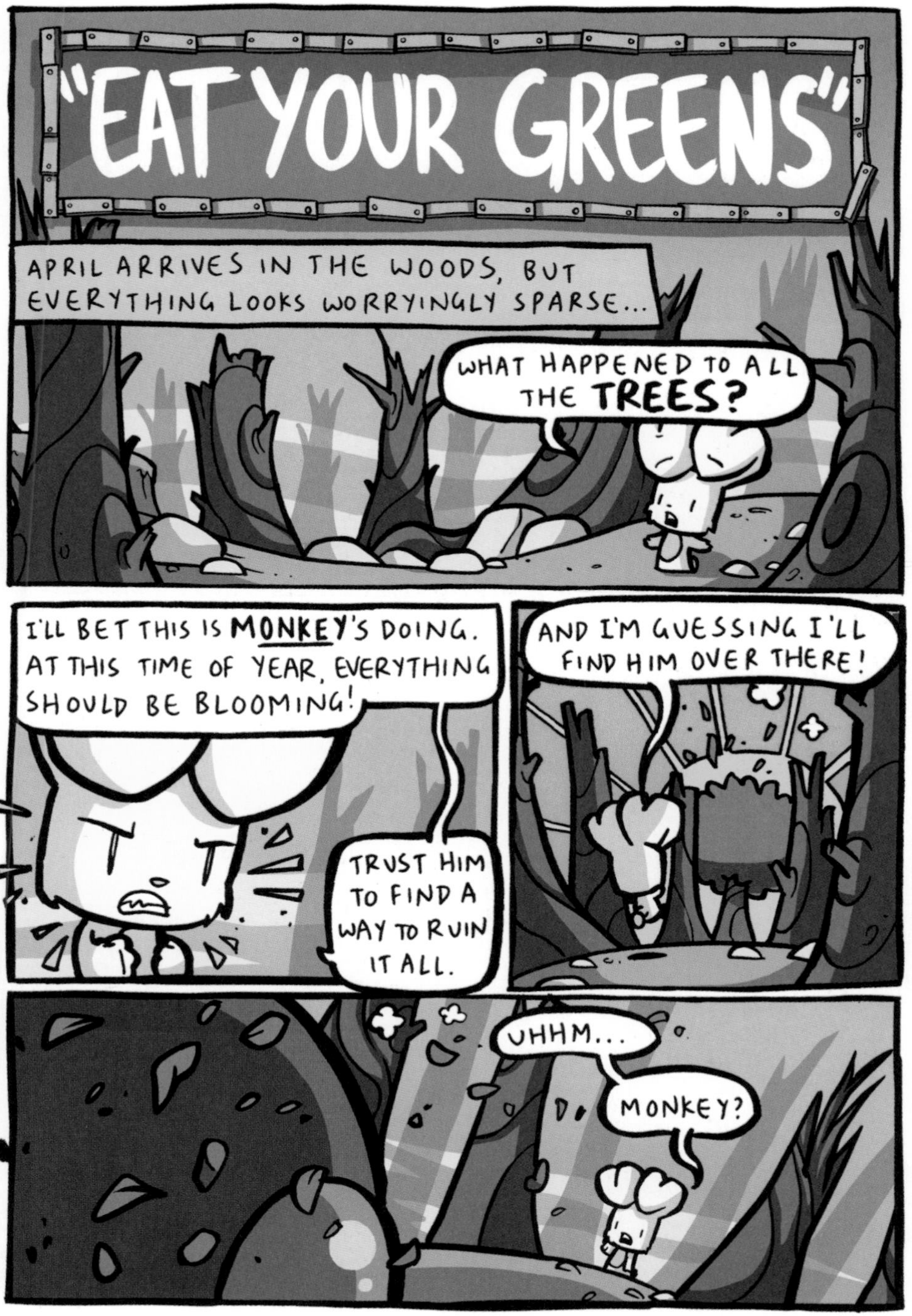
"EAT YOUR GREENS"
APRIL ARRIVES IN THE WOODS, BUT EVERYTHING LOOKS WORRYINGLY SPARSE...
WHAT HAPPENED TO ALL THE TREES?
I'LL BET THIS IS MONKEY'S DOING. AT THIS TIME OF YEAR, EVERYTHING SHOULD BE BLOOMING!
TRUST HIM TO FIND A WAY TO RUIN IT ALL.
AND I'M GUESSING I'LL FIND HIM OVER THERE!
UHHM...
MONKEY?

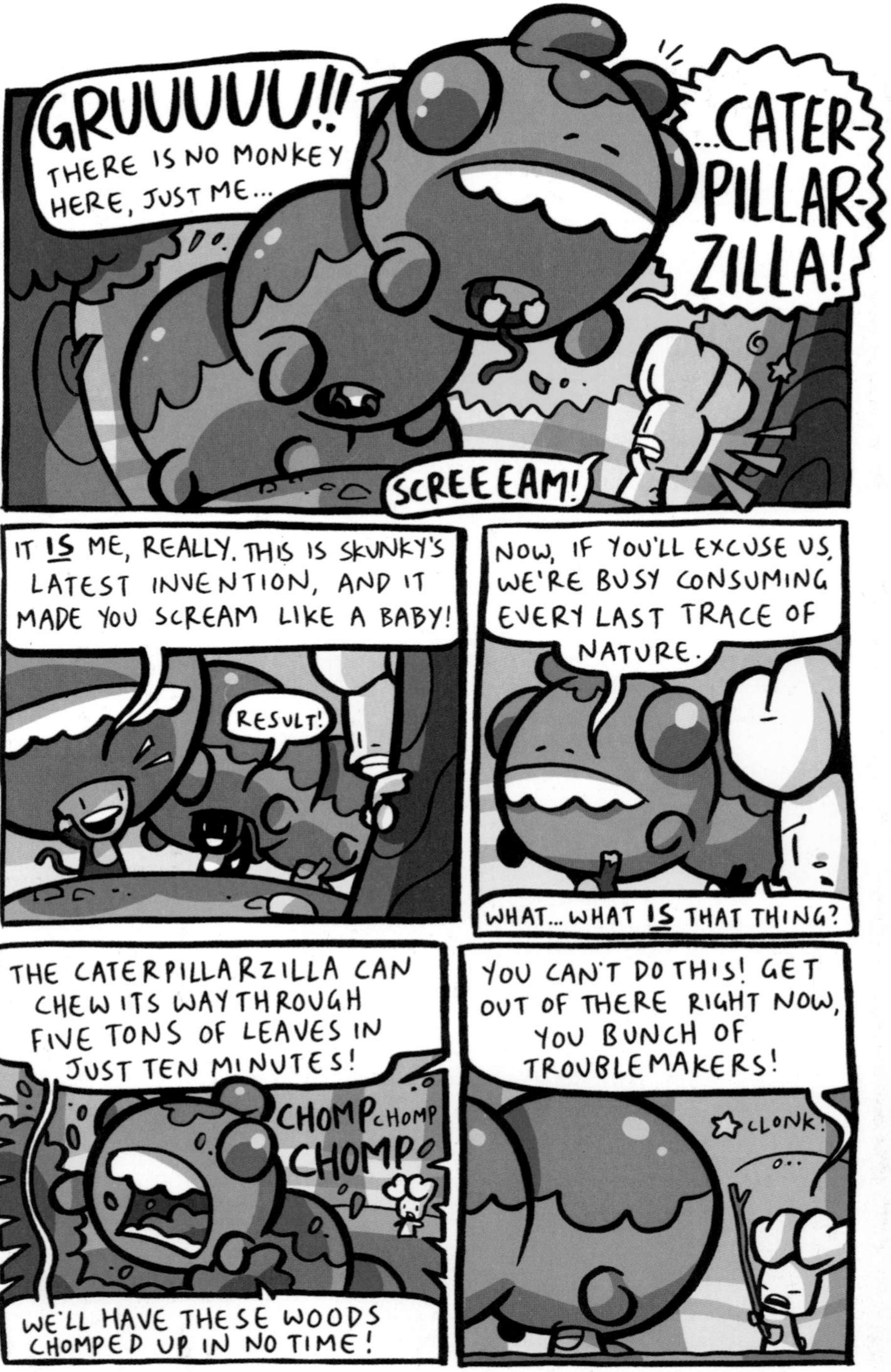
GRUUUUU!! THERE IS NO MONKEY HERE, JUST ME...
...CATER-PILLAR-ZILLA!
SCREEEAM!
IT IS ME, REALLY. THIS IS SKUNKY'S LATEST INVENTION, AND IT MADE YOU SCREAM LIKE A BABY!
RESULT!
NOW, IF YOU'LL EXCUSE US, WE'RE BUSY CONSUMING EVERY LAST TRACE OF NATURE.
WHAT... WHAT IS THAT THING?
THE CATERPILLARZILLA CAN CHEW ITS WAY THROUGH FIVE TONS OF LEAVES IN JUST TEN MINUTES!
CHOMP CHOMP CHOMP
WE'LL HAVE THESE WOODS CHOMPED UP IN NO TIME!
YOU CAN'T DO THIS! GET OUT OF THERE RIGHT NOW, YOU BUNCH OF TROUBLEMAKERS!
CLONK!

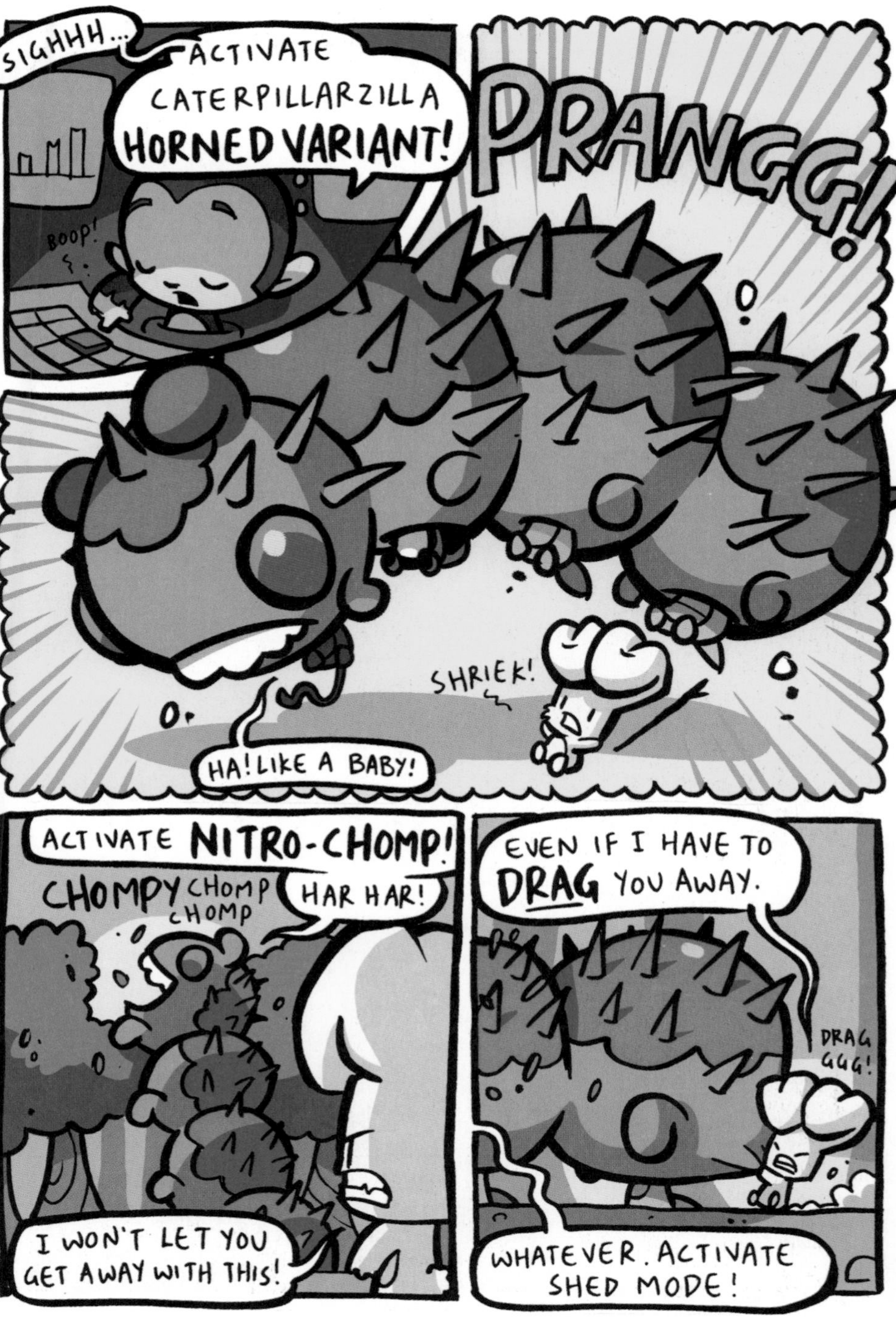
SIGHHH...
ACTIVATE CATERPILLARZILLA HORNED VARIANT!
BOOP!
PRANGG!
SHRIEK!
HA! LIKE A BABY!
ACTIVATE NITRO-CHOMP!
CHOMPY CHOMP CHOMP
HAR HAR!
I WON'T LET YOU GET AWAY WITH THIS!
EVEN IF I HAVE TO DRAG YOU AWAY.
DRAGGGG!
WHATEVER. ACTIVATE SHED MODE!

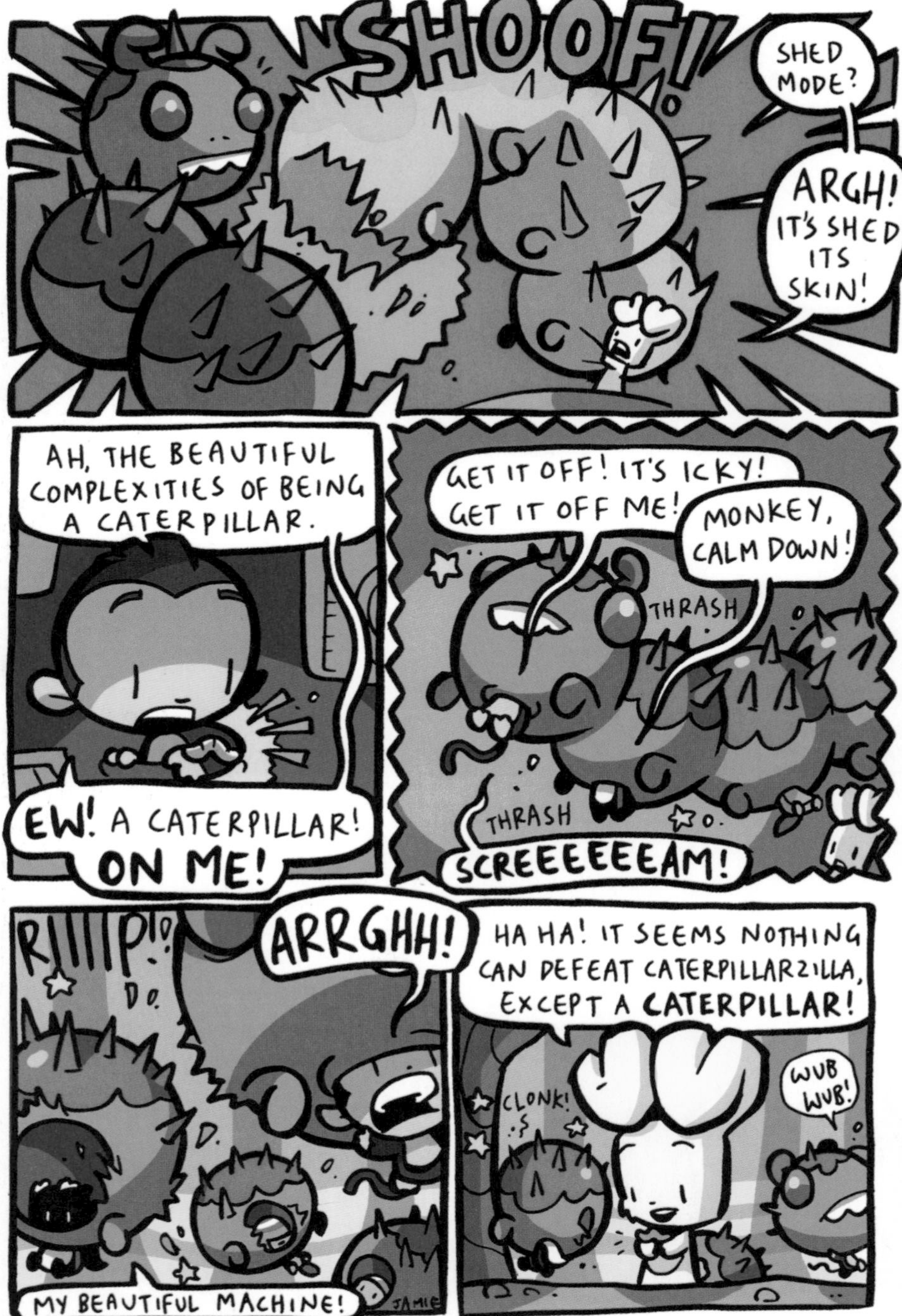
SHOOF!
SHED MODE?
ARGH! IT'S SHED ITS SKIN!
AH, THE BEAUTIFUL COMPLEXITIES OF BEING A CATERPILLAR.
EW! A CATERPILLAR! ON ME!
GET IT OFF! IT'S ICKY! GET IT OFF ME!
MONKEY, CALM DOWN!
THRASH
THRASH
SCREEEEEEEAM!
RIIIIP!
ARRGHH!
MY BEAUTIFUL MACHINE!
HA HA! IT SEEMS NOTHING CAN DEFEAT CATERPILLARZILLA, EXCEPT A CATERPILLAR!
CLONK!
WUB WUB!

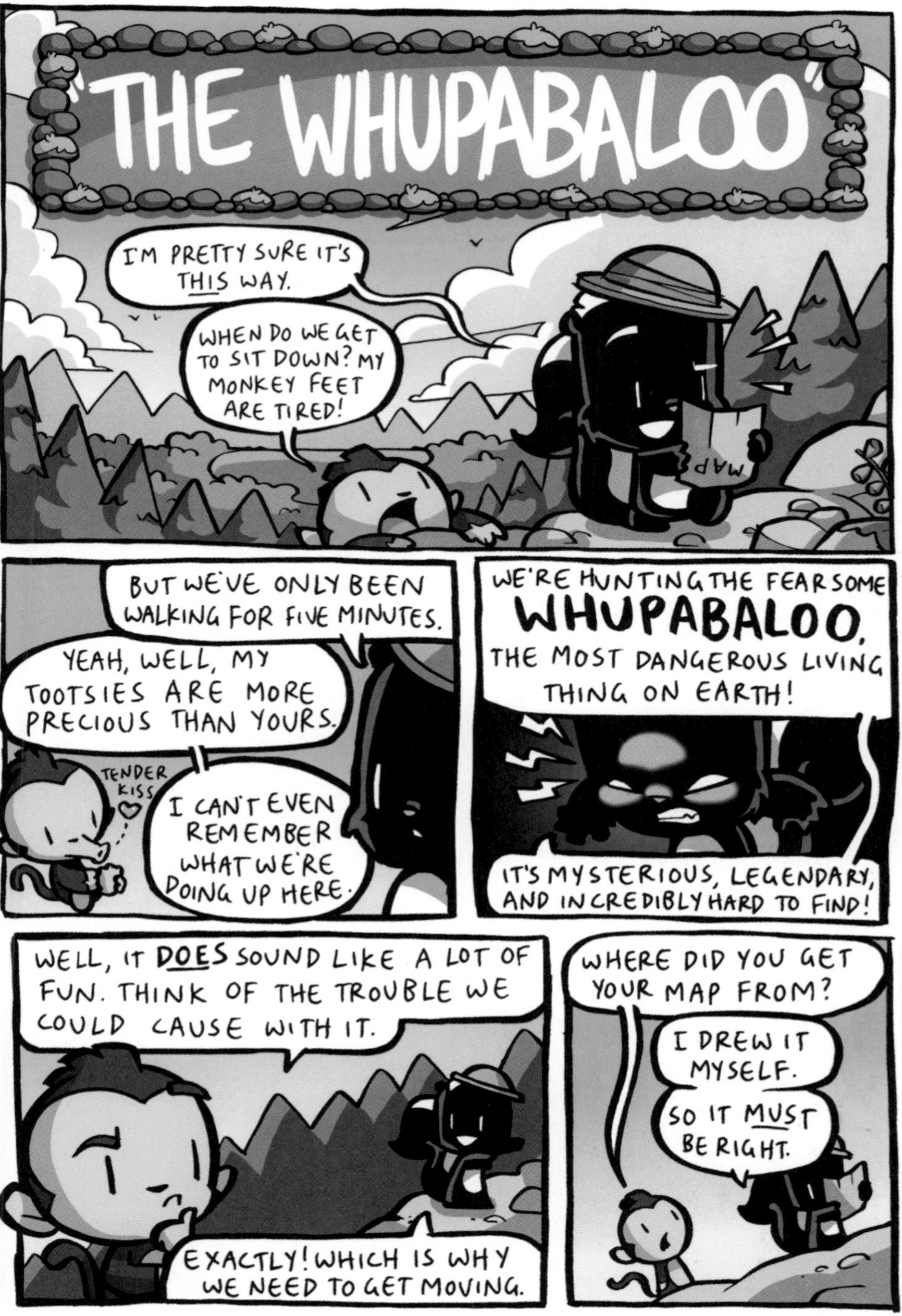
"THE WHUPABALOO"
I'M PRETTY SURE IT'S THIS WAY.
WHEN DO WE GET TO SIT DOWN? MY MONKEY FEET ARE TIRED!
MAP
BUT WE'VE ONLY BEEN WALKING FOR FIVE MINUTES.
YEAH, WELL, MY TOOTSIES ARE MORE PRECIOUS THAN YOURS.
TENDER KISS
I CAN'T EVEN REMEMBER WHAT WE'RE DOING UP HERE.
WE'RE HUNTING THE FEARSOME WHUPABALOO, THE MOST DANGEROUS LIVING THING ON EARTH!
IT'S MYSTERIOUS, LEGENDARY, AND INCREDIBLY HARD TO FIND!
WELL, IT DOES SOUND LIKE A LOT OF FUN. THINK OF THE TROUBLE WE COULD CAUSE WITH IT.
EXACTLY! WHICH IS WHY WE NEED TO GET MOVING.
WHERE DID YOU GET YOUR MAP FROM?
I DREW IT MYSELF.
SO IT MUST BE RIGHT.

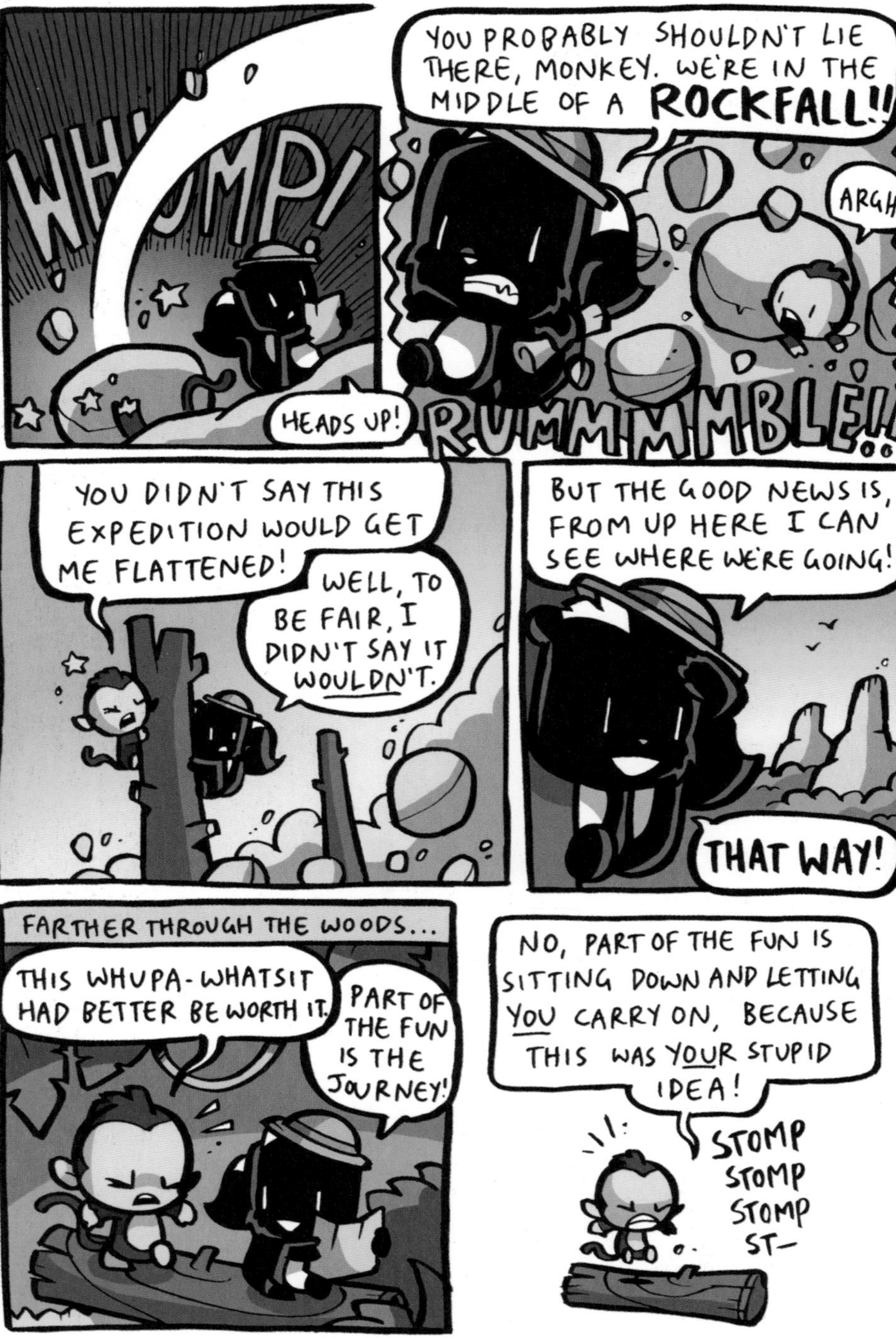
WHUMP!
YOU PROBABLY SHOULDN'T LIE THERE, MONKEY. WE'RE IN THE MIDDLE OF A ROCKFALL!!
ARGH!
HEADS UP!
RUMMMMMBLE!!
YOU DIDN'T SAY THIS EXPEDITION WOULD GET ME FLATTENED!
WELL, TO BE FAIR, I DIDN'T SAY IT WOULDN'T.
BUT THE GOOD NEWS IS, FROM UP HERE I CAN SEE WHERE WE'RE GOING!
THAT WAY!
FARTHER THROUGH THE WOODS...
THIS WHUPA-WHATSIT HAD BETTER BE WORTH IT.
PART OF THE FUN IS THE JOURNEY!
NO, PART OF THE FUN IS SITTING DOWN AND LETTING YOU CARRY ON, BECAUSE THIS WAS YOUR STUPID IDEA!
STOMP
STOMP
STOMP
ST—

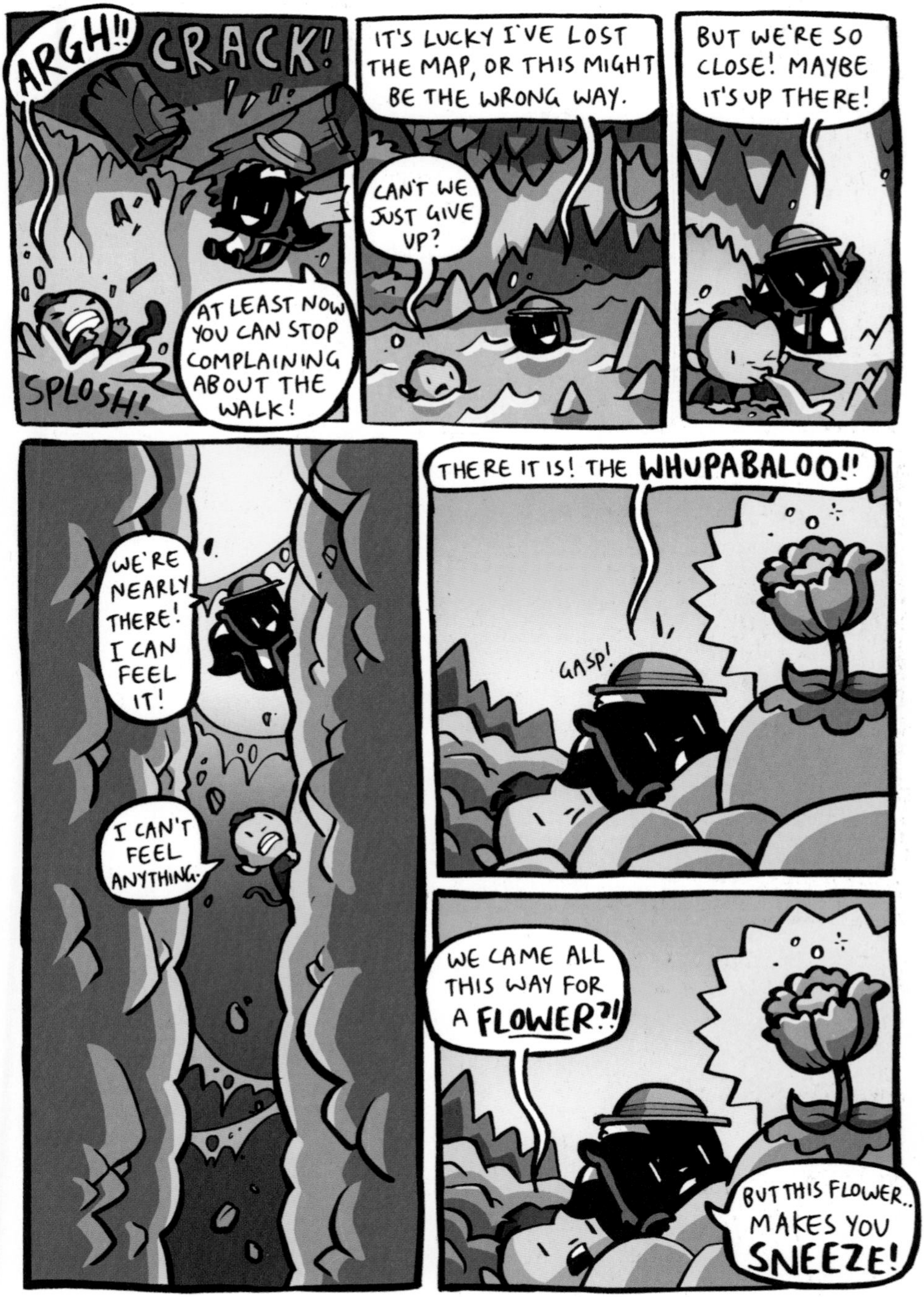
ARGH!!
CRACK!
SPLOSH!
AT LEAST NOW YOU CAN STOP COMPLAINING ABOUT THE WALK!
IT'S LUCKY I'VE LOST THE MAP, OR THIS MIGHT BE THE WRONG WAY.
CAN'T WE JUST GIVE UP?
BUT WE'RE SO CLOSE! MAYBE IT'S UP THERE!
WE'RE NEARLY THERE! I CAN FEEL IT!
I CAN'T FEEL ANYTHING.
THERE IT IS! THE WHUPABALOO!!
GASP!
WE CAME ALL THIS WAY FOR A FLOWER?!
BUT THIS FLOWER.. MAKES YOU SNEEZE!

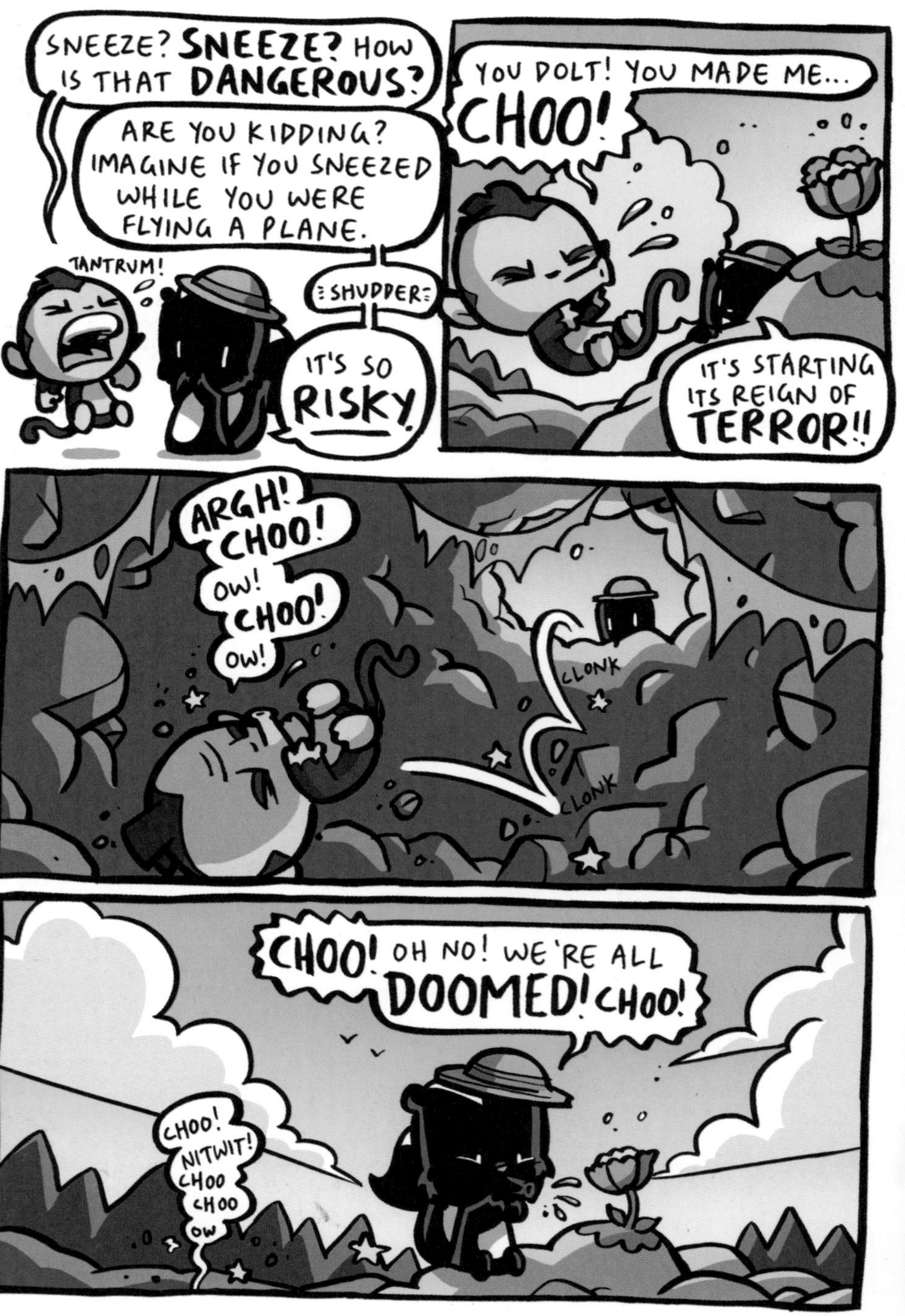
SNEEZE? SNEEZE? HOW IS THAT DANGEROUS?
ARE YOU KIDDING? IMAGINE IF YOU SNEEZED WHILE YOU WERE FLYING A PLANE.
TANTRUM!
=SHUDDER=
IT'S SO RISKY.
YOU DOLT! YOU MADE ME... CHOO!
IT'S STARTING ITS REIGN OF TERROR!!
ARGH! CHOO! OW! CHOO! OW!
CLONK
CLONK
CHOO! OH NO! WE'RE ALL DOOMED! CHOO!
CHOO! NITWIT! CHOO CHOO OW

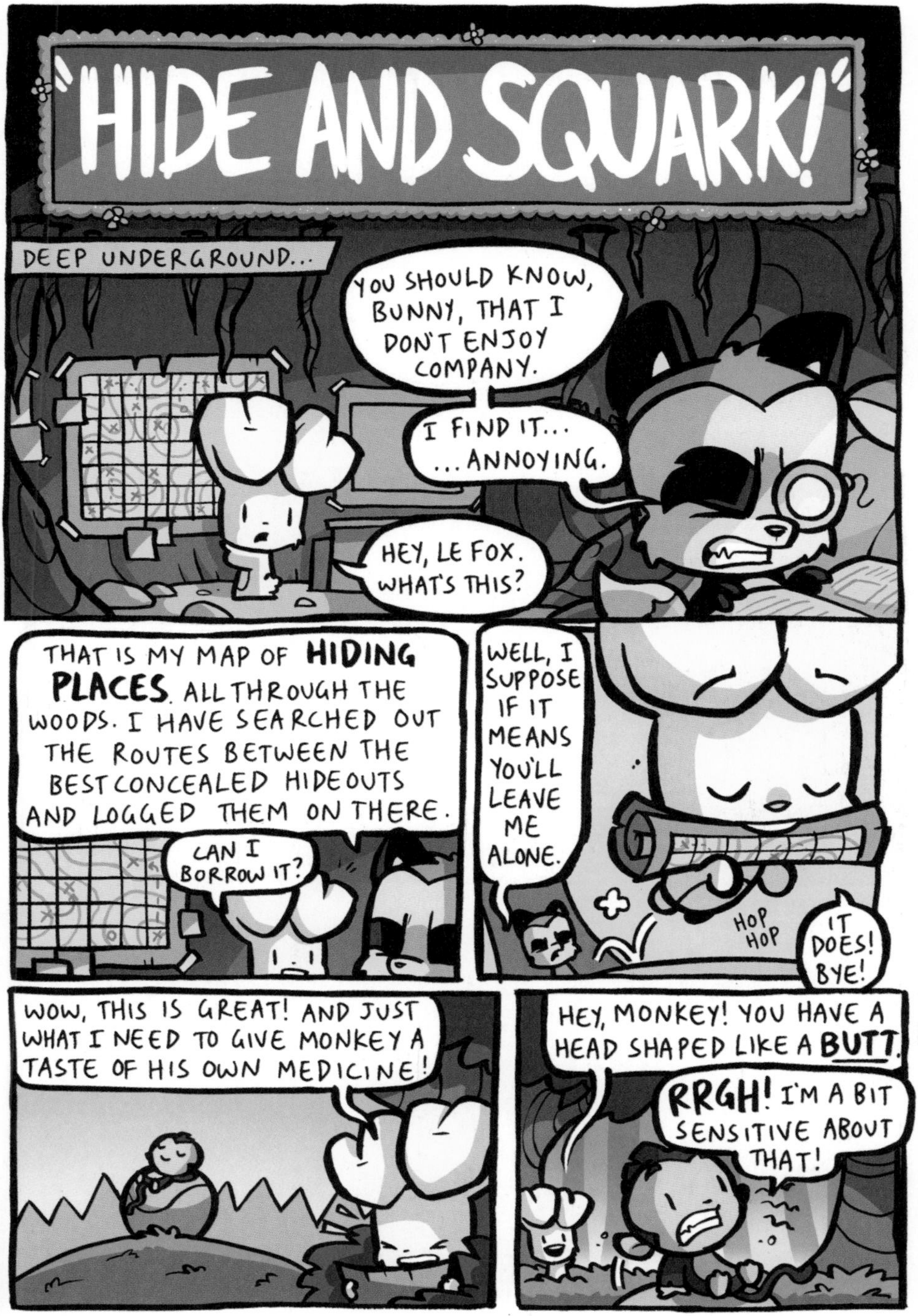
"HIDE AND SQUARK!"
DEEP UNDERGROUND...
YOU SHOULD KNOW, BUNNY, THAT I DON'T ENJOY COMPANY.
I FIND IT... ...ANNOYING.
HEY, LE FOX. WHAT'S THIS?
THAT IS MY MAP OF **HIDING PLACES**. ALL THROUGH THE WOODS. I HAVE SEARCHED OUT THE ROUTES BETWEEN THE BEST CONCEALED HIDEOUTS AND LOGGED THEM ON THERE.
CAN I BORROW IT?
WELL, I SUPPOSE IF IT MEANS YOU'LL LEAVE ME ALONE.
HOP HOP
IT DOES! BYE!
WOW, THIS IS GREAT! AND JUST WHAT I NEED TO GIVE MONKEY A TASTE OF HIS OWN MEDICINE!
HEY, MONKEY! YOU HAVE A HEAD SHAPED LIKE A **BUTT**.
RRGH! I'M A BIT SENSITIVE ABOUT THAT!

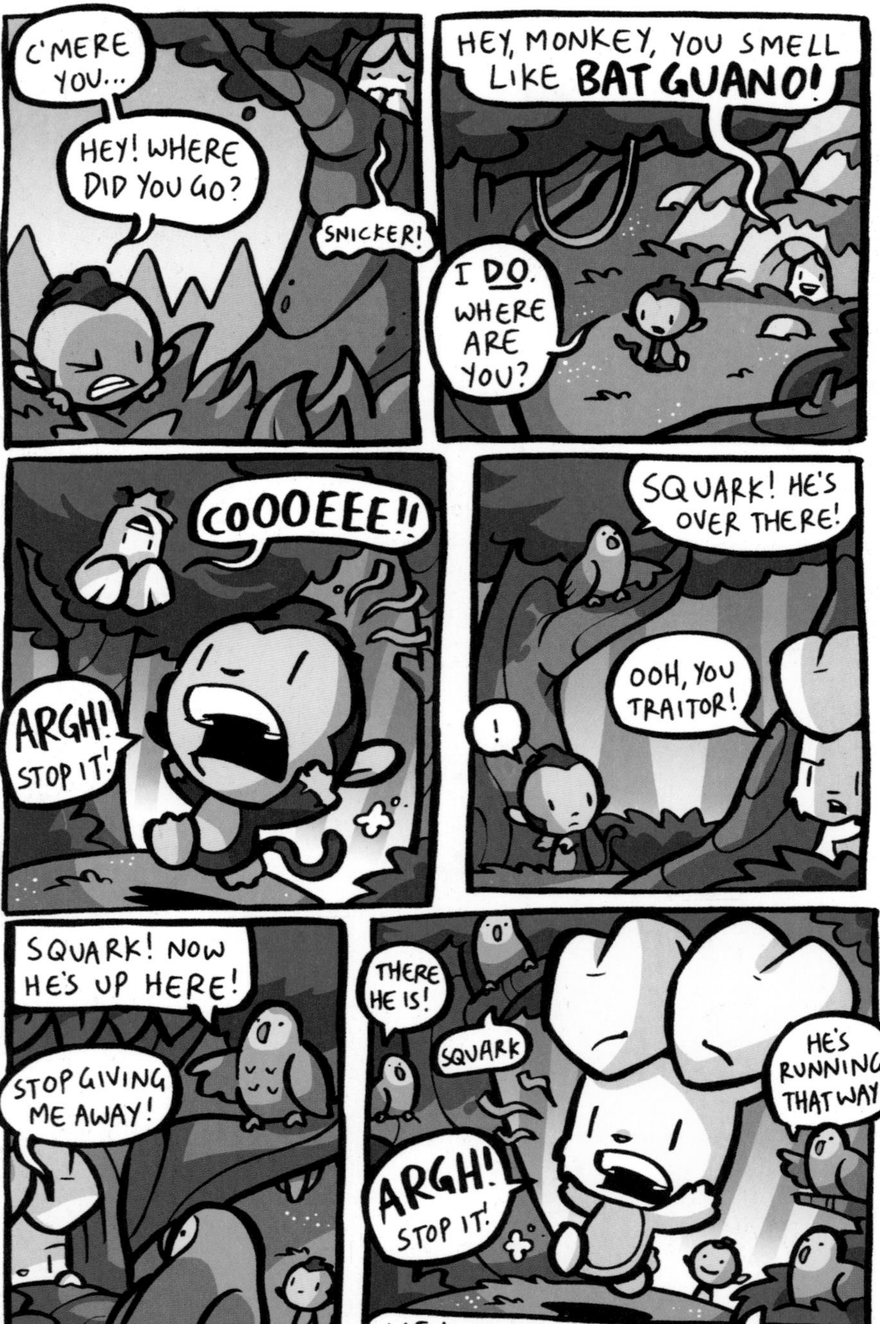
C'MERE YOU...
HEY! WHERE DID YOU GO?
SNICKER!
HEY, MONKEY, YOU SMELL LIKE BAT GUANO!
I DO. WHERE ARE YOU?
COOOEEE!!
ARGH! STOP IT!
SQUARK! HE'S OVER THERE!
!
OOH, YOU TRAITOR!
SQUARK! NOW HE'S UP HERE!
STOP GIVING ME AWAY!
THERE HE IS!
SQUARK
HE'S RUNNING THAT WAY!
ARGH! STOP IT!
WE KNOW YOUR SECRET! SQUARK!

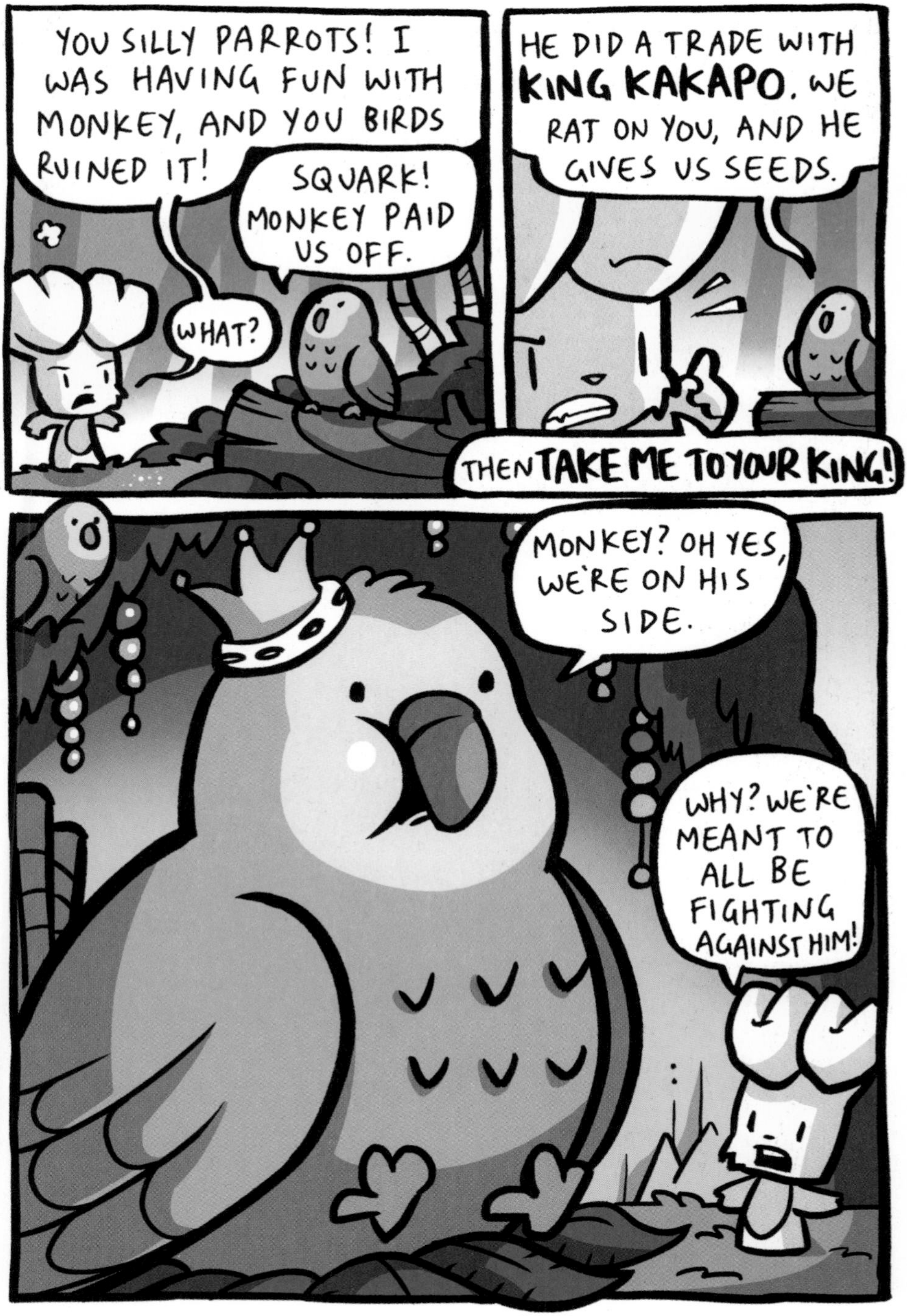
YOU SILLY PARROTS! I WAS HAVING FUN WITH MONKEY, AND YOU BIRDS RUINED IT!
SQUARK! MONKEY PAID US OFF.
WHAT?
HE DID A TRADE WITH **KING KAKAPO**. WE RAT ON YOU, AND HE GIVES US SEEDS.
THEN **TAKE ME TO YOUR KING!**
MONKEY? OH YES, WE'RE ON HIS SIDE.
WHY? WE'RE MEANT TO ALL BE FIGHTING AGAINST HIM!

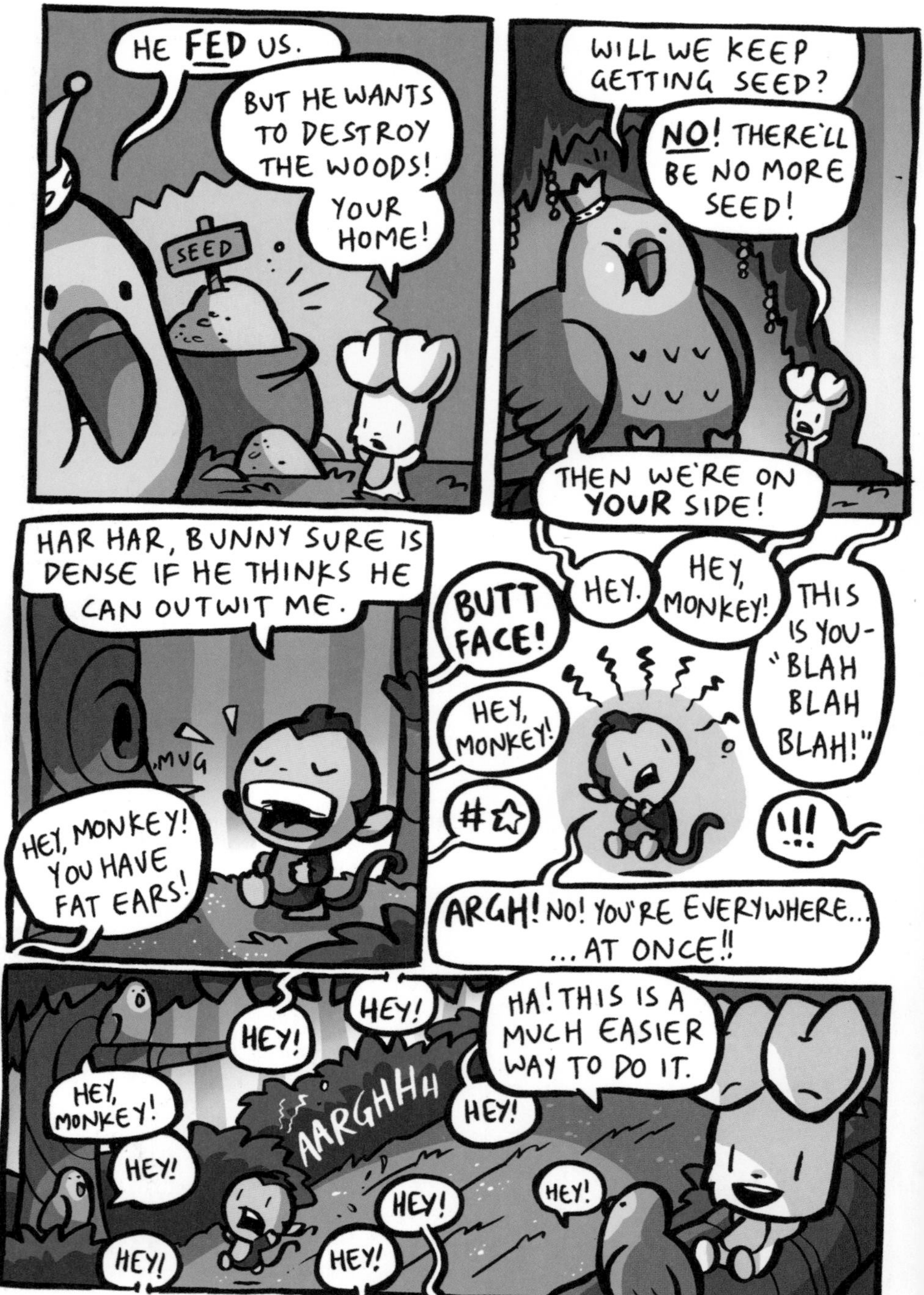
HE FED US.
BUT HE WANTS TO DESTROY THE WOODS!
YOUR HOME!
SEED
WILL WE KEEP GETTING SEED?
NO! THERE'LL BE NO MORE SEED!
THEN WE'RE ON YOUR SIDE!
HAR HAR, BUNNY SURE IS DENSE IF HE THINKS HE CAN OUTWIT ME.
MUG
HEY, MONKEY! YOU HAVE FAT EARS!
BUTT FACE!
HEY, MONKEY!
#☆
HEY.
HEY, MONKEY!
THIS IS YOU- "BLAH BLAH BLAH!"
!!!
ARGH! NO! YOU'RE EVERYWHERE... ...AT ONCE!!
HEY!
HEY!
HA! THIS IS A MUCH EASIER WAY TO DO IT.
HEY, MONKEY!
AARGHHH
HEY!
HEY!
HEY!
HEY!
HEY!
HEY!

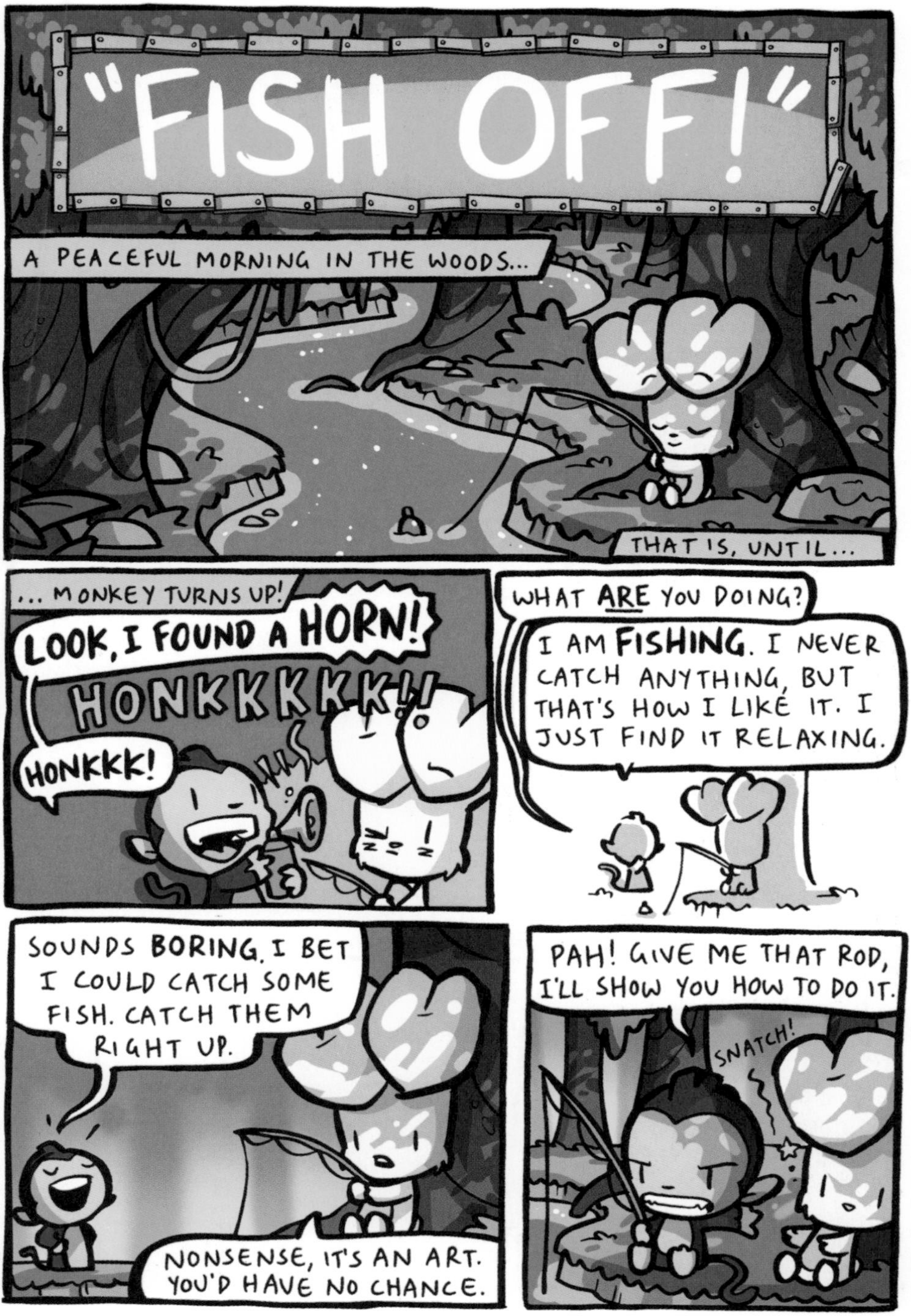

"FISH OFF!"
A PEACEFUL MORNING IN THE WOODS...
THAT IS, UNTIL...
... MONKEY TURNS UP!
LOOK, I FOUND A HORN!
HONKKKKKK!!
HONKKK!
WHAT ARE YOU DOING?
I AM FISHING. I NEVER CATCH ANYTHING, BUT THAT'S HOW I LIKE IT. I JUST FIND IT RELAXING.
SOUNDS BORING. I BET I COULD CATCH SOME FISH. CATCH THEM RIGHT UP.
NONSENSE, IT'S AN ART. YOU'D HAVE NO CHANCE.
PAH! GIVE ME THAT ROD, I'LL SHOW YOU HOW TO DO IT.
SNATCH!

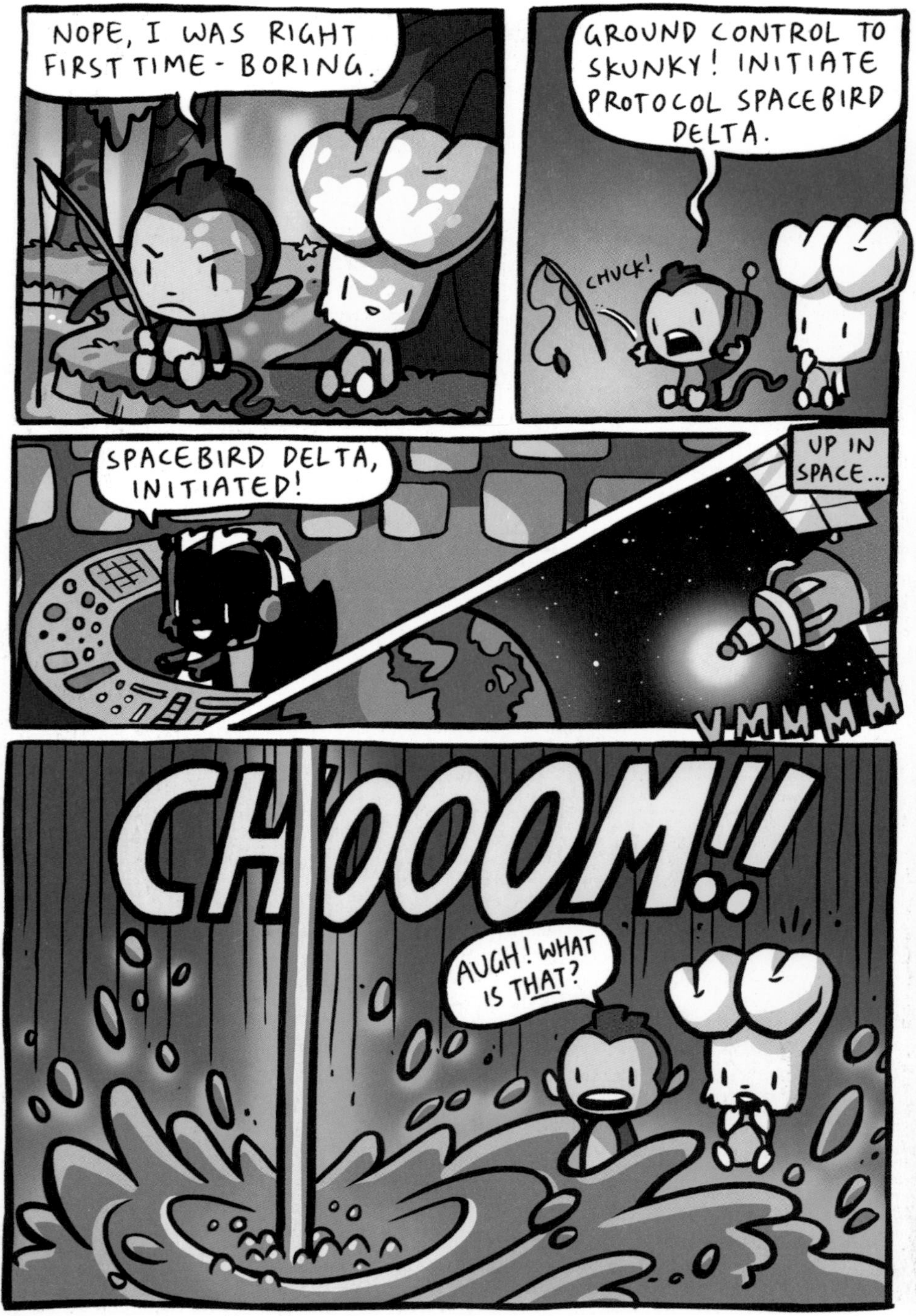
NOPE, I WAS RIGHT FIRST TIME - BORING.
GROUND CONTROL TO SKUNKY! INITIATE PROTOCOL SPACEBIRD DELTA.
CHUCK!
SPACEBIRD DELTA, INITIATED!
UP IN SPACE...
VMMMMM
CHOOOM!!
AUGH! WHAT IS THAT?

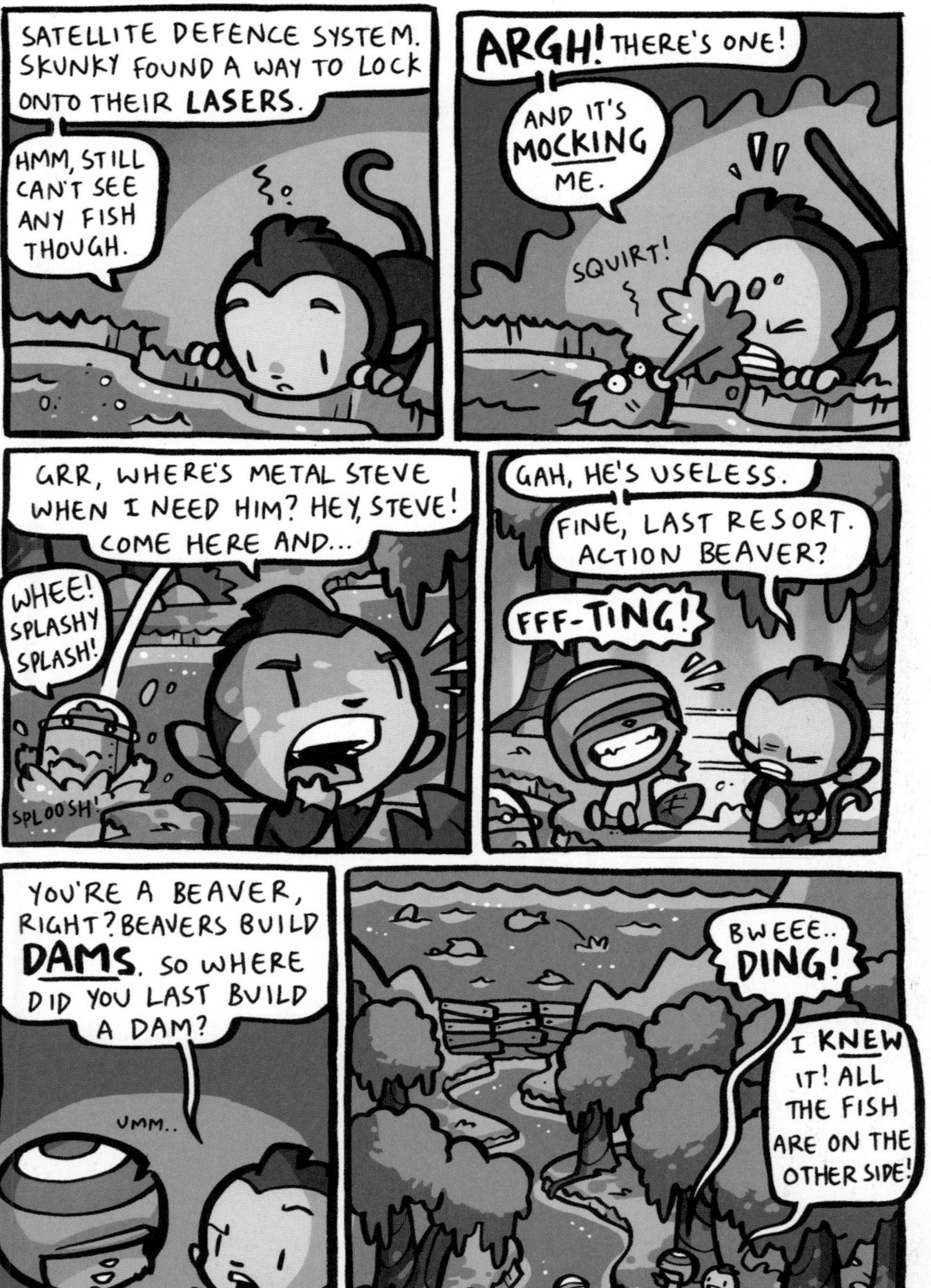

SATELLITE DEFENCE SYSTEM. SKUNKY FOUND A WAY TO LOCK ONTO THEIR **LASERS**.
HMM, STILL CAN'T SEE ANY FISH THOUGH.
ARGH! THERE'S ONE!
AND IT'S MOCKING ME.
SQUIRT!
GRR, WHERE'S METAL STEVE WHEN I NEED HIM? HEY, STEVE! COME HERE AND...
WHEE! SPLASHY SPLASH!
SPLOOSH!
GAH, HE'S USELESS.
FINE, LAST RESORT. ACTION BEAVER?
FFF-TING!
YOU'RE A BEAVER, RIGHT? BEAVERS BUILD **DAMS**. SO WHERE DID YOU LAST BUILD A DAM?
UMM..
BWEEE.. **DING!**
I KNEW IT! ALL THE FISH ARE ON THE OTHER SIDE!

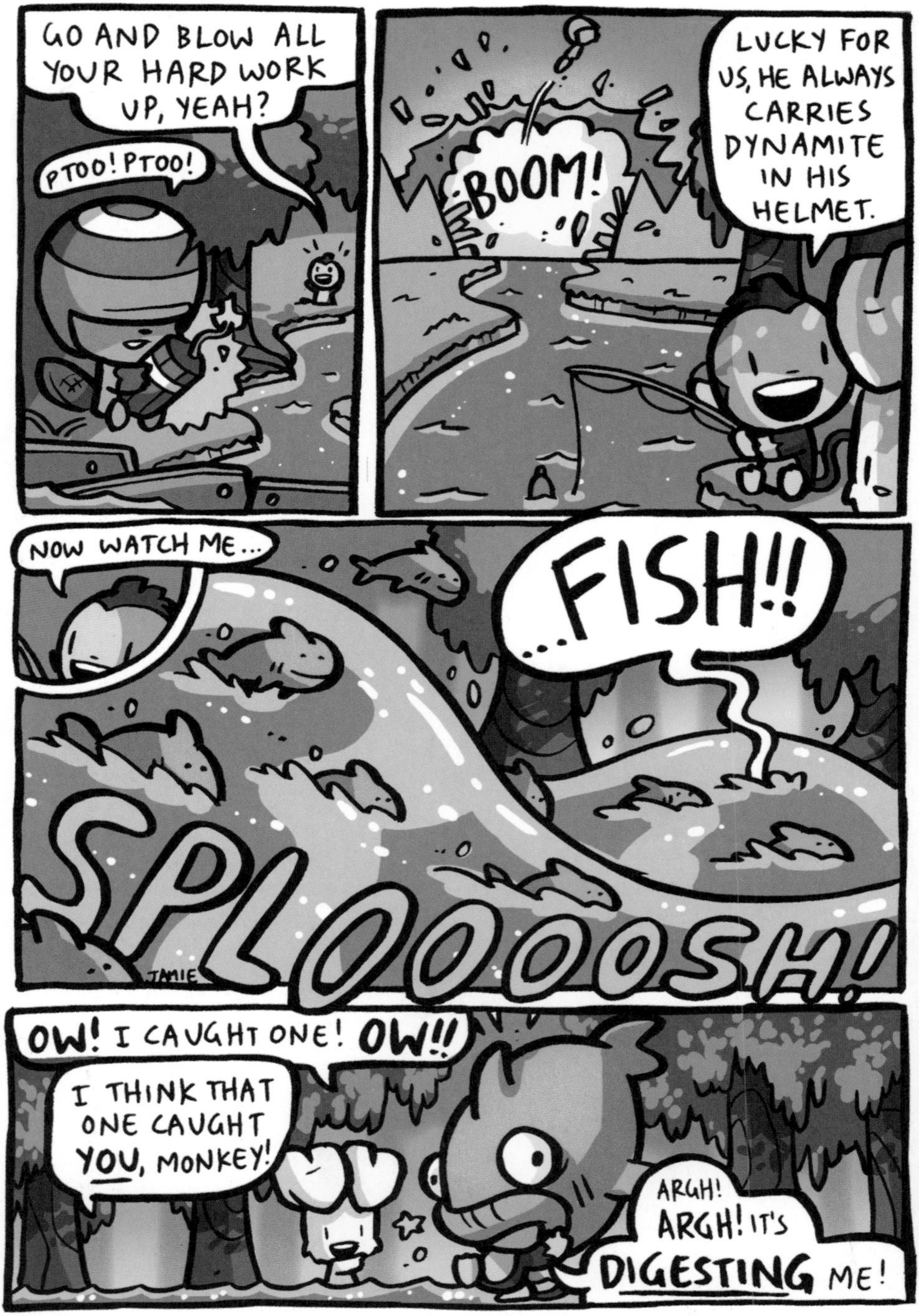

GO AND BLOW ALL YOUR HARD WORK UP, YEAH?
PTOO! PTOO!
BOOM!
LUCKY FOR US, HE ALWAYS CARRIES DYNAMITE IN HIS HELMET.
NOW WATCH ME...
...FISH!!
SPLOOOOSH!
JAMIE
OW! I CAUGHT ONE! OW!!
I THINK THAT ONE CAUGHT YOU, MONKEY!
ARGH! ARGH! IT'S DIGESTING ME!

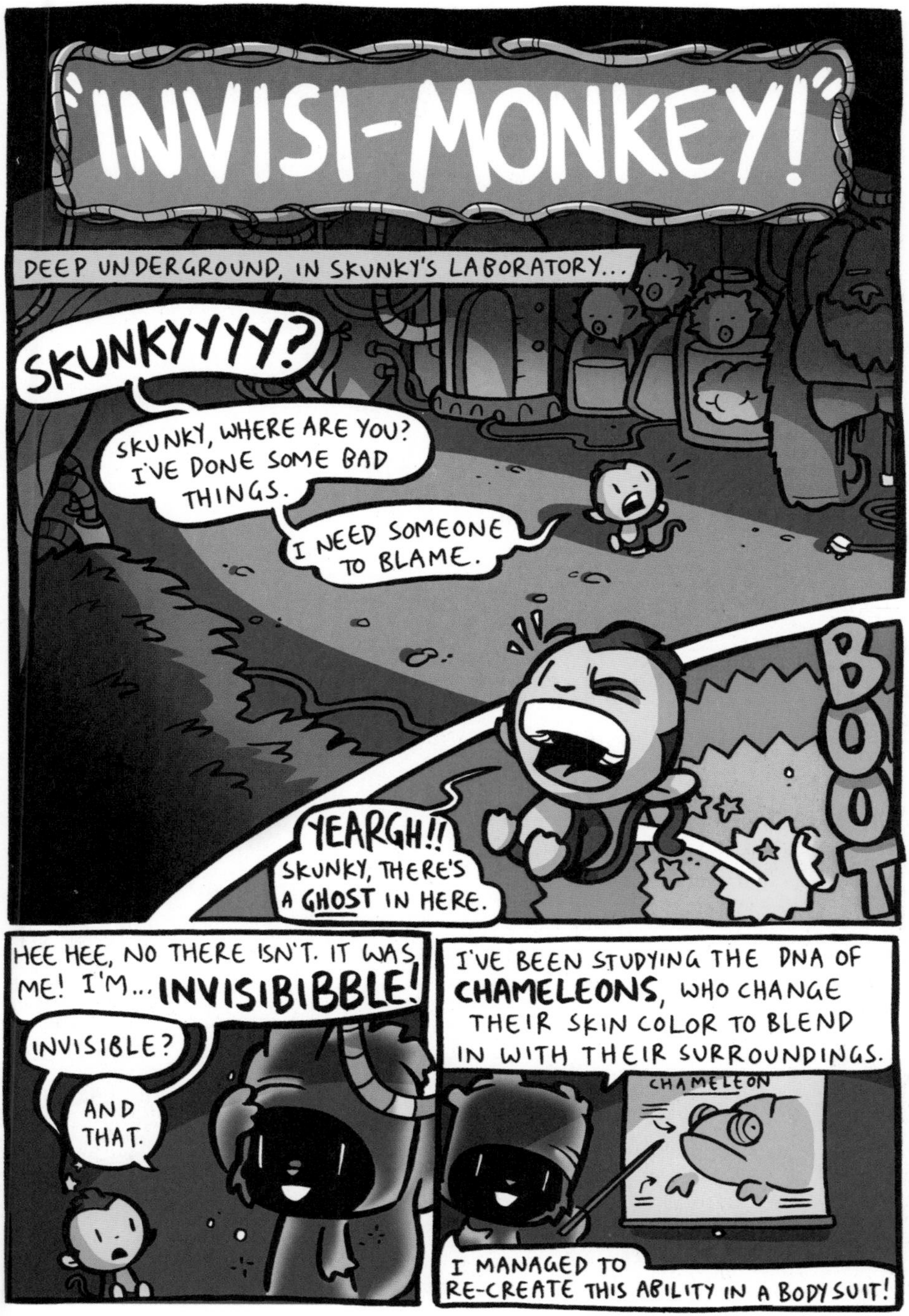
"INVISI-MONKEY!"
DEEP UNDERGROUND, IN SKUNKY'S LABORATORY...
SKUNKYYYY?
SKUNKY, WHERE ARE YOU? I'VE DONE SOME BAD THINGS.
I NEED SOMEONE TO BLAME.
BOOT
YEARGH!! SKUNKY, THERE'S A GHOST IN HERE.
HEE HEE, NO THERE ISN'T. IT WAS ME! I'M... INVISIBIBBLE!
INVISIBLE?
AND THAT.
I'VE BEEN STUDYING THE DNA OF CHAMELEONS, WHO CHANGE THEIR SKIN COLOR TO BLEND IN WITH THEIR SURROUNDINGS.
CHAMELEON
I MANAGED TO RE-CREATE THIS ABILITY IN A BODYSUIT!

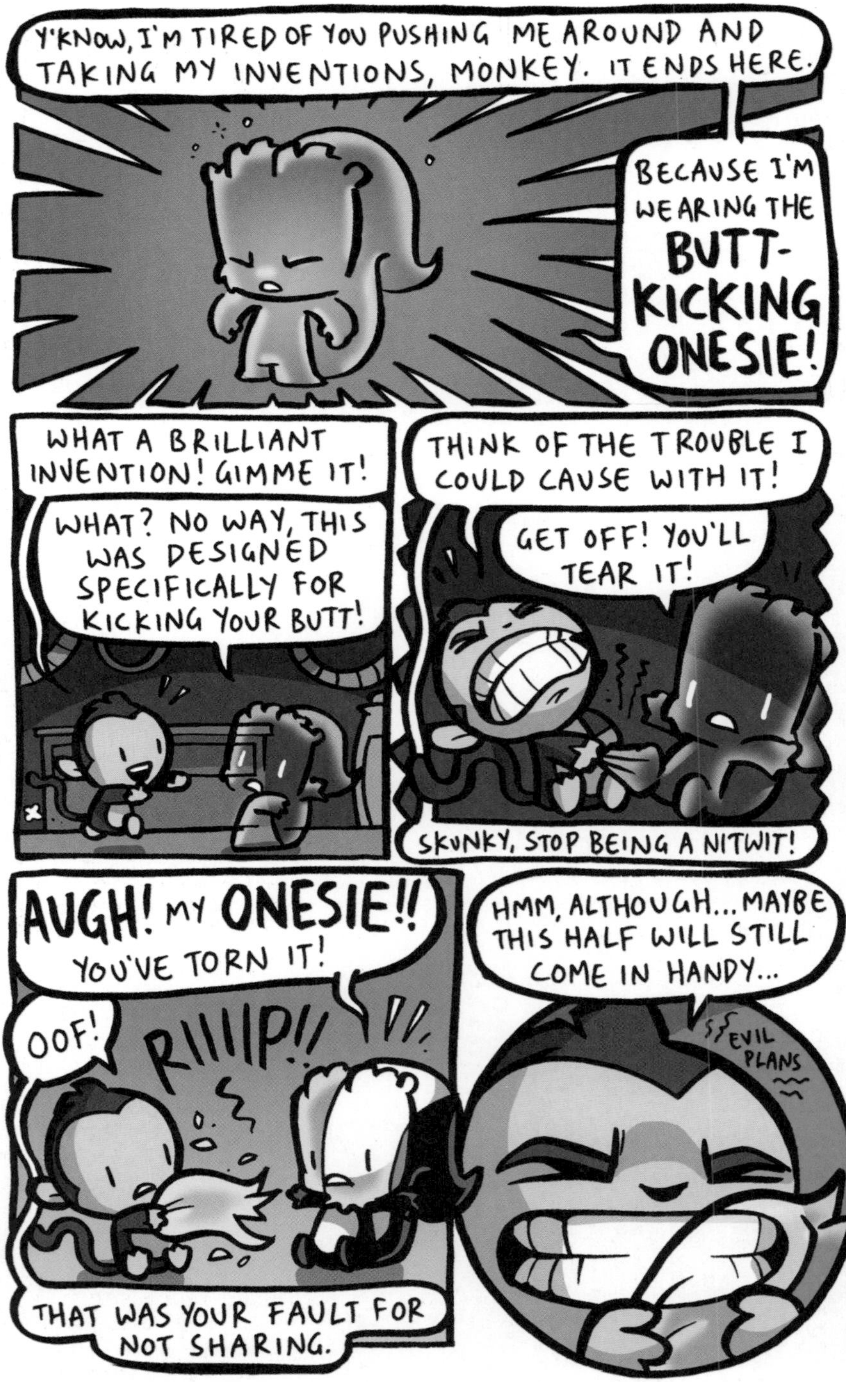
Y'KNOW, I'M TIRED OF YOU PUSHING ME AROUND AND TAKING MY INVENTIONS, MONKEY. IT ENDS HERE.
BECAUSE I'M WEARING THE BUTT-KICKING ONESIE!
WHAT A BRILLIANT INVENTION! GIMME IT!
WHAT? NO WAY, THIS WAS DESIGNED SPECIFICALLY FOR KICKING YOUR BUTT!
THINK OF THE TROUBLE I COULD CAUSE WITH IT!
GET OFF! YOU'LL TEAR IT!
SKUNKY, STOP BEING A NITWIT!
AUGH! MY ONESIE!! YOU'VE TORN IT!
OOF!
RIIIIP!!
THAT WAS YOUR FAULT FOR NOT SHARING.
HMM, ALTHOUGH... MAYBE THIS HALF WILL STILL COME IN HANDY...
EVIL PLANS

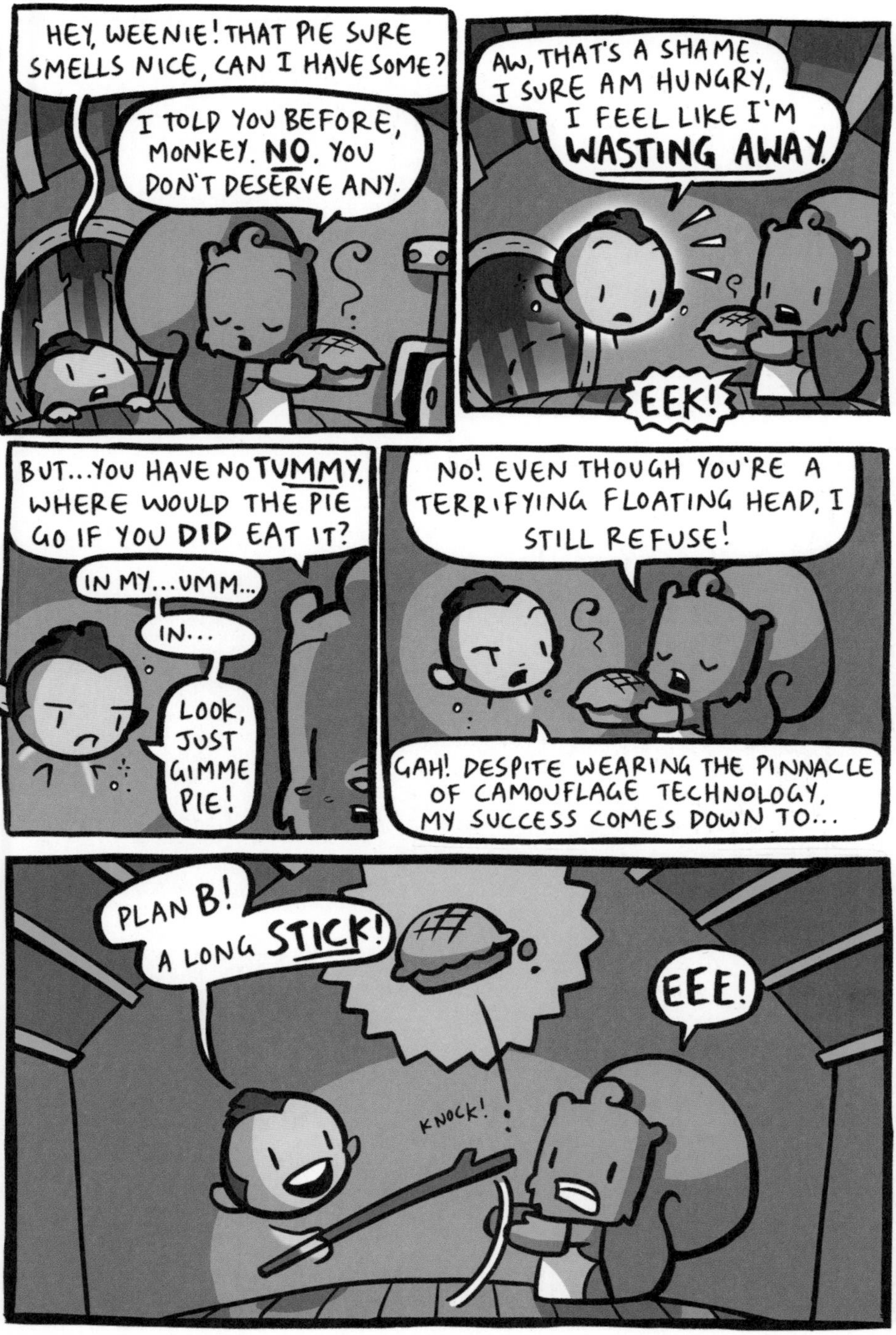
HEY, WEENIE! THAT PIE SURE SMELLS NICE, CAN I HAVE SOME?
I TOLD YOU BEFORE, MONKEY. NO. YOU DON'T DESERVE ANY.
AW, THAT'S A SHAME. I SURE AM HUNGRY, I FEEL LIKE I'M WASTING AWAY.
EEK!
BUT... YOU HAVE NO TUMMY. WHERE WOULD THE PIE GO IF YOU DID EAT IT?
IN MY... UMM...
IN...
LOOK, JUST GIMME PIE!
NO! EVEN THOUGH YOU'RE A TERRIFYING FLOATING HEAD, I STILL REFUSE!
GAH! DESPITE WEARING THE PINNACLE OF CAMOUFLAGE TECHNOLOGY, MY SUCCESS COMES DOWN TO...
PLAN B! A LONG STICK!
EEE!
KNOCK!

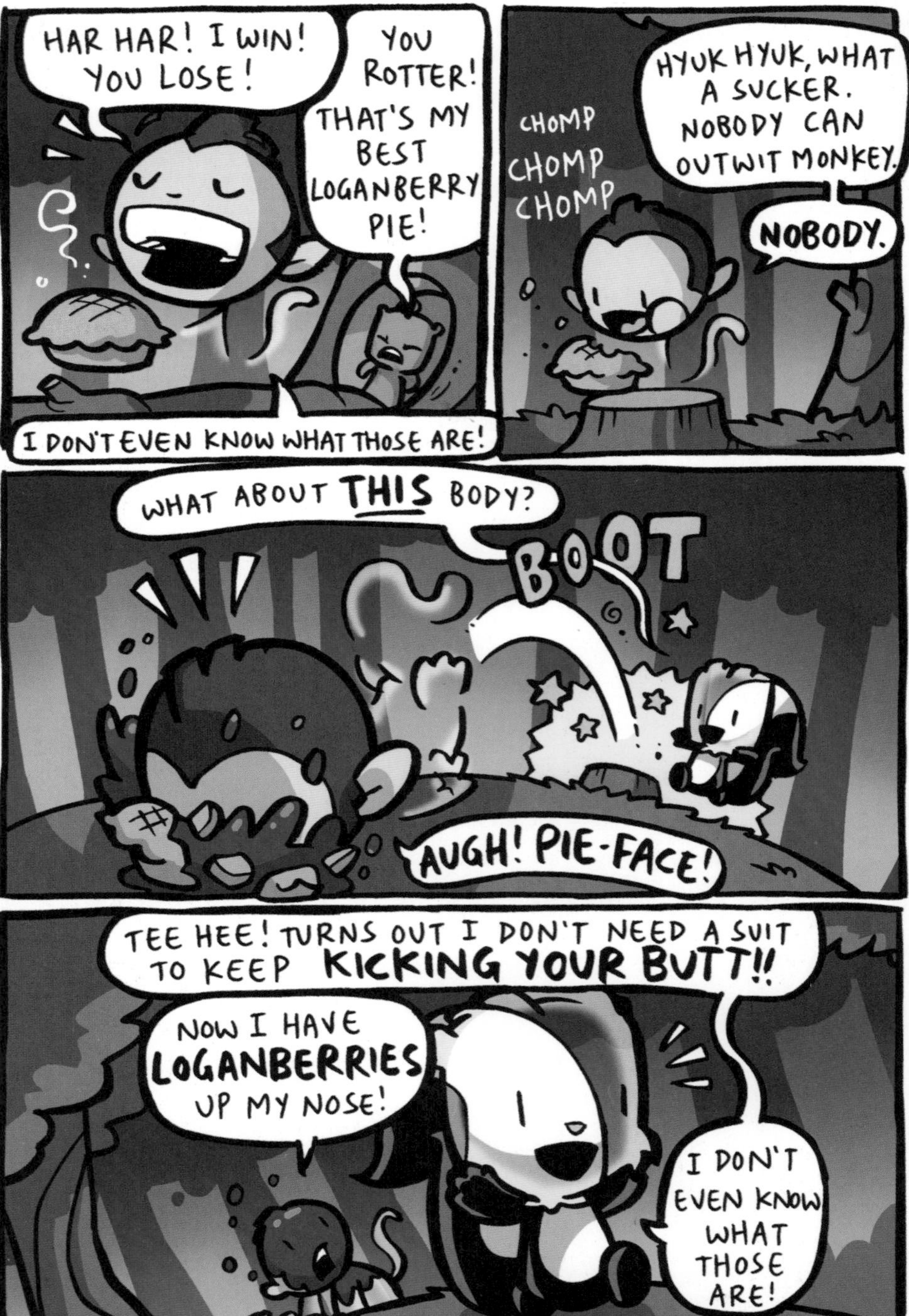
HAR HAR! I WIN! YOU LOSE!
YOU ROTTER! THAT'S MY BEST LOGANBERRY PIE!
I DON'T EVEN KNOW WHAT THOSE ARE!
CHOMP CHOMP CHOMP
HYUK HYUK, WHAT A SUCKER. NOBODY CAN OUTWIT MONKEY.
NOBODY.
WHAT ABOUT THIS BODY?
BOOT
AUGH! PIE-FACE!
TEE HEE! TURNS OUT I DON'T NEED A SUIT TO KEEP KICKING YOUR BUTT!!
NOW I HAVE LOGANBERRIES UP MY NOSE!
I DON'T EVEN KNOW WHAT THOSE ARE!

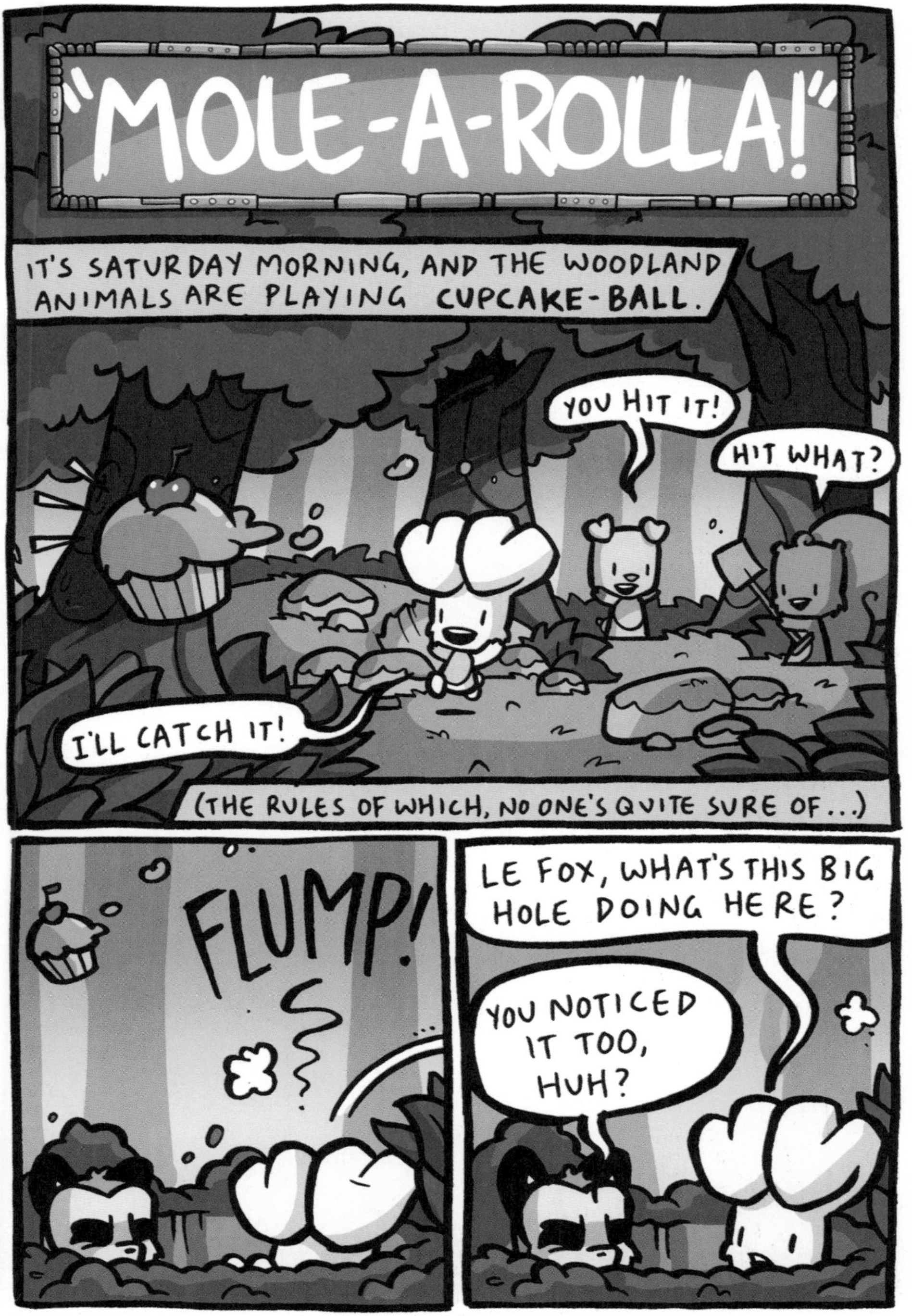
"MOLE-A-ROLLA!"
IT'S SATURDAY MORNING, AND THE WOODLAND ANIMALS ARE PLAYING CUPCAKE-BALL.
YOU HIT IT!
HIT WHAT?
I'LL CATCH IT!
(THE RULES OF WHICH, NO ONE'S QUITE SURE OF...)
FLUMP!
LE FOX, WHAT'S THIS BIG HOLE DOING HERE?
YOU NOTICED IT TOO, HUH?

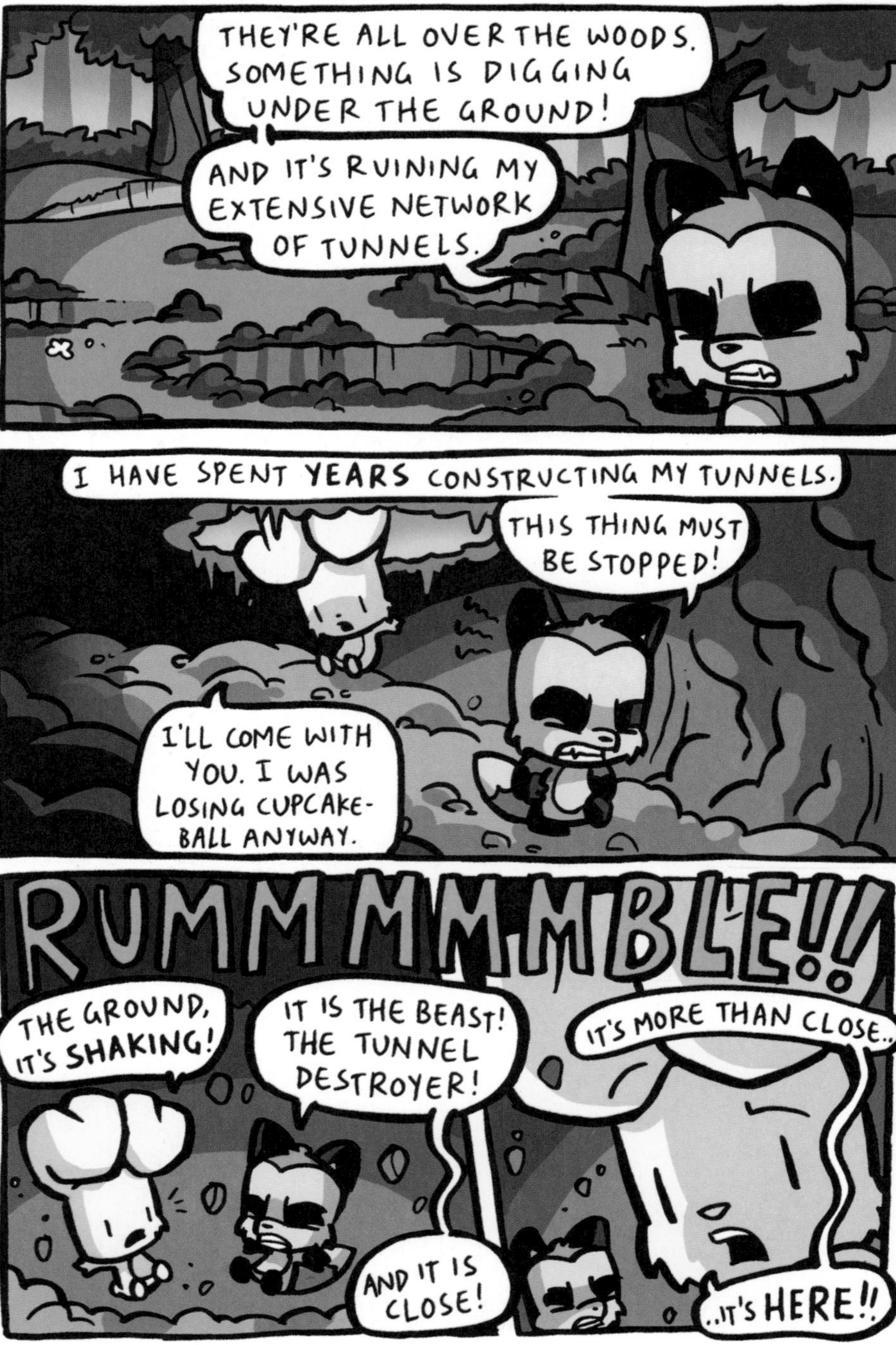
THEY'RE ALL OVER THE WOODS. SOMETHING IS DIGGING UNDER THE GROUND!
AND IT'S RUINING MY EXTENSIVE NETWORK OF TUNNELS.
I HAVE SPENT **YEARS** CONSTRUCTING MY TUNNELS.
THIS THING MUST BE STOPPED!
I'LL COME WITH YOU. I WAS LOSING CUPCAKE-BALL ANYWAY.
RUMMMMMMBLE!!!
THE GROUND, IT'S **SHAKING**!
IT IS THE BEAST! THE TUNNEL DESTROYER!
AND IT IS CLOSE!
IT'S MORE THAN CLOSE..
..IT'S **HERE**!!

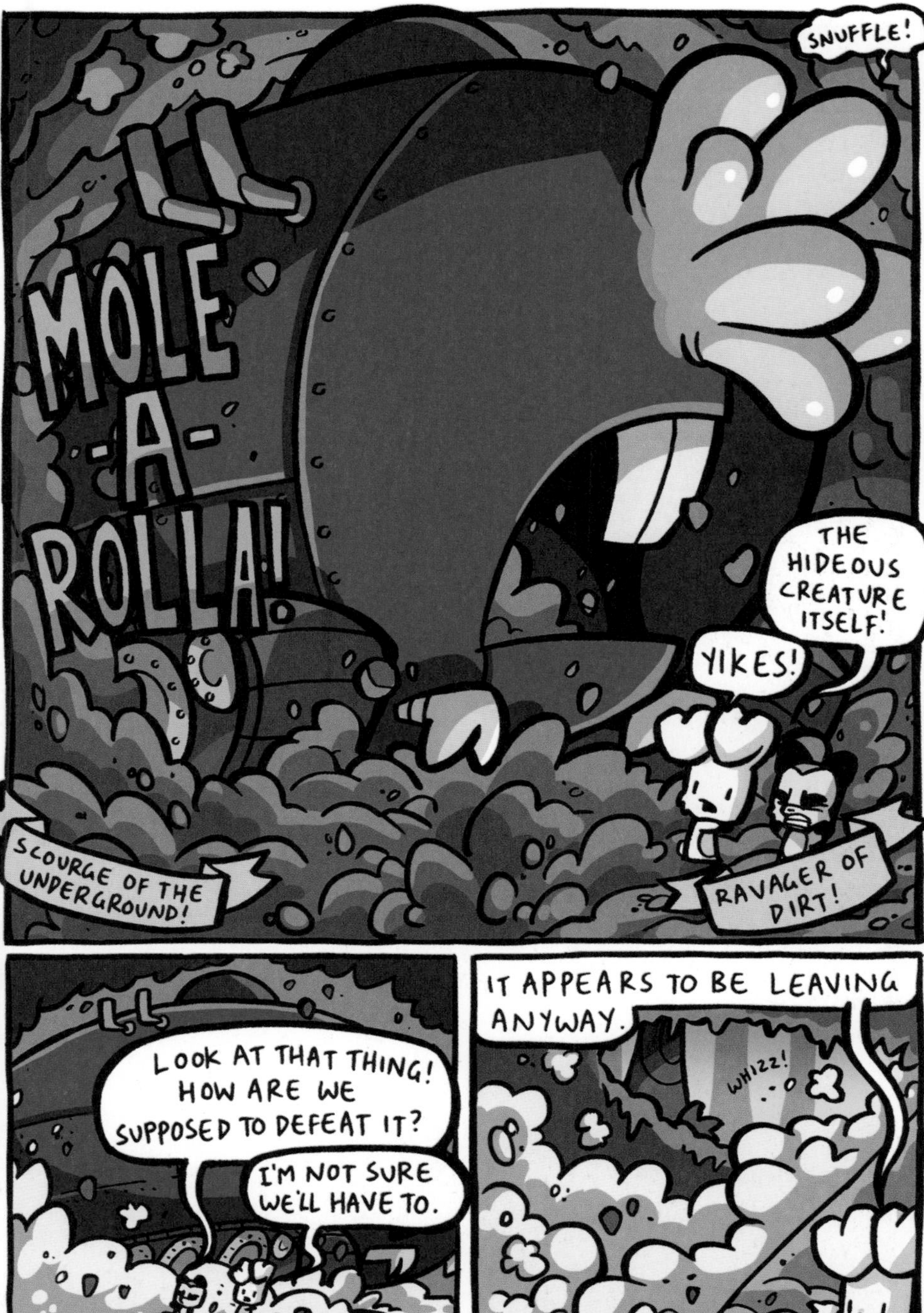
SNUFFLE!
MOLE-A-ROLLA!
THE HIDEOUS CREATURE ITSELF!
YIKES!
SCOURGE OF THE UNDERGROUND!
RAVAGER OF DIRT!
LOOK AT THAT THING! HOW ARE WE SUPPOSED TO DEFEAT IT?
I'M NOT SURE WE'LL HAVE TO.
IT APPEARS TO BE LEAVING ANYWAY.
WHIZZ!

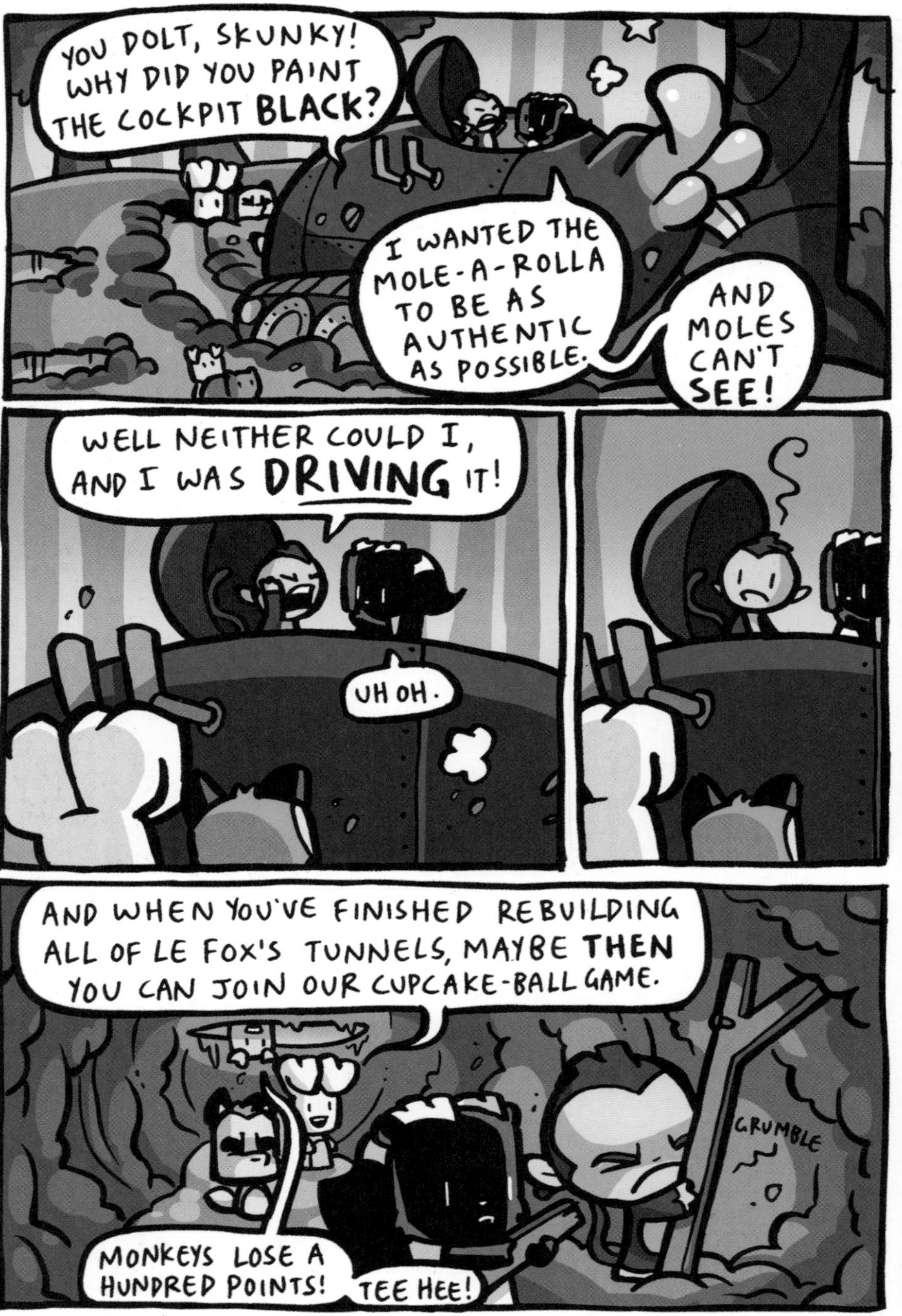
YOU DOLT, SKUNKY! WHY DID YOU PAINT THE COCKPIT BLACK?
I WANTED THE MOLE-A-ROLLA TO BE AS AUTHENTIC AS POSSIBLE.
AND MOLES CAN'T SEE!
WELL NEITHER COULD I, AND I WAS DRIVING IT!
UH OH.
AND WHEN YOU'VE FINISHED REBUILDING ALL OF LE FOX'S TUNNELS, MAYBE THEN YOU CAN JOIN OUR CUPCAKE-BALL GAME.
GRUMBLE
MONKEYS LOSE A HUNDRED POINTS!
TEE HEE!

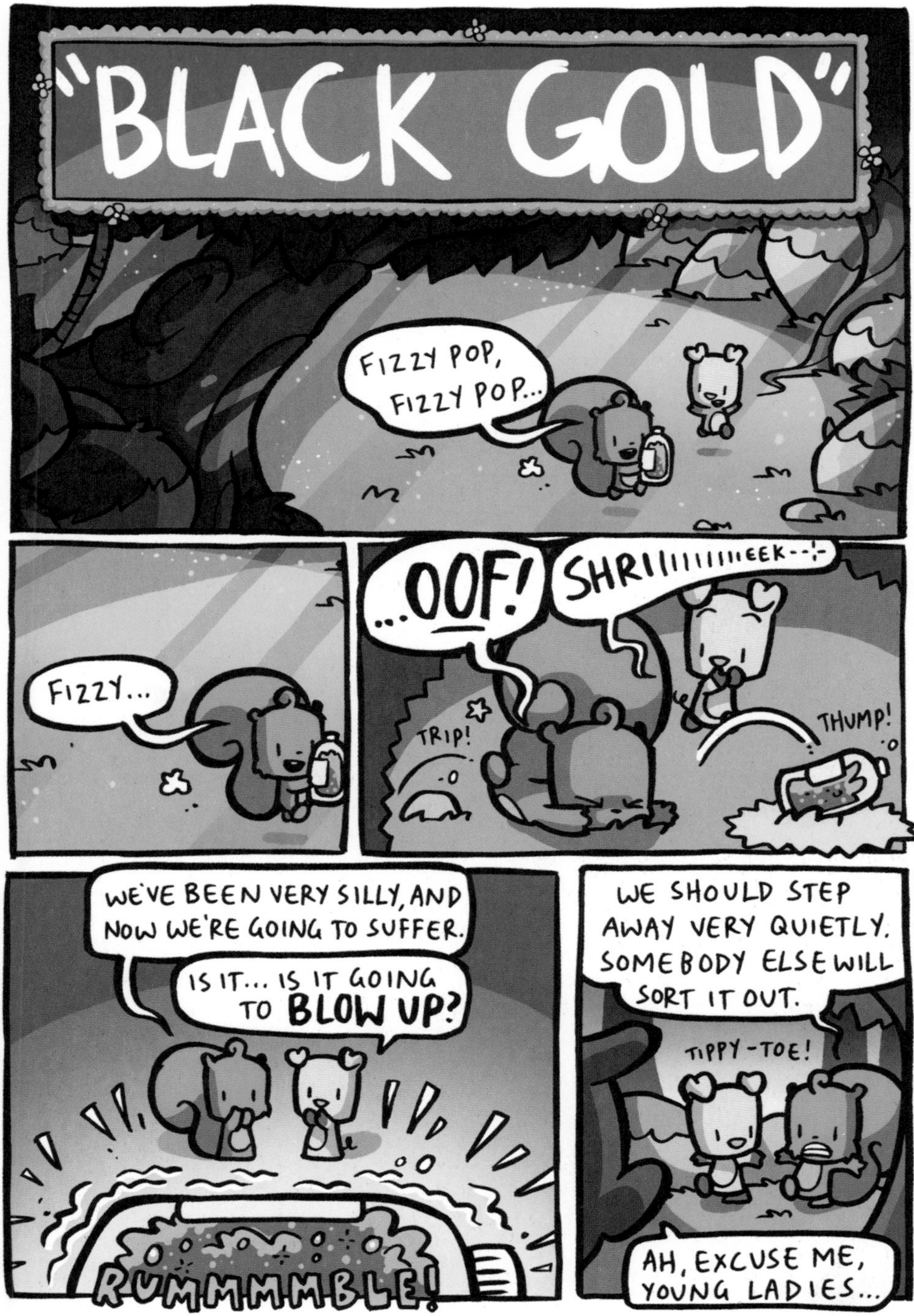
"BLACK GOLD"
FIZZY POP, FIZZY POP...
FIZZY...
...OOF!
SHRIIIIIIIIIEEK--
TRIP!
THUMP!
WE'VE BEEN VERY SILLY, AND NOW WE'RE GOING TO SUFFER.
IS IT... IS IT GOING TO BLOW UP?
RUMMMMMBLE!
WE SHOULD STEP AWAY VERY QUIETLY. SOMEBODY ELSE WILL SORT IT OUT.
TIPPY-TOE!
AH, EXCUSE ME, YOUNG LADIES...

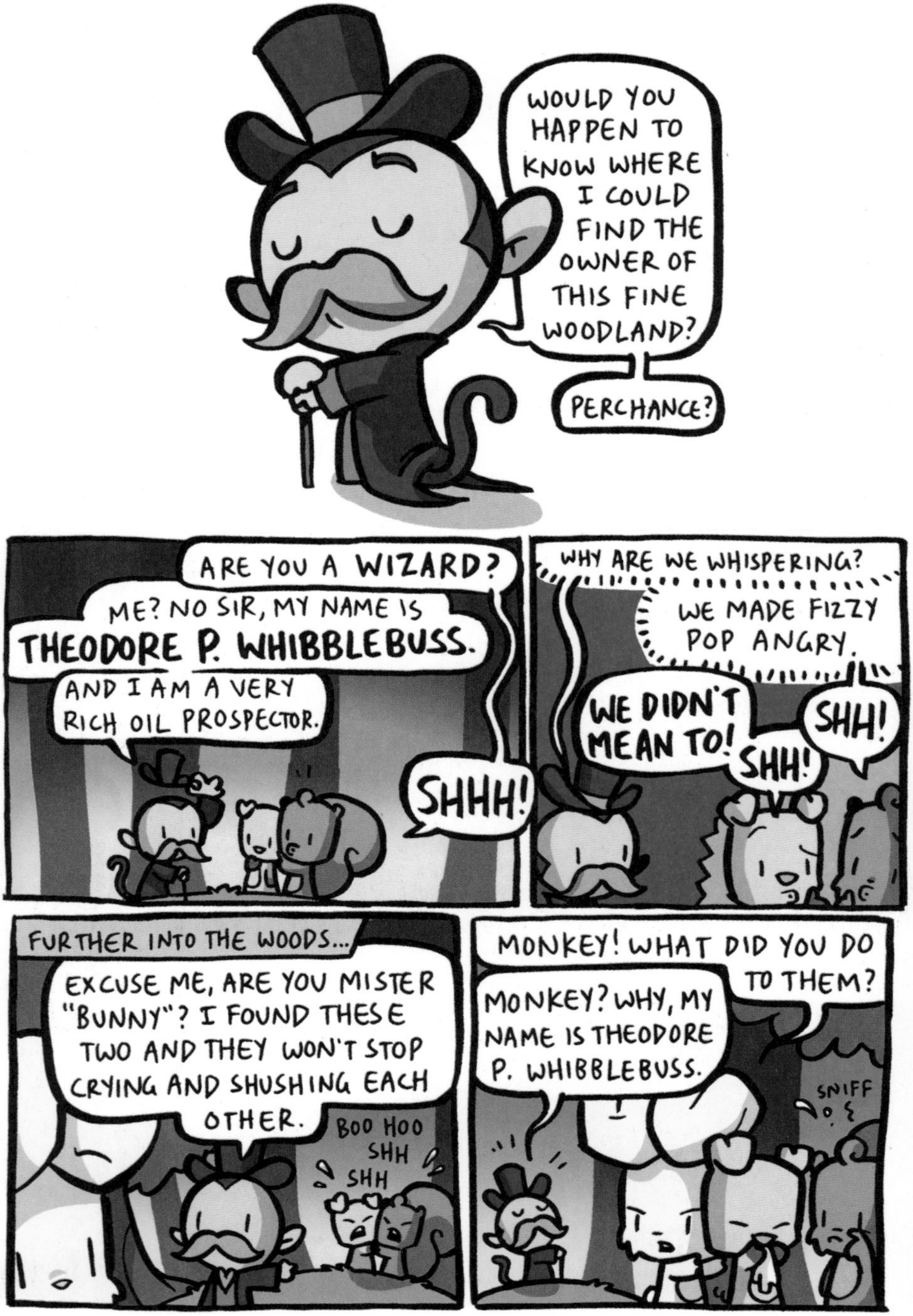
WOULD YOU HAPPEN TO KNOW WHERE I COULD FIND THE OWNER OF THIS FINE WOODLAND?
PERCHANCE?
ARE YOU A WIZARD?
ME? NO SIR, MY NAME IS THEODORE P. WHIBBLEBUSS.
AND I AM A VERY RICH OIL PROSPECTOR.
SHHH!
WHY ARE WE WHISPERING?
WE MADE FIZZY POP ANGRY.
WE DIDN'T MEAN TO!
SHH!
SHH!
FURTHER INTO THE WOODS...
EXCUSE ME, ARE YOU MISTER "BUNNY"? I FOUND THESE TWO AND THEY WON'T STOP CRYING AND SHUSHING EACH OTHER.
BOO HOO SHH SHH
MONKEY! WHAT DID YOU DO TO THEM?
MONKEY? WHY, MY NAME IS THEODORE P. WHIBBLEBUSS.
SNIFF

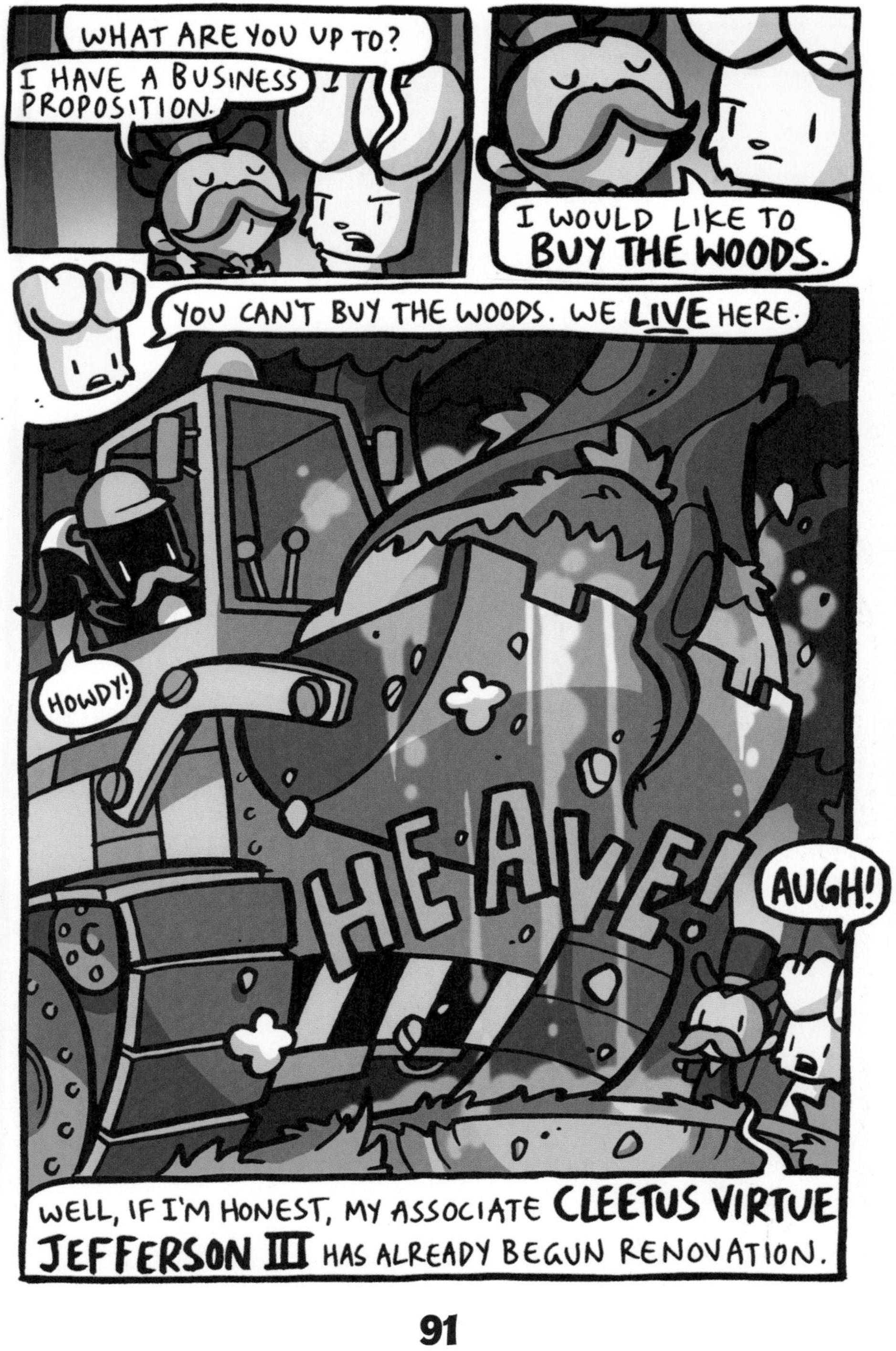

WHAT ARE YOU UP TO?
I HAVE A BUSINESS PROPOSITION.
I WOULD LIKE TO BUY THE WOODS.
YOU CAN'T BUY THE WOODS. WE LIVE HERE.
HOWDY!
HEAVE!
AUGH!
WELL, IF I'M HONEST, MY ASSOCIATE CLEETUS VIRTUE JEFFERSON III HAS ALREADY BEGUN RENOVATION.

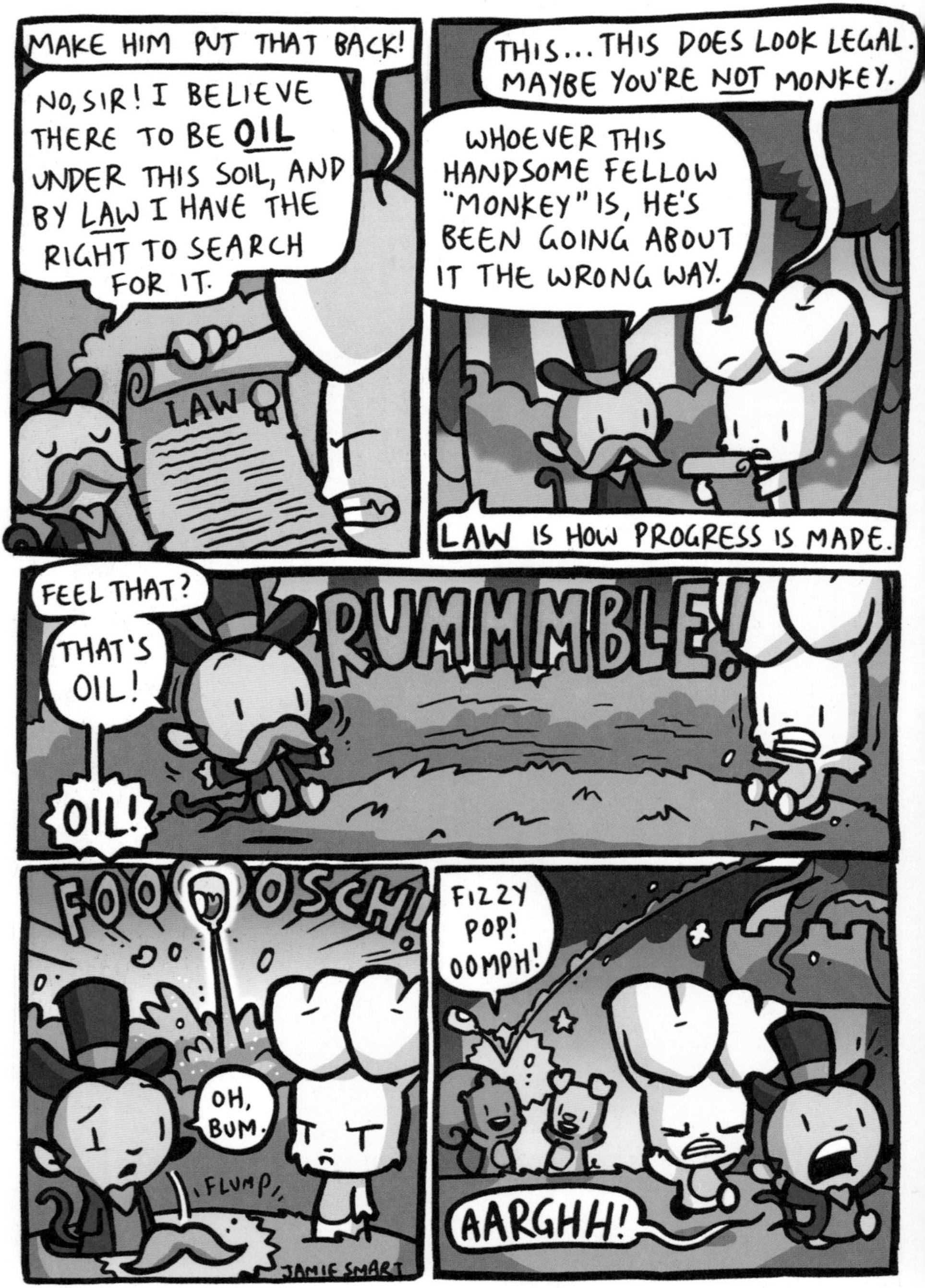
MAKE HIM PUT THAT BACK!
NO, SIR! I BELIEVE THERE TO BE OIL UNDER THIS SOIL, AND BY LAW I HAVE THE RIGHT TO SEARCH FOR IT.
LAW
THIS... THIS DOES LOOK LEGAL. MAYBE YOU'RE NOT MONKEY.
WHOEVER THIS HANDSOME FELLOW "MONKEY" IS, HE'S BEEN GOING ABOUT IT THE WRONG WAY.
LAW IS HOW PROGRESS IS MADE.
FEEL THAT?
THAT'S OIL!
OIL!
RUMMMBLE!
FOOOOSCH!
OH, BUM.
FLUMP
JAMIE SMART
FIZZY POP! OOMPH!
AARGHH!

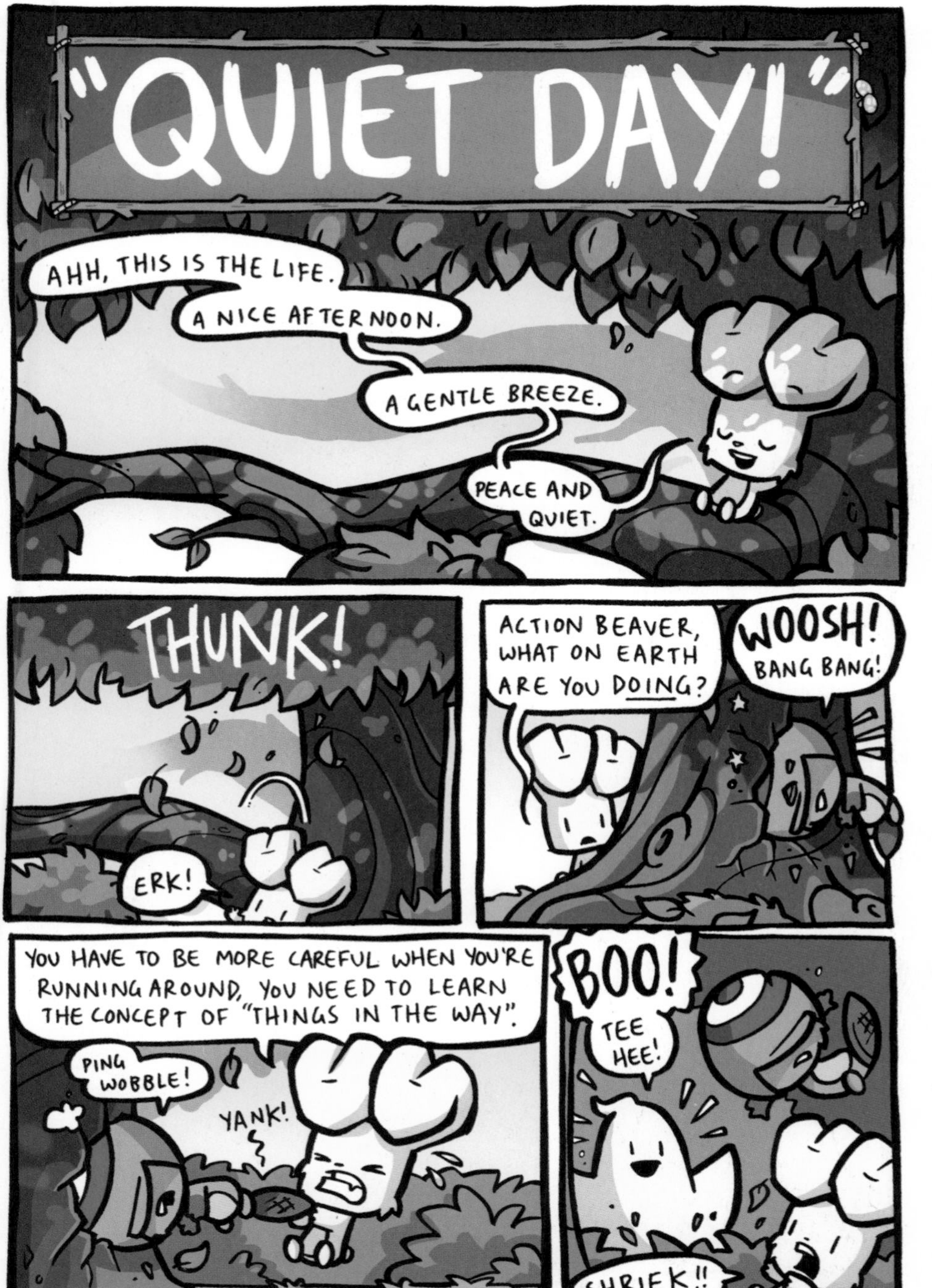
"QUIET DAY!"
AHH, THIS IS THE LIFE.
A NICE AFTERNOON.
A GENTLE BREEZE.
PEACE AND QUIET.
THUNK!
ERK!
ACTION BEAVER, WHAT ON EARTH ARE YOU DOING?
WOOSH! BANG BANG!
YOU HAVE TO BE MORE CAREFUL WHEN YOU'RE RUNNING AROUND, YOU NEED TO LEARN THE CONCEPT OF "THINGS IN THE WAY".
PING WOBBLE!
YANK!
BOO!
TEE HEE!
SHRIEK!!

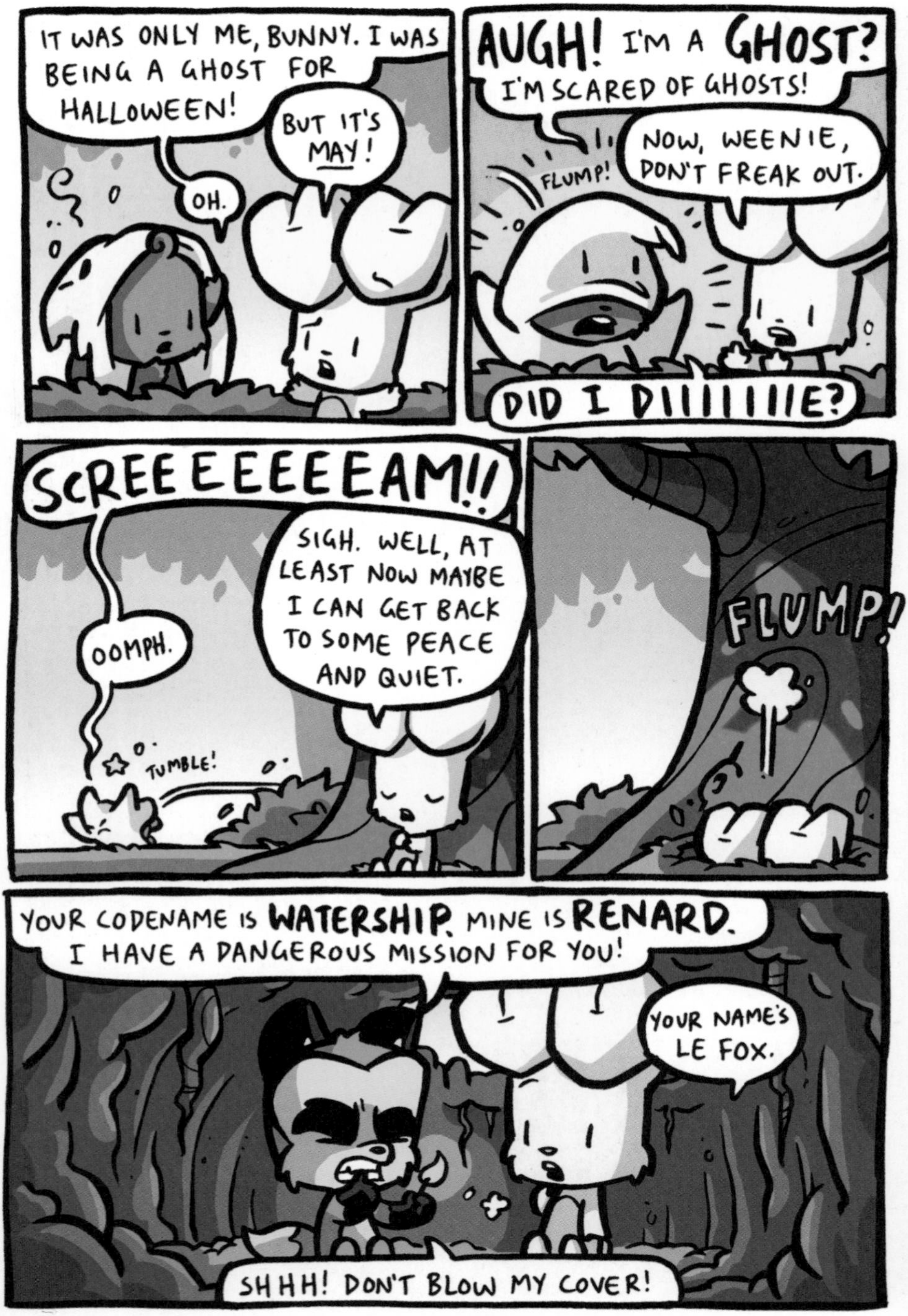
IT WAS ONLY ME, BUNNY. I WAS BEING A GHOST FOR HALLOWEEN!
BUT IT'S MAY!
OH.
AUGH! I'M A GHOST? I'M SCARED OF GHOSTS!
FLUMP!
NOW, WEENIE, DON'T FREAK OUT.
DID I DIIIIIIIE?
SCREEEEEEEEAM!!
OOMPH.
TUMBLE!
SIGH. WELL, AT LEAST NOW MAYBE I CAN GET BACK TO SOME PEACE AND QUIET.
FLUMP!
YOUR CODENAME IS WATERSHIP. MINE IS RENARD. I HAVE A DANGEROUS MISSION FOR YOU!
YOUR NAME'S LE FOX.
SHHH! DON'T BLOW MY COVER!

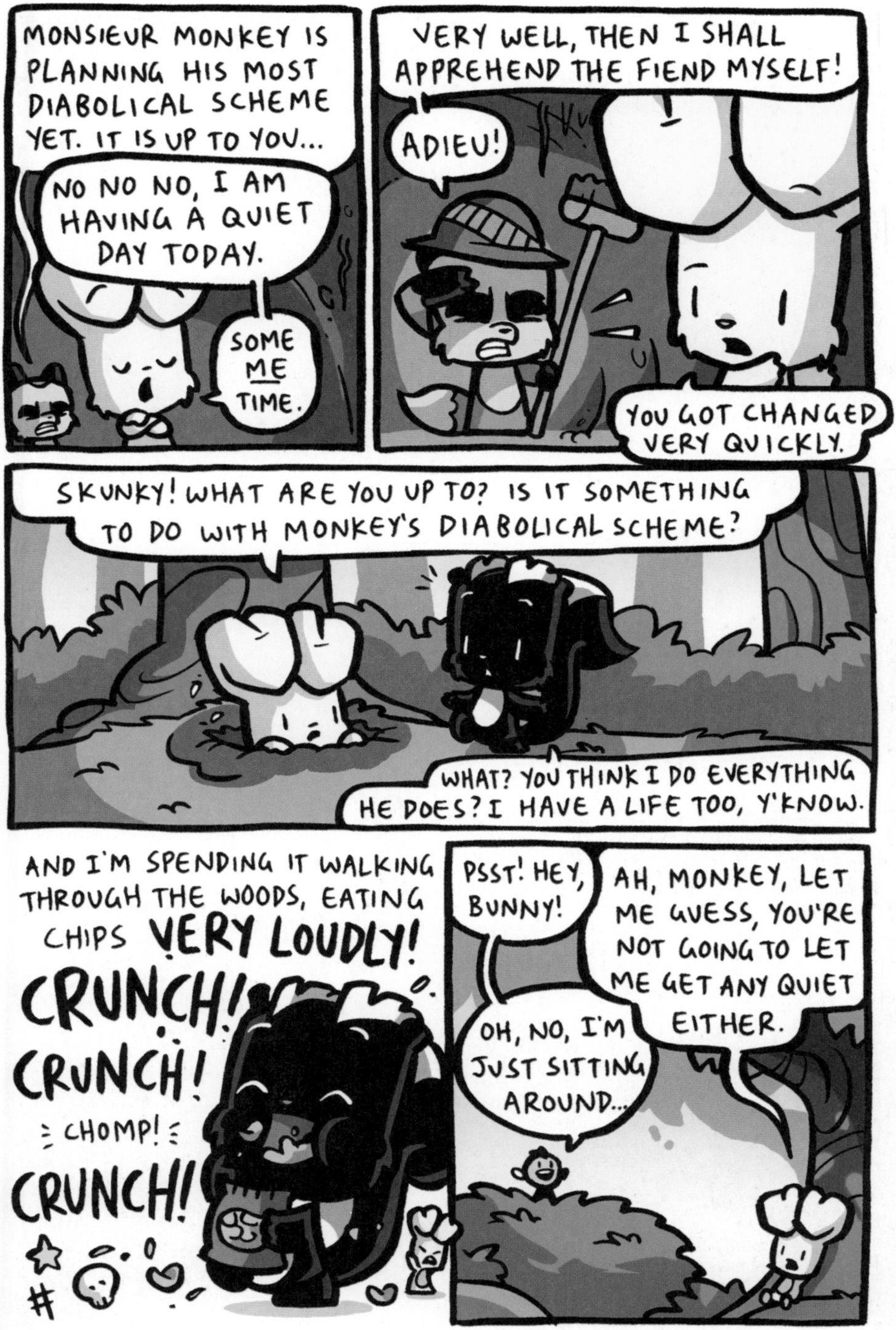
MONSIEUR MONKEY IS PLANNING HIS MOST DIABOLICAL SCHEME YET. IT IS UP TO YOU...
NO NO NO, I AM HAVING A QUIET DAY TODAY.
SOME ME TIME.
VERY WELL, THEN I SHALL APPREHEND THE FIEND MYSELF!
ADIEU!
YOU GOT CHANGED VERY QUICKLY.
SKUNKY! WHAT ARE YOU UP TO? IS IT SOMETHING TO DO WITH MONKEY'S DIABOLICAL SCHEME?
WHAT? YOU THINK I DO EVERYTHING HE DOES? I HAVE A LIFE TOO, Y'KNOW.
AND I'M SPENDING IT WALKING THROUGH THE WOODS, EATING CHIPS VERY LOUDLY!
CRUNCH!
CRUNCH!
CHOMP!
CRUNCH!
PSST! HEY, BUNNY!
AH, MONKEY, LET ME GUESS, YOU'RE NOT GOING TO LET ME GET ANY QUIET EITHER.
OH, NO, I'M JUST SITTING AROUND...

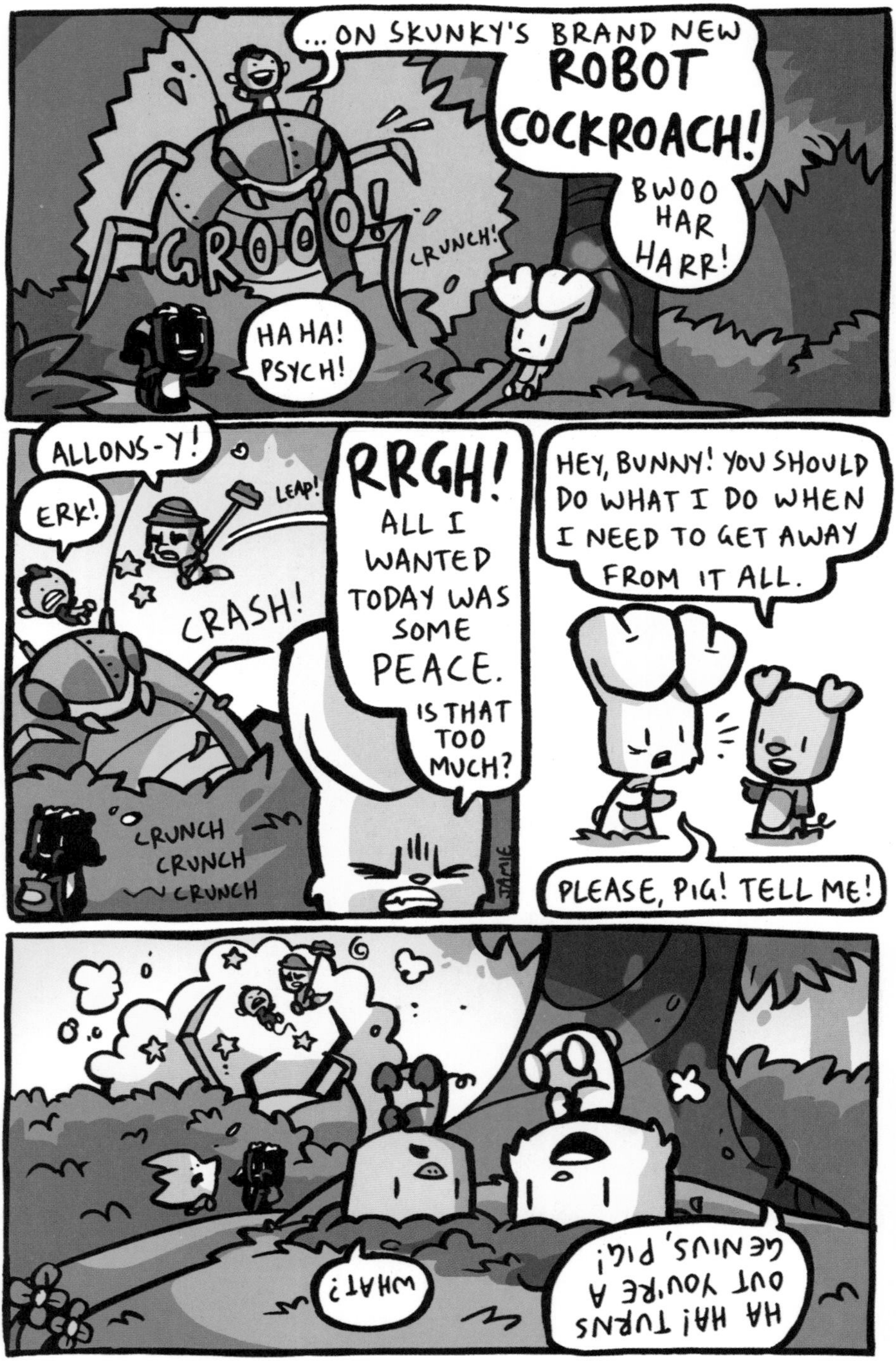
...ON SKUNKY'S BRAND NEW ROBOT COCKROACH!
BWOO HAR HARR!
GROOO!
CRUNCH!
HA HA! PSYCH!
ALLONS-Y!
ERK!
LEAP!
CRASH!
CRUNCH CRUNCH CRUNCH
RRGH! ALL I WANTED TODAY WAS SOME PEACE.
IS THAT TOO MUCH?
JAMIE
HEY, BUNNY! YOU SHOULD DO WHAT I DO WHEN I NEED TO GET AWAY FROM IT ALL.
PLEASE, PIG! TELL ME!
HA HA! TURNS OUT YOU'RE A GENIUS, PIG!
WHAT?

SUMMER

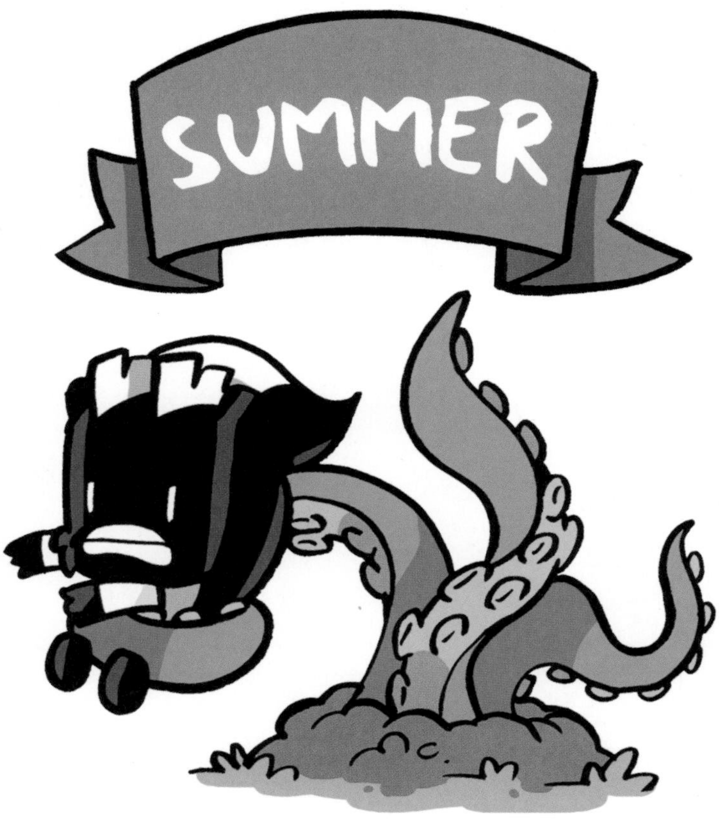

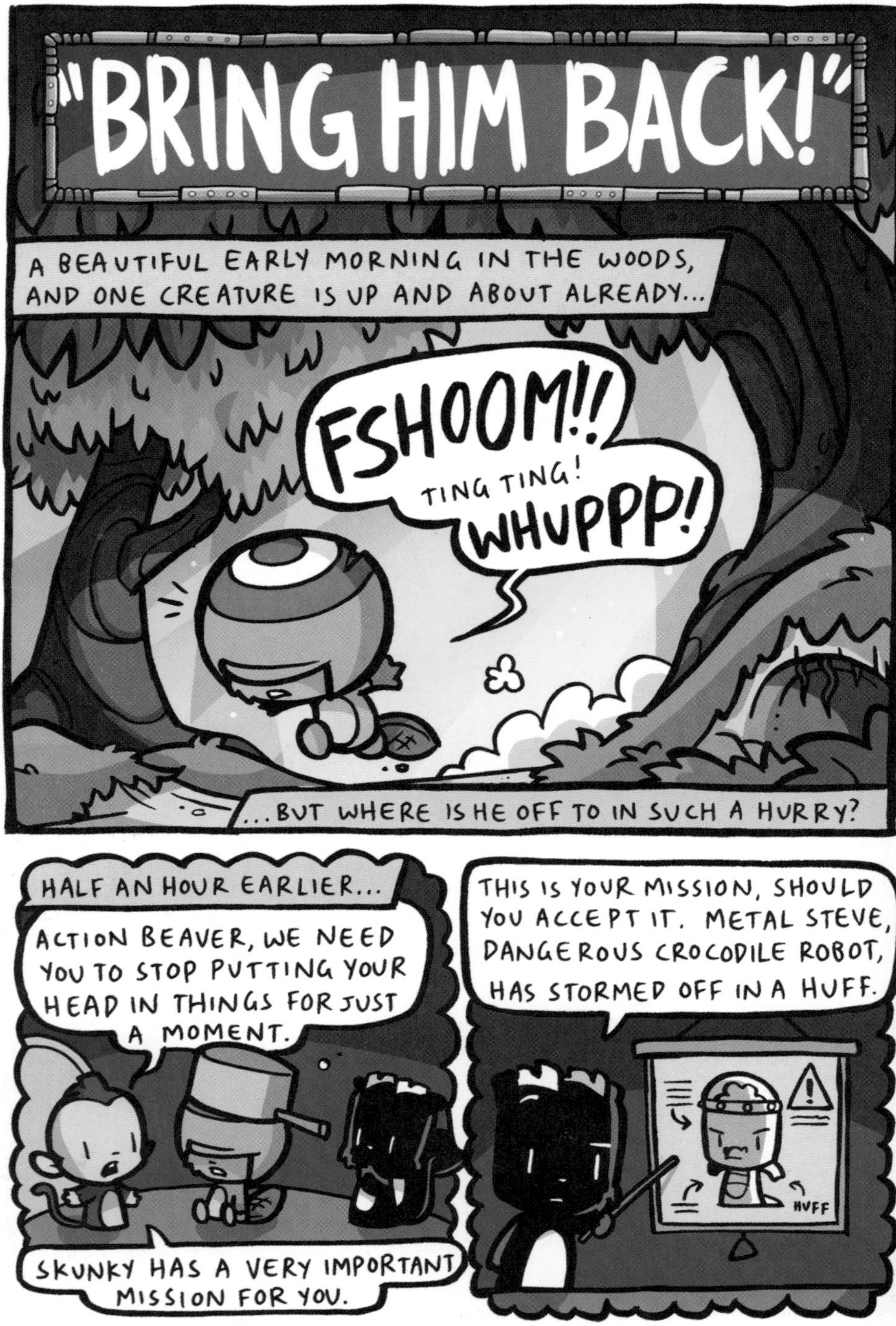

"BRING HIM BACK!"
A BEAUTIFUL EARLY MORNING IN THE WOODS, AND ONE CREATURE IS UP AND ABOUT ALREADY...
FSHOOM!!
TING TING!
WHUPPP!
...BUT WHERE IS HE OFF TO IN SUCH A HURRY?
HALF AN HOUR EARLIER...
ACTION BEAVER, WE NEED YOU TO STOP PUTTING YOUR HEAD IN THINGS FOR JUST A MOMENT.
SKUNKY HAS A VERY IMPORTANT MISSION FOR YOU.
THIS IS YOUR MISSION, SHOULD YOU ACCEPT IT. METAL STEVE, DANGEROUS CROCODILE ROBOT, HAS STORMED OFF IN A HUFF.
HUFF

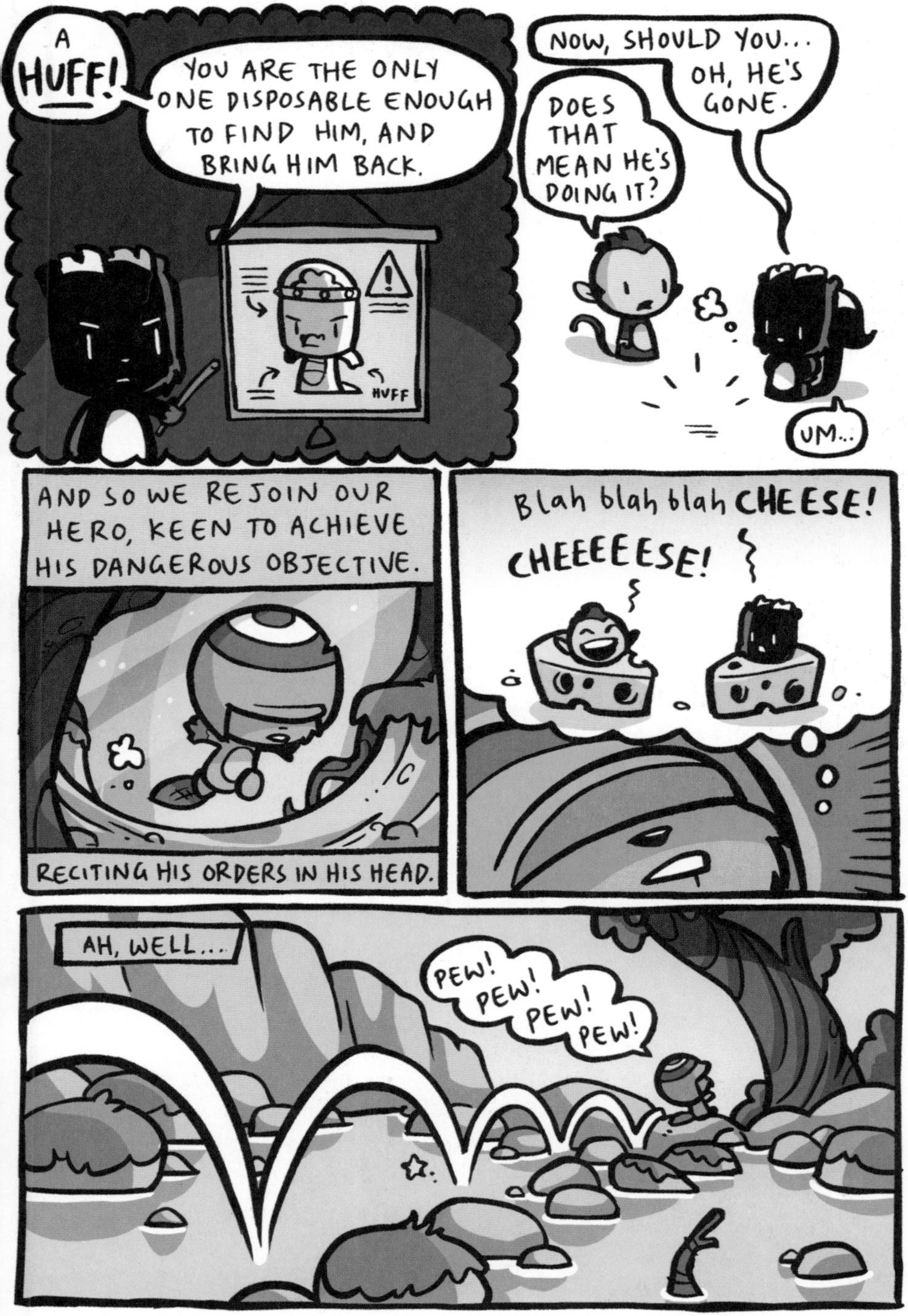
A HUFF!
YOU ARE THE ONLY ONE DISPOSABLE ENOUGH TO FIND HIM, AND BRING HIM BACK.
HUFF
NOW, SHOULD YOU... OH, HE'S GONE.
DOES THAT MEAN HE'S DOING IT?
UM...
AND SO WE REJOIN OUR HERO, KEEN TO ACHIEVE HIS DANGEROUS OBJECTIVE.
RECITING HIS ORDERS IN HIS HEAD.
Blah blah blah CHEESE!
CHEEEEESE!
AH, WELL...
PEW! PEW! PEW! PEW!

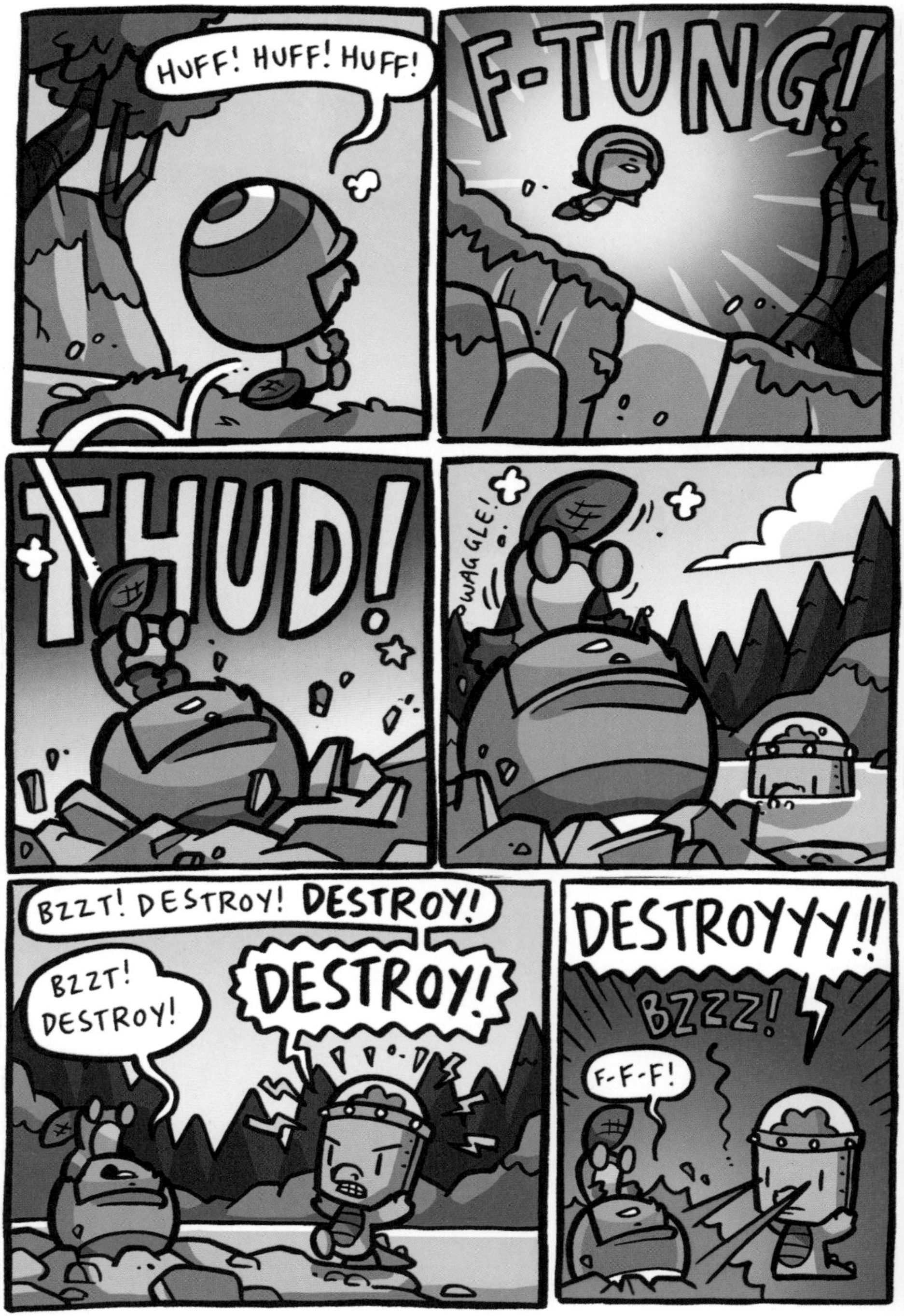

HUFF! HUFF! HUFF!
F-TUNG!
THUD!
WAGGLE!
BZZT! DESTROY! DESTROY!
BZZT! DESTROY!
DESTROY!
DESTROYYY!!
BZZZ!
F-F-F!

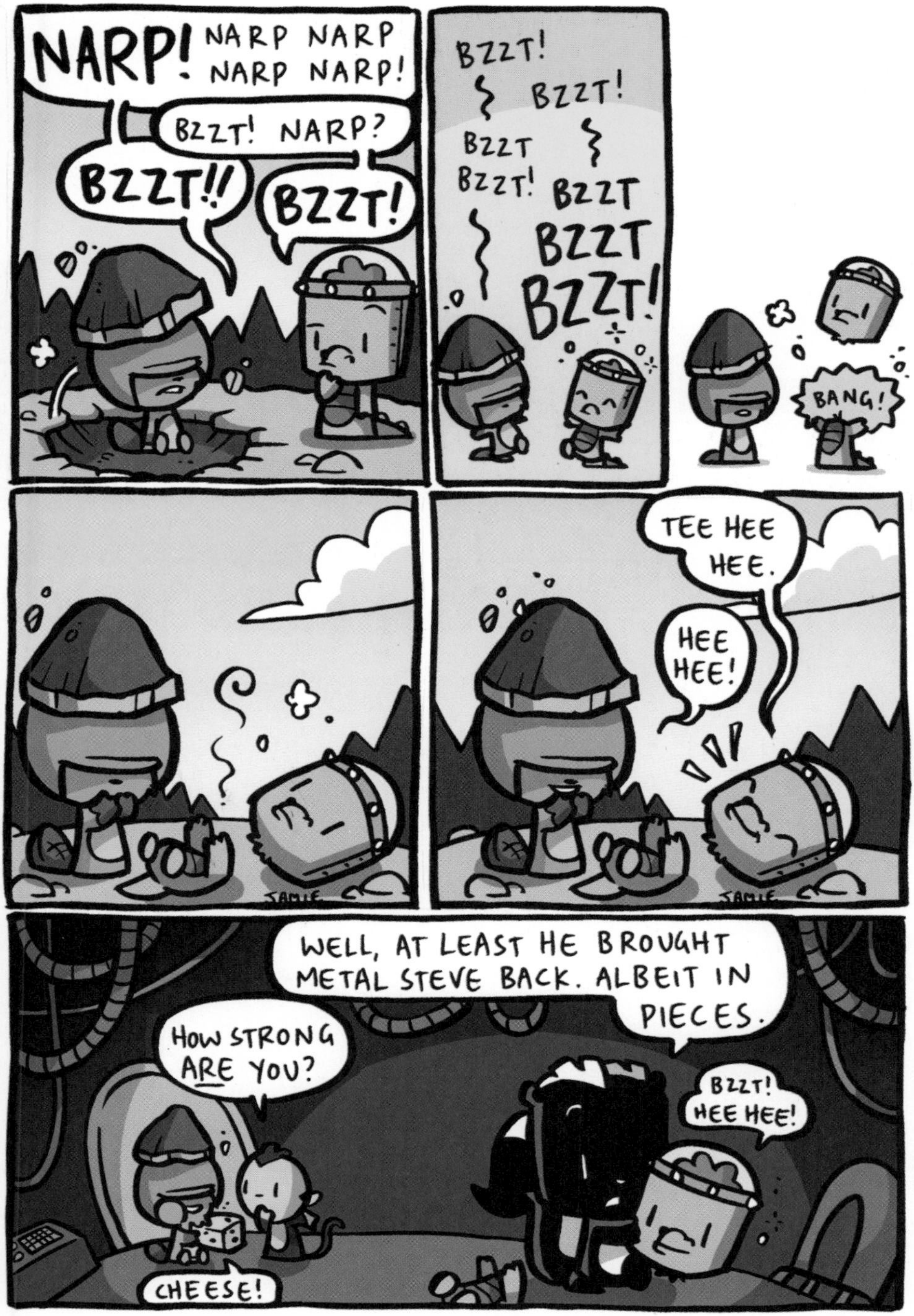
NARP! NARP NARP NARP NARP!
BZZT! NARP?
BZZT!!
BZZT!
BZZT!
BZZT!
BZZT BZZT!
BZZT
BZZT
BZZT!
BANG!
TEE HEE HEE.
HEE HEE!
WELL, AT LEAST HE BROUGHT METAL STEVE BACK. ALBEIT IN PIECES.
HOW STRONG ARE YOU?
BZZT! HEE HEE!
CHEESE!

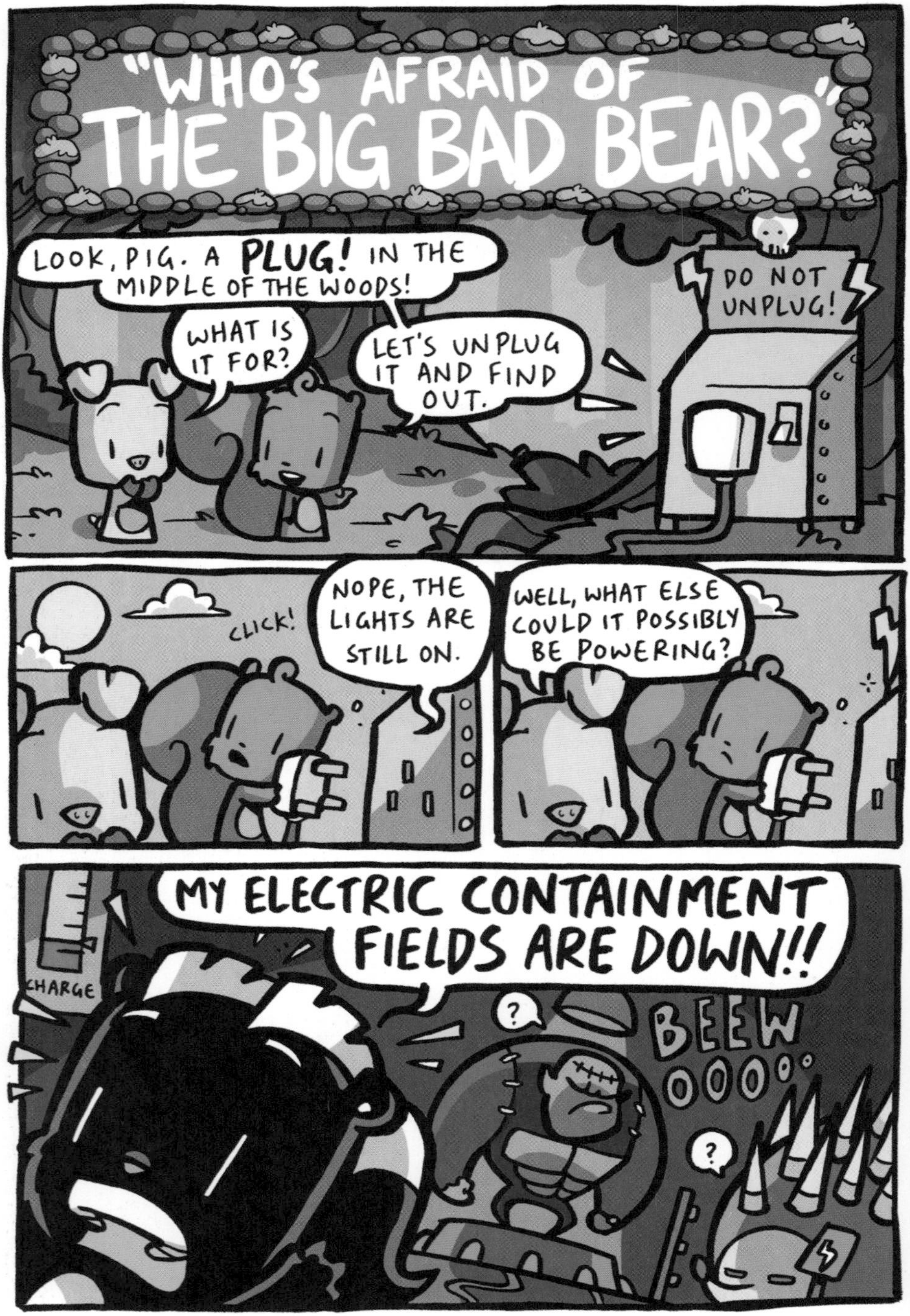
"WHO'S AFRAID OF THE BIG BAD BEAR?"
LOOK, PIG. A PLUG! IN THE MIDDLE OF THE WOODS!
WHAT IS IT FOR?
LET'S UNPLUG IT AND FIND OUT.
DO NOT UNPLUG!
CLICK!
NOPE, THE LIGHTS ARE STILL ON.
WELL, WHAT ELSE COULD IT POSSIBLY BE POWERING?
MY ELECTRIC CONTAINMENT FIELDS ARE DOWN!!
CHARGE
?
BEEWOOOO
?

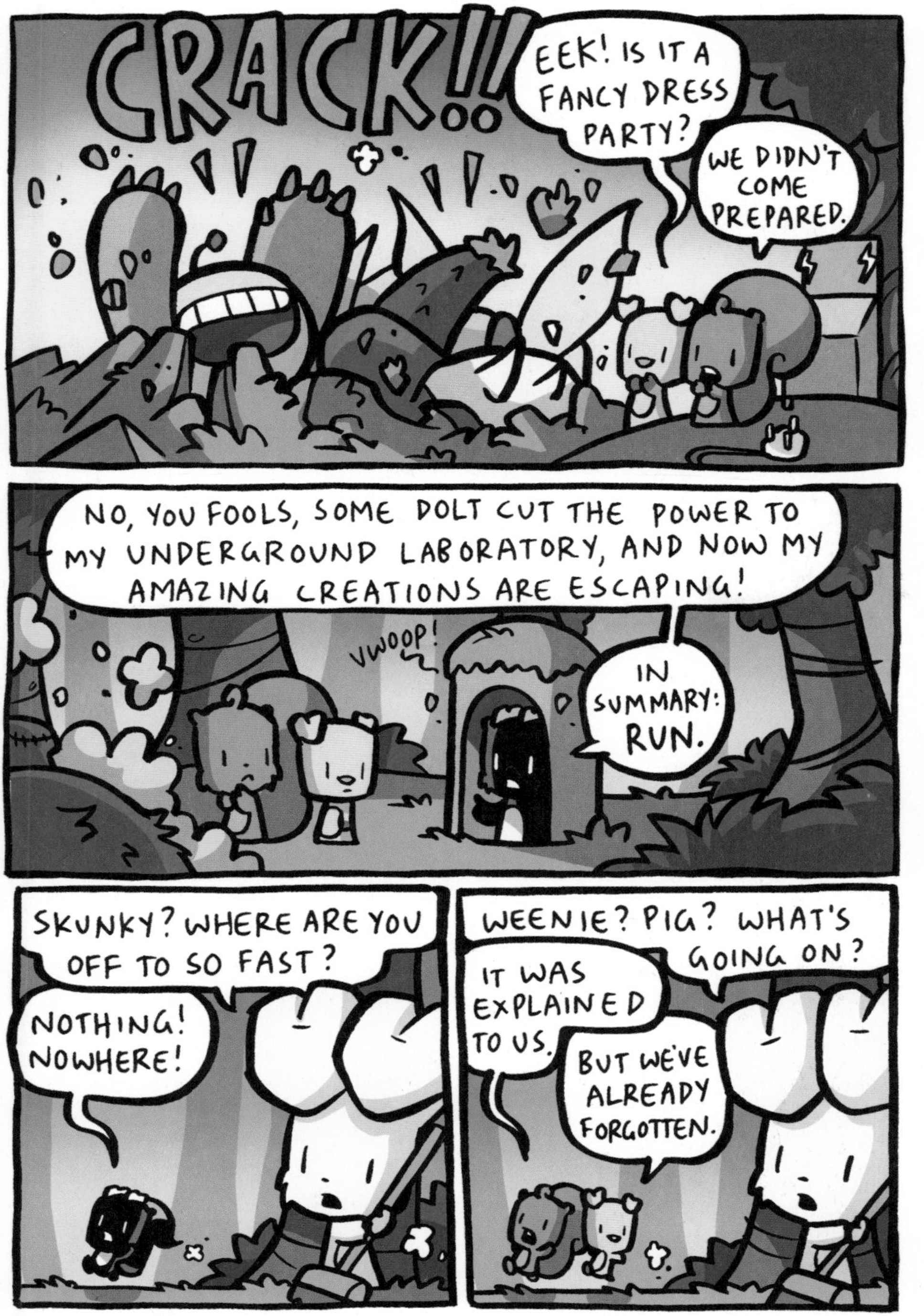
CRACK!!
EEK! IS IT A FANCY DRESS PARTY?
WE DIDN'T COME PREPARED.
NO, YOU FOOLS, SOME DOLT CUT THE POWER TO MY UNDERGROUND LABORATORY, AND NOW MY AMAZING CREATIONS ARE ESCAPING!
VWOOP!
IN SUMMARY: RUN.
SKUNKY? WHERE ARE YOU OFF TO SO FAST?
NOTHING! NOWHERE!
WEENIE? PIG? WHAT'S GOING ON?
IT WAS EXPLAINED TO US.
BUT WE'VE ALREADY FORGOTTEN.

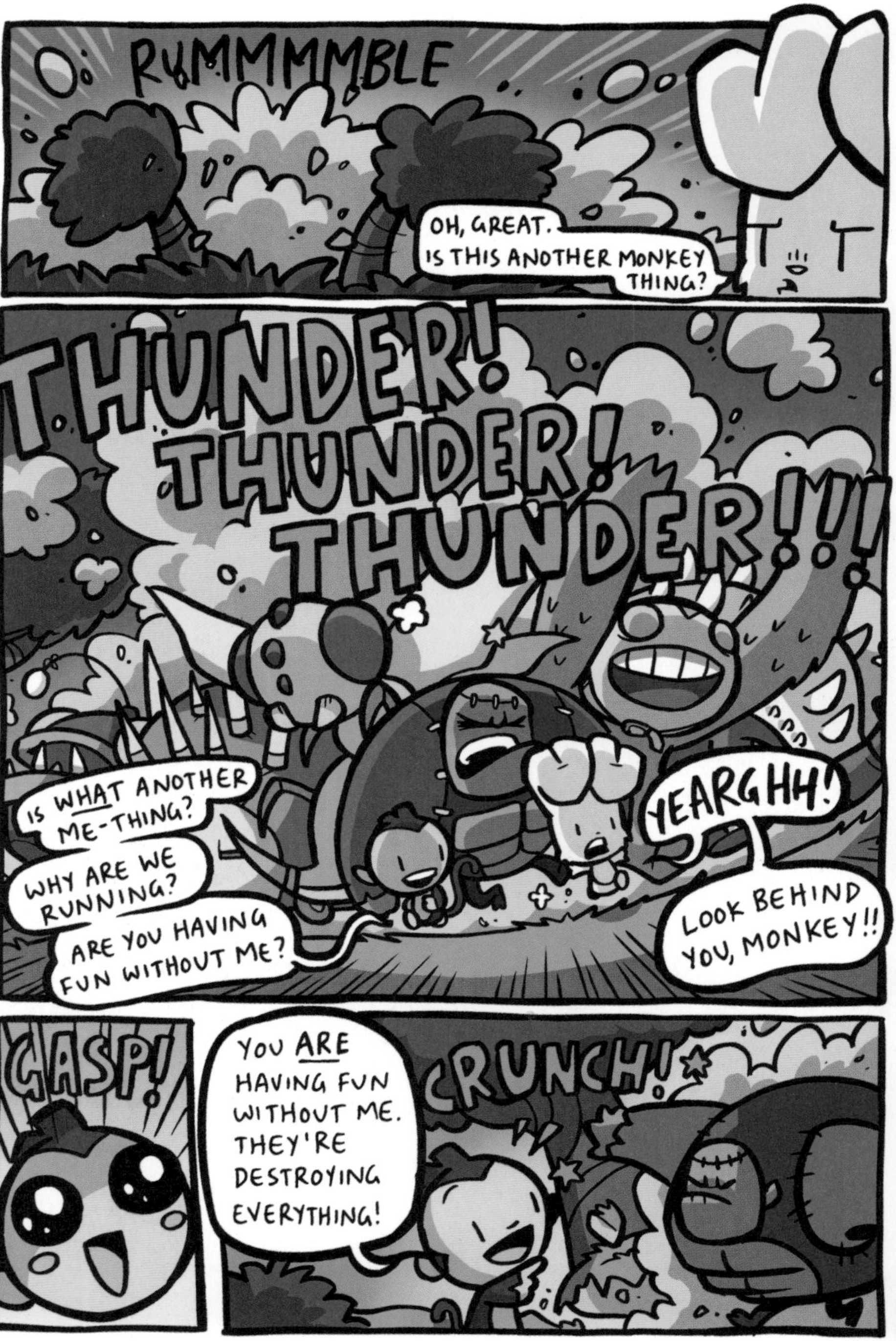
RUMMMMMBLE
OH, GREAT. IS THIS ANOTHER MONKEY THING?
THUNDER! THUNDER! THUNDER!!!
IS WHAT ANOTHER ME-THING?
WHY ARE WE RUNNING?
ARE YOU HAVING FUN WITHOUT ME?
YEARGHH!
LOOK BEHIND YOU, MONKEY!!
GASP!
YOU ARE HAVING FUN WITHOUT ME. THEY'RE DESTROYING EVERYTHING!
CRUNCH!

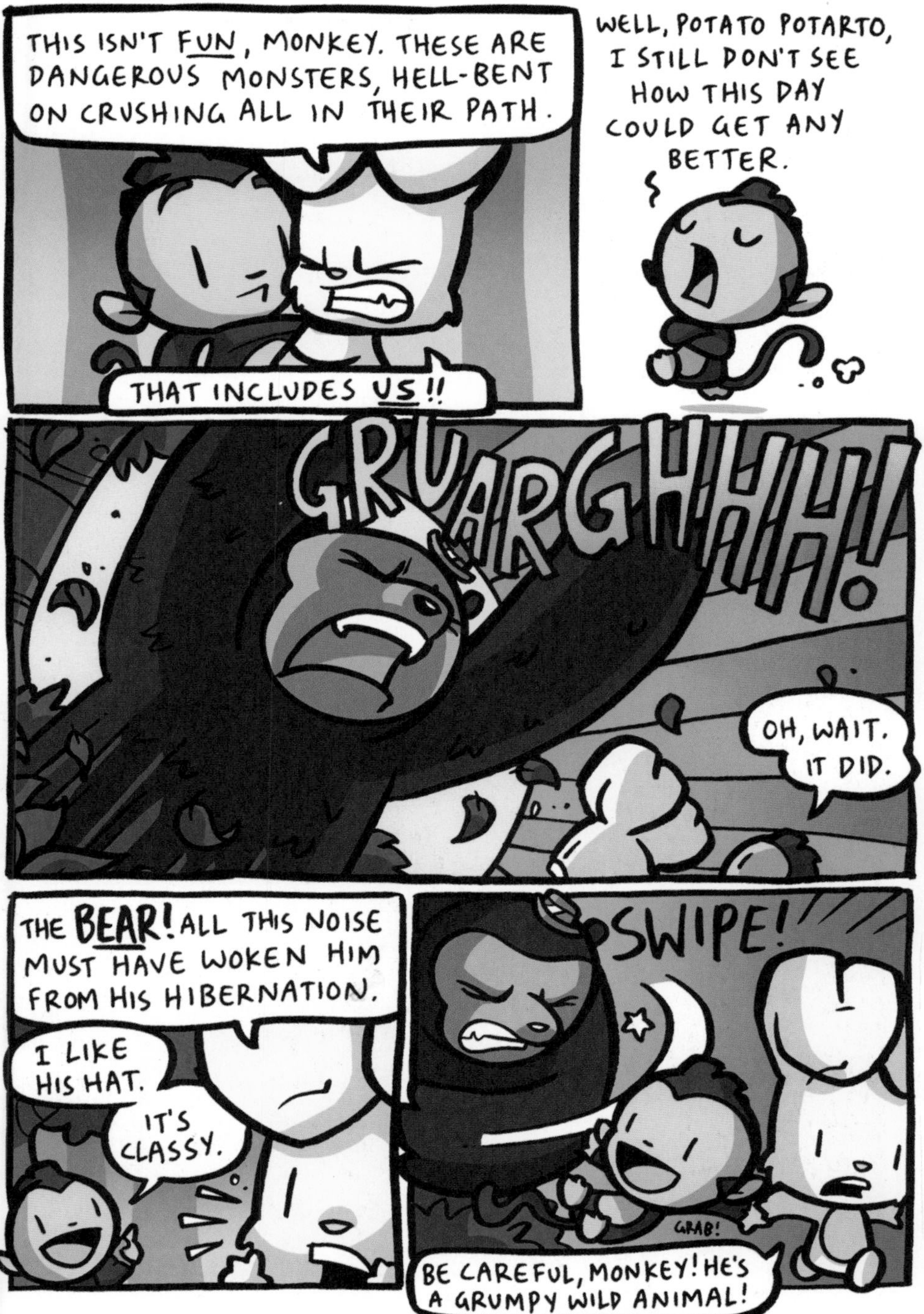

THIS ISN'T FUN, MONKEY. THESE ARE DANGEROUS MONSTERS, HELL-BENT ON CRUSHING ALL IN THEIR PATH.
THAT INCLUDES US!!
WELL, POTATO POTARTO, I STILL DON'T SEE HOW THIS DAY COULD GET ANY BETTER.
GRUARGHHHH!
OH, WAIT. IT DID.
THE BEAR! ALL THIS NOISE MUST HAVE WOKEN HIM FROM HIS HIBERNATION.
I LIKE HIS HAT.
IT'S CLASSY.
SWIPE!
GRAB!
BE CAREFUL, MONKEY! HE'S A GRUMPY WILD ANIMAL!

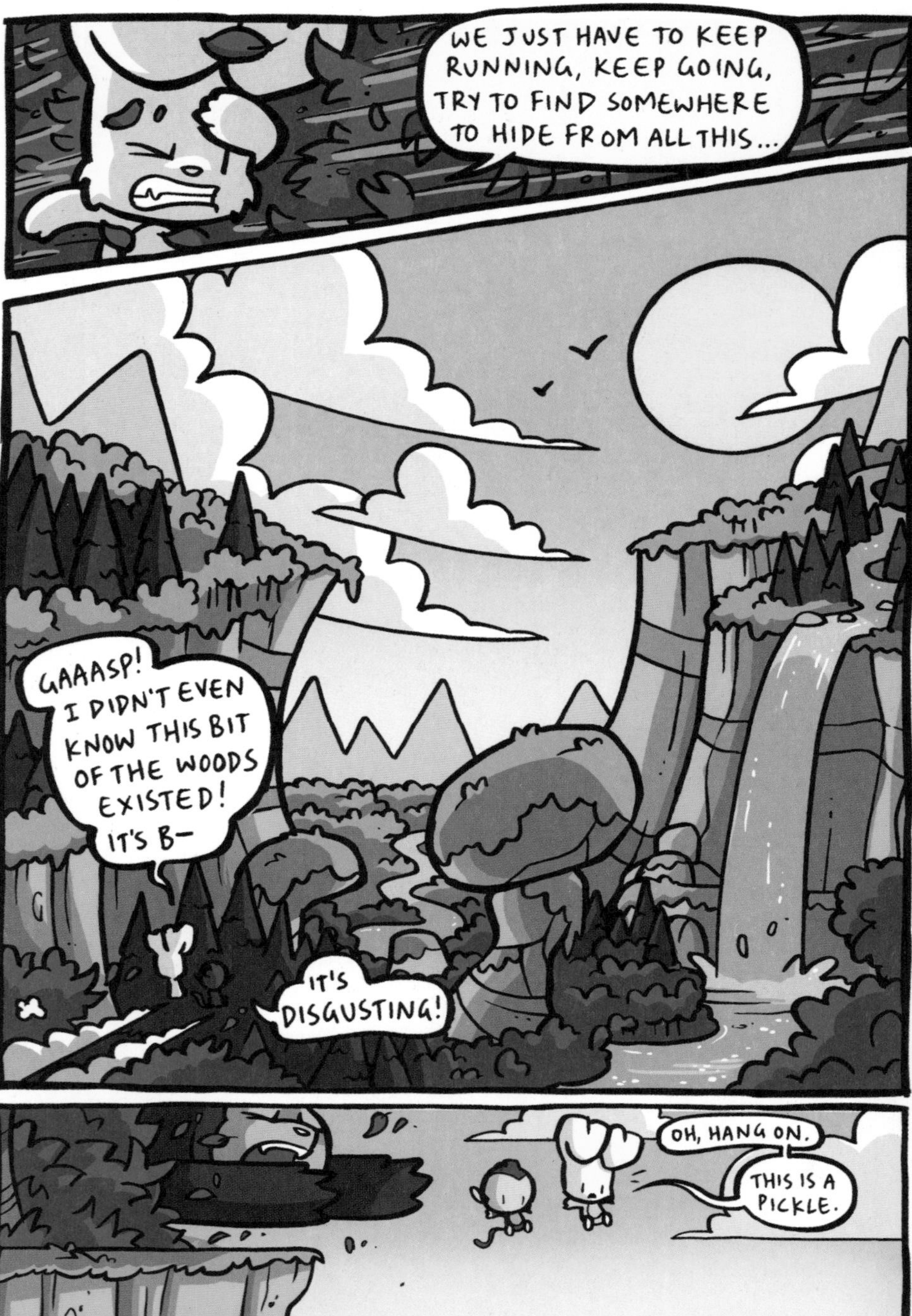
WE JUST HAVE TO KEEP RUNNING, KEEP GOING, TRY TO FIND SOMEWHERE TO HIDE FROM ALL THIS...
GAAASP! I DIDN'T EVEN KNOW THIS BIT OF THE WOODS EXISTED! IT'S B—
IT'S DISGUSTING!
OH, HANG ON.
THIS IS A PICKLE.

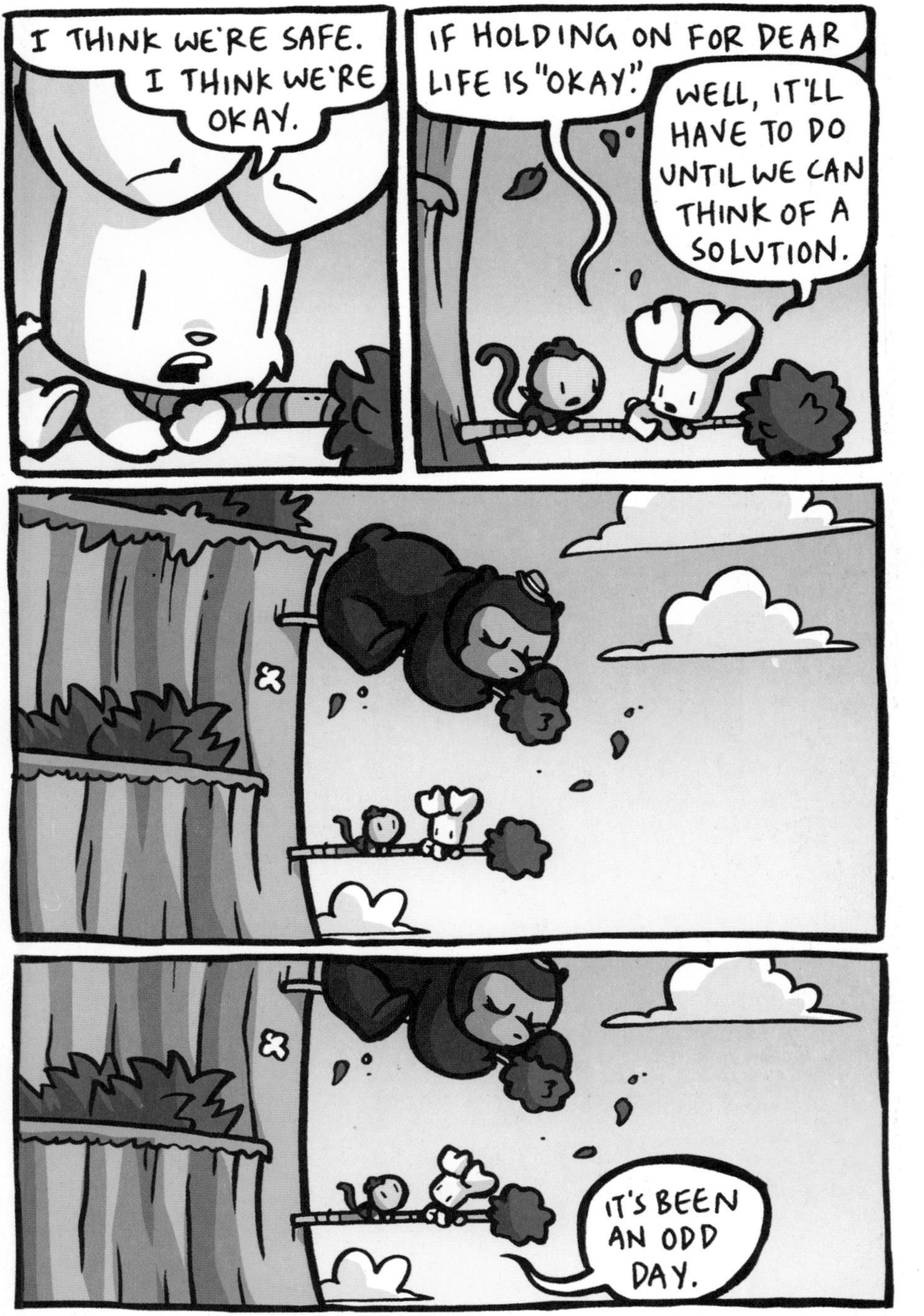
I THINK WE'RE SAFE.
I THINK WE'RE OKAY.
IF HOLDING ON FOR DEAR LIFE IS "OKAY."
WELL, IT'LL HAVE TO DO UNTIL WE CAN THINK OF A SOLUTION.
IT'S BEEN AN ODD DAY.

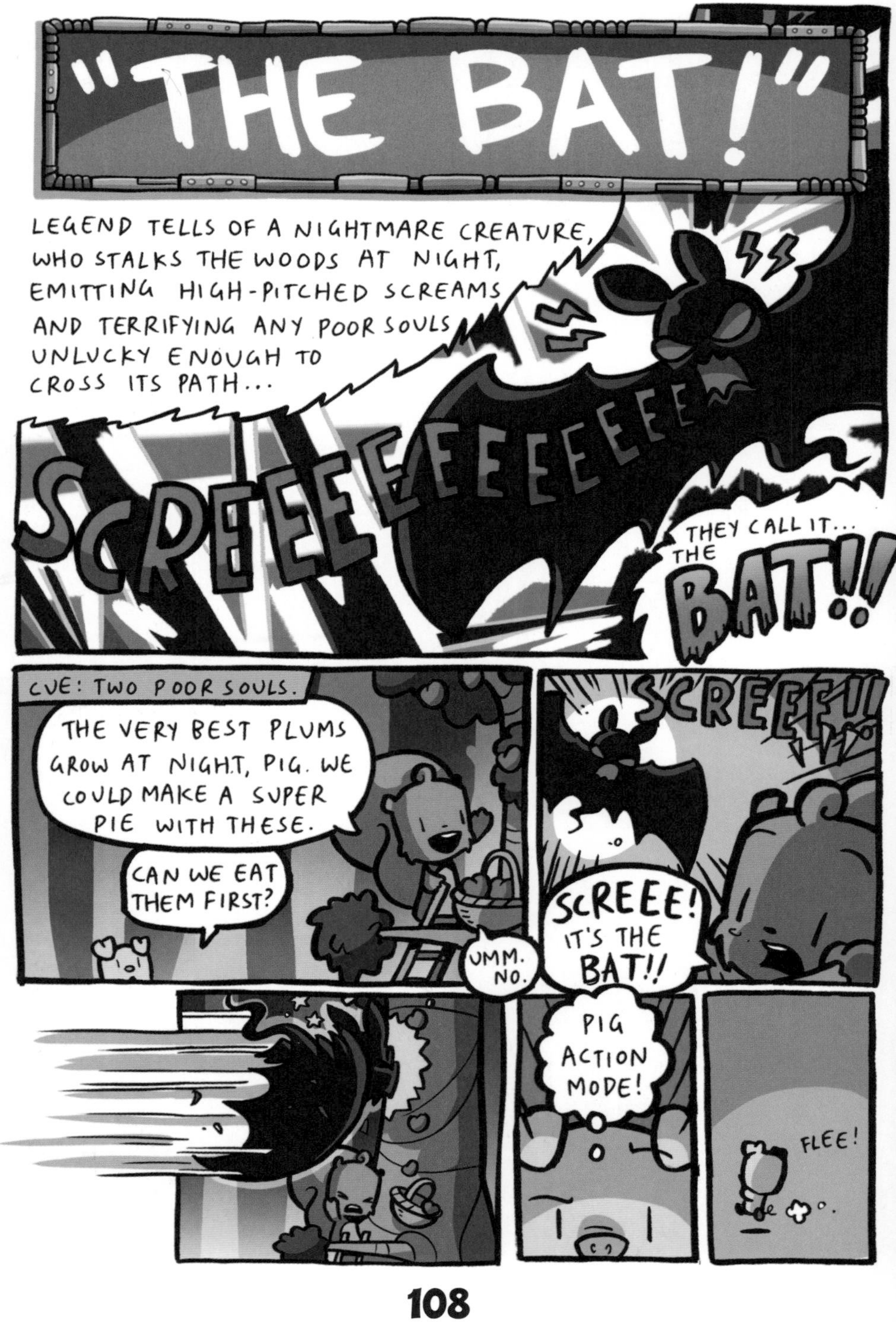
"THE BAT!"
LEGEND TELLS OF A NIGHTMARE CREATURE, WHO STALKS THE WOODS AT NIGHT, EMITTING HIGH-PITCHED SCREAMS AND TERRIFYING ANY POOR SOULS UNLUCKY ENOUGH TO CROSS ITS PATH...
SCREEEEEEEEEEE
THEY CALL IT... THE BAT!!
CUE: TWO POOR SOULS.
THE VERY BEST PLUMS GROW AT NIGHT, PIG. WE COULD MAKE A SUPER PIE WITH THESE.
CAN WE EAT THEM FIRST?
UMM. NO.
SCREEE!!
SCREEE! IT'S THE BAT!!
PIG ACTION MODE!
FLEE!

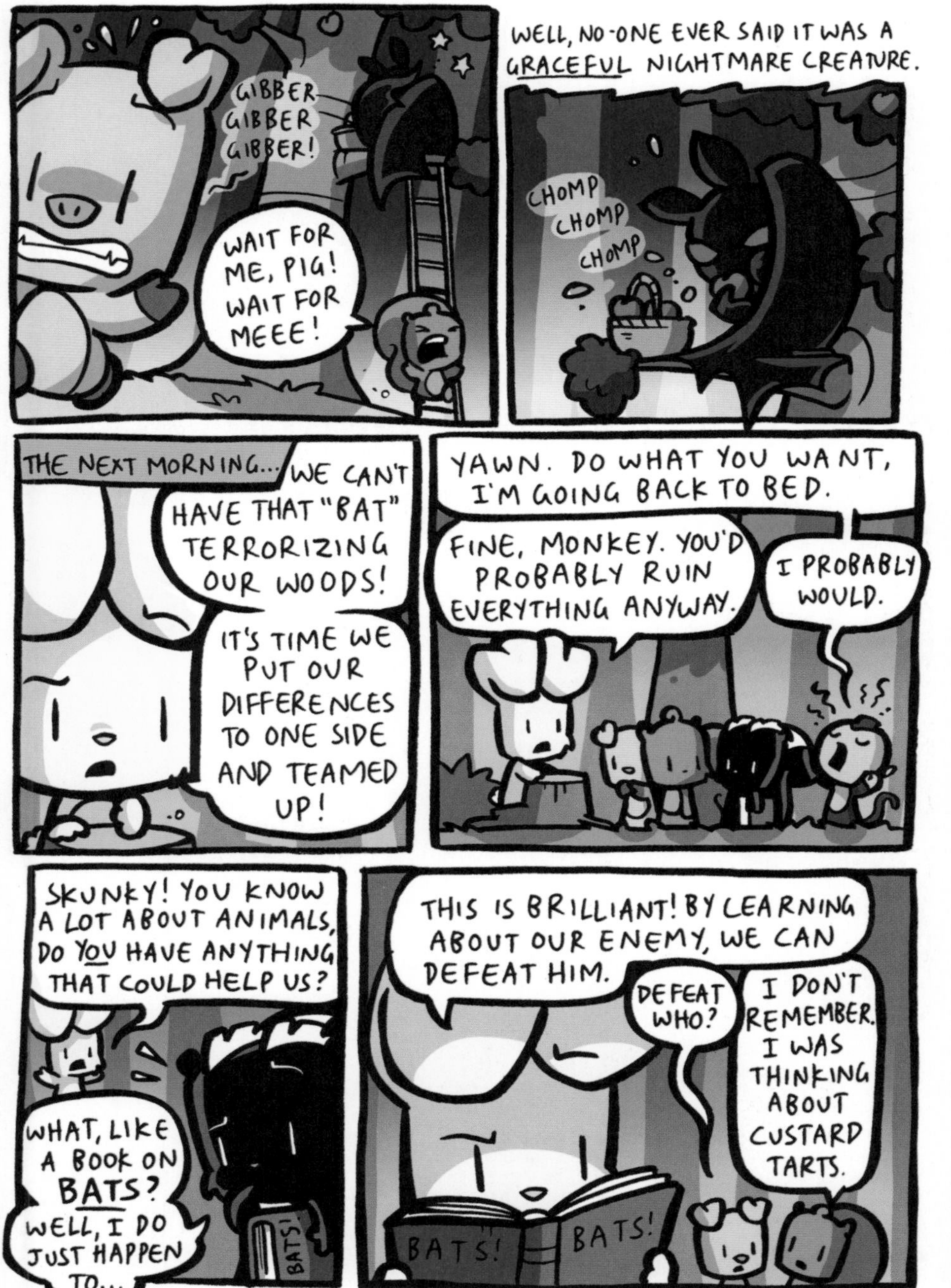
GIBBER GIBBER GIBBER!
WAIT FOR ME, PIG! WAIT FOR MEEE!
WELL, NO-ONE EVER SAID IT WAS A GRACEFUL NIGHTMARE CREATURE.
CHOMP CHOMP CHOMP
THE NEXT MORNING...
WE CAN'T HAVE THAT "BAT" TERRORIZING OUR WOODS!
IT'S TIME WE PUT OUR DIFFERENCES TO ONE SIDE AND TEAMED UP!
YAWN. DO WHAT YOU WANT, I'M GOING BACK TO BED.
FINE, MONKEY. YOU'D PROBABLY RUIN EVERYTHING ANYWAY.
I PROBABLY WOULD.
SKUNKY! YOU KNOW A LOT ABOUT ANIMALS, DO YOU HAVE ANYTHING THAT COULD HELP US?
WHAT, LIKE A BOOK ON BATS?
WELL, I DO JUST HAPPEN TO...
BATS!
THIS IS BRILLIANT! BY LEARNING ABOUT OUR ENEMY, WE CAN DEFEAT HIM.
DEFEAT WHO?
I DON'T REMEMBER. I WAS THINKING ABOUT CUSTARD TARTS.
BATS! BATS!

THAT NIGHT...

RIGHT, THE TRAP IS SET! FRUIT-FLAVORED JELLY WORMS AS BAIT.

WRIGGLY WORMS

WEENIE, DO YOU HAVE THE MUSIC READY?

RIGHT HERE, CAP'N!

ARE WE SINGING?

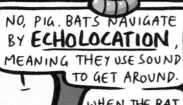

NO, PIG. BATS NAVIGATE BY **ECHOLOCATION**, MEANING THEY USE SOUND TO GET AROUND.

WHEN THE BAT SWOOPS DOWN TO GRAB A JELLY WORM, WE'LL BLAST THE MUSIC LOUD AND DISORIENTATE HIM!

PIG?

PIG, I WAS EXPLAINING SOMETHING.

WHERE DID YOU...?

PIG!!

CHOMP CHOMP

THAT'S OUR BAIT!

WORM

SCREEEEE!!

NOW, WEENIE! PLAY THE MUSIC!

IF YOU'RE HAPPY AND YOU KNOW IT, CLAP YOUR HANDS! CLAP CLAP!

CLICK!

OH! I LOVE THIS SONG!

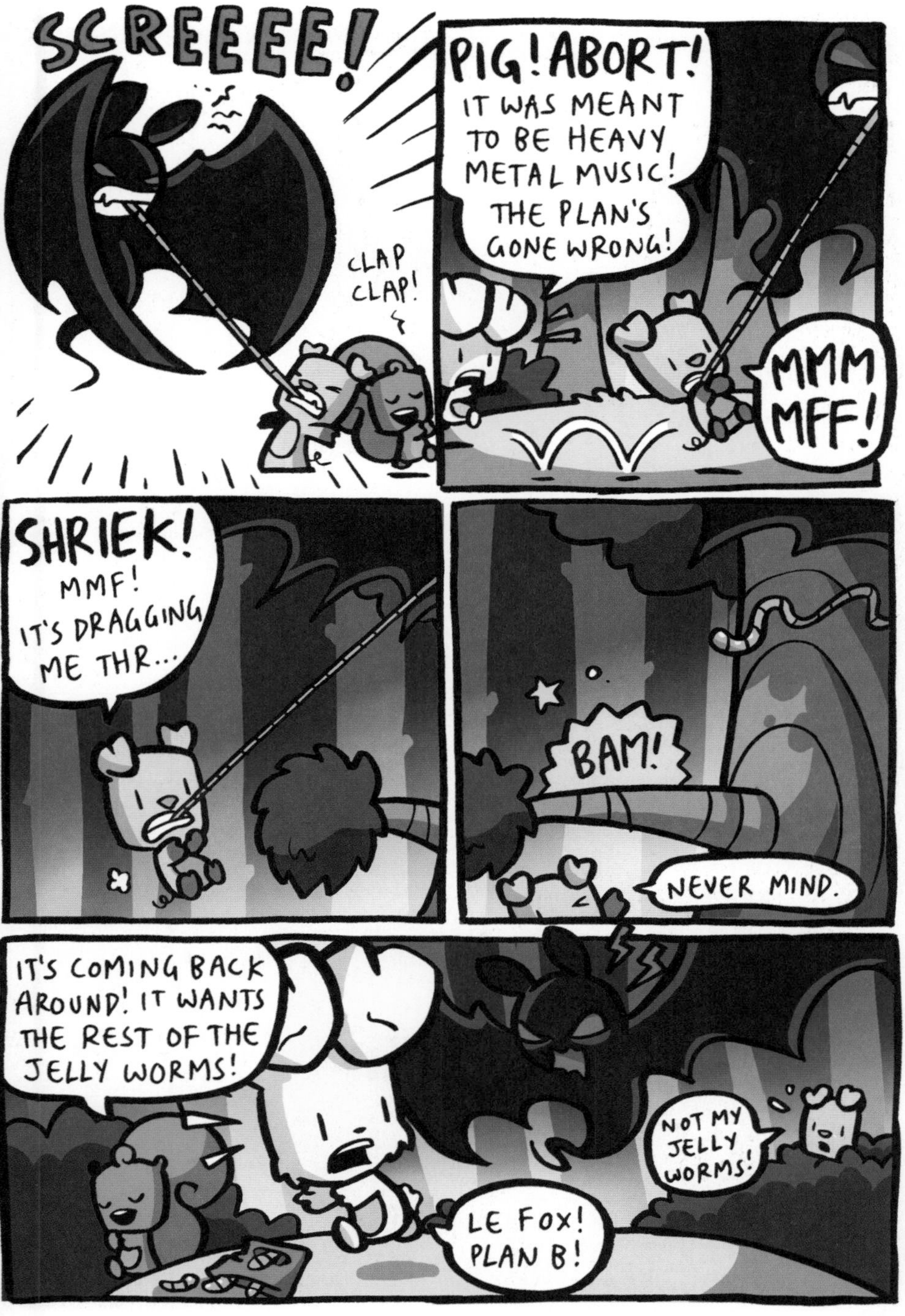
SCREEEE!
CLAP CLAP!
PIG! ABORT! IT WAS MEANT TO BE HEAVY METAL MUSIC! THE PLAN'S GONE WRONG!
MMM MFF!
SHRIEK! MMF! IT'S DRAGGING ME THR...
BAM!
NEVER MIND.
IT'S COMING BACK AROUND! IT WANTS THE REST OF THE JELLY WORMS!
NOT MY JELLY WORMS!
LE FOX! PLAN B!

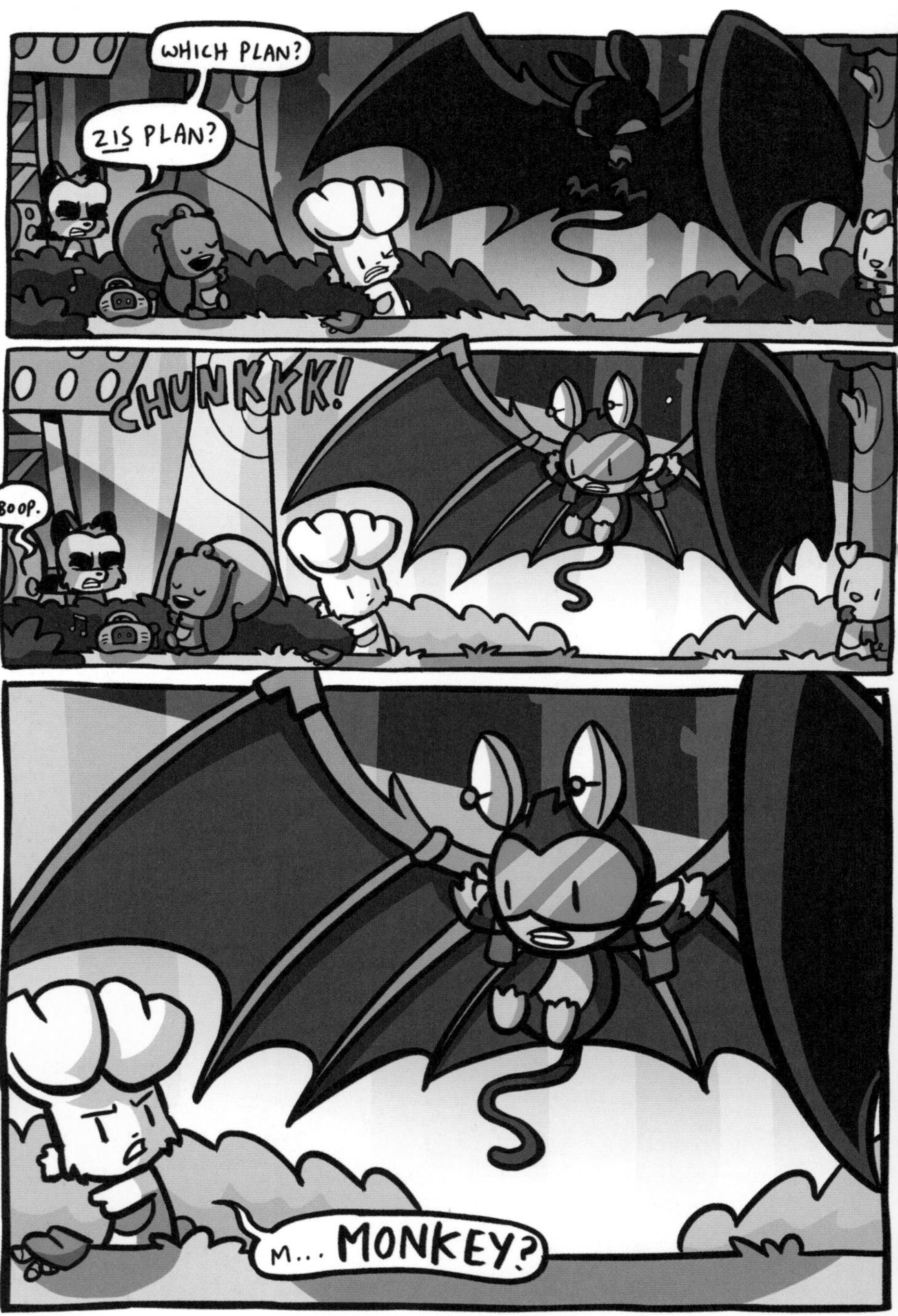
WHICH PLAN?
ZIS PLAN?
CHUNKKK!
BOOP.
M... MONKEY?

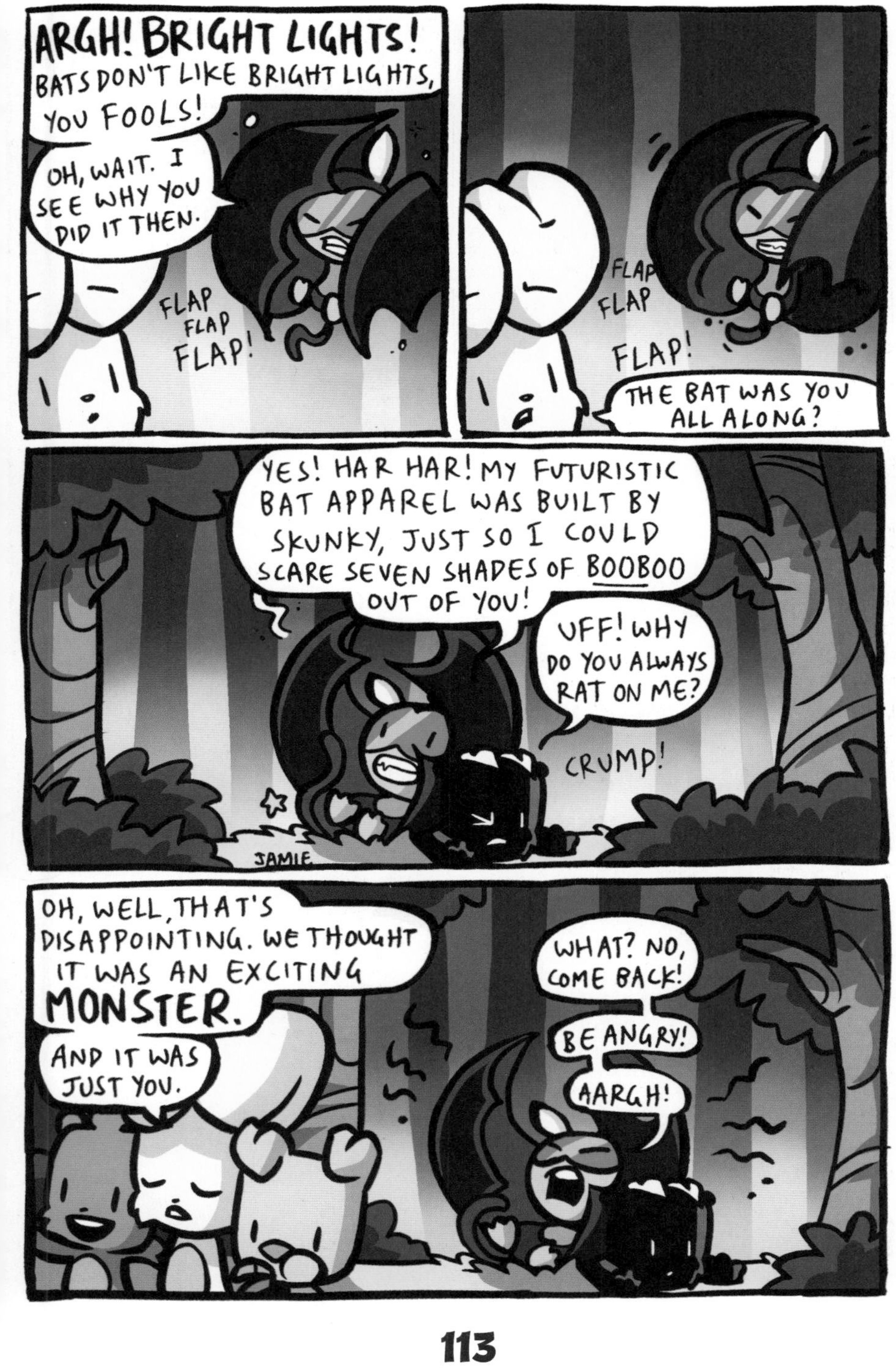
ARGH! BRIGHT LIGHTS! BATS DON'T LIKE BRIGHT LIGHTS, YOU FOOLS!
OH, WAIT. I SEE WHY YOU DID IT THEN.
FLAP FLAP FLAP!
FLAP FLAP FLAP!
THE BAT WAS YOU ALL ALONG?
YES! HAR HAR! MY FUTURISTIC BAT APPAREL WAS BUILT BY SKUNKY, JUST SO I COULD SCARE SEVEN SHADES OF BOOBOO OUT OF YOU!
UFF! WHY DO YOU ALWAYS RAT ON ME?
CRUMP!
JAMIE
OH, WELL, THAT'S DISAPPOINTING. WE THOUGHT IT WAS AN EXCITING MONSTER.
AND IT WAS JUST YOU.
WHAT? NO, COME BACK!
BE ANGRY!
AARGH!

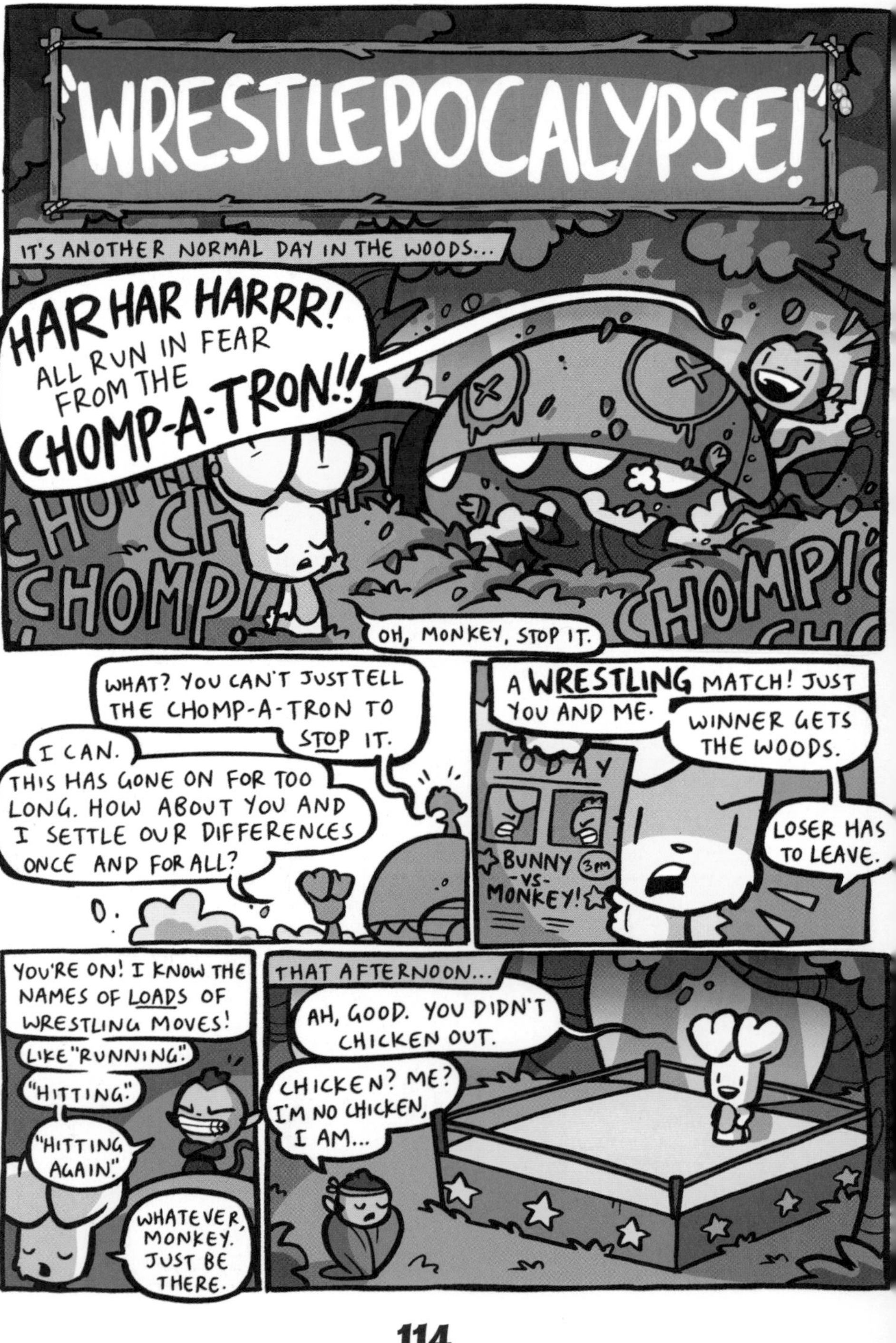
"WRESTLEPOCALYPSE!"
IT'S ANOTHER NORMAL DAY IN THE WOODS...
HAR HAR HARRR! ALL RUN IN FEAR FROM THE CHOMP-A-TRON!!
CHOMP! CHOMP! CHOMP! CHOMP!
OH, MONKEY, STOP IT.
WHAT? YOU CAN'T JUST TELL THE CHOMP-A-TRON TO STOP IT.
I CAN.
THIS HAS GONE ON FOR TOO LONG. HOW ABOUT YOU AND I SETTLE OUR DIFFERENCES ONCE AND FOR ALL?
A WRESTLING MATCH! JUST YOU AND ME.
WINNER GETS THE WOODS.
LOSER HAS TO LEAVE.
TODAY
BUNNY -VS- MONKEY!
3PM
YOU'RE ON! I KNOW THE NAMES OF LOADS OF WRESTLING MOVES!
LIKE "RUNNING."
"HITTING."
"HITTING AGAIN."
WHATEVER, MONKEY. JUST BE THERE.
THAT AFTERNOON...
AH, GOOD. YOU DIDN'T CHICKEN OUT.
CHICKEN? ME? I'M NO CHICKEN, I AM...

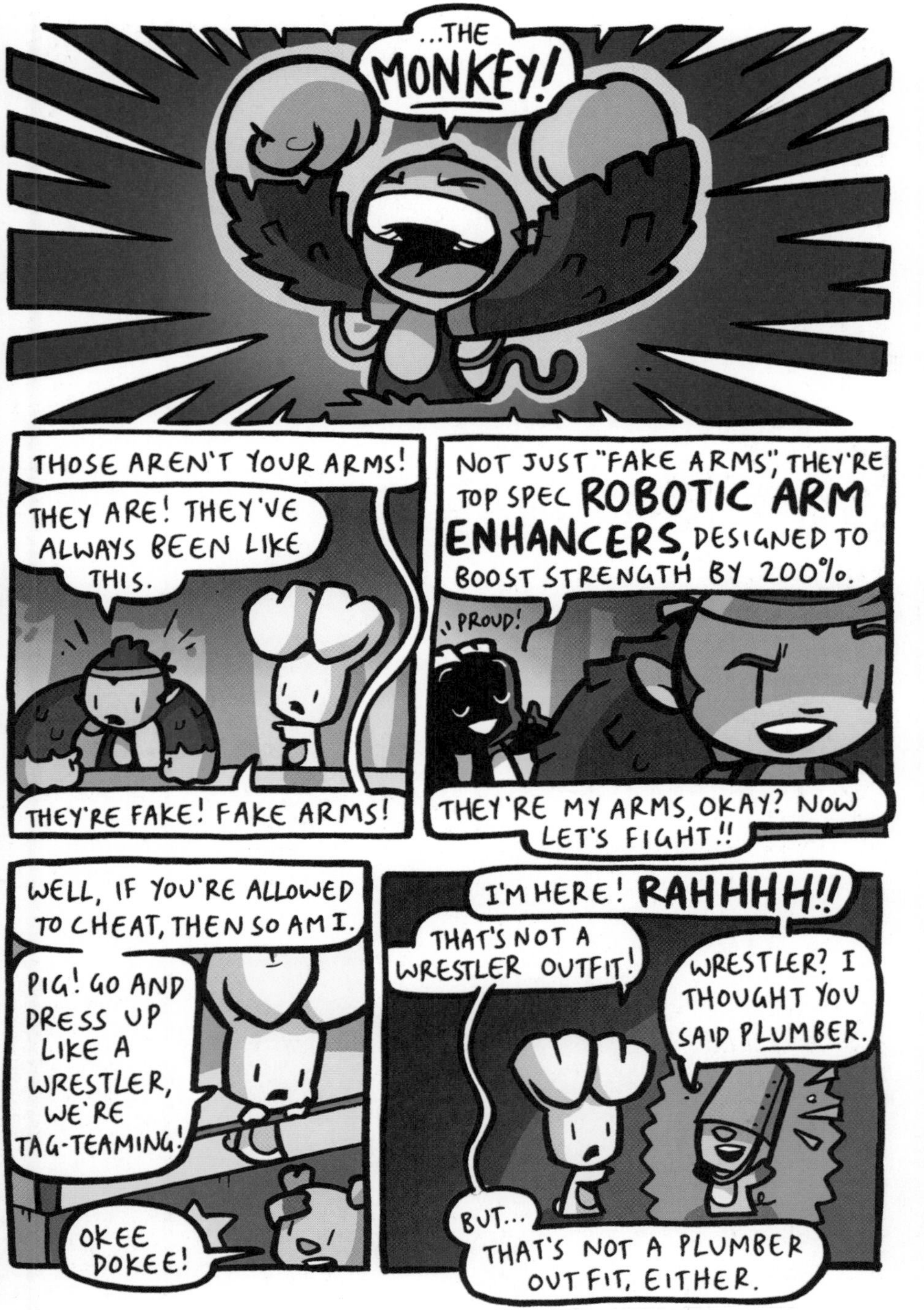
...THE MONKEY!
THOSE AREN'T YOUR ARMS!
THEY ARE! THEY'VE ALWAYS BEEN LIKE THIS.
THEY'RE FAKE! FAKE ARMS!
NOT JUST "FAKE ARMS", THEY'RE TOP SPEC ROBOTIC ARM ENHANCERS, DESIGNED TO BOOST STRENGTH BY 200%.
PROUD!
THEY'RE MY ARMS, OKAY? NOW LET'S FIGHT!!
WELL, IF YOU'RE ALLOWED TO CHEAT, THEN SO AM I.
PIG! GO AND DRESS UP LIKE A WRESTLER, WE'RE TAG-TEAMING!
OKEE DOKEE!
I'M HERE! RAHHHH!!
THAT'S NOT A WRESTLER OUTFIT!
WRESTLER? I THOUGHT YOU SAID PLUMBER.
BUT...
THAT'S NOT A PLUMBER OUTFIT, EITHER.

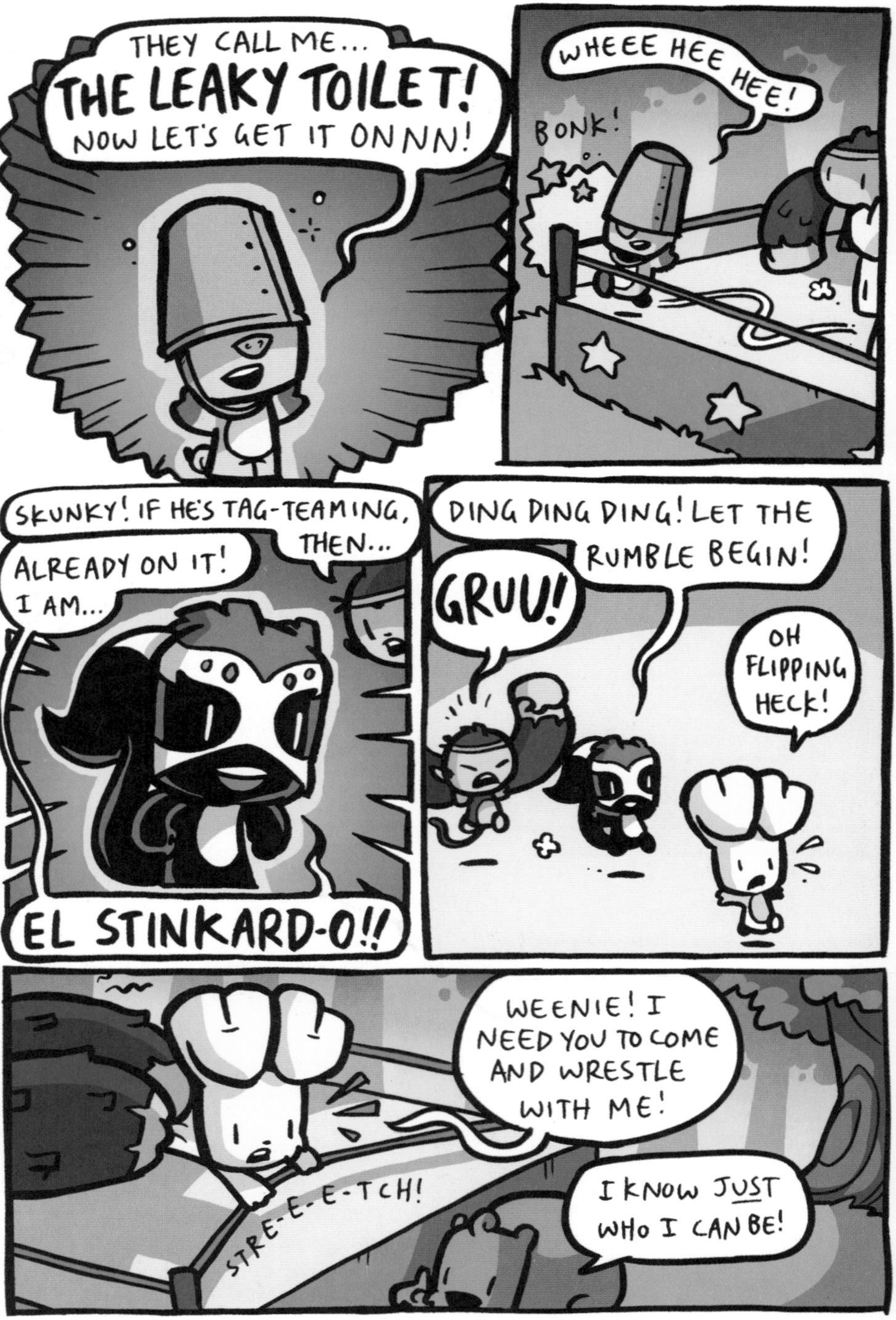
THEY CALL ME...
THE LEAKY TOILET!
NOW LET'S GET IT ONNN!
WHEEE HEE HEE!
BONK!
SKUNKY! IF HE'S TAG-TEAMING, THEN...
ALREADY ON IT! I AM...
EL STINKARD-O!!
DING DING DING! LET THE RUMBLE BEGIN!
GRUU!
OH FLIPPING HECK!
WEENIE! I NEED YOU TO COME AND WRESTLE WITH ME!
STRE-E-E-TCH!
I KNOW JUST WHO I CAN BE!

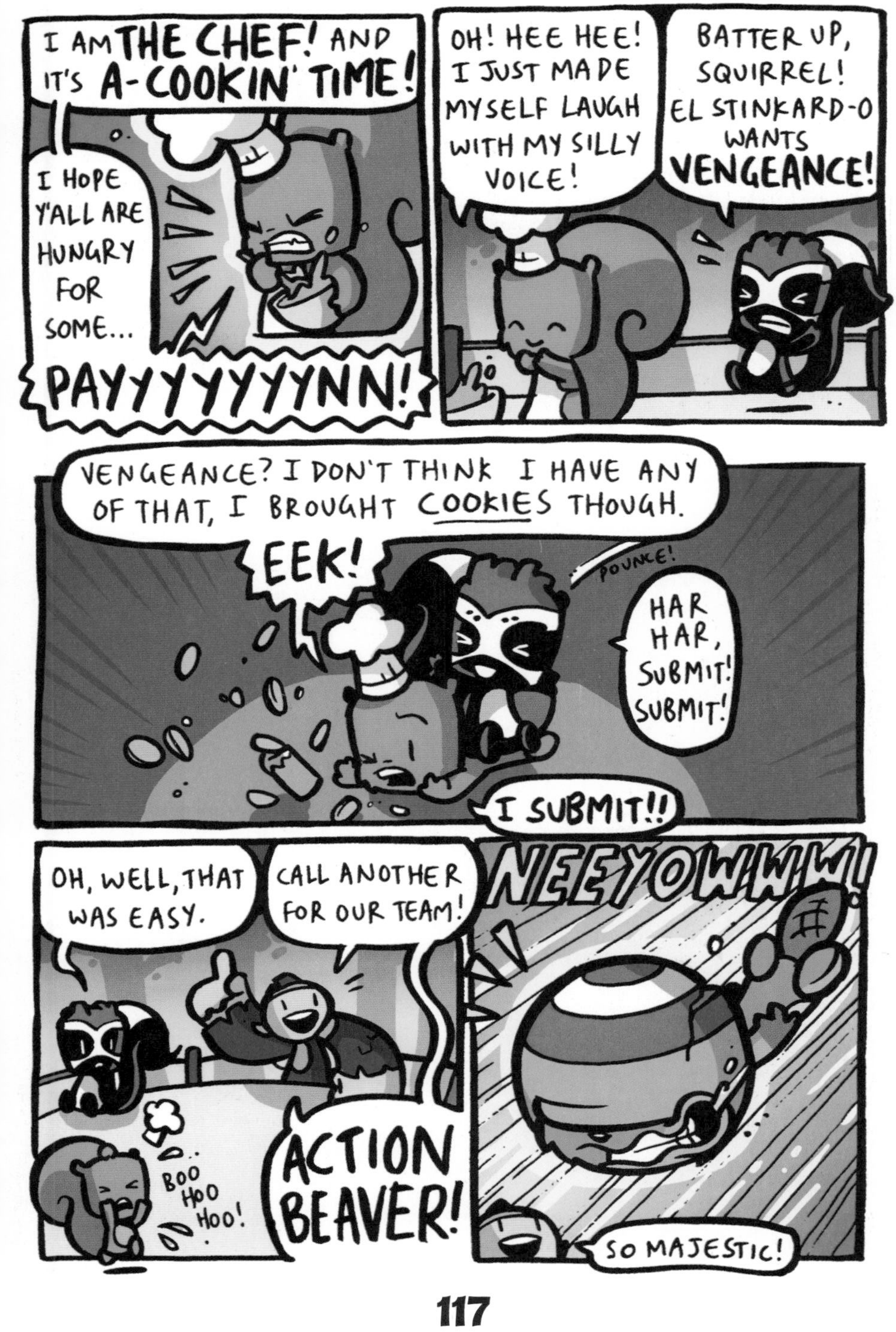

I AM THE CHEF! AND IT'S A-COOKIN' TIME!
I HOPE Y'ALL ARE HUNGRY FOR SOME...
PAYYYYYYYYNN!
OH! HEE HEE! I JUST MADE MYSELF LAUGH WITH MY SILLY VOICE!
BATTER UP, SQUIRREL! EL STINKARD-O WANTS VENGEANCE!
VENGEANCE? I DON'T THINK I HAVE ANY OF THAT, I BROUGHT COOKIES THOUGH.
EEK!
POUNCE!
HAR HAR, SUBMIT! SUBMIT!
I SUBMIT!!
OH, WELL, THAT WAS EASY.
CALL ANOTHER FOR OUR TEAM!
BOO HOO HOO!
ACTION BEAVER!
NEEYOWWW!
SO MAJESTIC!

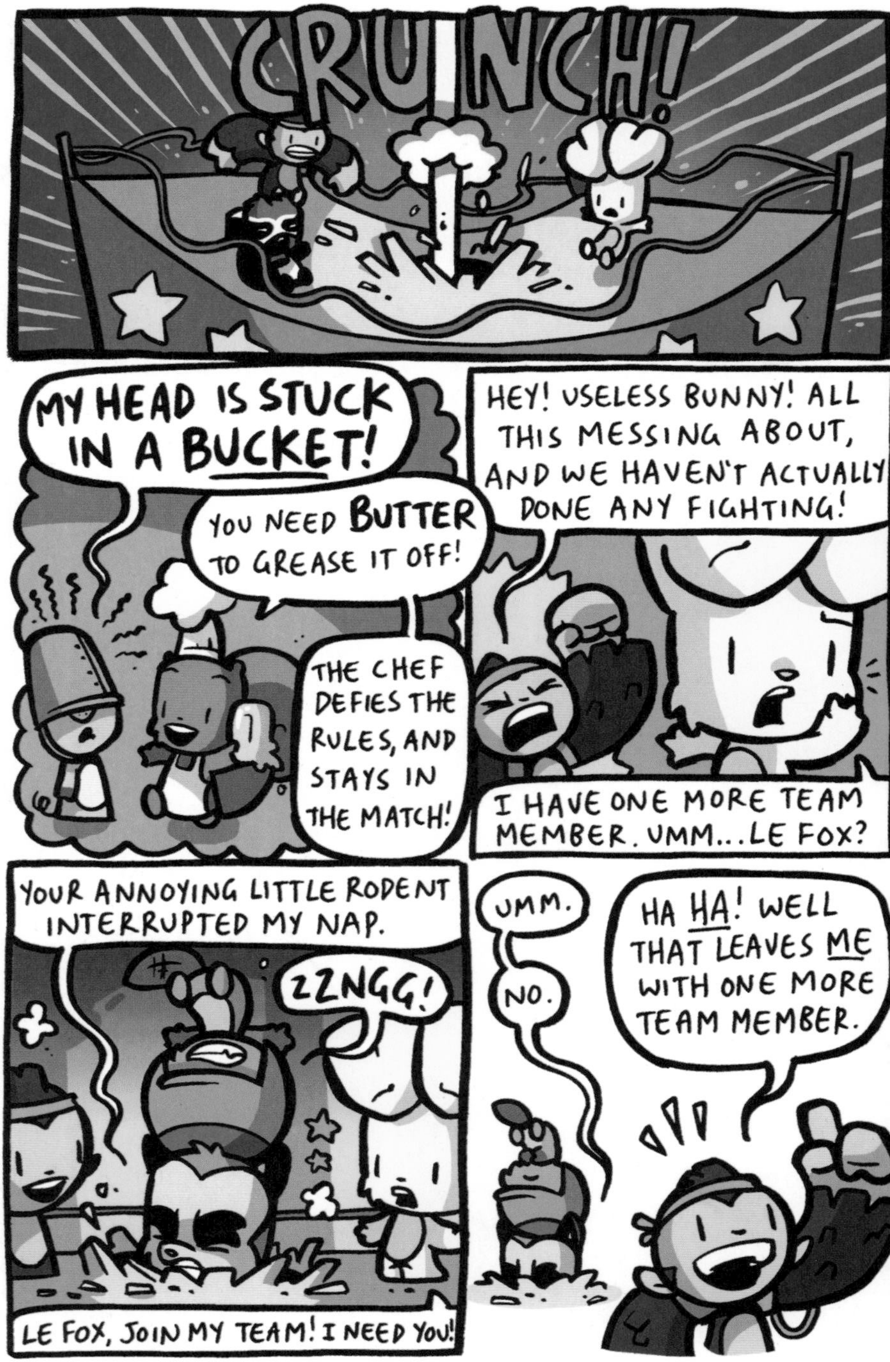
CRUNCH!
MY HEAD IS STUCK IN A BUCKET!
YOU NEED BUTTER TO GREASE IT OFF!
THE CHEF DEFIES THE RULES, AND STAYS IN THE MATCH!
HEY! USELESS BUNNY! ALL THIS MESSING ABOUT, AND WE HAVEN'T ACTUALLY DONE ANY FIGHTING!
I HAVE ONE MORE TEAM MEMBER. UMM... LE FOX?
YOUR ANNOYING LITTLE RODENT INTERRUPTED MY NAP.
ZZNGG!
LE FOX, JOIN MY TEAM! I NEED YOU!
UMM.
NO.
HA HA! WELL THAT LEAVES ME WITH ONE MORE TEAM MEMBER.

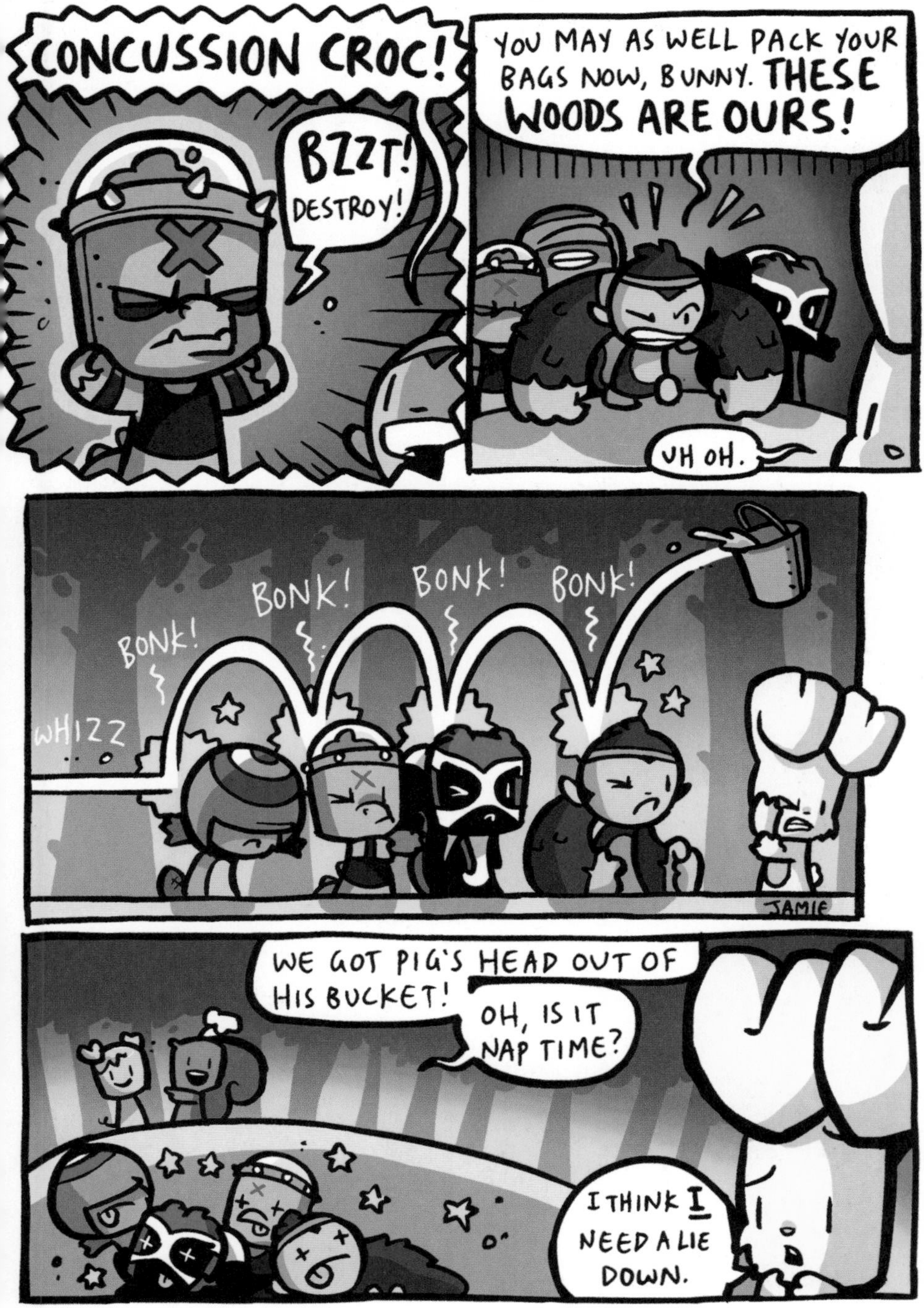
CONCUSSION CROC!
BZZT! DESTROY!
YOU MAY AS WELL PACK YOUR BAGS NOW, BUNNY. THESE WOODS ARE OURS!
UH OH.
WHIZZ
BONK!
BONK!
BONK!
BONK!
JAMIE
WE GOT PIG'S HEAD OUT OF HIS BUCKET!
OH, IS IT NAP TIME?
I THINK I NEED A LIE DOWN.

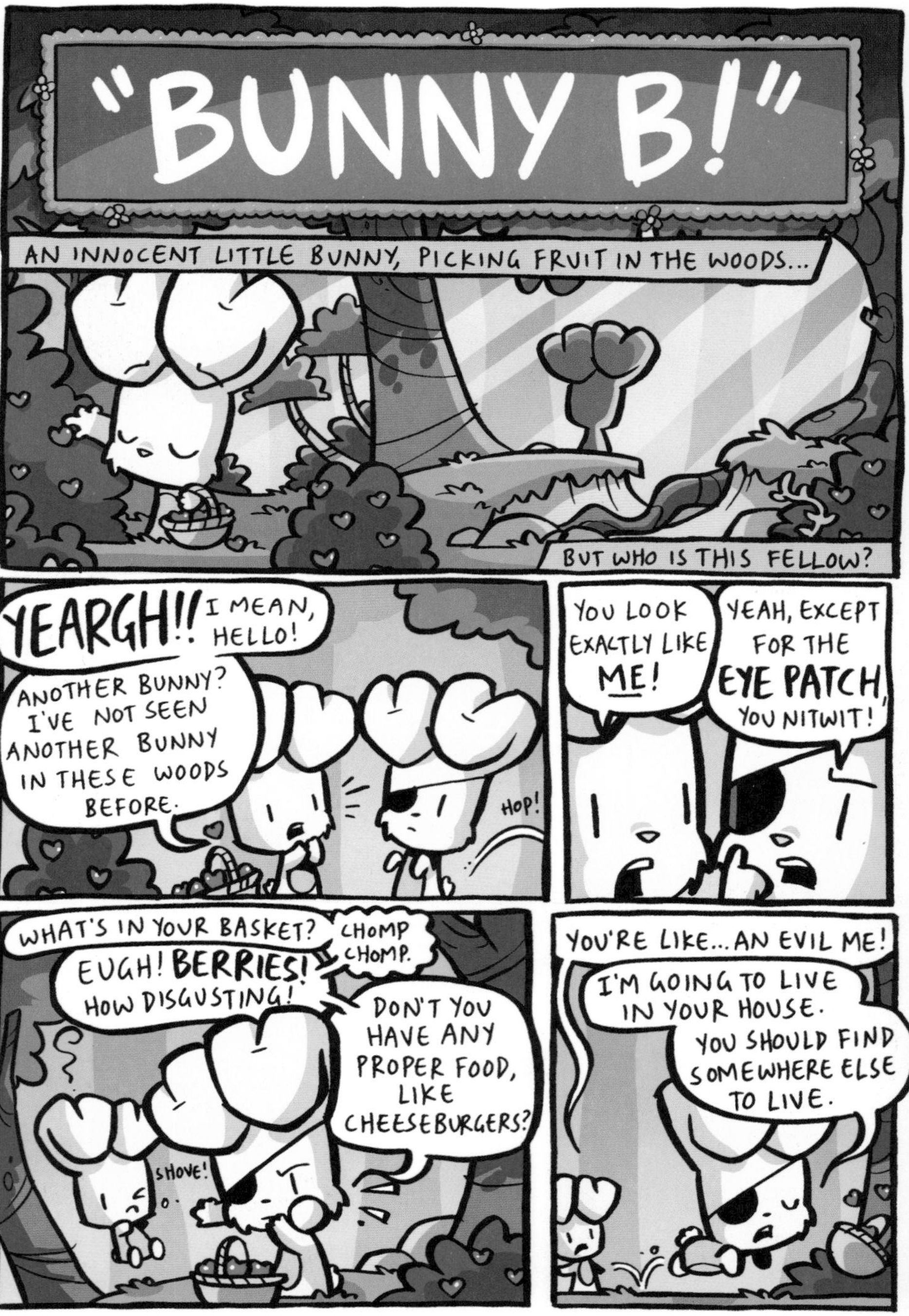
"BUNNY B!"
AN INNOCENT LITTLE BUNNY, PICKING FRUIT IN THE WOODS...
BUT WHO IS THIS FELLOW?
YEARGH!! I MEAN, HELLO!
ANOTHER BUNNY? I'VE NOT SEEN ANOTHER BUNNY IN THESE WOODS BEFORE.
HOP!
YOU LOOK EXACTLY LIKE ME!
YEAH, EXCEPT FOR THE EYE PATCH, YOU NITWIT!
WHAT'S IN YOUR BASKET?
CHOMP CHOMP.
EUGH! BERRIES! HOW DISGUSTING!
DON'T YOU HAVE ANY PROPER FOOD, LIKE CHEESEBURGERS?
SHOVE!
YOU'RE LIKE... AN EVIL ME!
I'M GOING TO LIVE IN YOUR HOUSE.
YOU SHOULD FIND SOMEWHERE ELSE TO LIVE.

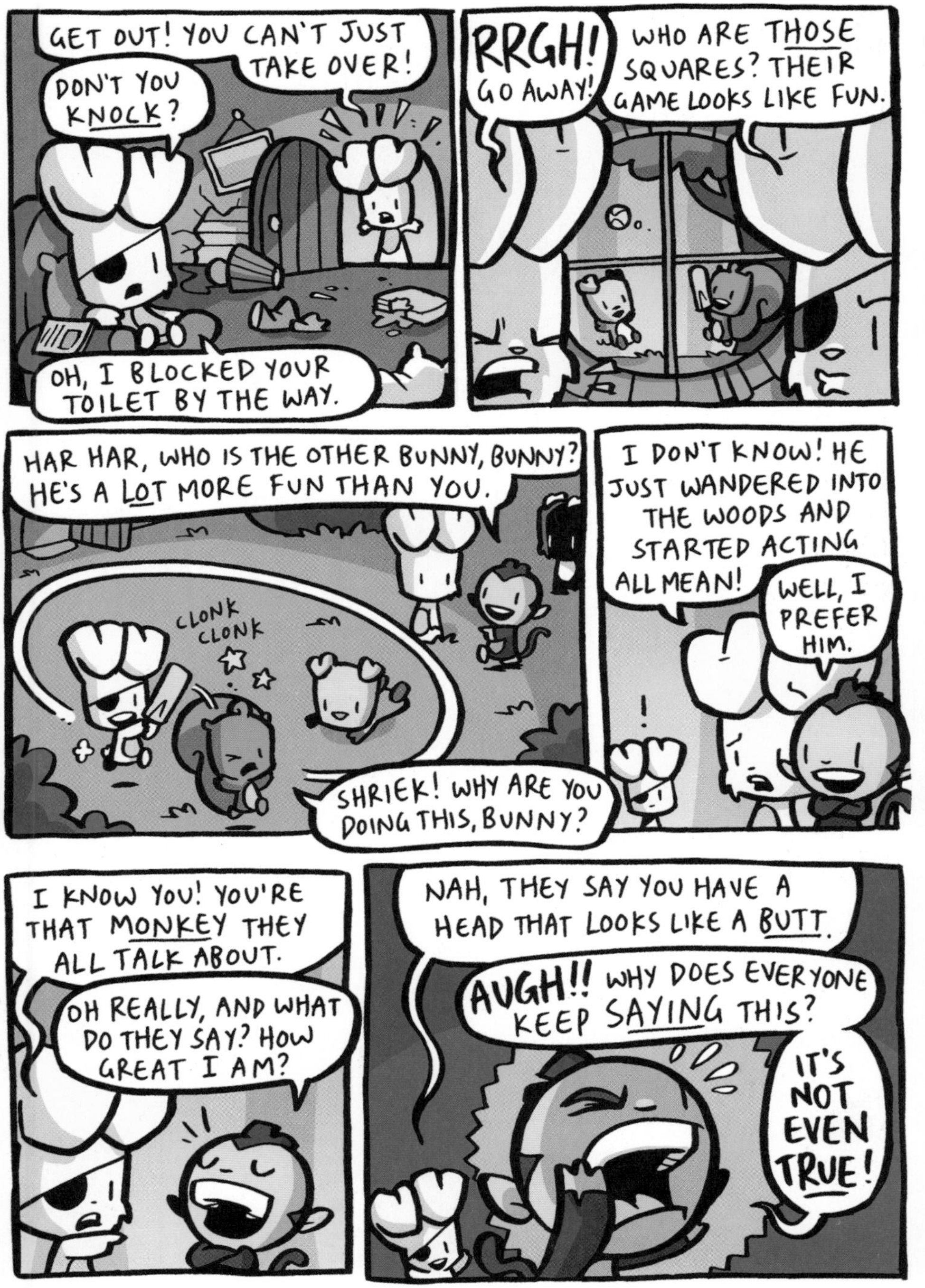
GET OUT! YOU CAN'T JUST TAKE OVER!
DON'T YOU KNOCK?
OH, I BLOCKED YOUR TOILET BY THE WAY.
RRGH! GO AWAY!
WHO ARE THOSE SQUARES? THEIR GAME LOOKS LIKE FUN.
HAR HAR, WHO IS THE OTHER BUNNY, BUNNY? HE'S A LOT MORE FUN THAN YOU.
CLONK CLONK
SHRIEK! WHY ARE YOU DOING THIS, BUNNY?
I DON'T KNOW! HE JUST WANDERED INTO THE WOODS AND STARTED ACTING ALL MEAN!
WELL, I PREFER HIM.
!
I KNOW YOU! YOU'RE THAT MONKEY THEY ALL TALK ABOUT.
OH REALLY, AND WHAT DO THEY SAY? HOW GREAT I AM?
NAH, THEY SAY YOU HAVE A HEAD THAT LOOKS LIKE A BUTT.
AUGH!! WHY DOES EVERYONE KEEP SAYING THIS?
IT'S NOT EVEN TRUE!

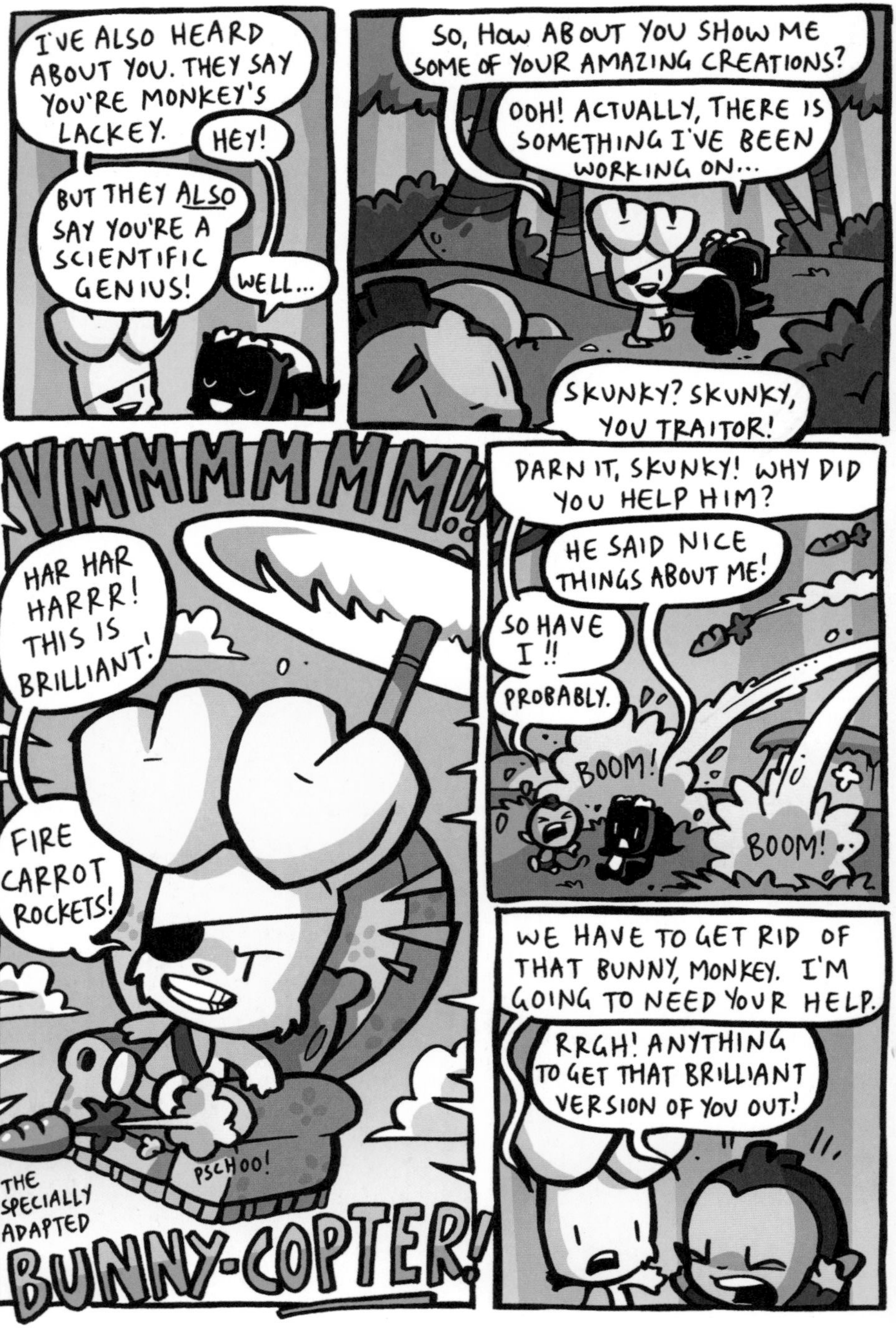
I'VE ALSO HEARD ABOUT YOU. THEY SAY YOU'RE MONKEY'S LACKEY.
HEY!
BUT THEY ALSO SAY YOU'RE A SCIENTIFIC GENIUS!
WELL...
SO, HOW ABOUT YOU SHOW ME SOME OF YOUR AMAZING CREATIONS?
OOH! ACTUALLY, THERE IS SOMETHING I'VE BEEN WORKING ON...
SKUNKY? SKUNKY, YOU TRAITOR!
VMMMMMMM!!
HAR HAR HARRR! THIS IS BRILLIANT!
FIRE CARROT ROCKETS!
PSCHOO!
THE SPECIALLY ADAPTED
BUNNY-COPTER!
DARN IT, SKUNKY! WHY DID YOU HELP HIM?
HE SAID NICE THINGS ABOUT ME!
SO HAVE I !!
PROBABLY.
BOOM!
BOOM!
WE HAVE TO GET RID OF THAT BUNNY, MONKEY. I'M GOING TO NEED YOUR HELP.
RRGH! ANYTHING TO GET THAT BRILLIANT VERSION OF YOU OUT!

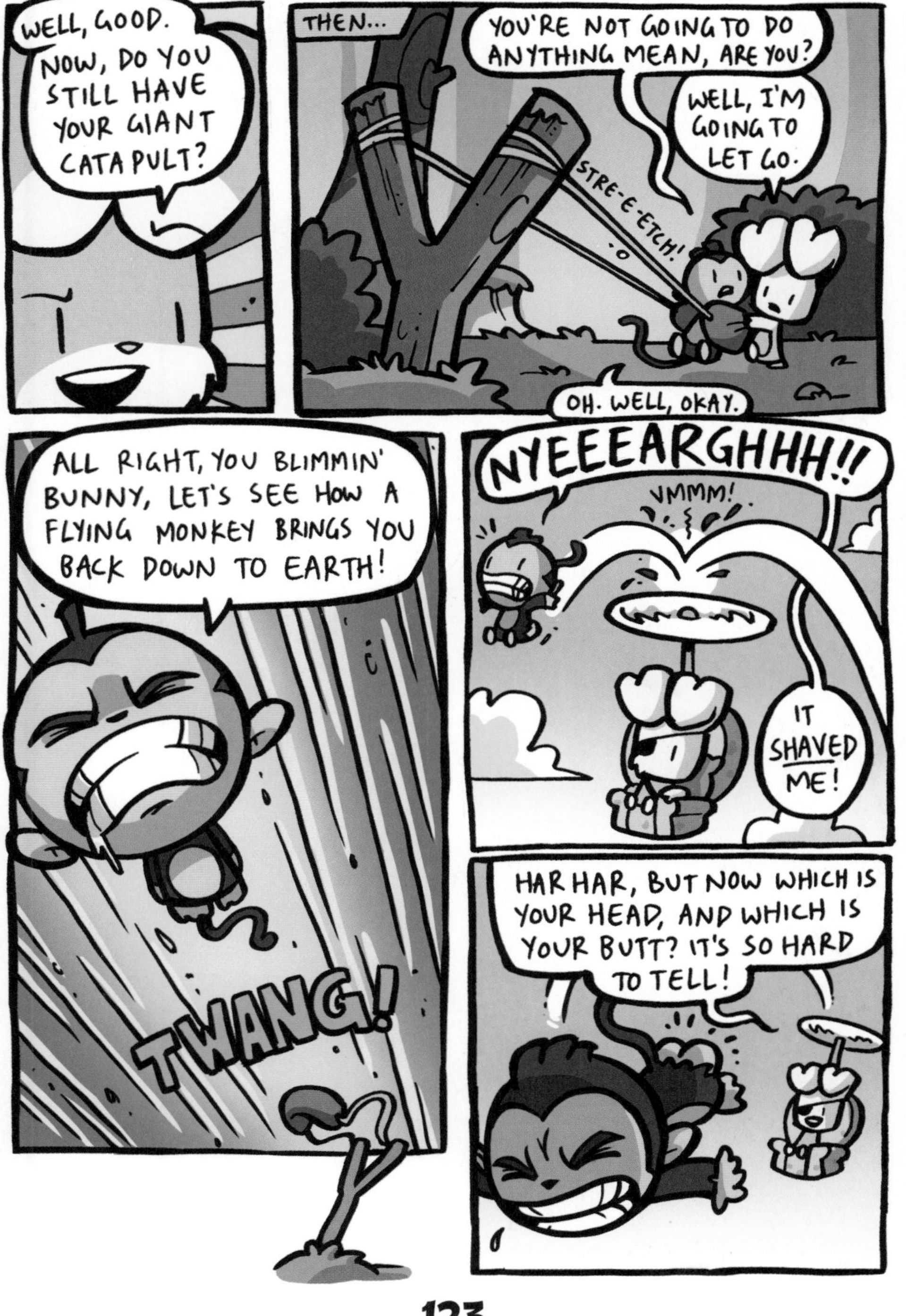
WELL, GOOD.
NOW, DO YOU STILL HAVE YOUR GIANT CATAPULT?
THEN...
YOU'RE NOT GOING TO DO ANYTHING MEAN, ARE YOU?
WELL, I'M GOING TO LET GO.
STRE-E-ETCH!
OH. WELL, OKAY.
ALL RIGHT, YOU BLIMMIN' BUNNY, LET'S SEE HOW A FLYING MONKEY BRINGS YOU BACK DOWN TO EARTH!
TWANG!
NYEEEARGHHH!!
VMMM!
IT SHAVED ME!
HAR HAR, BUT NOW WHICH IS YOUR HEAD, AND WHICH IS YOUR BUTT? IT'S SO HARD TO TELL!

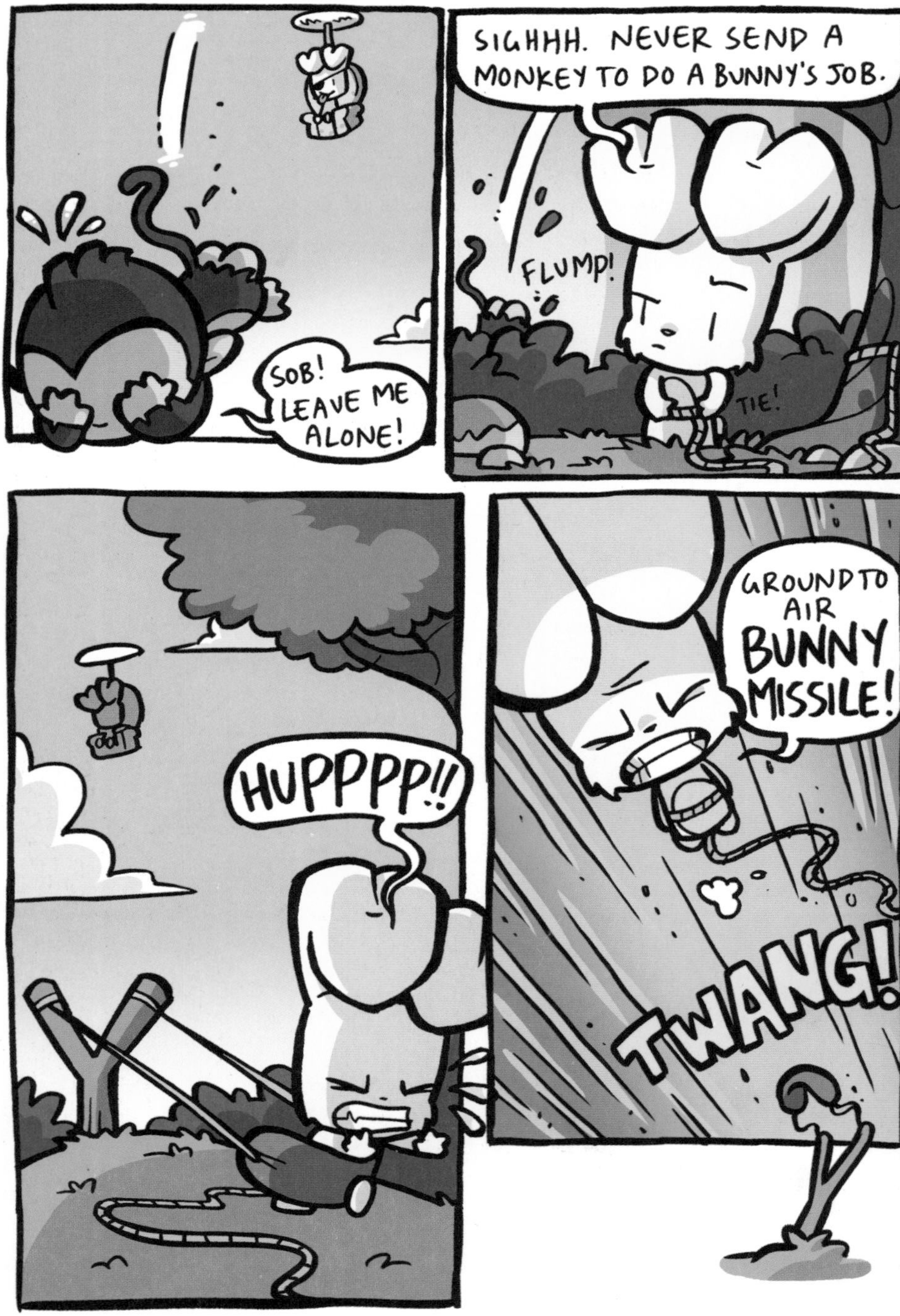
SOB! LEAVE ME ALONE!
SIGHHH. NEVER SEND A MONKEY TO DO A BUNNY'S JOB.
FLUMP!
TIE!
HUPPPP!!
GROUND TO AIR BUNNY MISSILE!
TWANG!

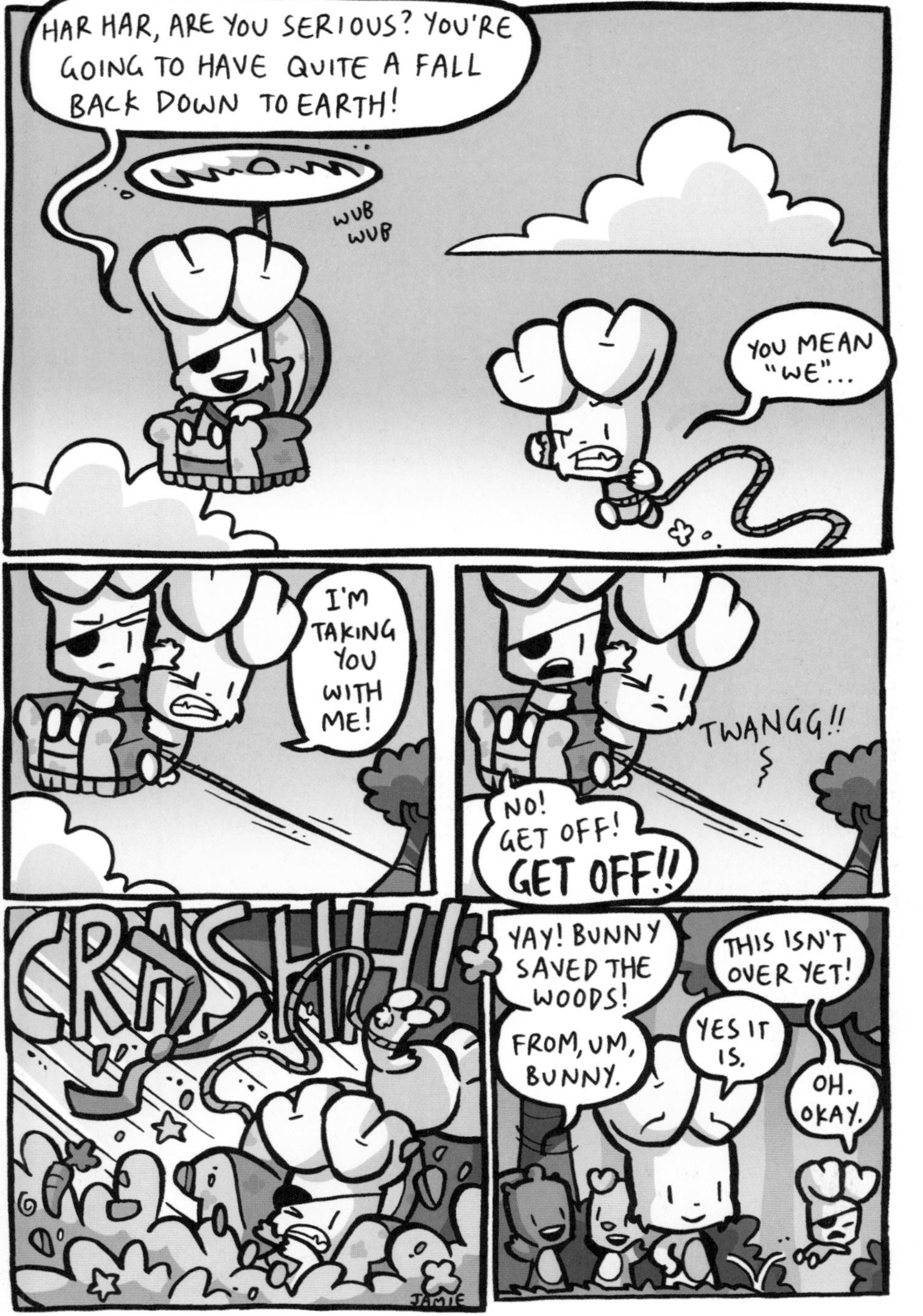
HAR HAR, ARE YOU SERIOUS? YOU'RE GOING TO HAVE QUITE A FALL BACK DOWN TO EARTH!
WUB WUB
YOU MEAN "WE"...
I'M TAKING YOU WITH ME!
TWANGG!!
NO! GET OFF! GET OFF!!
CRASHH!
JAMIE
YAY! BUNNY SAVED THE WOODS!
FROM, UM, BUNNY.
THIS ISN'T OVER YET!
YES IT IS.
OH. OKAY.

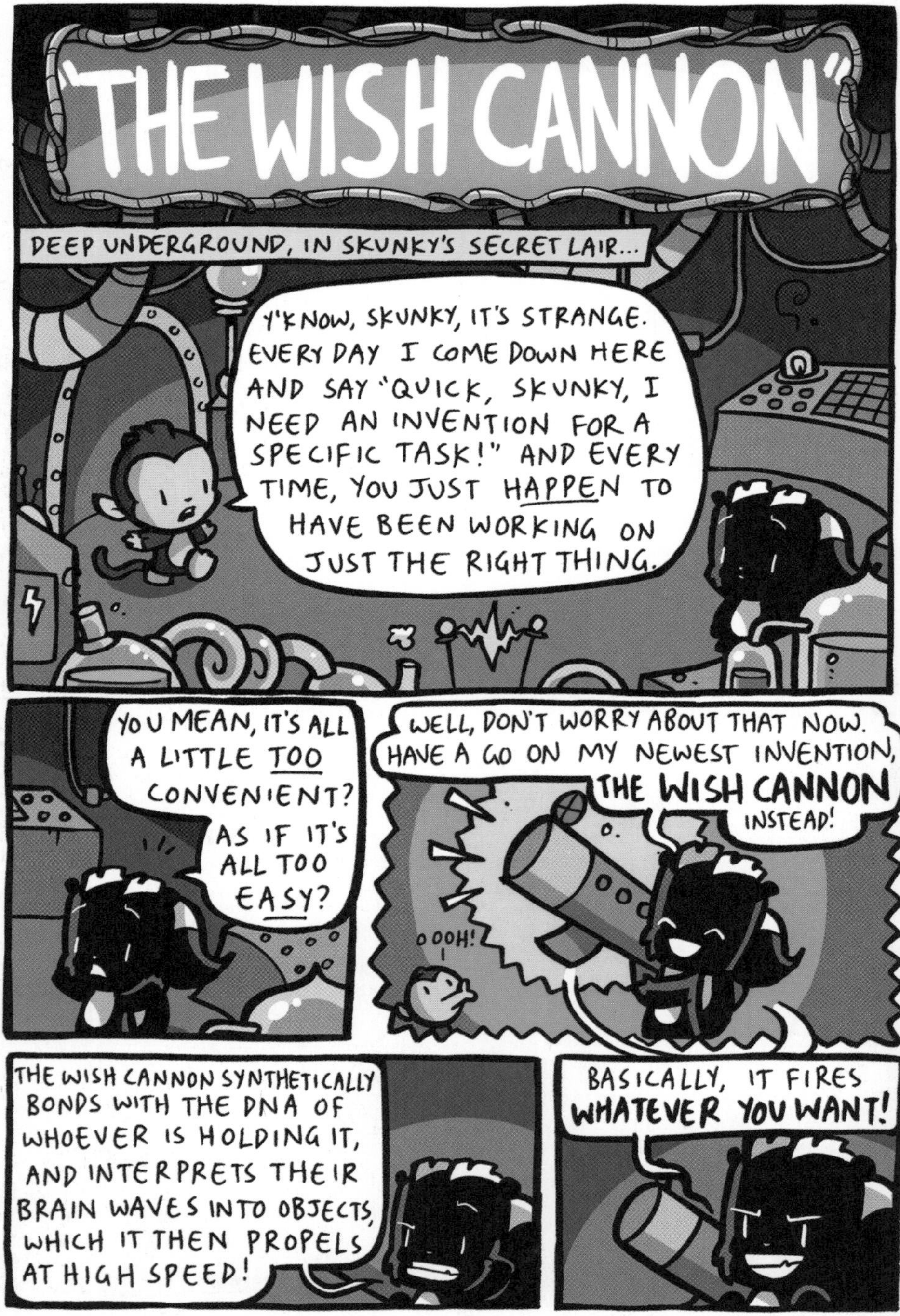
"THE WISH CANNON"
DEEP UNDERGROUND, IN SKUNKY'S SECRET LAIR...
Y'KNOW, SKUNKY, IT'S STRANGE. EVERY DAY I COME DOWN HERE AND SAY "QUICK, SKUNKY, I NEED AN INVENTION FOR A SPECIFIC TASK!" AND EVERY TIME, YOU JUST HAPPEN TO HAVE BEEN WORKING ON JUST THE RIGHT THING.
YOU MEAN, IT'S ALL A LITTLE TOO CONVENIENT?
AS IF IT'S ALL TOO EASY?
WELL, DON'T WORRY ABOUT THAT NOW. HAVE A GO ON MY NEWEST INVENTION, THE WISH CANNON INSTEAD!
OOOH!
THE WISH CANNON SYNTHETICALLY BONDS WITH THE DNA OF WHOEVER IS HOLDING IT, AND INTERPRETS THEIR BRAIN WAVES INTO OBJECTS, WHICH IT THEN PROPELS AT HIGH SPEED!
BASICALLY, IT FIRES WHATEVER YOU WANT!

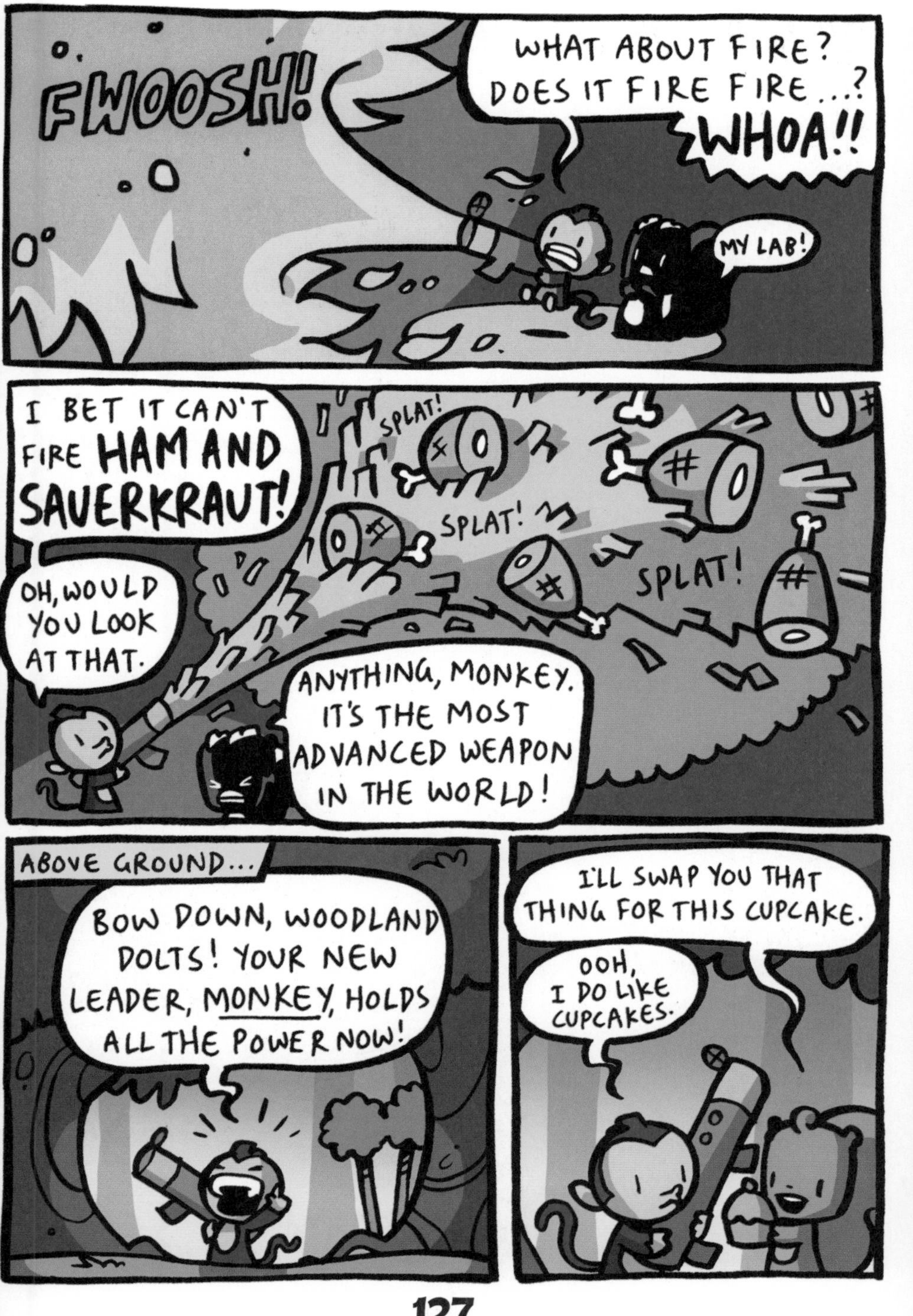
FWOOSH!
WHAT ABOUT FIRE? DOES IT FIRE FIRE...? WHOA!!
MY LAB!
I BET IT CAN'T FIRE HAM AND SAUERKRAUT!
SPLAT!
SPLAT!
SPLAT!
OH, WOULD YOU LOOK AT THAT.
ANYTHING, MONKEY. IT'S THE MOST ADVANCED WEAPON IN THE WORLD!
ABOVE GROUND...
BOW DOWN, WOODLAND DOLTS! YOUR NEW LEADER, MONKEY, HOLDS ALL THE POWER NOW!
I'LL SWAP YOU THAT THING FOR THIS CUPCAKE.
OOH, I DO LIKE CUPCAKES.

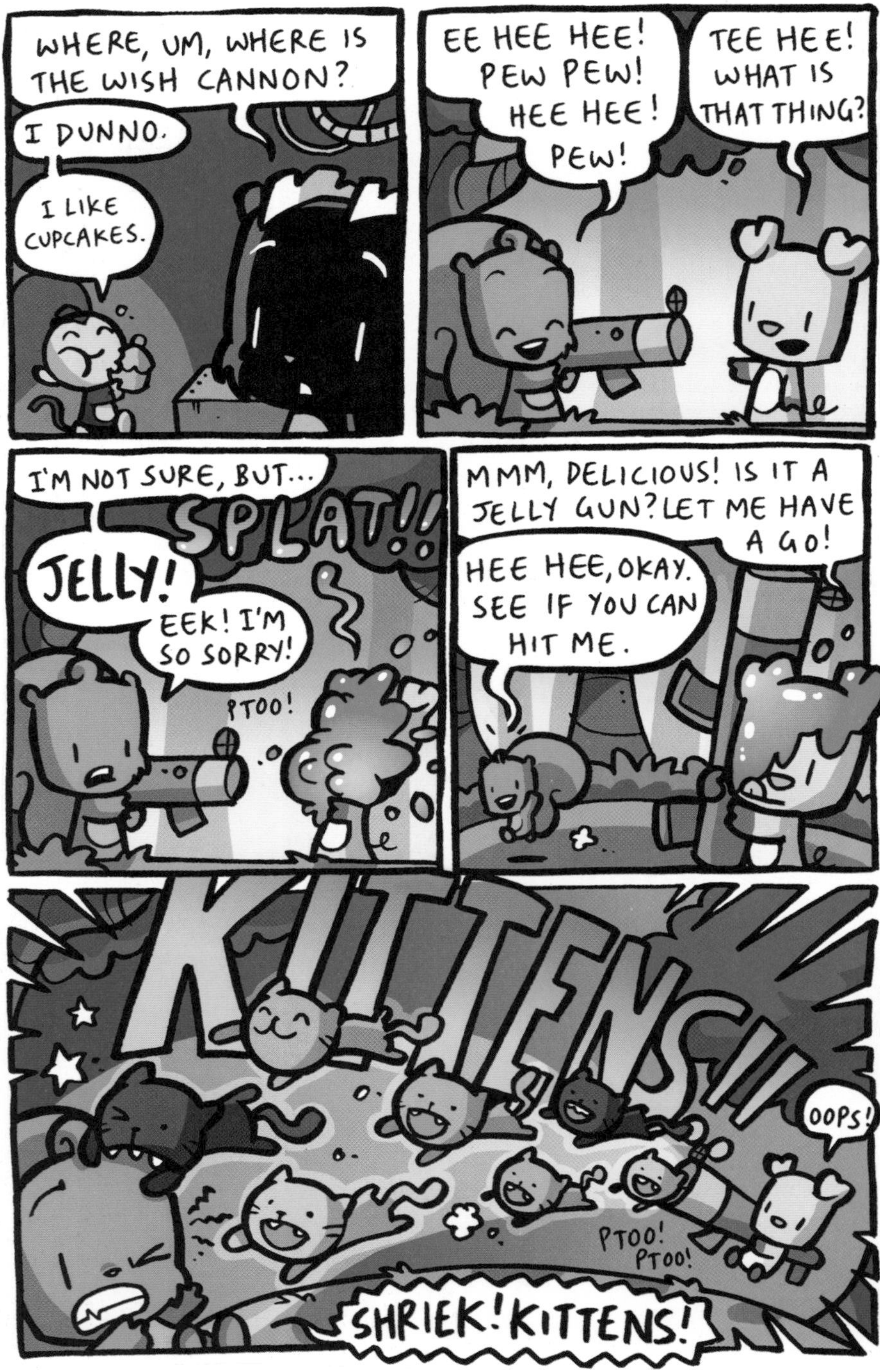
WHERE, UM, WHERE IS THE WISH CANNON?
I DUNNO.
I LIKE CUPCAKES.
EE HEE HEE! PEW PEW! HEE HEE! PEW!
TEE HEE! WHAT IS THAT THING?
I'M NOT SURE, BUT...
SPLAT!!
JELLY!
EEK! I'M SO SORRY!
PTOO!
MMM, DELICIOUS! IS IT A JELLY GUN? LET ME HAVE A GO!
HEE HEE, OKAY. SEE IF YOU CAN HIT ME.
KITTENS!!!
OOPS!
PTOO! PTOO!
SHRIEK! KITTENS!

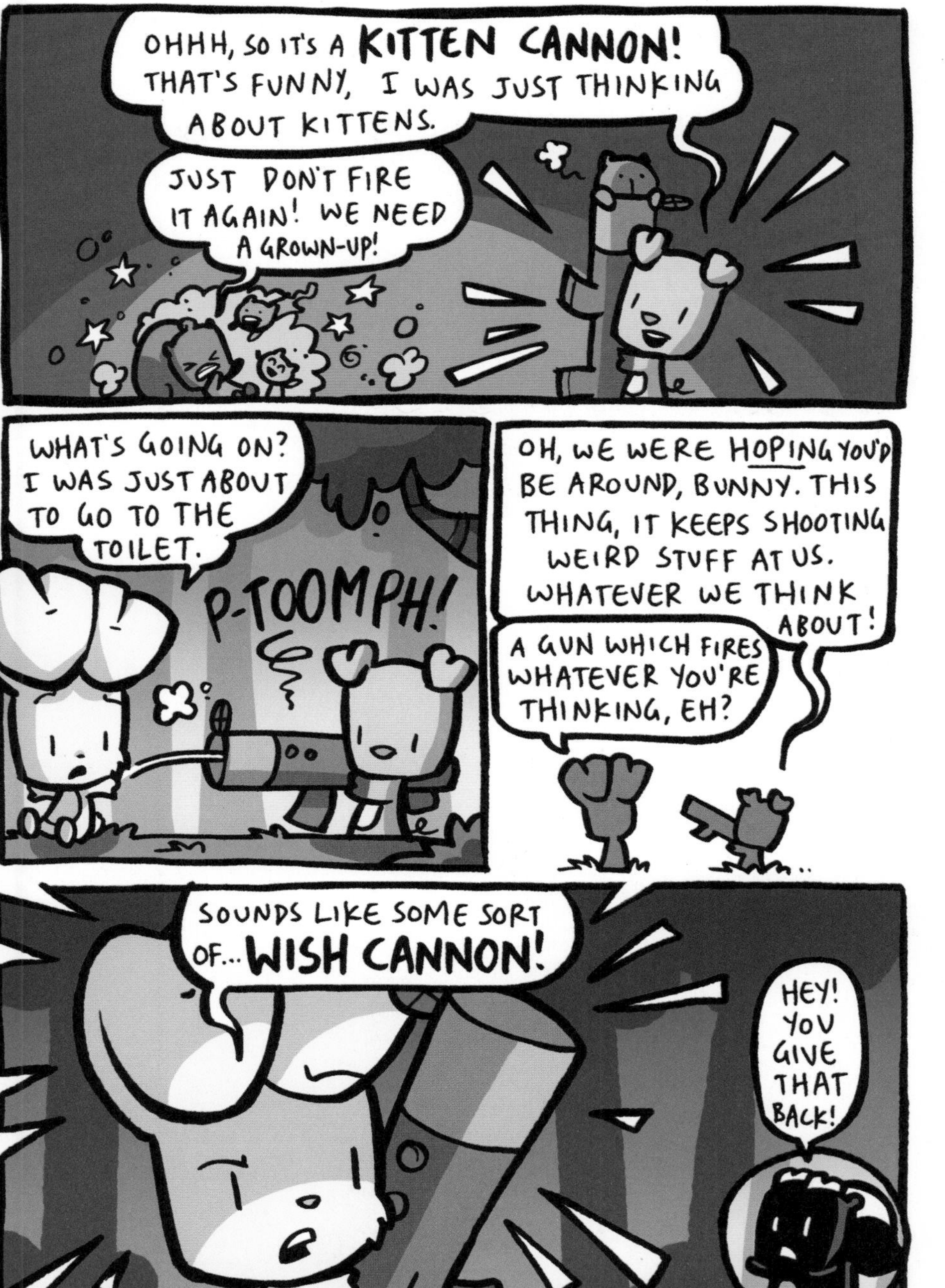
OHHH, SO IT'S A KITTEN CANNON! THAT'S FUNNY, I WAS JUST THINKING ABOUT KITTENS.
JUST DON'T FIRE IT AGAIN! WE NEED A GROWN-UP!
WHAT'S GOING ON? I WAS JUST ABOUT TO GO TO THE TOILET.
P-TOOMPH!
OH, WE WERE HOPING YOU'D BE AROUND, BUNNY. THIS THING, IT KEEPS SHOOTING WEIRD STUFF AT US. WHATEVER WE THINK ABOUT!
A GUN WHICH FIRES WHATEVER YOU'RE THINKING, EH?
SOUNDS LIKE SOME SORT OF... WISH CANNON!
HEY! YOU GIVE THAT BACK!

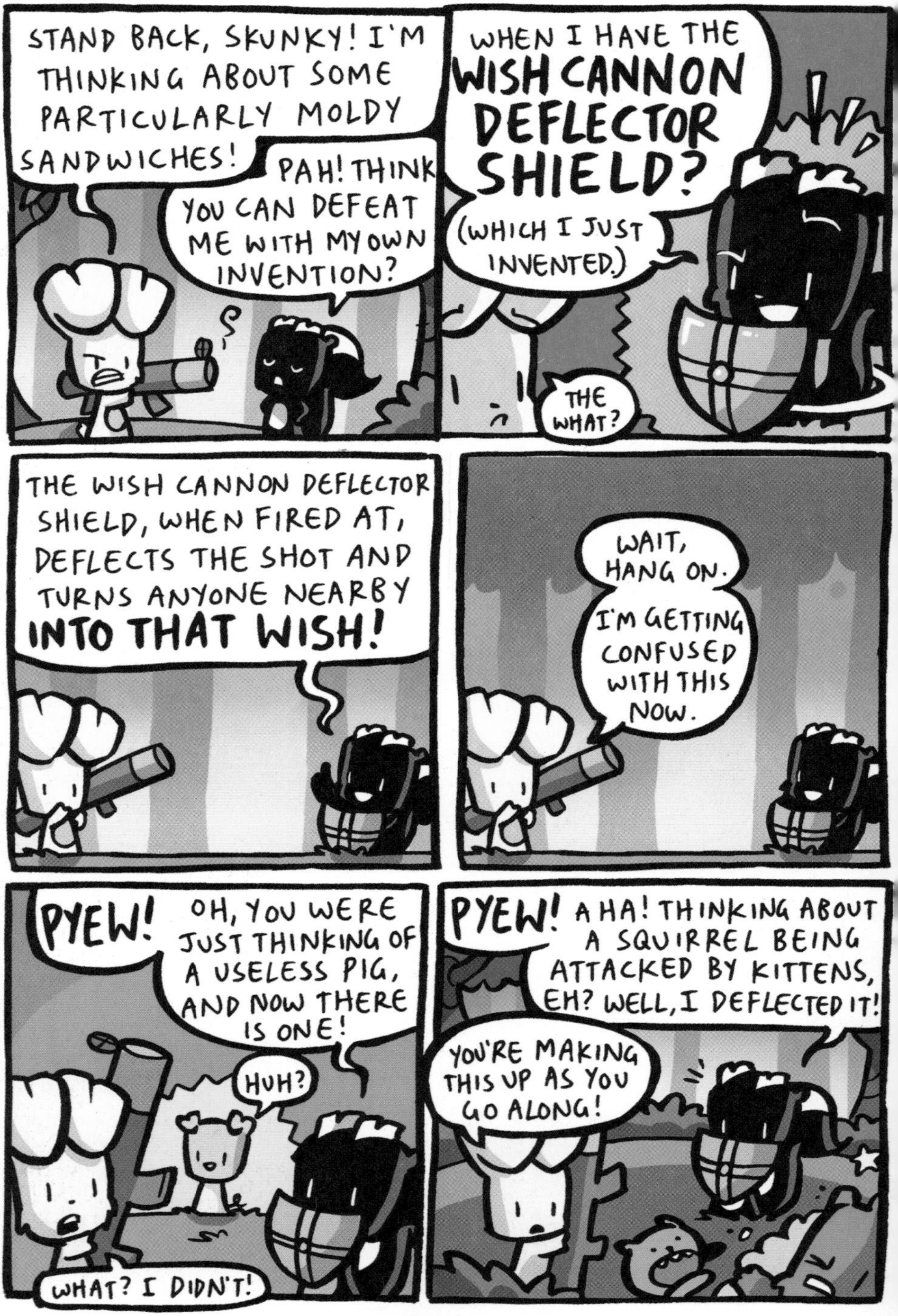
STAND BACK, SKUNKY! I'M THINKING ABOUT SOME PARTICULARLY MOLDY SANDWICHES!
PAH! THINK YOU CAN DEFEAT ME WITH MY OWN INVENTION?
WHEN I HAVE THE WISH CANNON DEFLECTOR SHIELD?
(WHICH I JUST INVENTED.)
THE WHAT?
THE WISH CANNON DEFLECTOR SHIELD, WHEN FIRED AT, DEFLECTS THE SHOT AND TURNS ANYONE NEARBY INTO THAT WISH!
WAIT, HANG ON.
I'M GETTING CONFUSED WITH THIS NOW.
PYEW!
OH, YOU WERE JUST THINKING OF A USELESS PIG, AND NOW THERE IS ONE!
HUH?
WHAT? I DIDN'T!
PYEW!
AHA! THINKING ABOUT A SQUIRREL BEING ATTACKED BY KITTENS, EH? WELL, I DEFLECTED IT!
YOU'RE MAKING THIS UP AS YOU GO ALONG!

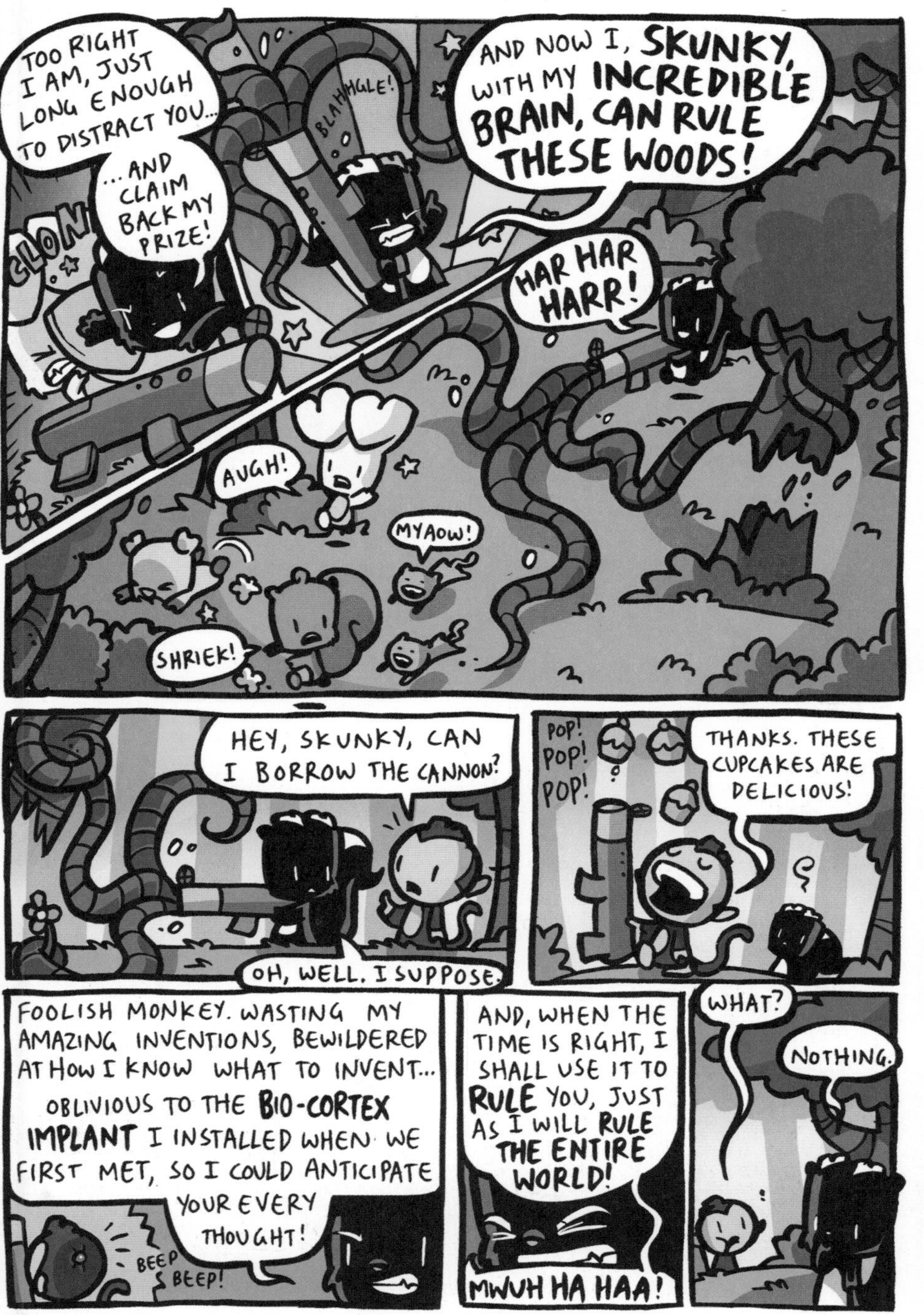
TOO RIGHT I AM, JUST LONG ENOUGH TO DISTRACT YOU...
...AND CLAIM BACK MY PRIZE!
CLON
BLAHHHGLE!
AND NOW I, SKUNKY, WITH MY INCREDIBLE BRAIN, CAN RULE THESE WOODS!
HAR HAR HARR!
AUGH!
MYAOW!
SHRIEK!
HEY, SKUNKY, CAN I BORROW THE CANNON?
OH, WELL. I SUPPOSE.
POP! POP! POP!
THANKS. THESE CUPCAKES ARE DELICIOUS!
FOOLISH MONKEY. WASTING MY AMAZING INVENTIONS, BEWILDERED AT HOW I KNOW WHAT TO INVENT...
OBLIVIOUS TO THE BIO-CORTEX IMPLANT I INSTALLED WHEN WE FIRST MET, SO I COULD ANTICIPATE YOUR EVERY THOUGHT!
BEEP BEEP!
AND, WHEN THE TIME IS RIGHT, I SHALL USE IT TO RULE YOU, JUST AS I WILL RULE THE ENTIRE WORLD!
MWUH HA HAA!
WHAT?
NOTHING.

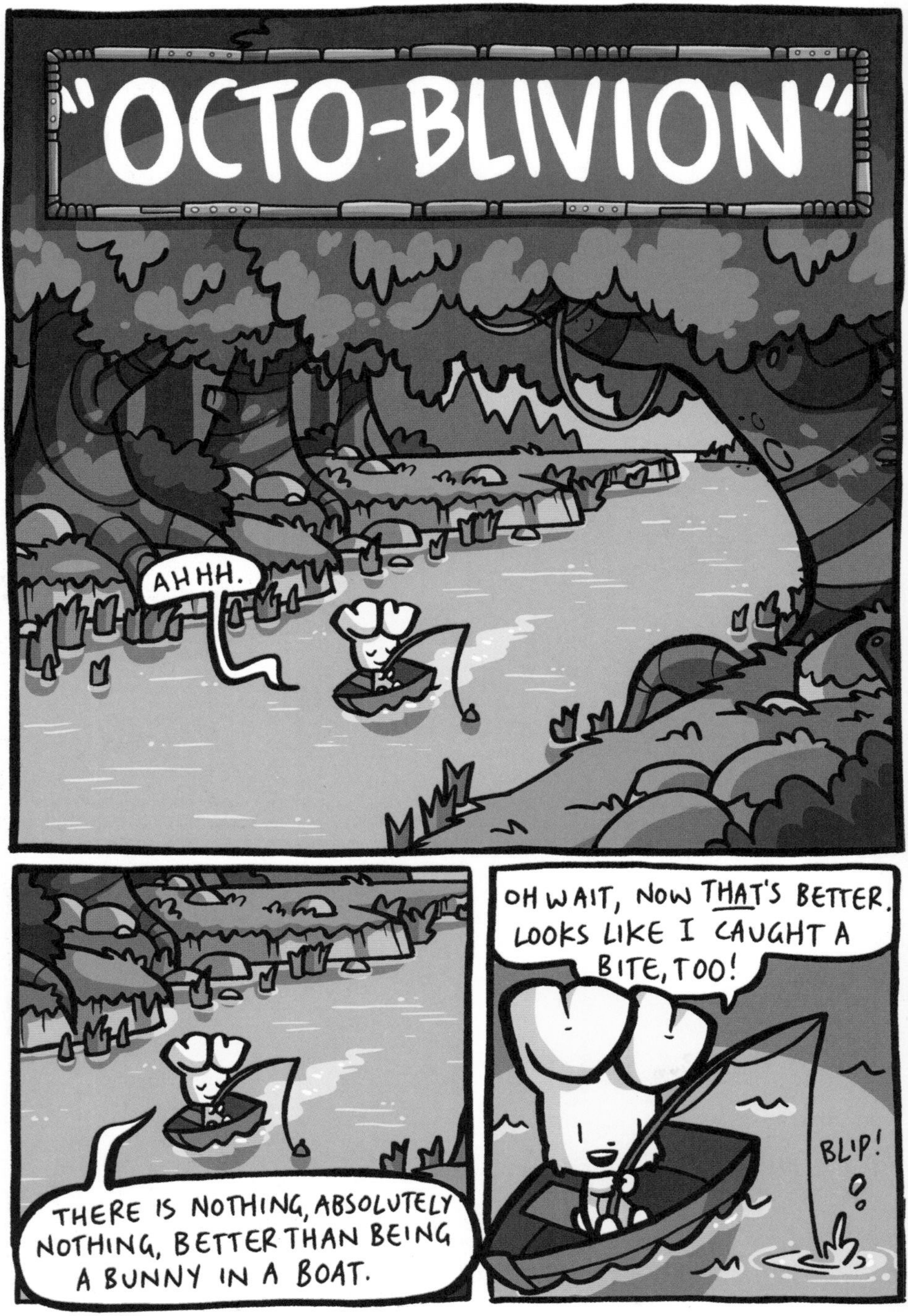
"OCTO-BLIVION"
AHHH.
THERE IS NOTHING, ABSOLUTELY NOTHING, BETTER THAN BEING A BUNNY IN A BOAT.
OH WAIT, NOW THAT'S BETTER. LOOKS LIKE I CAUGHT A BITE, TOO!
BLIP!

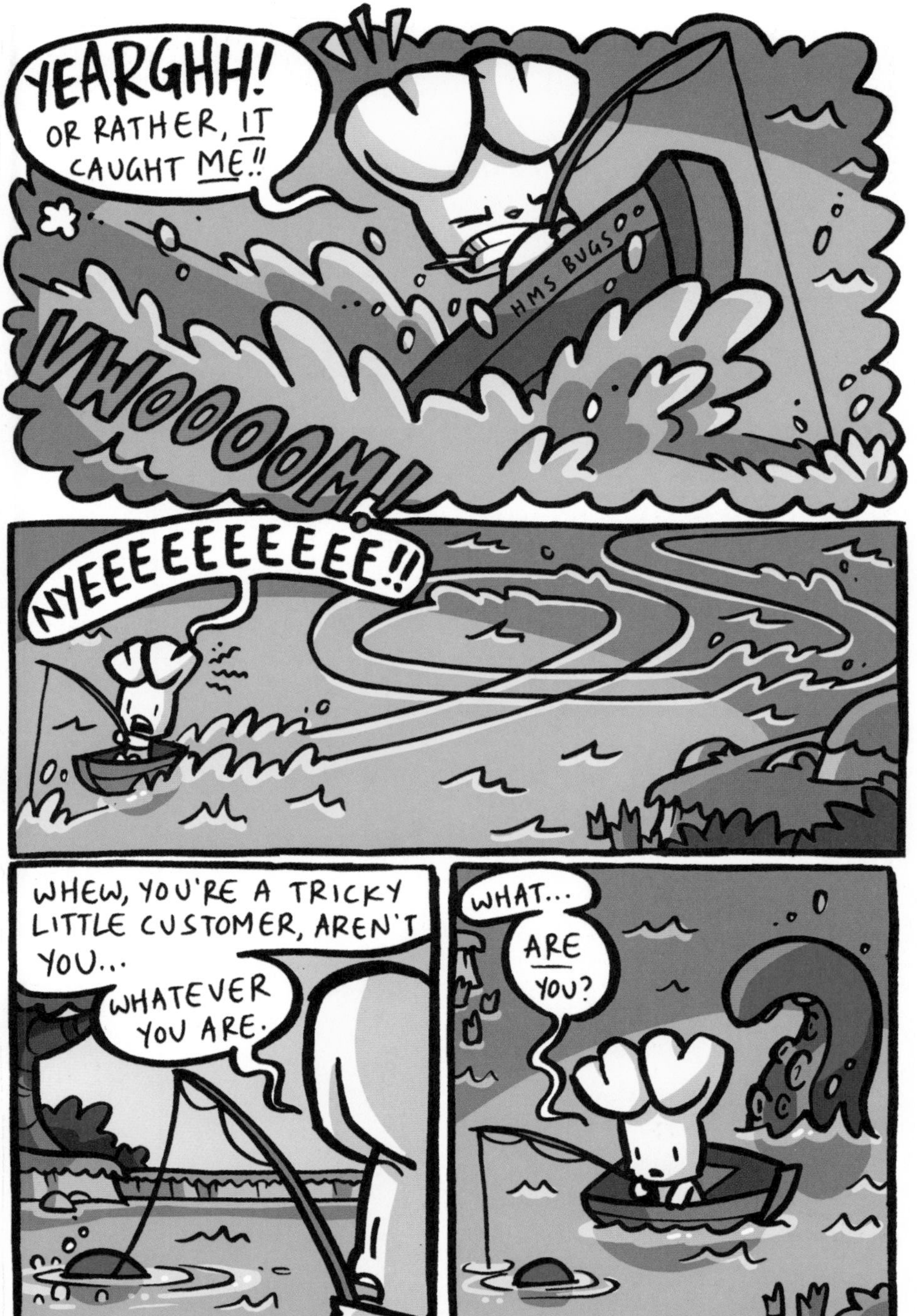
YEARGHH! OR RATHER, IT CAUGHT ME!!
HMS BUGS
VWOOOOOM!
NYEEEEEEEEEE!!
WHEW, YOU'RE A TRICKY LITTLE CUSTOMER, AREN'T YOU...
WHATEVER YOU ARE.
WHAT...
ARE YOU?

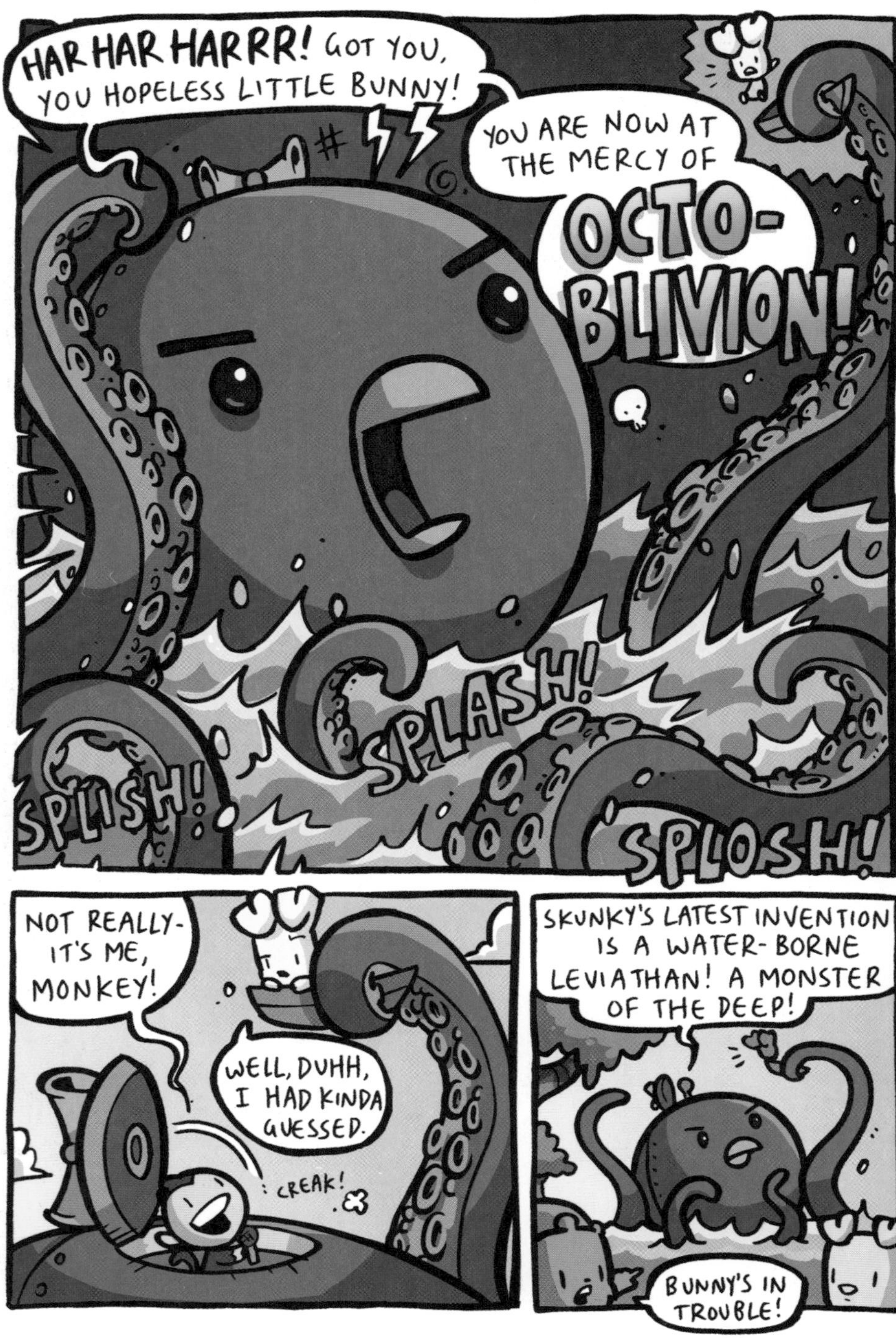

HAR HAR HARRR! GOT YOU, YOU HOPELESS LITTLE BUNNY!
YOU ARE NOW AT THE MERCY OF OCTO-BLIVION!
SPLISH!
SPLASH!
SPLOSH!
NOT REALLY-IT'S ME, MONKEY!
WELL, DUHH, I HAD KINDA GUESSED.
CREAK!
SKUNKY'S LATEST INVENTION IS A WATER-BORNE LEVIATHAN! A MONSTER OF THE DEEP!
BUNNY'S IN TROUBLE!

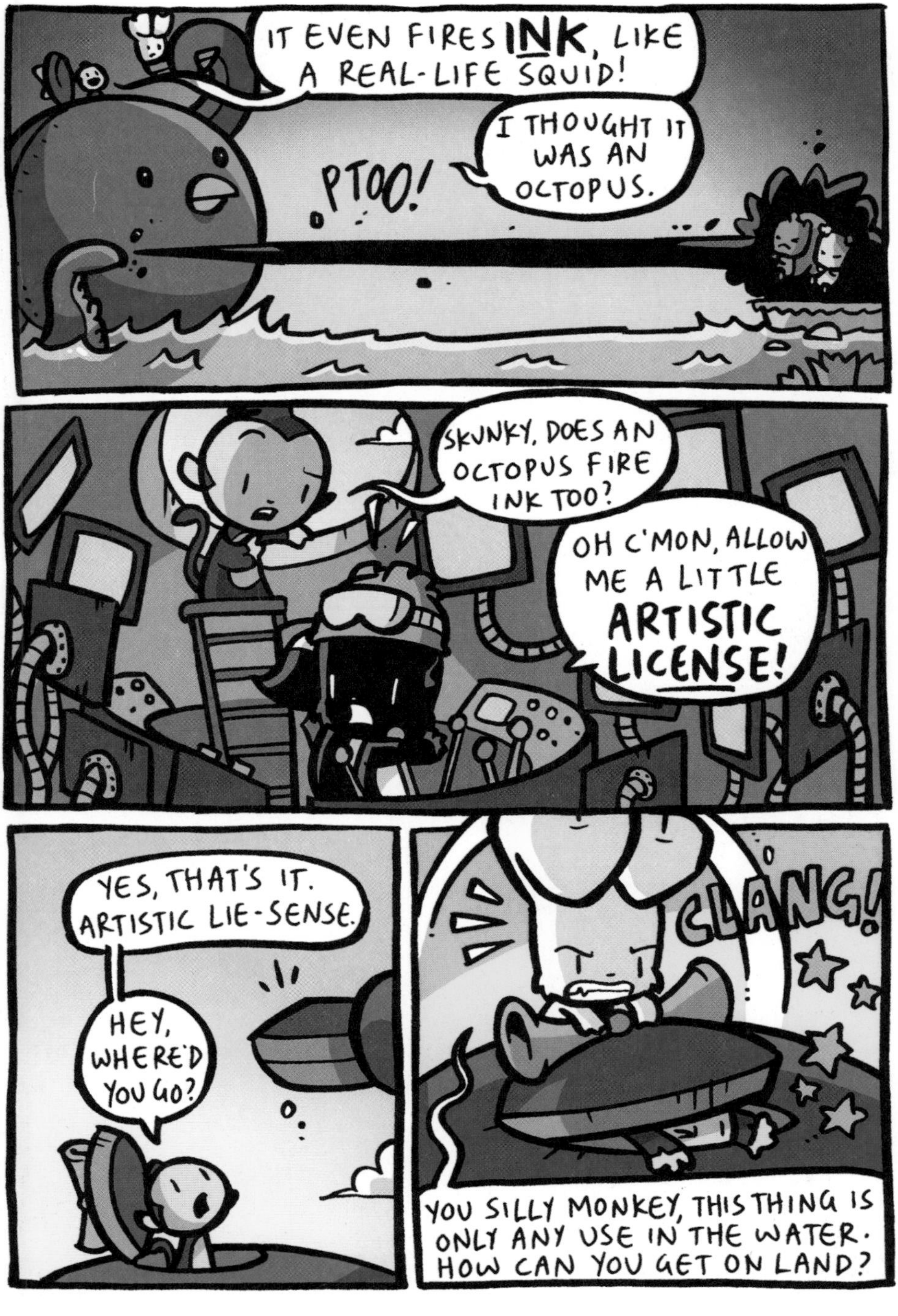
IT EVEN FIRES INK, LIKE A REAL-LIFE SQUID!
I THOUGHT IT WAS AN OCTOPUS.
PTOO!
SKUNKY, DOES AN OCTOPUS FIRE INK TOO?
OH C'MON, ALLOW ME A LITTLE ARTISTIC LICENSE!
YES, THAT'S IT. ARTISTIC LIE-SENSE.
HEY, WHERE'D YOU GO?
CLANG!
YOU SILLY MONKEY, THIS THING IS ONLY ANY USE IN THE WATER. HOW CAN YOU GET ON LAND?

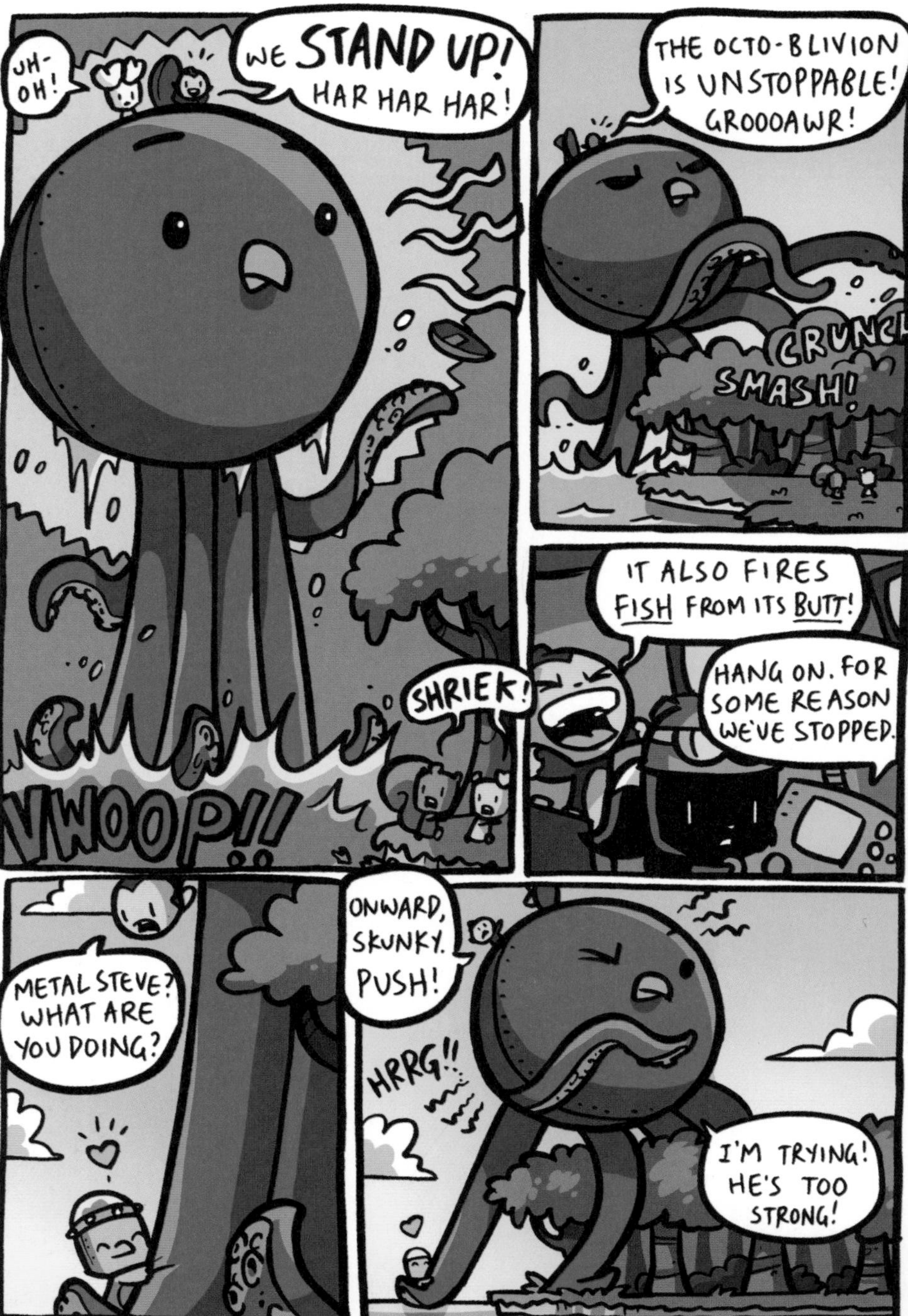

UH-OH!
WE STAND UP! HAR HAR HAR!
VWOOP!!
SHRIEK!
THE OCTO-BLIVION IS UNSTOPPABLE! GROOOAWR!
CRUNCH!
SMASH!
IT ALSO FIRES FISH FROM ITS BUTT!
HANG ON. FOR SOME REASON WE'VE STOPPED.
METAL STEVE? WHAT ARE YOU DOING?
ONWARD, SKUNKY. PUSH!
HRRG!!
I'M TRYING! HE'S TOO STRONG!

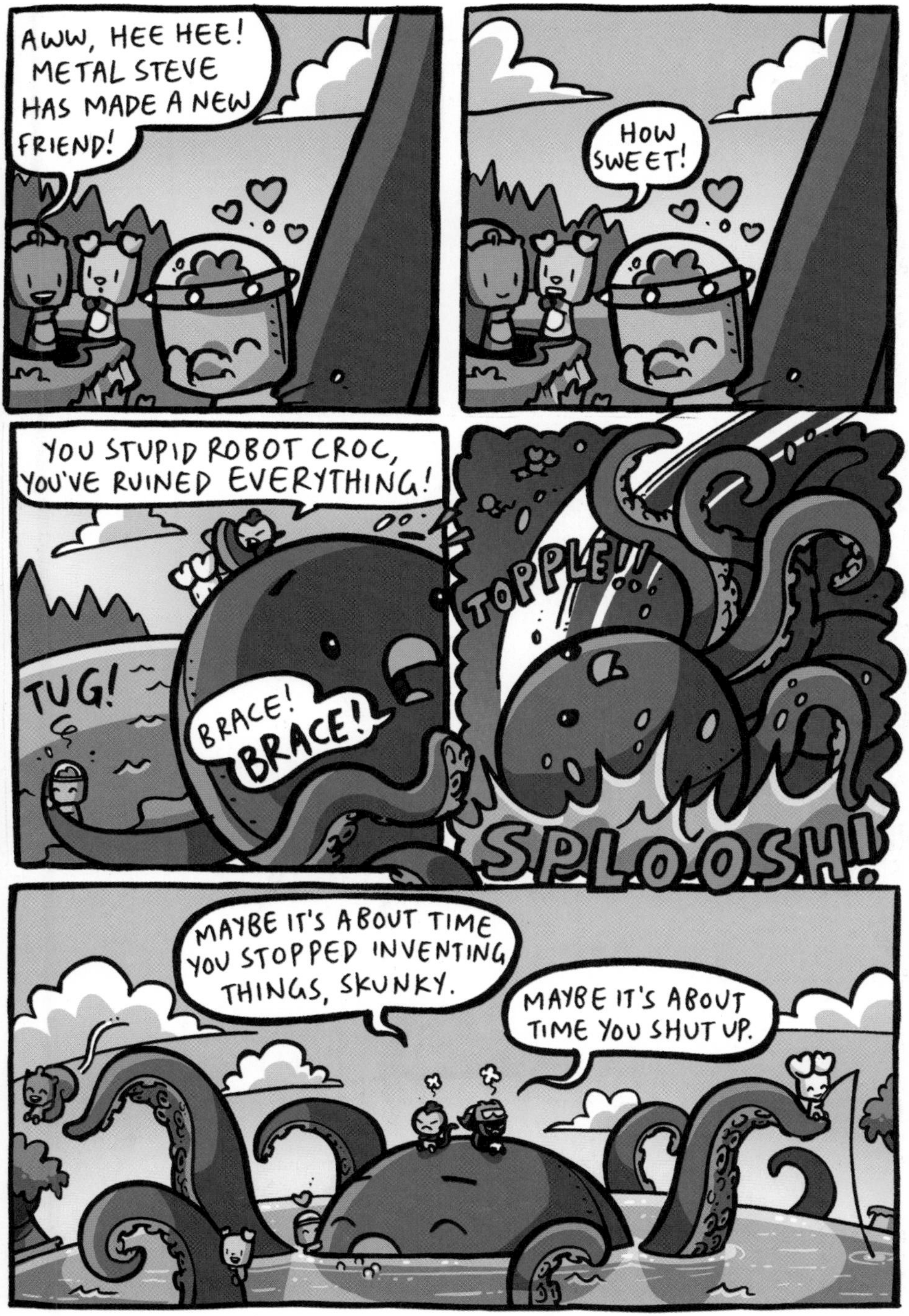
AWW, HEE HEE! METAL STEVE HAS MADE A NEW FRIEND!
HOW SWEET!
YOU STUPID ROBOT CROC, YOU'VE RUINED EVERYTHING!
TUG!
BRACE! BRACE!
TOPPLE!!
SPLOOSH!
MAYBE IT'S ABOUT TIME YOU STOPPED INVENTING THINGS, SKUNKY.
MAYBE IT'S ABOUT TIME YOU SHUT UP.

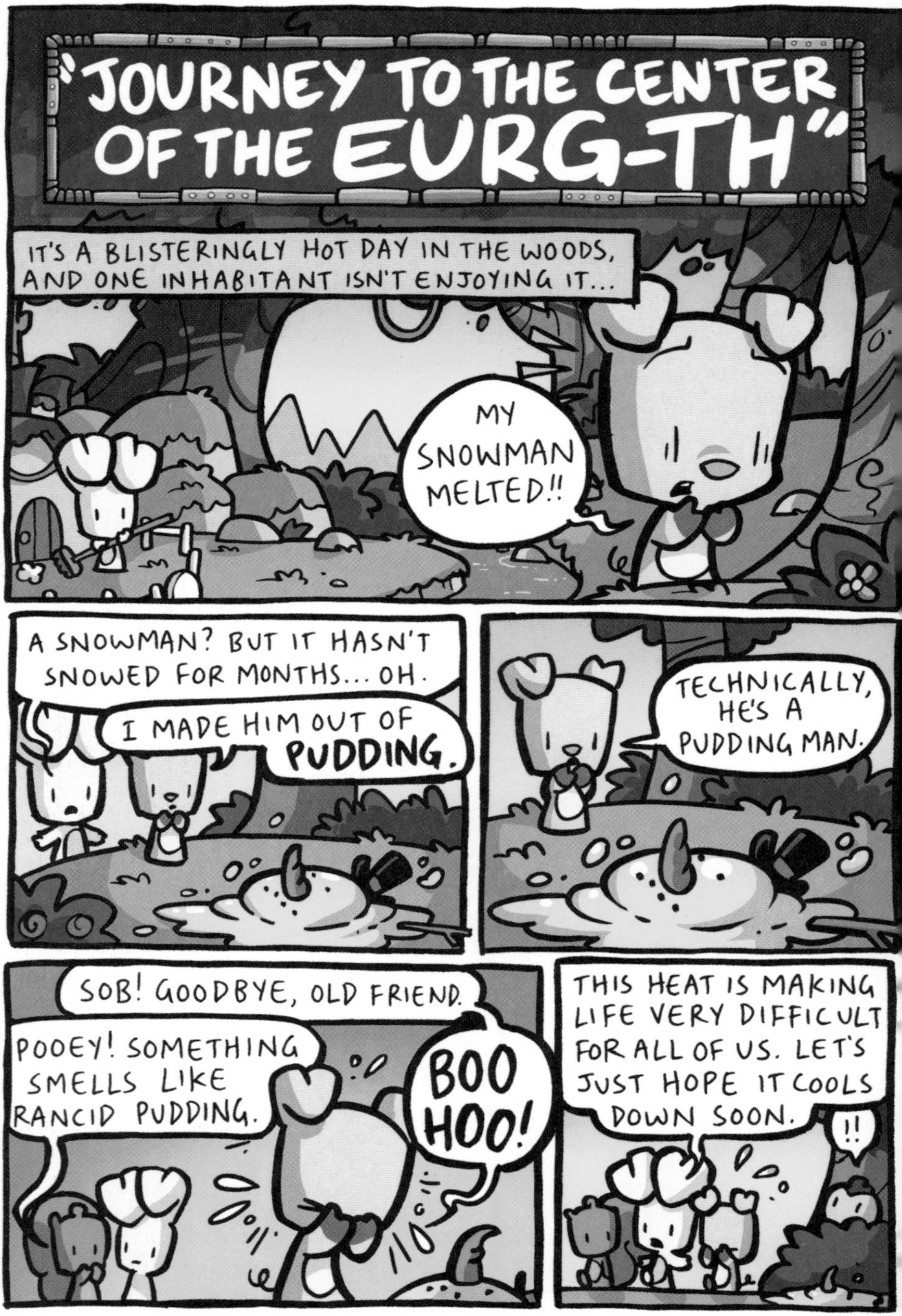
"JOURNEY TO THE CENTER OF THE EURG-TH"
IT'S A BLISTERINGLY HOT DAY IN THE WOODS, AND ONE INHABITANT ISN'T ENJOYING IT...
MY SNOWMAN MELTED!!
A SNOWMAN? BUT IT HASN'T SNOWED FOR MONTHS... OH.
I MADE HIM OUT OF PUDDING.
TECHNICALLY, HE'S A PUDDING MAN.
SOB! GOODBYE, OLD FRIEND.
BOO HOO!
POOEY! SOMETHING SMELLS LIKE RANCID PUDDING.
THIS HEAT IS MAKING LIFE VERY DIFFICULT FOR ALL OF US. LET'S JUST HOPE IT COOLS DOWN SOON.
!!

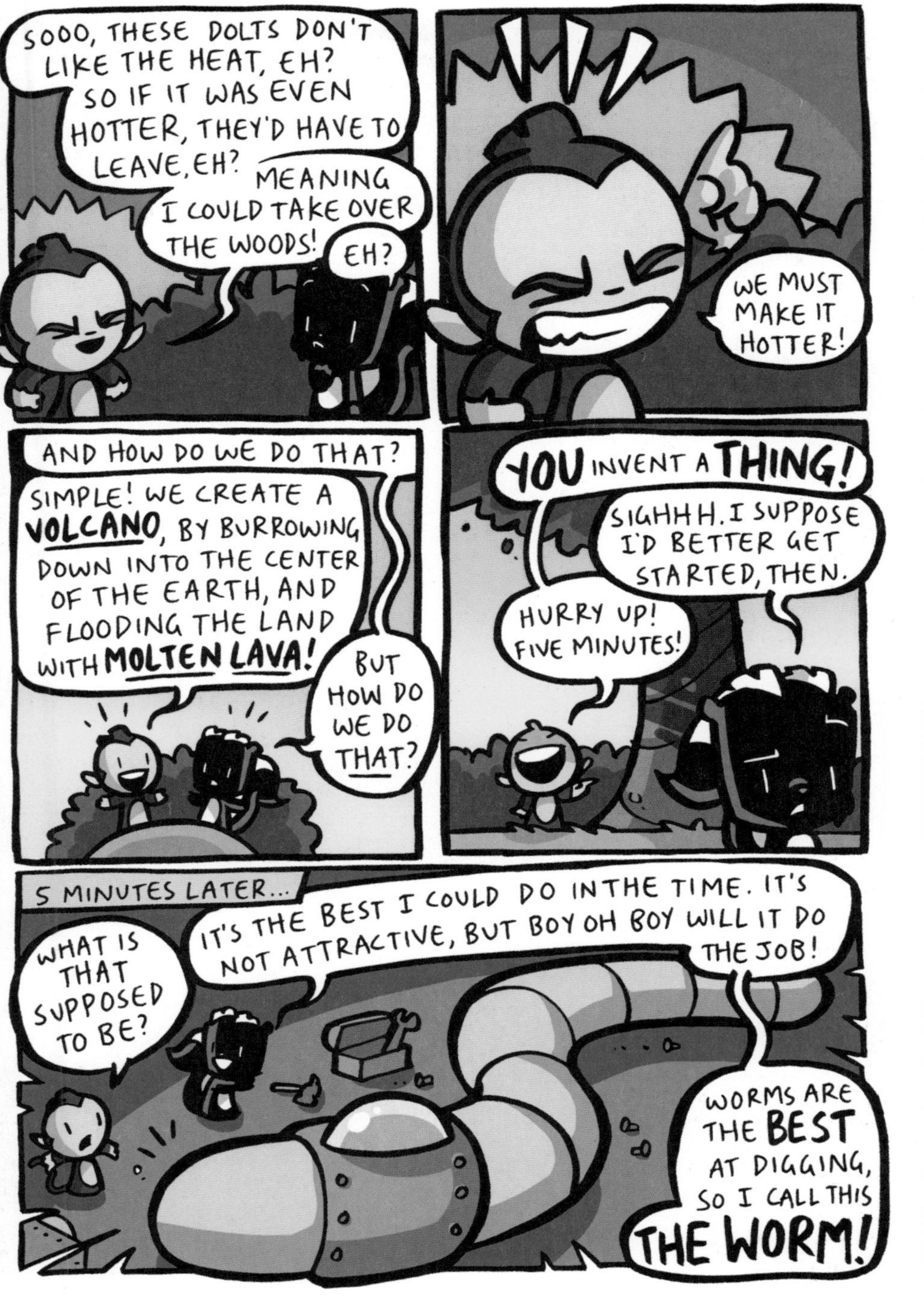
SOOO, THESE DOLTS DON'T LIKE THE HEAT, EH? SO IF IT WAS EVEN HOTTER, THEY'D HAVE TO LEAVE, EH?
MEANING I COULD TAKE OVER THE WOODS!
EH?
WE MUST MAKE IT HOTTER!
AND HOW DO WE DO THAT?
SIMPLE! WE CREATE A VOLCANO, BY BURROWING DOWN INTO THE CENTER OF THE EARTH, AND FLOODING THE LAND WITH MOLTEN LAVA!
BUT HOW DO WE DO THAT?
YOU INVENT A THING!
SIGHHH. I SUPPOSE I'D BETTER GET STARTED, THEN.
HURRY UP! FIVE MINUTES!
5 MINUTES LATER...
WHAT IS THAT SUPPOSED TO BE?
IT'S THE BEST I COULD DO IN THE TIME. IT'S NOT ATTRACTIVE, BUT BOY OH BOY WILL IT DO THE JOB!
WORMS ARE THE BEST AT DIGGING, SO I CALL THIS THE WORM!

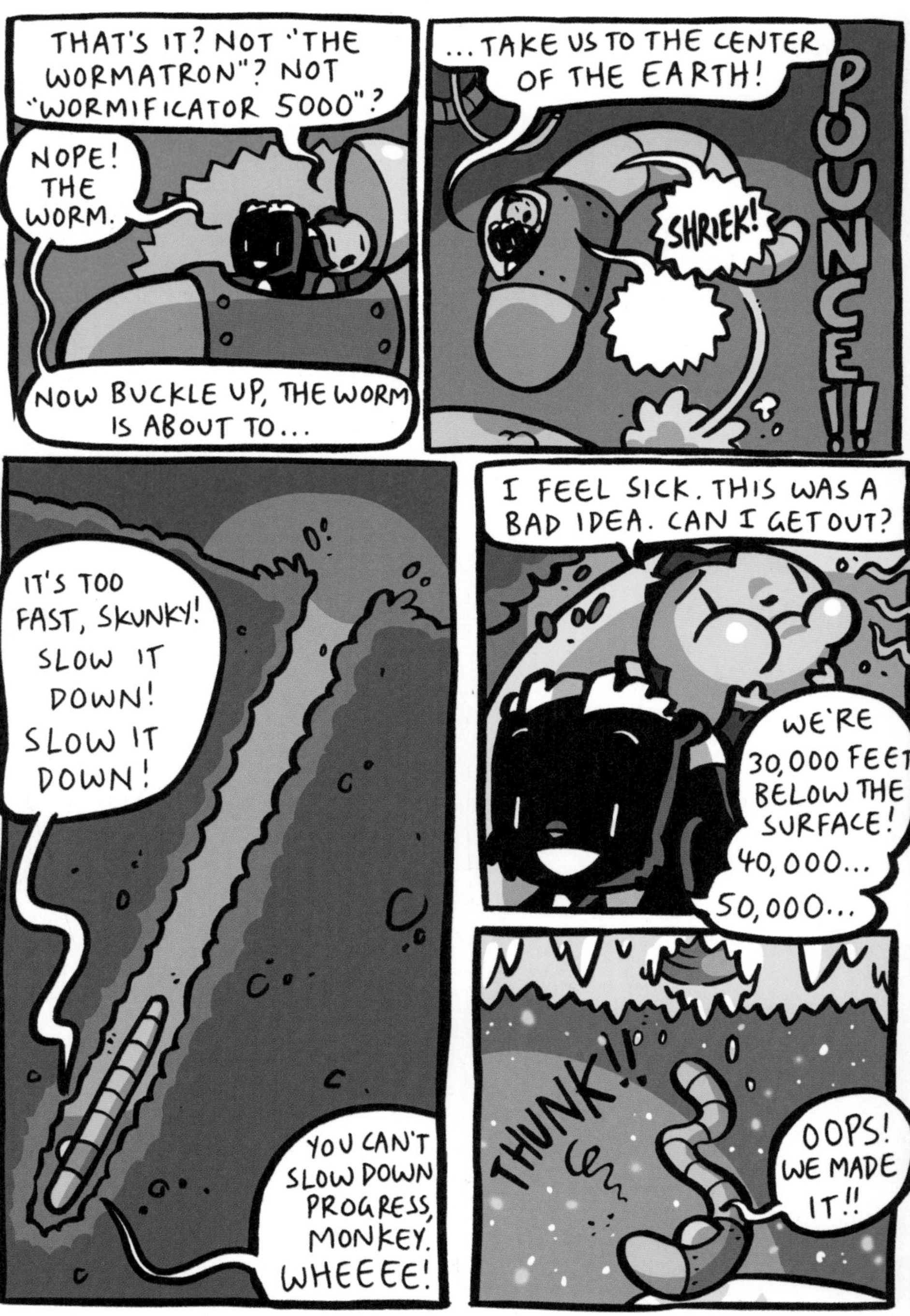
THAT'S IT? NOT "THE WORMATRON"? NOT "WORMIFICATOR 5000"?
NOPE! THE WORM.
NOW BUCKLE UP, THE WORM IS ABOUT TO...
...TAKE US TO THE CENTER OF THE EARTH!
POUNCE!!
SHRIEK!
IT'S TOO FAST, SKUNKY! SLOW IT DOWN! SLOW IT DOWN!
YOU CAN'T SLOW DOWN PROGRESS, MONKEY. WHEEEE!
I FEEL SICK. THIS WAS A BAD IDEA. CAN I GET OUT?
WE'RE 30,000 FEET BELOW THE SURFACE! 40,000... 50,000...
THUNK!!
OOPS! WE MADE IT!!

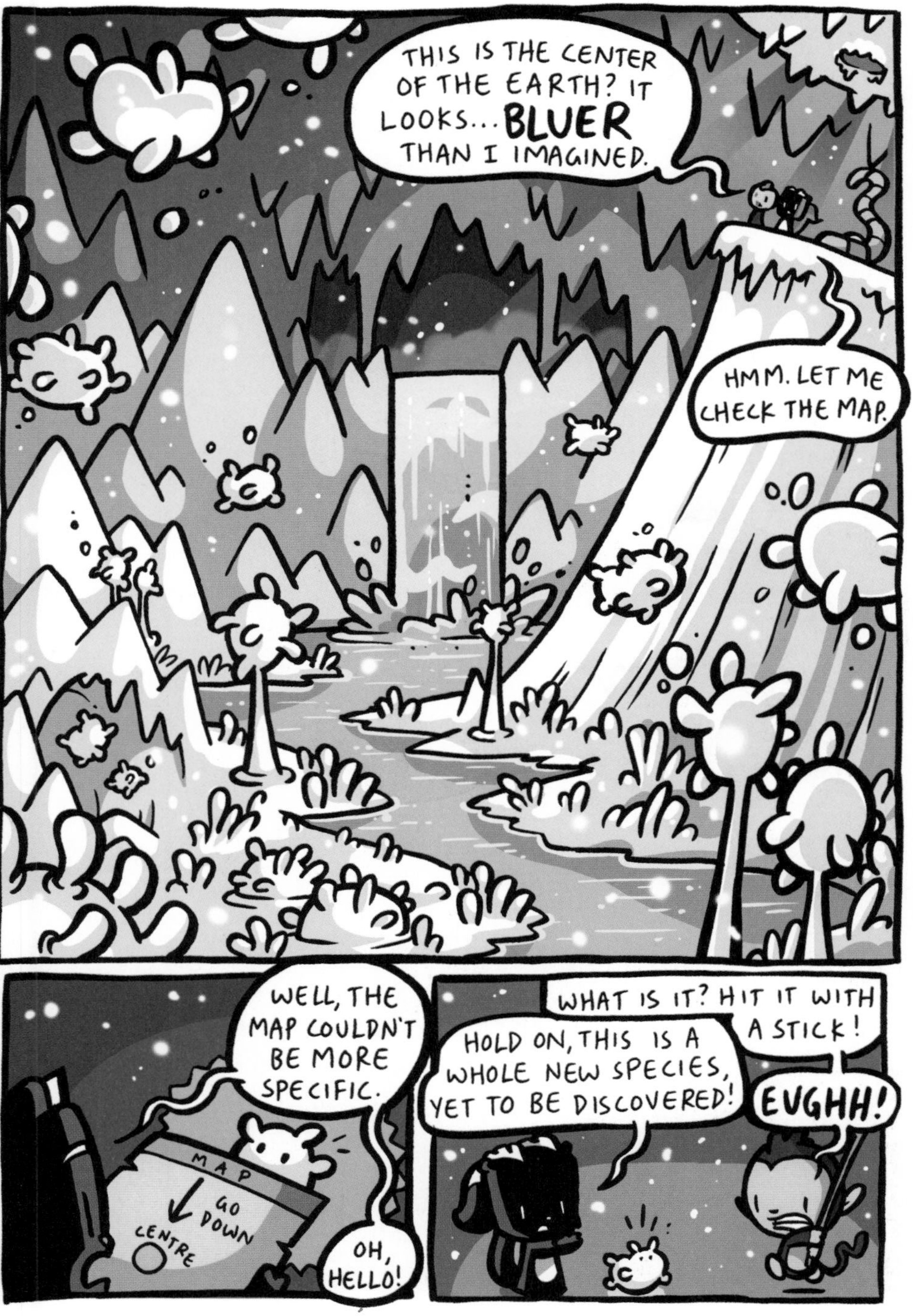
THIS IS THE CENTER OF THE EARTH? IT LOOKS... BLUER THAN I IMAGINED.
HMM. LET ME CHECK THE MAP.
WELL, THE MAP COULDN'T BE MORE SPECIFIC.
MAP
GO DOWN
CENTRE
OH, HELLO!
WHAT IS IT? HIT IT WITH A STICK!
HOLD ON, THIS IS A WHOLE NEW SPECIES, YET TO BE DISCOVERED!
EUGHH!

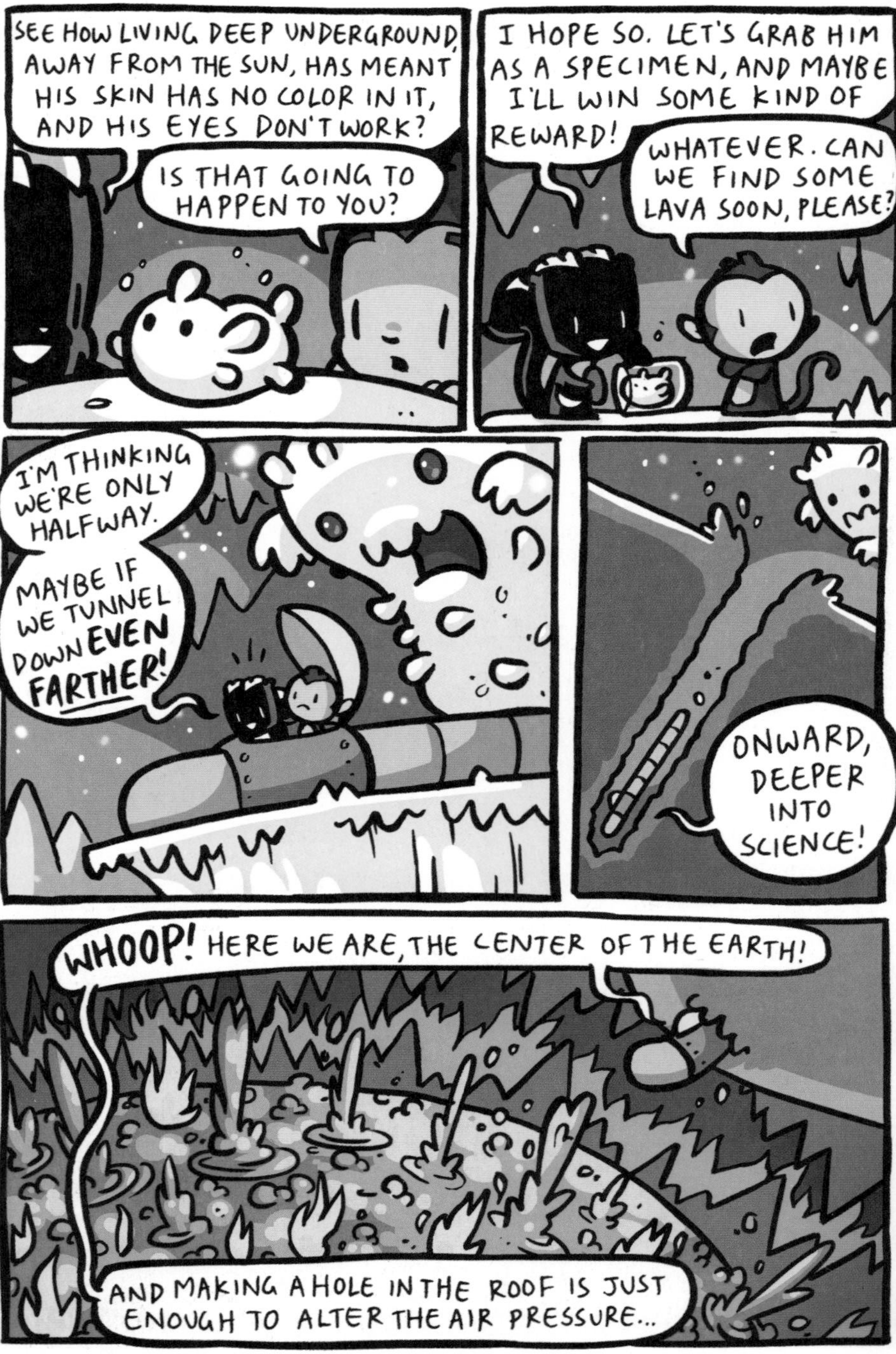
SEE HOW LIVING DEEP UNDERGROUND, AWAY FROM THE SUN, HAS MEANT HIS SKIN HAS NO COLOR IN IT, AND HIS EYES DON'T WORK?
IS THAT GOING TO HAPPEN TO YOU?
I HOPE SO. LET'S GRAB HIM AS A SPECIMEN, AND MAYBE I'LL WIN SOME KIND OF REWARD!
WHATEVER. CAN WE FIND SOME LAVA SOON, PLEASE?
I'M THINKING WE'RE ONLY HALFWAY.
MAYBE IF WE TUNNEL DOWN EVEN FARTHER!
ONWARD, DEEPER INTO SCIENCE!
WHOOP! HERE WE ARE, THE CENTER OF THE EARTH!
AND MAKING A HOLE IN THE ROOF IS JUST ENOUGH TO ALTER THE AIR PRESSURE...

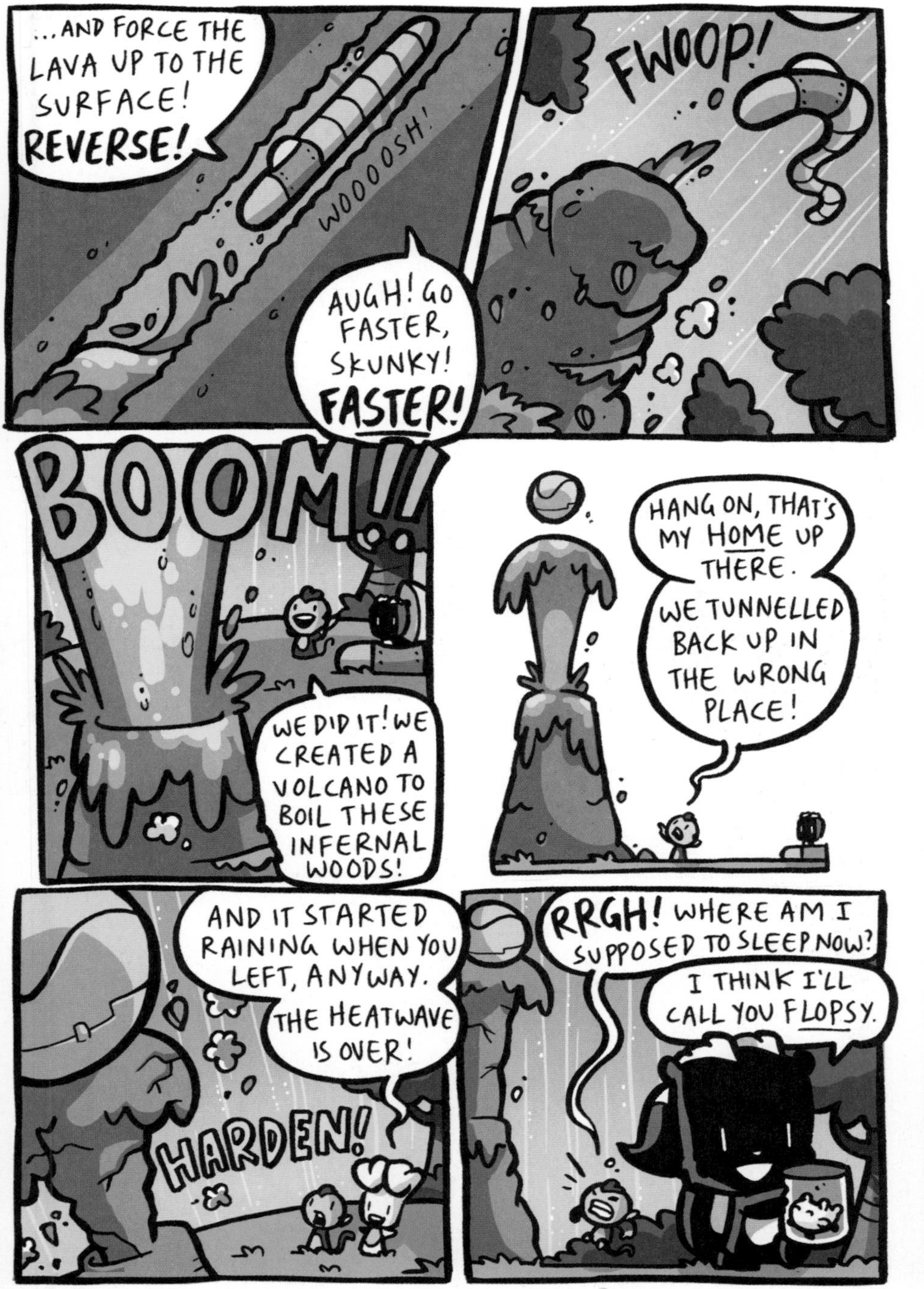
...AND FORCE THE LAVA UP TO THE SURFACE! REVERSE!
WOOOOOSH!
FWOOP!
AUGH! GO FASTER, SKUNKY! FASTER!
BOOM!!!
WE DID IT! WE CREATED A VOLCANO TO BOIL THESE INFERNAL WOODS!
HANG ON, THAT'S MY HOME UP THERE.
WE TUNNELLED BACK UP IN THE WRONG PLACE!
AND IT STARTED RAINING WHEN YOU LEFT, ANYWAY.
THE HEATWAVE IS OVER!
HARDEN!
RRGH! WHERE AM I SUPPOSED TO SLEEP NOW?
I THINK I'LL CALL YOU FLOPSY.

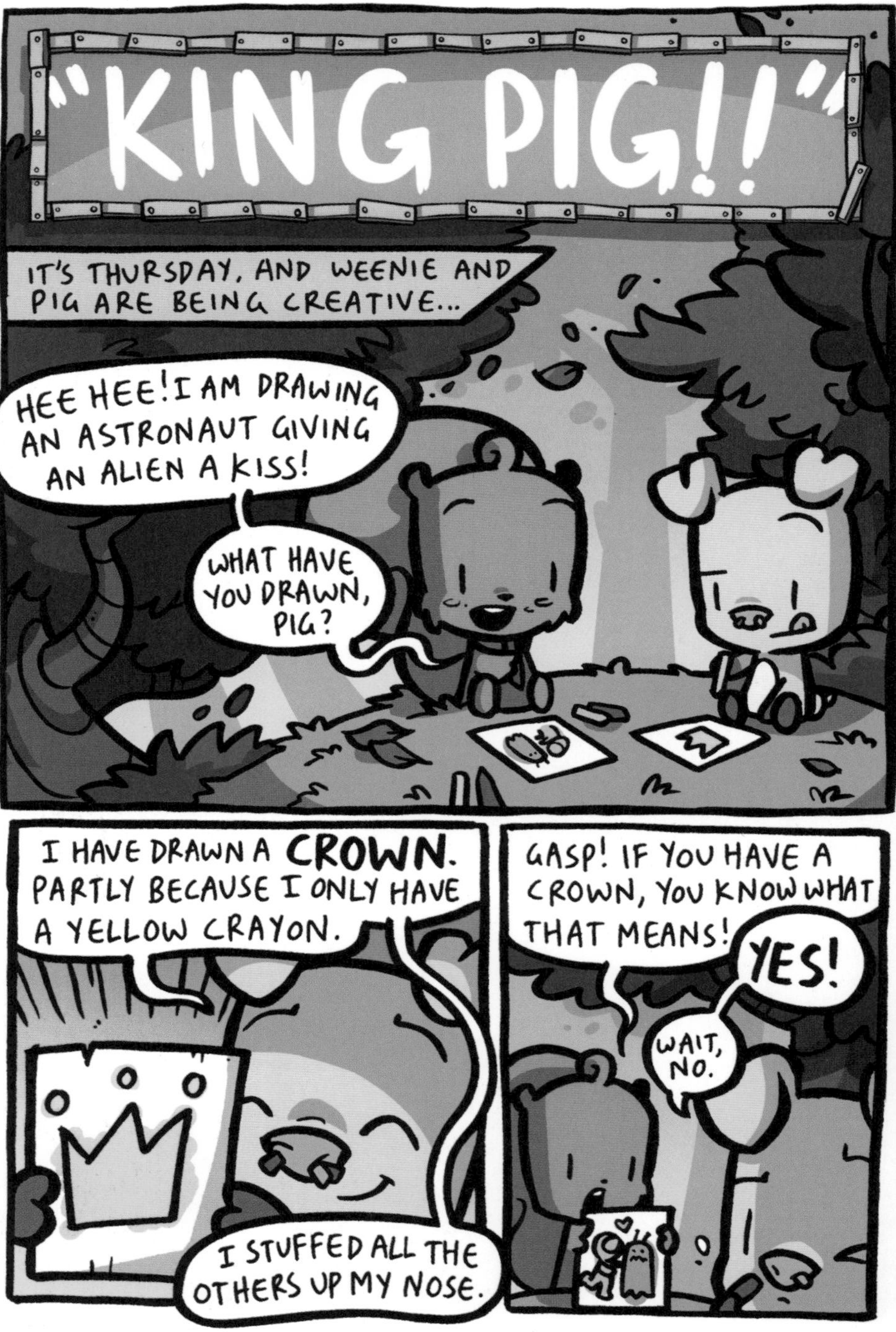
"KING PIG!!"
IT'S THURSDAY, AND WEENIE AND PIG ARE BEING CREATIVE...
HEE HEE! I AM DRAWING AN ASTRONAUT GIVING AN ALIEN A KISS!
WHAT HAVE YOU DRAWN, PIG?
I HAVE DRAWN A CROWN. PARTLY BECAUSE I ONLY HAVE A YELLOW CRAYON.
I STUFFED ALL THE OTHERS UP MY NOSE.
GASP! IF YOU HAVE A CROWN, YOU KNOW WHAT THAT MEANS!
YES!
WAIT, NO.

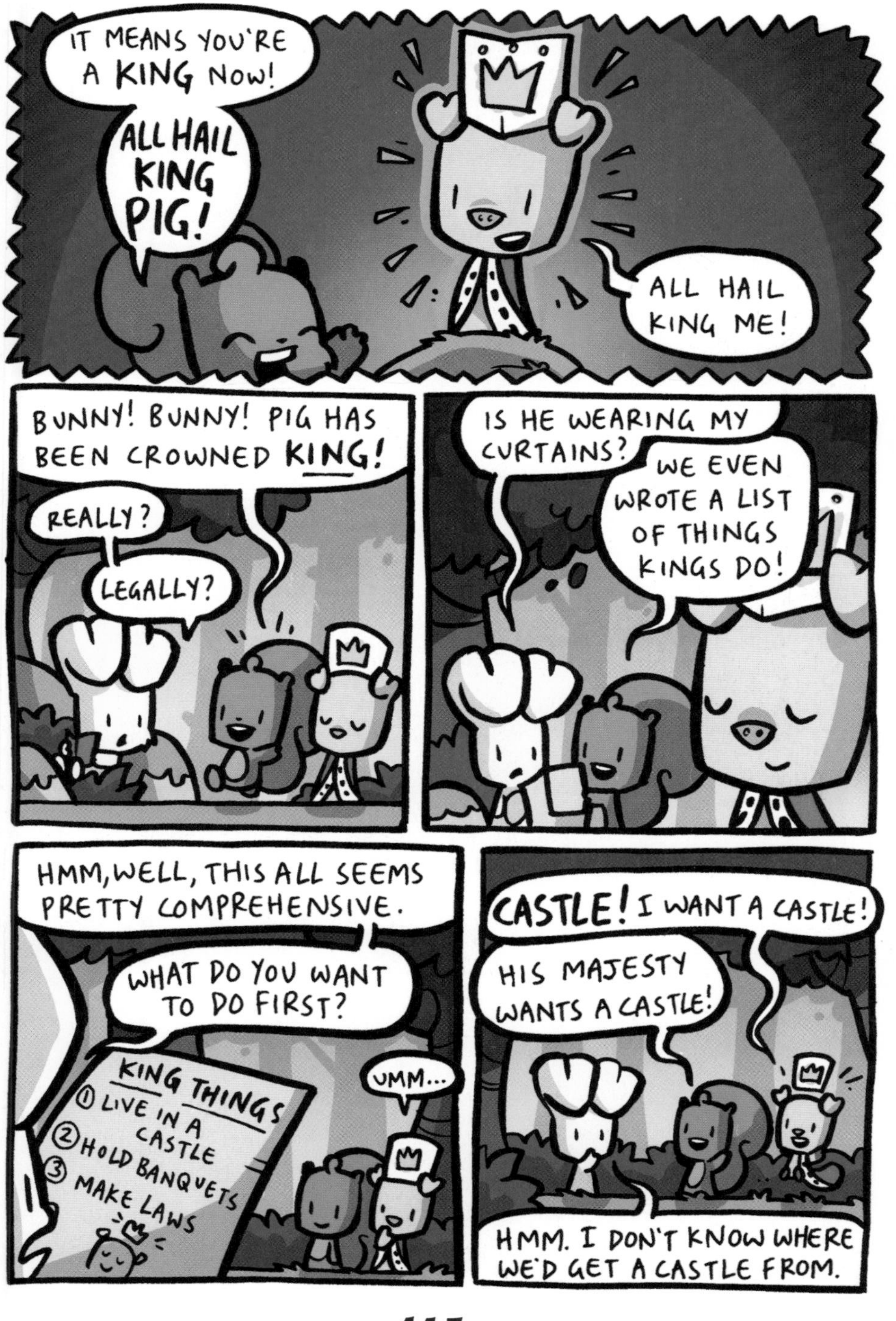
IT MEANS YOU'RE A KING NOW!
ALL HAIL KING PIG!
ALL HAIL KING ME!
BUNNY! BUNNY! PIG HAS BEEN CROWNED KING!
REALLY?
LEGALLY?
IS HE WEARING MY CURTAINS?
WE EVEN WROTE A LIST OF THINGS KINGS DO!
HMM, WELL, THIS ALL SEEMS PRETTY COMPREHENSIVE.
WHAT DO YOU WANT TO DO FIRST?
KING THINGS
① LIVE IN A CASTLE
② HOLD BANQUETS
③ MAKE LAWS
UMM...
CASTLE! I WANT A CASTLE!
HIS MAJESTY WANTS A CASTLE!
HMM. I DON'T KNOW WHERE WE'D GET A CASTLE FROM.

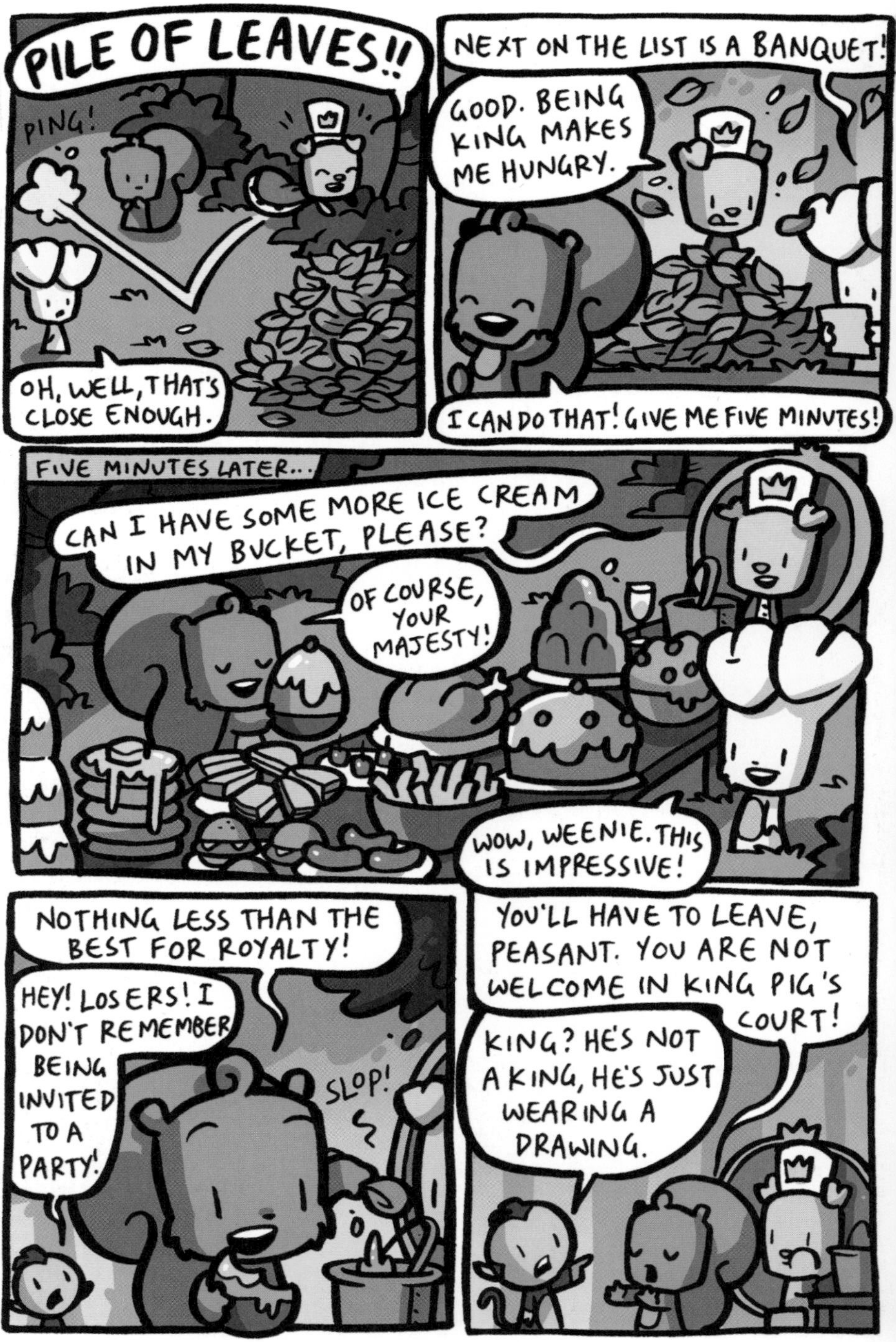
PILE OF LEAVES!!
PING!
OH, WELL, THAT'S CLOSE ENOUGH.
NEXT ON THE LIST IS A BANQUET!
GOOD. BEING KING MAKES ME HUNGRY.
I CAN DO THAT! GIVE ME FIVE MINUTES!
FIVE MINUTES LATER...
CAN I HAVE SOME MORE ICE CREAM IN MY BUCKET, PLEASE?
OF COURSE, YOUR MAJESTY!
WOW, WEENIE. THIS IS IMPRESSIVE!
NOTHING LESS THAN THE BEST FOR ROYALTY!
HEY! LOSERS! I DON'T REMEMBER BEING INVITED TO A PARTY!
SLOP!
YOU'LL HAVE TO LEAVE, PEASANT. YOU ARE NOT WELCOME IN KING PIG'S COURT!
KING? HE'S NOT A KING, HE'S JUST WEARING A DRAWING.

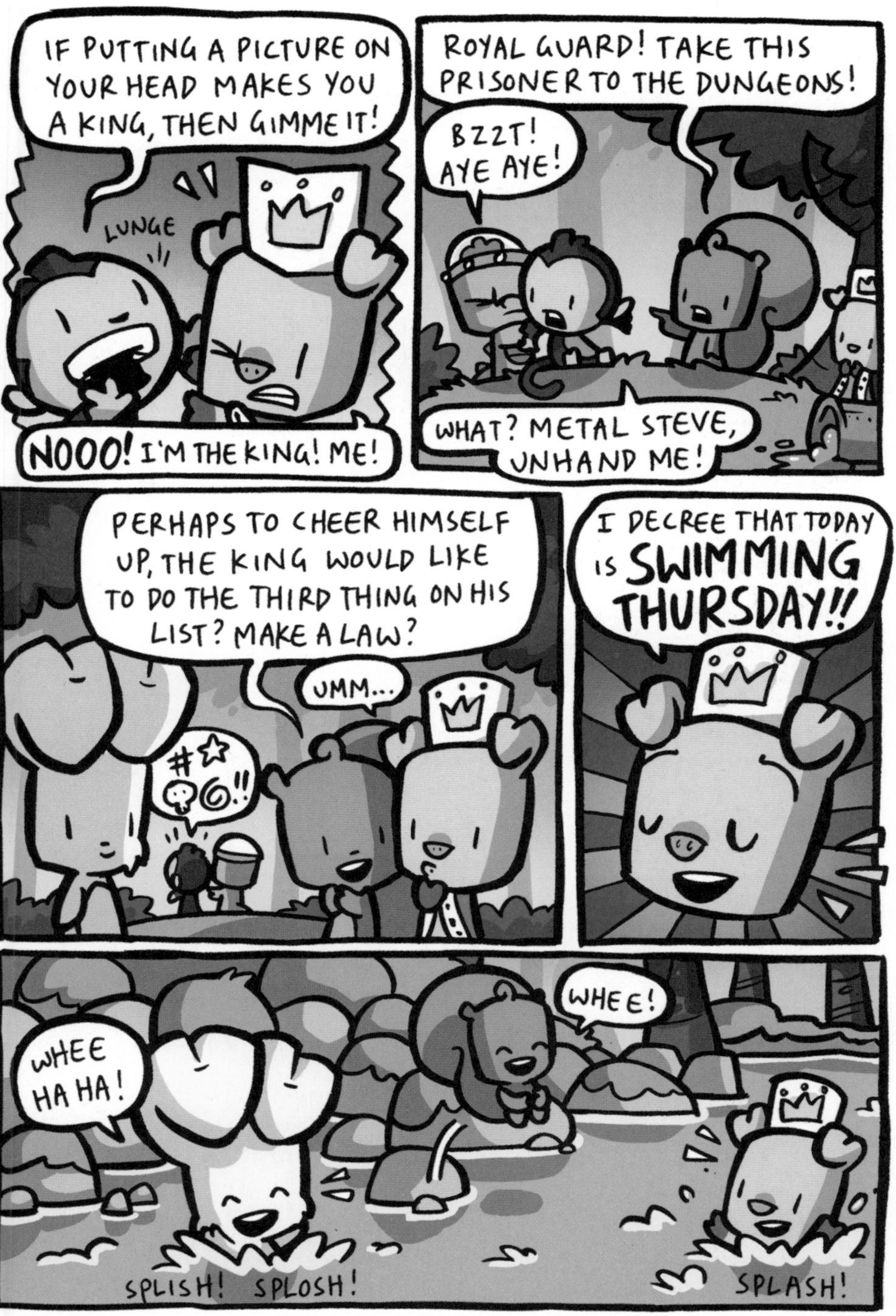
IF PUTTING A PICTURE ON YOUR HEAD MAKES YOU A KING, THEN GIMME IT!
LUNGE
NOOO! I'M THE KING! ME!
ROYAL GUARD! TAKE THIS PRISONER TO THE DUNGEONS!
BZZT! AYE AYE!
WHAT? METAL STEVE, UNHAND ME!
PERHAPS TO CHEER HIMSELF UP, THE KING WOULD LIKE TO DO THE THIRD THING ON HIS LIST? MAKE A LAW?
UMM...
I DECREE THAT TODAY IS SWIMMING THURSDAY!!
WHEE HA HA!
WHEE!
SPLISH! SPLOSH!
SPLASH!

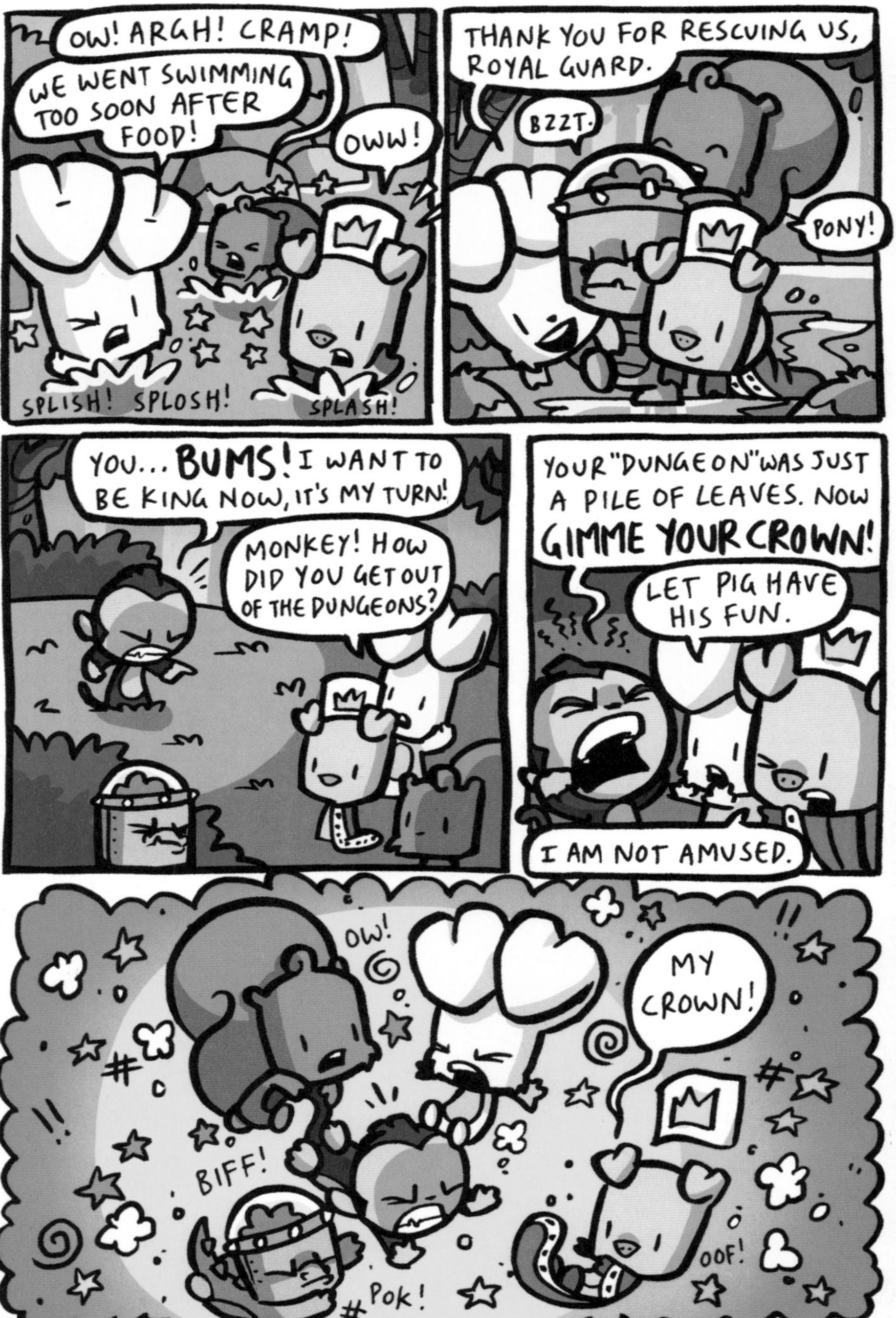
OW! ARGH! CRAMP!
WE WENT SWIMMING TOO SOON AFTER FOOD!
OWW!
SPLISH! SPLOSH!
SPLASH!
THANK YOU FOR RESCUING US, ROYAL GUARD.
BZZT.
PONY!
YOU... BUMS! I WANT TO BE KING NOW, IT'S MY TURN!
MONKEY! HOW DID YOU GET OUT OF THE DUNGEONS?
YOUR "DUNGEON" WAS JUST A PILE OF LEAVES. NOW GIMME YOUR CROWN!
LET PIG HAVE HIS FUN.
I AM NOT AMUSED.
OW!
MY CROWN!
BIFF!
OOF!
POK!

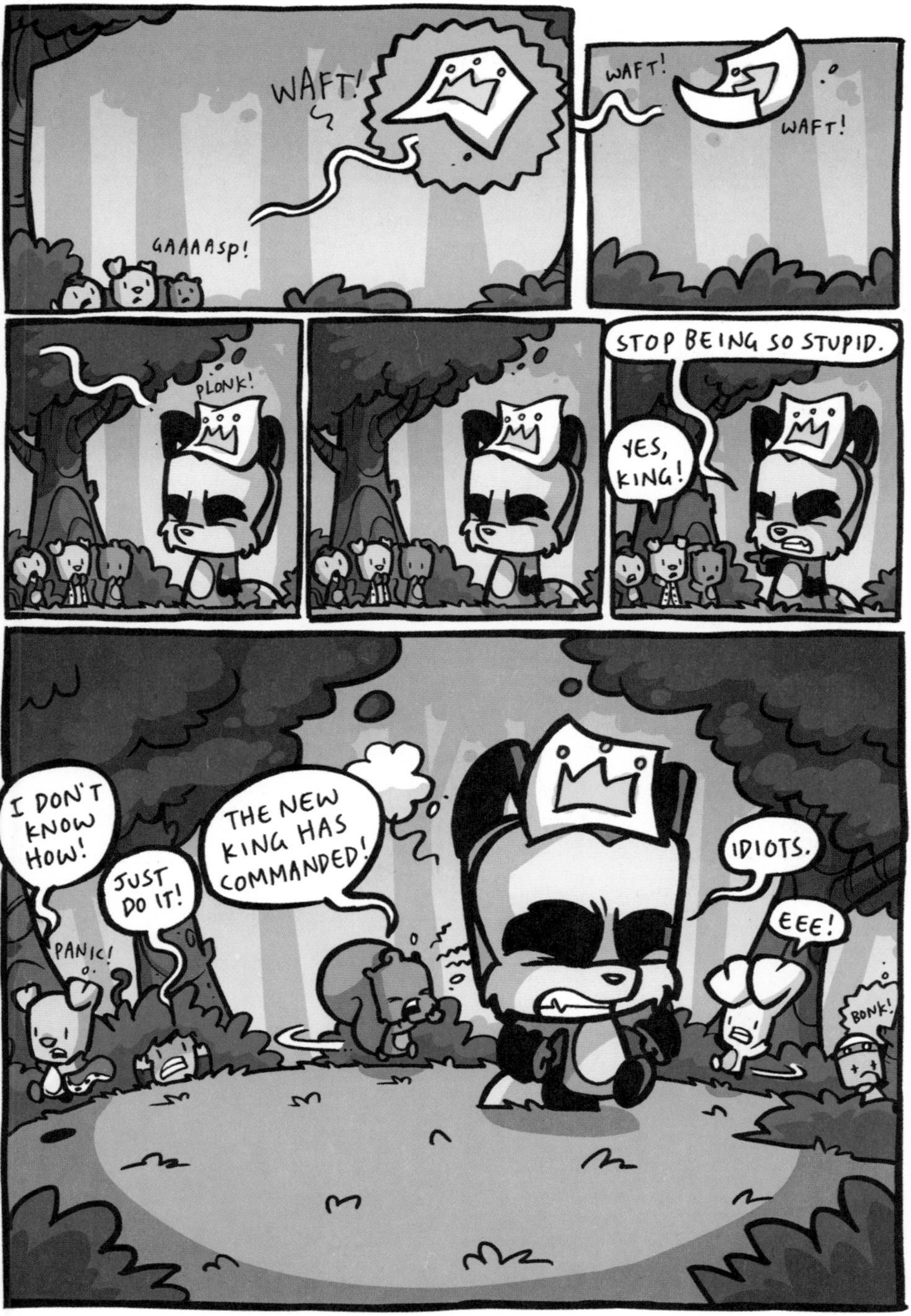
WAFT!
GAAAASP!
WAFT!
WAFT!
PLONK!
STOP BEING SO STUPID.
YES, KING!
I DON'T KNOW HOW!
JUST DO IT!
PANIC!
THE NEW KING HAS COMMANDED!
IDIOTS.
EEE!
BONK!

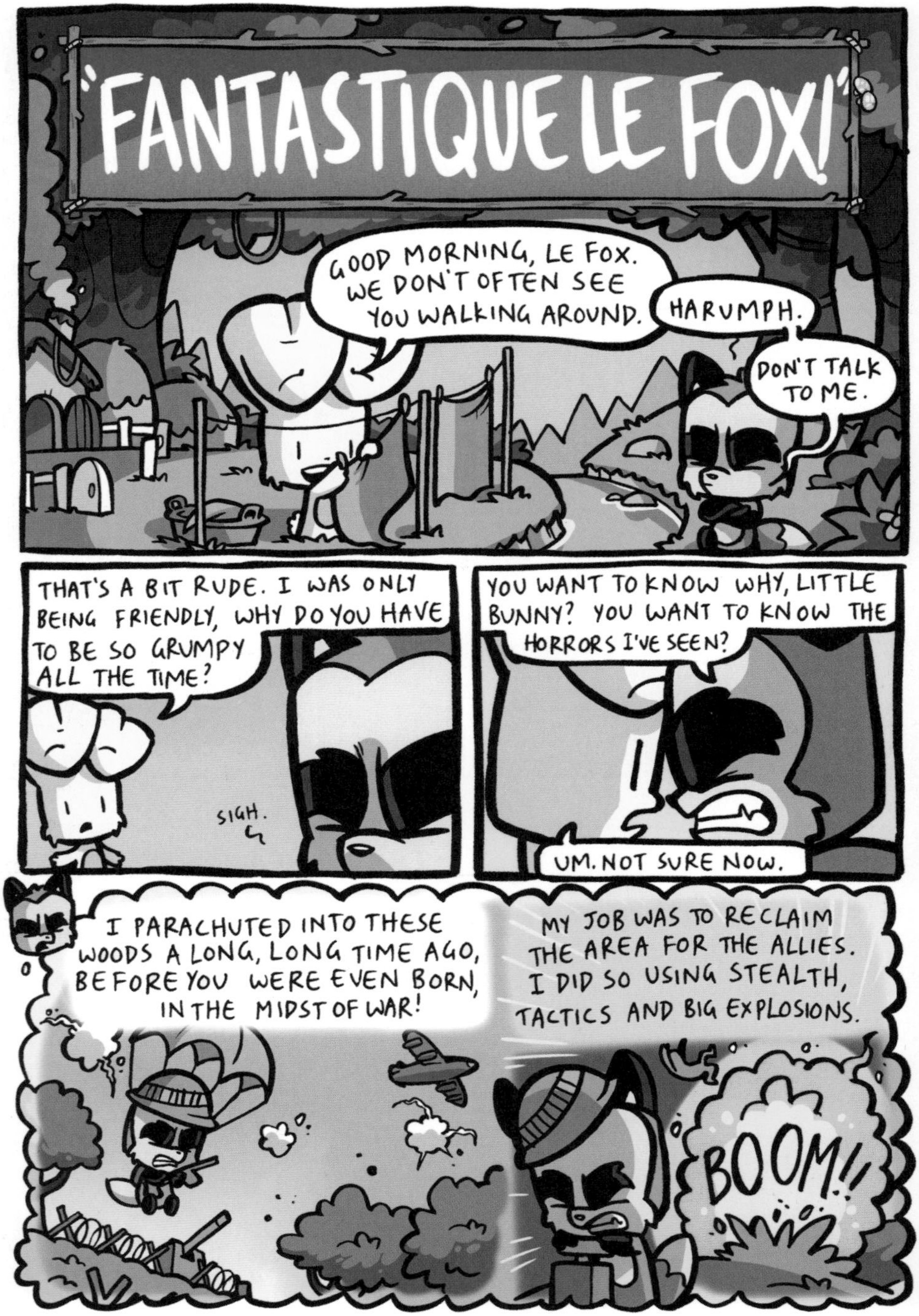
"FANTASTIQUE LE FOX!"
GOOD MORNING, LE FOX. WE DON'T OFTEN SEE YOU WALKING AROUND.
HARUMPH.
DON'T TALK TO ME.
THAT'S A BIT RUDE. I WAS ONLY BEING FRIENDLY, WHY DO YOU HAVE TO BE SO GRUMPY ALL THE TIME?
SIGH.
YOU WANT TO KNOW WHY, LITTLE BUNNY? YOU WANT TO KNOW THE HORRORS I'VE SEEN?
UM. NOT SURE NOW.
I PARACHUTED INTO THESE WOODS A LONG, LONG TIME AGO, BEFORE YOU WERE EVEN BORN, IN THE MIDST OF WAR!
MY JOB WAS TO RECLAIM THE AREA FOR THE ALLIES. I DID SO USING STEALTH, TACTICS AND BIG EXPLOSIONS.
BOOM!!

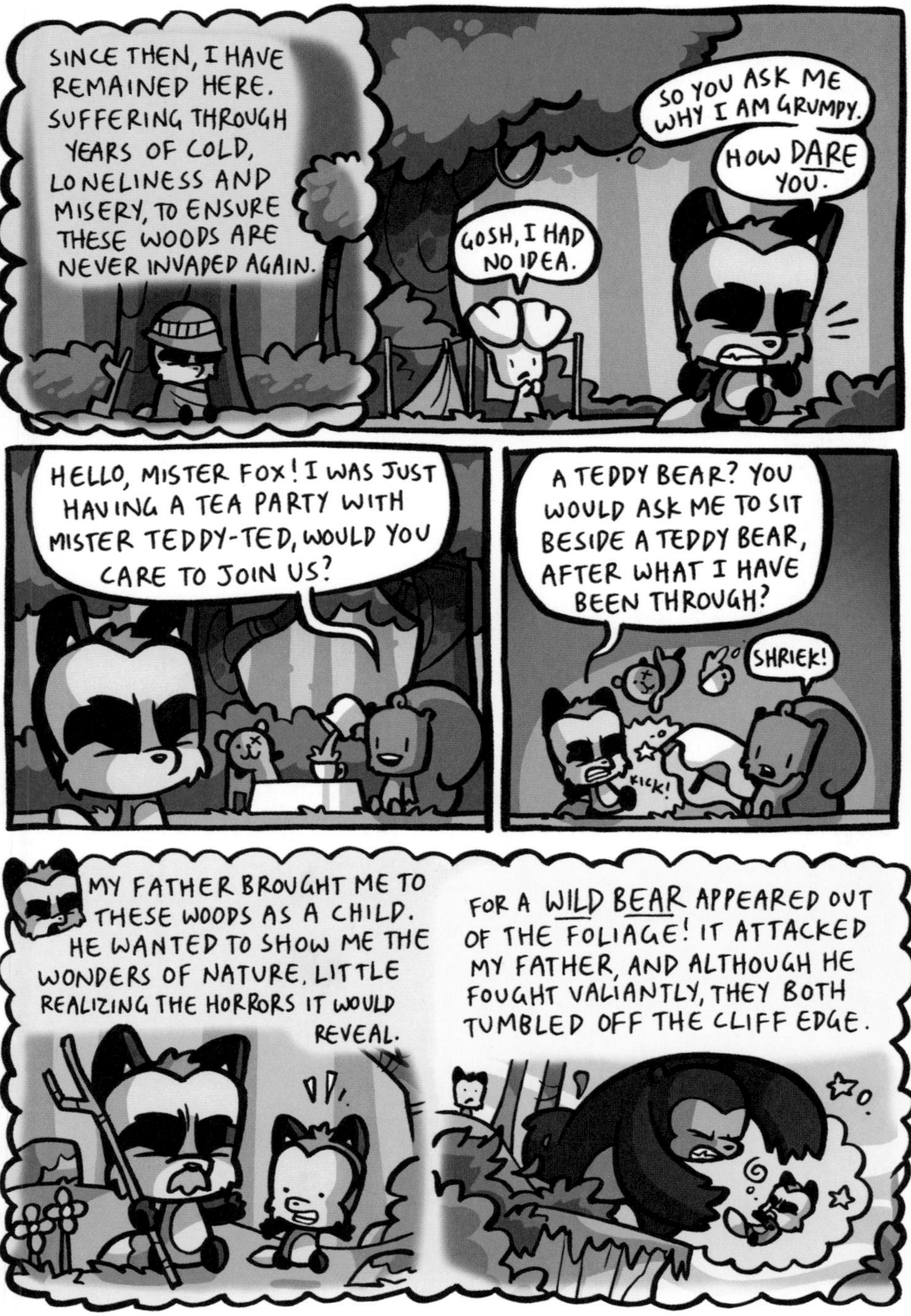

SINCE THEN, I HAVE REMAINED HERE. SUFFERING THROUGH YEARS OF COLD, LONELINESS AND MISERY, TO ENSURE THESE WOODS ARE NEVER INVADED AGAIN.
SO YOU ASK ME WHY I AM GRUMPY.
HOW DARE YOU.
GOSH, I HAD NO IDEA.
HELLO, MISTER FOX! I WAS JUST HAVING A TEA PARTY WITH MISTER TEDDY-TED, WOULD YOU CARE TO JOIN US?
A TEDDY BEAR? YOU WOULD ASK ME TO SIT BESIDE A TEDDY BEAR, AFTER WHAT I HAVE BEEN THROUGH?
SHRIEK!
KICK!
MY FATHER BROUGHT ME TO THESE WOODS AS A CHILD. HE WANTED TO SHOW ME THE WONDERS OF NATURE. LITTLE REALIZING THE HORRORS IT WOULD REVEAL.
FOR A WILD BEAR APPEARED OUT OF THE FOLIAGE! IT ATTACKED MY FATHER, AND ALTHOUGH HE FOUGHT VALIANTLY, THEY BOTH TUMBLED OFF THE CLIFF EDGE.

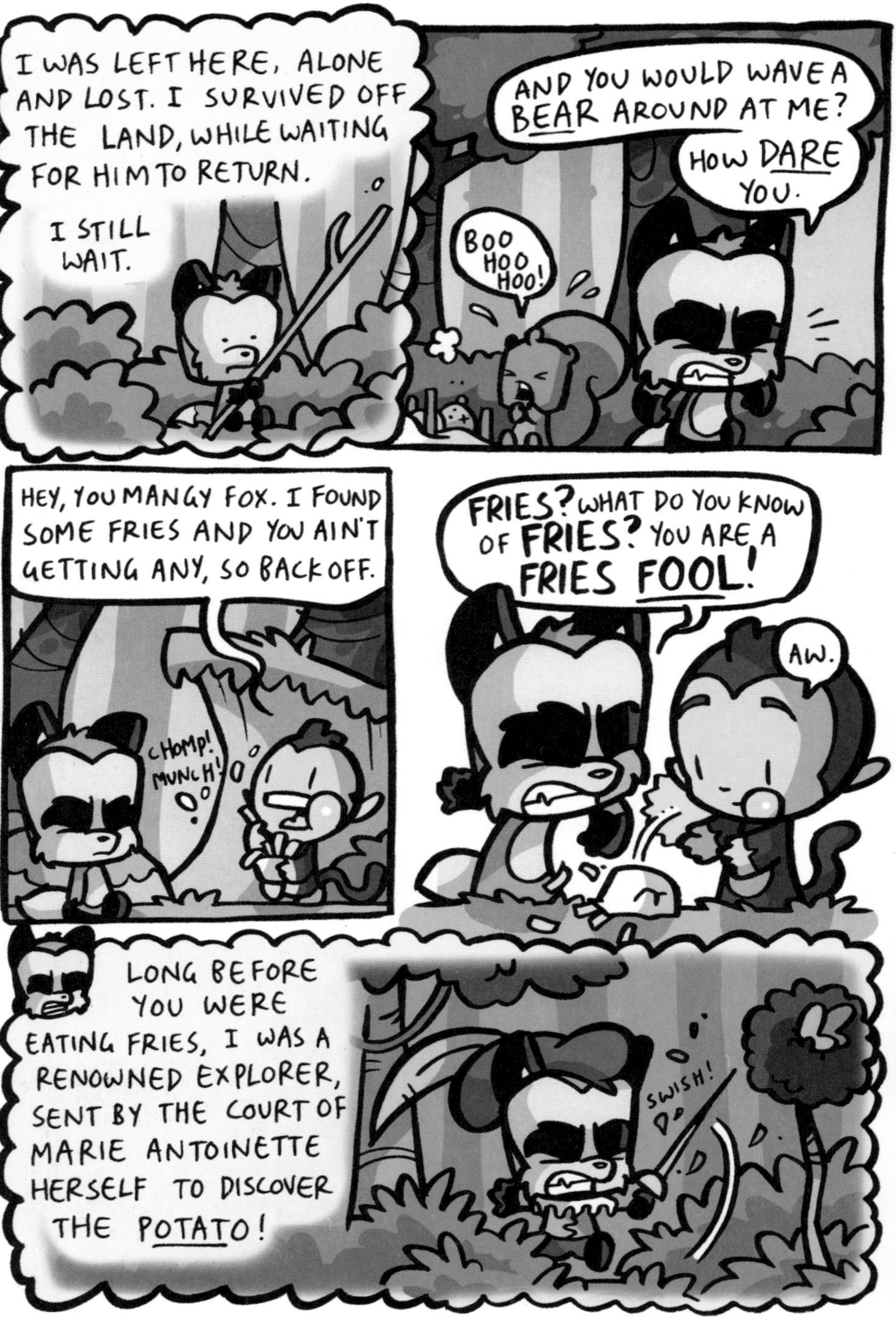

I WAS LEFT HERE, ALONE AND LOST. I SURVIVED OFF THE LAND, WHILE WAITING FOR HIM TO RETURN.
I STILL WAIT.
AND YOU WOULD WAVE A BEAR AROUND AT ME?
HOW DARE YOU.
BOO HOO HOO!
HEY, YOU MANGY FOX. I FOUND SOME FRIES AND YOU AIN'T GETTING ANY, SO BACK OFF.
CHOMP! MUNCH!
FRIES? WHAT DO YOU KNOW OF FRIES? YOU ARE A FRIES FOOL!
AW.
LONG BEFORE YOU WERE EATING FRIES, I WAS A RENOWNED EXPLORER, SENT BY THE COURT OF MARIE ANTOINETTE HERSELF TO DISCOVER THE POTATO!
SWISH!

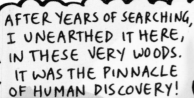
AFTER YEARS OF SEARCHING, I UNEARTHED IT HERE, IN THESE VERY WOODS. IT WAS THE PINNACLE OF HUMAN DISCOVERY!

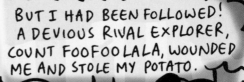
BUT I HAD BEEN FOLLOWED! A DEVIOUS RIVAL EXPLORER, COUNT FOOFOOLALA, WOUNDED ME AND STOLE MY POTATO.

HE CLAIMED ALL MY GLORY. I REMAINED HERE, TOO WEAK TO RETURN HOME.

SO NOW NEITHER OF US CAN ENJOY THE POTATO.

I'M STILL GOING TO EAT THEM OFF THE FLOOR.

HOW DARE YOU.

HEE HEE, LOOK, MISTER FOX! BUNNY TIED A BALLOON AROUND ME SO I WOULDN'T KEEP GETTING LOST.

THE BALLOON.

I REMEMBER IT WELL.

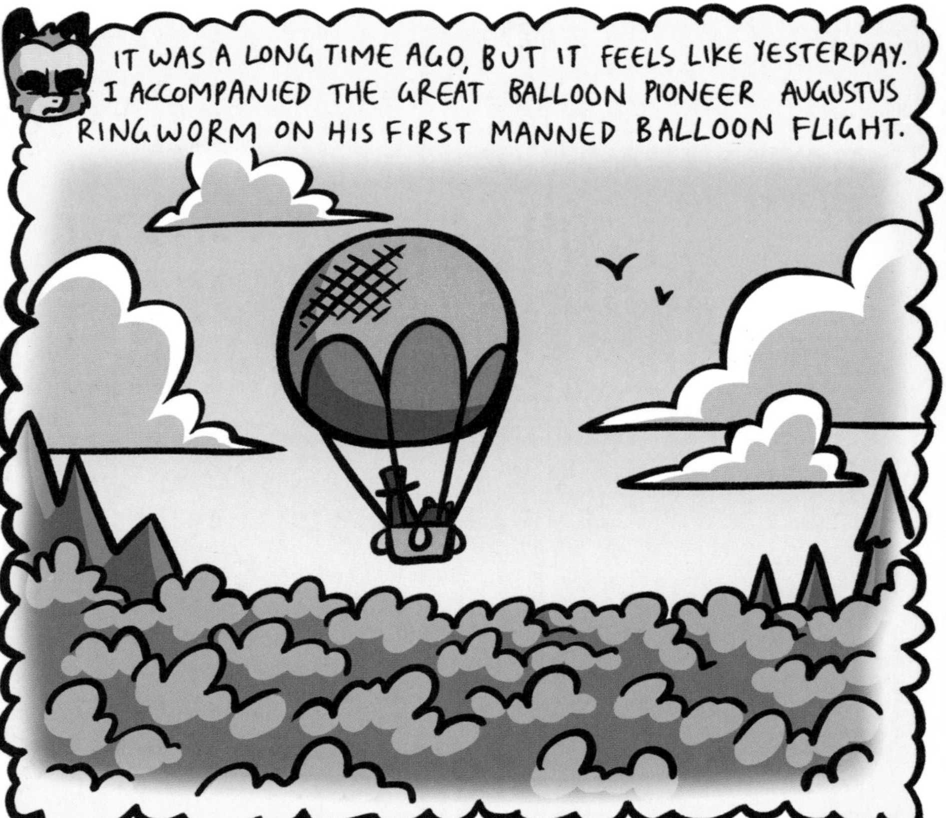
IT WAS A LONG TIME AGO, BUT IT FEELS LIKE YESTERDAY. I ACCOMPANIED THE GREAT BALLOON PIONEER AUGUSTUS RINGWORM ON HIS FIRST MANNED BALLOON FLIGHT.

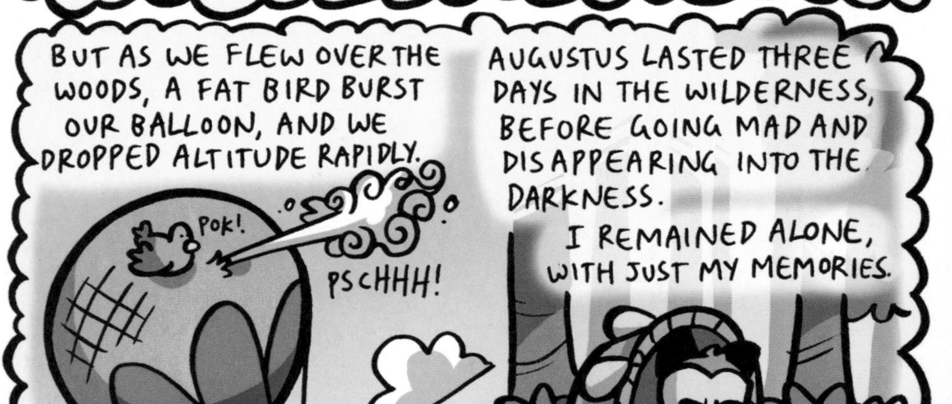
BUT AS WE FLEW OVER THE WOODS, A FAT BIRD BURST OUR BALLOON, AND WE DROPPED ALTITUDE RAPIDLY.
POK!
PSCHHH!
AUGUSTUS LASTED THREE DAYS IN THE WILDERNESS, BEFORE GOING MAD AND DISAPPEARING INTO THE DARKNESS.
I REMAINED ALONE, WITH JUST MY MEMORIES.

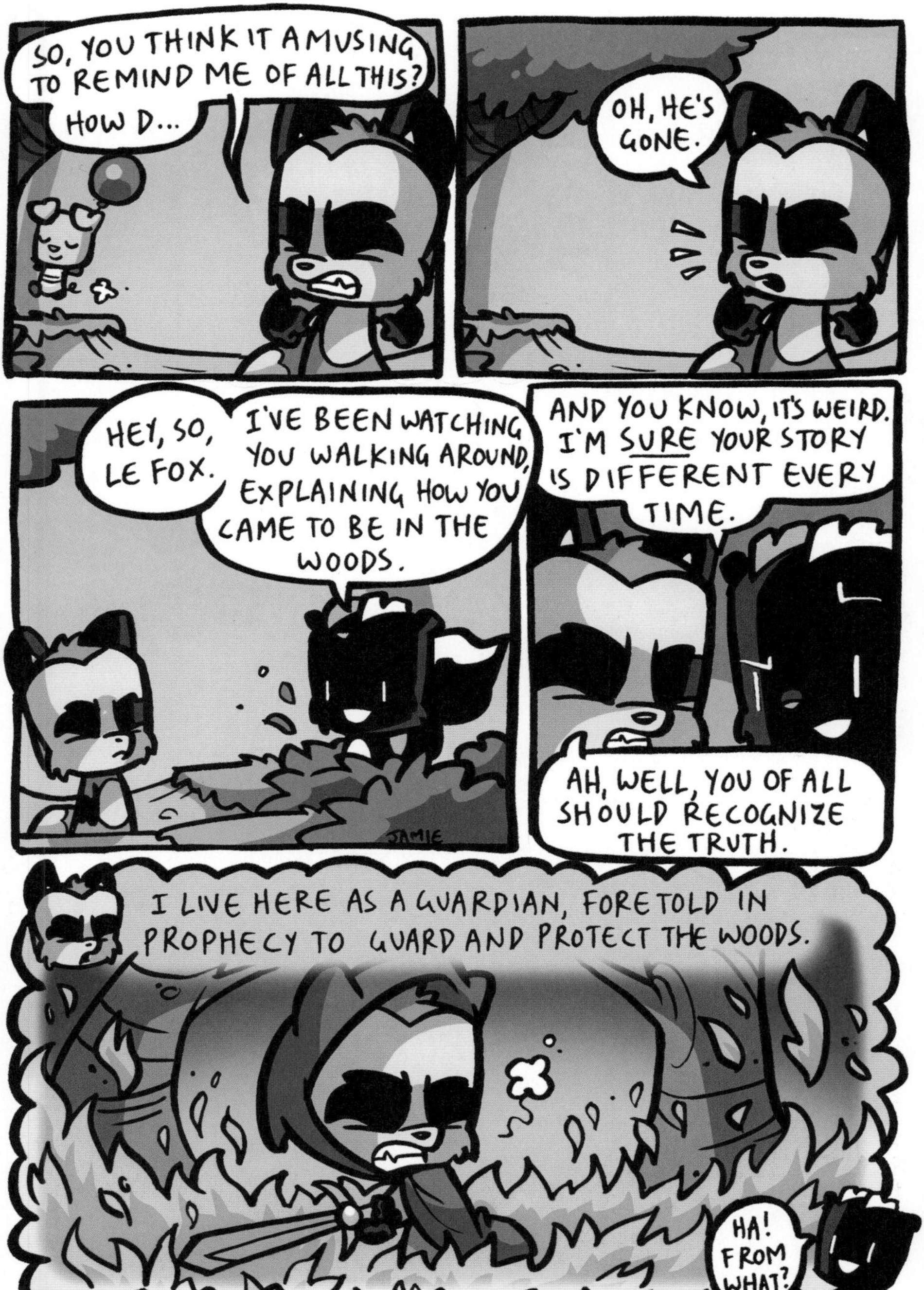
SO, YOU THINK IT AMUSING TO REMIND ME OF ALL THIS? HOW D...
OH, HE'S GONE.
HEY, SO, LE FOX.
I'VE BEEN WATCHING YOU WALKING AROUND, EXPLAINING HOW YOU CAME TO BE IN THE WOODS.
AND YOU KNOW, IT'S WEIRD. I'M SURE YOUR STORY IS DIFFERENT EVERY TIME.
AH, WELL, YOU OF ALL SHOULD RECOGNIZE THE TRUTH.
JAMIE
I LIVE HERE AS A GUARDIAN, FORETOLD IN PROPHECY TO GUARD AND PROTECT THE WOODS.
HA! FROM WHAT?

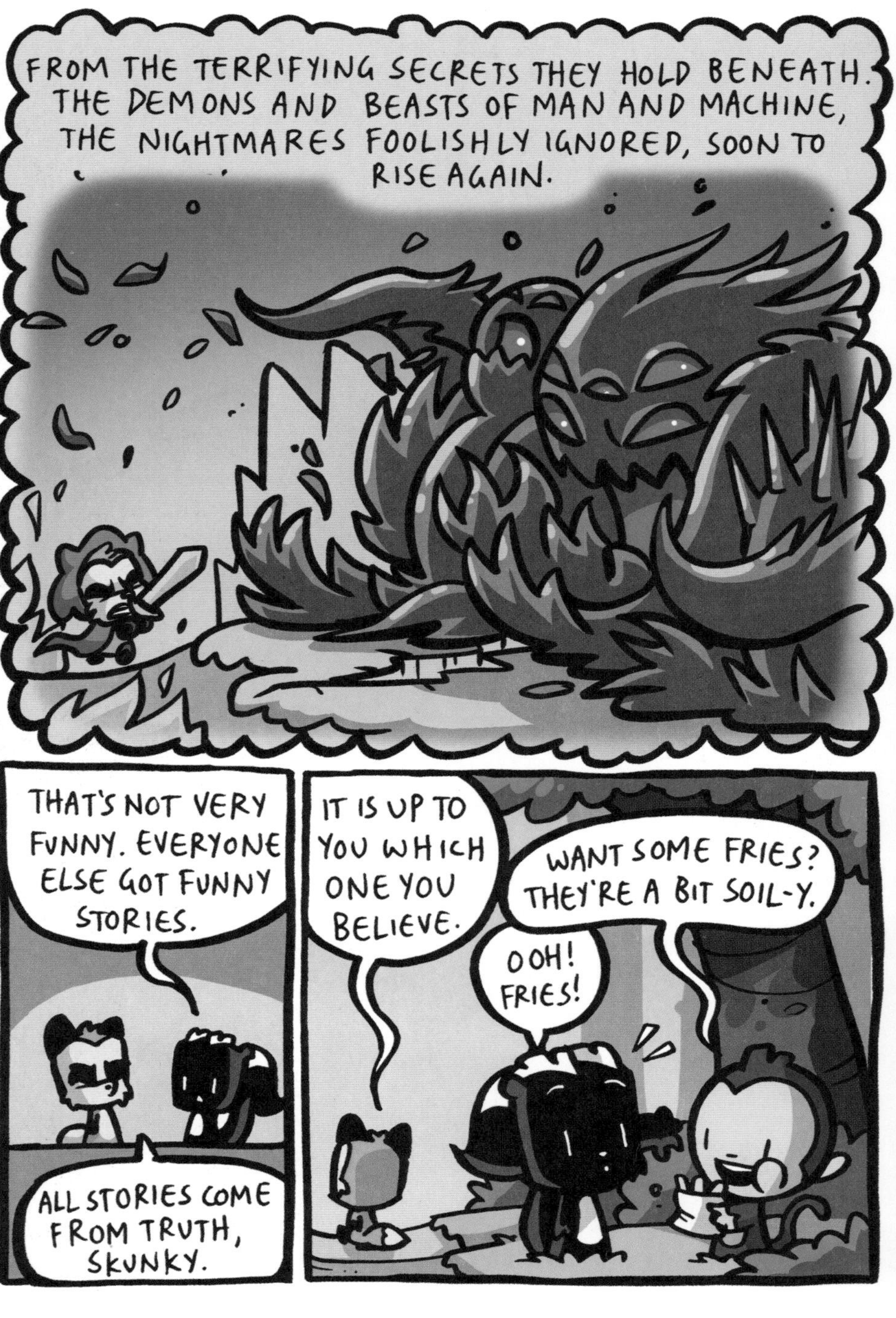
FROM THE TERRIFYING SECRETS THEY HOLD BENEATH. THE DEMONS AND BEASTS OF MAN AND MACHINE, THE NIGHTMARES FOOLISHLY IGNORED, SOON TO RISE AGAIN.
THAT'S NOT VERY FUNNY. EVERYONE ELSE GOT FUNNY STORIES.
ALL STORIES COME FROM TRUTH, SKUNKY.
IT IS UP TO YOU WHICH ONE YOU BELIEVE.
WANT SOME FRIES? THEY'RE A BIT SOIL-Y.
OOH! FRIES!

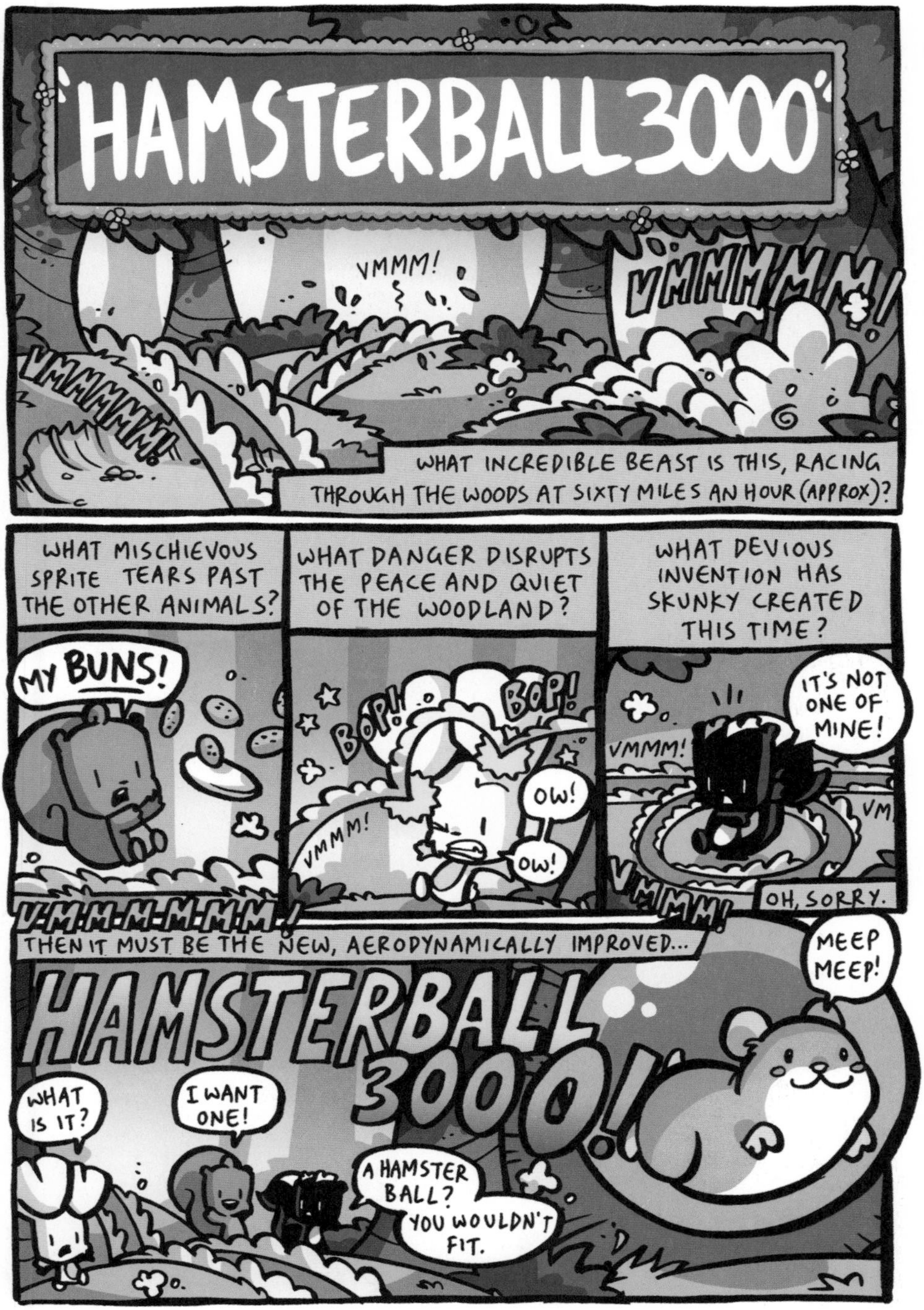
HAMSTERBALL 3000
VMMM!
VMMMMMM!
VMMMMMM!
WHAT INCREDIBLE BEAST IS THIS, RACING THROUGH THE WOODS AT SIXTY MILES AN HOUR (APPROX)?
WHAT MISCHIEVOUS SPRITE TEARS PAST THE OTHER ANIMALS?
MY BUNS!
WHAT DANGER DISRUPTS THE PEACE AND QUIET OF THE WOODLAND?
BOP!
BOP!
OW!
OW!
VMMM!
WHAT DEVIOUS INVENTION HAS SKUNKY CREATED THIS TIME?
IT'S NOT ONE OF MINE!
VMMM!
VM
VMMMM!
OH, SORRY.
V-M-M-M-M-M-M!
THEN IT MUST BE THE NEW, AERODYNAMICALLY IMPROVED...
MEEP MEEP!
HAMSTERBALL 3000!
WHAT IS IT?
I WANT ONE!
A HAMSTER BALL?
YOU WOULDN'T FIT.

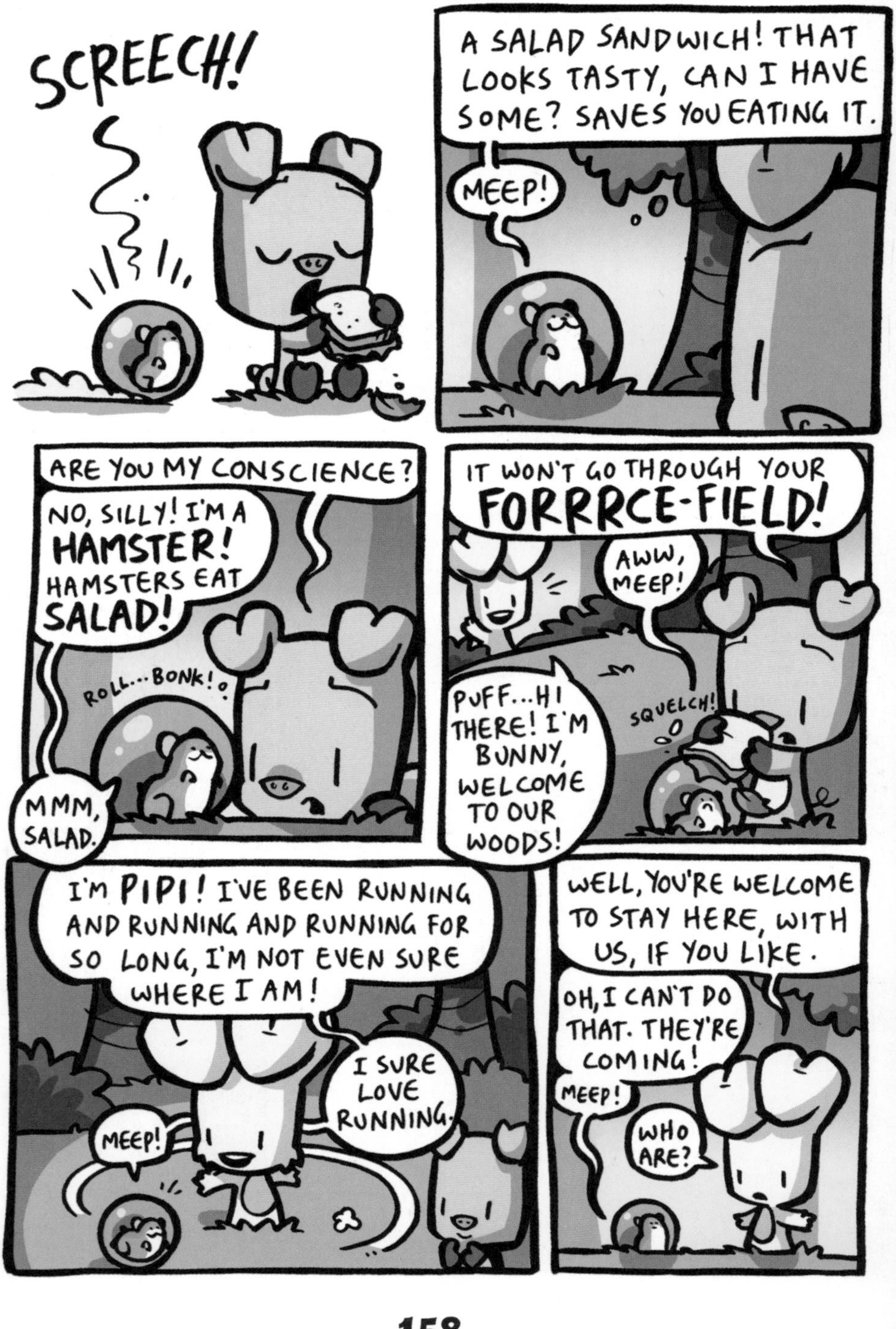
SCREECH!
A SALAD SANDWICH! THAT LOOKS TASTY, CAN I HAVE SOME? SAVES YOU EATING IT.
MEEP!
ARE YOU MY CONSCIENCE?
NO, SILLY! I'M A HAMSTER! HAMSTERS EAT SALAD!
ROLL...BONK!
MMM, SALAD.
IT WON'T GO THROUGH YOUR FORRRCE-FIELD!
AWW, MEEP!
SQUELCH!
PUFF...HI THERE! I'M BUNNY, WELCOME TO OUR WOODS!
I'M PIPI! I'VE BEEN RUNNING AND RUNNING AND RUNNING FOR SO LONG, I'M NOT EVEN SURE WHERE I AM!
I SURE LOVE RUNNING.
MEEP!
WELL, YOU'RE WELCOME TO STAY HERE, WITH US, IF YOU LIKE.
OH, I CAN'T DO THAT. THEY'RE COMING!
MEEP!
WHO ARE?

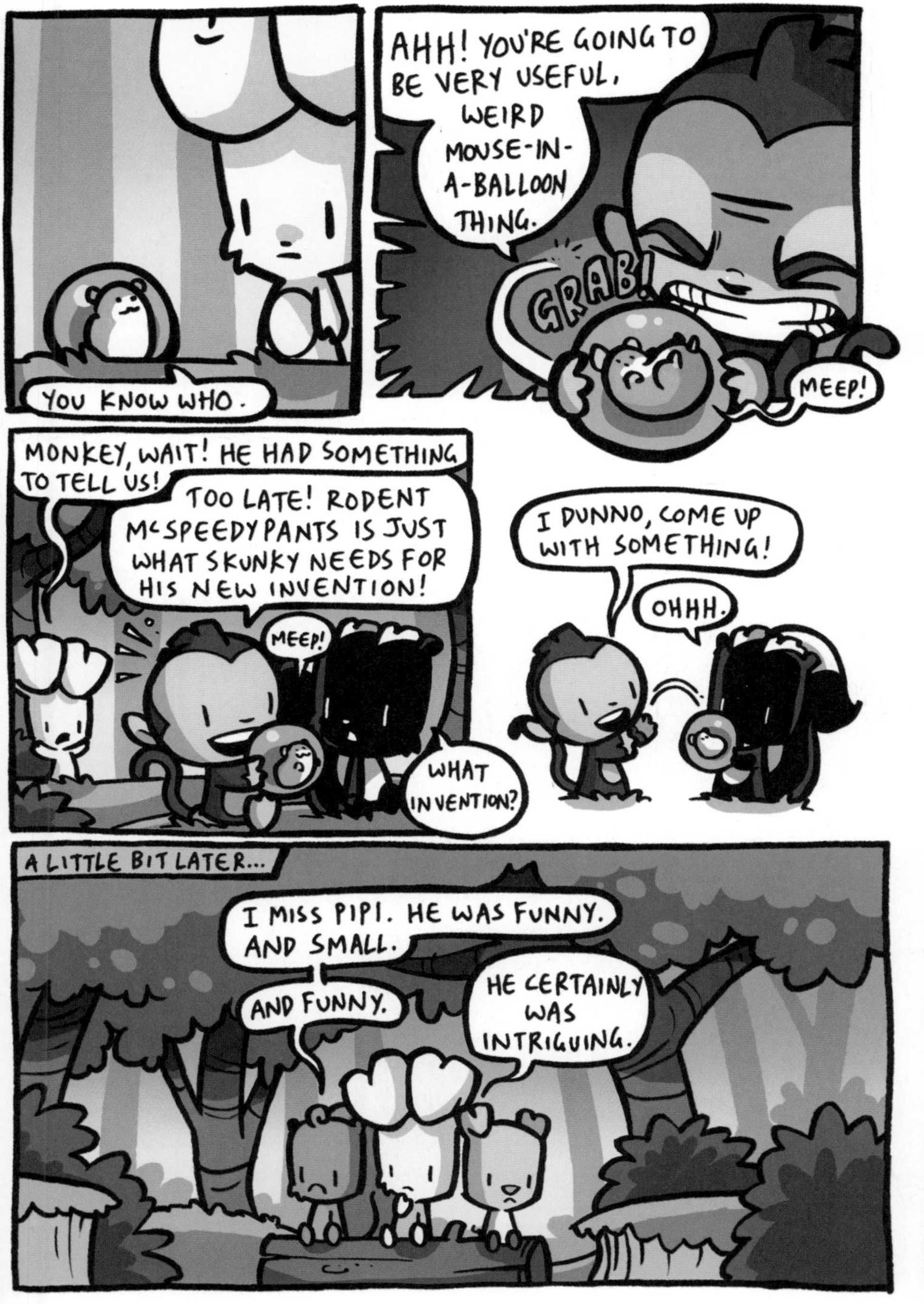
YOU KNOW WHO.
AHH! YOU'RE GOING TO BE VERY USEFUL, WEIRD MOUSE-IN-A-BALLOON THING.
GRAB!
MEEP!
MONKEY, WAIT! HE HAD SOMETHING TO TELL US!
TOO LATE! RODENT McSPEEDYPANTS IS JUST WHAT SKUNKY NEEDS FOR HIS NEW INVENTION!
MEEP!
WHAT INVENTION?
I DUNNO, COME UP WITH SOMETHING!
OHHH.
A LITTLE BIT LATER...
I MISS PIPI. HE WAS FUNNY. AND SMALL.
AND FUNNY.
HE CERTAINLY WAS INTRIGUING.

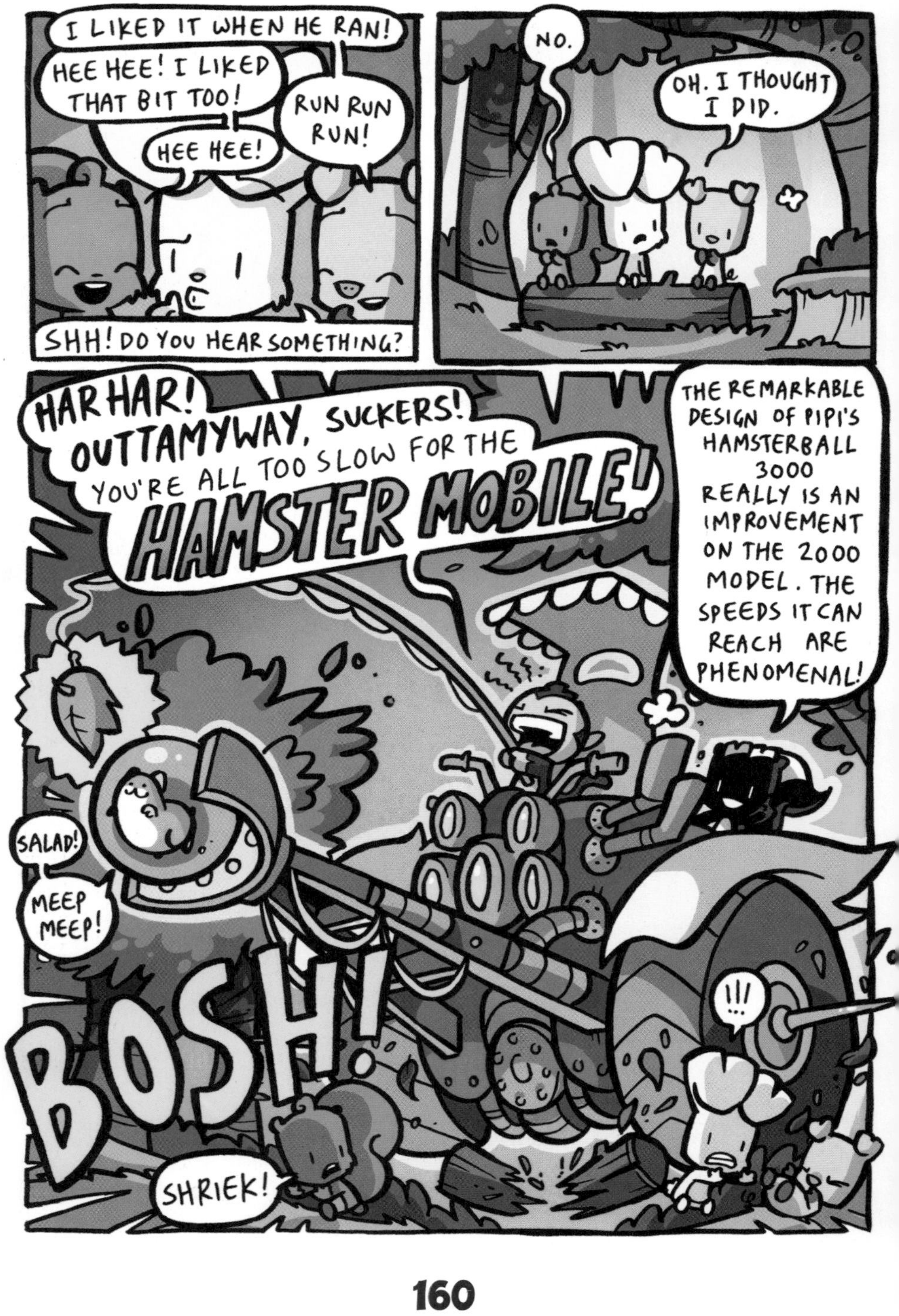
I LIKED IT WHEN HE RAN!
HEE HEE! I LIKED THAT BIT TOO!
RUN RUN RUN!
HEE HEE!
SHH! DO YOU HEAR SOMETHING?
NO.
OH. I THOUGHT I DID.
HAR HAR! OUTTAMYWAY, SUCKERS! YOU'RE ALL TOO SLOW FOR THE HAMSTER MOBILE!
THE REMARKABLE DESIGN OF PIPI'S HAMSTERBALL 3000 REALLY IS AN IMPROVEMENT ON THE 2000 MODEL. THE SPEEDS IT CAN REACH ARE PHENOMENAL!
SALAD!
MEEP MEEP!
BOSH!
!!!
...
SHRIEK!

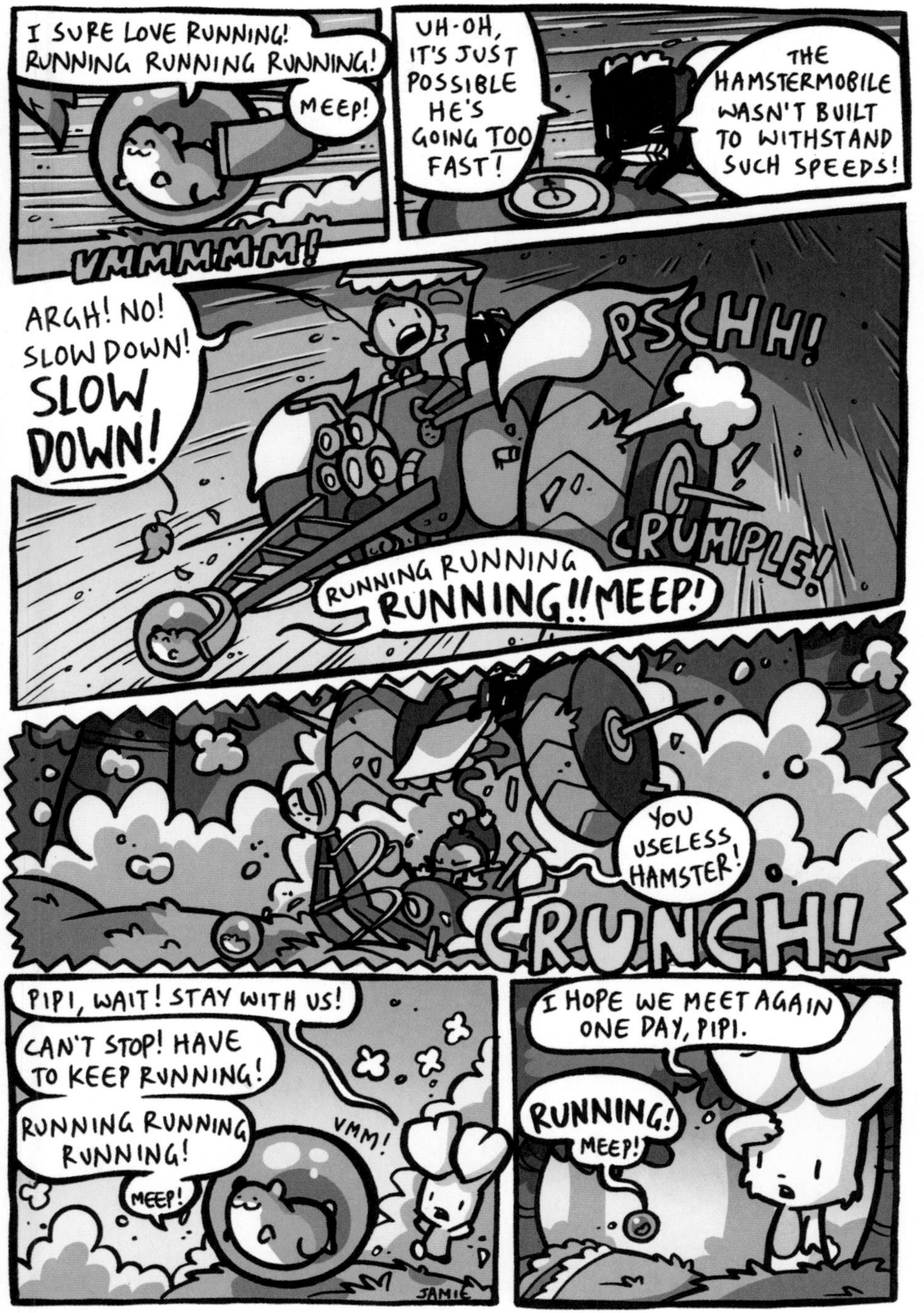
I SURE LOVE RUNNING! RUNNING RUNNING RUNNING!
MEEP!
UH-OH, IT'S JUST POSSIBLE HE'S GOING TOO FAST!
THE HAMSTERMOBILE WASN'T BUILT TO WITHSTAND SUCH SPEEDS!
VMMMMMM!
ARGH! NO! SLOW DOWN! SLOW DOWN!
PSCHH!
CRUMPLE!
RUNNING RUNNING RUNNING!! MEEP!
YOU USELESS HAMSTER!
CRUNCH!
PIPI, WAIT! STAY WITH US!
CAN'T STOP! HAVE TO KEEP RUNNING!
RUNNING RUNNING RUNNING!
VMM!
MEEP!
JAMIE
I HOPE WE MEET AGAIN ONE DAY, PIPI.
RUNNING!
MEEP!

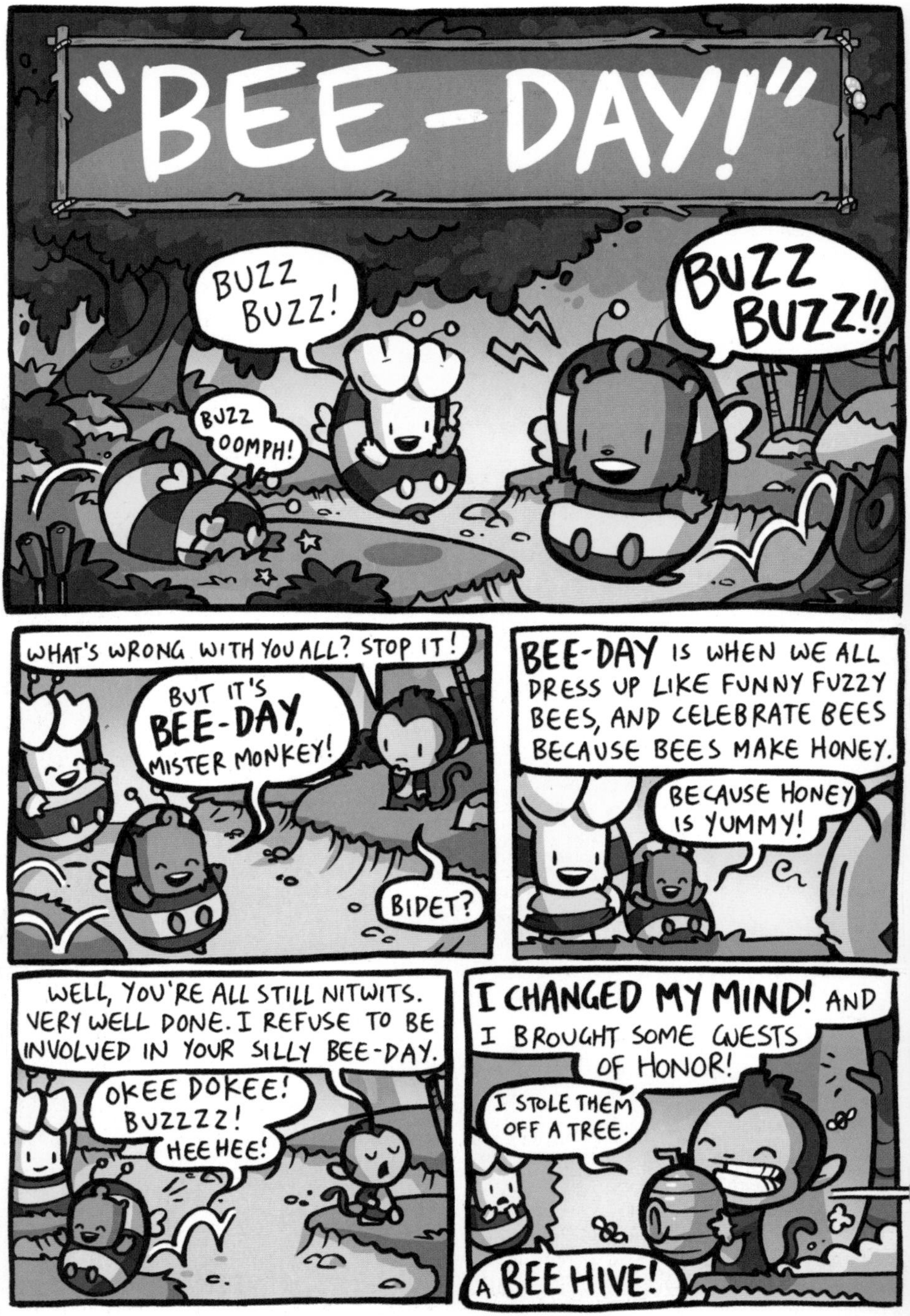
"BEE-DAY!"
BUZZ BUZZ!
BUZZ BUZZ!!
BUZZ OOMPH!
WHAT'S WRONG WITH YOU ALL? STOP IT!
BUT IT'S BEE-DAY, MISTER MONKEY!
BIDET?
BEE-DAY IS WHEN WE ALL DRESS UP LIKE FUNNY FUZZY BEES, AND CELEBRATE BEES BECAUSE BEES MAKE HONEY.
BECAUSE HONEY IS YUMMY!
WELL, YOU'RE ALL STILL NITWITS. VERY WELL DONE. I REFUSE TO BE INVOLVED IN YOUR SILLY BEE-DAY.
OKEE DOKEE! BUZZZZ! HEE HEE!
I CHANGED MY MIND! AND I BROUGHT SOME GUESTS OF HONOR!
I STOLE THEM OFF A TREE.
A BEE HIVE!

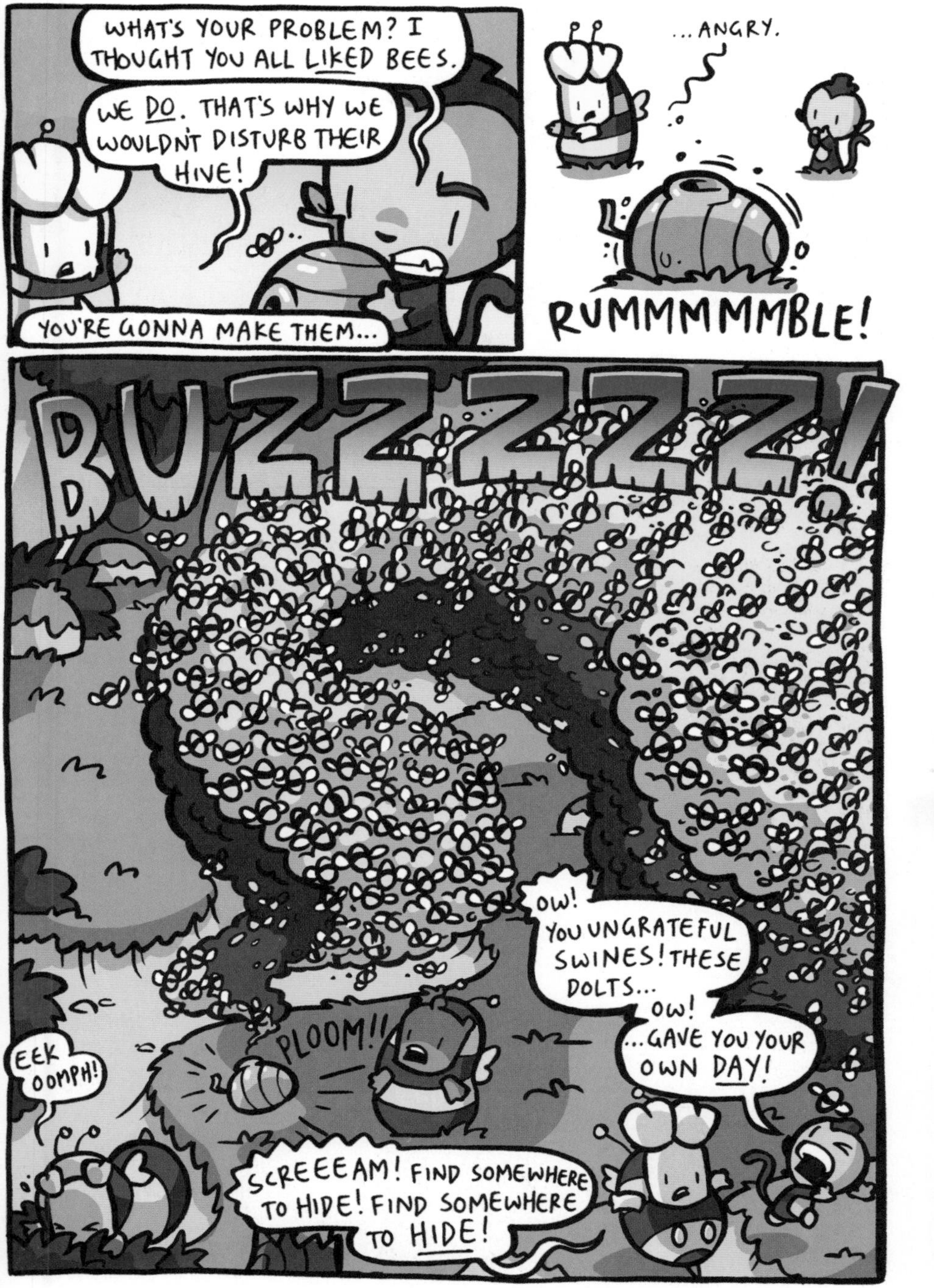
WHAT'S YOUR PROBLEM? I THOUGHT YOU ALL LIKED BEES.
WE DO. THAT'S WHY WE WOULDN'T DISTURB THEIR HIVE!
YOU'RE GONNA MAKE THEM...
...ANGRY.
RUMMMMMMBLE!
BUZZZZZ!
OW! YOU UNGRATEFUL SWINES! THESE DOLTS...
OW!
...GAVE YOU YOUR OWN DAY!
PLOOM!!
EEK OOMPH!
SCREEEAM! FIND SOMEWHERE TO HIDE! FIND SOMEWHERE TO HIDE!

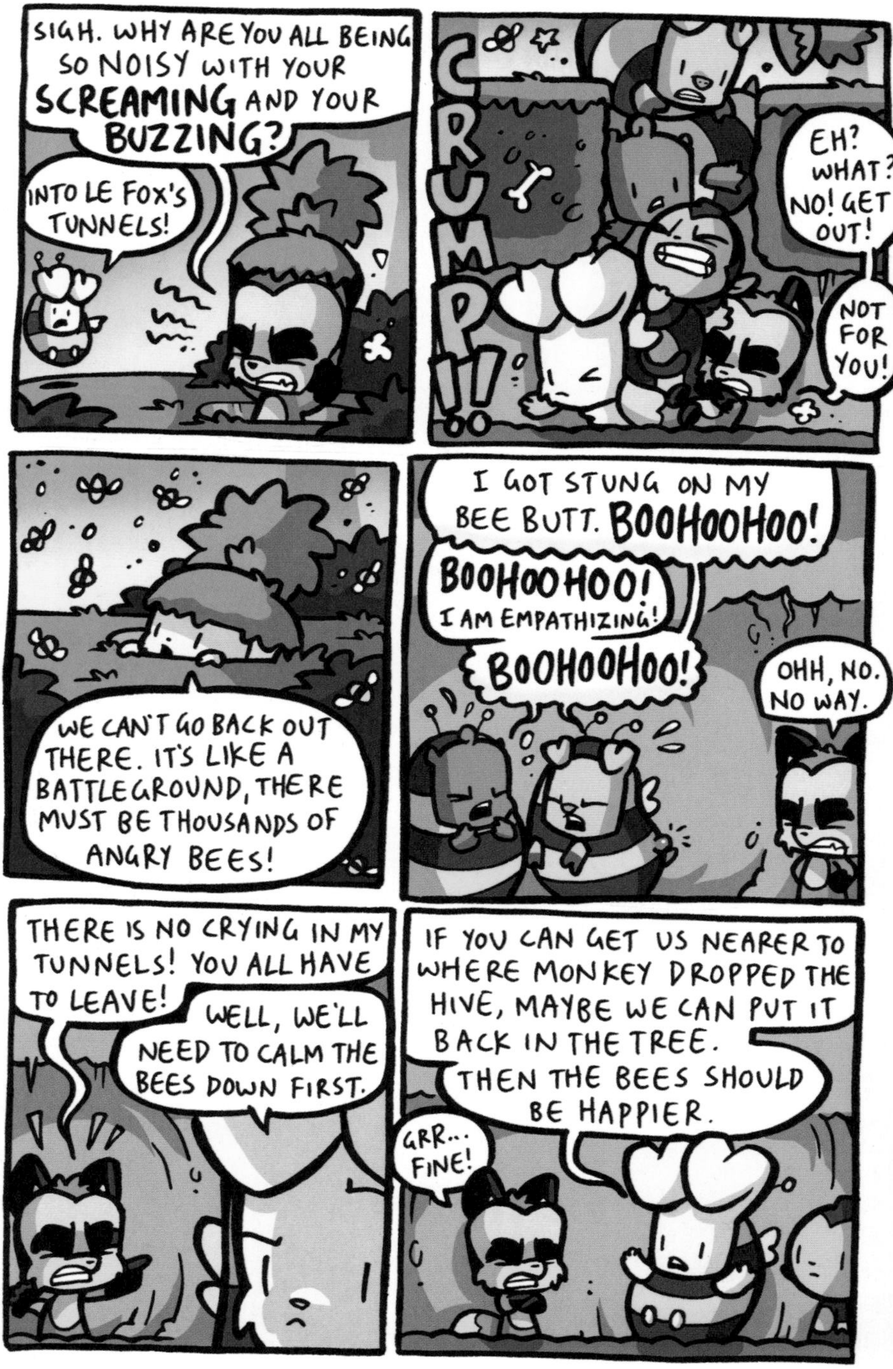
SIGH. WHY ARE YOU ALL BEING SO NOISY WITH YOUR SCREAMING AND YOUR BUZZING?
INTO LE FOX'S TUNNELS!
CRUMP!!
EH? WHAT? NO! GET OUT!
NOT FOR YOU!
WE CAN'T GO BACK OUT THERE. IT'S LIKE A BATTLEGROUND, THERE MUST BE THOUSANDS OF ANGRY BEES!
I GOT STUNG ON MY BEE BUTT. BOOHOOHOO!
BOOHOOHOO! I AM EMPATHIZING!
BOOHOOHOO!
OHH, NO. NO WAY.
THERE IS NO CRYING IN MY TUNNELS! YOU ALL HAVE TO LEAVE!
WELL, WE'LL NEED TO CALM THE BEES DOWN FIRST.
IF YOU CAN GET US NEARER TO WHERE MONKEY DROPPED THE HIVE, MAYBE WE CAN PUT IT BACK IN THE TREE.
THEN THE BEES SHOULD BE HAPPIER.
GRR... FINE!

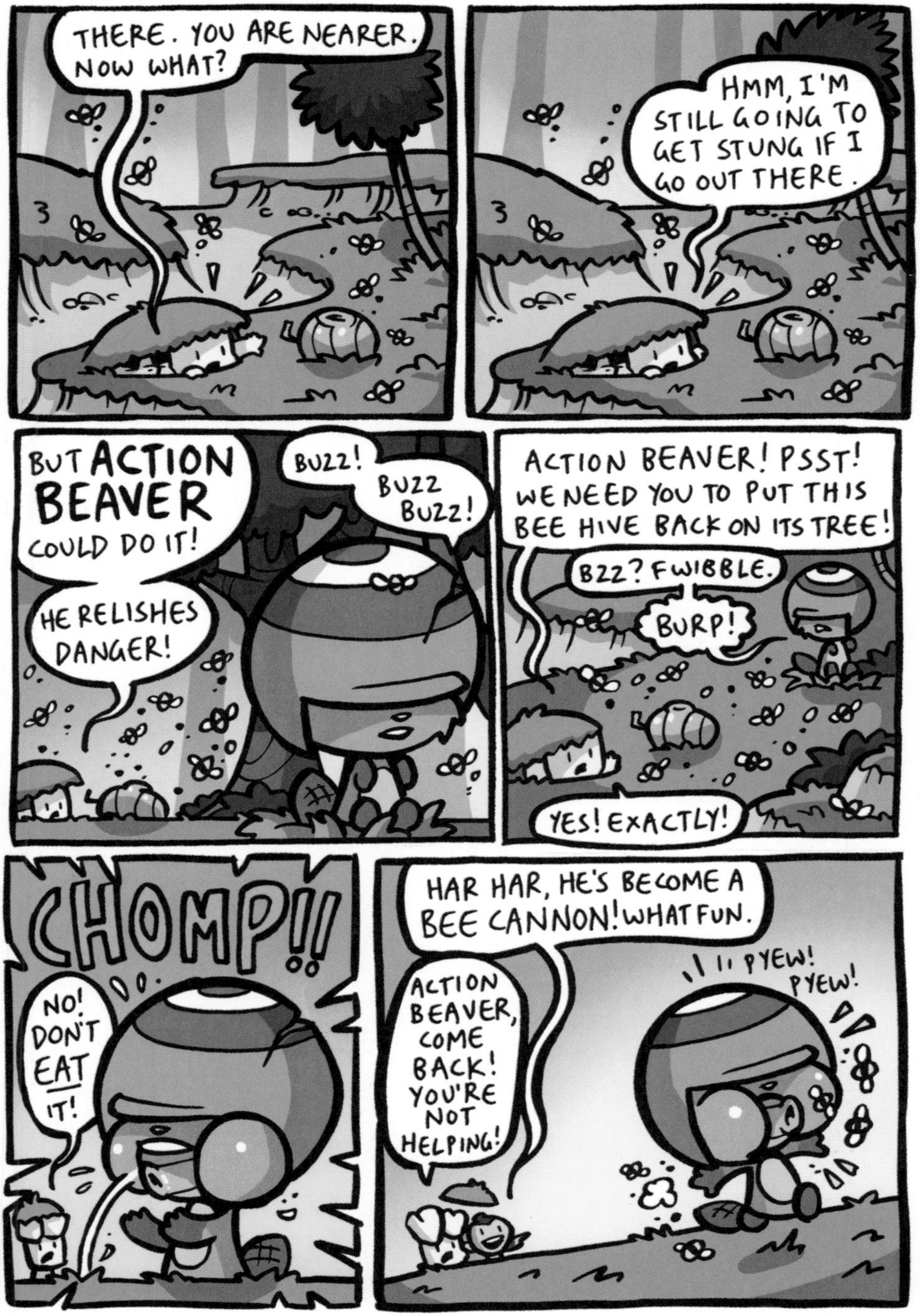
THERE. YOU ARE NEARER. NOW WHAT?
HMM, I'M STILL GOING TO GET STUNG IF I GO OUT THERE.
BUT ACTION BEAVER COULD DO IT!
HE RELISHES DANGER!
BUZZ!
BUZZ BUZZ!
ACTION BEAVER! PSST! WE NEED YOU TO PUT THIS BEE HIVE BACK ON ITS TREE!
BZZ? FWIBBLE.
BURP!
YES! EXACTLY!
CHOMP!!
NO! DON'T EAT IT!
HAR HAR, HE'S BECOME A BEE CANNON! WHAT FUN.
ACTION BEAVER, COME BACK! YOU'RE NOT HELPING!
PYEW! PYEW!

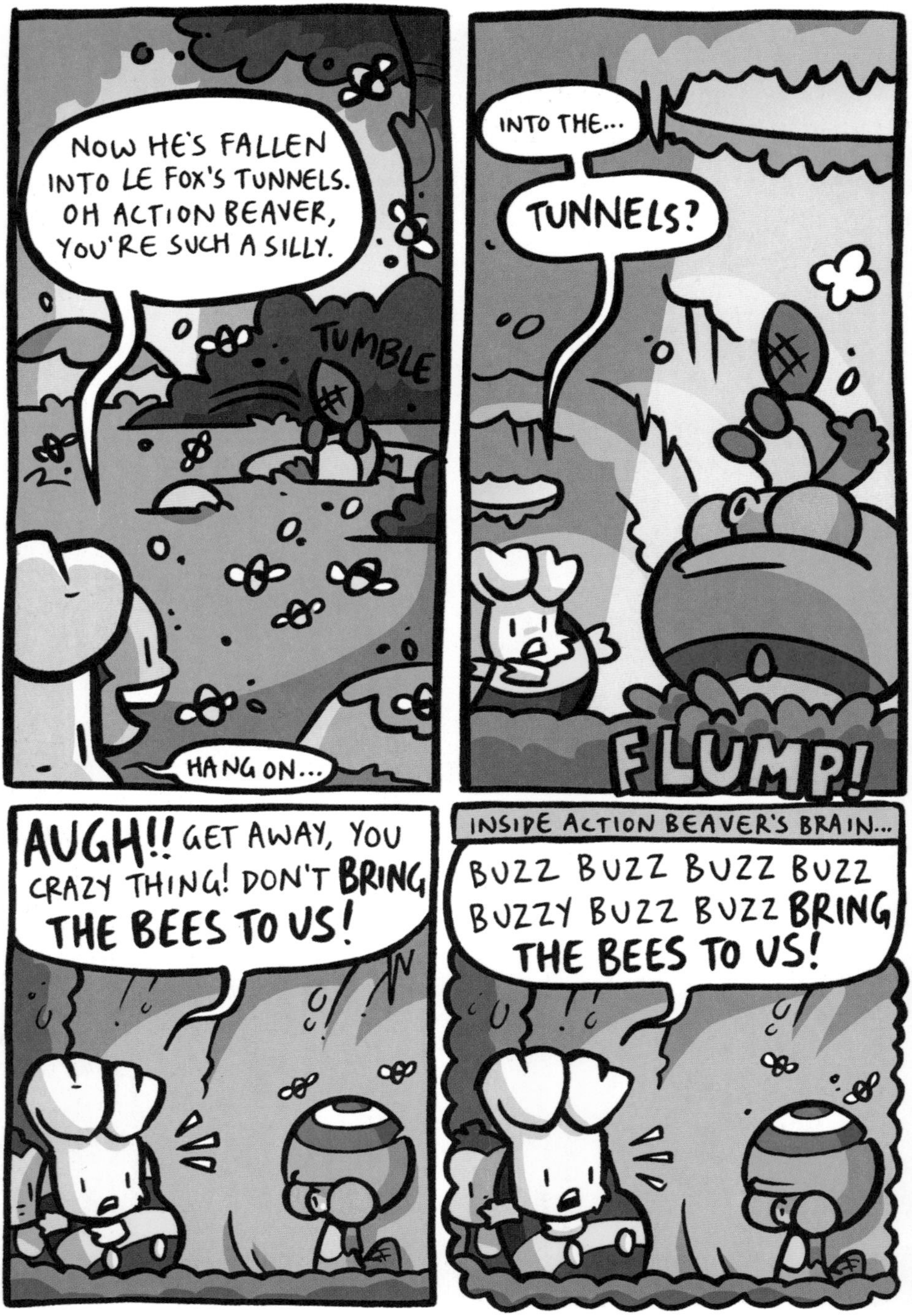
NOW HE'S FALLEN INTO LE FOX'S TUNNELS. OH ACTION BEAVER, YOU'RE SUCH A SILLY.
TUMBLE
HANG ON...
INTO THE...
TUNNELS?
FLUMP!
AUGH!! GET AWAY, YOU CRAZY THING! DON'T BRING THE BEES TO US!
INSIDE ACTION BEAVER'S BRAIN...
BUZZ BUZZ BUZZ BUZZ BUZZY BUZZ BUZZ BRING THE BEES TO US!

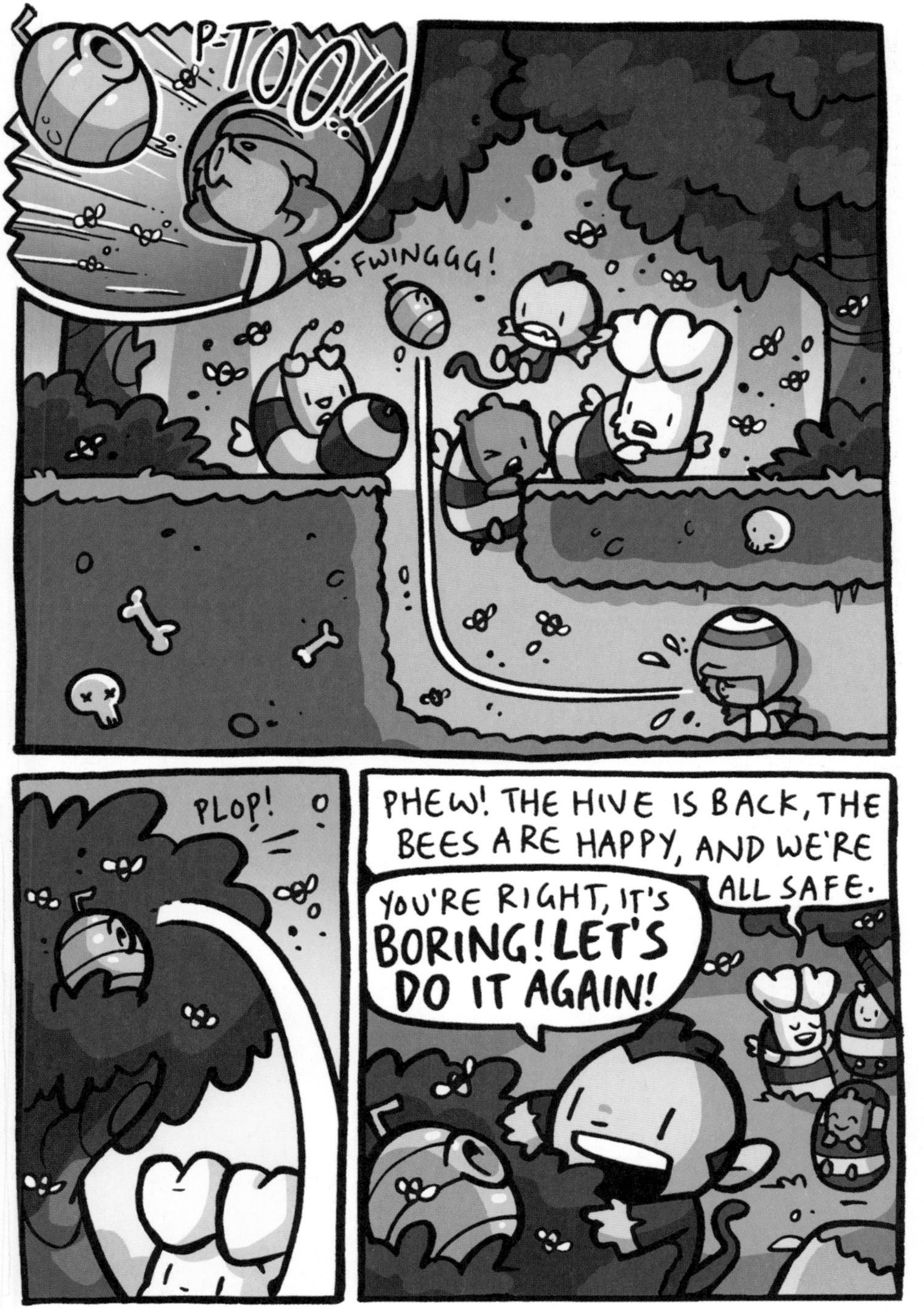
P-TOO!!
FWINGGG!
PLOP!
PHEW! THE HIVE IS BACK, THE BEES ARE HAPPY, AND WE'RE ALL SAFE.
YOU'RE RIGHT, IT'S BORING! LET'S DO IT AGAIN!

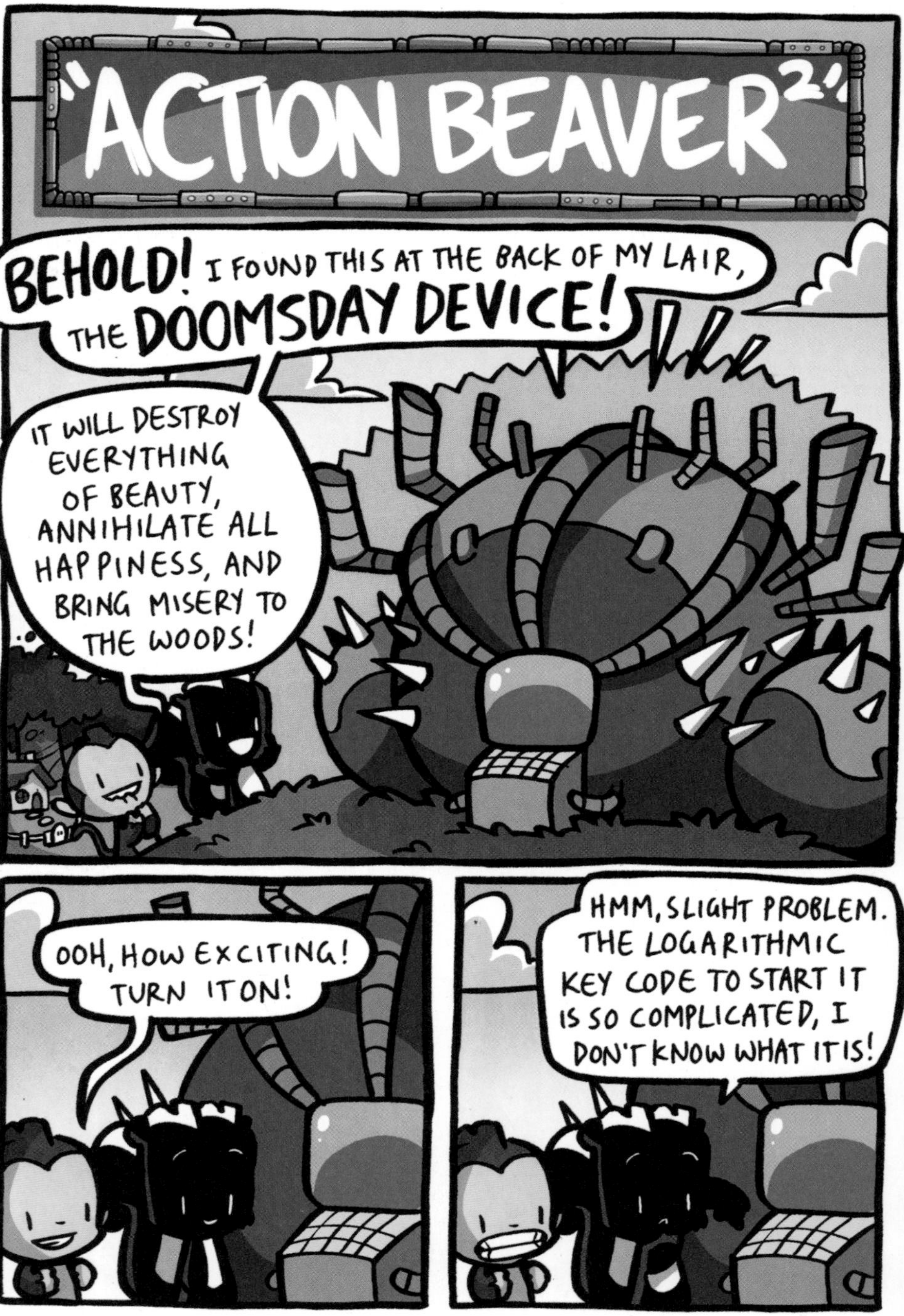
"ACTION BEAVER²"
BEHOLD! I FOUND THIS AT THE BACK OF MY LAIR, THE DOOMSDAY DEVICE!
IT WILL DESTROY EVERYTHING OF BEAUTY, ANNIHILATE ALL HAPPINESS, AND BRING MISERY TO THE WOODS!
OOH, HOW EXCITING! TURN IT ON!
HMM, SLIGHT PROBLEM. THE LOGARITHMIC KEY CODE TO START IT IS SO COMPLICATED, I DON'T KNOW WHAT IT IS!

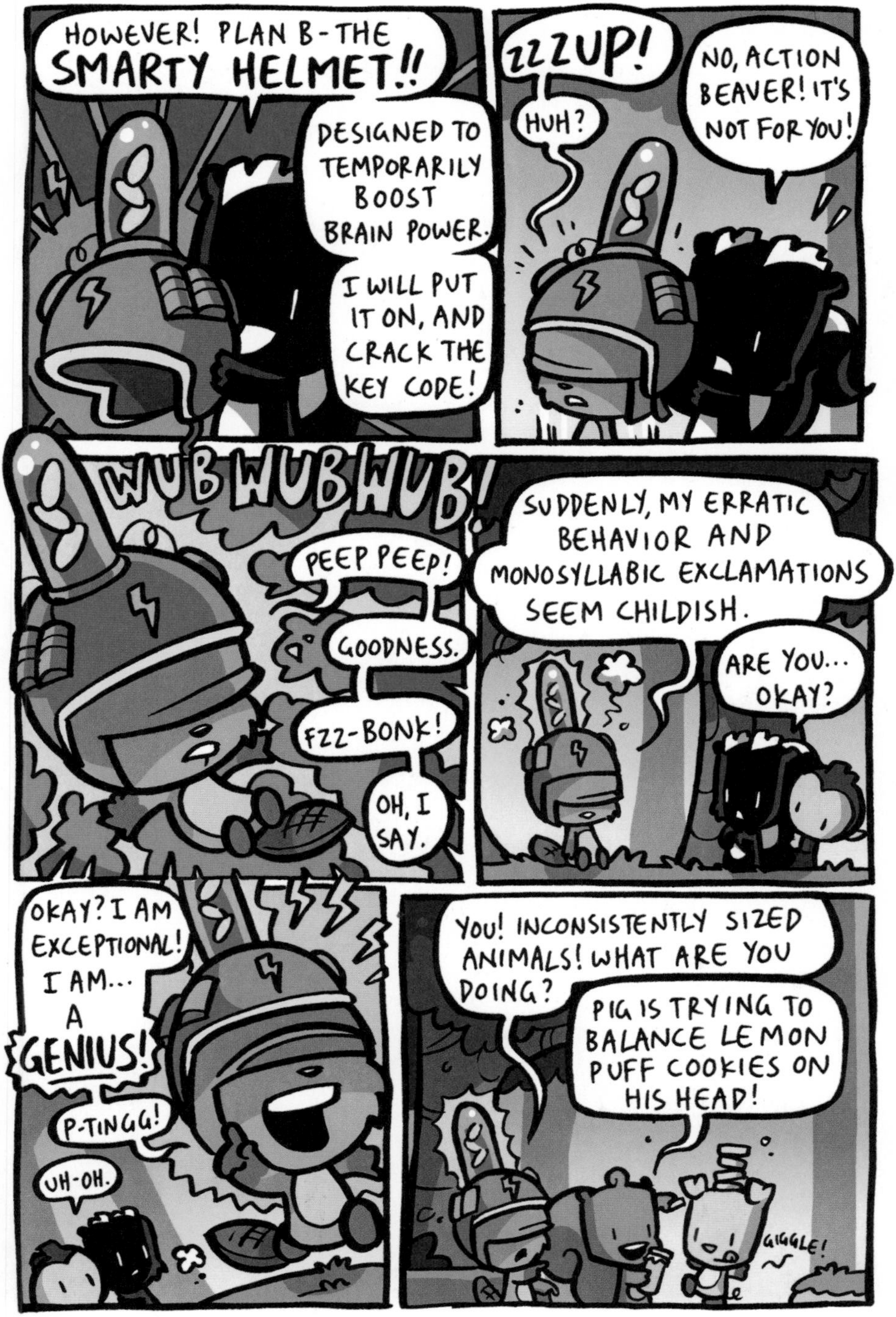
HOWEVER! PLAN B-THE SMARTY HELMET!!
DESIGNED TO TEMPORARILY BOOST BRAIN POWER.
I WILL PUT IT ON, AND CRACK THE KEY CODE!
ZZZUP!
HUH?
NO, ACTION BEAVER! IT'S NOT FOR YOU!
WUBWUBWUB!
PEEP PEEP!
GOODNESS.
FZZ-BONK!
OH, I SAY.
SUDDENLY, MY ERRATIC BEHAVIOR AND MONOSYLLABIC EXCLAMATIONS SEEM CHILDISH.
ARE YOU... OKAY?
OKAY? I AM EXCEPTIONAL! I AM... A GENIUS!
P-TINGG!
UH-OH.
YOU! INCONSISTENTLY SIZED ANIMALS! WHAT ARE YOU DOING?
PIG IS TRYING TO BALANCE LEMON PUFF COOKIES ON HIS HEAD!
GIGGLE!

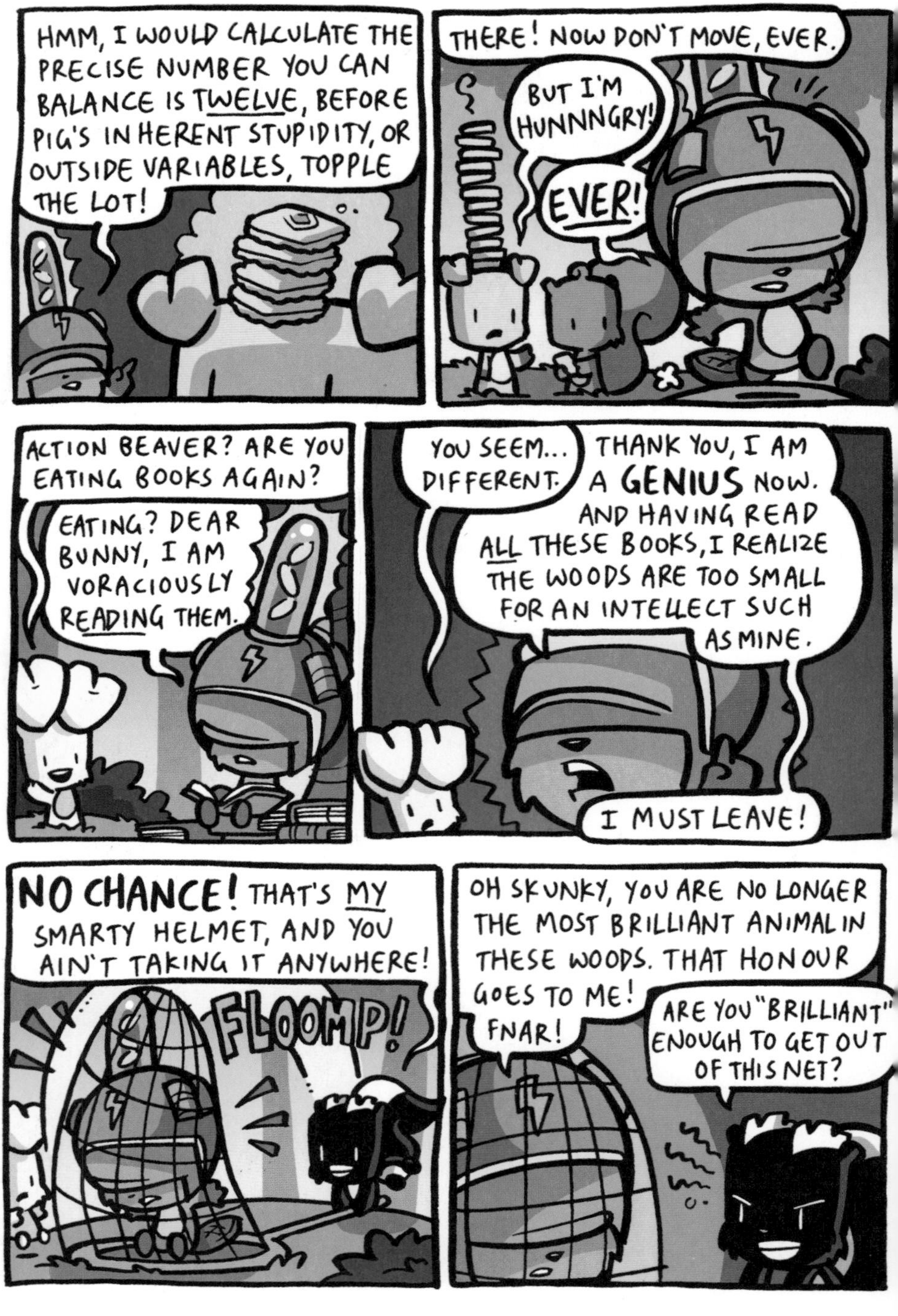

HMM, I WOULD CALCULATE THE PRECISE NUMBER YOU CAN BALANCE IS TWELVE, BEFORE PIG'S INHERENT STUPIDITY, OR OUTSIDE VARIABLES, TOPPLE THE LOT!
THERE! NOW DON'T MOVE, EVER.
BUT I'M HUNNNGRY!
EVER!
ACTION BEAVER? ARE YOU EATING BOOKS AGAIN?
EATING? DEAR BUNNY, I AM VORACIOUSLY READING THEM.
YOU SEEM... DIFFERENT.
THANK YOU, I AM A GENIUS NOW.
AND HAVING READ ALL THESE BOOKS, I REALIZE THE WOODS ARE TOO SMALL FOR AN INTELLECT SUCH AS MINE.
I MUST LEAVE!
NO CHANCE! THAT'S MY SMARTY HELMET, AND YOU AIN'T TAKING IT ANYWHERE!
FLOOMP!
OH SKUNKY, YOU ARE NO LONGER THE MOST BRILLIANT ANIMAL IN THESE WOODS. THAT HONOUR GOES TO ME!
FNAR!
ARE YOU "BRILLIANT" ENOUGH TO GET OUT OF THIS NET?

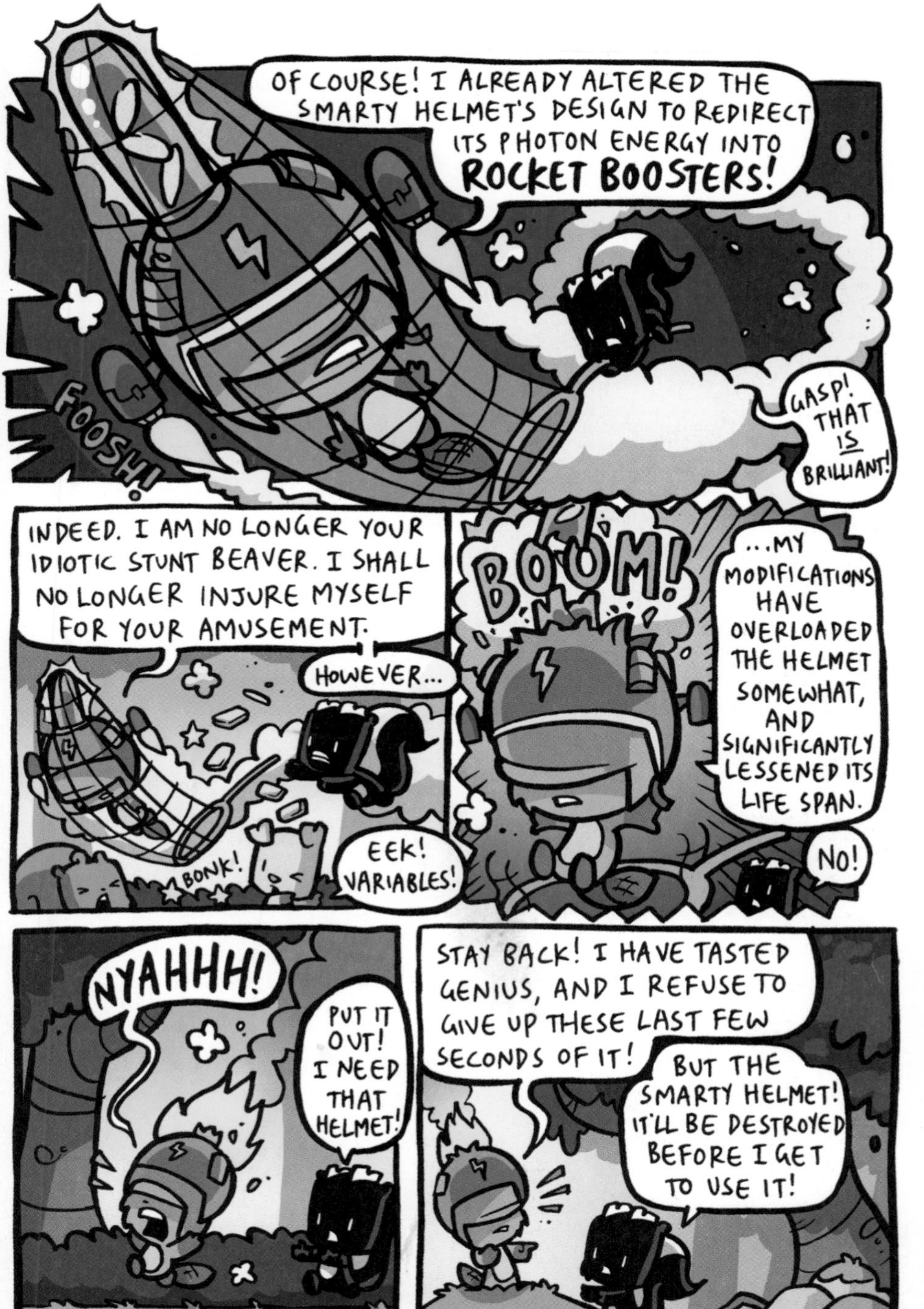
OF COURSE! I ALREADY ALTERED THE SMARTY HELMET'S DESIGN TO REDIRECT ITS PHOTON ENERGY INTO ROCKET BOOSTERS!
FOOSH!
GASP! THAT IS BRILLIANT!
INDEED. I AM NO LONGER YOUR IDIOTIC STUNT BEAVER. I SHALL NO LONGER INJURE MYSELF FOR YOUR AMUSEMENT.
HOWEVER...
BONK!
EEK! VARIABLES!
BOOM!
...MY MODIFICATIONS HAVE OVERLOADED THE HELMET SOMEWHAT, AND SIGNIFICANTLY LESSENED ITS LIFE SPAN.
NO!
NYAHHH!
PUT IT OUT! I NEED THAT HELMET!
STAY BACK! I HAVE TASTED GENIUS, AND I REFUSE TO GIVE UP THESE LAST FEW SECONDS OF IT!
BUT THE SMARTY HELMET! IT'LL BE DESTROYED BEFORE I GET TO USE IT!

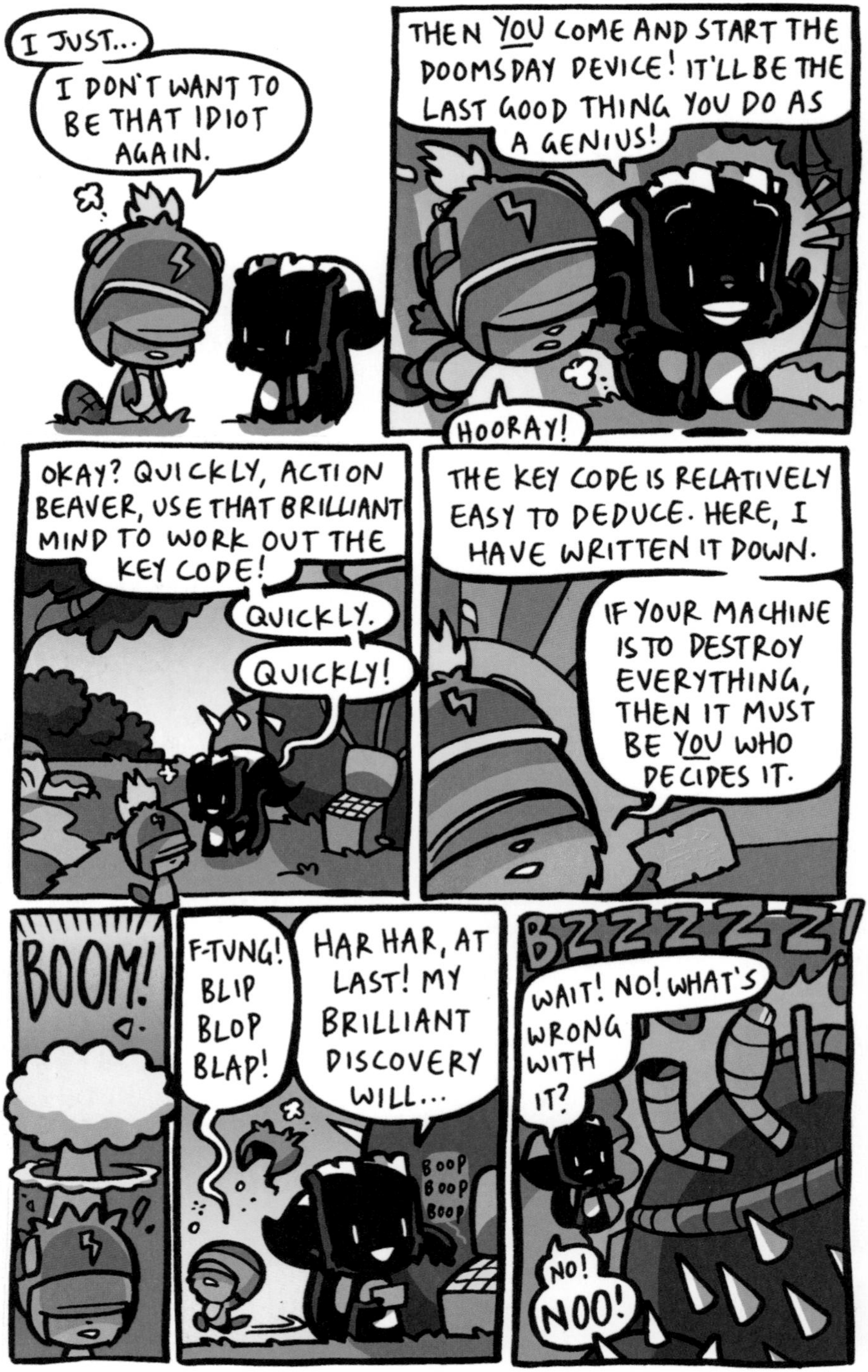
I JUST...
I DON'T WANT TO BE THAT IDIOT AGAIN.
THEN YOU COME AND START THE DOOMSDAY DEVICE! IT'LL BE THE LAST GOOD THING YOU DO AS A GENIUS!
HOORAY!
OKAY? QUICKLY, ACTION BEAVER, USE THAT BRILLIANT MIND TO WORK OUT THE KEY CODE!
QUICKLY.
QUICKLY!
THE KEY CODE IS RELATIVELY EASY TO DEDUCE. HERE, I HAVE WRITTEN IT DOWN.
IF YOUR MACHINE IS TO DESTROY EVERYTHING, THEN IT MUST BE YOU WHO DECIDES IT.
BOOM!
F-TUNG! BLIP BLOP BLAP!
HAR HAR, AT LAST! MY BRILLIANT DISCOVERY WILL...
BOOP BOOP BOOP
BZZZZZZ!
WAIT! NO! WHAT'S WRONG WITH IT?
NO! NOO!

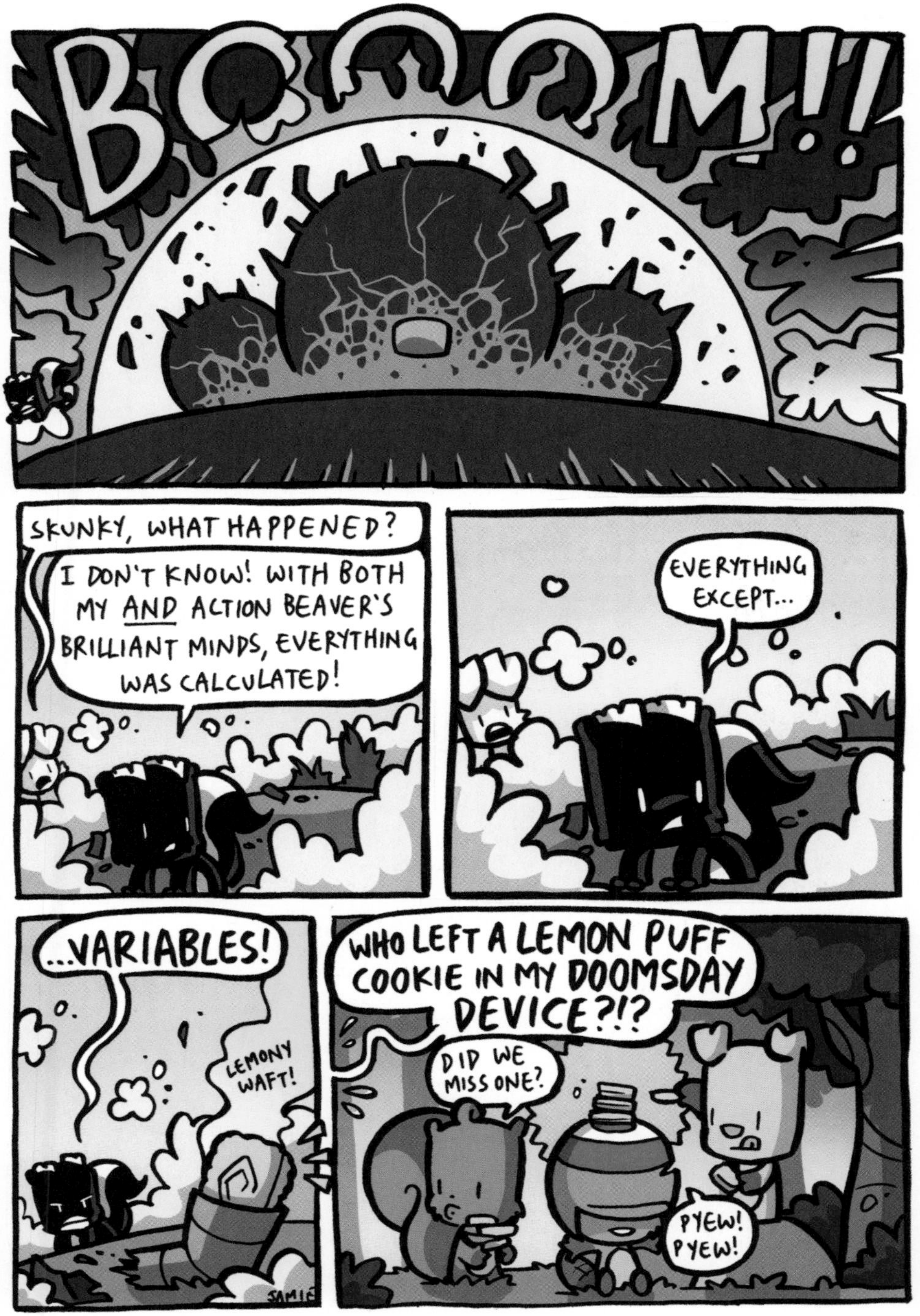
BOOOOM!!
SKUNKY, WHAT HAPPENED?
I DON'T KNOW! WITH BOTH MY AND ACTION BEAVER'S BRILLIANT MINDS, EVERYTHING WAS CALCULATED!
EVERYTHING EXCEPT...
...VARIABLES!
LEMONY WAFT!
WHO LEFT A LEMON PUFF COOKIE IN MY DOOMSDAY DEVICE?!?
DID WE MISS ONE?
PYEW! PYEW!
SAMIE

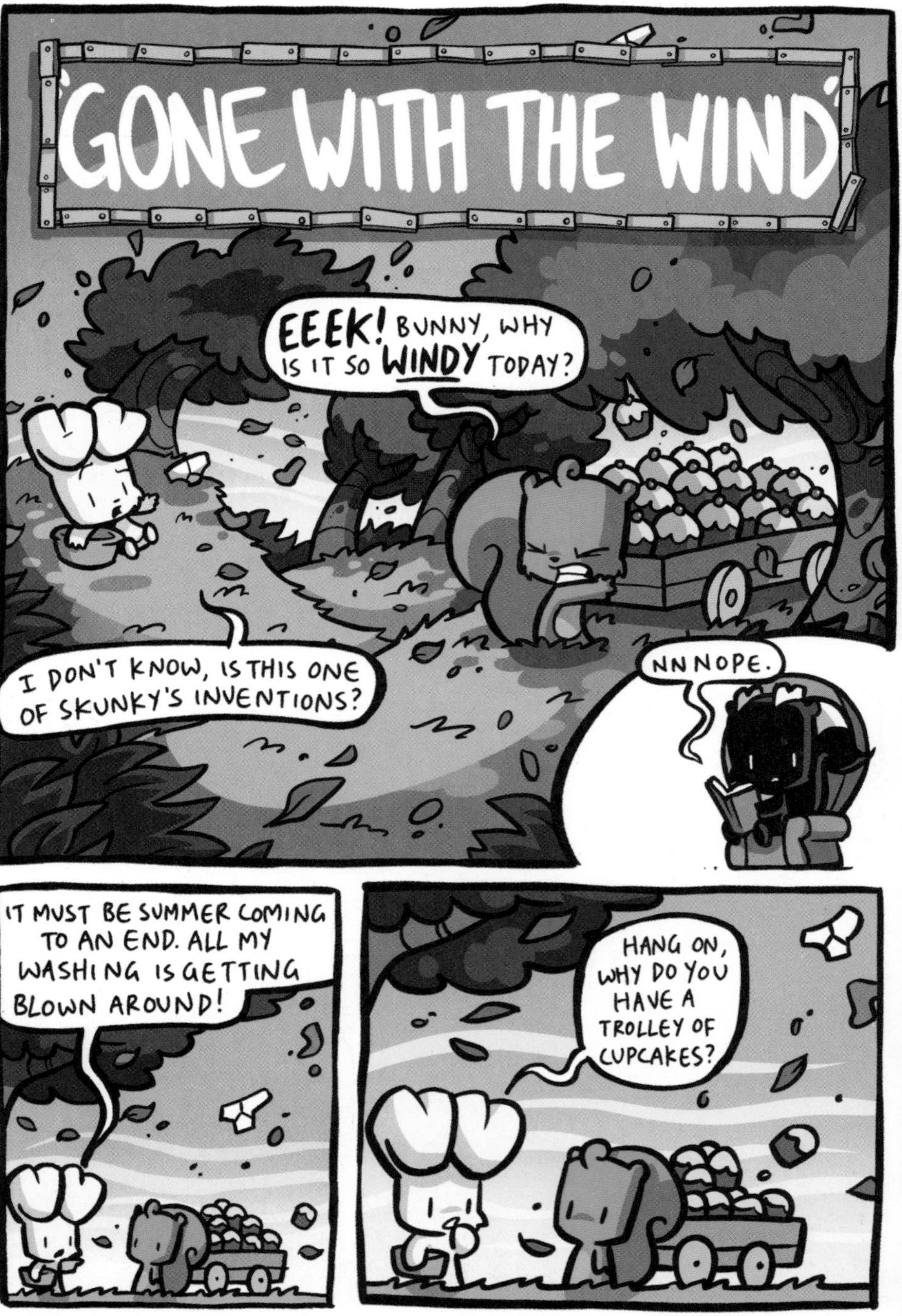
GONE WITH THE WIND
EEEK! BUNNY, WHY IS IT SO WINDY TODAY?
I DON'T KNOW, IS THIS ONE OF SKUNKY'S INVENTIONS?
NNNOPE.
IT MUST BE SUMMER COMING TO AN END. ALL MY WASHING IS GETTING BLOWN AROUND!
HANG ON, WHY DO YOU HAVE A TROLLEY OF CUPCAKES?

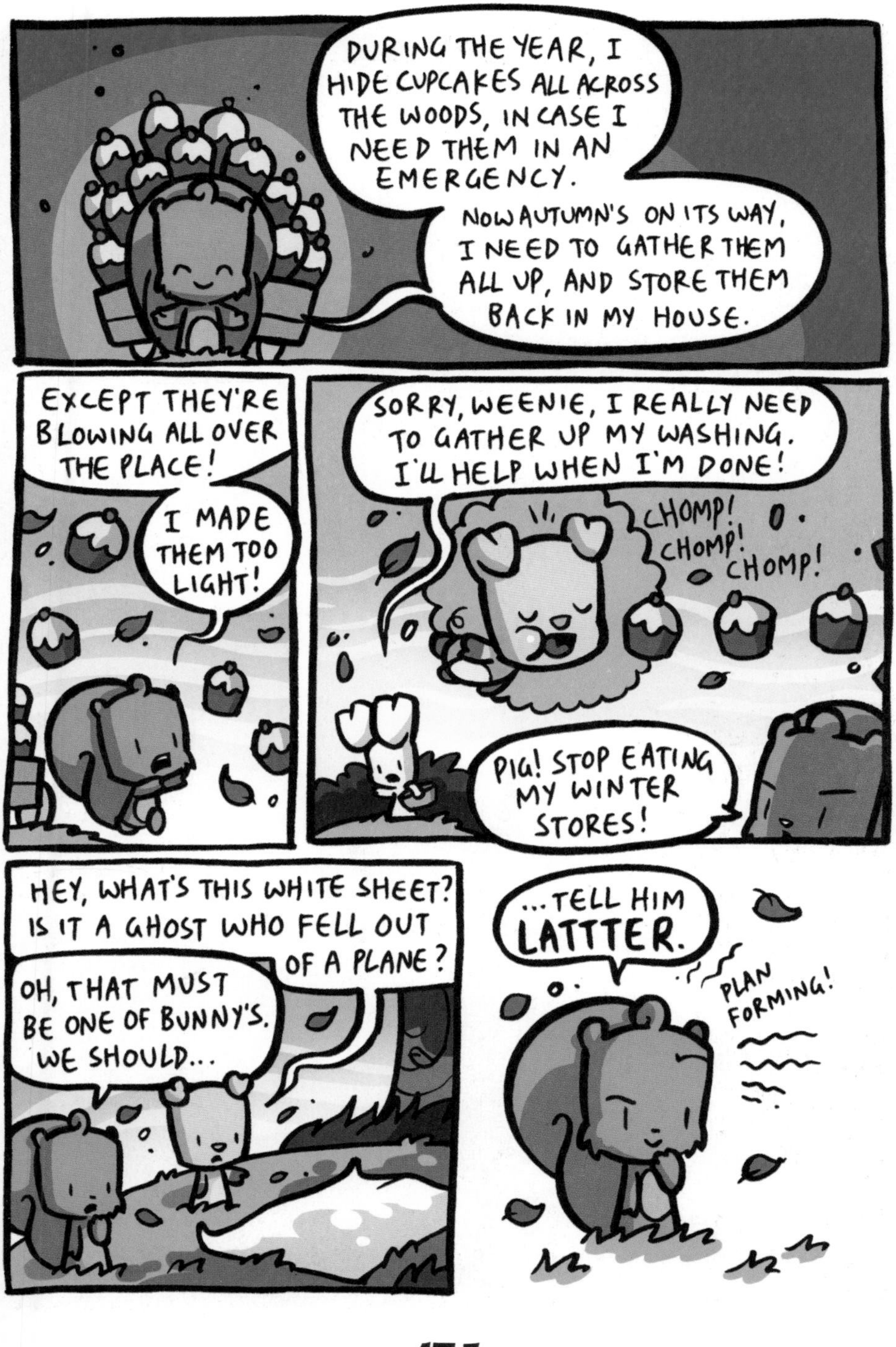
DURING THE YEAR, I HIDE CUPCAKES ALL ACROSS THE WOODS, IN CASE I NEED THEM IN AN EMERGENCY.
NOW AUTUMN'S ON ITS WAY, I NEED TO GATHER THEM ALL UP, AND STORE THEM BACK IN MY HOUSE.
EXCEPT THEY'RE BLOWING ALL OVER THE PLACE!
I MADE THEM TOO LIGHT!
SORRY, WEENIE, I REALLY NEED TO GATHER UP MY WASHING. I'LL HELP WHEN I'M DONE!
CHOMP! CHOMP! CHOMP!
PIG! STOP EATING MY WINTER STORES!
HEY, WHAT'S THIS WHITE SHEET? IS IT A GHOST WHO FELL OUT OF A PLANE?
OH, THAT MUST BE ONE OF BUNNY'S. WE SHOULD...
...TELL HIM LATTTER.
PLAN FORMING!

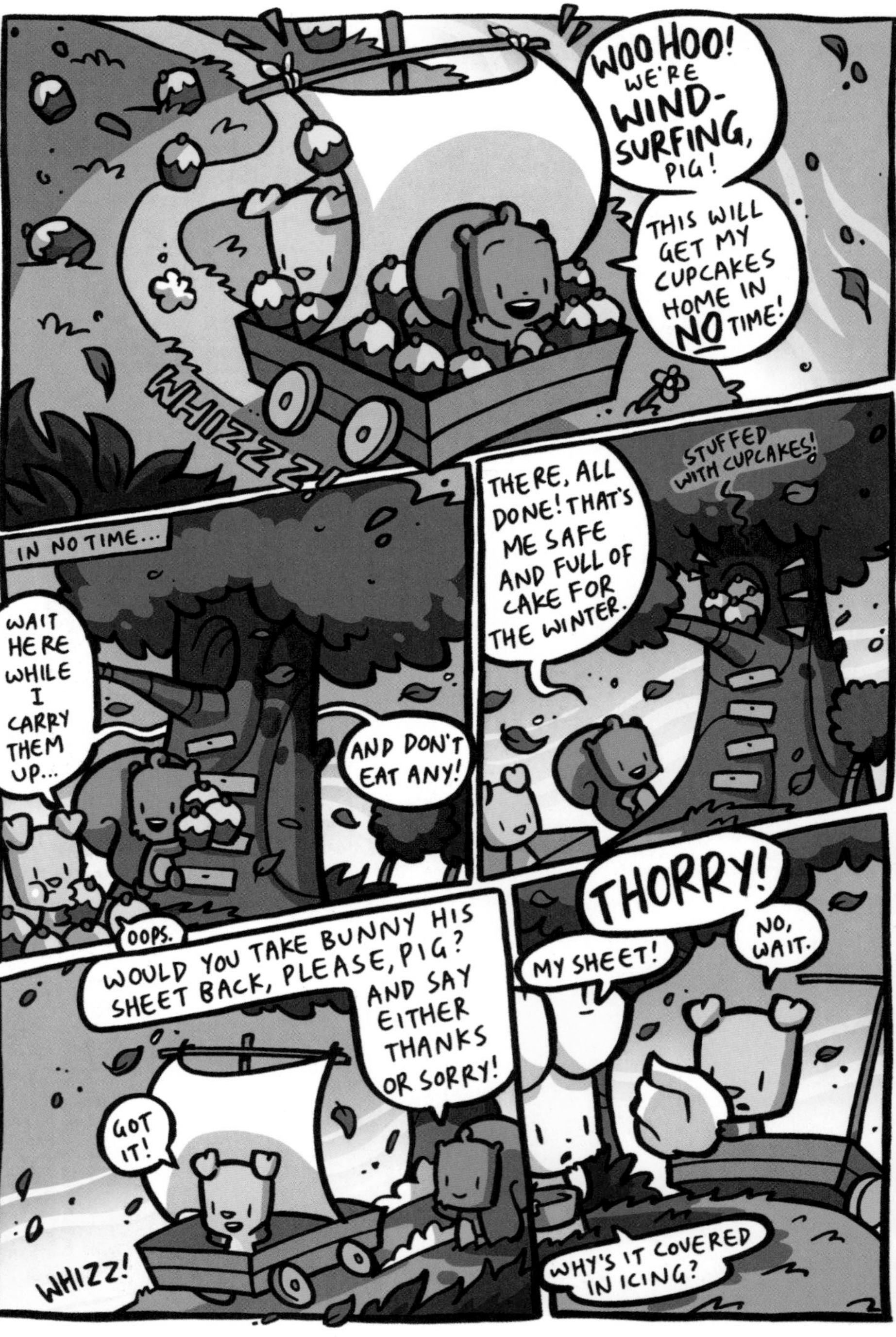
WOO HOO! WE'RE WIND-SURFING, PIG!
THIS WILL GET MY CUPCAKES HOME IN NO TIME!
WHIZZZZ!
IN NO TIME...
WAIT HERE WHILE I CARRY THEM UP...
AND DON'T EAT ANY!
OOPS.
THERE, ALL DONE! THAT'S ME SAFE AND FULL OF CAKE FOR THE WINTER.
STUFFED WITH CUPCAKES!
WOULD YOU TAKE BUNNY HIS SHEET BACK, PLEASE, PIG?
AND SAY EITHER THANKS OR SORRY!
GOT IT!
WHIZZ!
THORRY!
MY SHEET!
NO, WAIT.
WHY'S IT COVERED IN ICING?

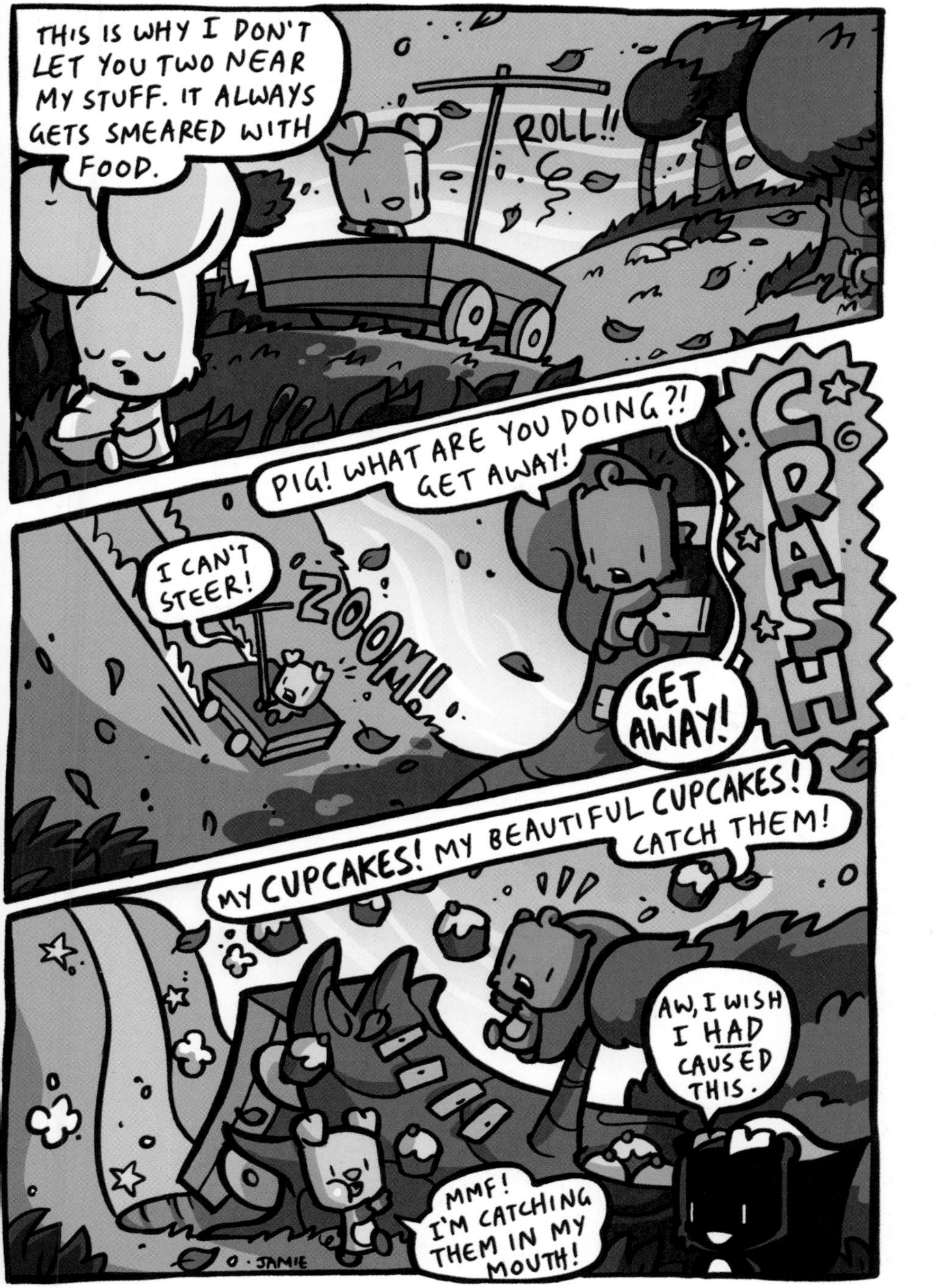
THIS IS WHY I DON'T LET YOU TWO NEAR MY STUFF. IT ALWAYS GETS SMEARED WITH FOOD.
ROLL!!
PIG! WHAT ARE YOU DOING?! GET AWAY!
CRASH
I CAN'T STEER!
ZOOM!
GET AWAY!
MY CUPCAKES! MY BEAUTIFUL CUPCAKES!
CATCH THEM!
AW, I WISH I HAD CAUSED THIS.
MMF! I'M CATCHING THEM IN MY MOUTH!
JAMIE

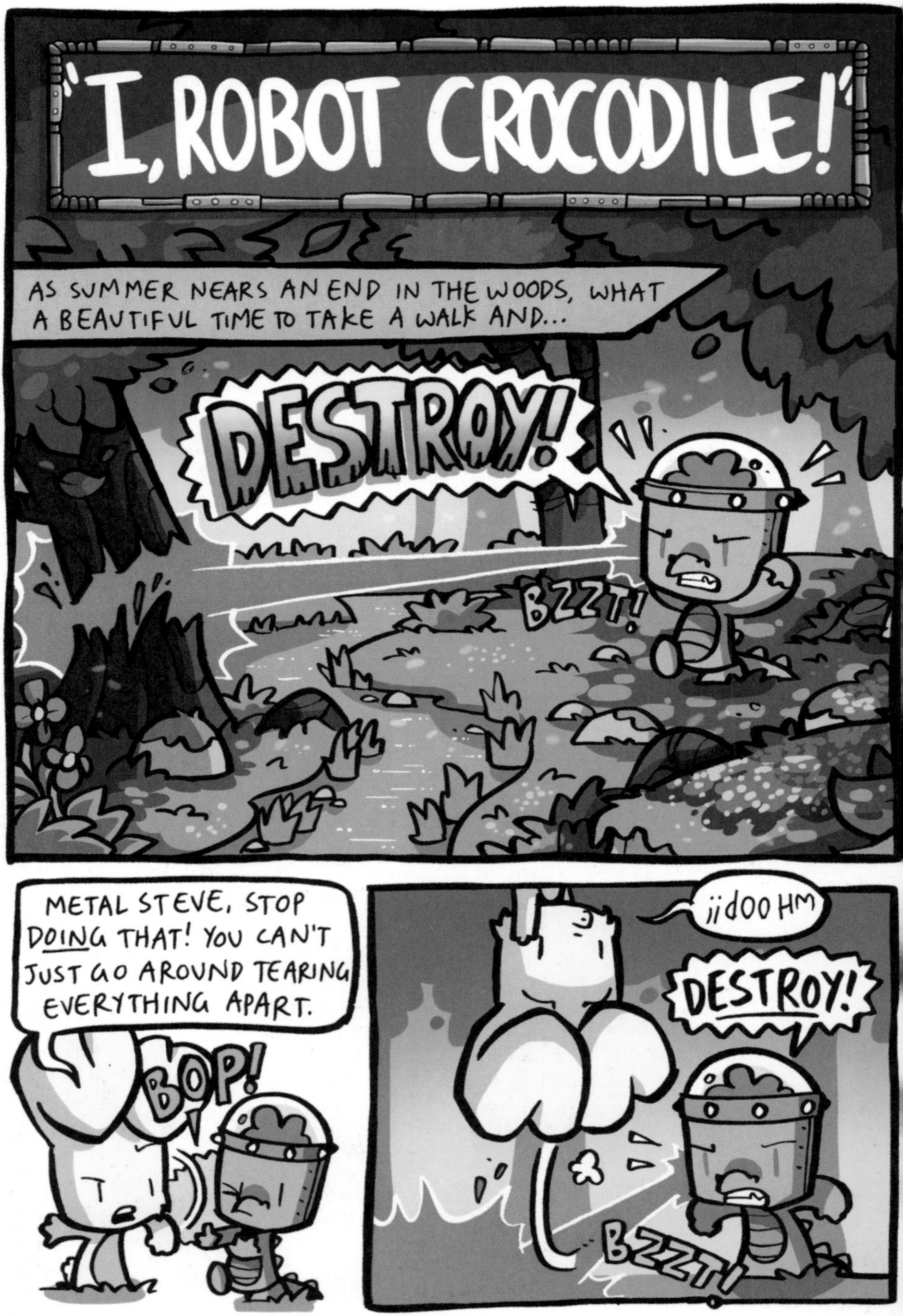
"I, ROBOT CROCODILE!"
AS SUMMER NEARS AN END IN THE WOODS, WHAT A BEAUTIFUL TIME TO TAKE A WALK AND...
DESTROY!
BZZT!
METAL STEVE, STOP DOING THAT! YOU CAN'T JUST GO AROUND TEARING EVERYTHING APART.
BOP!
¡¡dOOHM
DESTROY!
BZZT!

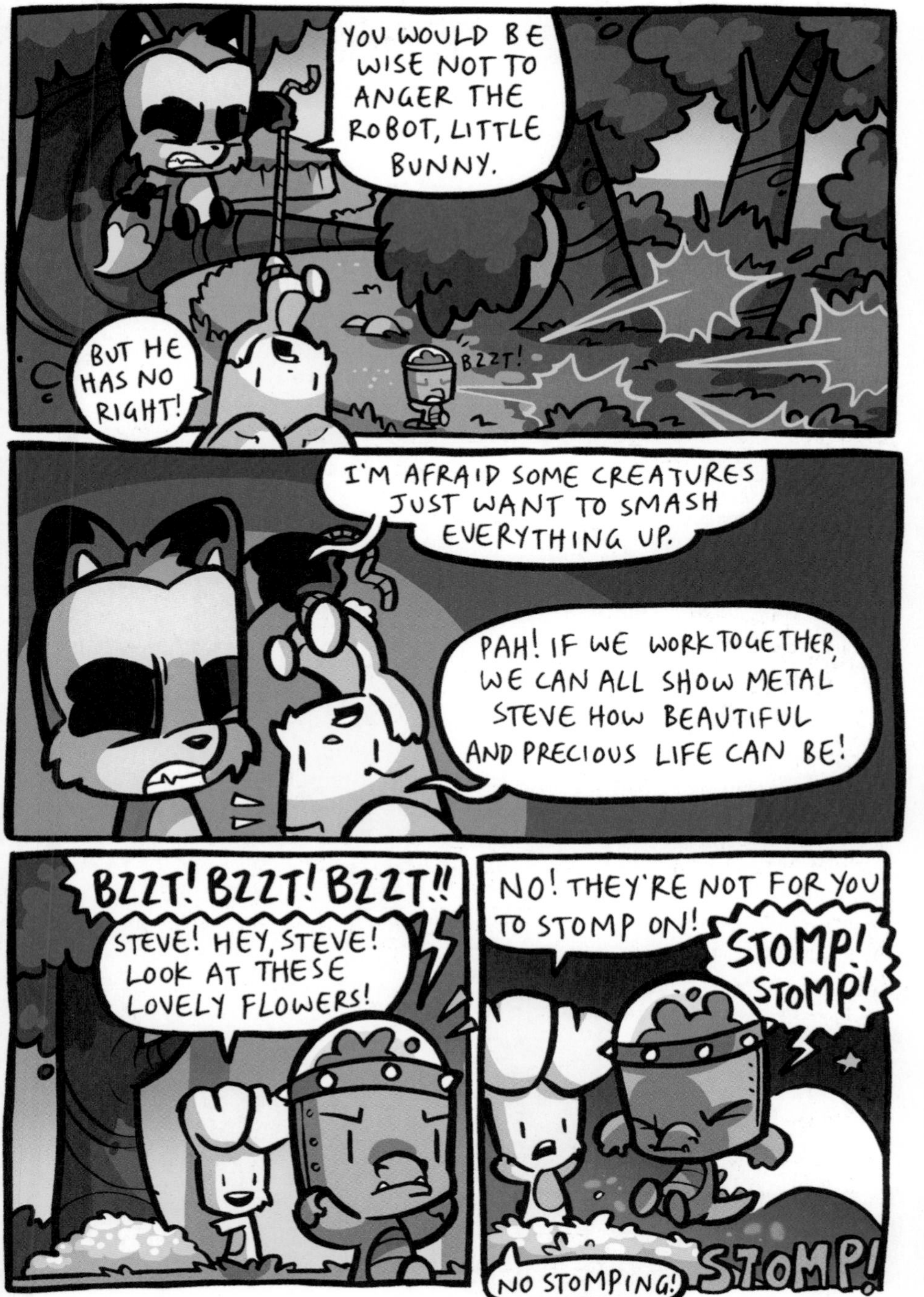
YOU WOULD BE WISE NOT TO ANGER THE ROBOT, LITTLE BUNNY.
BUT HE HAS NO RIGHT!
BZZT!
I'M AFRAID SOME CREATURES JUST WANT TO SMASH EVERYTHING UP.
PAH! IF WE WORK TOGETHER, WE CAN ALL SHOW METAL STEVE HOW BEAUTIFUL AND PRECIOUS LIFE CAN BE!
BZZT! BZZT! BZZT!!
STEVE! HEY, STEVE! LOOK AT THESE LOVELY FLOWERS!
NO! THEY'RE NOT FOR YOU TO STOMP ON!
STOMP! STOMP!
NO STOMPING!
STOMP!

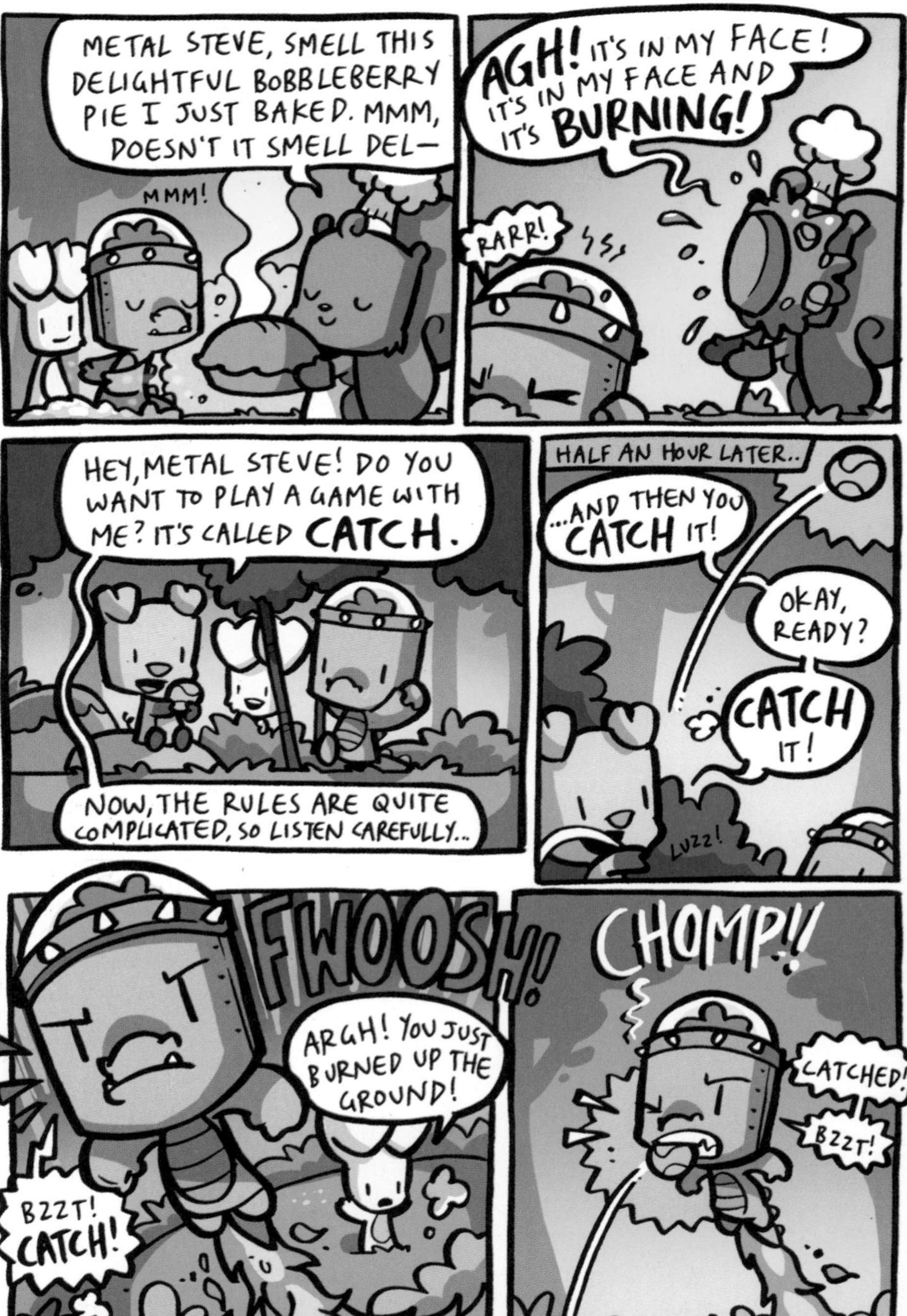
METAL STEVE, SMELL THIS DELIGHTFUL BOBBLEBERRY PIE I JUST BAKED. MMM, DOESN'T IT SMELL DEL—
MMM!
AGH! IT'S IN MY FACE! IT'S IN MY FACE AND IT'S BURNING!
RARR!
HEY, METAL STEVE! DO YOU WANT TO PLAY A GAME WITH ME? IT'S CALLED CATCH.
NOW, THE RULES ARE QUITE COMPLICATED, SO LISTEN CAREFULLY...
HALF AN HOUR LATER..
...AND THEN YOU CATCH IT!
OKAY, READY?
CATCH IT!
LUZZ!
FWOOSH!
BZZT! CATCH!
ARGH! YOU JUST BURNED UP THE GROUND!
CHOMP!!
CATCHED!
BZZT!

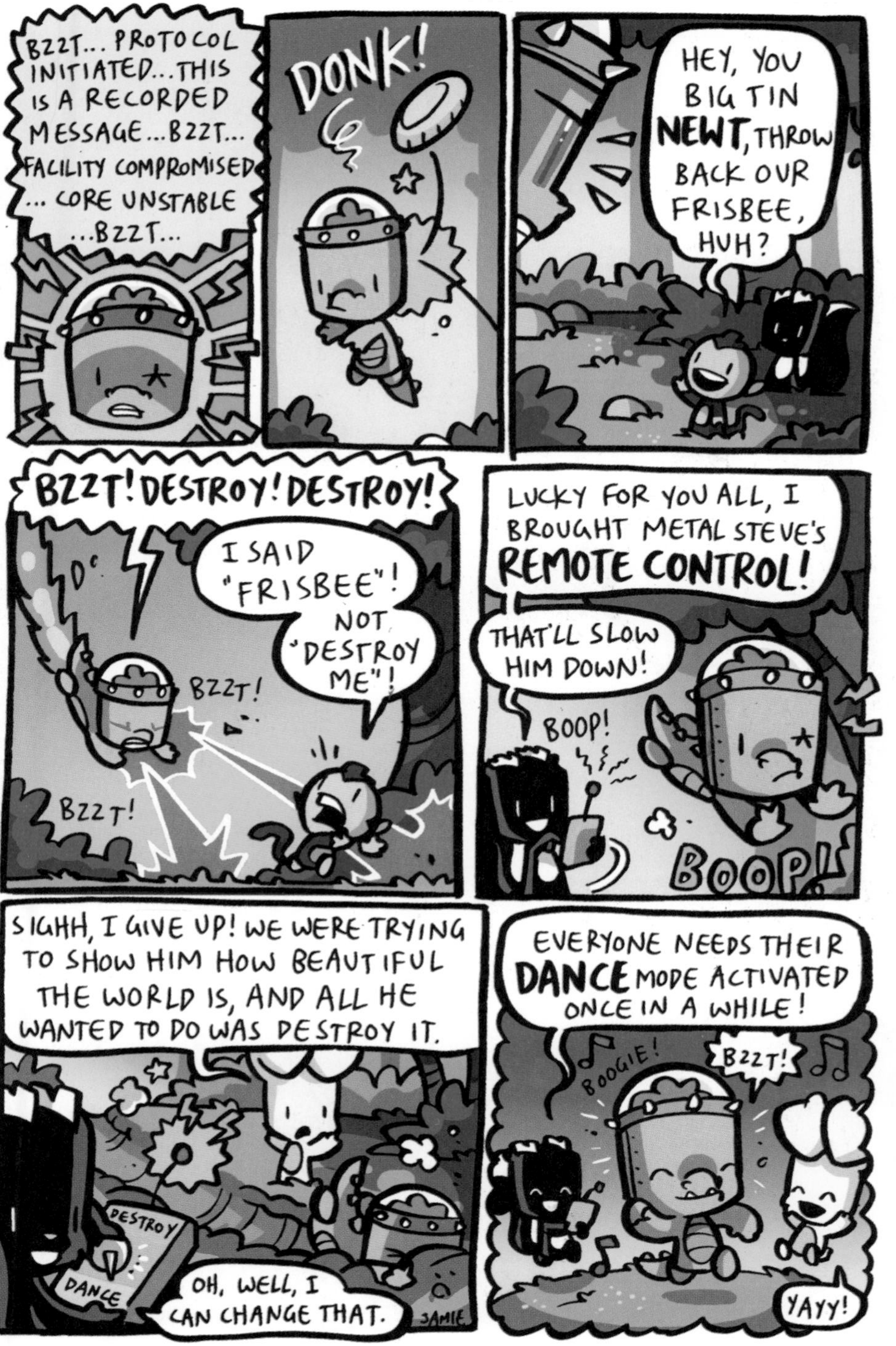
BZZT... PROTOCOL INITIATED... THIS IS A RECORDED MESSAGE... BZZT... FACILITY COMPROMISED ... CORE UNSTABLE ...BZZT...
DONK!
HEY, YOU BIG TIN NEWT, THROW BACK OUR FRISBEE, HUH?
BZZT! DESTROY! DESTROY!
D:
I SAID "FRISBEE"!
NOT "DESTROY ME"!
BZZT!
BZZT!
LUCKY FOR YOU ALL, I BROUGHT METAL STEVE'S REMOTE CONTROL!
THAT'LL SLOW HIM DOWN!
BOOP!
BOOP!
SIGHH, I GIVE UP! WE WERE TRYING TO SHOW HIM HOW BEAUTIFUL THE WORLD IS, AND ALL HE WANTED TO DO WAS DESTROY IT.
DESTROY
DANCE
OH, WELL, I CAN CHANGE THAT.
JAMIE
EVERYONE NEEDS THEIR DANCE MODE ACTIVATED ONCE IN A WHILE!
BOOGIE!
BZZT!
YAYY!

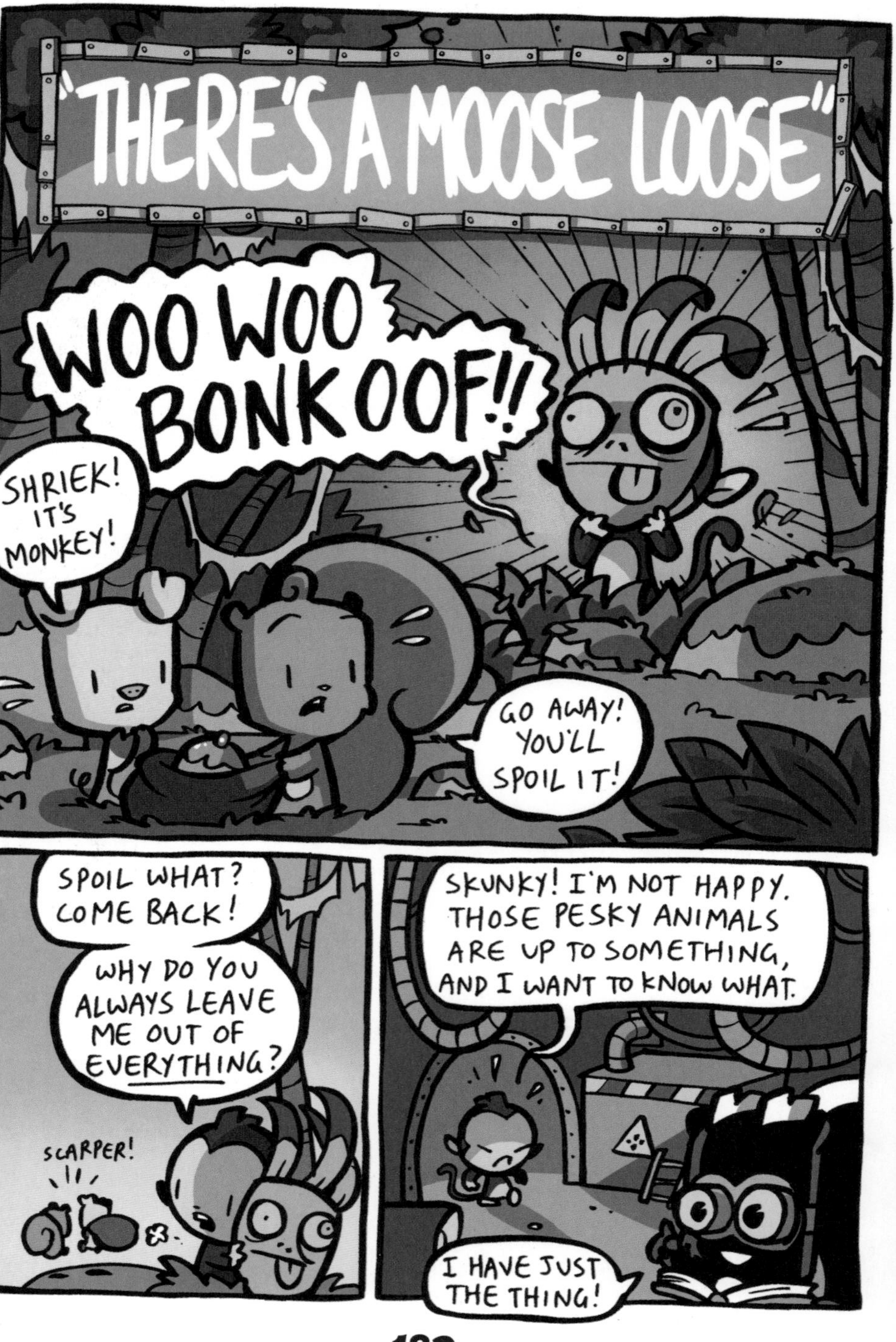
"THERE'S A MOOSE LOOSE"
WOO WOO BONKOOF!!
SHRIEK! IT'S MONKEY!
GO AWAY! YOU'LL SPOIL IT!
SPOIL WHAT? COME BACK!
WHY DO YOU ALWAYS LEAVE ME OUT OF EVERYTHING?
SCARPER!
SKUNKY! I'M NOT HAPPY. THOSE PESKY ANIMALS ARE UP TO SOMETHING, AND I WANT TO KNOW WHAT.
I HAVE JUST THE THING!

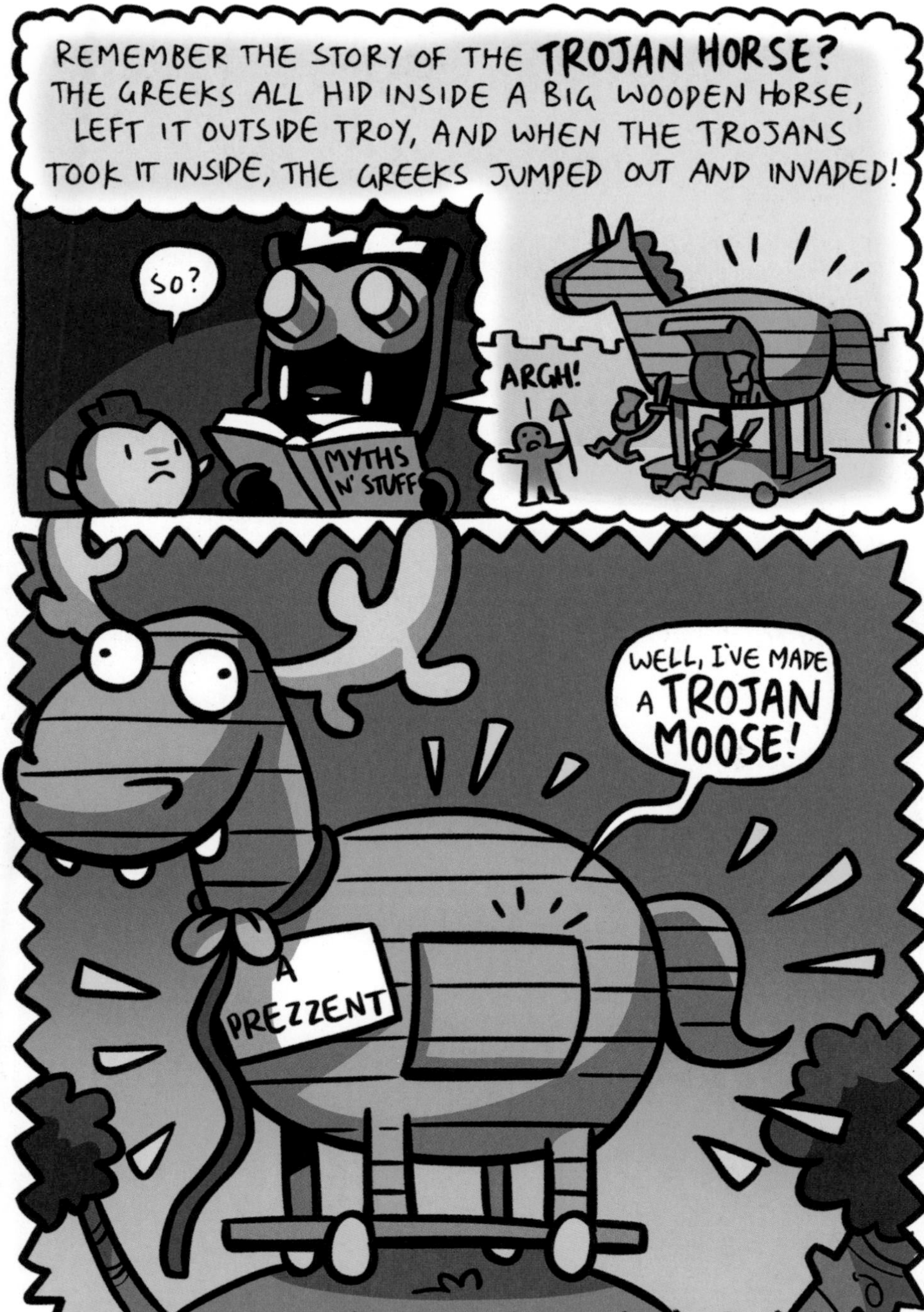
REMEMBER THE STORY OF THE TROJAN HORSE? THE GREEKS ALL HID INSIDE A BIG WOODEN HORSE, LEFT IT OUTSIDE TROY, AND WHEN THE TROJANS TOOK IT INSIDE, THE GREEKS JUMPED OUT AND INVADED!
SO?
MYTHS N' STUFF
ARGH!
WELL, I'VE MADE A TROJAN MOOSE!
A PREZZENT

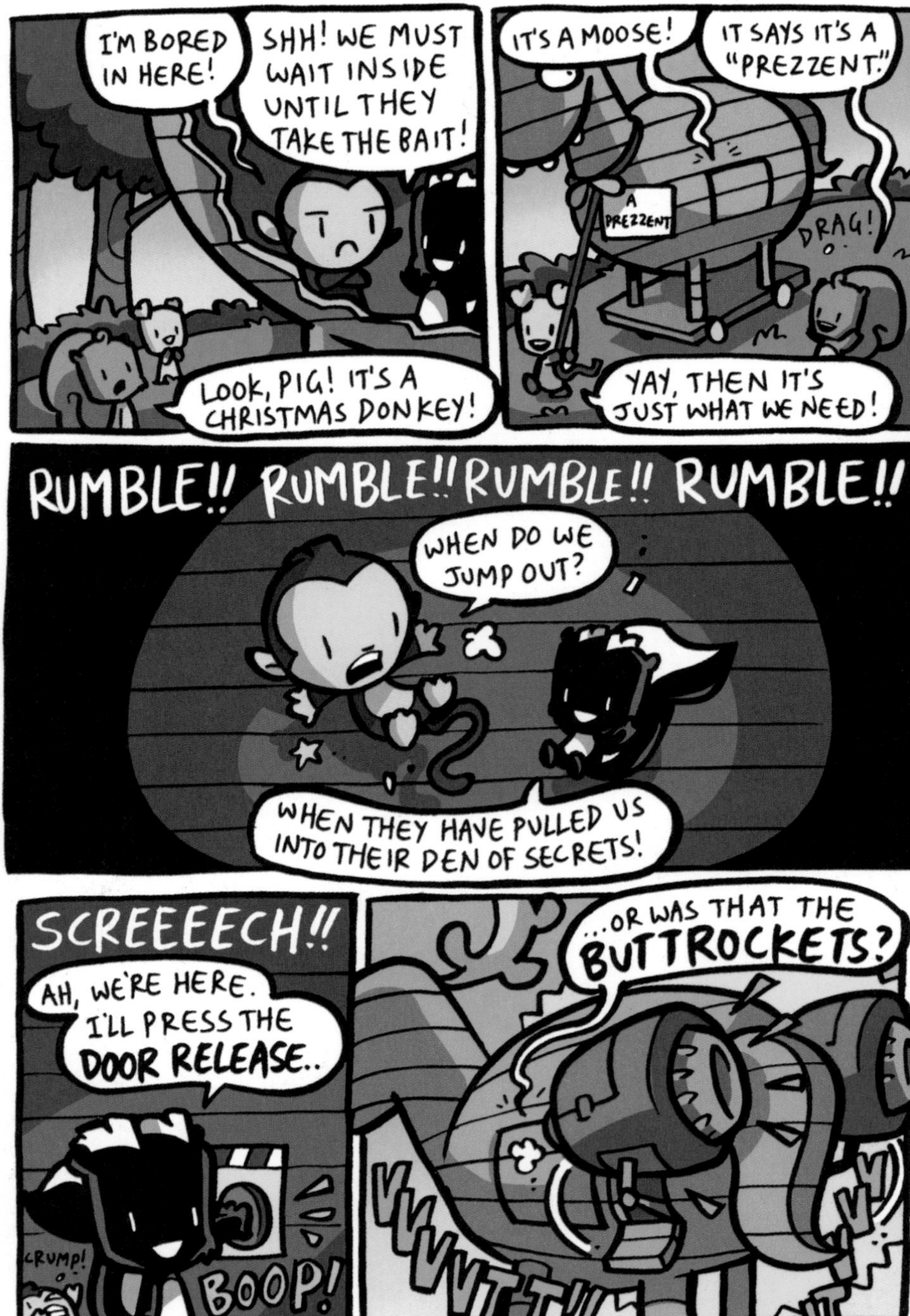
I'M BORED IN HERE!
SHH! WE MUST WAIT INSIDE UNTIL THEY TAKE THE BAIT!
LOOK, PIG! IT'S A CHRISTMAS DONKEY!
IT'S A MOOSE!
IT SAYS IT'S A "PREZZENT."
A PREZZENT
DRAG!
YAY, THEN IT'S JUST WHAT WE NEED!
RUMBLE!! RUMBLE!! RUMBLE!! RUMBLE!!
WHEN DO WE JUMP OUT?
WHEN THEY HAVE PULLED US INTO THEIR DEN OF SECRETS!
SCREEEECH!!
AH, WE'RE HERE. I'LL PRESS THE DOOR RELEASE..
CRUMP!
BOOP!
...OR WAS THAT THE BUTTROCKETS?
VVVVVTTT!!!

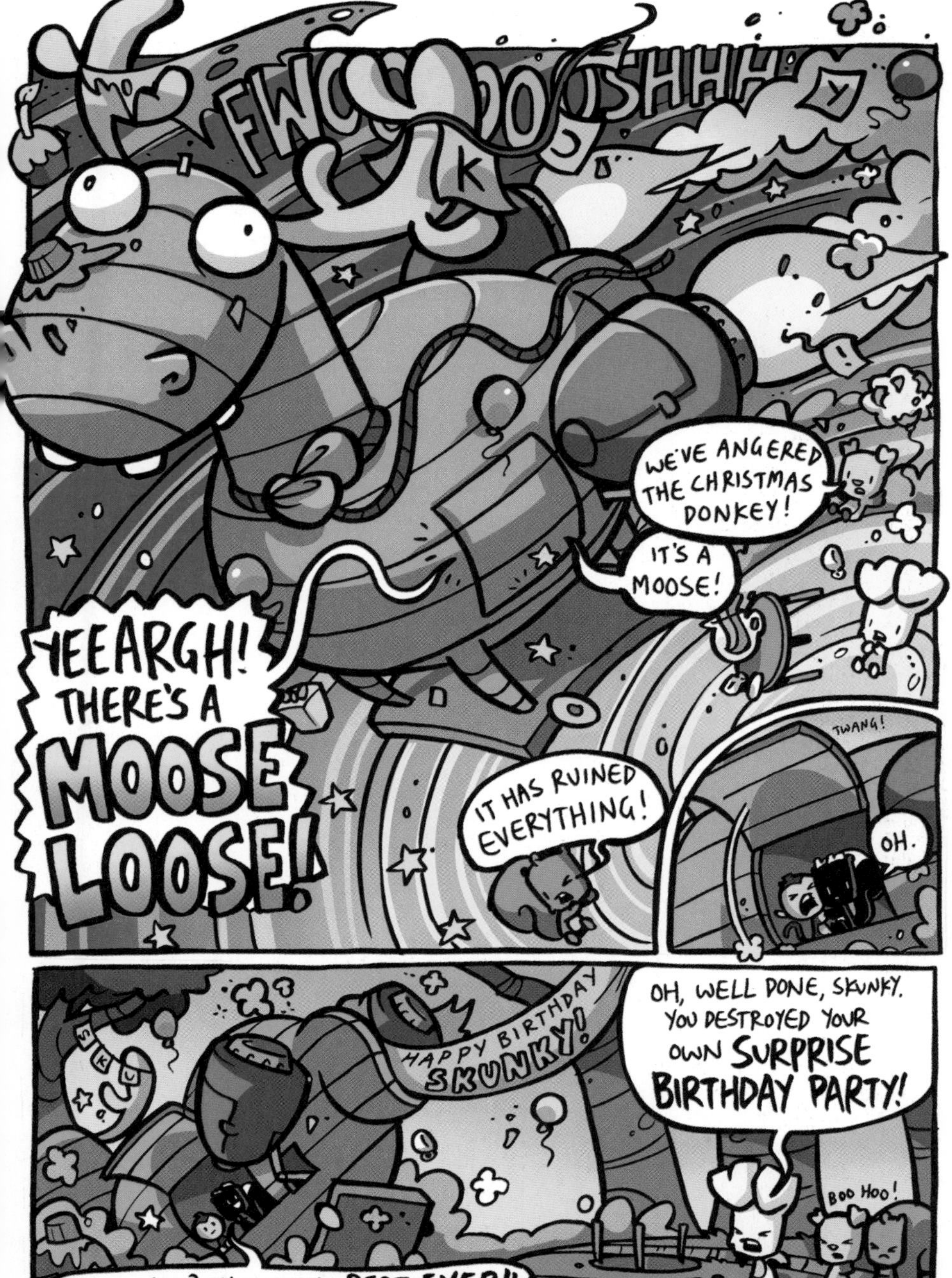

FWOOOOOSHHH
WE'VE ANGERED THE CHRISTMAS DONKEY!
IT'S A MOOSE!
YEEARGH! THERE'S A MOOSE LOOSE!
TWANG!
IT HAS RUINED EVERYTHING!
OH.
HAPPY BIRTHDAY SKUNKY!
OH, WELL DONE, SKUNKY. YOU DESTROYED YOUR OWN SURPRISE BIRTHDAY PARTY!
BOO HOO!
DESTROYED? THIS IS THE BEST EVER!!

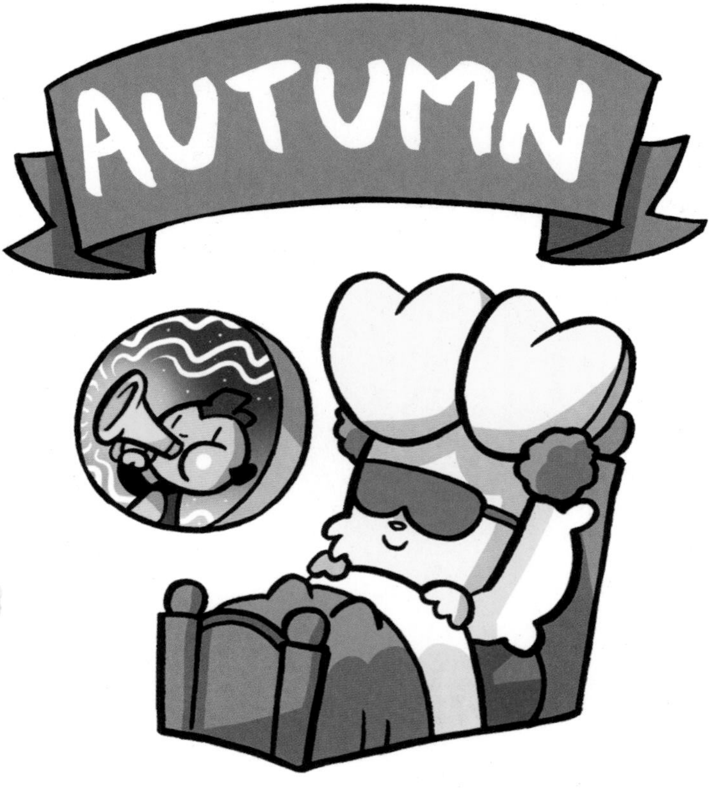
AUTUMN

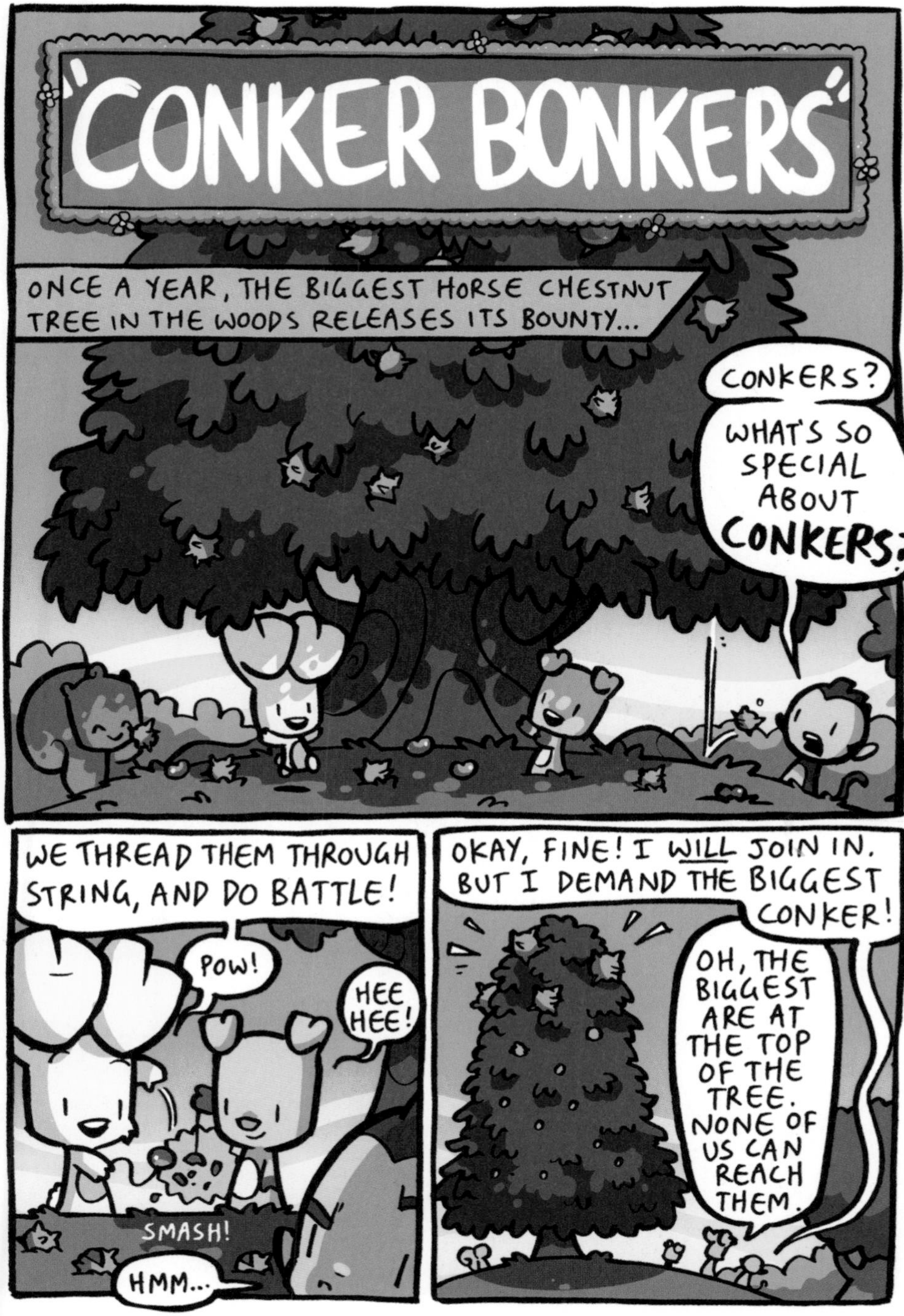
"CONKER BONKERS"
ONCE A YEAR, THE BIGGEST HORSE CHESTNUT TREE IN THE WOODS RELEASES ITS BOUNTY...
CONKERS?
WHAT'S SO SPECIAL ABOUT CONKERS?
WE THREAD THEM THROUGH STRING, AND DO BATTLE!
POW!
HEE HEE!
SMASH!
HMM...
OKAY, FINE! I WILL JOIN IN. BUT I DEMAND THE BIGGEST CONKER!
OH, THE BIGGEST ARE AT THE TOP OF THE TREE. NONE OF US CAN REACH THEM.

CONKERS ARE THE BIG SEEDS OF CHESTNUT TREES. THE GAME "CONKERS" IS PLAYED IN GREAT BRITAIN, IRELAND, AND NOVA SCOTIA, CANADA. AND IN THESE WOODS APPARENTLY.

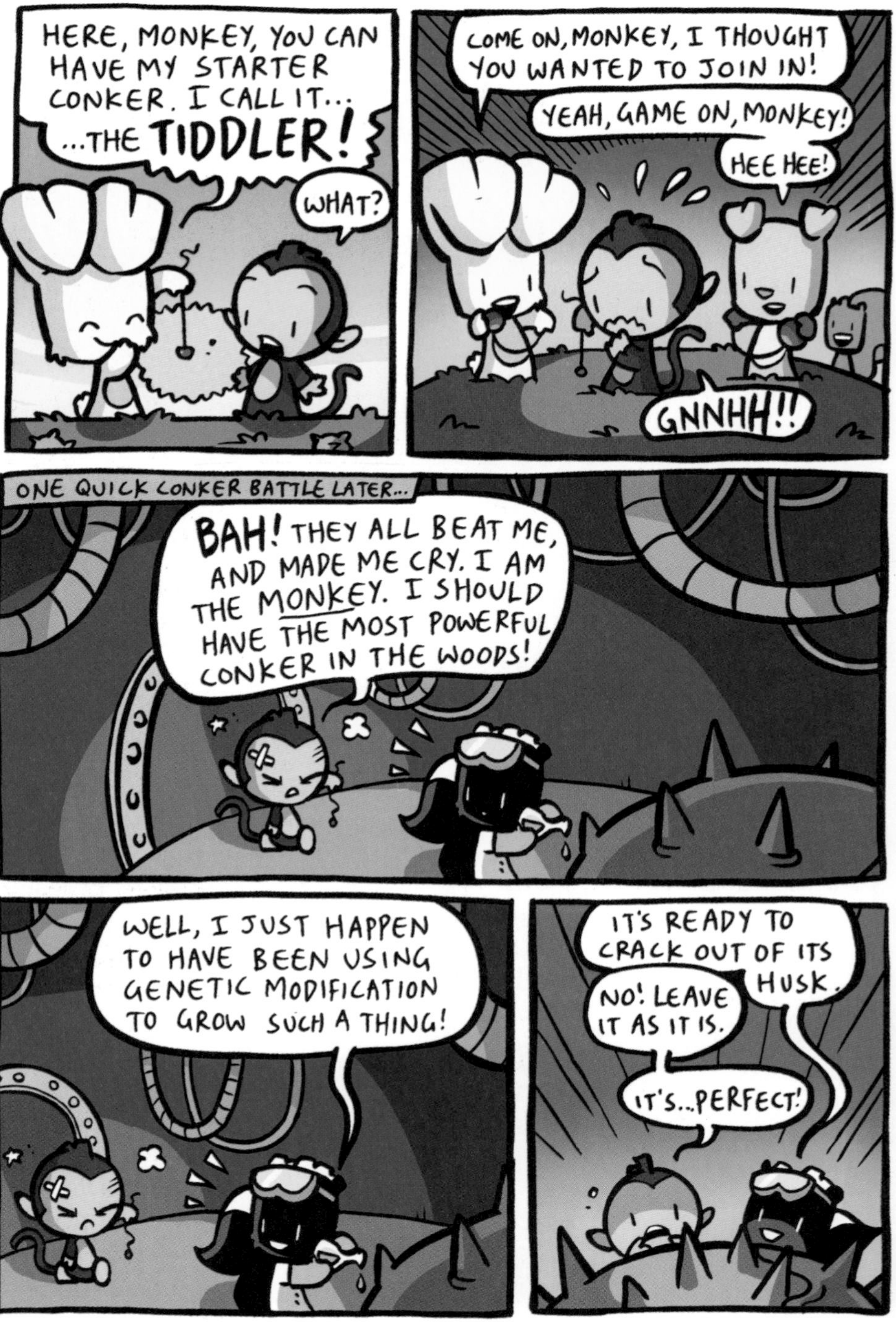

HERE, MONKEY, YOU CAN HAVE MY STARTER CONKER. I CALL IT...
...THE TIDDLER!
WHAT?
COME ON, MONKEY, I THOUGHT YOU WANTED TO JOIN IN!
YEAH, GAME ON, MONKEY!
HEE HEE!
GNNHH!!
ONE QUICK CONKER BATTLE LATER...
BAH! THEY ALL BEAT ME, AND MADE ME CRY. I AM THE MONKEY. I SHOULD HAVE THE MOST POWERFUL CONKER IN THE WOODS!
WELL, I JUST HAPPEN TO HAVE BEEN USING GENETIC MODIFICATION TO GROW SUCH A THING!
IT'S READY TO CRACK OUT OF ITS HUSK.
NO! LEAVE IT AS IT IS.
IT'S...PERFECT!

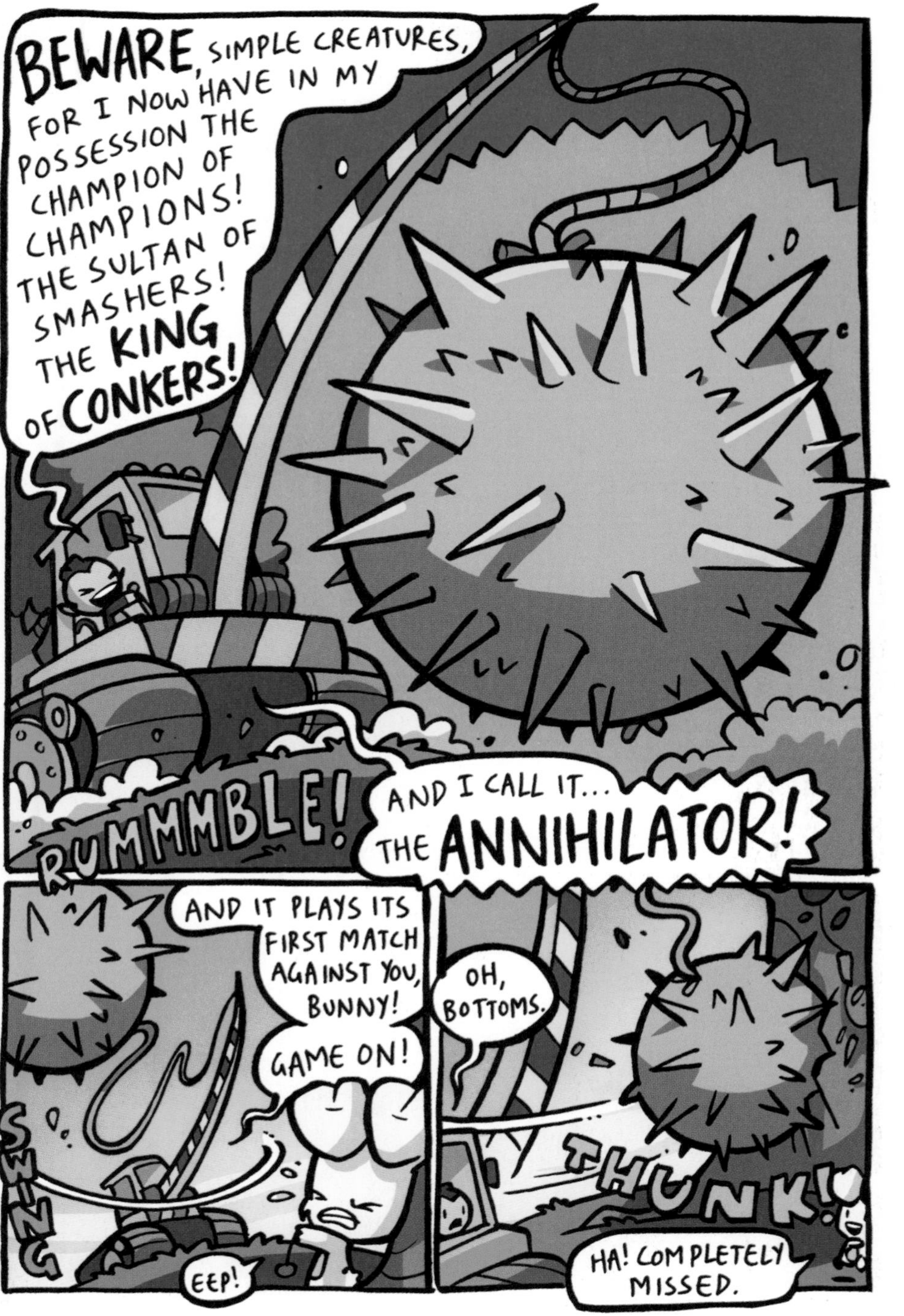
BEWARE, SIMPLE CREATURES, FOR I NOW HAVE IN MY POSSESSION THE CHAMPION OF CHAMPIONS! THE SULTAN OF SMASHERS! THE KING OF CONKERS!
RUMMMBLE!
AND I CALL IT... THE ANNIHILATOR!
AND IT PLAYS ITS FIRST MATCH AGAINST YOU, BUNNY!
GAME ON!
SWING
EEP!
OH, BOTTOMS.
THUNK!
HA! COMPLETELY MISSED.

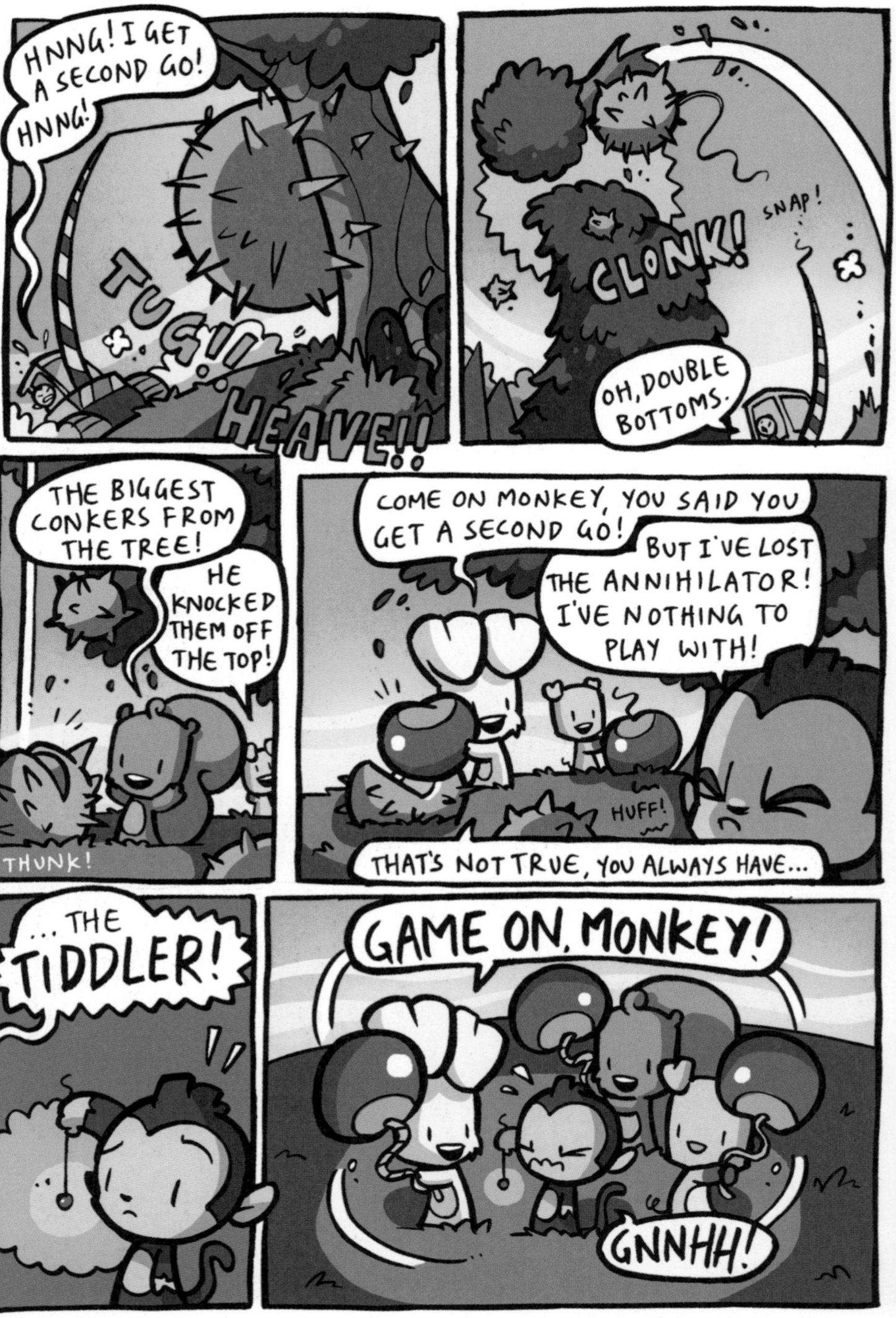
HNNG! I GET A SECOND GO! HNNG!
TUG!!
HEAVE!!
CLONK!
SNAP!
OH, DOUBLE BOTTOMS.
THE BIGGEST CONKERS FROM THE TREE!
HE KNOCKED THEM OFF THE TOP!
THUNK!
COME ON MONKEY, YOU SAID YOU GET A SECOND GO!
BUT I'VE LOST THE ANNIHILATOR! I'VE NOTHING TO PLAY WITH!
HUFF!
THAT'S NOT TRUE, YOU ALWAYS HAVE...
... THE TIDDLER!
GAME ON, MONKEY!
GNNHH!

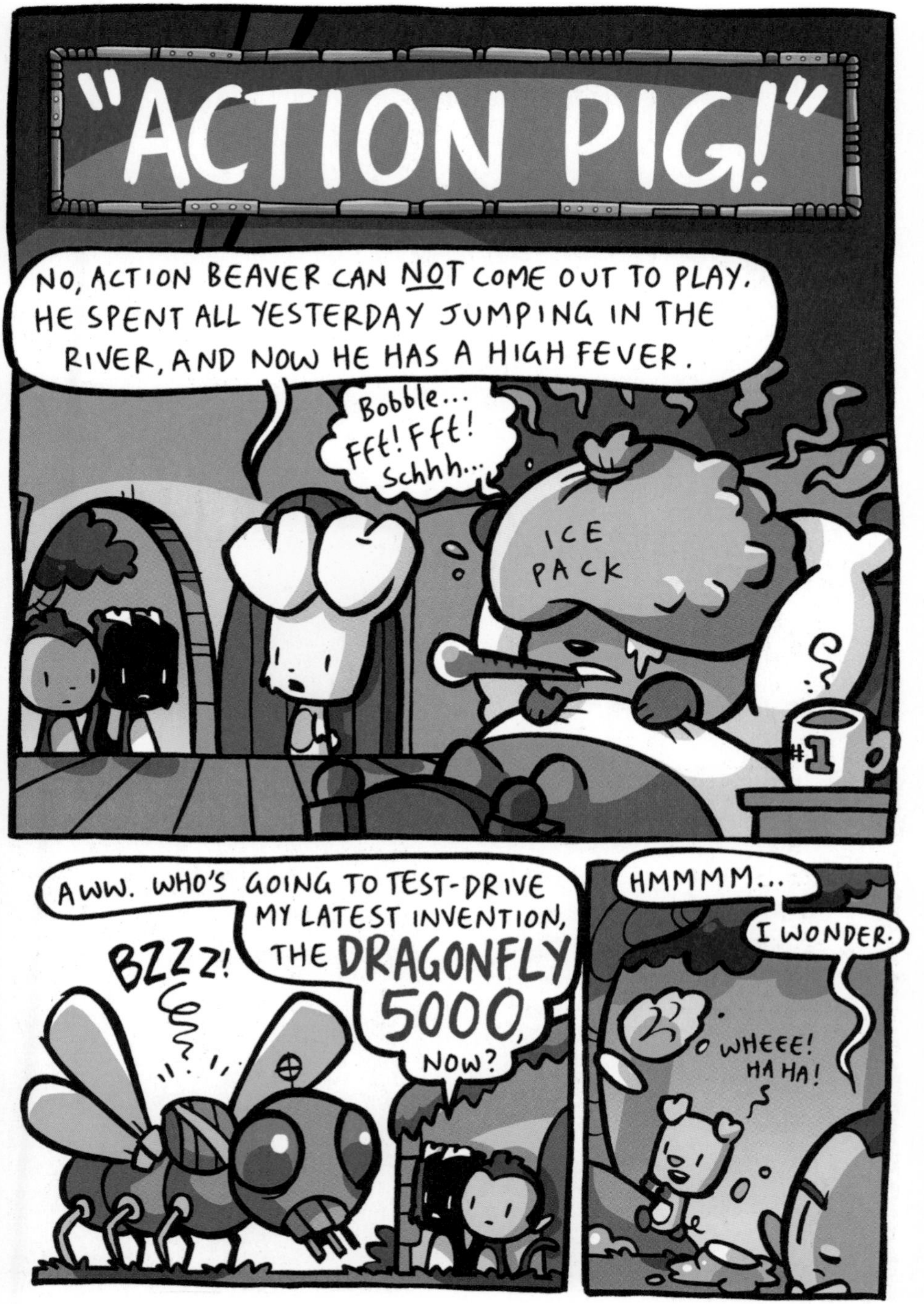
"ACTION PIG!"
NO, ACTION BEAVER CAN NOT COME OUT TO PLAY. HE SPENT ALL YESTERDAY JUMPING IN THE RIVER, AND NOW HE HAS A HIGH FEVER.
Bobble... Fft! Fft! Schhh...
ICE PACK
#1
AWW. WHO'S GOING TO TEST-DRIVE MY LATEST INVENTION, THE DRAGONFLY 5000, NOW?
BZZz!
HMMMM...
I WONDER.
WHEEE! HA HA!

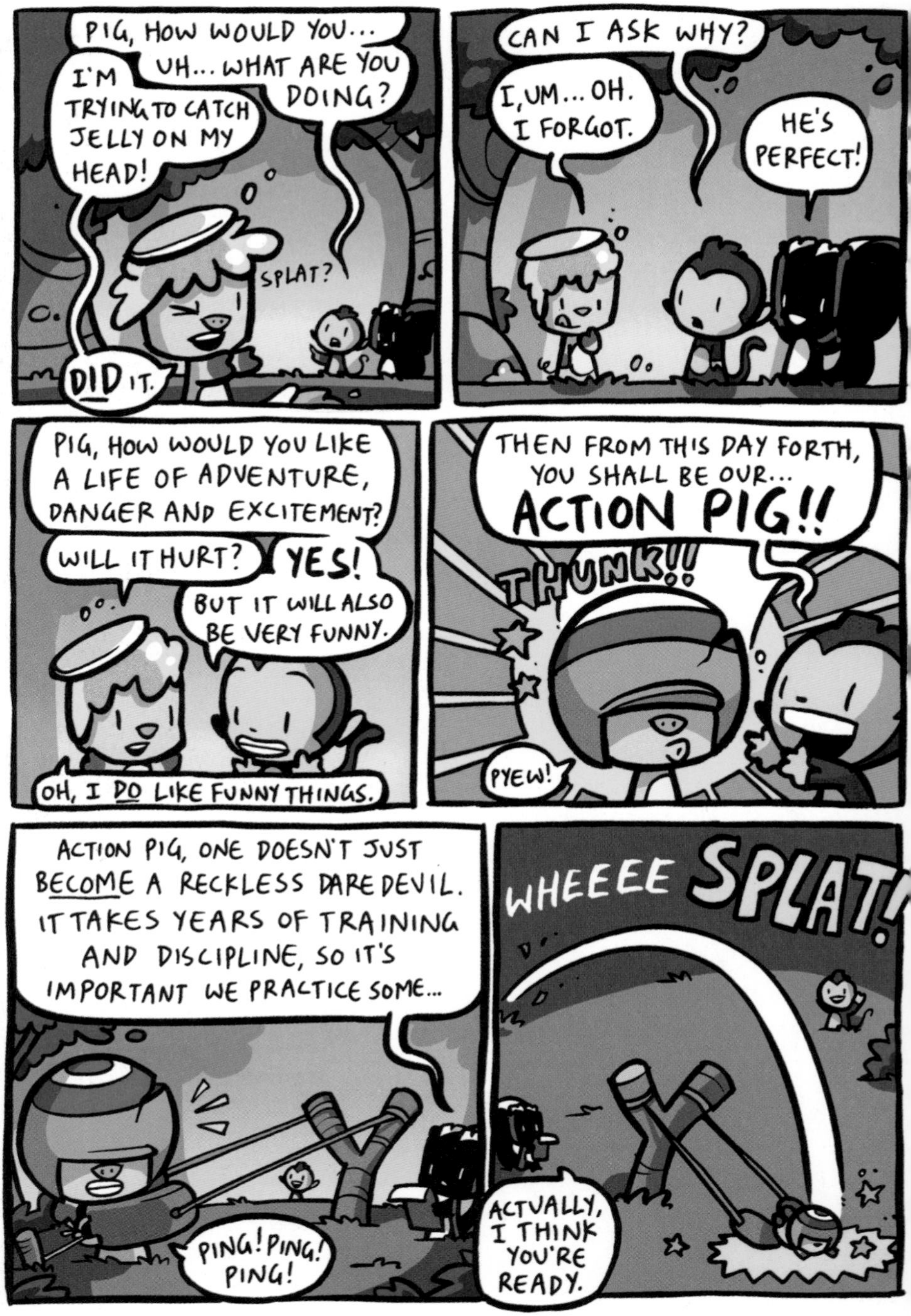
PIG, HOW WOULD YOU...
UH... WHAT ARE YOU DOING?
I'M TRYING TO CATCH JELLY ON MY HEAD!
SPLAT?
DID IT.
CAN I ASK WHY?
I, UM... OH. I FORGOT.
HE'S PERFECT!
PIG, HOW WOULD YOU LIKE A LIFE OF ADVENTURE, DANGER AND EXCITEMENT?
WILL IT HURT?
YES!
BUT IT WILL ALSO BE VERY FUNNY.
OH, I DO LIKE FUNNY THINGS.
THEN FROM THIS DAY FORTH, YOU SHALL BE OUR...
ACTION PIG!!
THUNK!!
PYEW!
ACTION PIG, ONE DOESN'T JUST BECOME A RECKLESS DAREDEVIL. IT TAKES YEARS OF TRAINING AND DISCIPLINE, SO IT'S IMPORTANT WE PRACTICE SOME...
PING! PING! PING!
WHEEEE SPLAT!
ACTUALLY, I THINK YOU'RE READY.

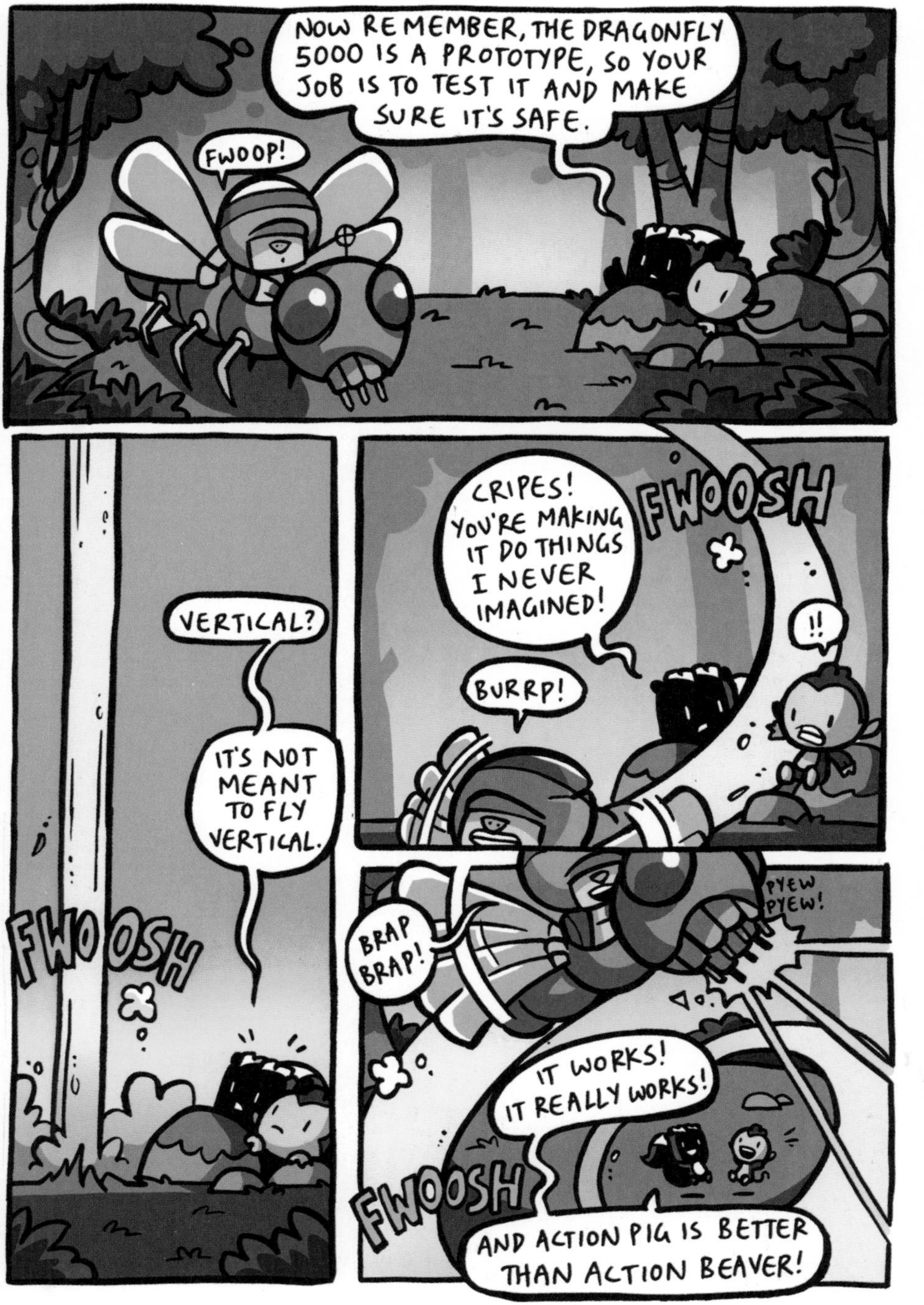
NOW REMEMBER, THE DRAGONFLY 5000 IS A PROTOTYPE, SO YOUR JOB IS TO TEST IT AND MAKE SURE IT'S SAFE.
FWOOP!
VERTICAL?
IT'S NOT MEANT TO FLY VERTICAL.
FWOOSH
CRIPES! YOU'RE MAKING IT DO THINGS I NEVER IMAGINED!
FWOOSH
!!
BURRP!
BRAP BRAP!
PYEW PYEW!
IT WORKS! IT REALLY WORKS!
FWOOSH
AND ACTION PIG IS BETTER THAN ACTION BEAVER!

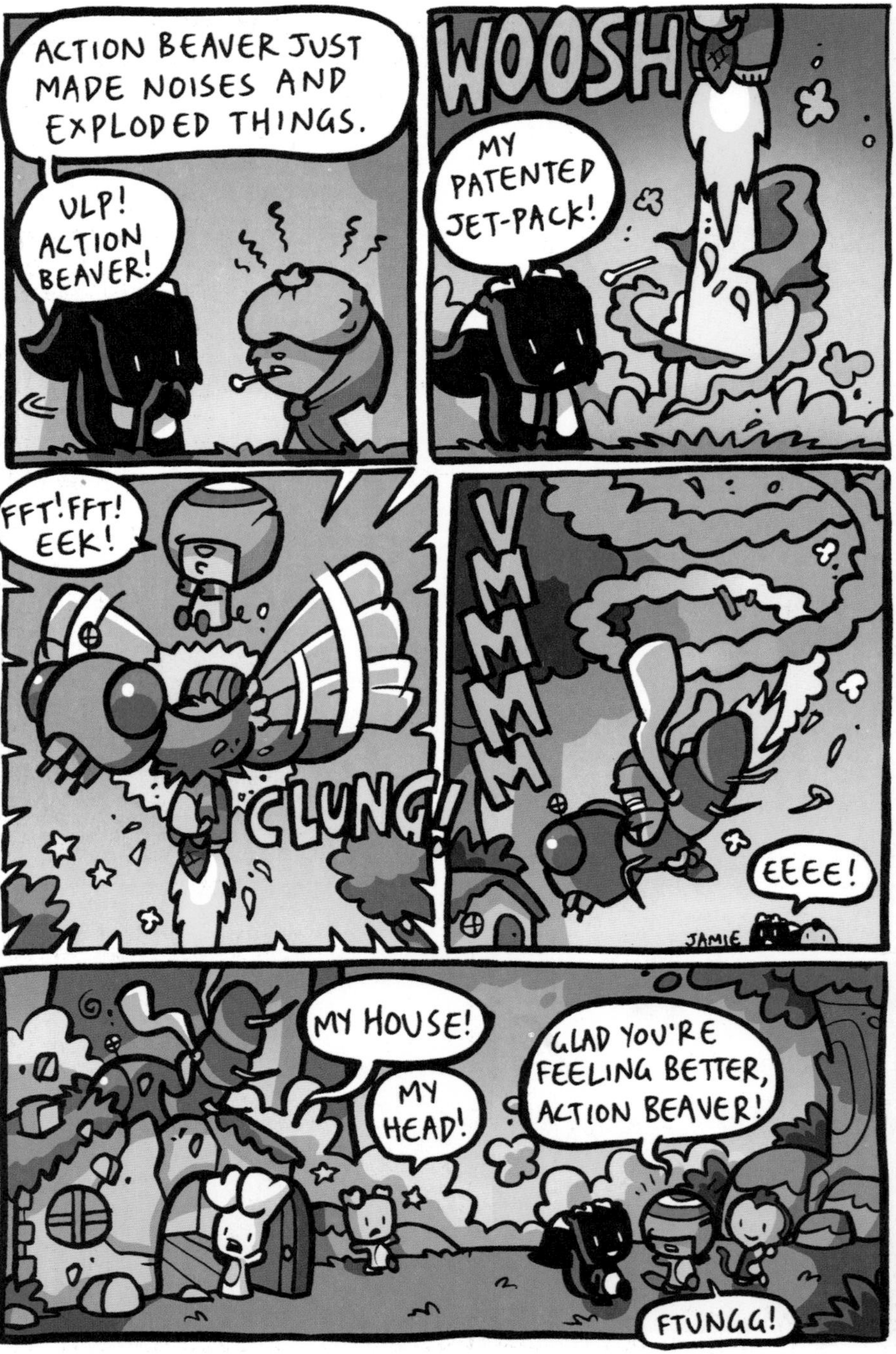
ACTION BEAVER JUST MADE NOISES AND EXPLODED THINGS.
ULP! ACTION BEAVER!
WOOSH
MY PATENTED JET-PACK!
FFT! FFT! EEK!
CLUNG!
VMMMMMM
EEEE!
JAMIE
MY HOUSE!
MY HEAD!
GLAD YOU'RE FEELING BETTER, ACTION BEAVER!
FTUNGG!

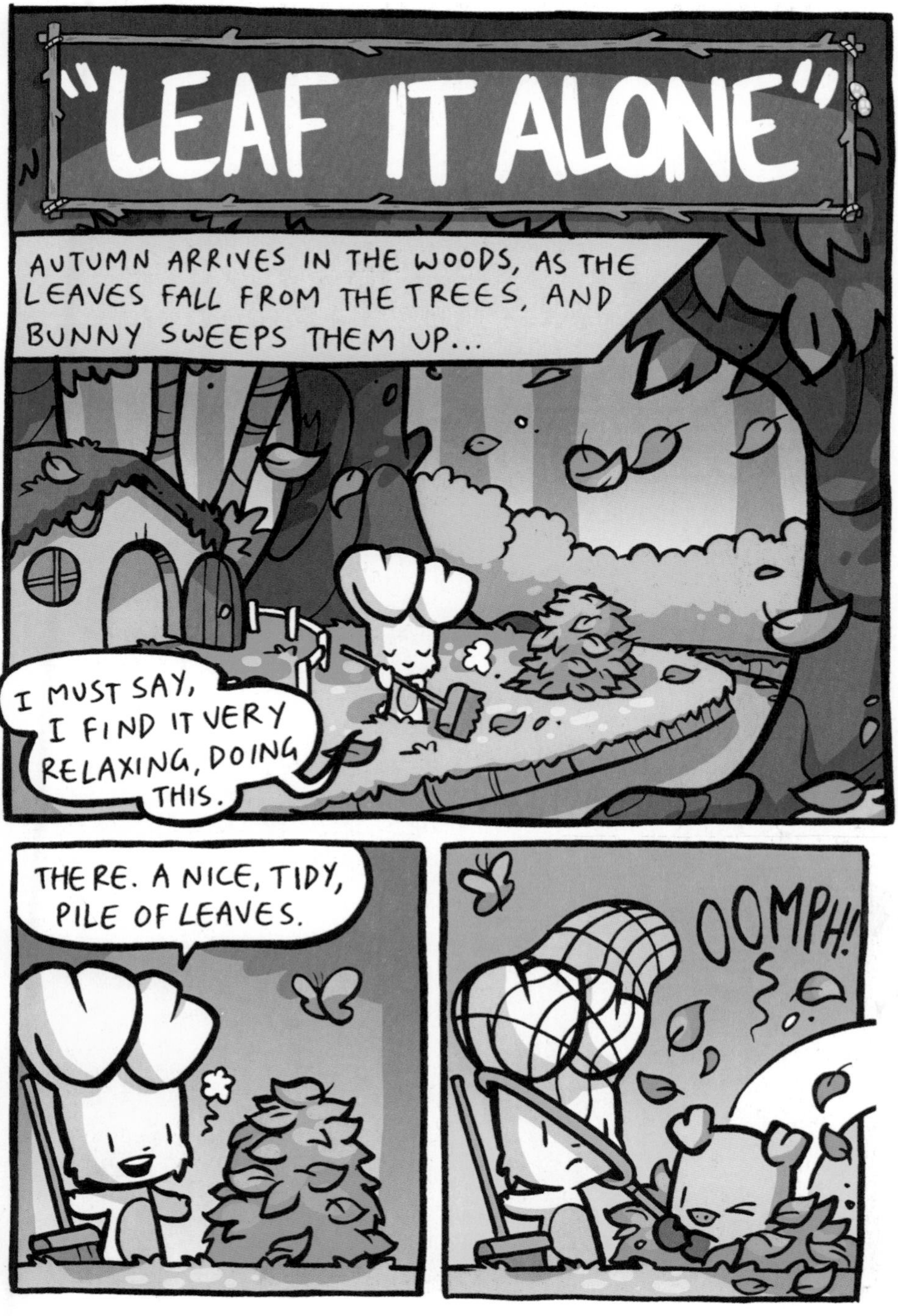
"LEAF IT ALONE"
AUTUMN ARRIVES IN THE WOODS, AS THE LEAVES FALL FROM THE TREES, AND BUNNY SWEEPS THEM UP...
I MUST SAY, I FIND IT VERY RELAXING, DOING THIS.
THERE. A NICE, TIDY, PILE OF LEAVES.
OOMPH!

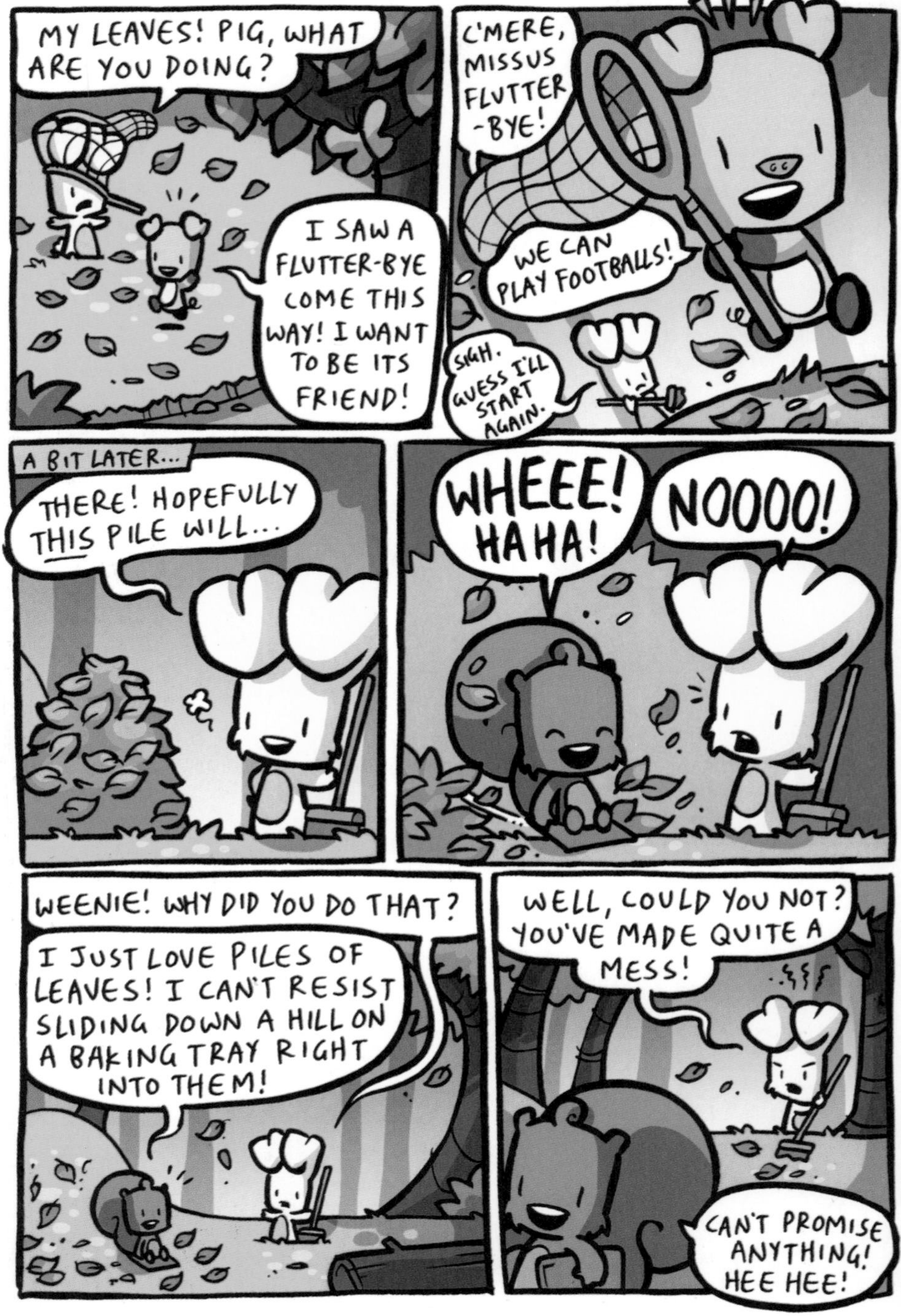

MY LEAVES! PIG, WHAT ARE YOU DOING?
I SAW A FLUTTER-BYE COME THIS WAY! I WANT TO BE ITS FRIEND!
C'MERE, MISSUS FLUTTER-BYE!
WE CAN PLAY FOOTBALLS!
SIGH. GUESS I'LL START AGAIN.
A BIT LATER...
THERE! HOPEFULLY THIS PILE WILL...
WHEEE! HAHA!
NOOOO!
WEENIE! WHY DID YOU DO THAT?
I JUST LOVE PILES OF LEAVES! I CAN'T RESIST SLIDING DOWN A HILL ON A BAKING TRAY RIGHT INTO THEM!
WELL, COULD YOU NOT? YOU'VE MADE QUITE A MESS!
CAN'T PROMISE ANYTHING! HEE HEE!

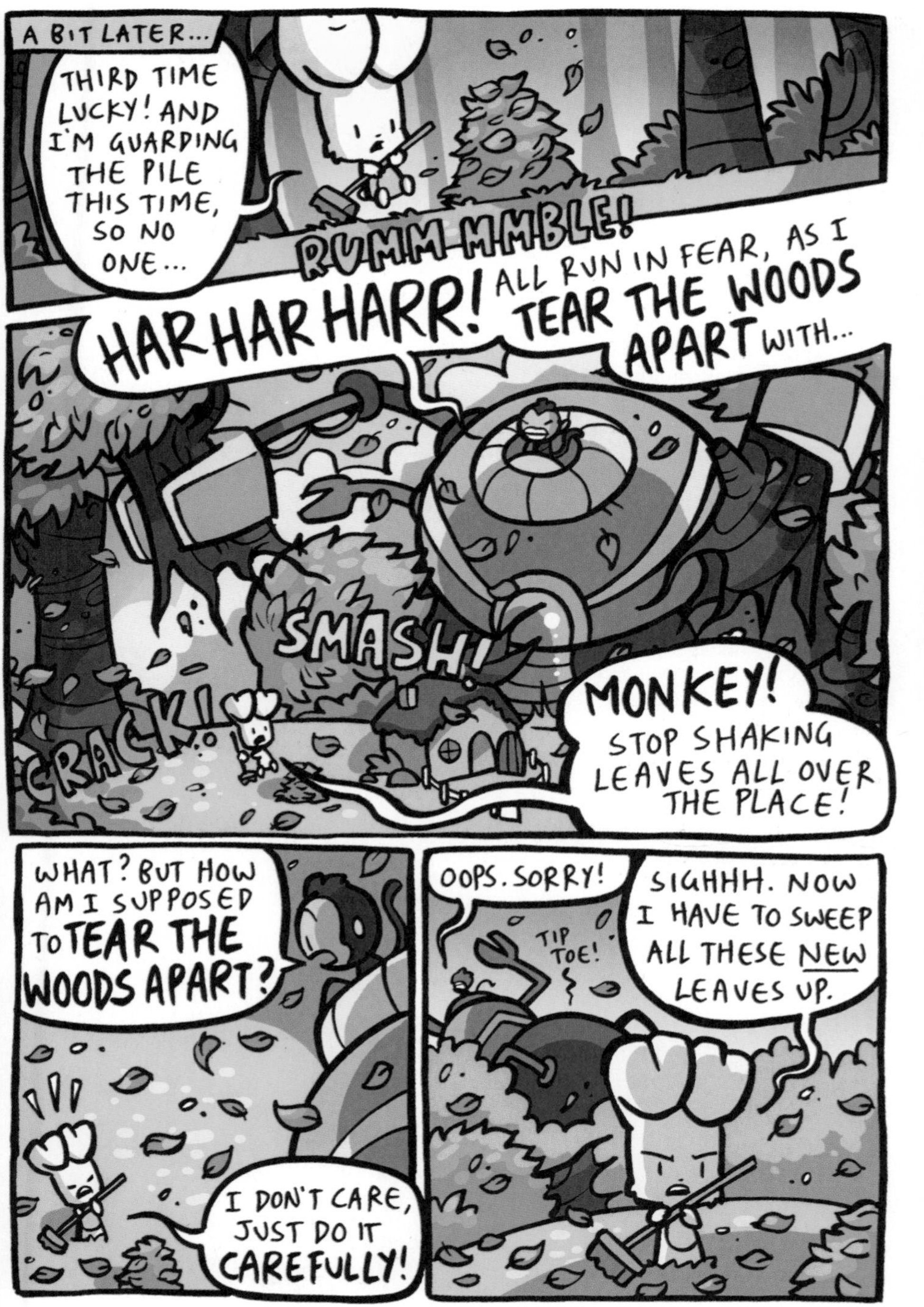
A BIT LATER...
THIRD TIME LUCKY! AND I'M GUARDING THE PILE THIS TIME, SO NO ONE...
RUMMMMMBLE!
HAR HAR HARR! ALL RUN IN FEAR, AS I TEAR THE WOODS APART WITH...
SMASH!
CRACK!
MONKEY! STOP SHAKING LEAVES ALL OVER THE PLACE!
WHAT? BUT HOW AM I SUPPOSED TO TEAR THE WOODS APART?
I DON'T CARE, JUST DO IT CAREFULLY!
OOPS. SORRY!
TIP TOE!
SIGHHH. NOW I HAVE TO SWEEP ALL THESE NEW LEAVES UP.

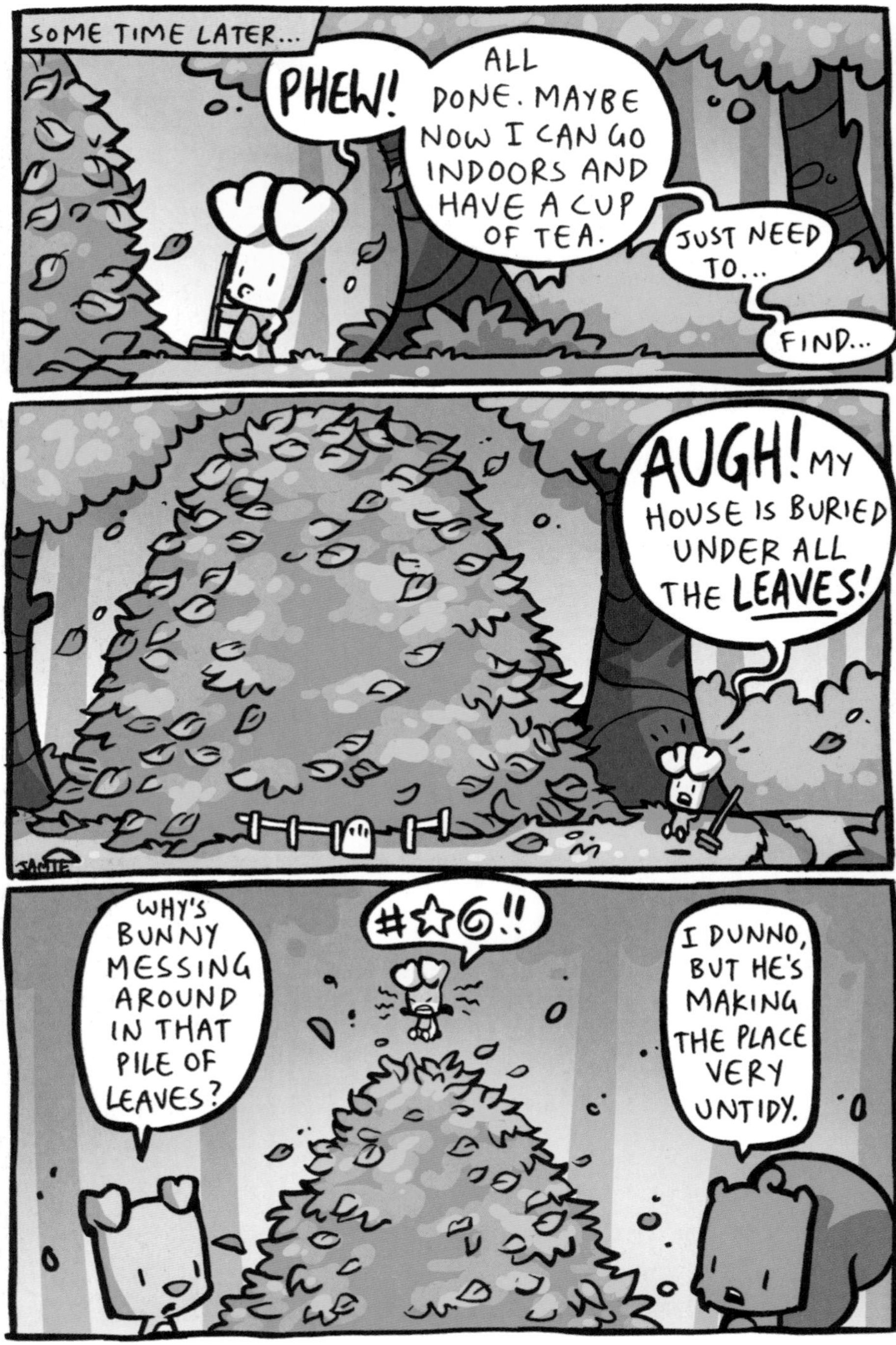
SOME TIME LATER...
PHEW!
ALL DONE. MAYBE NOW I CAN GO INDOORS AND HAVE A CUP OF TEA.
JUST NEED TO...
FIND...
AUGH! MY HOUSE IS BURIED UNDER ALL THE LEAVES!
WHY'S BUNNY MESSING AROUND IN THAT PILE OF LEAVES?
#☆@!!
I DUNNO, BUT HE'S MAKING THE PLACE VERY UNTIDY.

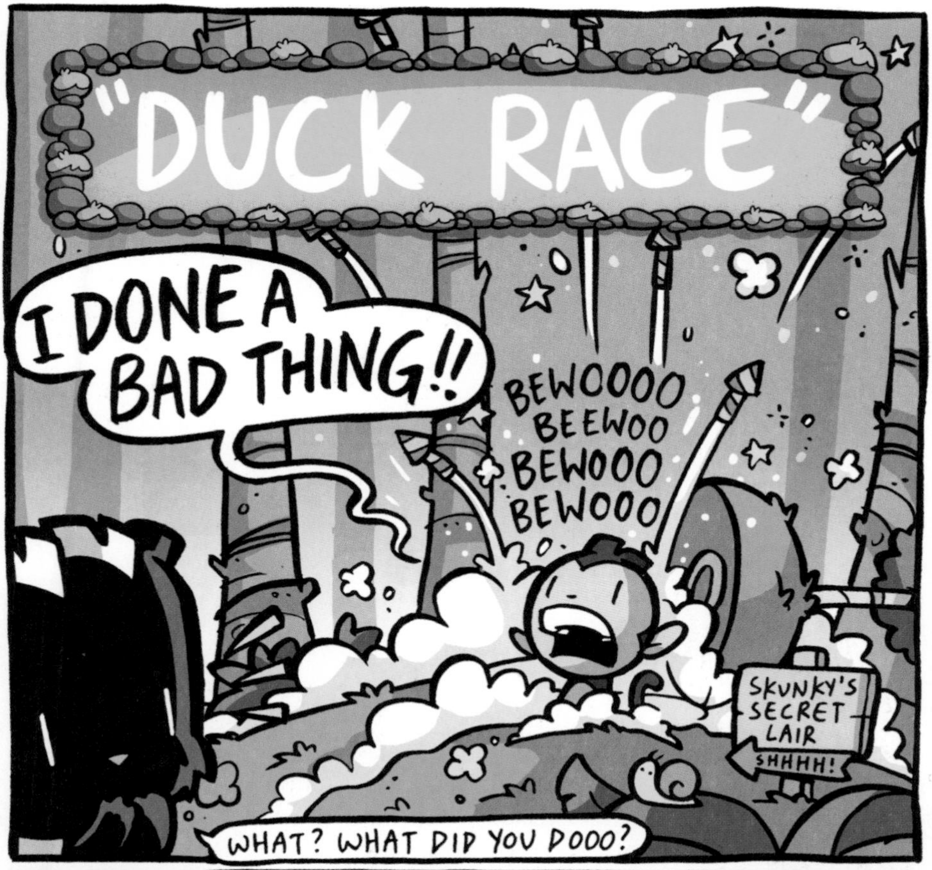
"DUCK RACE"
I DONE A BAD THING!!
BEWOOOO BEEWOO BEWOOO BEWOOO
SKUNKY'S SECRET LAIR
SHHHH!
WHAT? WHAT DID YOU DOOO?

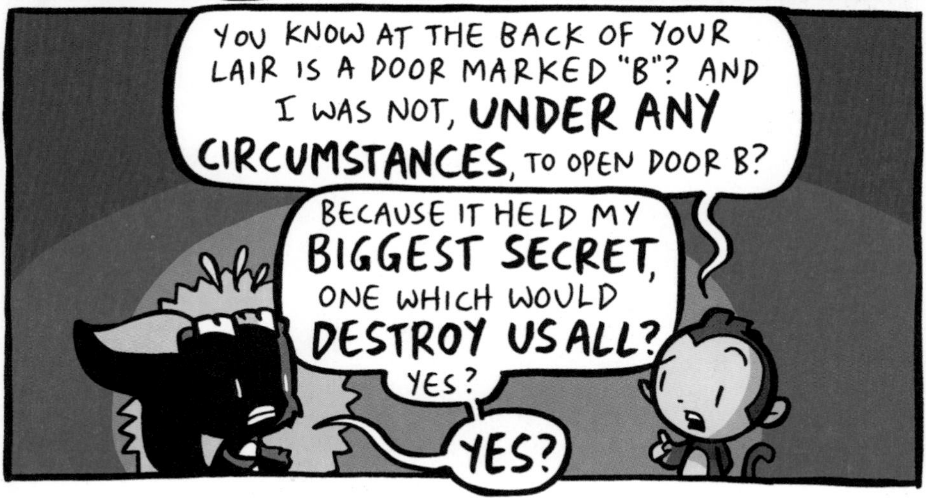
YOU KNOW AT THE BACK OF YOUR LAIR IS A DOOR MARKED "B"? AND I WAS NOT, UNDER ANY CIRCUMSTANCES, TO OPEN DOOR B?
BECAUSE IT HELD MY BIGGEST SECRET, ONE WHICH WOULD DESTROY US ALL? YES?
YES?

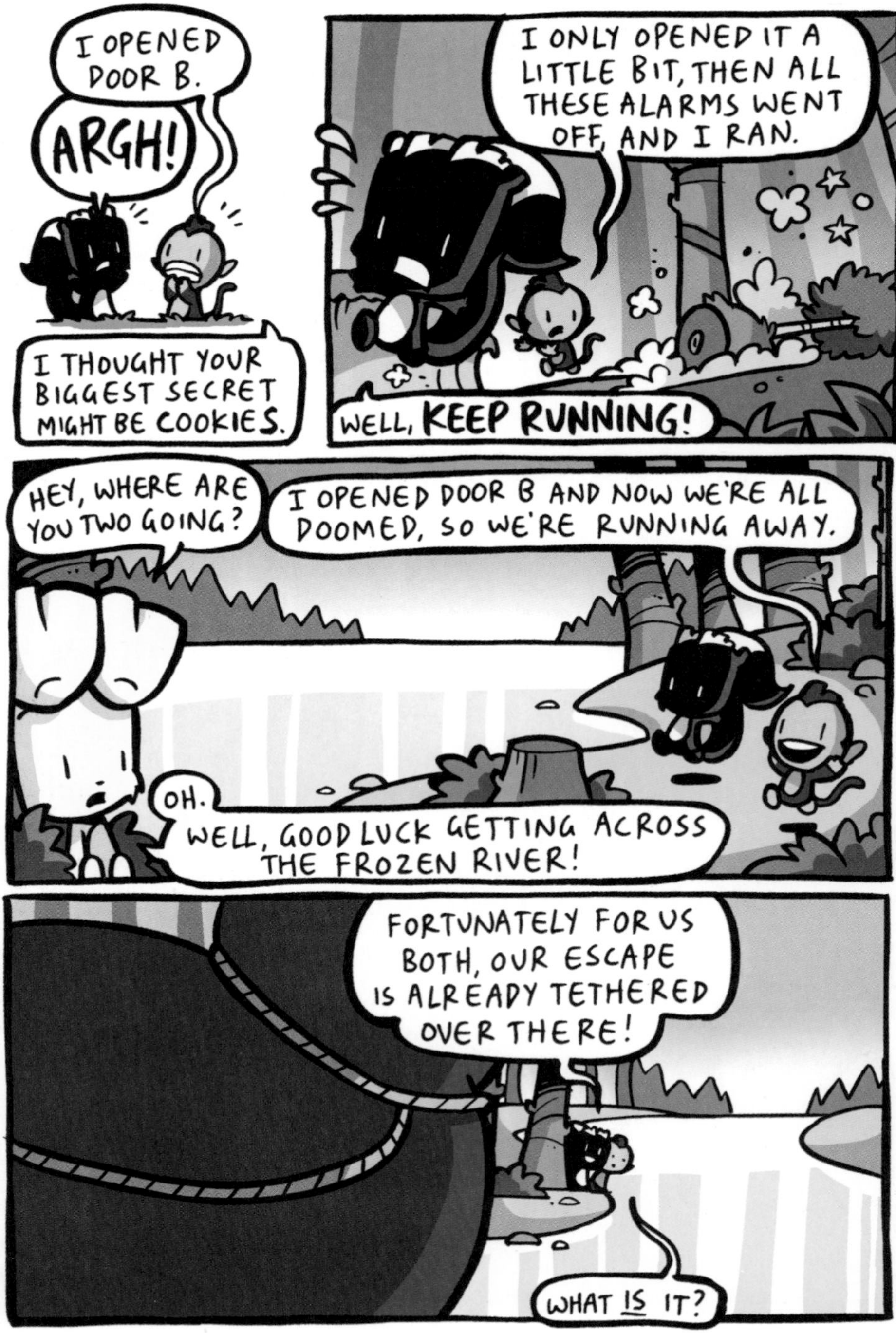
I OPENED DOOR B.
ARGH!
I THOUGHT YOUR BIGGEST SECRET MIGHT BE COOKIES.
I ONLY OPENED IT A LITTLE BIT, THEN ALL THESE ALARMS WENT OFF, AND I RAN.
WELL, KEEP RUNNING!
HEY, WHERE ARE YOU TWO GOING?
I OPENED DOOR B AND NOW WE'RE ALL DOOMED, SO WE'RE RUNNING AWAY.
OH.
WELL, GOOD LUCK GETTING ACROSS THE FROZEN RIVER!
FORTUNATELY FOR US BOTH, OUR ESCAPE IS ALREADY TETHERED OVER THERE!
WHAT IS IT?

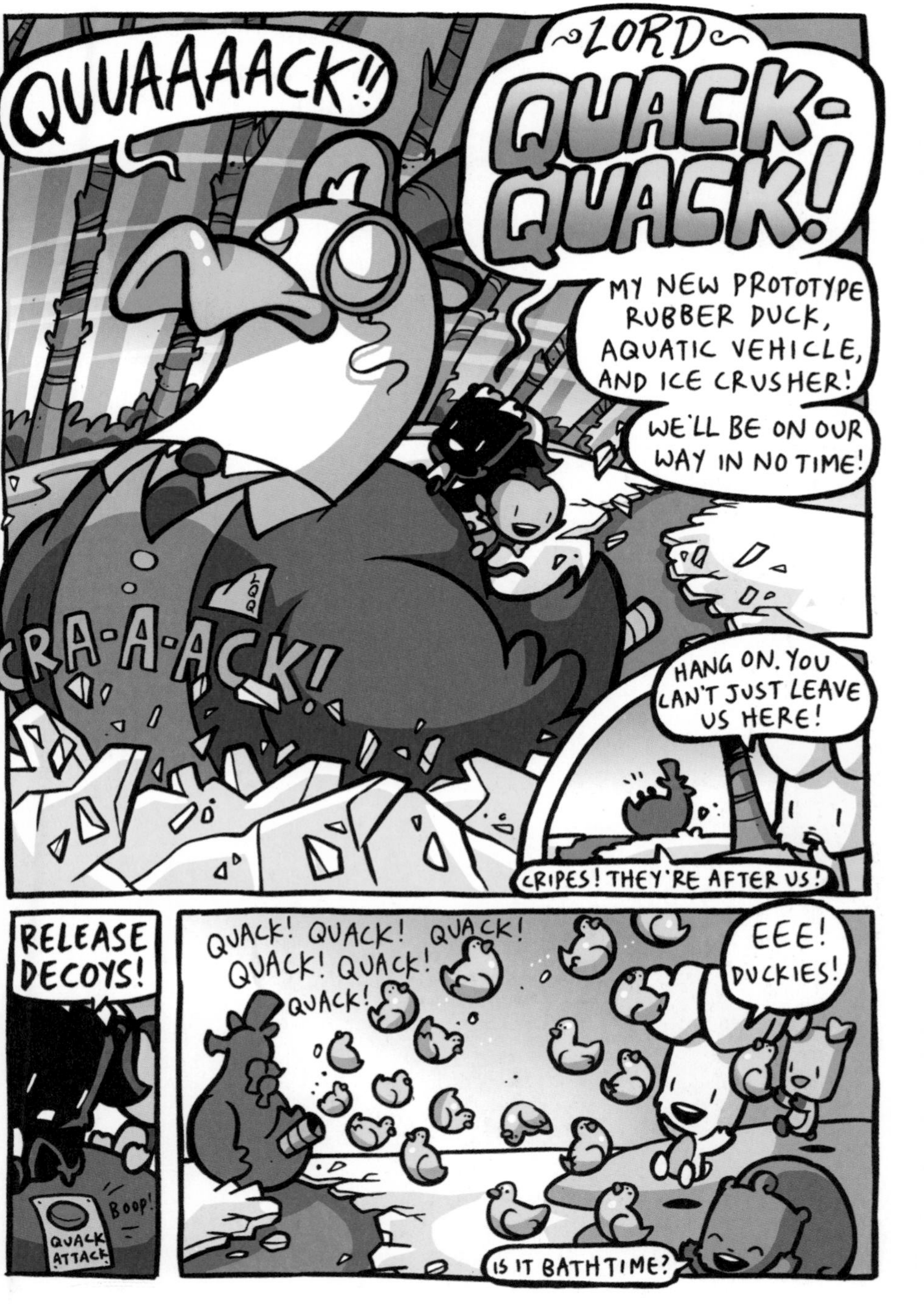
QUUAAAACK!!
LORD QUACK-QUACK!
MY NEW PROTOTYPE RUBBER DUCK, AQUATIC VEHICLE, AND ICE CRUSHER!
WE'LL BE ON OUR WAY IN NO TIME!
CRA-A-ACK!
HANG ON. YOU CAN'T JUST LEAVE US HERE!
CRIPES! THEY'RE AFTER US!
RELEASE DECOYS!
BOOP!
QUACK ATTACK
QUACK! QUACK! QUACK! QUACK! QUACK! QUACK!
EEE! DUCKIES!
IS IT BATH TIME?

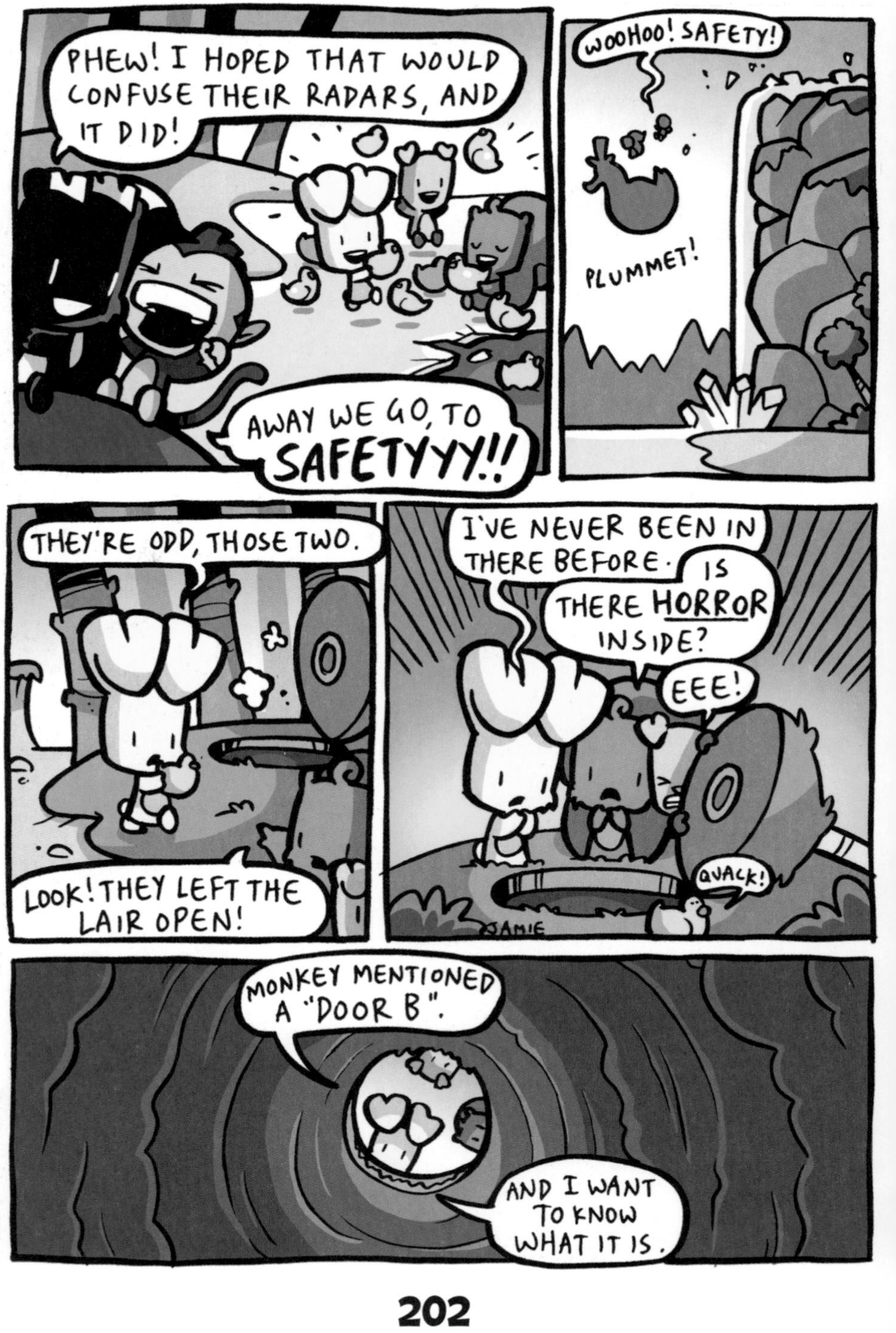
PHEW! I HOPED THAT WOULD CONFUSE THEIR RADARS, AND IT DID!
AWAY WE GO, TO SAFETYYY!!
WOOHOO! SAFETY!
PLUMMET!
THEY'RE ODD, THOSE TWO.
LOOK! THEY LEFT THE LAIR OPEN!
I'VE NEVER BEEN IN THERE BEFORE.
IS THERE HORROR INSIDE?
EEE!
QUACK!
JAMIE
MONKEY MENTIONED A "DOOR B".
AND I WANT TO KNOW WHAT IT IS.

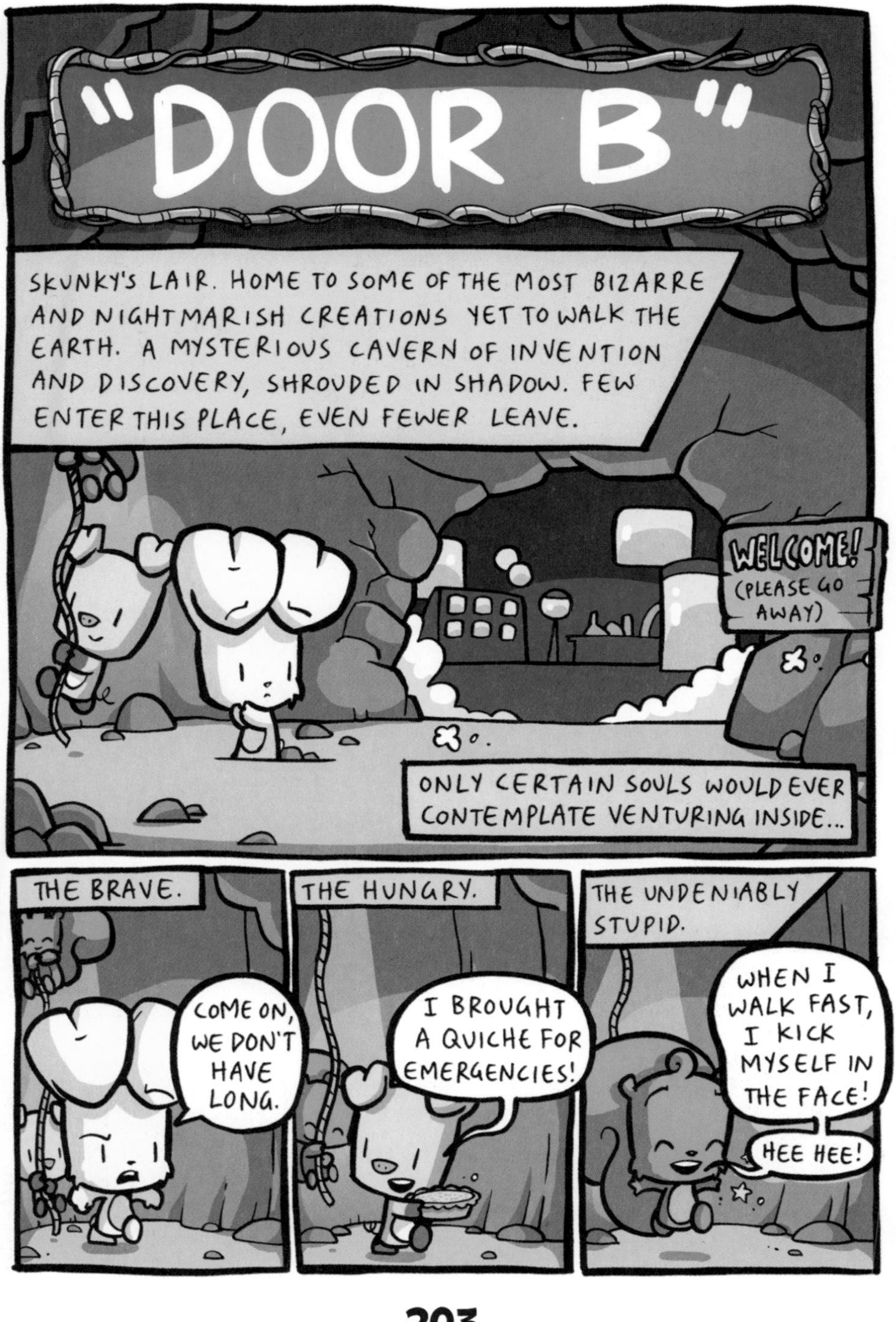
"DOOR B"
SKUNKY'S LAIR. HOME TO SOME OF THE MOST BIZARRE AND NIGHTMARISH CREATIONS YET TO WALK THE EARTH. A MYSTERIOUS CAVERN OF INVENTION AND DISCOVERY, SHROUDED IN SHADOW. FEW ENTER THIS PLACE, EVEN FEWER LEAVE.
WELCOME! (PLEASE GO AWAY)
ONLY CERTAIN SOULS WOULD EVER CONTEMPLATE VENTURING INSIDE...
THE BRAVE.
COME ON, WE DON'T HAVE LONG.
THE HUNGRY.
I BROUGHT A QUICHE FOR EMERGENCIES!
THE UNDENIABLY STUPID.
WHEN I WALK FAST, I KICK MYSELF IN THE FACE!
HEE HEE!

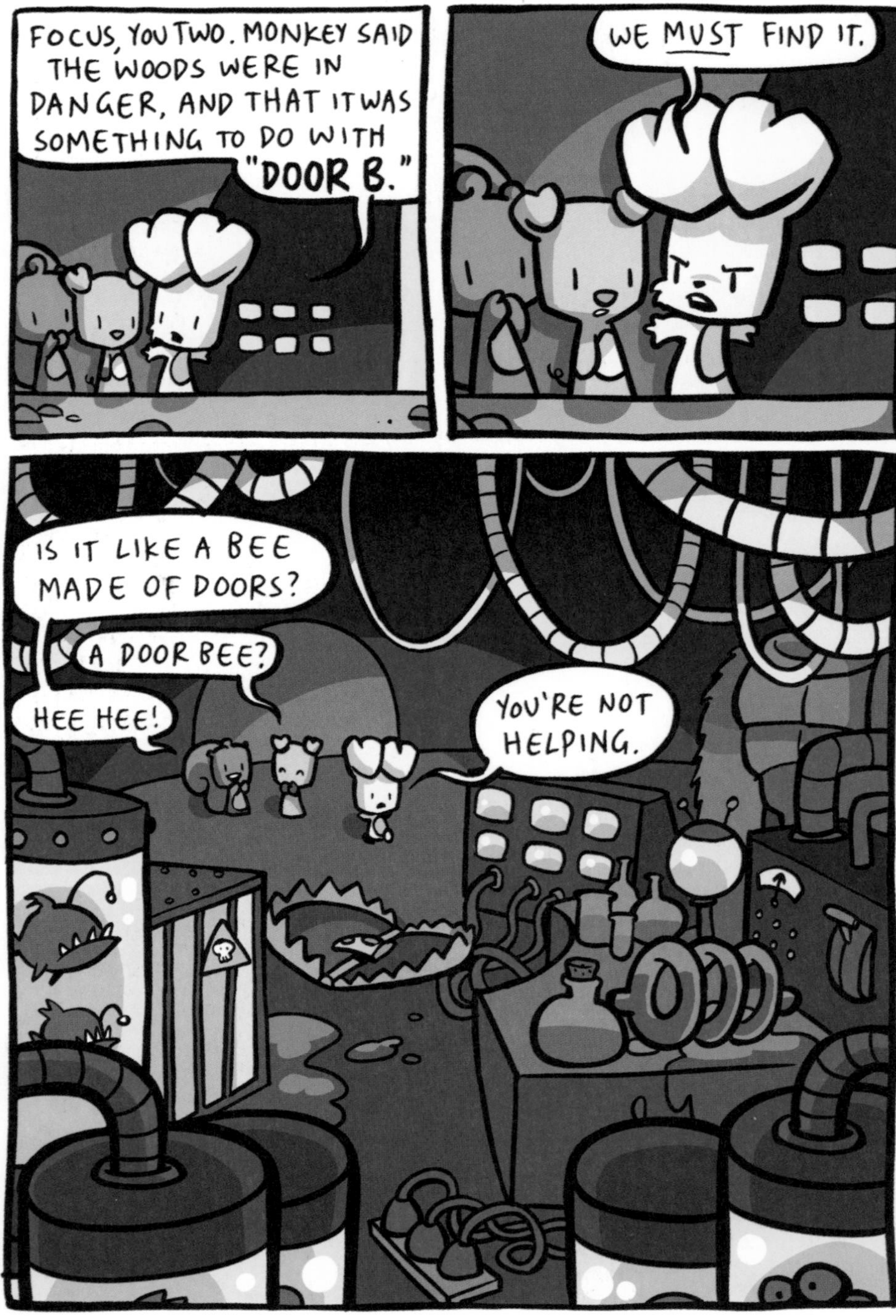
FOCUS, YOU TWO. MONKEY SAID THE WOODS WERE IN DANGER, AND THAT IT WAS SOMETHING TO DO WITH "DOOR B."
WE MUST FIND IT.
IS IT LIKE A BEE MADE OF DOORS?
A DOOR BEE?
HEE HEE!
YOU'RE NOT HELPING.

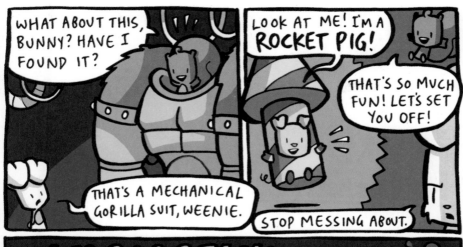

WHAT ABOUT THIS, BUNNY? HAVE I FOUND IT?

THAT'S A MECHANICAL GORILLA SUIT, WEENIE.

LOOK AT ME! I'M A ROCKET PIG!

THAT'S SO MUCH FUN! LET'S SET YOU OFF!

STOP MESSING ABOUT.

WOOOOOSH!!

WOOSH.

WOOSH.

RIGHT, BUNNY. LOOKS LIKE IT'S JUST UP TO YOU TO FIND "DOOR B."

OH.

THERE IT IS.

B

WHAT'S IN HERE THAT SCARED EVEN SKUNKY SO MUCH?

WHAT HORRIBLE SECRET LIES INSIDE?

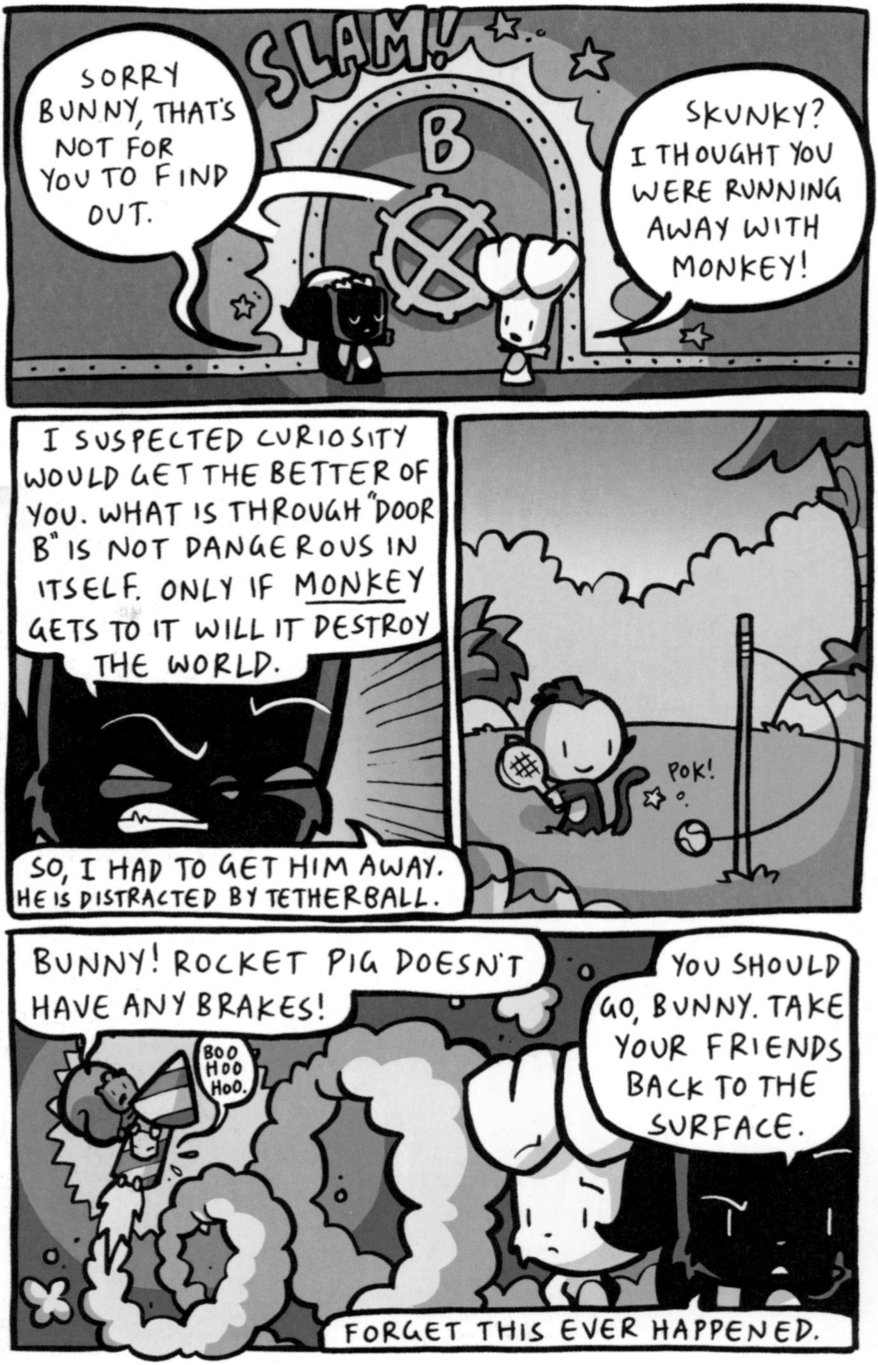
SLAM!
SORRY BUNNY, THAT'S NOT FOR YOU TO FIND OUT.
B
SKUNKY? I THOUGHT YOU WERE RUNNING AWAY WITH MONKEY!
I SUSPECTED CURIOSITY WOULD GET THE BETTER OF YOU. WHAT IS THROUGH "DOOR B" IS NOT DANGEROUS IN ITSELF. ONLY IF MONKEY GETS TO IT WILL IT DESTROY THE WORLD.
SO, I HAD TO GET HIM AWAY. HE IS DISTRACTED BY TETHERBALL.
POK!
BUNNY! ROCKET PIG DOESN'T HAVE ANY BRAKES!
BOO HOO HOO.
YOU SHOULD GO, BUNNY. TAKE YOUR FRIENDS BACK TO THE SURFACE.
FORGET THIS EVER HAPPENED.

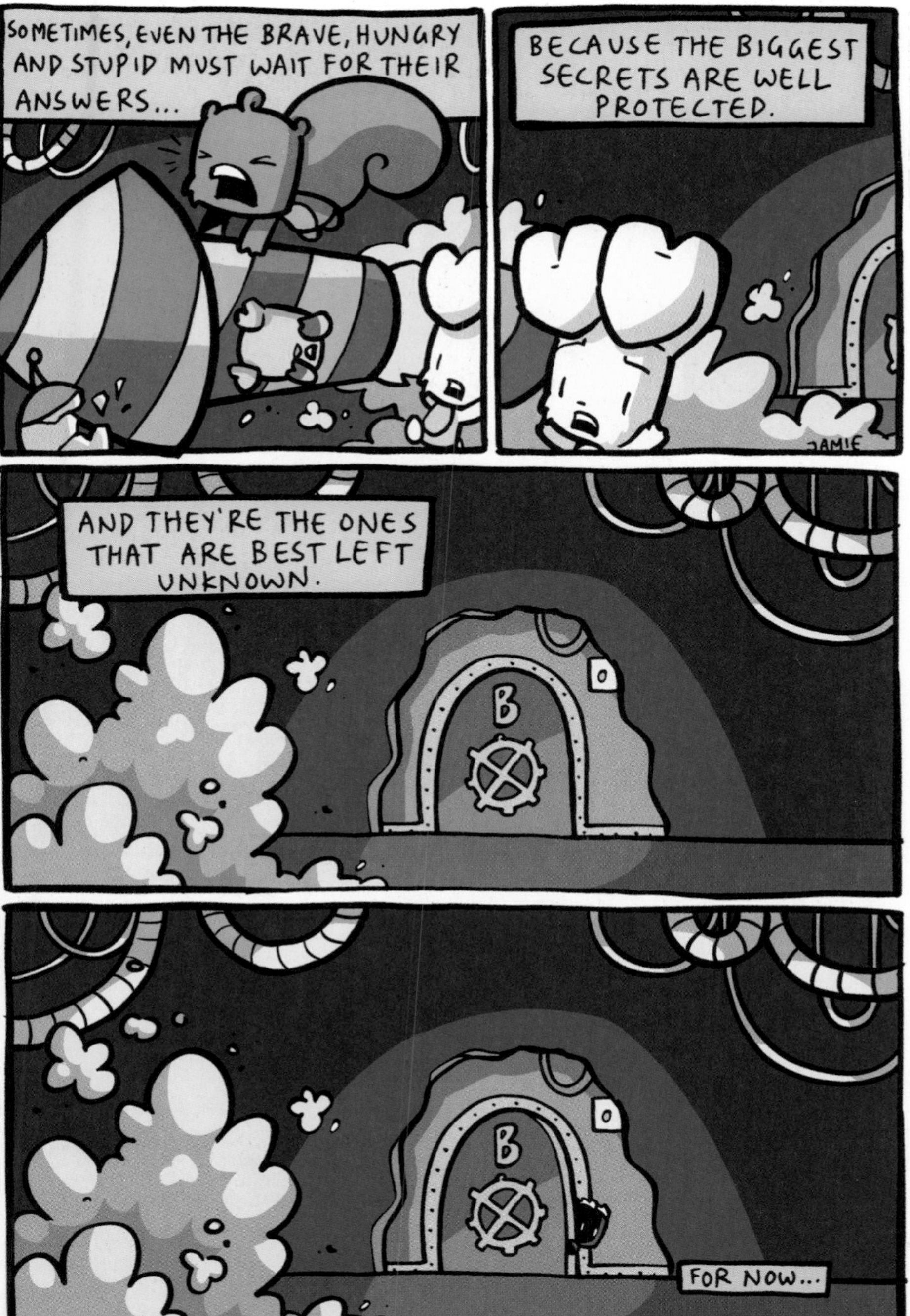
SOMETIMES, EVEN THE BRAVE, HUNGRY AND STUPID MUST WAIT FOR THEIR ANSWERS...
BECAUSE THE BIGGEST SECRETS ARE WELL PROTECTED.
JAMIE
AND THEY'RE THE ONES THAT ARE BEST LEFT UNKNOWN.
B
O
FOR NOW...

'HYPNO-MONKEY'

IT'S A RARE SUNNY DAY FOR THIS TIME OF YEAR, SO SKUNKY HAS DECIDED TO TAKE HIS WORK OUTSIDE...

HEY, SKUNKY, WHAT'S THIS? I FOUND IT. CAN I KICK IT?

HMM?

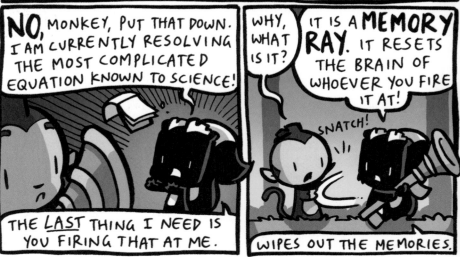

NO, MONKEY, PUT THAT DOWN. I AM CURRENTLY RESOLVING THE MOST COMPLICATED EQUATION KNOWN TO SCIENCE!

THE LAST THING I NEED IS YOU FIRING THAT AT ME.

WHY, WHAT IS IT?

IT IS A MEMORY RAY. IT RESETS THE BRAIN OF WHOEVER YOU FIRE IT AT!

SNATCH!

WIPES OUT THE MEMORIES.

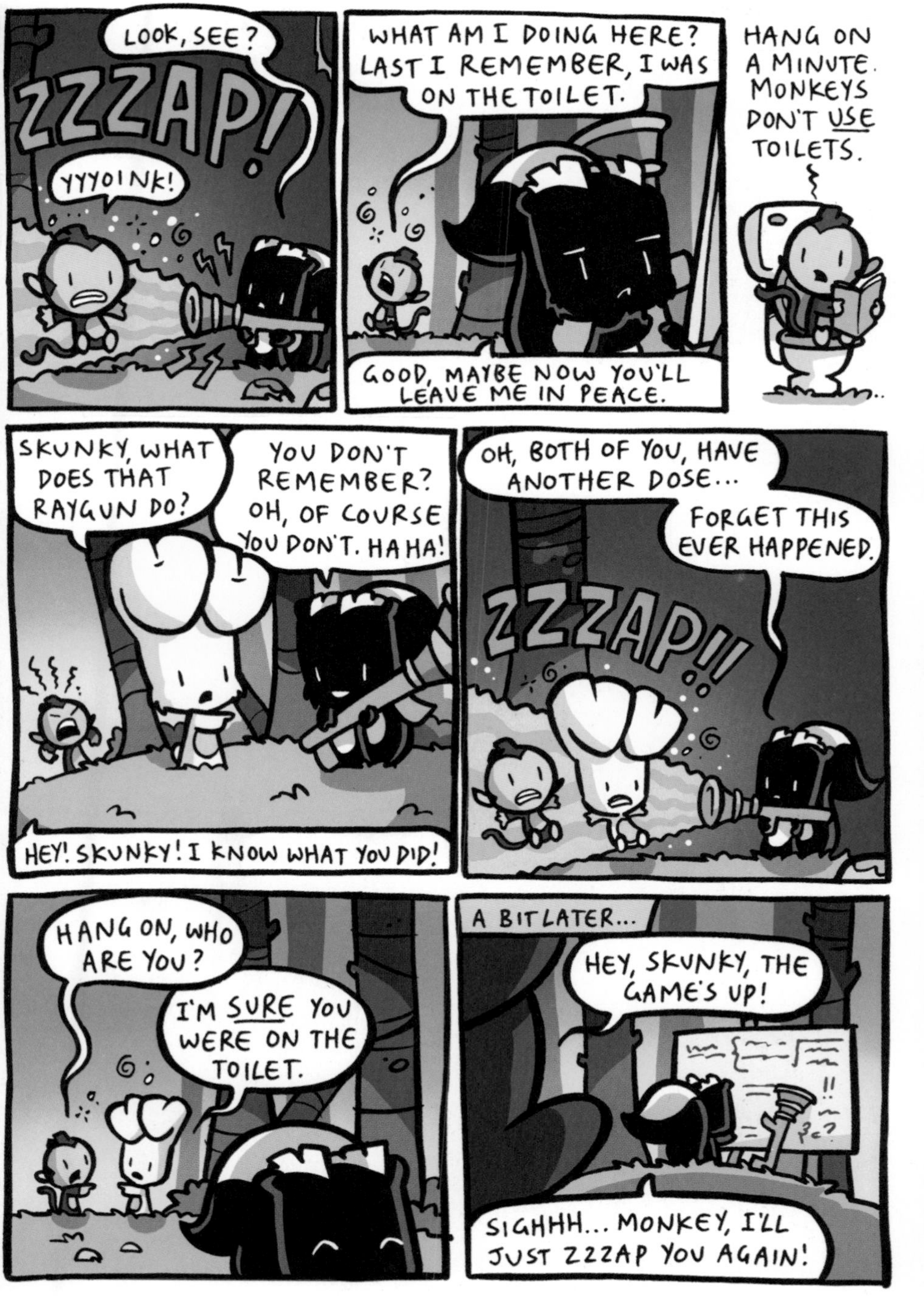
LOOK, SEE?
ZZZAP!
YYYOINK!
WHAT AM I DOING HERE? LAST I REMEMBER, I WAS ON THE TOILET.
GOOD, MAYBE NOW YOU'LL LEAVE ME IN PEACE.
HANG ON A MINUTE. MONKEYS DON'T USE TOILETS.
SKUNKY, WHAT DOES THAT RAYGUN DO?
YOU DON'T REMEMBER? OH, OF COURSE YOU DON'T. HA HA!
HEY! SKUNKY! I KNOW WHAT YOU DID!
OH, BOTH OF YOU, HAVE ANOTHER DOSE...
FORGET THIS EVER HAPPENED.
ZZZAP!!
HANG ON, WHO ARE YOU?
I'M SURE YOU WERE ON THE TOILET.
A BIT LATER...
HEY, SKUNKY, THE GAME'S UP!
SIGHHH... MONKEY, I'LL JUST ZZZAP YOU AGAIN!

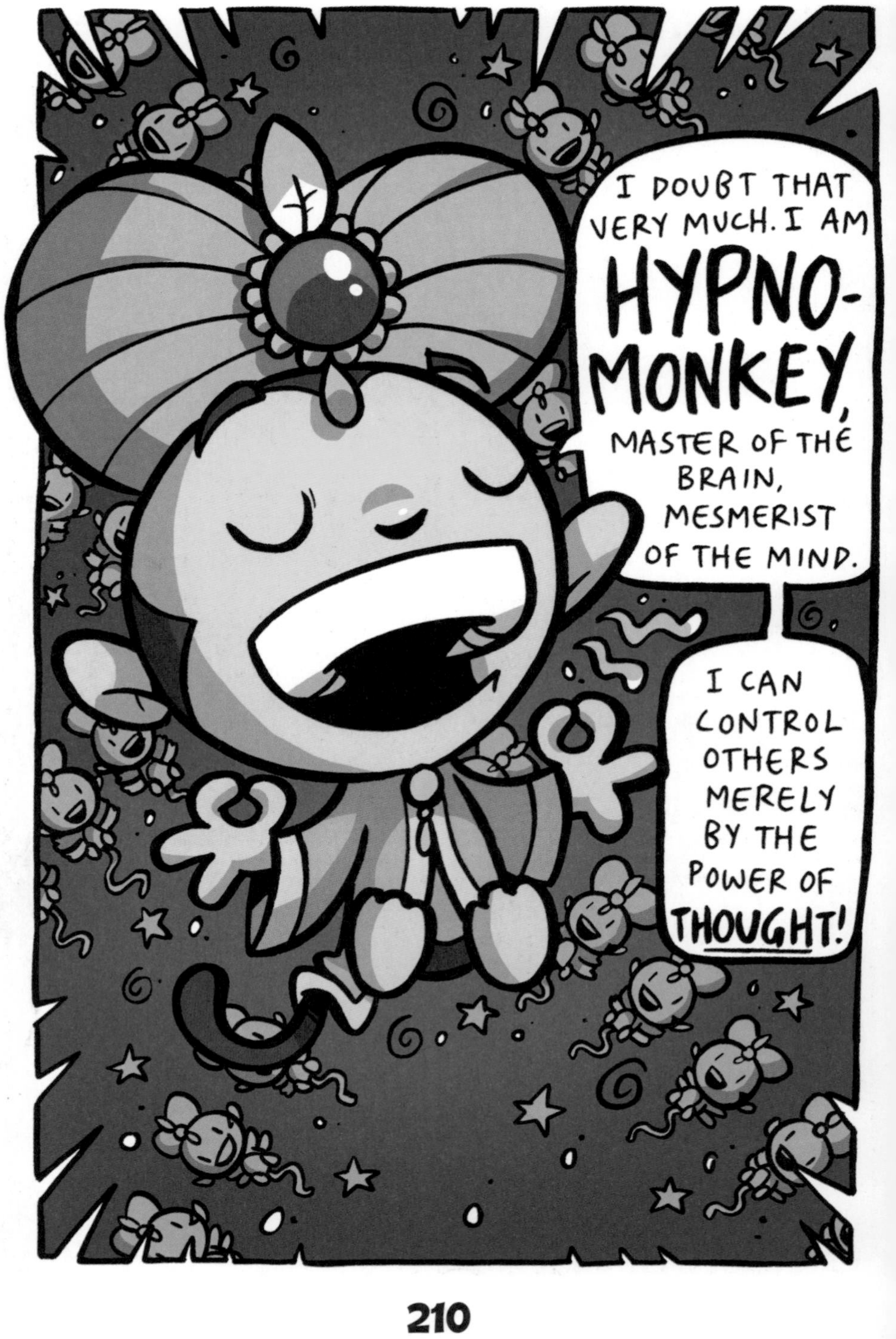
I DOUBT THAT VERY MUCH. I AM HYPNO-MONKEY, MASTER OF THE BRAIN, MESMERIST OF THE MIND.
I CAN CONTROL OTHERS MERELY BY THE POWER OF THOUGHT!

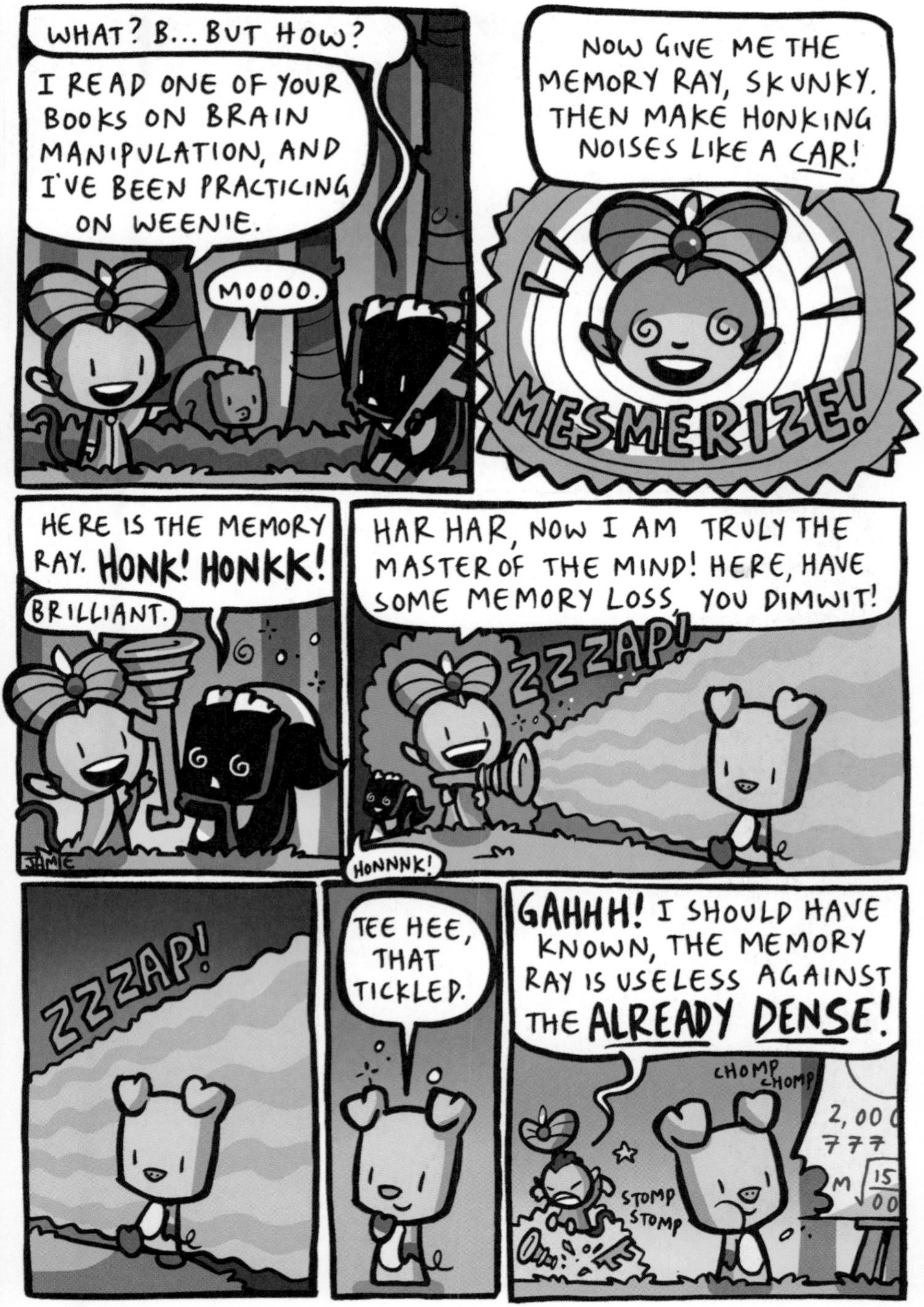
WHAT? B... BUT HOW?
I READ ONE OF YOUR BOOKS ON BRAIN MANIPULATION, AND I'VE BEEN PRACTICING ON WEENIE.
MOOOO.
NOW GIVE ME THE MEMORY RAY, SKUNKY. THEN MAKE HONKING NOISES LIKE A CAR!
MESMERIZE!
HERE IS THE MEMORY RAY. HONK! HONKK!
BRILLIANT.
HAR HAR, NOW I AM TRULY THE MASTER OF THE MIND! HERE, HAVE SOME MEMORY LOSS, YOU DIMWIT!
ZZZAP!
HONNNK!
ZZZAP!
TEE HEE, THAT TICKLED.
GAHHH! I SHOULD HAVE KNOWN, THE MEMORY RAY IS USELESS AGAINST THE ALREADY DENSE!
CHOMP CHOMP
STOMP STOMP

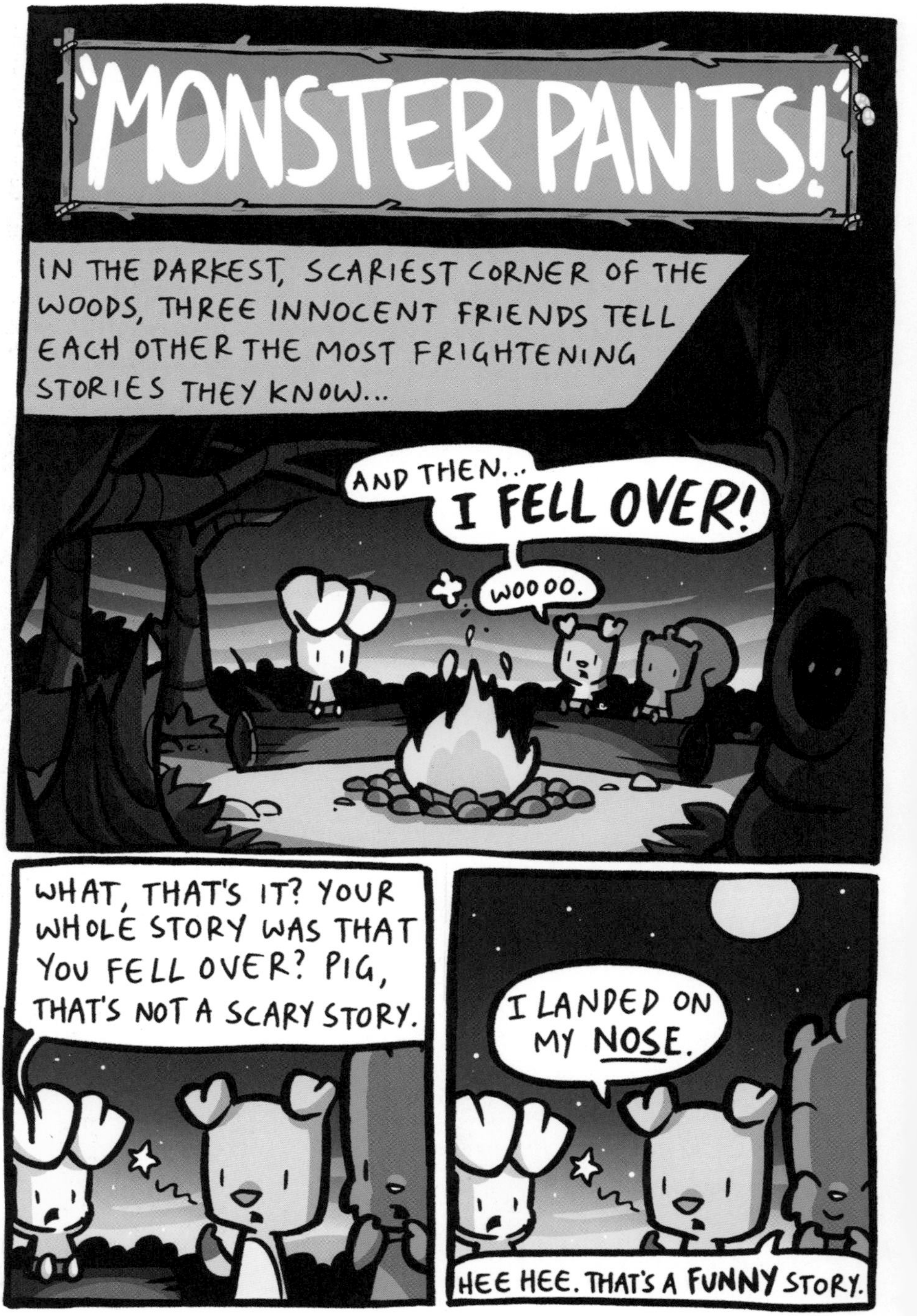
"MONSTER PANTS!"
IN THE DARKEST, SCARIEST CORNER OF THE WOODS, THREE INNOCENT FRIENDS TELL EACH OTHER THE MOST FRIGHTENING STORIES THEY KNOW...
AND THEN... I FELL OVER!
WOOOO.
WHAT, THAT'S IT? YOUR WHOLE STORY WAS THAT YOU FELL OVER? PIG, THAT'S NOT A SCARY STORY.
I LANDED ON MY NOSE.
HEE HEE. THAT'S A FUNNY STORY.

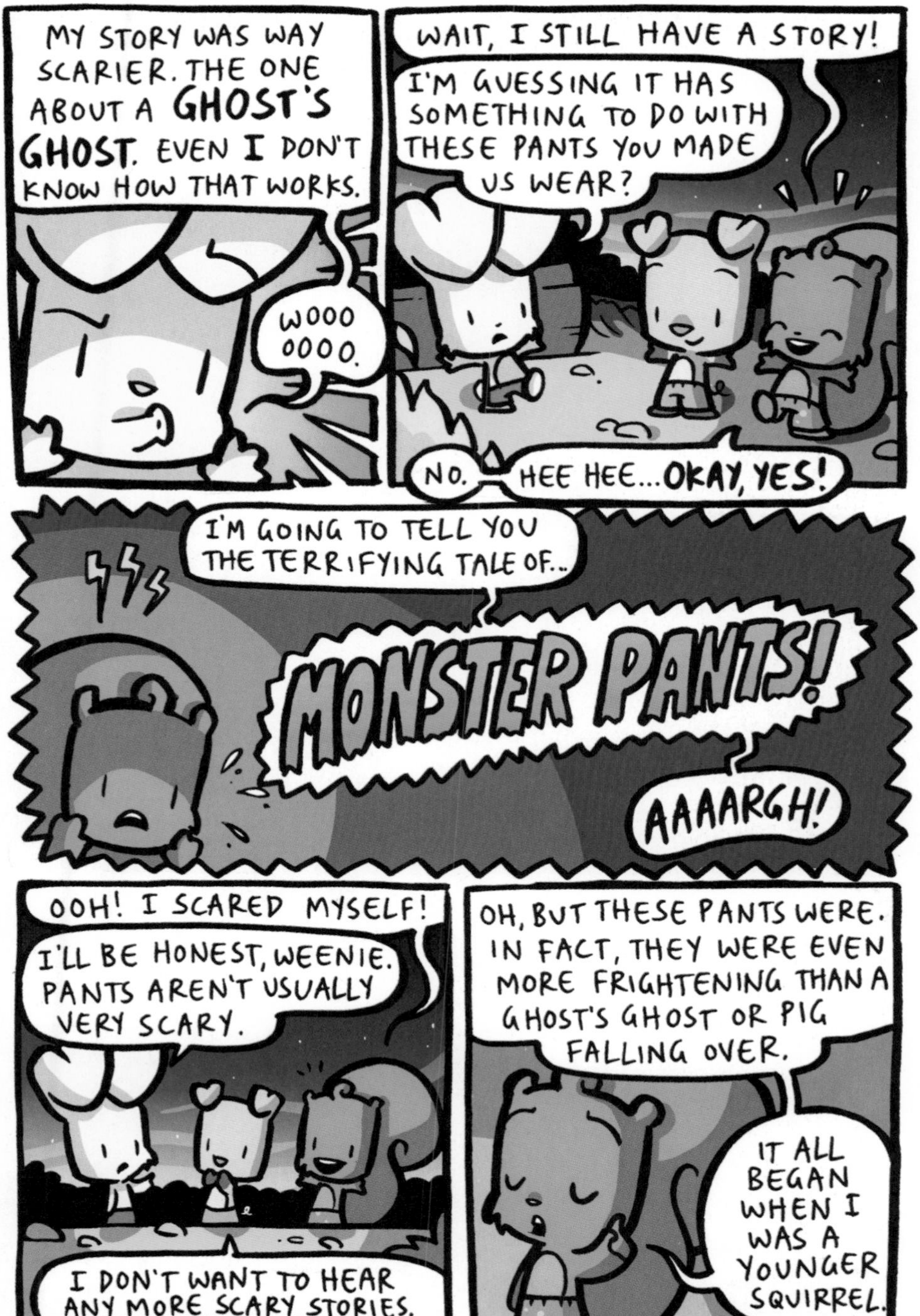
MY STORY WAS WAY SCARIER. THE ONE ABOUT A GHOST'S GHOST. EVEN I DON'T KNOW HOW THAT WORKS.
WOOO OOOO.
WAIT, I STILL HAVE A STORY!
I'M GUESSING IT HAS SOMETHING TO DO WITH THESE PANTS YOU MADE US WEAR?
NO.
HEE HEE... OKAY, YES!
I'M GOING TO TELL YOU THE TERRIFYING TALE OF...
MONSTER PANTS!
AAAARGH!
OOH! I SCARED MYSELF!
I'LL BE HONEST, WEENIE. PANTS AREN'T USUALLY VERY SCARY.
I DON'T WANT TO HEAR ANY MORE SCARY STORIES.
OH, BUT THESE PANTS WERE. IN FACT, THEY WERE EVEN MORE FRIGHTENING THAN A GHOST'S GHOST OR PIG FALLING OVER.
IT ALL BEGAN WHEN I WAS A YOUNGER SQUIRREL.

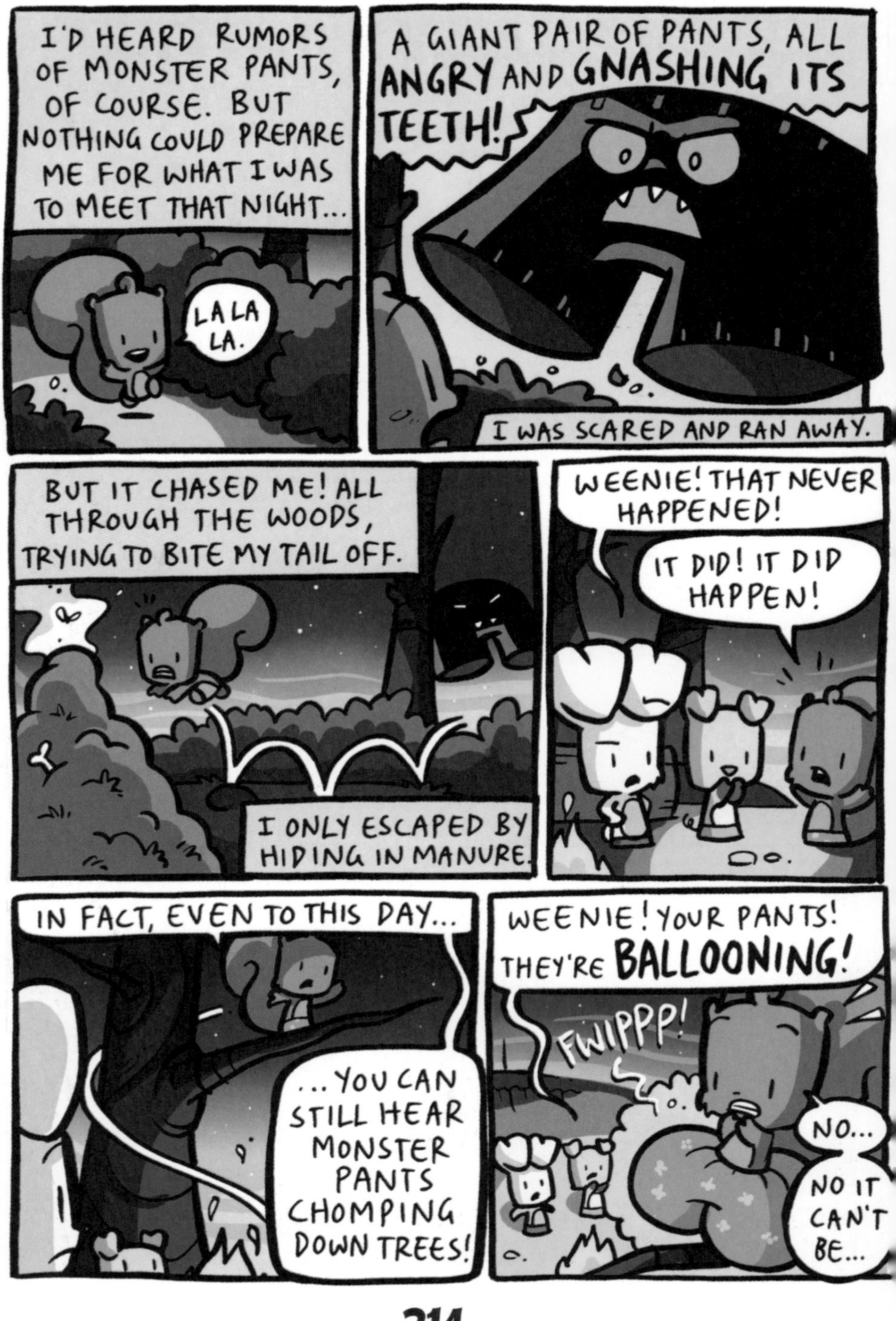
I'D HEARD RUMORS OF MONSTER PANTS, OF COURSE. BUT NOTHING COULD PREPARE ME FOR WHAT I WAS TO MEET THAT NIGHT...
LA LA LA.
A GIANT PAIR OF PANTS, ALL ANGRY AND GNASHING ITS TEETH!
I WAS SCARED AND RAN AWAY.
BUT IT CHASED ME! ALL THROUGH THE WOODS, TRYING TO BITE MY TAIL OFF.
I ONLY ESCAPED BY HIDING IN MANURE.
WEENIE! THAT NEVER HAPPENED!
IT DID! IT DID HAPPEN!
IN FACT, EVEN TO THIS DAY...
...YOU CAN STILL HEAR MONSTER PANTS CHOMPING DOWN TREES!
WEENIE! YOUR PANTS! THEY'RE BALLOONING!
FWIPPP!
NO...
NO IT CAN'T BE...

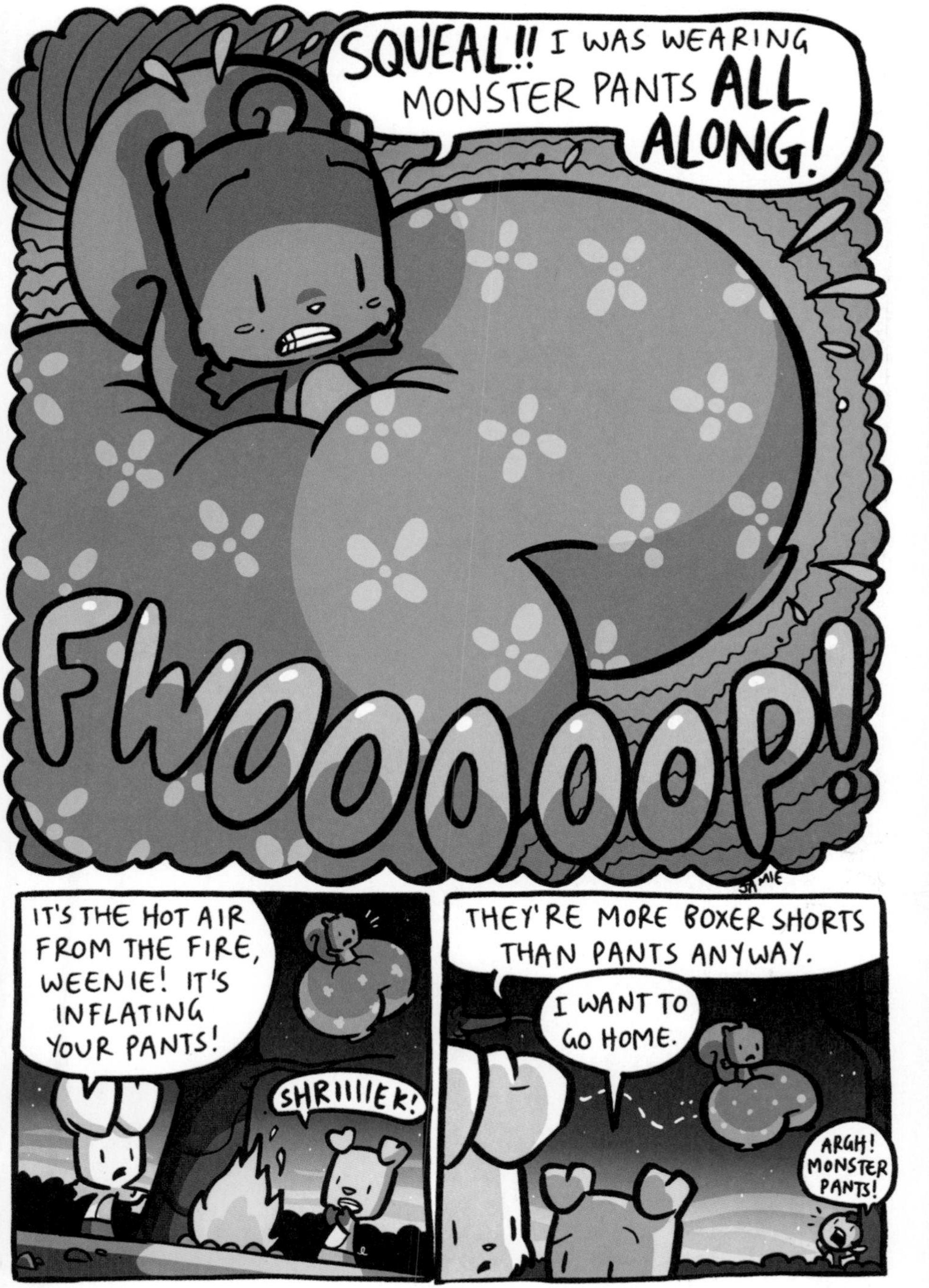

SQUEAL!! I WAS WEARING MONSTER PANTS ALL ALONG!
FWOOOOOP!
IT'S THE HOT AIR FROM THE FIRE, WEENIE! IT'S INFLATING YOUR PANTS!
SHRIIIIEK!
THEY'RE MORE BOXER SHORTS THAN PANTS ANYWAY.
I WANT TO GO HOME.
ARGH! MONSTER PANTS!

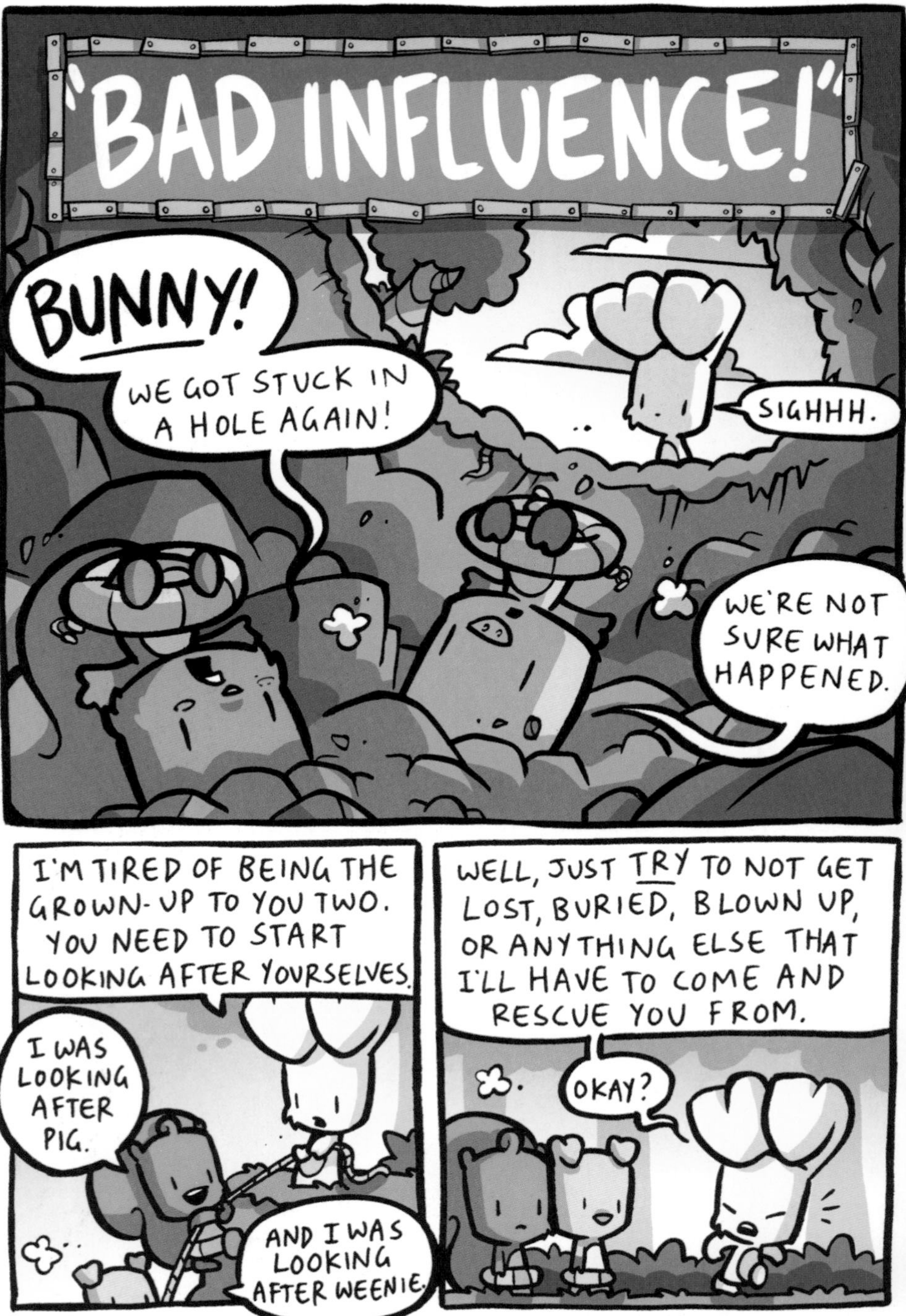
"BAD INFLUENCE!"
BUNNY!
WE GOT STUCK IN A HOLE AGAIN!
SIGHHH.
WE'RE NOT SURE WHAT HAPPENED.
I'M TIRED OF BEING THE GROWN-UP TO YOU TWO. YOU NEED TO START LOOKING AFTER YOURSELVES.
I WAS LOOKING AFTER PIG.
AND I WAS LOOKING AFTER WEENIE.
WELL, JUST TRY TO NOT GET LOST, BURIED, BLOWN UP, OR ANYTHING ELSE THAT I'LL HAVE TO COME AND RESCUE YOU FROM.
OKAY?

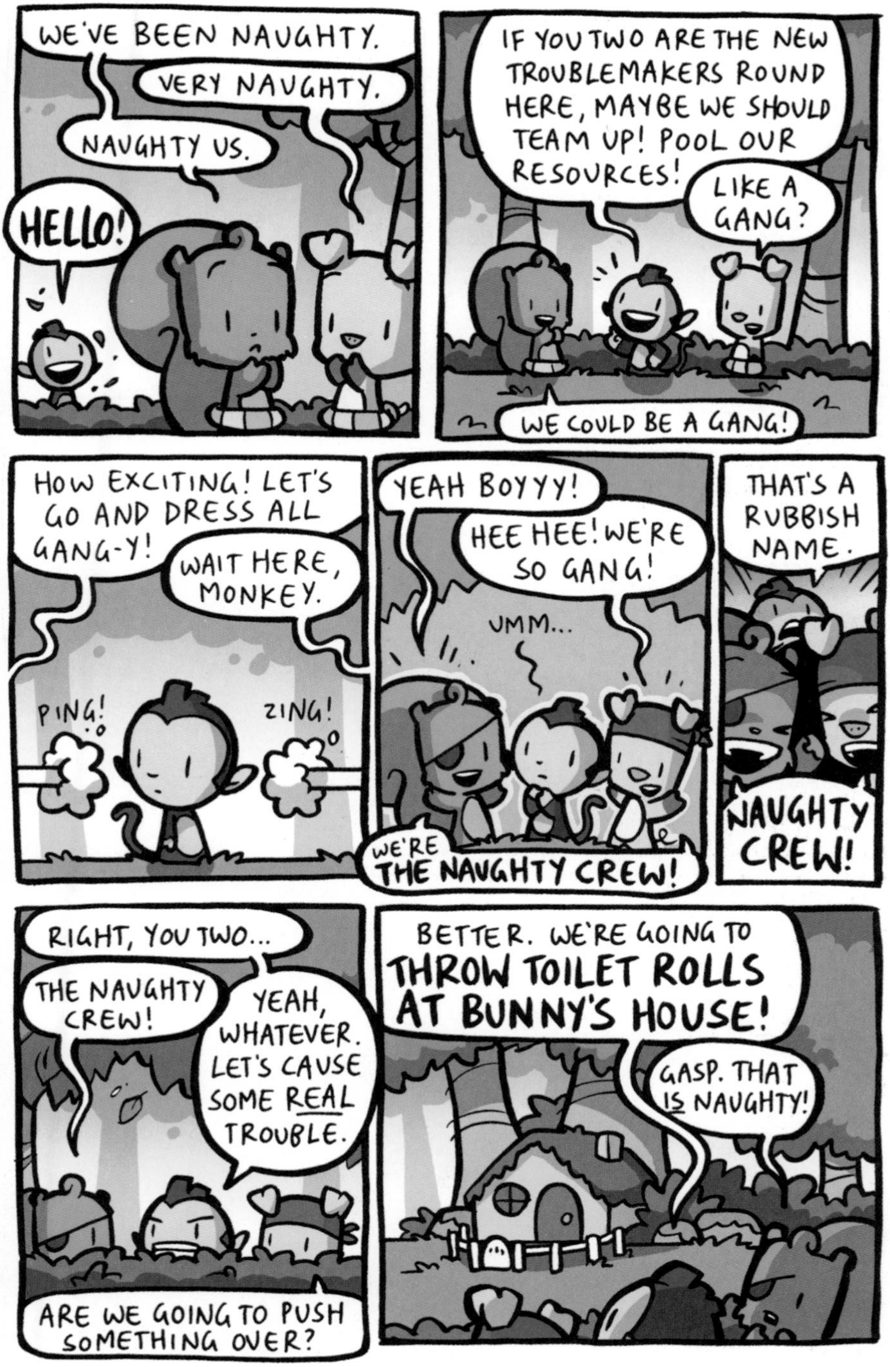
WE'VE BEEN NAUGHTY.
VERY NAUGHTY.
NAUGHTY US.
HELLO!
IF YOU TWO ARE THE NEW TROUBLEMAKERS ROUND HERE, MAYBE WE SHOULD TEAM UP! POOL OUR RESOURCES!
LIKE A GANG?
WE COULD BE A GANG!
HOW EXCITING! LET'S GO AND DRESS ALL GANG-Y!
WAIT HERE, MONKEY.
PING!
ZING!
YEAH BOYYY!
HEE HEE! WE'RE SO GANG!
UMM...
WE'RE THE NAUGHTY CREW!
THAT'S A RUBBISH NAME.
NAUGHTY CREW!
RIGHT, YOU TWO...
THE NAUGHTY CREW!
YEAH, WHATEVER. LET'S CAUSE SOME REAL TROUBLE.
ARE WE GOING TO PUSH SOMETHING OVER?
BETTER. WE'RE GOING TO THROW TOILET ROLLS AT BUNNY'S HOUSE!
GASP. THAT IS NAUGHTY!

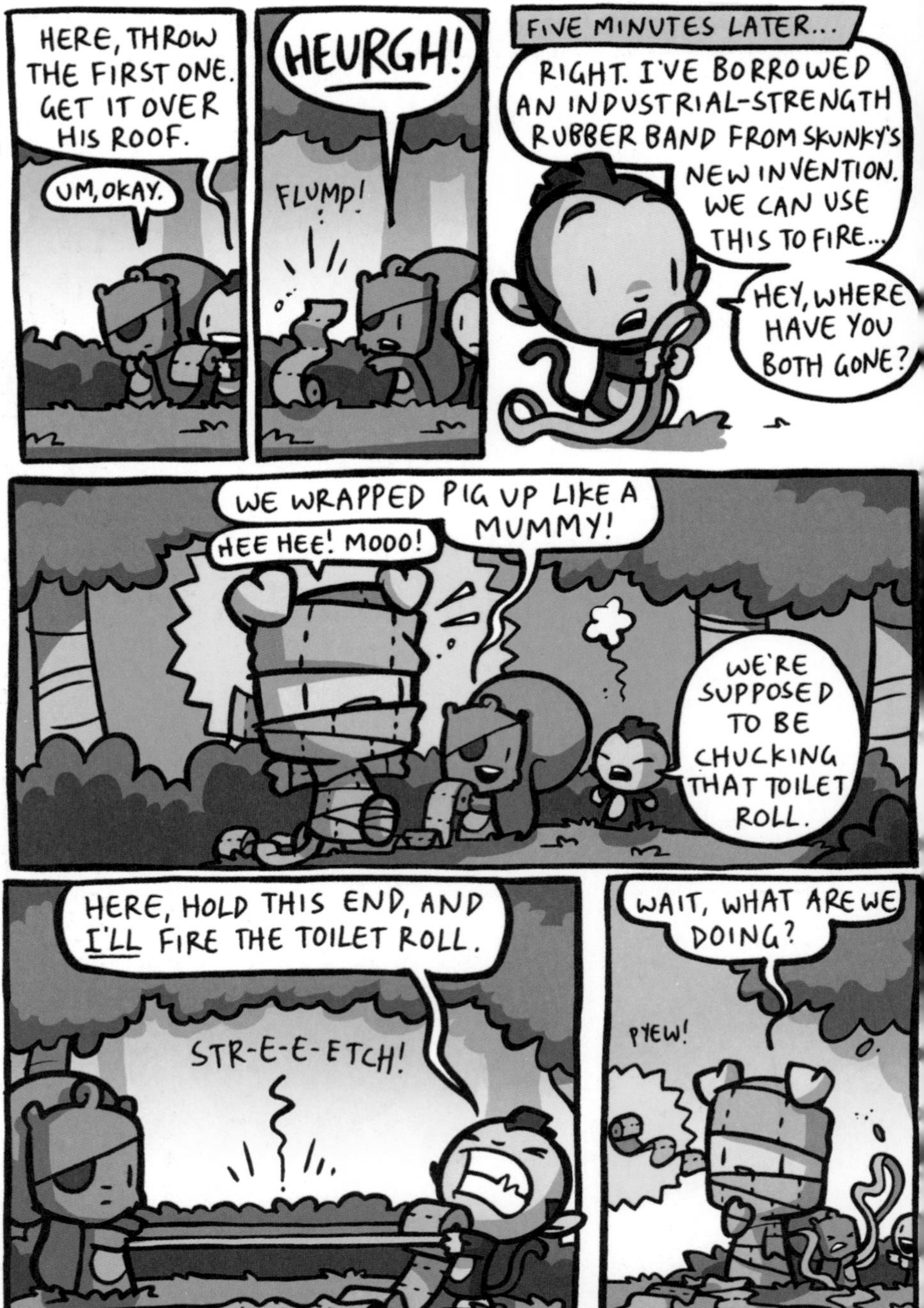
HERE, THROW THE FIRST ONE. GET IT OVER HIS ROOF.
UM, OKAY.
HEURGH!
FLUMP!
FIVE MINUTES LATER...
RIGHT. I'VE BORROWED AN INDUSTRIAL-STRENGTH RUBBER BAND FROM SKUNKY'S NEW INVENTION. WE CAN USE THIS TO FIRE...
HEY, WHERE HAVE YOU BOTH GONE?
WE WRAPPED PIG UP LIKE A MUMMY!
HEE HEE! MOOO!
WE'RE SUPPOSED TO BE CHUCKING THAT TOILET ROLL.
HERE, HOLD THIS END, AND I'LL FIRE THE TOILET ROLL.
STR-E-E-ETCH!
WAIT, WHAT ARE WE DOING?
PYEW!

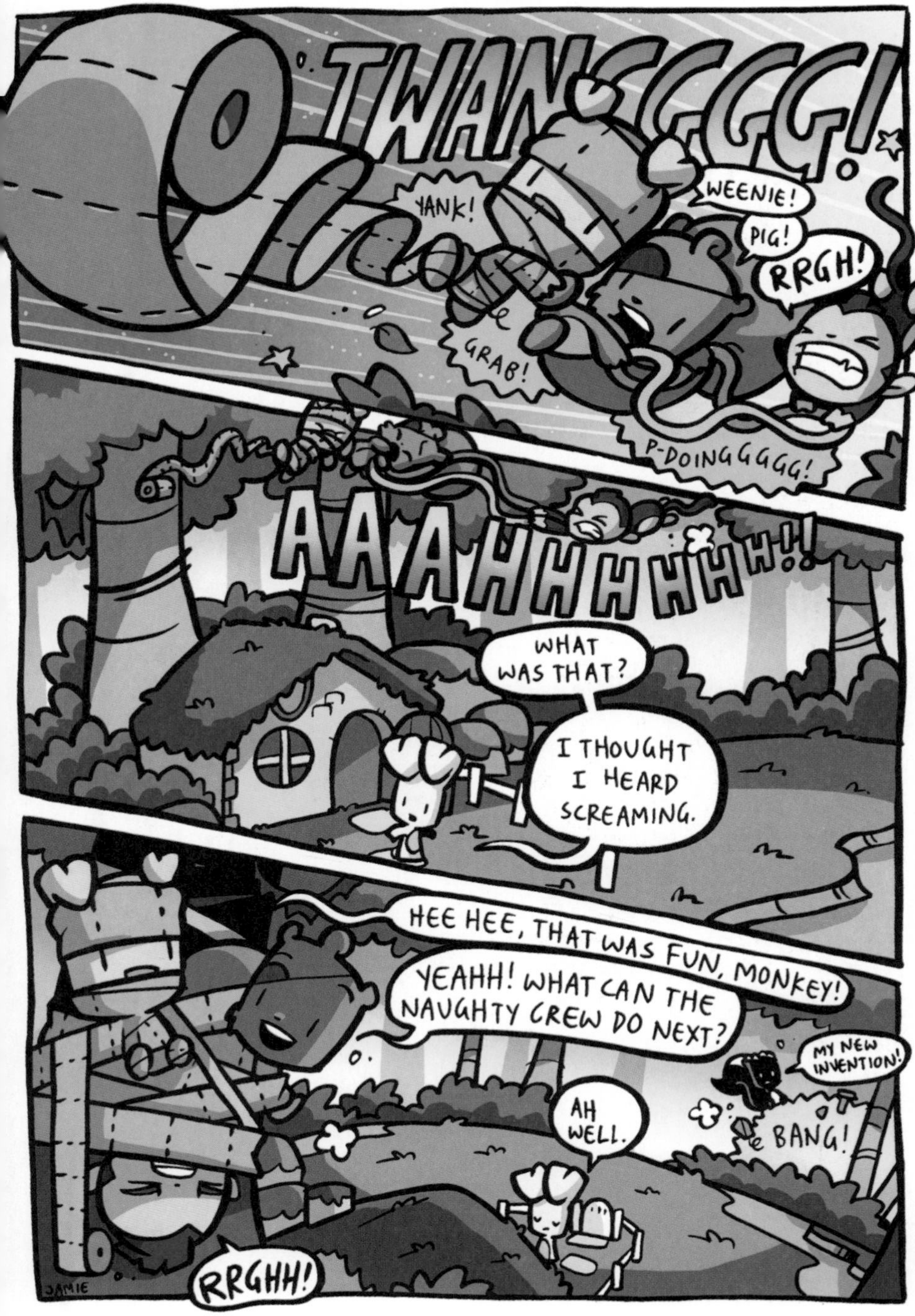
TWANGGGG!
YANK!
WEENIE!
PIG!
RRGH!
GRAB!
P-DOINGGGGG!
AAAHHHHHHH!!
WHAT WAS THAT?
I THOUGHT I HEARD SCREAMING.
HEE HEE, THAT WAS FUN, MONKEY!
YEAHH! WHAT CAN THE NAUGHTY CREW DO NEXT?
MY NEW INVENTION!
BANG!
AH WELL.
RRGHH!
JAMIE

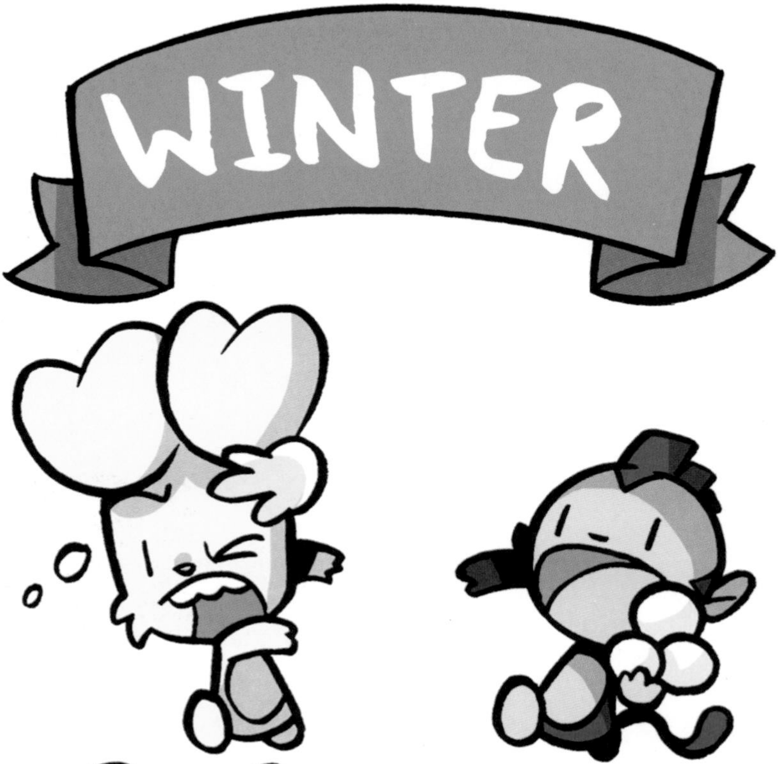
WINTER

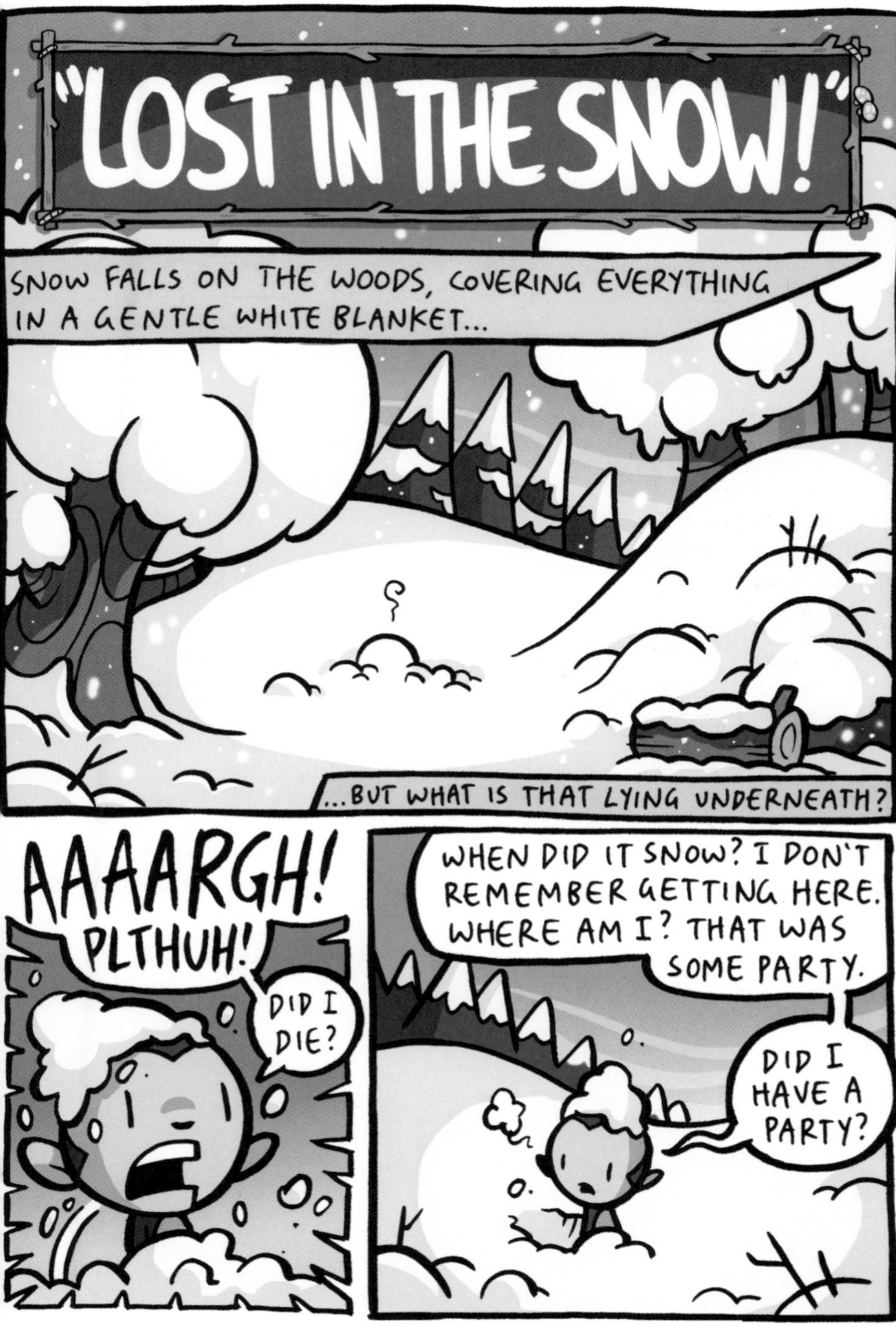
"LOST IN THE SNOW!"
SNOW FALLS ON THE WOODS, COVERING EVERYTHING IN A GENTLE WHITE BLANKET...
...BUT WHAT IS THAT LYING UNDERNEATH?
AAAARGH! PLTHUH!
DID I DIE?
WHEN DID IT SNOW? I DON'T REMEMBER GETTING HERE. WHERE AM I? THAT WAS SOME PARTY.
DID I HAVE A PARTY?

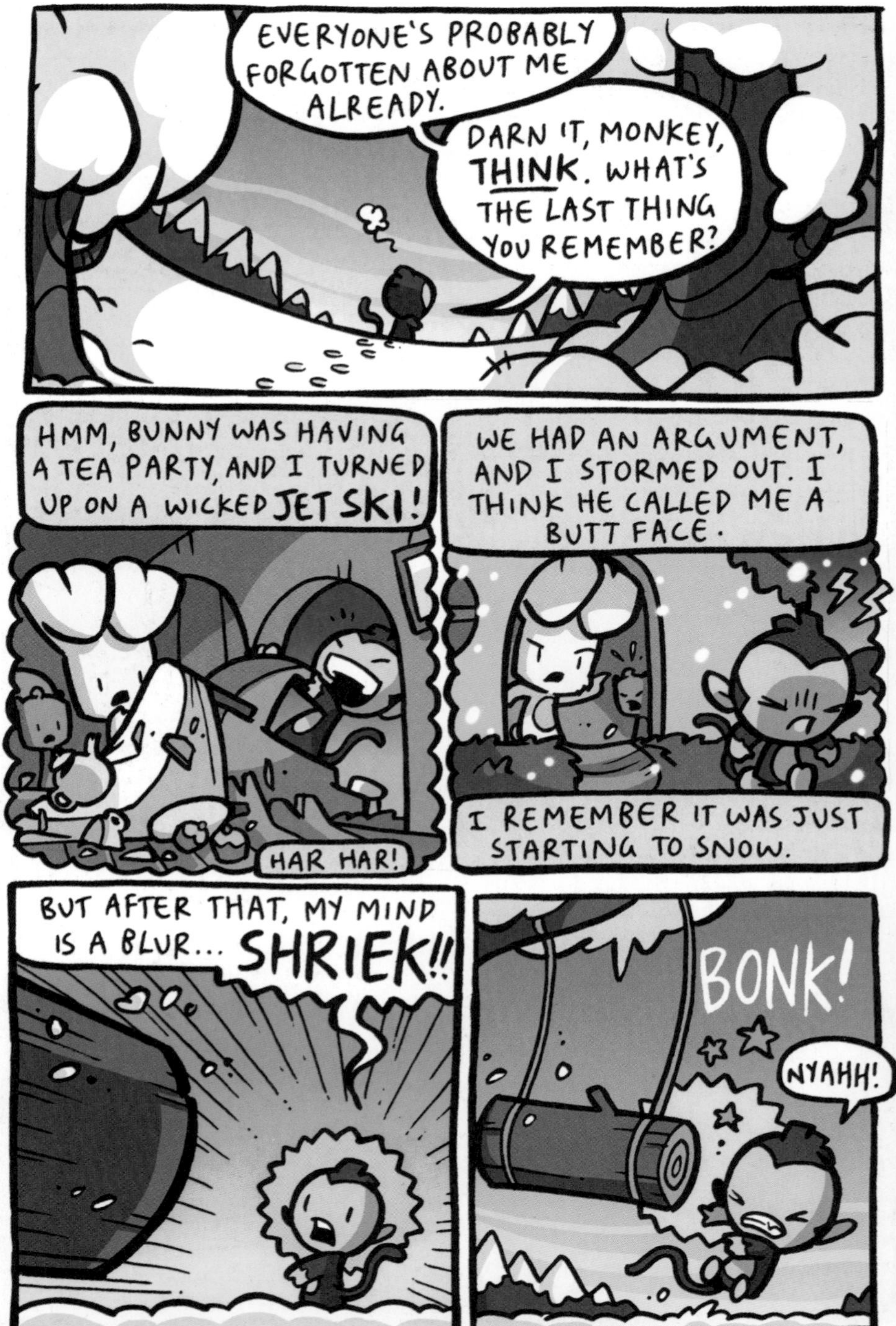
EVERYONE'S PROBABLY FORGOTTEN ABOUT ME ALREADY.
DARN IT, MONKEY, THINK. WHAT'S THE LAST THING YOU REMEMBER?
HMM, BUNNY WAS HAVING A TEA PARTY, AND I TURNED UP ON A WICKED JET SKI!
HAR HAR!
WE HAD AN ARGUMENT, AND I STORMED OUT. I THINK HE CALLED ME A BUTT FACE.
I REMEMBER IT WAS JUST STARTING TO SNOW.
BUT AFTER THAT, MY MIND IS A BLUR...
SHRIEK!!
BONK!
NYAHH!

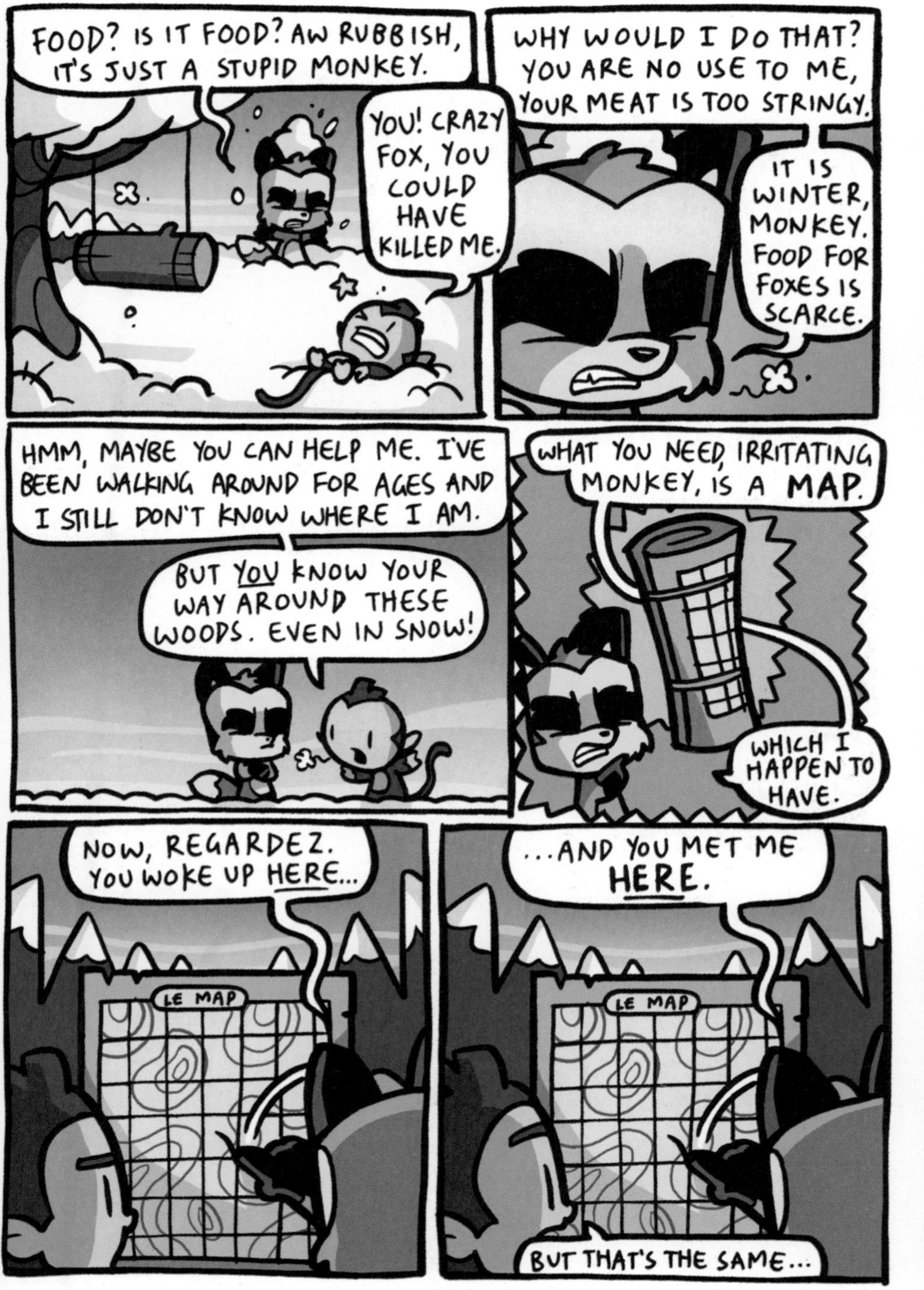
FOOD? IS IT FOOD? AW RUBBISH, IT'S JUST A STUPID MONKEY.
YOU! CRAZY FOX, YOU COULD HAVE KILLED ME.
WHY WOULD I DO THAT? YOU ARE NO USE TO ME, YOUR MEAT IS TOO STRINGY.
IT IS WINTER, MONKEY. FOOD FOR FOXES IS SCARCE.
HMM, MAYBE YOU CAN HELP ME. I'VE BEEN WALKING AROUND FOR AGES AND I STILL DON'T KNOW WHERE I AM.
BUT YOU KNOW YOUR WAY AROUND THESE WOODS. EVEN IN SNOW!
WHAT YOU NEED, IRRITATING MONKEY, IS A MAP.
WHICH I HAPPEN TO HAVE.
NOW, REGARDEZ. YOU WOKE UP HERE...
LE MAP
...AND YOU MET ME HERE.
LE MAP
BUT THAT'S THE SAME...

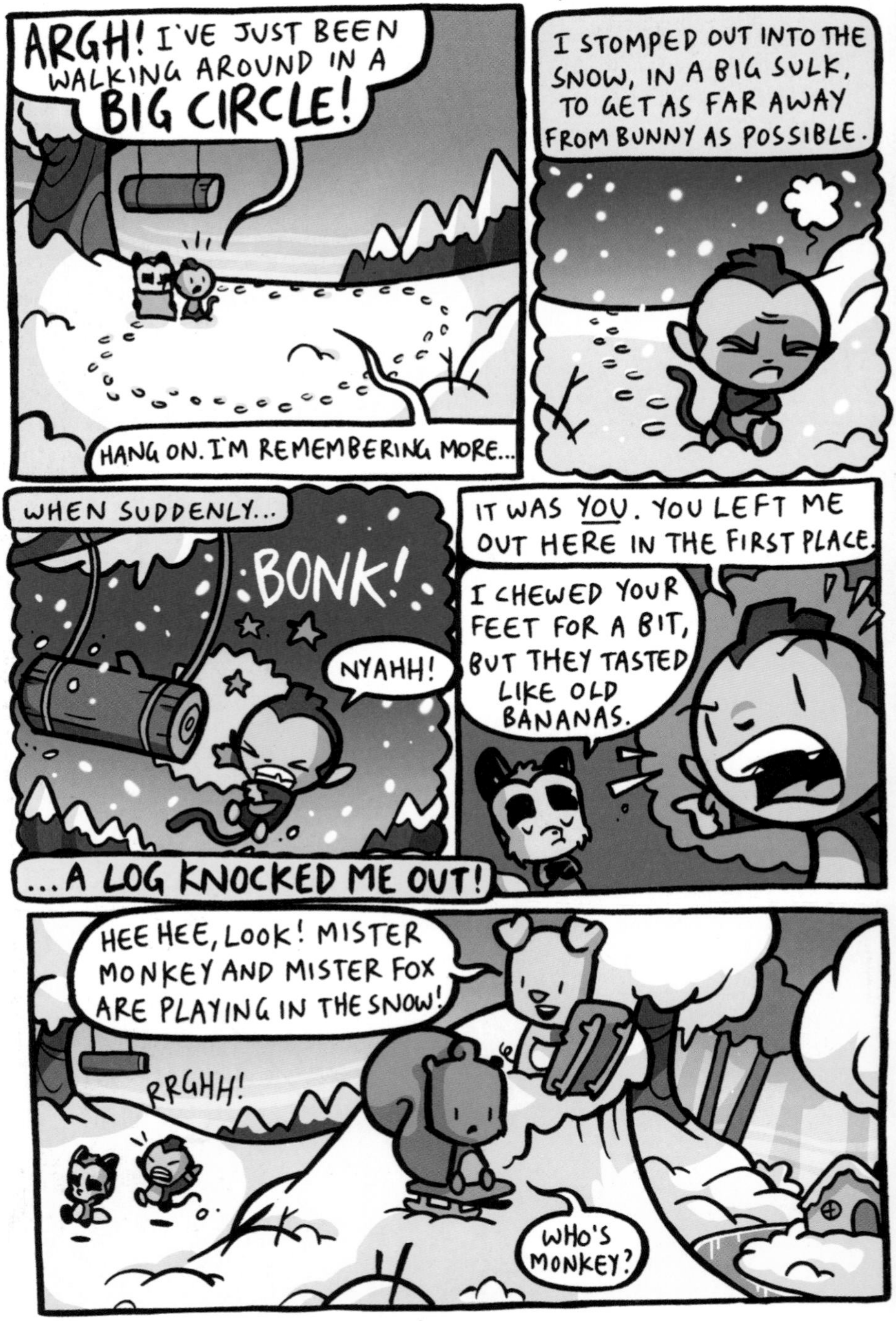
ARGH! I'VE JUST BEEN WALKING AROUND IN A BIG CIRCLE!
HANG ON. I'M REMEMBERING MORE...
I STOMPED OUT INTO THE SNOW, IN A BIG SULK, TO GET AS FAR AWAY FROM BUNNY AS POSSIBLE.
WHEN SUDDENLY...
BONK!
NYAHH!
...A LOG KNOCKED ME OUT!
IT WAS YOU. YOU LEFT ME OUT HERE IN THE FIRST PLACE.
I CHEWED YOUR FEET FOR A BIT, BUT THEY TASTED LIKE OLD BANANAS.
HEE HEE, LOOK! MISTER MONKEY AND MISTER FOX ARE PLAYING IN THE SNOW!
RRGHH!
WHO'S MONKEY?

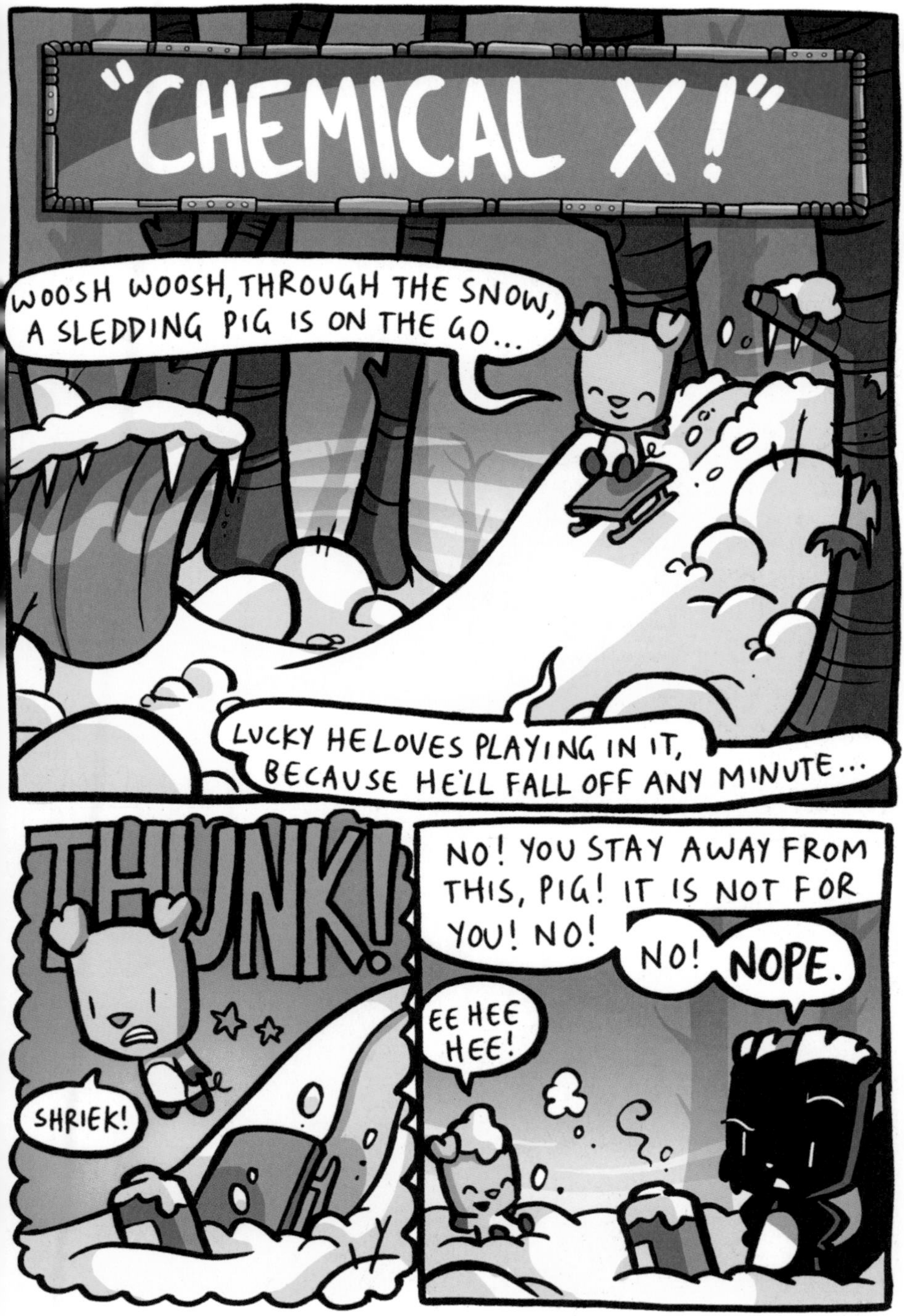
"CHEMICAL X!"
WOOSH WOOSH, THROUGH THE SNOW, A SLEDDING PIG IS ON THE GO...
LUCKY HE LOVES PLAYING IN IT, BECAUSE HE'LL FALL OFF ANY MINUTE...
THUNK!
SHRIEK!
NO! YOU STAY AWAY FROM THIS, PIG! IT IS NOT FOR YOU! NO!
NO!
NOPE.
EE HEE HEE!

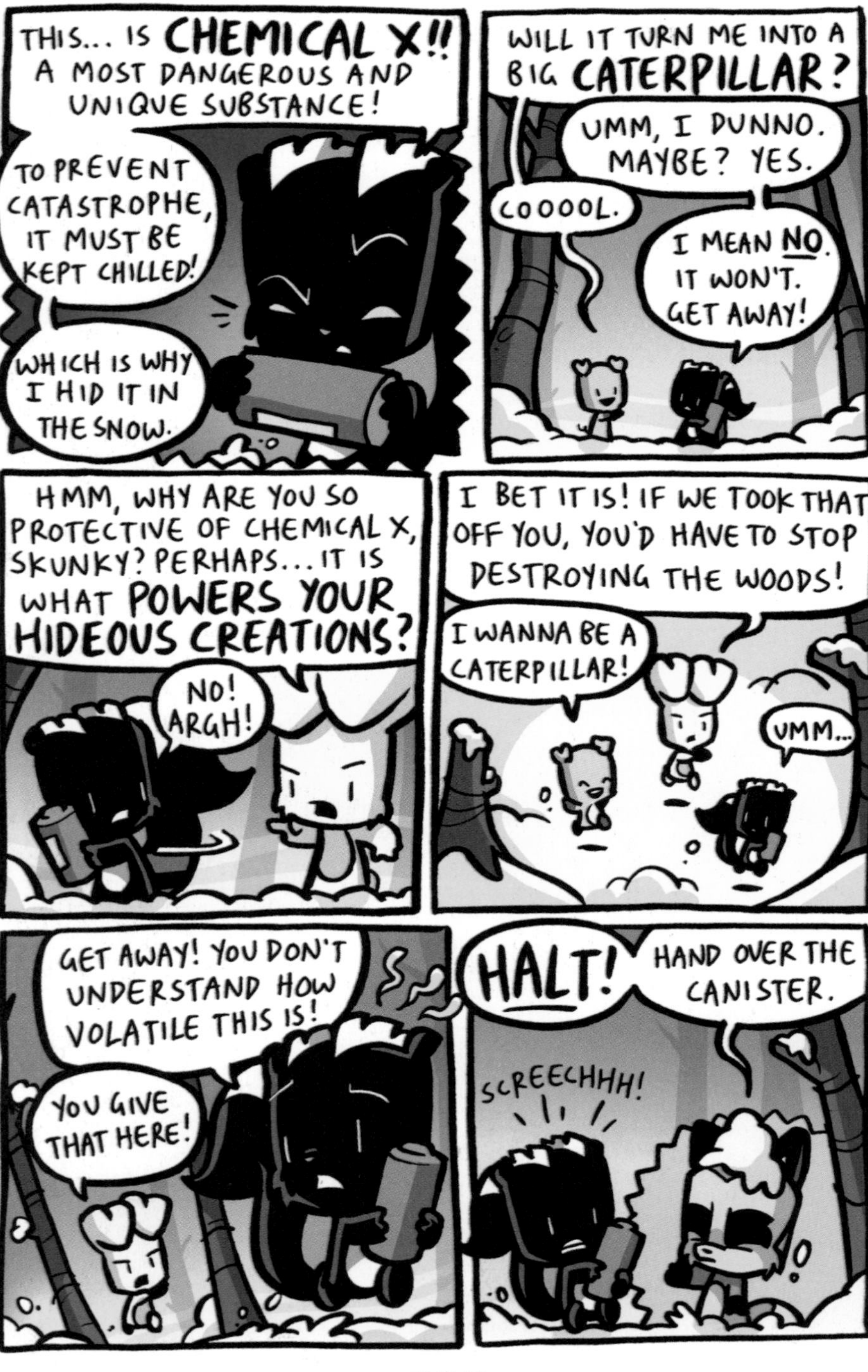
THIS... IS CHEMICAL X!! A MOST DANGEROUS AND UNIQUE SUBSTANCE!
TO PREVENT CATASTROPHE, IT MUST BE KEPT CHILLED!
WHICH IS WHY I HID IT IN THE SNOW.
WILL IT TURN ME INTO A BIG CATERPILLAR?
UMM, I DUNNO. MAYBE? YES.
COOOOL.
I MEAN NO. IT WON'T. GET AWAY!
HMM, WHY ARE YOU SO PROTECTIVE OF CHEMICAL X, SKUNKY? PERHAPS... IT IS WHAT POWERS YOUR HIDEOUS CREATIONS?
NO! ARGH!
I BET IT IS! IF WE TOOK THAT OFF YOU, YOU'D HAVE TO STOP DESTROYING THE WOODS!
I WANNA BE A CATERPILLAR!
UMM...
GET AWAY! YOU DON'T UNDERSTAND HOW VOLATILE THIS IS!
YOU GIVE THAT HERE!
HALT!
HAND OVER THE CANISTER.
SCREECHHH!

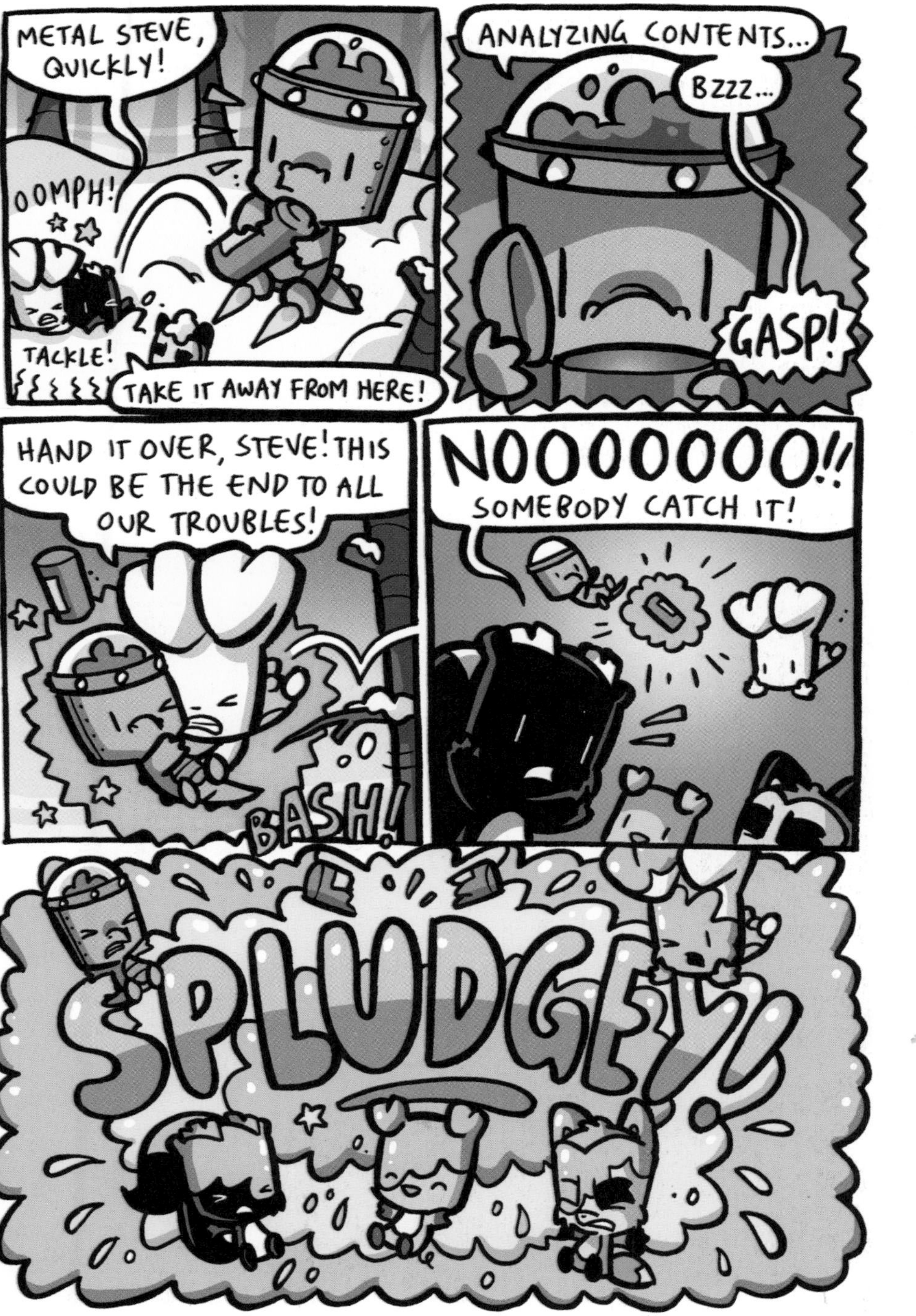
METAL STEVE, QUICKLY!
OOMPH!
TACKLE!
TAKE IT AWAY FROM HERE!
ANALYZING CONTENTS...
BZZZ...
GASP!
HAND IT OVER, STEVE! THIS COULD BE THE END TO ALL OUR TROUBLES!
BASH!
NOOOOOOO!!
SOMEBODY CATCH IT!
SPLUDGE!!

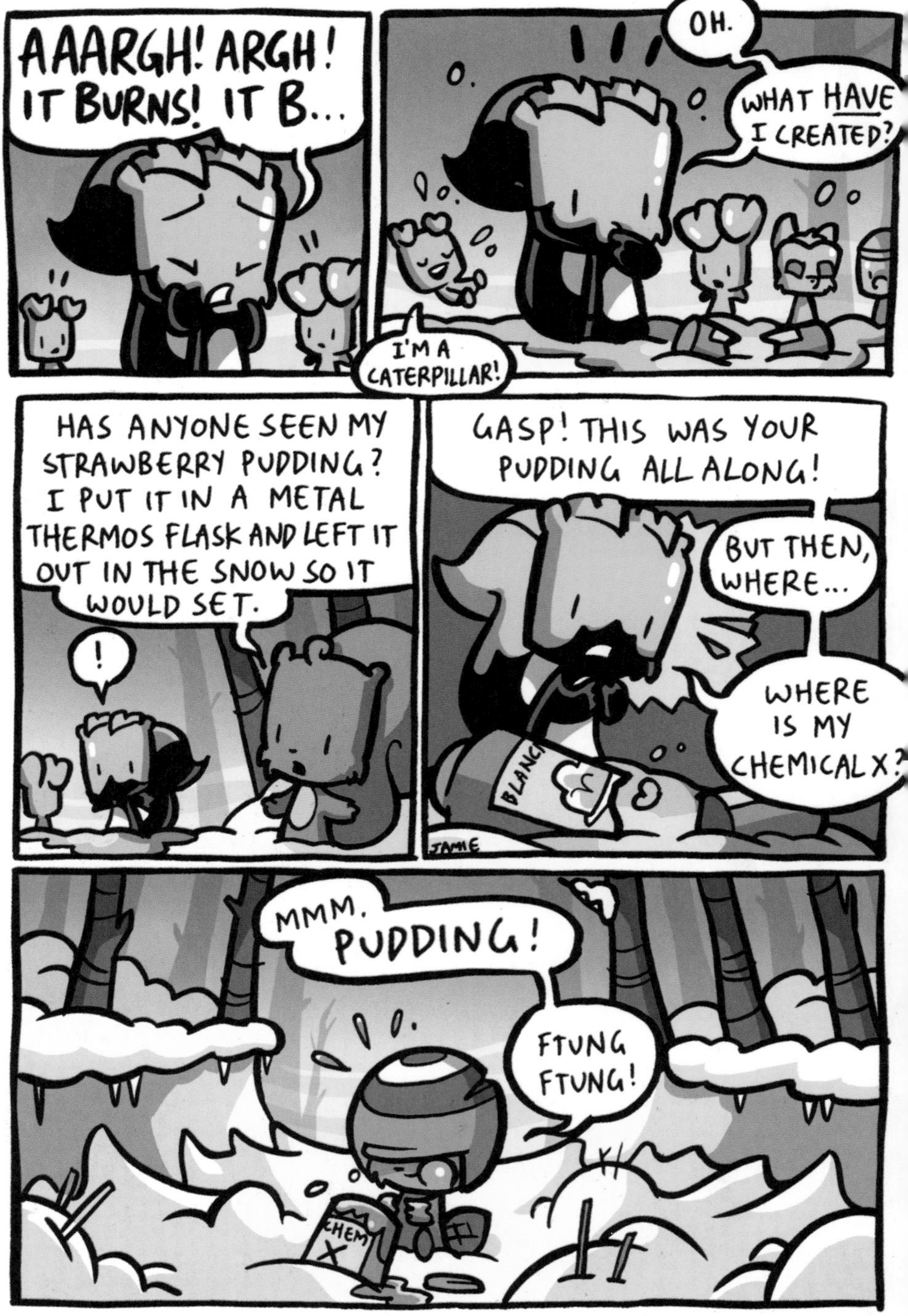
AAARGH! ARGH! IT BURNS! IT B...
OH.
WHAT HAVE I CREATED?
I'M A CATERPILLAR!
HAS ANYONE SEEN MY STRAWBERRY PUDDING? I PUT IT IN A METAL THERMOS FLASK AND LEFT IT OUT IN THE SNOW SO IT WOULD SET.
!
GASP! THIS WAS YOUR PUDDING ALL ALONG!
BUT THEN, WHERE...
WHERE IS MY CHEMICAL X?
BLANC
JAMIE
MMM. PUDDING!
FTUNG FTUNG!
CHEM X

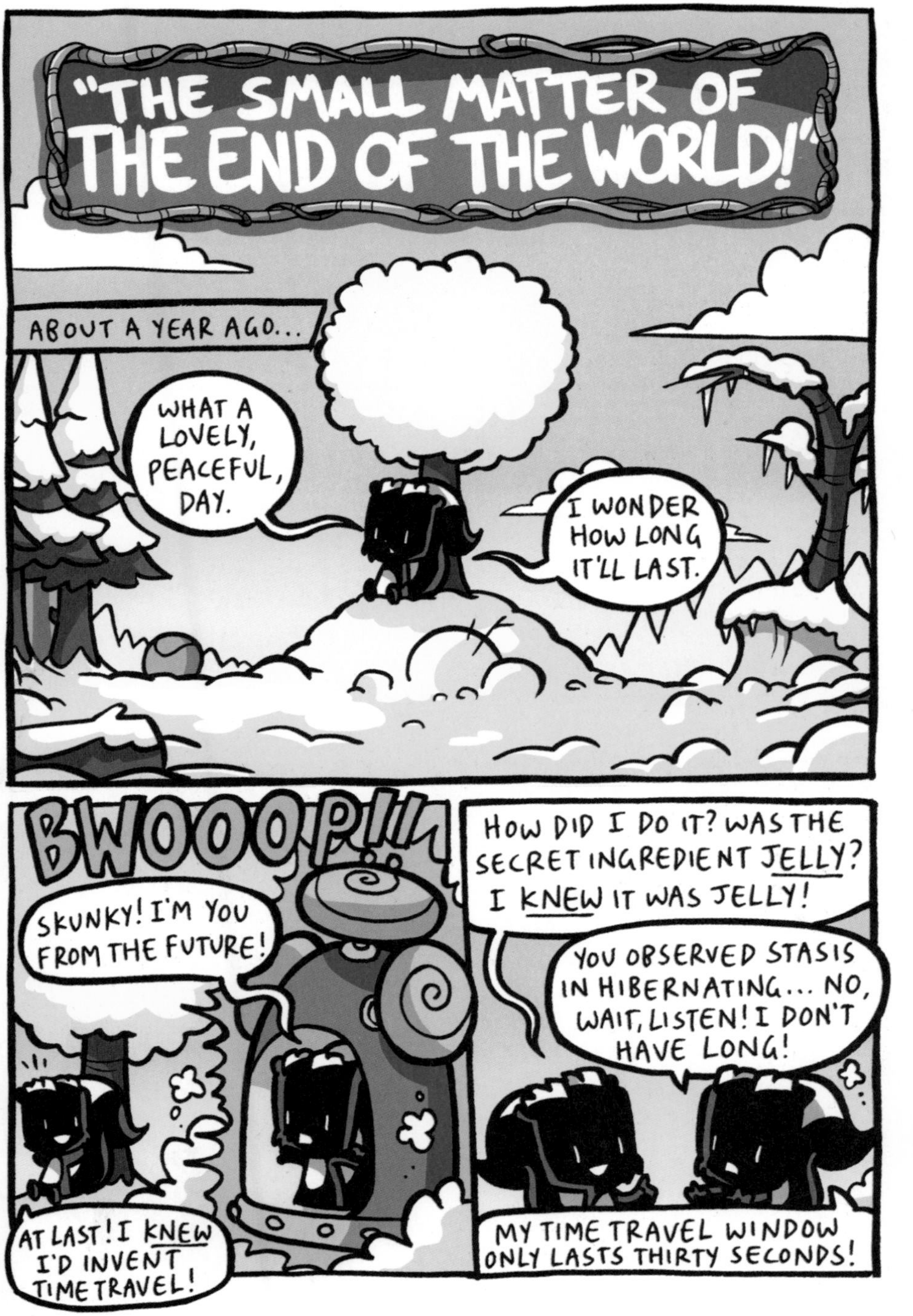
"THE SMALL MATTER OF THE END OF THE WORLD!"
ABOUT A YEAR AGO...
WHAT A LOVELY, PEACEFUL, DAY.
I WONDER HOW LONG IT'LL LAST.
BWOOOP!!!
SKUNKY! I'M YOU FROM THE FUTURE!
AT LAST! I KNEW I'D INVENT TIME TRAVEL!
HOW DID I DO IT? WAS THE SECRET INGREDIENT JELLY? I KNEW IT WAS JELLY!
YOU OBSERVED STASIS IN HIBERNATING... NO, WAIT, LISTEN! I DON'T HAVE LONG!
MY TIME TRAVEL WINDOW ONLY LASTS THIRTY SECONDS!

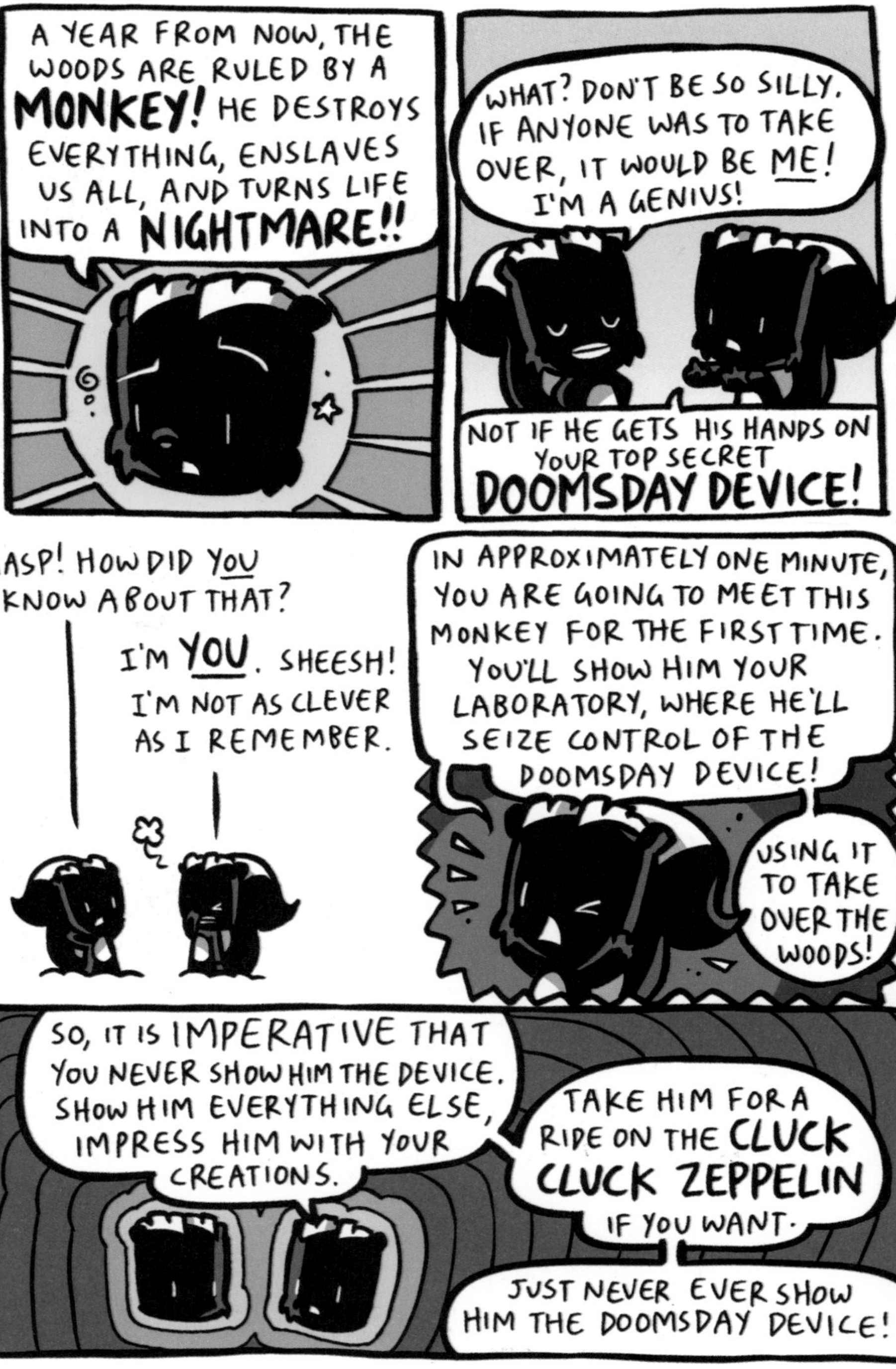
A YEAR FROM NOW, THE WOODS ARE RULED BY A MONKEY! HE DESTROYS EVERYTHING, ENSLAVES US ALL, AND TURNS LIFE INTO A NIGHTMARE!!
WHAT? DON'T BE SO SILLY. IF ANYONE WAS TO TAKE OVER, IT WOULD BE ME! I'M A GENIUS!
NOT IF HE GETS HIS HANDS ON YOUR TOP SECRET DOOMSDAY DEVICE!
GASP! HOW DID YOU KNOW ABOUT THAT?
I'M YOU. SHEESH! I'M NOT AS CLEVER AS I REMEMBER.
IN APPROXIMATELY ONE MINUTE, YOU ARE GOING TO MEET THIS MONKEY FOR THE FIRST TIME. YOU'LL SHOW HIM YOUR LABORATORY, WHERE HE'LL SEIZE CONTROL OF THE DOOMSDAY DEVICE!
USING IT TO TAKE OVER THE WOODS!
SO, IT IS IMPERATIVE THAT YOU NEVER SHOW HIM THE DEVICE. SHOW HIM EVERYTHING ELSE, IMPRESS HIM WITH YOUR CREATIONS.
TAKE HIM FOR A RIDE ON THE CLUCK CLUCK ZEPPELIN IF YOU WANT.
JUST NEVER EVER SHOW HIM THE DOOMSDAY DEVICE!

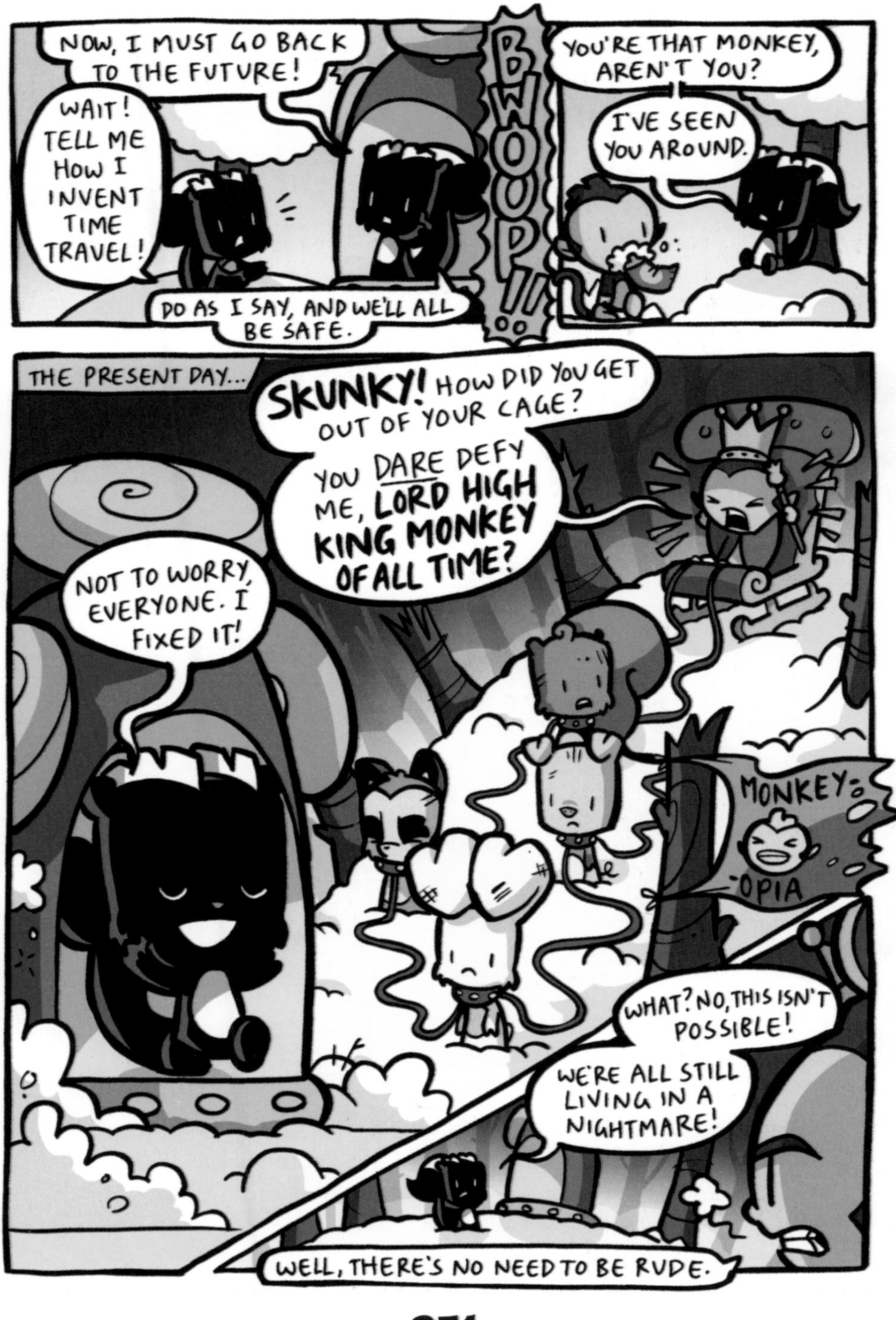
NOW, I MUST GO BACK TO THE FUTURE!
WAIT! TELL ME HOW I INVENT TIME TRAVEL!
DO AS I SAY, AND WE'LL ALL BE SAFE.
BWOOP!!
YOU'RE THAT MONKEY, AREN'T YOU?
I'VE SEEN YOU AROUND.
THE PRESENT DAY...
SKUNKY! HOW DID YOU GET OUT OF YOUR CAGE?
YOU DARE DEFY ME, LORD HIGH KING MONKEY OF ALL TIME?
NOT TO WORRY, EVERYONE. I FIXED IT!
MONKEY-OPIA
WHAT? NO, THIS ISN'T POSSIBLE!
WE'RE ALL STILL LIVING IN A NIGHTMARE!
WELL, THERE'S NO NEED TO BE RUDE.

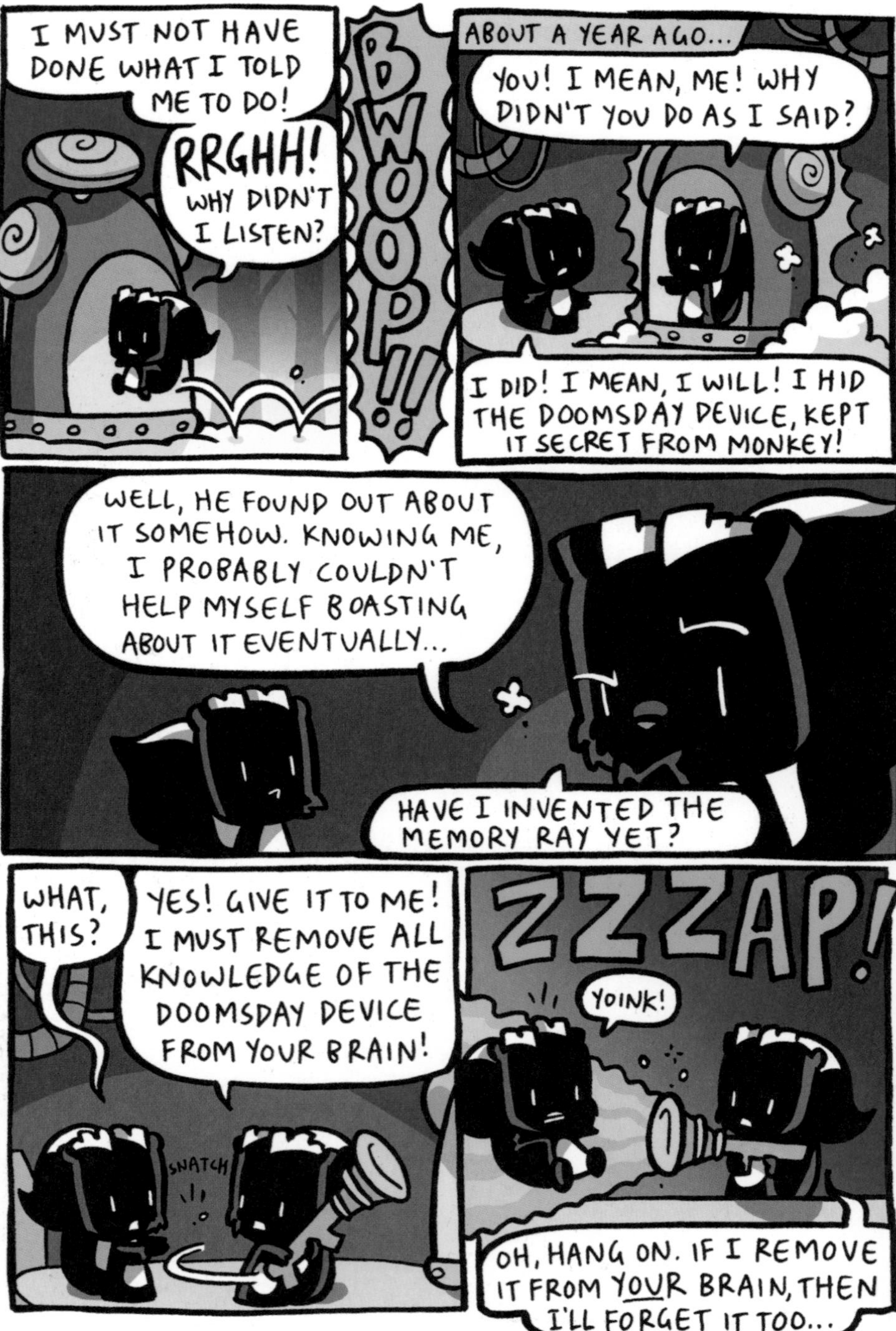
I MUST NOT HAVE DONE WHAT I TOLD ME TO DO!
RRGHH! WHY DIDN'T I LISTEN?
BWOOP!!
ABOUT A YEAR AGO...
YOU! I MEAN, ME! WHY DIDN'T YOU DO AS I SAID?
I DID! I MEAN, I WILL! I HID THE DOOMSDAY DEVICE, KEPT IT SECRET FROM MONKEY!
WELL, HE FOUND OUT ABOUT IT SOMEHOW. KNOWING ME, I PROBABLY COULDN'T HELP MYSELF BOASTING ABOUT IT EVENTUALLY...
HAVE I INVENTED THE MEMORY RAY YET?
WHAT, THIS?
YES! GIVE IT TO ME! I MUST REMOVE ALL KNOWLEDGE OF THE DOOMSDAY DEVICE FROM YOUR BRAIN!
SNATCH
ZZZAP!
YOINK!
OH, HANG ON. IF I REMOVE IT FROM YOUR BRAIN, THEN I'LL FORGET IT TOO...

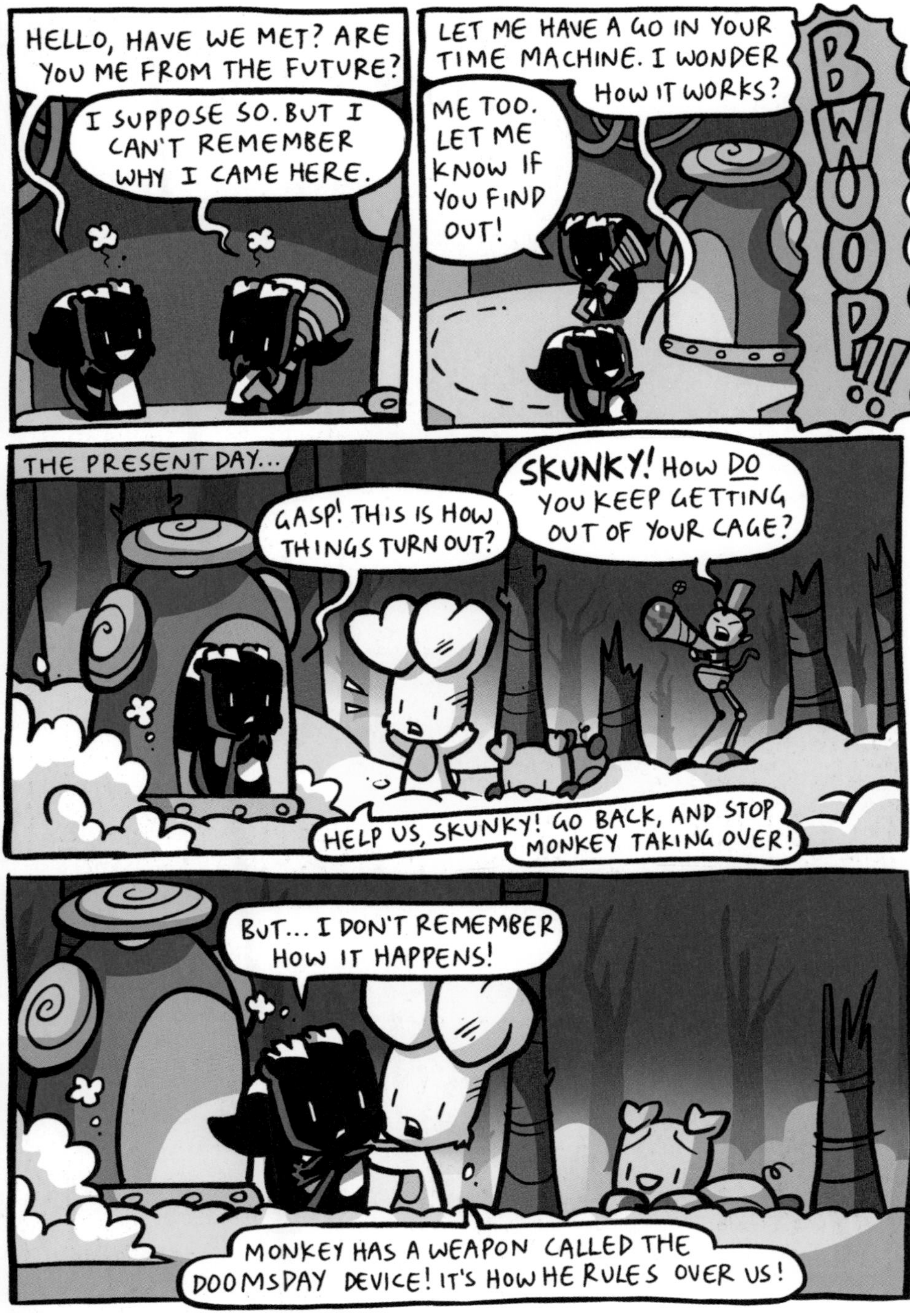
HELLO, HAVE WE MET? ARE YOU ME FROM THE FUTURE?
I SUPPOSE SO. BUT I CAN'T REMEMBER WHY I CAME HERE.
LET ME HAVE A GO IN YOUR TIME MACHINE. I WONDER HOW IT WORKS?
ME TOO. LET ME KNOW IF YOU FIND OUT!
BWOOOP!!!
THE PRESENT DAY...
GASP! THIS IS HOW THINGS TURN OUT?
SKUNKY! HOW DO YOU KEEP GETTING OUT OF YOUR CAGE?
HELP US, SKUNKY! GO BACK, AND STOP MONKEY TAKING OVER!
BUT... I DON'T REMEMBER HOW IT HAPPENS!
MONKEY HAS A WEAPON CALLED THE DOOMSDAY DEVICE! IT'S HOW HE RULES OVER US!

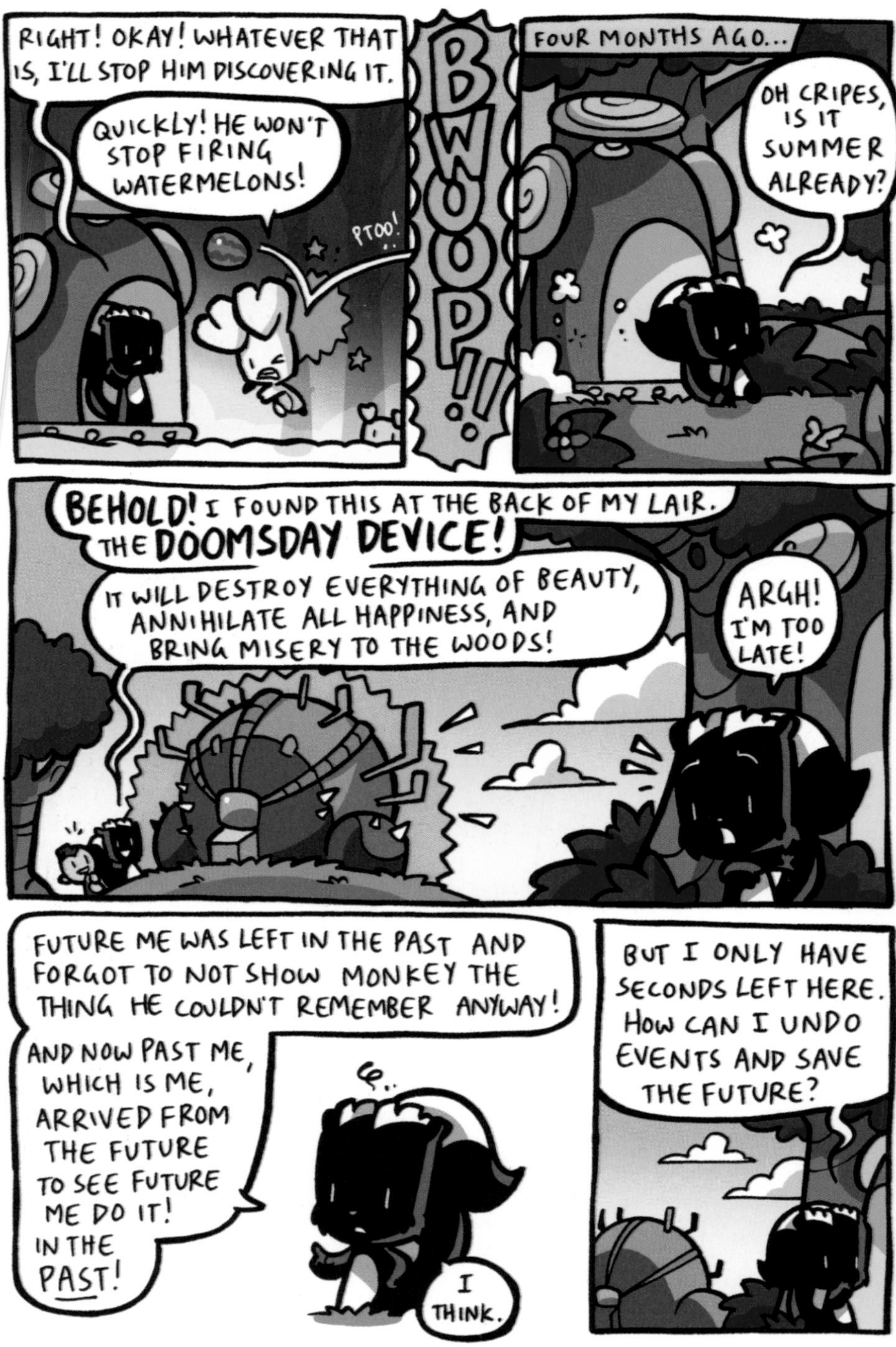
RIGHT! OKAY! WHATEVER THAT IS, I'LL STOP HIM DISCOVERING IT.
QUICKLY! HE WON'T STOP FIRING WATERMELONS!
PTOO!
BWOOP!!
FOUR MONTHS AGO...
OH CRIPES, IS IT SUMMER ALREADY?
BEHOLD! I FOUND THIS AT THE BACK OF MY LAIR. THE DOOMSDAY DEVICE!
IT WILL DESTROY EVERYTHING OF BEAUTY, ANNIHILATE ALL HAPPINESS, AND BRING MISERY TO THE WOODS!
ARGH! I'M TOO LATE!
FUTURE ME WAS LEFT IN THE PAST AND FORGOT TO NOT SHOW MONKEY THE THING HE COULDN'T REMEMBER ANYWAY!
AND NOW PAST ME, WHICH IS ME, ARRIVED FROM THE FUTURE TO SEE FUTURE ME DO IT! IN THE PAST!
I THINK.
BUT I ONLY HAVE SECONDS LEFT HERE. HOW CAN I UNDO EVENTS AND SAVE THE FUTURE?

HELLO, MISTER SKUNKY. WE'RE TRYING TO BALANCE LEMON PUFF COOKIES ON PIG'S HEAD.

NOT NOW, I AM TRYING TO USE MY GEN<u>IU</u>S BRAIN!

ALTHOUGH, PERHAPS WHAT'S IN MY HEAD ISN'T THE SOLUTION. PERHAPS IT'S WHAT'S...**ON YOURS!**

SORRY! RIGHT NOW I NEED THIS MORE THAN YOU DO!

AWW, NOW WE HAVE TO START FROM THE BEGINNING!

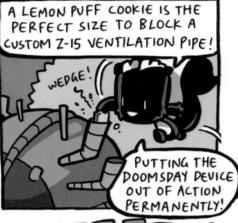

A LEMON PUFF COOKIE IS THE PERFECT SIZE TO BLOCK A CUSTOM Z-15 VENTILATION PIPE!

WEDGE!

PUTTING THE DOOMSDAY DEVICE OUT OF ACTION PERMANENTLY!

AND BACK, JUST IN TIME!

QUICKLY, ACTION BEAVER, USE THAT BRILLIANT MIND TO WORK OUT THE KEY CODE!

BZZZZZZZZ!

WAIT! NO! WHAT'S WRONG WITH IT?

NO! NOO!

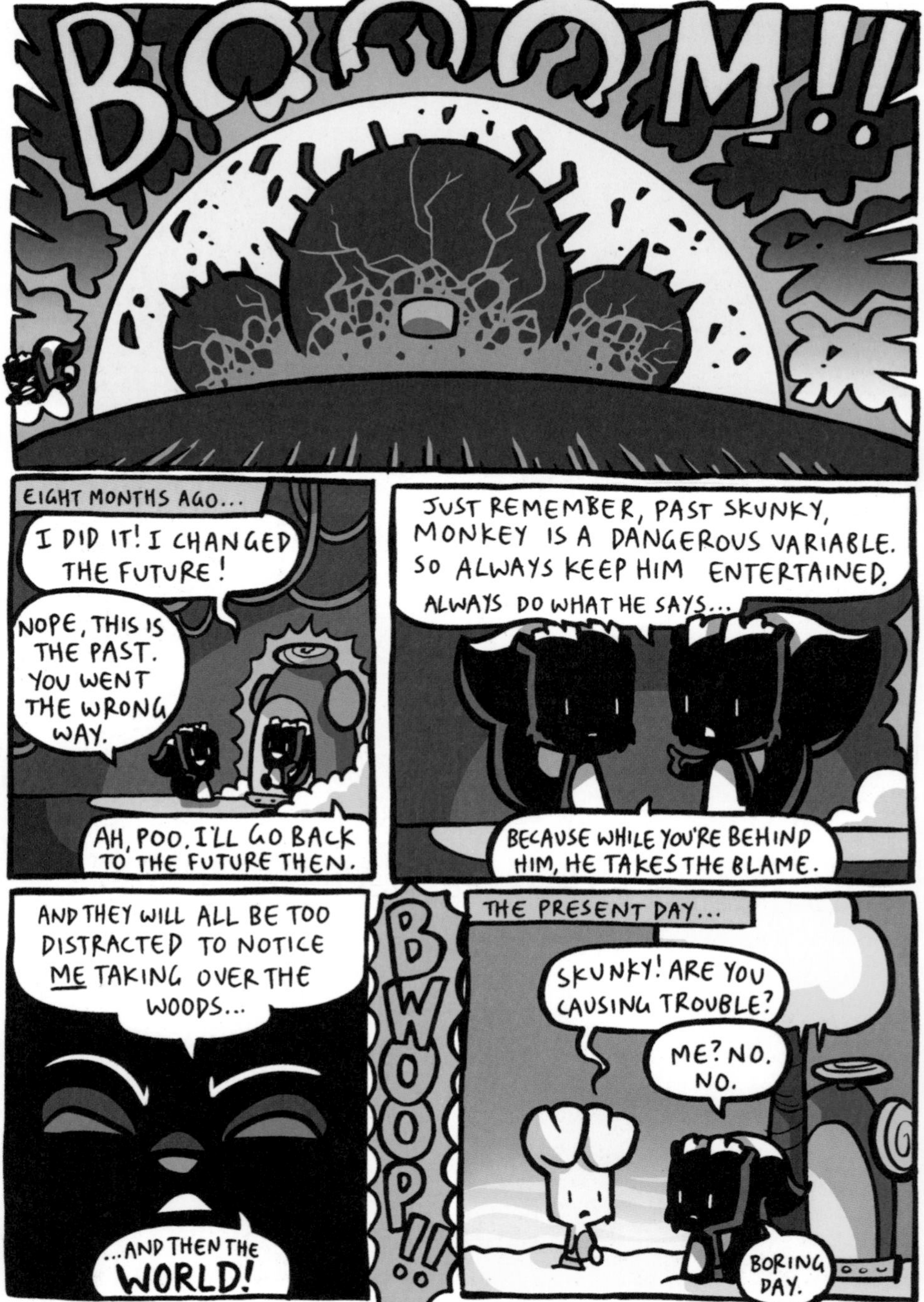
BOOOOM!!
EIGHT MONTHS AGO...
I DID IT! I CHANGED THE FUTURE!
NOPE, THIS IS THE PAST. YOU WENT THE WRONG WAY.
AH, POO. I'LL GO BACK TO THE FUTURE THEN.
JUST REMEMBER, PAST SKUNKY, MONKEY IS A DANGEROUS VARIABLE. SO ALWAYS KEEP HIM ENTERTAINED. ALWAYS DO WHAT HE SAYS...
BECAUSE WHILE YOU'RE BEHIND HIM, HE TAKES THE BLAME.
AND THEY WILL ALL BE TOO DISTRACTED TO NOTICE ME TAKING OVER THE WOODS...
...AND THEN THE WORLD!
BWOOP!!
THE PRESENT DAY...
SKUNKY! ARE YOU CAUSING TROUBLE?
ME? NO. NO.
BORING DAY.

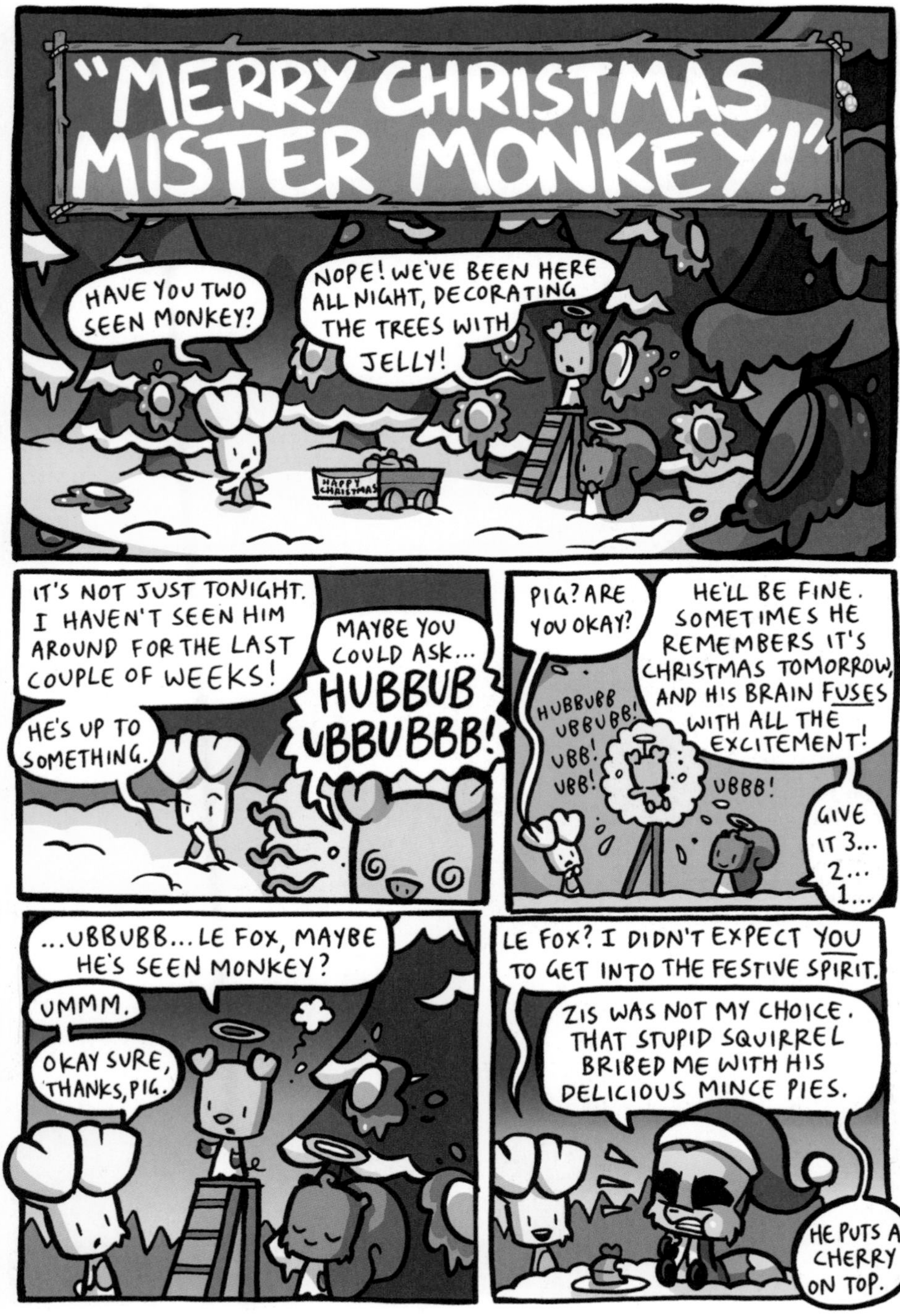
"MERRY CHRISTMAS MISTER MONKEY!"
HAVE YOU TWO SEEN MONKEY?
NOPE! WE'VE BEEN HERE ALL NIGHT, DECORATING THE TREES WITH JELLY!
HAPPY CHRISTMAS
IT'S NOT JUST TONIGHT. I HAVEN'T SEEN HIM AROUND FOR THE LAST COUPLE OF WEEKS!
HE'S UP TO SOMETHING.
MAYBE YOU COULD ASK...
HUBBUB UBBUBBB!
PIG? ARE YOU OKAY?
HE'LL BE FINE. SOMETIMES HE REMEMBERS IT'S CHRISTMAS TOMORROW, AND HIS BRAIN FUSES WITH ALL THE EXCITEMENT!
HUBBUBB UBBUBB! UBB! UBB!
UBBB!
GIVE IT 3... 2... 1...
...UBBUBB... LE FOX, MAYBE HE'S SEEN MONKEY?
UMMM.
OKAY SURE, THANKS, PIG.
LE FOX? I DIDN'T EXPECT YOU TO GET INTO THE FESTIVE SPIRIT.
ZIS WAS NOT MY CHOICE. THAT STUPID SQUIRREL BRIBED ME WITH HIS DELICIOUS MINCE PIES.
HE PUTS A CHERRY ON TOP.

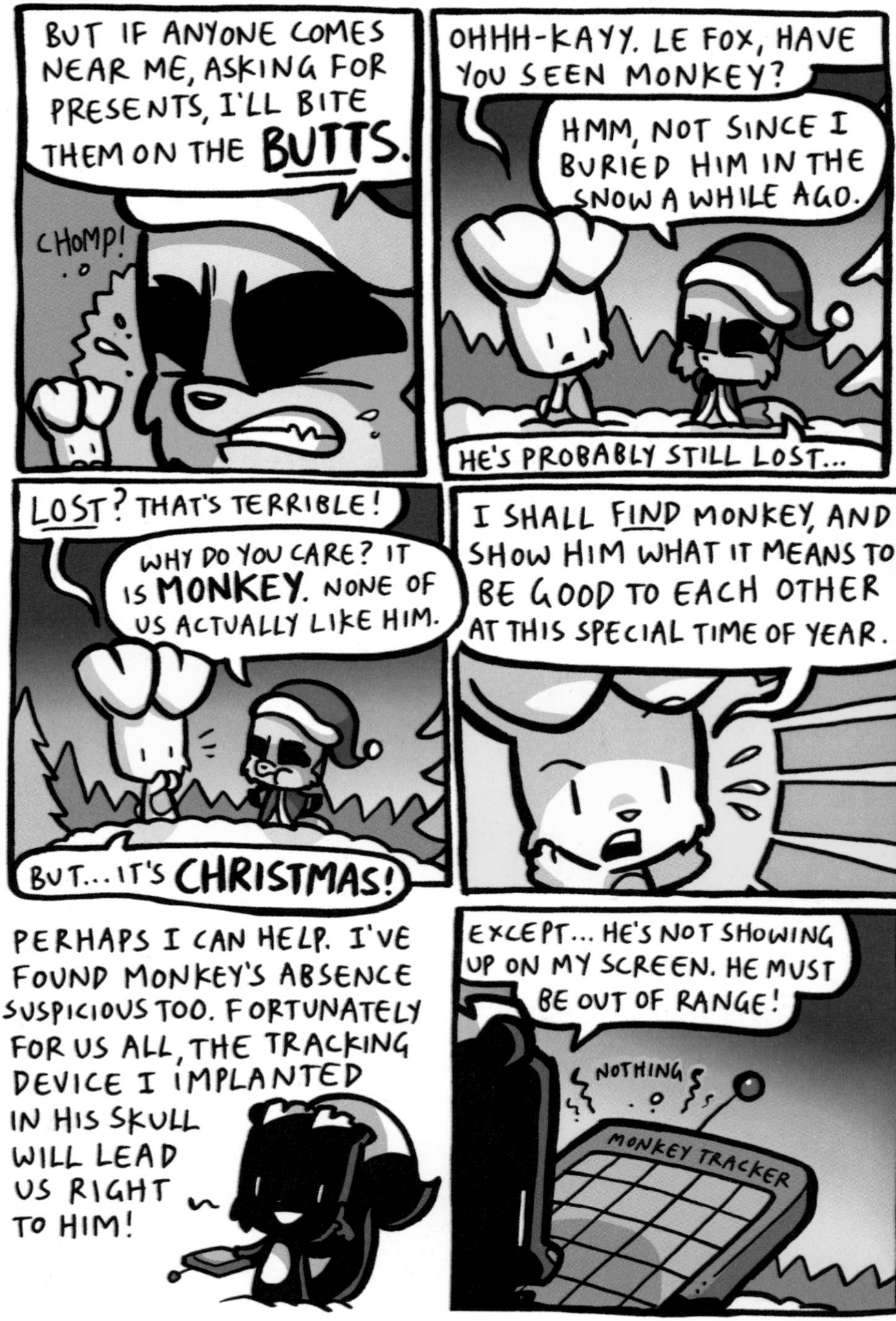

BUT IF ANYONE COMES NEAR ME, ASKING FOR PRESENTS, I'LL BITE THEM ON THE BUTTS.
CHOMP!
OHHH-KAYY. LE FOX, HAVE YOU SEEN MONKEY?
HMM, NOT SINCE I BURIED HIM IN THE SNOW A WHILE AGO.
HE'S PROBABLY STILL LOST...
LOST? THAT'S TERRIBLE!
WHY DO YOU CARE? IT IS MONKEY. NONE OF US ACTUALLY LIKE HIM.
BUT... IT'S CHRISTMAS!
I SHALL FIND MONKEY, AND SHOW HIM WHAT IT MEANS TO BE GOOD TO EACH OTHER AT THIS SPECIAL TIME OF YEAR.
PERHAPS I CAN HELP. I'VE FOUND MONKEY'S ABSENCE SUSPICIOUS TOO. FORTUNATELY FOR US ALL, THE TRACKING DEVICE I IMPLANTED IN HIS SKULL WILL LEAD US RIGHT TO HIM!
EXCEPT... HE'S NOT SHOWING UP ON MY SCREEN. HE MUST BE OUT OF RANGE!
NOTHING
MONKEY TRACKER

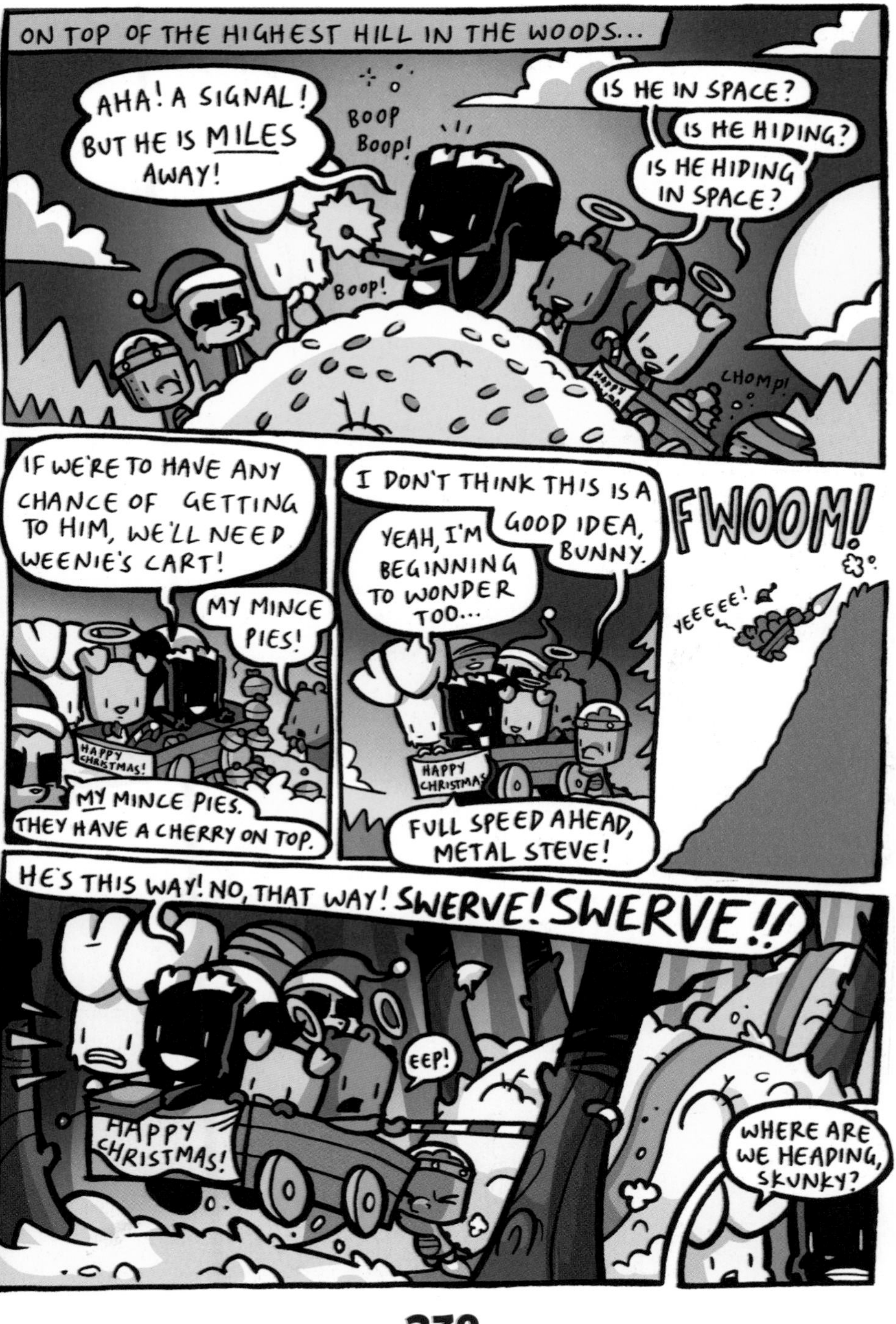

ON TOP OF THE HIGHEST HILL IN THE WOODS...
AHA! A SIGNAL! BUT HE IS MILES AWAY!
BOOP BOOP!
BOOP!
IS HE IN SPACE?
IS HE HIDING?
IS HE HIDING IN SPACE?
CHOMP!
IF WE'RE TO HAVE ANY CHANCE OF GETTING TO HIM, WE'LL NEED WEENIE'S CART!
MY MINCE PIES!
HAPPY CHRISTMAS!
MY MINCE PIES. THEY HAVE A CHERRY ON TOP.
I DON'T THINK THIS IS A GOOD IDEA, BUNNY.
YEAH, I'M BEGINNING TO WONDER TOO...
HAPPY CHRISTMAS
FULL SPEED AHEAD, METAL STEVE!
FWOOM!
YEEEEE!
HE'S THIS WAY! NO, THAT WAY! SWERVE! SWERVE!!
EEP!
HAPPY CHRISTMAS!
WHERE ARE WE HEADING, SKUNKY?

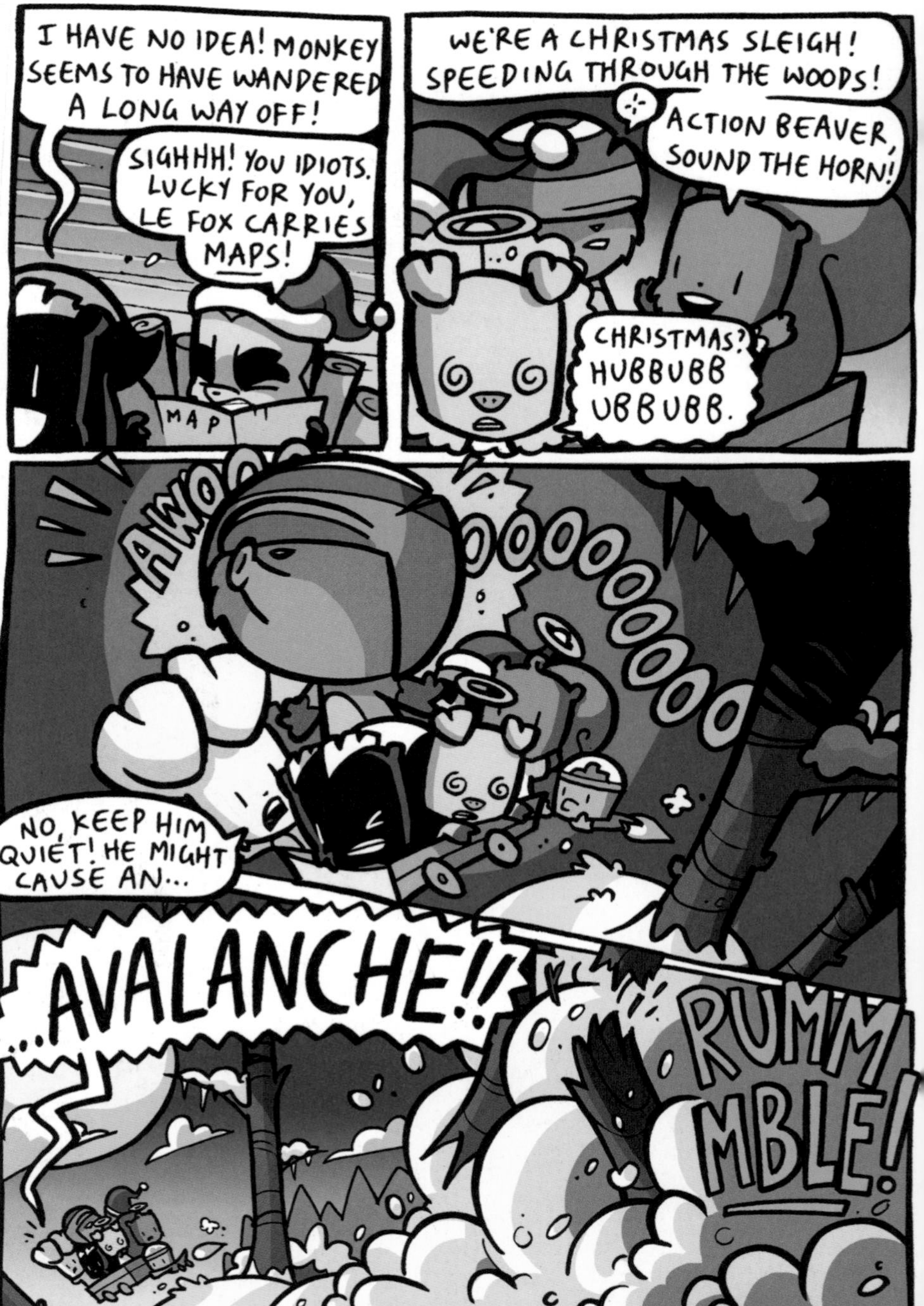
I HAVE NO IDEA! MONKEY SEEMS TO HAVE WANDERED A LONG WAY OFF!
SIGHHH! YOU IDIOTS. LUCKY FOR YOU, LE FOX CARRIES MAPS!
MAP
WE'RE A CHRISTMAS SLEIGH! SPEEDING THROUGH THE WOODS!
ACTION BEAVER, SOUND THE HORN!
CHRISTMAS? HUBBUBB UBBUBB.
AWOOOOOOOOOOOOOOOO
NO, KEEP HIM QUIET! HE MIGHT CAUSE AN...
...AVALANCHE!!
RUMMMBLE!

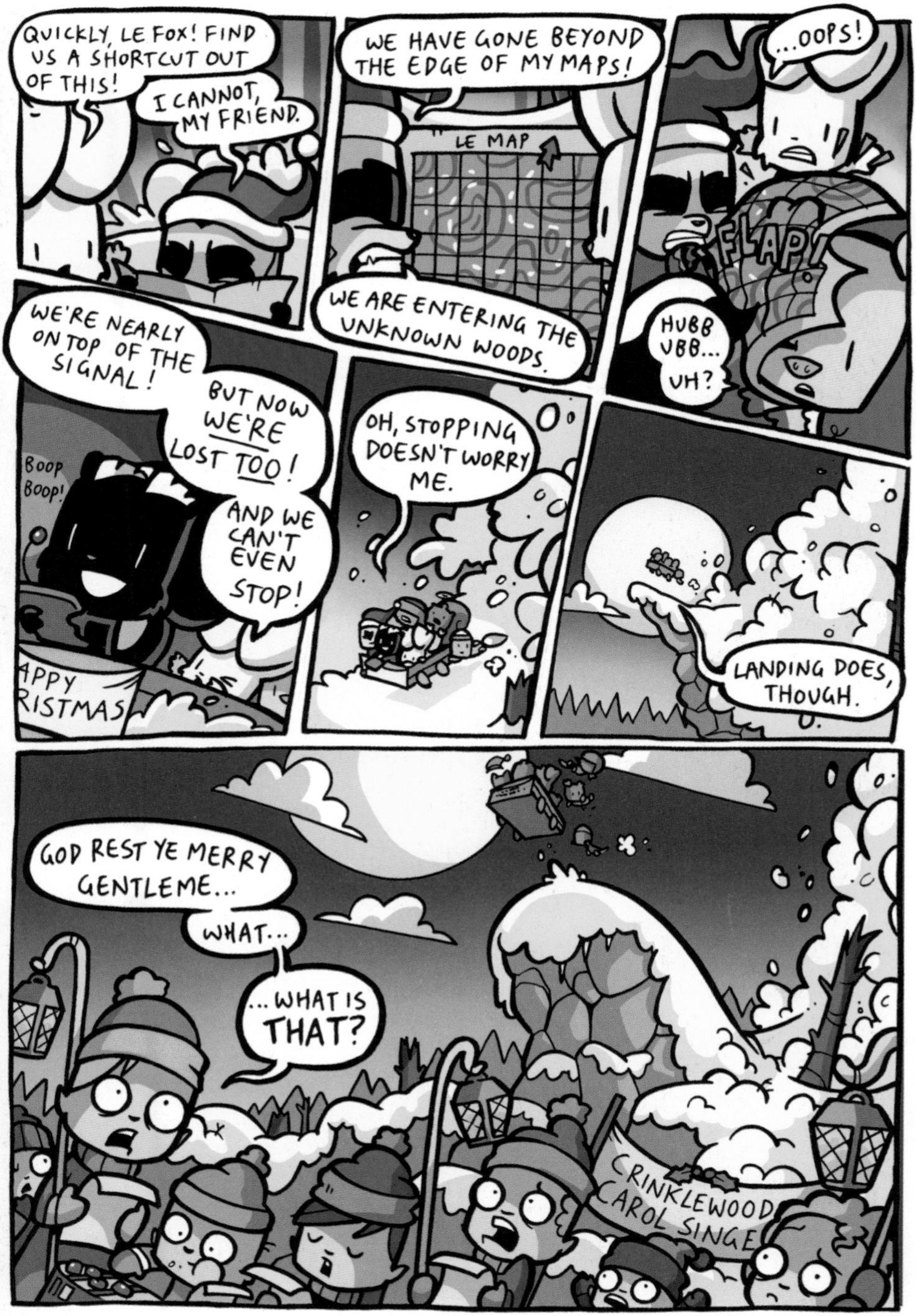
QUICKLY, LE FOX! FIND US A SHORTCUT OUT OF THIS!
I CANNOT, MY FRIEND.
WE HAVE GONE BEYOND THE EDGE OF MY MAPS!
LE MAP
...OOPS!
FLAP!
WE ARE ENTERING THE UNKNOWN WOODS.
HUBB UBB... UH?
WE'RE NEARLY ON TOP OF THE SIGNAL!
BUT NOW WE'RE LOST TOO!
AND WE CAN'T EVEN STOP!
BOOP BOOP!
APPY RISTMAS
OH, STOPPING DOESN'T WORRY ME.
LANDING DOES, THOUGH.
GOD REST YE MERRY GENTLEME...
WHAT...
...WHAT IS THAT?
CRINKLEWOOD CAROL SINGE

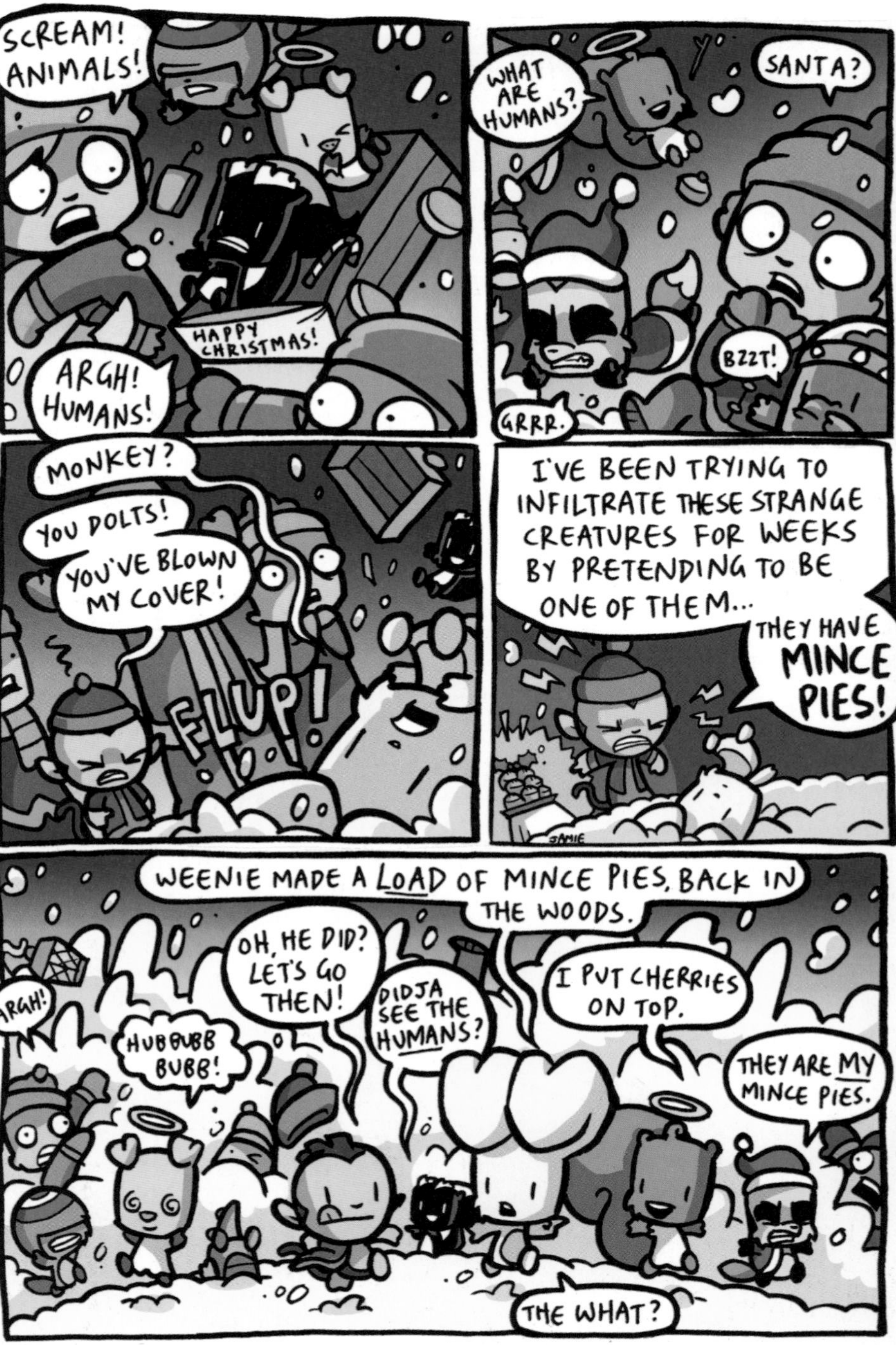
SCREAM! ANIMALS!
HAPPY CHRISTMAS!
ARGH! HUMANS!
WHAT ARE HUMANS?
SANTA?
BZZT!
GRRR.
MONKEY?
YOU DOLTS!
YOU'VE BLOWN MY COVER!
FLUP!
I'VE BEEN TRYING TO INFILTRATE THESE STRANGE CREATURES FOR WEEKS BY PRETENDING TO BE ONE OF THEM...
THEY HAVE MINCE PIES!
JAMIE
WEENIE MADE A LOAD OF MINCE PIES, BACK IN THE WOODS.
ARGH!
HUBBUBB BUBB!
OH, HE DID? LET'S GO THEN!
DIDJA SEE THE HUMANS?
I PUT CHERRIES ON TOP.
THEY ARE MY MINCE PIES.
THE WHAT?

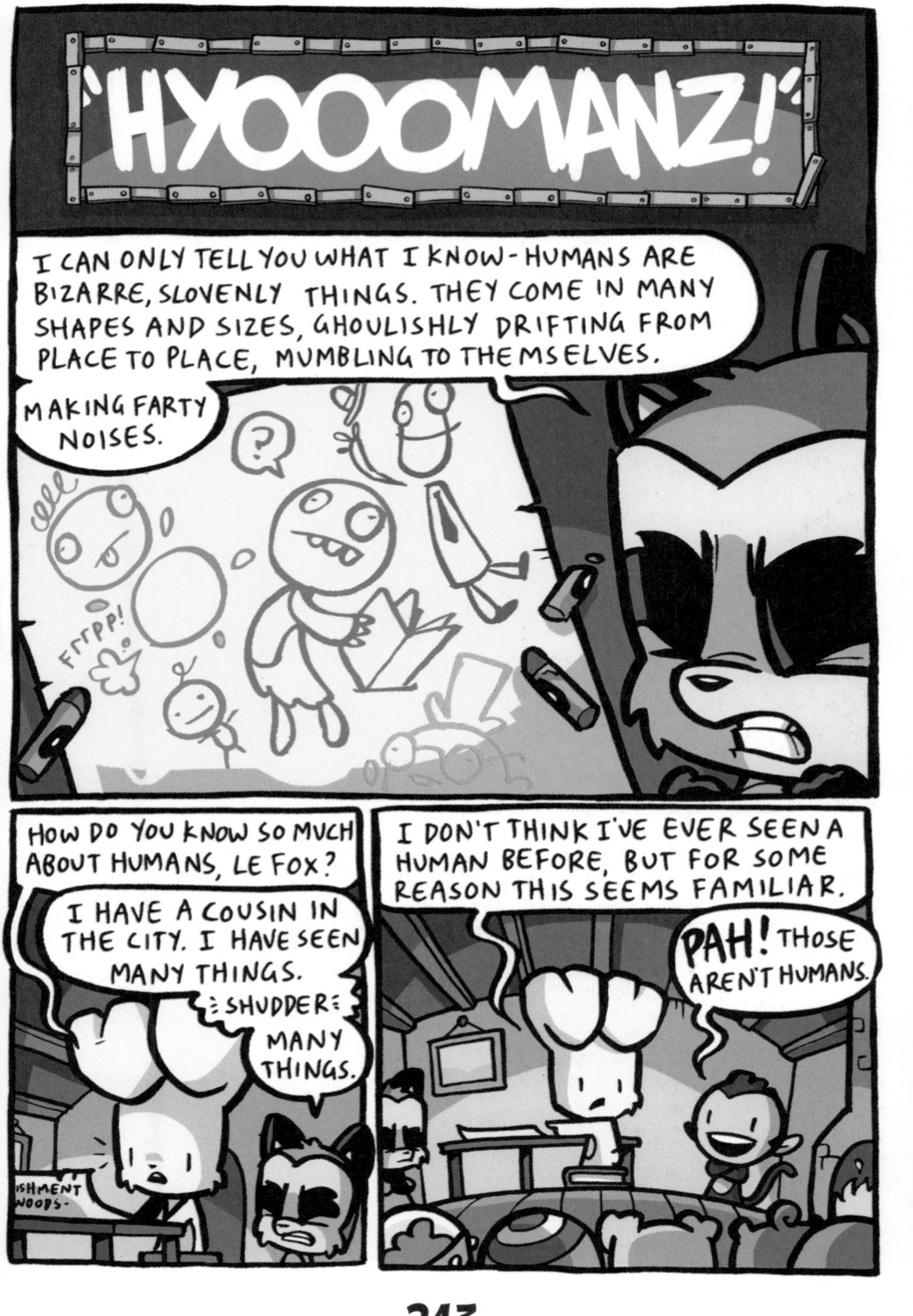
"HYOOOMANZ!"
I CAN ONLY TELL YOU WHAT I KNOW - HUMANS ARE BIZARRE, SLOVENLY THINGS. THEY COME IN MANY SHAPES AND SIZES, GHOULISHLY DRIFTING FROM PLACE TO PLACE, MUMBLING TO THEMSELVES.
MAKING FARTY NOISES.
FRRPP!
HOW DO YOU KNOW SO MUCH ABOUT HUMANS, LE FOX?
I HAVE A COUSIN IN THE CITY. I HAVE SEEN MANY THINGS.
SHUDDER
MANY THINGS.
ISHMENT
WOODS-
I DON'T THINK I'VE EVER SEEN A HUMAN BEFORE, BUT FOR SOME REASON THIS SEEMS FAMILIAR.
PAH! THOSE AREN'T HUMANS.

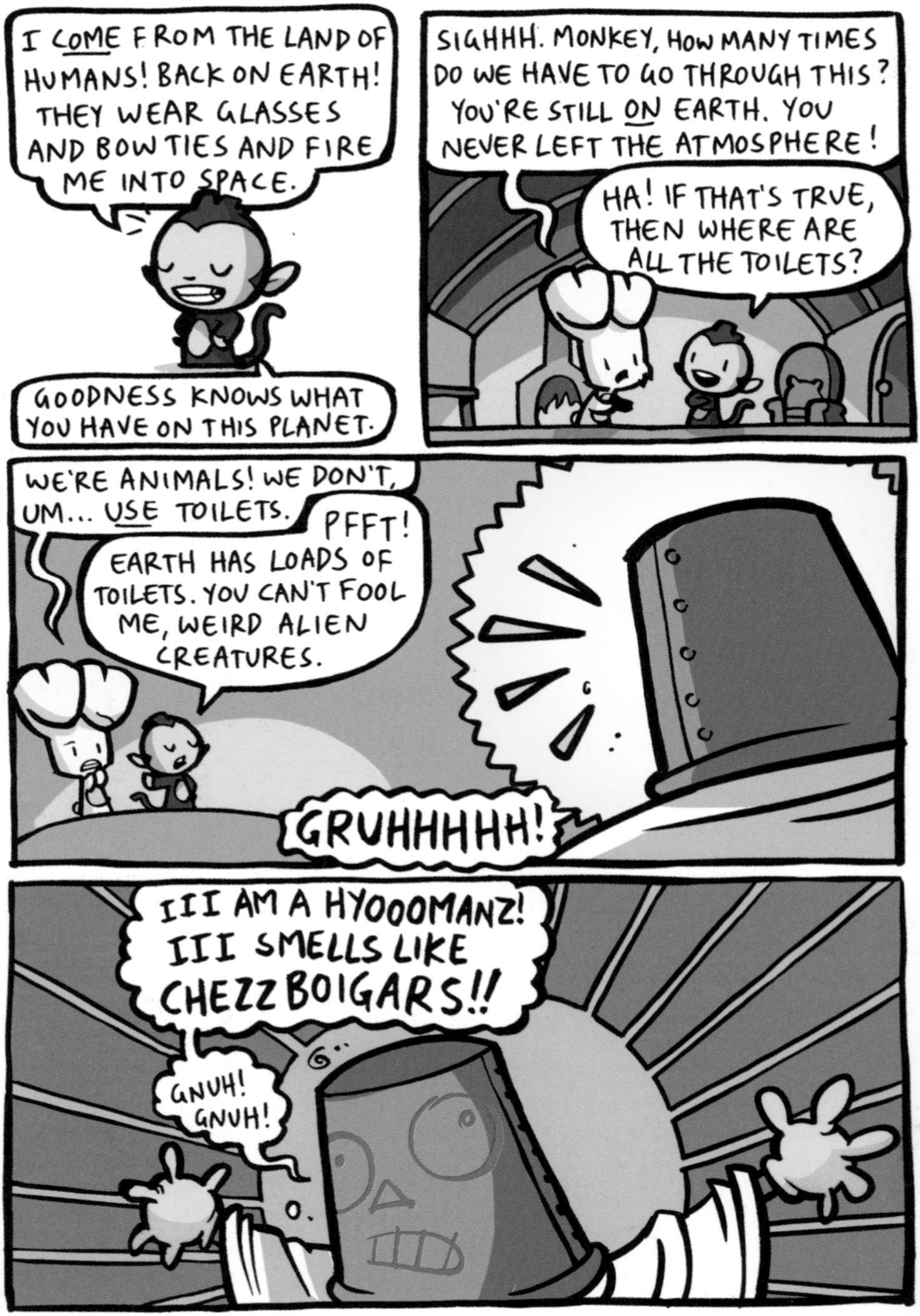
I COME FROM THE LAND OF HUMANS! BACK ON EARTH! THEY WEAR GLASSES AND BOW TIES AND FIRE ME INTO SPACE.
GOODNESS KNOWS WHAT YOU HAVE ON THIS PLANET.
SIGHHH. MONKEY, HOW MANY TIMES DO WE HAVE TO GO THROUGH THIS? YOU'RE STILL ON EARTH. YOU NEVER LEFT THE ATMOSPHERE!
HA! IF THAT'S TRUE, THEN WHERE ARE ALL THE TOILETS?
WE'RE ANIMALS! WE DON'T, UM... USE TOILETS.
PFFT! EARTH HAS LOADS OF TOILETS. YOU CAN'T FOOL ME, WEIRD ALIEN CREATURES.
GRUHHHHH!
III AM A HYOOOMANZ! III SMELLS LIKE CHEZZBOIGARS!!
GNUH! GNUH!

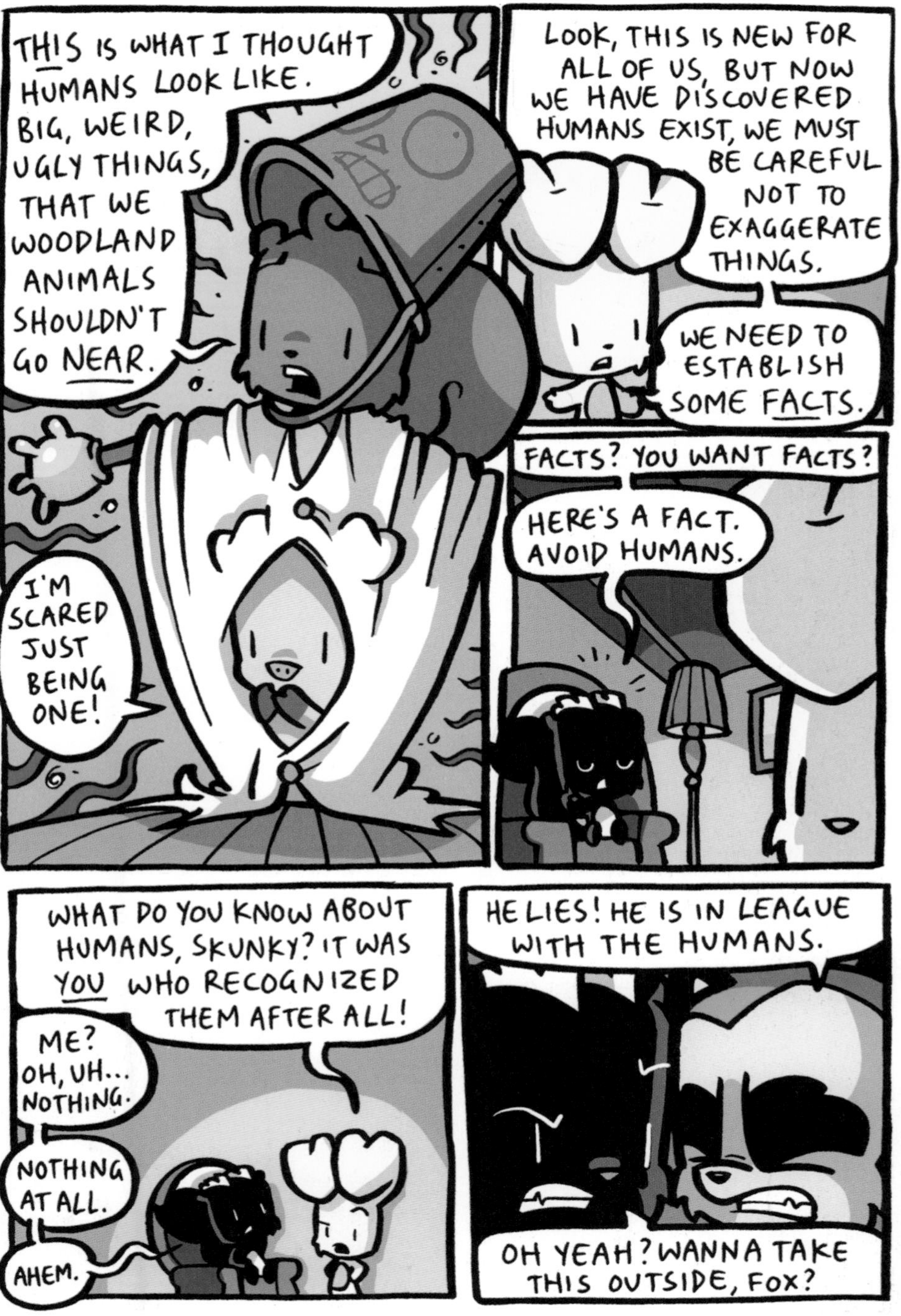
THIS IS WHAT I THOUGHT HUMANS LOOK LIKE. BIG, WEIRD, UGLY THINGS, THAT WE WOODLAND ANIMALS SHOULDN'T GO NEAR.
I'M SCARED JUST BEING ONE!
LOOK, THIS IS NEW FOR ALL OF US, BUT NOW WE HAVE DISCOVERED HUMANS EXIST, WE MUST BE CAREFUL NOT TO EXAGGERATE THINGS.
WE NEED TO ESTABLISH SOME FACTS.
FACTS? YOU WANT FACTS?
HERE'S A FACT. AVOID HUMANS.
WHAT DO YOU KNOW ABOUT HUMANS, SKUNKY? IT WAS YOU WHO RECOGNIZED THEM AFTER ALL!
ME? OH, UH... NOTHING.
NOTHING AT ALL.
AHEM.
HE LIES! HE IS IN LEAGUE WITH THE HUMANS.
OH YEAH? WANNA TAKE THIS OUTSIDE, FOX?

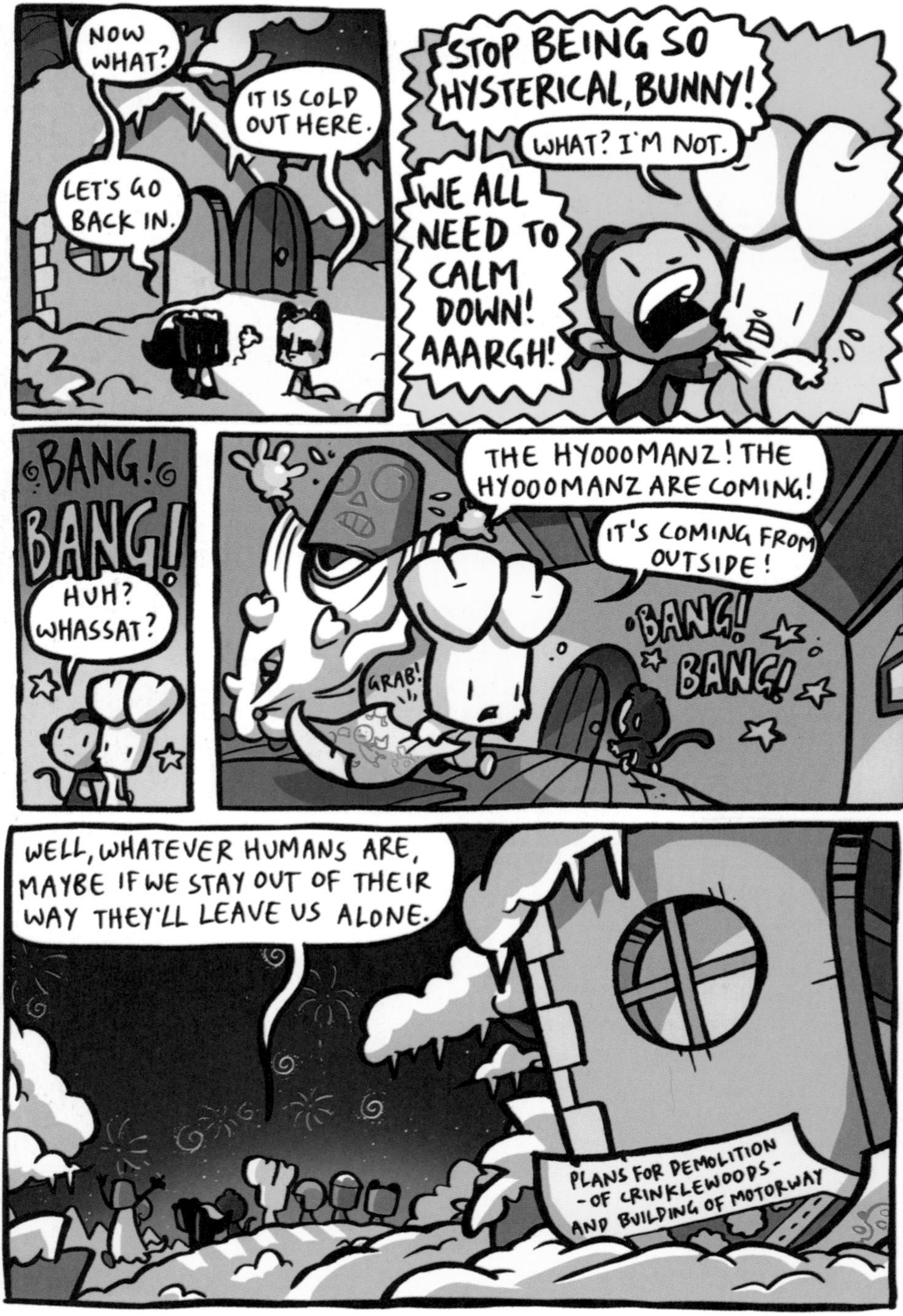
NOW WHAT?
IT IS COLD OUT HERE.
LET'S GO BACK IN.
STOP BEING SO HYSTERICAL, BUNNY!
WHAT? I'M NOT.
WE ALL NEED TO CALM DOWN! AAARGH!
BANG! BANG!
HUH? WHASSAT?
THE HYOOOMANZ! THE HYOOOMANZ ARE COMING!
IT'S COMING FROM OUTSIDE!
GRAB!
BANG! BANG!
WELL, WHATEVER HUMANS ARE, MAYBE IF WE STAY OUT OF THEIR WAY THEY'LL LEAVE US ALONE.
PLANS FOR DEMOLITION - OF CRINKLEWOODS - AND BUILDING OF MOTORWAY

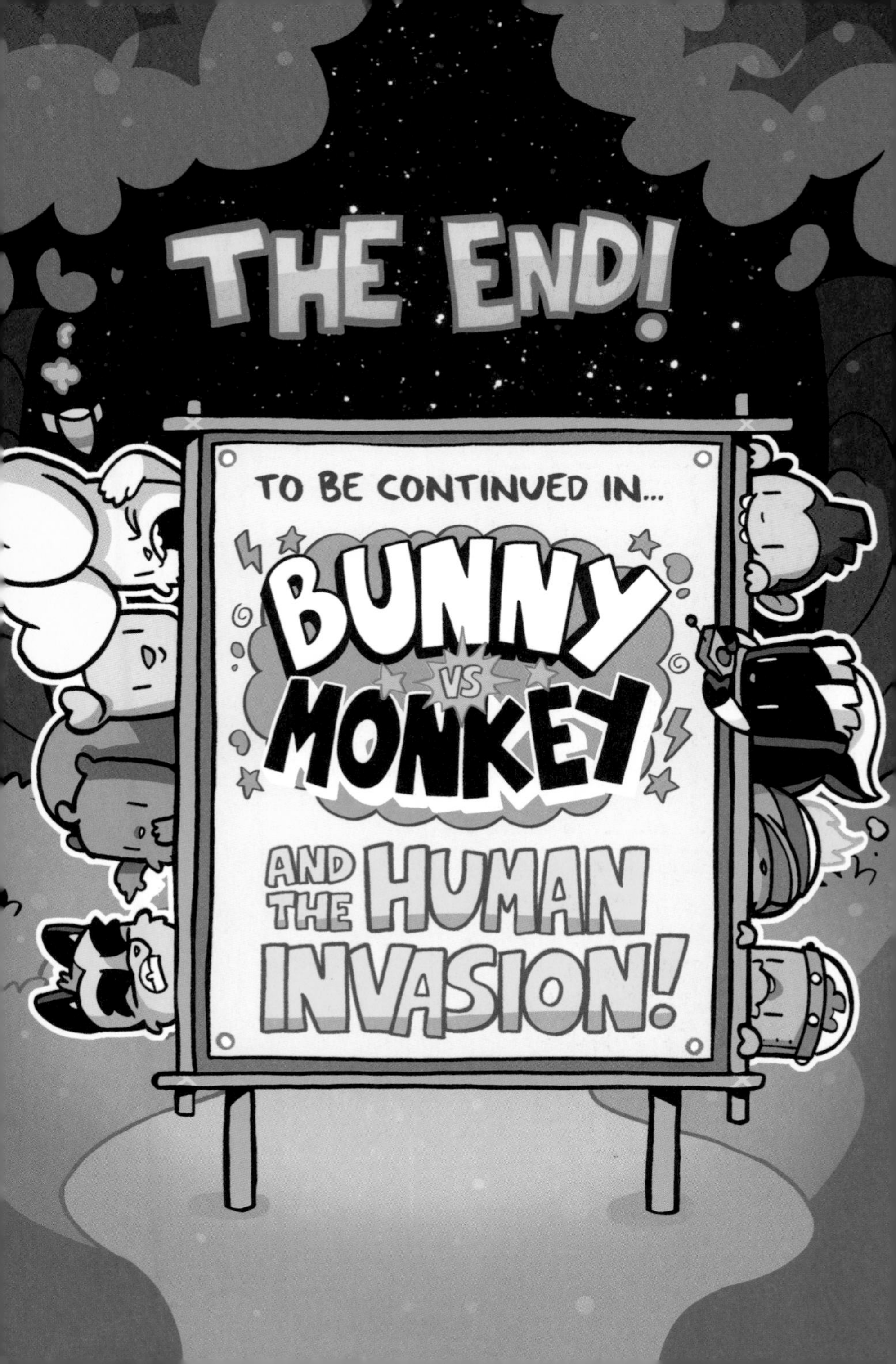
THE END!
TO BE CONTINUED IN...
BUNNY VS MONKEY
AND THE HUMAN INVASION!

HOW TO DRAW BUNNY

①

FIRST, LET'S DRAW **THE HEAD!** BUNNY'S HEAD LOOKS LIKE A **BULGING SQUARE!**

②

ADD AN **EAR!** TRY DRAWING A **HEART SHAPE** FOR BUNNY'S EAR.

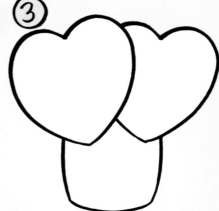

③

ADD **ANOTHER EAR!** DRAW A SECOND HEART TUCKED BEHIND THE FIRST.

now... BUNNY'S FACE!

①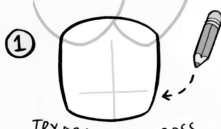

TRY DRAWING A CROSS - THIS WILL HELP YOU TO WORK OUT WHERE BUNNY'S FACE FITS ON HIS HEAD!

②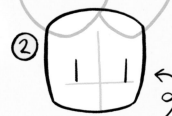

FOR INSTANCE, HIS **EYES** SIT ON THE HORIZONTAL LINE!

③

ABOVE HIS EYES, ADD TWO CURVED LINES FOR **EYEBROWS!**

④

A LITTLE TRIANGLE FOR A **NOSE...**

⑤

ANOTHER CURVED LINE FOR A **SMILING MOUTH...**

⑥

AND FINALLY A LITTLE TUFT OF **CHEEK HAIR!**

AND THEN... THE BODY!

ALL THE CHARACTERS IN BUNNY VS. MONKEY HAVE A **LUMP** FOR A BODY. IT MIGHT HELP TO IMAGINE IT LIKE A **CURVED TRIANGLE**, OR EVEN A **SHARK'S FIN!**

① WE THEN ADD A CIRCULAR PATCH OF **TUMMY FUR...**

② A SAUSAGE SHAPE FOR HIS **ARM...**

③ ANOTHER SAUSAGE FOR THE **OTHER ARM.** (TRY ADDING FINGERS TO THE END OF IT!)

④ A **BOBBLE TAIL!**

⑤ AND THAT'S **BUNNY!**

THESE ARE THE BASIC STEPS FOR DRAWING BUNNY. ONCE YOU'VE MASTERED THESE, IT'S IMPORTANT TO KEEP PRACTICING! IT WILL BECOME EASIER AND EASIER, AND THE BUNNIES YOU DRAW WILL LOOK MORE AND MORE NATURAL! TRY GIVING HIM DIFFERENT POSES, TOO! DIFFERENT EXPRESSIONS! STRETCH HIS FIGURE OUT AND SEE WHAT YOU CAN MAKE HIM DO!

NOTICE THE **FEET** ON THIS BUNNY — JUST TWO LITTLE CIRCLES!

HOW TO DRAW
MONKEY

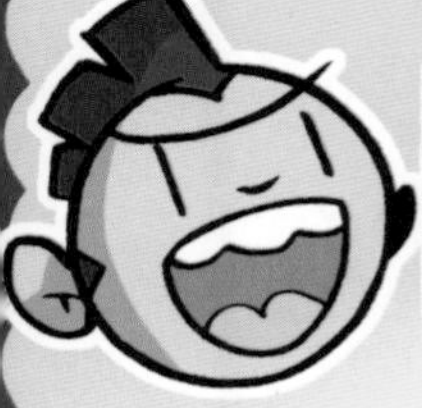

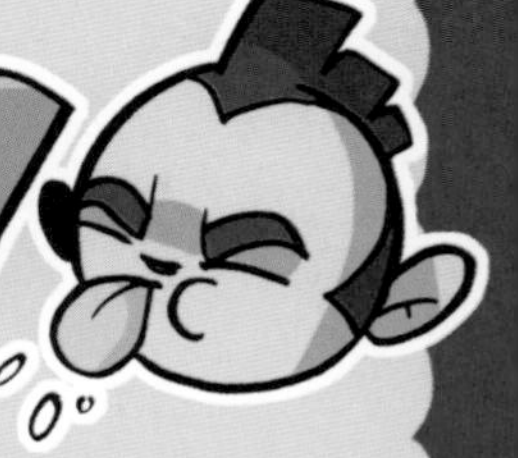

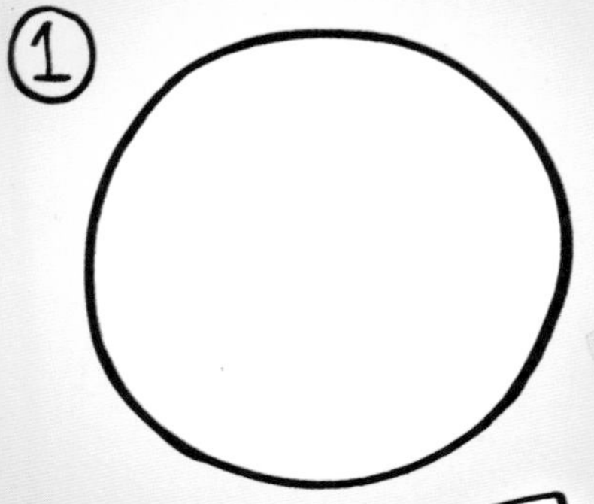

MONKEY'S HEAD STARTS WITH A **GREAT BIG CIRCLE!**

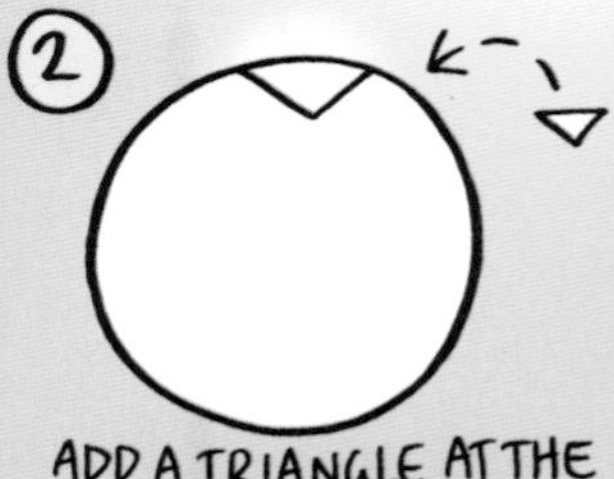

ADD A TRIANGLE AT THE TOP. THIS IS THE **PEAK** OF HIS FUR!

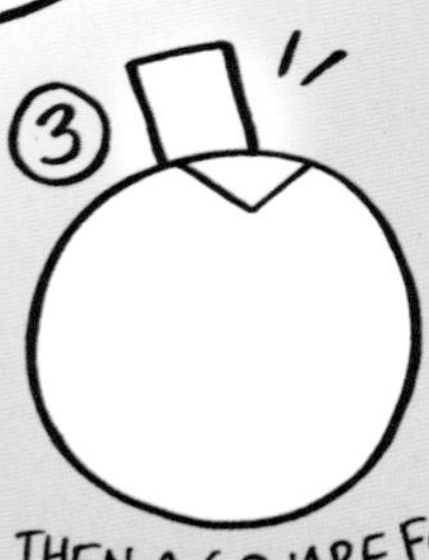

THEN A SQUARE FOR THE FIRST TUFT...

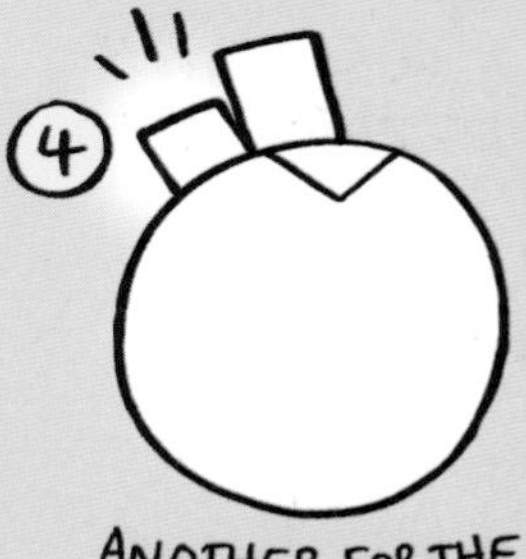

ANOTHER FOR THE SECOND TUFT...

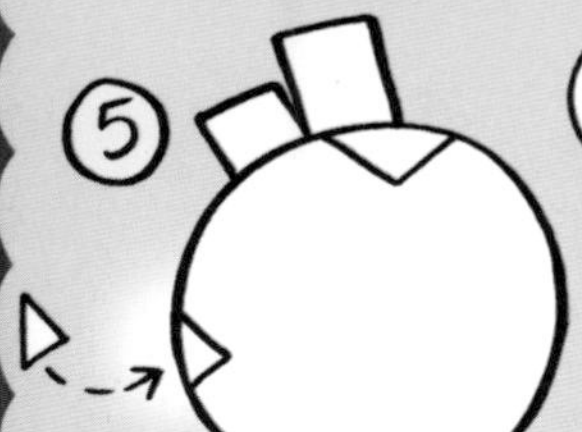

ONE MORE TRIANGLE ON THE SIDE...

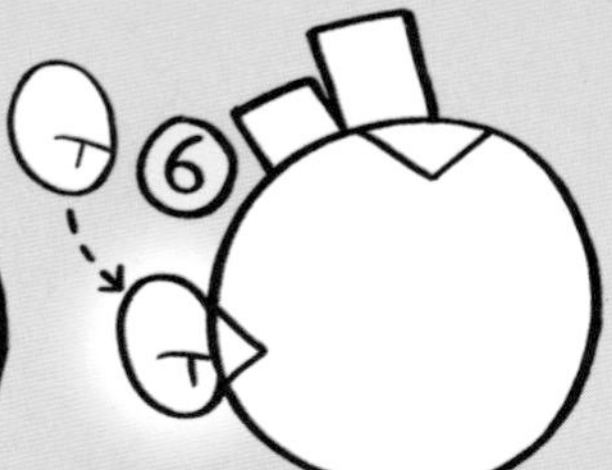

AND THEN MONKEY'S **EAR** NEXT TO IT. HIS EARS ARE **EGG-SHAPED**, WITH A LITTLE "T" SQUIGGLED INSIDE!

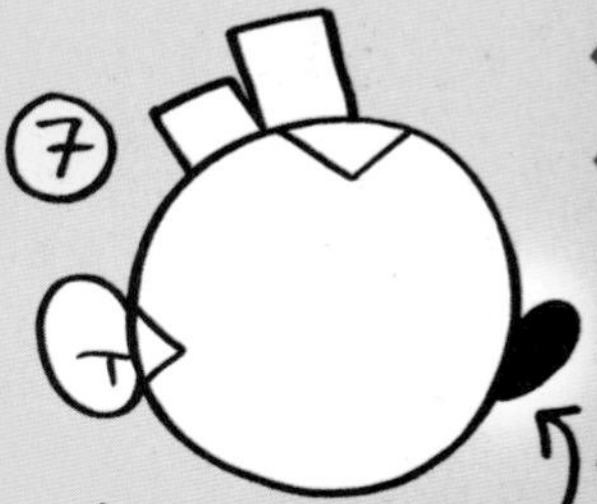

ADD A LITTLE DARK LUMP FOR THE EAR ON THE OTHER SIDE!

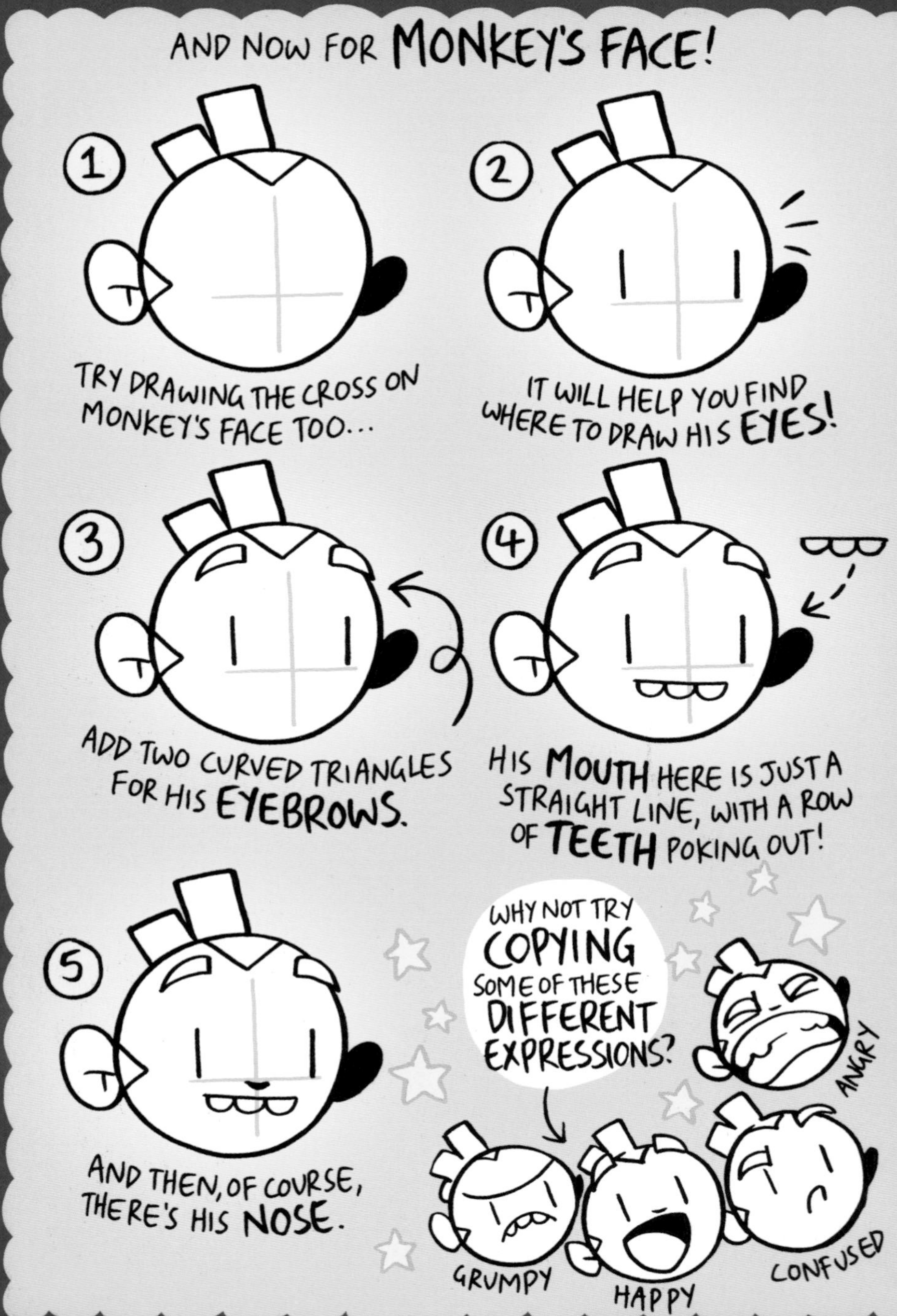
AND NOW FOR MONKEY'S FACE!
1
TRY DRAWING THE CROSS ON MONKEY'S FACE TOO...
2
IT WILL HELP YOU FIND WHERE TO DRAW HIS EYES!
3
ADD TWO CURVED TRIANGLES FOR HIS EYEBROWS.
4
HIS MOUTH HERE IS JUST A STRAIGHT LINE, WITH A ROW OF TEETH POKING OUT!
5
AND THEN, OF COURSE, THERE'S HIS NOSE.
WHY NOT TRY COPYING SOME OF THESE DIFFERENT EXPRESSIONS?
ANGRY
GRUMPY
HAPPY
CONFUSED

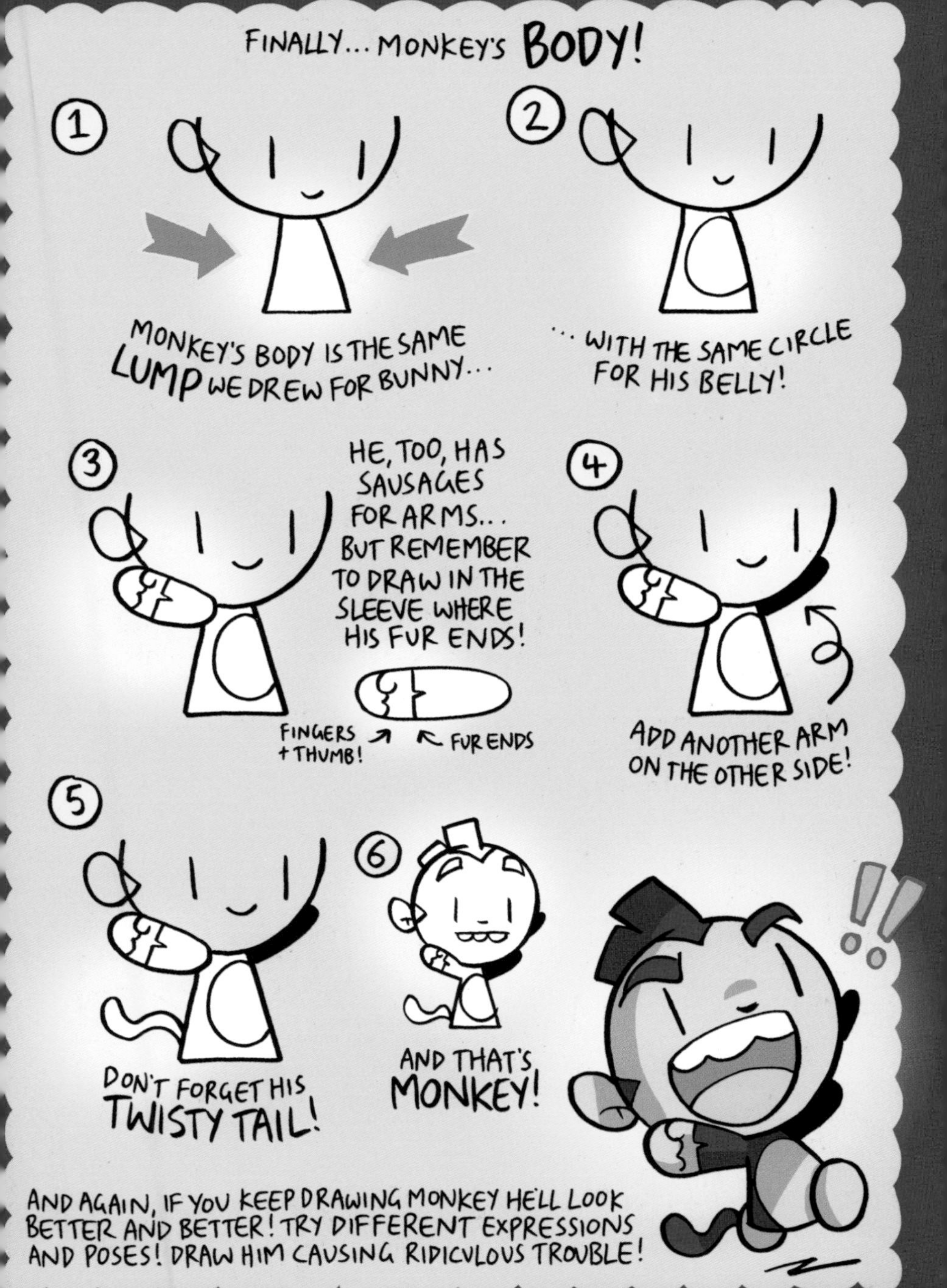
FINALLY... MONKEY'S BODY!
1
MONKEY'S BODY IS THE SAME LUMP WE DREW FOR BUNNY...
2
...WITH THE SAME CIRCLE FOR HIS BELLY!
3
HE, TOO, HAS SAUSAGES FOR ARMS... BUT REMEMBER TO DRAW IN THE SLEEVE WHERE HIS FUR ENDS!
FINGERS + THUMB!
FUR ENDS
4
ADD ANOTHER ARM ON THE OTHER SIDE!
5
DON'T FORGET HIS TWISTY TAIL!
6
AND THAT'S MONKEY!
!!
AND AGAIN, IF YOU KEEP DRAWING MONKEY HE'LL LOOK BETTER AND BETTER! TRY DIFFERENT EXPRESSIONS AND POSES! DRAW HIM CAUSING RIDICULOUS TROUBLE!

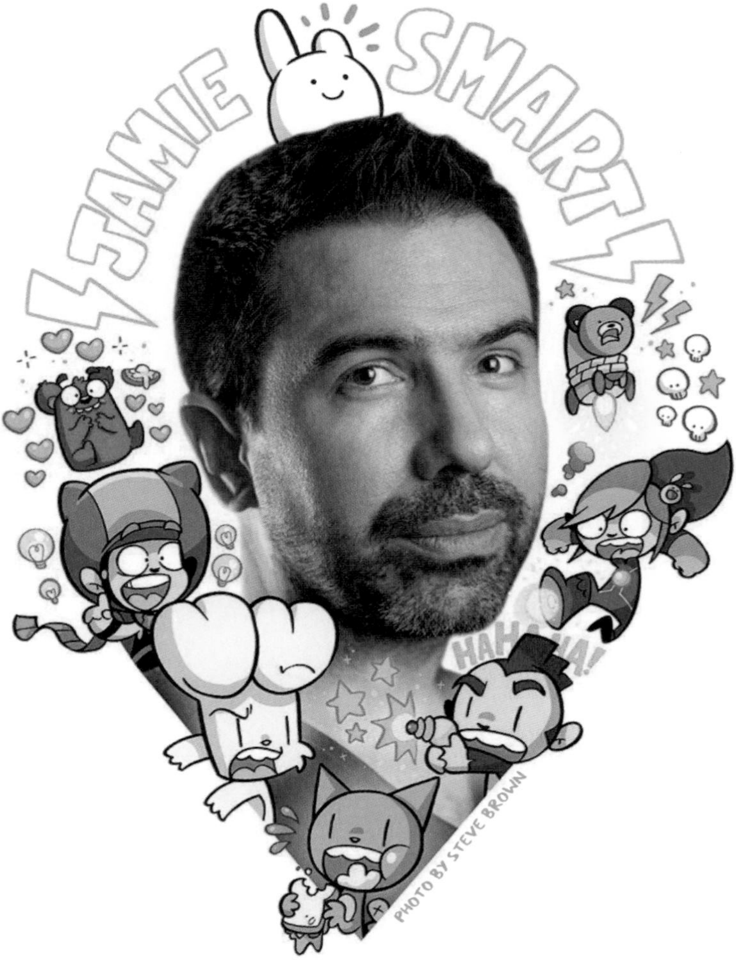
JAMIE SMART
HAHAHA!
PHOTO BY STEVE BROWN

JAMIE SMART HAS BEEN CREATING CHILDREN'S COMICS FOR MANY YEARS, WITH POPULAR TITLES INCLUDING *BUNNY VS MONKEY*, *LOOSHKIN*, AND *FISH-HEAD STEVE*, WHICH BECAME THE FIRST WORK OF ITS SORT TO BE SHORTLISTED FOR THE ROALD DAHL FUNNY PRIZE.

JAMIE LIVES IN THE SOUTH-EAST OF ENGLAND, WHERE HE SPENDS HIS TIME THINKING UP STORIES AND GETTING LOST ON DOG WALKS.